She needs him; he wants her!

Passionate Protectors?

Three passionate and exciting romances
from top Mills & Boon authors!

D0313081

Passionate Protectors?

ANNE MATHER

SARA CRAVEN

MAGGIE COX

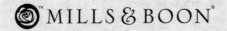
™ MILLS & BOON®

First published in Great Britain 2010
Harlequin Mills & Boon Limited,
Eton House, 18-24 Paradise Road, Richmond, Surrey TW9 1SR

PASSIONATE PROTECTORS?
© by Harlequin Enterprises II B.V./S.à.r.l 2010

Hot Pursuit, The Bedroom Barter and *A Passionate Protector* were first
published in Great Britain by Harlequin Mills & Boon Limited in separate,
single volumes.

Hot Pursuit © Anne Mather 2002
The Bedroom Barter © Sara Craven 2003
A Passionate Protector © Maggie Cox 2003

ISBN: 978 0 263 88110 3

05-0910

Printed and bound in Spain
by Litografia Rosés S.A., Barcelona

HOT PURSUIT

BY
ANNE MATHER

Anne Mather says: "I've always wanted to write – which is not to say I've always wanted to be a professional writer. On the contrary, for years I wrote only for my own pleasure, and it wasn't until my husband suggested that I ought to send one of my stories to a publisher that we put several publishers' names into a hat and pulled one out. The rest, as they say, is history. And now, more than a hundred and fifty books later, I'm literally – excuse the pun – staggered by what happened.

I had written all through my infant and junior years, and on into my teens. The trouble was, I never used to finish any of the stories, and *Caroline*, my first published book, was the first book I'd actually completed. I was newly married then and my daughter was just a baby. It was quite a job, juggling my household chores and scribbling away in exercise books every chance I got. Not very professional, as you can see, but that's the way it was.

I now have two grown-up children, a son and daughter, and two adorable grandchildren, Abigail and Ben. My e-mail address is: mystic-am@msn.com and I'd be happy to hear from any of my readers."

CHAPTER ONE

'WE'RE going to be late, Daddy.'

'I know that.'

Matt Seton managed not to sound as frustrated as he felt. It wasn't Rosie's fault that he'd overslept on the very morning that Mrs Webb wasn't here, or that his head was still buzzing with the effort of falling out of bed just a couple of hours after he'd flaked out.

'Mrs Sanders says that there's no excuse for sleeping in these days,' continued Rosie primly, and Matt could hear the echo of his ex-wife Carol's peevish tones in his daughter's voice.

'I know. I know. I'm sorry.' Clenching his teeth, Matt tightened his hands on the wheel of the powerful Range Rover. The temptation was to step down hard on the accelerator, but he didn't think that risking another ticket for speeding would improve his standing with Mrs Sanders either.

'So who's going to pick me up this afternoon?' Rosie asked, a little anxiously now, and Matt turned to give his daughter a reassuring look.

'I will,' he told the seven-year-old firmly. 'And if I can't make it I'll ask Auntie Emma to collect you. How's that?'

Rosie seemed slightly mollified, but as her small hands curved around the bag containing her pencil case and schoolbooks she cast her father an appealing look. 'You won't forget, will you, Daddy? I don't like having to ask Mrs Sanders to ring you.'

Matt expelled a long sigh. 'You've only had to do that once, Rosie,' he protested. And then, because it was obviously a cause of some concern to the child, his lean mouth parted in a rueful grin. 'I'll be there,' he promised. 'I can't have my best girl waiting around in the playground.'

'Mrs Sanders doesn't let us wait in the playground,' Rosie

5

told him pedantically. 'We have to stay in school if our Mummys or Daddys aren't there when school's over.'

'Right.' Matt's mouth compressed. 'Well, as I say, I won't let you down. Okay?'

'Okay!'

Rosie's eyes brightened in anticipation and Matt felt a heel for even comparing her to her mother. Rosemary was nothing like Carol, thank God, and it was up to him to organise a more stable structure in his daughter's life.

And he was trying, goodness knew. Since ill-health had forced Rosie's original nanny to retire he had interviewed a number of applicants for the position without any lasting success. Few younger women wanted to live in a remote area of Northumbria, far from the nearest town, and the older nannies who'd applied had, for the most part, appeared far too strict for his taste. He didn't want Rosie's confidence, already fragile because of her mother's abandonment, shattered by some fire-breathing dragon who saw the unconventionality of Matt's life-style as an opportunity to terrorise the little girl.

In consequence, he was seriously considering contacting an agency in London, in the hope that someone there might be professional enough about their career not to care about living in such rural surroundings. Saviour's Bay wasn't the back of beyond, after all. It was a wild and beautiful area of the Northumbrian coast, whose history was as turbulent as the seas that lashed the rocks below the cliffs. Its moors and hamlets were the haunt of archaeologists and naturalists, and from Matt's point of view it was the ideal place to escape the demands that being a successful writer had put on him. Few people knew where he lived these days, and that suited him very well.

But it didn't suit everyone, he acknowledged, and until the day came when he was forced to consider sending Rosie away to school he had to persist in his search for a suitable replacement for the woman who had virtually brought her up.

Not her mother, needless to say, he added to himself. Carol's indifference, not just to him but also to their daughter, had long since lost its power to hurt him. There were times when he wondered why they'd ever married at all, but Carol had given him Rosie, and he could never regret that. He adored his small daughter and he'd do whatever it took to keep her with him.

Matt appreciated that his success had given him certain advantages. When Carol had left him for another man he'd been the author of two moderately successful novels, but that was all. It was his third book that had hit the big time, and his fourth and fifth novels had sold in their millions. Subsequent sales of screen rights to a hotshot Hollywood director had helped, and these days he could virtually name his price.

But being photographed wherever he went, having his picture exhibited in magazines and periodicals, being invited onto television talk shows and the like, was not what he'd had in mind when he'd written his first book. As a doctor, specialising in psychology, he knew exactly what other people thought he'd expected from his change of career. The truth was, he had never been interested in becoming famous. And these days he just wanted to be left alone to get on with his next manuscript.

Which was why he'd bought Seadrift, the sprawling house overlooking the bay that he'd fallen in love with the first time he'd seen it. It served the dual purpose of giving him the peace he needed to work and the opportunity to put several hundred miles between him and the London media.

The gates of St Winifred's Primary loomed ahead and Matt breathed a sigh of relief. A glance at his watch told him it was still a minute or two to nine o'clock, and if Rosie got her skates on she should make it into class in time for registration.

'Have a good day, angel,' he said, exchanging a swift kiss with his daughter before she thrust open her door and clambered down onto the kerb.

'Bye, Daddy,' she called, her face briefly exhibiting a little of the anxiety she'd exhibited earlier. Then, cramming her grey hat with its upturned brim and distinctive red band down onto her sooty bob, to prevent the wind from taking it, she raised a hand in farewell and raced across the playground to the doors, where one or two stragglers were still entering the building.

Matt waited until the swirling hem of Rosie's pleated skirt had disappeared from view before putting the Range Rover into drive again and moving away. He couldn't prevent the sigh of relief he felt at knowing that she was in safe hands for a few hours at least. When he was working he could easily forget the time, and it wasn't fair on his daughter that she should have to spend her days worrying that he might not be there when she came out of school.

That was why he needed someone—nursemaid, nanny, whatever—to take up the slack. He had a housekeeper, Mrs Webb, who came in most days to cook and clean and do the ironing, but he'd never realised how much he'd depended on Hester Gibson until she'd been forced to retire. But then, Hester had been so much more than a nanny. From the very beginning she'd been more of a mother to Rosie than Carol had ever been, and when Carol had moved in with her lover Hester had taken Matt under her wing, too.

They had been living in London at that time, but Hester had had no qualms when Matt had suggested moving to the wilds of Northumbria. Like Matt, she had been an exile from the northeast of England herself, only living in the south because she hadn't been able to find suitable employment in her home town of Newcastle. It had been like coming home for both of them, and the house at Saviour's Bay had offered space and comfort.

Matt sighed again, and, turning the heavy vehicle in the yard of the village pub, drove back the way he'd come. The roads between Saviour's Bay and the village of Ellsmoor, where Rosie's school was situated, were narrow, with high, untrimmed hedges on either side. He supposed the state of the hedges was due to the local farmers, who were having a hard time of it at present, but it meant it was impossible to see far enough ahead to overtake the slow-moving hay wagon in front of him. But Matt was in no hurry now. He had the rest of the morning and the early part of the afternoon to himself, and as he'd worked half the night he thought he deserved a break.

Of course, he needed a shave, he conceded, running a hand over the stubble on his jawline. And some coffee, he thought eagerly, having only had time to pour milk onto Rosie's cornflakes and fill her glass with fresh orange juice before charging out to the car. Yes, some strong caffeine was just what he needed. It might clear his head and provide him with the impetus to get this nanny business sorted.

He made reasonably good time back to the house. Saviour's Bay was a village, too, but a much smaller community than that of Ellsmoor. In recent weeks he'd toyed with the idea of buying an apartment in Newcastle that they could use in term time. A would-be employee would obviously find the city more appealing. But the idea of living in town—any town—even for a limited period wasn't appealing to him. He loved Seadrift, loved its isolation too much to consider any alternative at present. And Rosie loved it, too. She couldn't remember living anywhere else.

As he swung onto the private road that led up to the house he noticed a car parked at an angle at the side of the road just before the turning. He slowed, wondering if the driver had missed his way, but the vehicle appeared to be deserted. Whoever owned the car had either abandoned it to walk back to the village, or had gone up to the house, he decided. There were no other houses along this stretch of the cliffs, which was why he'd bought Seadrift in the first place.

He frowned, looking back the way he'd come, but there was no one in sight. He wasn't worried. He'd had too many skirmishes with the press in the past to be concerned about some rogue reporter who might have hopes of finding a novel perspective on his present situation. Thankfully the press in this area accepted his presence without much hassle, and were usually too busy following up local issues to trouble him. But the car was there and it had to belong to someone.

So who?

Scowling, he pressed his foot down on the accelerator and quickened his pace. The pleasant anticipation he'd been feeling of making coffee and reading his mail was dissipating, and he resented whoever it was for ruining his mood.

The gates to the house appeared on the right. They were open, as usual, and Matt drove straight through and up the white gravelled drive to the house. Long and low and sprawling, Seadrift looked solidly inviting, even on this overcast June morning. Its walls were shadowed with wisteria, its tall windows reflecting the light of the watery sun that was trying to push between the clouds.

There was a block-paved turning circle in front of the double doors, flanked by outbuildings that had now been put to a variety of uses. A triple garage had been converted from a low barn, and another of the sheds was used to store gardening equipment.

Parking the Range Rover to one side of the doors, Matt sat for a moment, waiting to see if his arrival elicited any response from whoever it was he suspected had invaded his territory. And, sure enough, a figure did appear from around the corner of the barn. But it wasn't the man he'd expected; it was a woman. And as far as he could see she was carrying nothing more incriminating than the handbag-size haversack that was looped over one shoulder.

She was young, too, he noticed, watching her as she saw the car and after only a momentary hesitation came towards him. She was reasonably tall and slim, with long light brown hair streaked with blonde and confined in a chunky braid. She didn't look any older than her mid-twenties, and he wondered what she was doing, wandering around a stranger's property. Hadn't she heard of the dangers that could face young women like her in remote areas? Hell, in not so remote ones, too. For God's sake, she knew nothing about him.

Of course, she might have expected there to be a woman at the house, he was reminding himself, when another thought struck him. She could be from the agency. Just because he hadn't heard from them recently it didn't mean they didn't still have his name on their books. Here he was, suspecting the worst, and she could be the best thing that had happened to him in weeks. A nanny for Rosie. Someone to look after her and care for her; to give her her meals and be company for her when he was working. Someone to take her to school and pick her up again on those occasions when he couldn't. Could he be that lucky?

Collecting his thoughts, Matt pushed open the door of the Range Rover and stepped out onto the forecourt. Then, replacing his scowl with a polite look of enquiry, he went towards her and said, 'Are you looking for me?'

'Oh—' The girl seemed taken aback by his sudden appearance and Matt had a moment to assess the quality of the cream leather jacket she had slung about her shoulders. It had obviously not been bought off the peg at some department store, and the voile dress she was wearing with it seemed unsuitable for a morning interview with a prospective employer. But what the hell? he thought. Professionally trained nannies could command generous salaries these days, and what did he know about women's fashions anyway?

Apparently deciding he meant her no harm, in spite of the stubble on his chin, she gave a nervous smile. 'I—yes,' she said, answering his question. 'Yes, I suppose I am. If—if you live here.'

'I do.' Matt held out his hand. 'Matt Seton. And you are…?'

She seemed disconcerted by his introduction. Had she recognised his name? Whatever, she was definitely reluctant to shake his hand. But eventually she allowed him to enclose her fingers in his much larger ones and said, 'I'm—Sara.' And, when he arched his brow, 'Um—Sara Victor.'

'Ah.' Matt liked her name. It sounded solid; old-fashioned. Having interviewed a series of Hollys and Jades and Pippas, it was refreshing to meet someone whose parents hadn't been influenced by television soaps. 'So, Miss Victor: have you come far?'

She seemed surprised at his question, withdrawing her hand from his with unflattering haste. Dammit, surely she wasn't scared of him.

'Er—not far,' she said at last. Then, when it was obvious that something more was expected, she added, 'I—I stayed at a guesthouse in Morpeth last night.'

'Really?' Matt revised his opinion. The agency must have cast its net far and wide. She'd hardly have stayed in Morpeth if she lived in Newcastle. There was only a handful of miles between the two.

'Is that your car at the end of the road?' he asked now, and she nodded.

'It's a hired car,' she told him swiftly. 'But there seems to be something wrong with it. It gave up down there, as you can see.'

'Lucky you made it this far, then,' remarked Matt neutrally. 'I'll have the garage in Saviour's Bay pick it up later. They can return it to the agency when it's fixed.'

'But I don't—' She broke off, staring at him as if he was speaking in a foreign language. 'There's no need for you to do that. If I could just use your phone—'

Her voice trailed away and Matt's brows drew together in sudden suspicion. 'You're not from the agency, are you?' he exclaimed. 'I should have known. You're another bloody reporter, aren't you?' He gave her a scathing look. 'They must be desperate if they're sending bimbos to do the job!'

'I am not a bimbo!' For once he had stung her into an unconsidered retort. She straightened her spine, as if she could add to her height. But she was still several inches shorter than Matt's six feet plus and her frustration showed in her face. 'And I never claimed to be from any agency.'

'Whatever.' Matt's jaw compressed. 'So, what are you doing here? I notice you haven't denied being a reporter.'

'A reporter?' She stared at him, thick blonde lashes shading eyes of a misty grey-green. 'I don't understand. Were you expecting a reporter?' Her face paled a little. 'Why would a reporter come here?'

'Don't pretend you don't know who I am.'

'I don't.' She frowned. 'Well, I know your name is Seton. You told me that.'

'Matt Seton?' prompted Matt caustically. 'Ring any bells?'

'Actually, no.' She looked troubled. 'Who are you?'

Matt swayed back on his heels. Was she serious? She certainly looked as if she was, and if he'd had any conceit to speak of she'd have certainly exploded it with her innocent words. If they were innocent, he amended. Or could she really be that good?

'You don't go to bookshops, then?' he enquired drily, aware of a totally unfamiliar sensation of pique. 'You've never heard of my work?'

'I'm afraid not.' She looked a little relieved now, but hardly apologetic. 'Are you famous?'

Matt couldn't prevent an ironic laugh. 'Moderately so,' he said mildly. 'So...' He lifted his shoulders. 'What are you doing here?'

'I told you. My car broke down.' She paused. 'I was hoping to use your phone, as I said.'

'Really?' Matt considered her.

'Yes, really.' She shivered suddenly, and, although it was hardly a cold morning, Matt noticed how pale she was. 'Um, would you mind?'

Matt hesitated. It could still be a clever ruse on her part to get inside his house. But he was beginning to doubt that. Nevertheless, no one apart from his friends and family had ever got beyond his door, and he was loath to invite any stranger, however convincing, into his home.

'Don't you have a mobile?' he said, and she gave a weary sigh.

'I don't have my mobile with me,' she told him tiredly. 'But if helping me is a problem just tell me where I can find the nearest garage. I assume the one you mentioned isn't far away.'

'Far enough,' muttered Matt heavily. 'Can you walk the best part of three miles?'

'If I have to,' she replied, lifting her head. 'Just point me in the right direction.'

But he couldn't do it. Berating himself for being a fool, he slammed the door of the Range Rover and gestured towards the house. 'You can use the phone,' he said, striding past her. He led the way through an archway that gave access to the back of the building, hoping he wasn't making the biggest mistake of his life. 'Follow me.'

Immediately, his two retrievers set up an excited barking, and he wondered if she'd heard them earlier. Although the dogs themselves were just big pussy-cats, really, the noise they made had scared off tougher intruders than her.

'Do you like dogs?' he asked, glancing over his shoulder, and she gave an uncertain shrug.

'I don't know,' she said. 'Are yours dangerous?'

'Oh, yeah!' Matt gave a wry grin. Then, realising she was taking him literally, he added. 'Dangerously friendly, I mean. If you're not careful they'll lick you to death.'

Her smile appeared again, a more open one this time, and Matt was amazed at the difference it made to her thin features. For a moment she looked really beautiful, but then the smile disappeared again and he was left with the knowledge that for someone who had supposedly only been driving for about an hour that morning she looked exhausted.

Opening the door into the boot room, Matt weathered the assault of the two golden retrievers with good-natured indulgence. They were Rosie's dogs, really, but as they spent as much time with him as they did with her they tended to share their affections equally.

It took them only a few moments to discover he wasn't alone, however, and he had to grab them by the scruffs of their necks before they knocked his guest over. As it was, she swayed a little under the onslaught, and he was forced to lock the dogs in their compound in the yard before opening the door into the kitchen.

'Sorry about that,' he said, glancing ruefully about him. Their plates from the previous night's supper still lay on the drainer, waiting to be put into the dishwasher, and Rosie's breakfast bowl and glass occupied a prominent position on the island bar. If Mrs Webb had been working that morning the place would have looked much different, and Matt thought how typical it was that the one morning he had a visitor the kitchen should look like a tip.

'They're very friendly, aren't they?' she said, speaking about the dogs, but he knew she'd noticed the mess. 'Are they yours or your wife's?'

Matt's mouth turned down. 'My daughter's, actually,' he said. Then, because she was looking as if the next puff of wind would knock her over, he added, 'I was just about to make myself some coffee. Would you like a cup?'

'Oh, please!'

If he was to speculate, Matt would have said she spoke like someone who hadn't had anything to eat or drink in some time.

There was such eagerness in her response, and once again he felt a renewal of his doubts about her. Who was she really? Where had she been heading on the coast road, which was usually only used by locals and holidaymakers? What did she really want?

'I've got the number of the garage in Saviour's Bay,' he said as he spooned coffee into the filter. 'I'll just get this going and then I'll find it for you.'

'Thank you.'

She hovered by the door, one hand clutching the strap of her haversack, the other braced against the wall unit nearest to her. He couldn't be sure, but he thought she was trembling, though whether that was because she was cold, despite the warmth of the Aga, or apprehensive, he wouldn't like to say.

It was quite a novelty for Matt to face the fact that she might not trust him. Her question about whether the dogs belonged to him or his wife might just have been a rather clumsy attempt to discover if he was married. For the first time he realised how vulnerable she might feel.

'Hey, why don't you sit down?' he suggested, pointing towards the two stools that were set at either side of the island bar. 'This is going to take a few minutes.'

'O—kay.'

With evident reluctance she crossed the room and, dropping her haversack onto the floor beside her, levered herself onto one of the tall stools. But he noticed she chose the one that put the width of the bar between them, before treating him to another of those polite smiles.

Matt pulled a wry face but he didn't say anything. She'd learn soon enough that he wasn't interested in her or anyone else. That was, if she bothered to check him out in whatever place she was heading for. Despite his fame, and the monetary success it had brought him, Matt had declined all opportunities to replace his ex-wife.

And he had had opportunities, he conceded without conceit. A man in his position always attracted a certain type of woman, even if he was as ugly as sin, and he wasn't that. His features were harsh, maybe, but they weren't totally unappealing. He'd been told when he was younger and less cynical that deep-set eyes, olive skin, and a nose that had been broken playing rugby were far more interesting than pretty-boy looks.

But who knew what the real truth was? He no longer cared. So long as Rosie loved him, that was all that mattered.

When he turned back to his visitor, however, he got a surprise. While he'd been speculating on the possibilities of her being afraid of him, she'd slumped in her seat, shoulders hunched, head resting on the arms she'd folded on the counter. She was either asleep or exhausted, he realised in amazement. And he'd bet money on the former. What the hell was going on?

The phone rang at that moment and at once she jerked awake. Cursing, Matt went to answer it, not knowing whether his irritation was caused by the fact that she'd fallen asleep or that the sound had awakened her. Looping the receiver off the wall, he jammed it to his ear. 'Yeah?'

'Matt?'

'Emma!' Matt expelled a long breath. 'Hi! What can I do for you?'

'I'm not disturbing you, am I?'

It would be all the same if she was, thought Matt ruefully. He owed Emma Proctor too much to resent the interruption and, aware that Sara was watching him with wary grey-green eyes, he said swiftly, 'No, I just got back from taking Rosie to school. I'm in the middle of making some coffee, actually. I'm afraid we slept in this morning.'

Emma made a sympathetic sound. 'Of course, it's Mrs Webb's day off, isn't it? I gather you've had no luck with the agency?'

'No.' Matt didn't particularly want to get into that now. 'No luck at all.'

'What about trying the local employment agency?' Emma suggested helpfully. 'They sometimes have childminders on their books.'

'But I don't want a childminder,' declared Matt mildly. 'I want someone with the proper training, not a girl who only wants to work here on a part-time basis. I need someone in the evenings, too, when I'm working. You know that.'

'What you need is a surrogate mother for Rosie,' said Emma a little tersely. 'And the chances of finding someone like that who's also prepared to live in rural Northumbria—'

'I know, I know.' He and Emma had had this conversation too many times for Matt to show much patience with it now. 'Look, thanks for caring, but I've really got to work this out for myself.'

'If you can,' muttered Emma huffily. 'Anyway, that wasn't why I rang. I wondered if you wanted me to collect Rosie from school this afternoon. I've got to go to Berwick this morning, but I should be back by—'

'It's okay. I've told Rosie I'll pick her up myself this afternoon,' replied Matt quickly, wondering what his visitor was making of the one-sided conversation. He hesitated. 'I appreciate the offer, Em. I really do. Some other time, yeah?'

'I suppose so.' To his relief, she didn't pursue it. 'Well, I'd better go. There's nothing you want from Berwick, is there? I can always drop it off on my way home.'

'Not that I can think of,' said Matt politely. 'Have a good day, Em. Speak to you soon.'

When he replaced the receiver he noticed that his visitor dropped her gaze, as if afraid of being caught out watching him. Frowning slightly, he turned back to the filter and saw that the jug was now full and steaming on the hotplate. Unhooking a couple of mugs from the rack, he looked at Sara again.

'Black? White? With sugar or without?'

'White with no sugar,' she answered at once. 'It smells delicious.'

Matt poured some for her and pushed the mug across the counter. Then, taking a carton of milk from the fridge, he passed that over, too. 'Help yourself.'

'Thank you.'

Matt drew a breath. 'You hungry?'

'Hungry?' For a moment she looked almost eager. Then those thick blonde lashes shaded her eyes again. 'No,' she responded carefully. 'This is fine.'

Matt considered, and then pulled a large biscuit tin towards him. It was where Mrs Webb stored the muffins she made for his breakfast and, although these had been made the day before, they still smelled fresh and appetising. Heated in the microwave, they often made a meal for someone who often forgot about food altogether, and Matt offered the tin to Sara now.

'Sure?' he asked. 'I usually heat a couple of these for my breakfast. I can recommend them.'

She looked as if she wanted to take one, but after a pregnant pause she shook her head. 'The coffee is all I need,' she assured him. And then, perhaps to divert herself, she added, 'I gather you're looking for a nursemaid for your daughter?' Faint colour entered her cheeks. 'How old is she?'

'Rosie?'

Matt hesitated, closing the tin again. Then, deciding there was no harm in telling her, he added, 'Seven.' He shook his head. 'I can hardly believe it. Time goes so fast.'

Sara moistened her lips. 'Is your wife dead?' she asked, and then lifted her hand in a gesture of remorse. 'No. Don't answer that. I had no right to ask.'

'No, you didn't.' But Matt answered her just the same. 'Carol left me when Rosie was a baby,' he said flatly. 'Don't worry. It's not a secret.'

'I see.' Sara cradled her coffee mug between her palms. 'I'm sorry.'

'Yeah.' Matt gave a wry smile. 'But, believe me, it was the best thing for both of us.'

Sara looked up at him. 'For you and your wife?'

'For me and my daughter,' Matt amended, hooking his heel around the stool opposite and straddling it to face her. He nodded to her cup. 'Coffee all right?'

She drew back when he was seated, as if his nearness—or his bulk—intimidated her. It crossed his mind that someone must have done a number on her, must be responsible for her lack of confidence, but he didn't say anything. In his professional experience it was wiser not to probe another person's psyche. Not unless you had a reason for doing so, at least.

'So you live here alone?' she said at last, apparently deciding to pursue her enquiries, and he pulled a wry face.

'I have Rosie,' he said, his lips twitching. 'Hey, are you sure you're not a journalist? That's the kind of question they ask.'

Her face fell. 'No!' she exclaimed. And then, as if realising he was only teasing her, she continued, 'I was thinking about the job.'

'What job?' For a moment he was nonplussed, and she took advantage of his silence.

'Your daughter's nanny,' she declared quickly. 'Would you consider me for the post?'

CHAPTER TWO

HE LOOKED stunned. That was the only description Sara could find to fit the expression on his lean tanned face. An expression that was definitely at odds with his harsh compelling features. At least a day's growth of stubble roughened his jawline and there were dark pouches beneath the deep-set hollows of his eyes.

And why shouldn't he be shocked at her announcement? thought Sara uneasily. It wasn't every day that a strange woman turned up on your doorstep asking for work. After all, he knew nothing about her. She didn't even have the backing of an employment agency. She could be a con artist, living on her wits. Though any con artist worth her salt would surely not try and dupe a man like him.

Sara wished now that she hadn't made the offer. She didn't know anything about him either, and just because he had been kind to her that was no reason to trust him. Besides, she wasn't a nanny. She wasn't a nursemaid. Her experience with children had been confined to the classroom, but he'd never believe that she'd once been a primary school teacher. That had been at another time; sometimes now it seemed like another life. When she'd been young—and so naïve.

'You're offering to become Rosie's nanny?' Matt Seton asked at last, and she could tell he was suspicious of her offer. 'You didn't say you were looking for work.'

I'm not. I'm looking for sanctuary, thought Sara wildly, but she couldn't tell him that. And when she'd left London the previous evening she'd had no plans beyond the need to get away. To put as many miles between her and Max as possible.

But she couldn't think about that now. She needed time to come to terms with what she'd done. 'I might be,' she said, taking a sip of her coffee to avoid his penetrating gaze. 'Are you interested?'

'"I might be",' he mocked, echoing her words. 'Are you used to working with children.'

'I was.' Sara chose her words with care. She didn't like lying but she really didn't have a choice. And, the more she thought about it, the more the idea appealed to her. A job like this might be exactly what she needed. Somewhere to stay; a means of earning money; a chance to disappear without leaving a trail. She hesitated, and then stated bravely, 'I used to be a primary school teacher.'

'Used to be?' Dark brows arched interrogatively.

'Yes.'

'But not any more?'

'Not recently, no.'

'Why?' The question was innocent enough but she had the feeling he was baiting her.

'Because I gave up teaching some time ago,' she admitted. 'But it's not something you forget.'

'So what have you been doing?'

Fighting for my life!

Somehow she managed to keep her voice steady as she replied, 'I—got married. My hus—my ex-husband, that is, didn't like me having a job.'

And that must be the understatement of the year!

'I see.' Matt Seton was regarding her so intently she was almost sure he could see into her mind. And if he could he'd know that she wasn't being completely honest, that she was only telling him as much of the truth as she needed to sound sincere. 'Do you come from around here?'

He asked a lot of questions. Sara swallowed and considered the option of saying yes. But he'd know she didn't sound like a local. So, after a moment, she said, 'I used to live in the south of England until quite recently.'

'Until you decided to hire a car and drive three hundred miles up the motorway?' suggested Matt laconically. 'What happened, Sara? Did your husband ditch you for someone else, so you decided to disappear and make the bastard sweat?'

'No!' She was horrified. If Max had turned his attentions elsewhere she wouldn't be in this state now. 'I—I told you, we're—

we're divorced. I just fancied a change of scene, that's all. I didn't know where I wanted to stay until I got here.'

'And decided that because I needed a nanny, you'd be it,' he commented cynically. 'Forgive me if I sound sceptical, but I've never heard such a load of garbage in my life.'

'It's not garbage.' Sara suspected she was beginning to sound desperate but she couldn't help it. She really wanted this job. 'Do you want a nanny or don't you? You sounded fairly sure about it when you were on the phone.'

Matt tipped his stool onto its back legs, balancing himself with one hand on the counter. 'So you were listening?'

'How could I not?' Sara knew there was no point in denying it. 'All I'm asking is that you consider me for the position.'

'Really?' He didn't look convinced. 'So what qualifications do you have?'

Sara hesitated. 'Well, two years of working at a primary school in—in London.' She'd almost mentioned the school's name and that would have been foolish. 'Like I say, I left when I got married.'

'And you can prove this? You've got certification, references?'

Sara bent her head. 'Not with me.'

'But you could get them?'

Her shoulders slumped. 'Not easily, no.'

'Surprise, surprise.' He was sardonic. 'Hey, I may live in the sticks, but I haven't got straw in my ears, Mrs Victor.'

'It's Miss Victor,' she muttered unnecessarily. If he wasn't going to employ her, what did it matter what he thought her name was? It wasn't her real one. She lifted her head, deciding to make one last plea for his understanding. 'Look, I'm not going to pretend that working for you wouldn't suit my purposes. It would. And, although I can't prove it, I was a primary school teacher. A damn good one, as it happens.' She gazed at him. 'You could give me a week's trial, at least. What have you got to lose?'

'Plenty.' The feet of the stool thudded down onto the tiled floor as he leaned almost threateningly towards her. 'I don't just leave my daughter with anyone, *Miss* Victor. She's far too important to me. I'm sorry.'

He didn't look sorry. On the contrary, he looked as if he'd be glad to see the back of her, and she pushed the remains of her coffee aside and got to her feet.

'So am I,' she said, barely audibly, bending to pick up her bag. 'If—if I could just use your phone…'

'Wait.' To her dismay he stood also, successfully putting himself between her and the door. 'Tell me something: did you really spend the night in Morpeth, or was that a lie, too?'

'Does it matter?'

She was trying to remain calm, but she was suddenly conscious of how vulnerable she was here. So long as they'd been discussing the job she'd felt a certain amount of control over the situation. But he'd made it plain that he didn't believe her and now she was uneasily aware that he held her fate in his hands. What did he intend to do with that knowledge? What if he decided to report her to the authorities? How long would she remain free if he gave her description to the police?

'Humour me,' he said, pushing his hands into the back pockets of his jeans. Jeans that fit him so closely that they were worn almost white in places, she noticed inconsequentially, running her tongue over her dry lips.

'I—all right, no,' she conceded unwillingly. 'May I use the phone now?'

'So—you've been driving since late last night or early this morning?'

Sara sighed. 'Something like that.'

'You must be exhausted.'

She gave a mirthless laugh. 'What's it to you?'

He was silent for so long that she thought he wasn't going to answer her. Then he said flatly, 'I'm not completely heartless. I know a runaway when I see one. Why don't you sit down again and I'll make you some breakfast? You might even like to rest for a while before contacting the garage about your car.'

Sara stared at him. 'I didn't come down with the last shower either,' she exclaimed scornfully. 'And where do you get off, calling me a runaway? I told you, I decided I needed a change of scene—'

'I know what you said,' he interrupted her blandly. 'But you don't really expect me to believe that, do you?'

'I don't give a—a flying flea what you believe!'

'Oh, I think you do.' He was smug.

'Why should I?'

'Because it must have occurred to you that I could decide to keep you here until I had your story checked out.'

Sara gasped. 'You wouldn't do that!'

'Give me one reason why I shouldn't.'

'Because—because you have no right. I'm not a child; I'm not even a teenager. I can please myself what I do.'

'Possibly.' He paused. 'But you must admit that someone who suddenly decides they need a change of scene wouldn't leave in the middle of the night. Particularly as you appear to have left without bringing any papers, any references, anything to prove you are who you say you are.'

Sara felt totally defeated. 'Just let me go,' she said wearily. 'Please.' She paused. 'Forget the phone. I'll check the car myself, and if it still doesn't start I'll make some other arrangement. Just forget you ever saw me.'

Matt sighed. 'I can't do that.'

'Why not?'

'Because I think you need some help,' he said gently. 'Why don't you tell me what really happened? My guess is that you had a row with your husband and decided to take off. I don't know where the hired car comes in, but that's not important. Am I somewhere near the truth?'

'I told you.' She spoke doggedly. 'I don't have a husband.'

'Right.' His mouth thinned. 'So why are you still wearing both your wedding and engagement rings? For sentimental reasons?'

Sara sagged. She'd forgotten about the rings. She was so used to wearing them, so used to Max's anger if she ever dared to take them off, that she hadn't even thought about them or what they might mean to someone else.

She swayed. She felt so dizzy suddenly. When had she last had anything to eat? she wondered. Not today, certainly. And she couldn't recall eating much the previous day either. She'd missed dinner, of course, but had she had any lunch? She wished she could remember. But everything that had happened before Max came home remained a blank.

Not the memory of Max lying at the foot of the stairs, however. She recalled that, and recalled herself rushing down the stairs after him, kneeling at his side, desperately trying to find a pulse. But her hand had been shaking so much she hadn't been able to feel anything. In any case, he hadn't been breathing. And surely that could mean only one thing.

He was dead!

She swayed again, and saw Matt put out his hand towards her. He was going to touch her, she thought, jerking back from the contact as if she was stung. Her legs felt like jelly. Dear God, what was happening to her? She mustn't pass out here. She knew nothing about this man except that he was threatening to expose her.

She should never have come here; never have asked for his help. She was on her own now. That was what she wanted. The only person she could rely on was herself…

Sara opened her eyes to curtains moving in the breeze from the open window behind them. Sunlight dappled peach-coloured walls, laid yellow fingers over a tall armoire and a matching chest of drawers, added warmth to the lime-green quilted bedspread that covered her. Somewhere a tractor was droning its way across a field, a dog was barking, and the plaintive sound of gulls was overlaid by the dull thunder of the sea.

Where was she?

Propping herself up on her elbows, she frowned as she looked around the pretty bedroom. Nothing was familiar to her—except her jacket folded over the back of a rose-pink loveseat, and her strappy high heels standing beside the chair.

Then it all came rushing back. Max's fall, and her escape; the car she'd hired that had stalled just after she'd turned onto the sea road; the many futile attempts she'd made to start it again.

A shiver crept down her spine. But that still didn't explain how she came to be here, lying in a strange bed, fully clothed except for her jacket and shoes. What had happened? She put a confused hand to her head. She had to remember.

There'd been a house, she thought, her head throbbing with the effort to recall the morning's events. She'd been so relieved to find it on this lonely stretch of the coast. She'd hoped that whoever owned the house might let her use their phone to call a garage. She'd doubted she'd find a phone box this far from the village.

But the house had appeared to be empty. She remembered hearing dogs barking, and she'd been on her way back to the road when one of those big Range Rovers had pulled into the yard. Even then she'd hoped that it might be a woman driving the vehicle. At that time of the morning mothers were often employed on the school run. But the man who'd swung open the door and pushed jean-clad legs out of the car had been anything but feminine.

Matt Seton.

She swallowed, wondering if Max would have heard of him. Probably, she decided. Max had always prided himself on being familiar with every facet of the arts, and although she'd never read any of his books Seton had projected such an image of power and self-confidence that she was sure that anything he produced would be a success.

But Max was dead, she reminded herself once more, feeling a sense of panic creeping over her. In any case, she wasn't supposed to be thinking about Max right now. She was trying to work out how she came to be in Matt Seton's bedroom.

Well, maybe not his bedroom, she conceded, determinedly concentrating on the room instead of letting her thoughts numb her mind to the exclusion of anything else. She had the feeling that Matt Seton's bedroom would look nothing like this. This room was too light, too feminine. His daughter's, perhaps? He'd said he had a daughter. Did she really want to know?

Still, he had been kind to her, she acknowledged. Initially, anyway. Despite the fact that when he'd emerged from the Range Rover her primary instinct had been to run. She hadn't wanted to speak to him, hadn't wanted to put her trust—however fleetingly—into another man's hands. But common sense had won out over panic and she'd been quite proud of the way she'd handled herself then.

Until the idea of asking him for a job had occurred to her. That had been a crazy notion. She realised it now, had realised it as soon as he'd started asking questions she couldn't—or wouldn't—answer. But the thought of staying here, of blending into the landscape so that no one would find her until she wanted them to, had seemed, momentarily at least, the perfect solution.

A dog barked again. Closer at hand this time. She guessed it must be just beneath the window and she heard a man bidding it to be quiet. The man's voice was familiar, strong and attractive, and she had no difficulty in identifying it as belonging to her unwilling host.

Which brought the realisation that Matt Seton must have carried her upstairs and put her to bed. He must have removed her shoes and jacket and covered her with the quilted spread. Why? Had she fainted? Had she fallen and hit her head? No, that simply wouldn't happen. Not today. Not after...

Her bag? Alarm gripped her again. Where was her bag? Her haversack? She'd had it with her when she'd been feeling so dizzy downstairs, but she couldn't see it now. What was in it? What could Matt Seton have found if he'd looked through it? Anything incriminating? Oh, she hated that word. But was there anything to prove that her name wasn't really Sara Victor?

Throwing the coverlet aside, she swung her legs over the side of the bed and choked back a gasp of pain. Her hip throbbed abominably, and even if the room hadn't spun briefly about her she'd still have had to remain motionless until the pain subsided.

Finally it did, and, drawing up the skirt of her dress, she examined the ugly bruise that was visible below the high-cut hem of her briefs. Circles of black and blue spread out from a central contusion where ruptured blood vessels were discernible beneath the skin. It was nasty, but not life-threatening, and she touched it with cold, unsteady fingers before pulling her skirt down again.

'So you're awake!'

The voice she'd heard a few minutes before seemed to be right behind her, and she swung apprehensively towards the sound. Matt Seton was standing in the open doorway, one shoulder propped against the jamb, his eyes dark and shrewd, surveying her. How long had he been there? she wondered anxiously. Had he seen—?

She expelled an uneven breath. She was unwillingly aware that long ago, before her marriage to Max, she'd have considered Matt Seton quite a dish. Even wary and suspicious of her as he was, he still possessed the kind of animal magnetism that most women found irresistible. He wasn't handsome, though his lean hard features did have a rough appeal. But it was more than that. A combination of strength and vulnerability that she was sure had all his female acquaintances falling over themselves to help him. A subtle power that was all about sex.

She bent her head, and, as if sensing she was still not entirely recovered from her loss of consciousness, he went on, 'When did you last have a meal?'

Sara's eyes went automatically to her watch, but she saw to her dismay that it wasn't working. A crack bisected the glass and one of the hands was bent. She must have done it when she fell against the table the night before, but because until now she hadn't wanted to know what time it was she hadn't noticed.

'I—what time is it?' she asked, without answering him, and Matt pulled a wry face.

'Why? Will that change anything?' Then, when her eyes registered some anxiety, he added shortly, 'It's after one o'clock. I was about to make myself some lunch. Do you want some?'

One o'clock! Sara was horrified. She must have been unconscious for over three hours.

'You fainted,' he said, as if reading the consternation in her face. 'And then I guess, because you were exhausted, you fell asleep. Do you feel better?'

Did she? Sara had the feeling she'd never feel better again. What was going on back home? Did Hugo know Max was dead yet? Of course he must. He had been going to join them for supper after the show...

'Hello? Are you still with us?'

She must have been staring into space for several seconds, because she realised that her host had moved to the foot of the bed and was now regarding her with narrowed assessing eyes. What was he thinking? she pondered apprehensively. Why couldn't she stop giving him reasons to suspect her of God knew what? Yet, whatever he suspected, it couldn't be worse than the truth.

'I'm sorry.' She eased herself to the edge of the bed, trying not to jar her injured hip. 'When I asked to use the phone I didn't expect to make such a nuisance of myself.'

He didn't argue with her. There was no insincere attempt to put her at her ease. Just a silent acknowledgement of the statement she had made and a patient anticipation of an answer to the question he had asked earlier.

'Lunch,' he prompted her at last. 'I think we need to talk, and I'll be happier doing it when you've got some solid food inside you.'

'Perhaps I don't want to talk to you,' she retorted, getting to her feet. Without her heels he seemed that much taller, easily six feet, with a powerful muscular body that bore no resemblance to Max's more bulky frame. 'Where's my bag?'

His expression was cynical. 'There,' he said flatly, indicating a spot beside the loveseat. 'Don't worry. I haven't been rummaging through your belongings while you've been unconscious. What do you take me for?'

Sara's pale cheeks deepened with embarrassed colour. 'I—I don't know what you mean.' But she did. Max wouldn't have hesitated in using any situation to his advantage. 'I—just wanted a tissue.'

'Yeah, right.' He was sardonic. Then his brows drew together as she stepped rather stiffly into her shoes. 'Are you sure you're all right?'

'I'm fine.' But she wasn't. She'd been stiff getting out of the car, but she'd still been running on adrenalin and the ache in her hip had been bearable. Now, after resting, after giving in to her exhaustion, her senses were no longer dulled by over-active hormones and she could hardly move without wincing. 'I'm still a bit unsteady, that's all.'

Matt regarded her dourly. 'I'd say that was the understatement of the year,' he remarked, forestalling her when she would have reached for her jacket. 'You won't be needing this. Not yet, anyway. You're going to have something to eat, even if I have to feed you myself.'

Sara's cheeks flushed. 'You can't force me!'

'Don't make me prove it,' remarked Matt, making for the door, her jacket looped over one shoulder. He nodded towards a door beside the armoire. 'There's a bathroom through there. Why don't you freshen up before the meal?' He paused. 'Oh, and there are tissues in there, too. If you really need them.'

Sara pressed her lips together as he left the room. Once again, he'd caught her out in a lie. But then, she was no good at lying. She never had been. It might have been easier for her if she had. If Max—

But she had to stop thinking about Max. Had to stop remembering how he'd humiliated and terrified her for almost three years. Why had she stayed with him? Why had she put up with his moods, his tempers? Because she'd been too much of a coward to break away from him? Or because she'd known what he'd do to her and her mother if she dared to try and leave him?

And now he was dead…

Her throat felt dry, and after ensuring that Matt had left the room she shuffled across to the bathroom. Like the bedroom, it was predominantly peach and green in colour. Pale green bath and basin; cream tiles with a peach flower decorating the centre; thick peach and green towels set on a stainless steel rack.

There was a mirror above the basin and Sara examined her reflection with critical eyes. Fortunately, her face was unmarked. Max never left any visible signs of his cruelty, at least none that couldn't be covered by her clothes. There had never been any obvious signs that he was anything other than an ideal husband. Even Hugo—gentle, bumbling Hugo—had never suspected what a monster his brother really was. And as for her mother…

Sara trembled. She was doing it again, concentrating all her attention on the past. She'd done what she could. She'd phoned the emergency services before she'd fled from the apartment. She'd ensured that Max was attended to. The only thing she hadn't done was stay and be charged with his murder…

Expelling an unsteady breath, Sara ran some water into the basin and washed her face and hands with the creamy soap she found there. It was so good to get rid of the stale make-up she'd been wearing since the night before, and, after rescuing her haversack from the other room, she spent a few minutes applying moisturiser to her skin. She didn't use any lipstick or mascara, but an eyeliner was necessary to draw attention away from the dark circles around her eyes. She looked pale, but she couldn't help that. She had the feeling she'd never look normal again.

She found her brush and, loosening her hair, she got rid of the tangles before plaiting it again. Then, satisfied that she'd repaired the damage, she went back into the bedroom.

She found her hip was easier now that she was moving about again. In a few days the bruises would disappear, as they had done before. She'd be able to look at herself and pretend, as she had pretended so many times before, that Max had left no scars upon her. But the real scars went deeper, were longer lasting. Those scars were incapable of being destroyed.

She closed her eyes for a moment, preparing herself to meet the questions Matt Seton wasn't going to forget he hadn't had answers to. And, before she left the room, she took off her watch and her rings and slipped them into the bottom of her bag. One way or another she was no longer Max's possession. She was on her own now, and, until she decided what she was going to do, she had to think on her feet.

There was still her mother, of course. But she doubted she would have any sympathy for her daughter. They had never been close, and in the older woman's eyes the only sensible thing Sara had ever done was to marry Max Bradbury. It had always been the same. Max could do no wrong. And, because when they'd got married Max had moved her mother out of her run-down house in Greenwich and into a luxury apartment in Bloomsbury, Sara had never been able to appeal to her for help. God knew what she'd think when she discovered Max was dead and her daughter was missing. Sara doubted she would ever forgive her.

CHAPTER THREE

SARA looked even paler when she came downstairs, and Matt felt a heel for upsetting her. But, dammit, he hadn't been born yesterday, and it was obvious that the story she'd told him wasn't even close to the truth.

He had already beaten eggs for omelettes, and he set a bowl of freshly washed salad on the breakfast bar. Fresh coffee was simmering on the hob, and there was nearly half a bottle of Chardonnay in the fridge—a hangover from his working jag of the night before.

'Sit down,' he said, indicating the stool she had occupied before. He had considered laying the table in the dining room, but that had seemed too formal. Besides, if he had any sense he'd feed her and send her on her way without any further nonsense. It wasn't his problem if she was running away. He had been a fool to get involved. 'How do you feel?'

'Better,' she said, with another of her guarded smiles. She edged onto the stool. 'You didn't have to do this, you know.'

Yes, I did, thought Matt wryly, but he contented himself with a careless, 'No problem.' The eggs sizzled as he poured them into a hot pan. 'There's wine in the fridge, if you want it.'

'Not for me, thank you.' She was evidently trying to relax, but although she propped her elbows on the bar and looped her fingers together he could see she was on edge. Then, as if determined to behave naturally, she added, 'You said you were a writer?'

Matt cast her a sardonic glance. 'Did I say that?'

'Well, you implied as much,' she said, looking embarrassed, and he took pity on her.

'Yeah,' he agreed. 'I write.'

Her eyes widened, and he was struck anew at how lucid they were. But now that she'd removed her make-up he could see the dark shadows that surrounded them, noticed with his professional eye for observation that her skin was porcelain-fragile and almost transparent.

Who the hell was she? he wondered. What was she really doing in this part of the country? And why did he feel such an unwarranted sense of responsibility for her?

'What do you write?' she asked, apparently hoping to prevent him from asking her any more questions, and he drew a breath.

'Thrillers,' he replied at last, deciding not to elaborate. She wouldn't be interested in his background in psychology, or in the fact that the main character in his last three novels had used psychological profiling to catch his villains. Carol hadn't been. She'd thought she'd married a doctor. She'd never been interested in his writing. He tipped half the cooked eggs onto Sara's plate. 'Okay?'

She nodded her thanks for the golden-brown omelette he'd set in front of her. 'Mmm, this looks delicious.'

'So eat it,' he advised, straddling the stool opposite as he'd done before. He pulled his own plate towards him and set a board with newly sliced French bread beside them. 'Help yourself.'

He noticed how long it took her to swallow just a few mouthfuls of the omelette. She asked if she could have a glass of water and punctuated every forkful with several generous gulps so that the glass was empty long before the eggs were eaten. Much against his better judgement, Matt refilled the glass and added a handful of ice cubes from the freezer. For that she offered him a smile that for once was totally sincere.

'So—are you writing at the moment?' she asked at last, seemingly conscious of the fact that he was watching her every move. She managed to meet his eyes, if only briefly. 'It must be a fascinating occupation.'

'It's a living.' Matt helped himself to a wedge of bread and spread it thickly with butter. He offered it to her, but she declined, and, taking a bite, he chewed thoughtfully before continuing, 'I'm lucky. I enjoy it. Not all writers do, you know.'

'They don't?'

He wondered if her ingenuity was real or feigned. She certainly appeared to be interested. But then, he'd been flattered too many times before to take anything at face value. 'No,' he answered her now, forking the last of his omelette into his mouth. 'To some people, it's just a job. For me, it was a hobby long before I started to take it seriously.'

Sara looked impressed. 'It must be great to do something you really enjoy.' She cupped her chin in her hand. 'I envy you.'

'You didn't enjoy teaching, then?' suggested Matt mildly, and saw the way the colour seeped into her face at his words.

'That's different,' she said tightly. 'I meant, it must be wonderful to have a—vocation.'

'Well, I wouldn't call it that. But I know what you mean.' Matt shrugged and then directed his attention to her plate. 'Is something wrong with your eggs?'

'Oh—no.' She hurried to reassure him. 'You're a good cook. I just—er—I don't have much of an appetite, I'm afraid. I'm sorry.'

Matt collected the plates and got up to pour the coffee. Then, setting a mug of the steaming liquid in front of her, he said, 'So what are you going to do now?'

She glanced half apprehensively towards the door and he wondered if she was remembering the argument they'd had before she'd collapsed. But as far as she was concerned her vehicle was unusable. Was she thinking she would have to make other arrangements before she could continue with her journey?

'I—I suppose I should ring the garage in—where was it you said? Saviour?'

'Saviour's Bay.' Matt regarded her levelly. 'Actually, I did ring them myself.'

'You did?' The relief in her eyes made him regret the lie he'd just told her. 'What did they say? Are they sending somebody out?'

Matt ignored his twingeing conscience. 'Not until tomorrow. They're pretty strapped today.'

'Oh, no!' Her disappointment was evident. She ran slim fingers up into the hair at her temples, dragging several strands to curl about her jawline. 'God, what am I going to do now?'

He guessed the question was rhetorical, but he answered her anyway. 'You could stay here overnight,' he suggested, wondering why he was doing this. 'I have a spare room. You've just spent a couple of hours in it.'

'No!'

'Why not?' He hardened his tone. 'You were quite prepared to stay if I offered you a job. What's the difference?'

She flushed. 'That was a mistake.'

'What was?'

'Asking you for a job. I don't know what possessed me.'

'Try desperation?' he suggested flatly. 'Come on, Sara, we both know you don't have anywhere else to go. And until your car's fixed…'

She shook her head. 'I'll find a hotel. A guesthouse. Something.'

'Around here? I don't think so. Not unless you're prepared to hike several miles, as I said. And somehow, in those heels, I don't think you'd make it.'

'You don't know what shoes I've brought with me. I have a suitcase in my car—'

'No, you don't. I checked.' Matt didn't go on to add that he'd started her car, too. She must have flooded the carburettor when it had stalled and she'd tried to start it again. 'There's nothing in the boot.'

Her indignation was appealing. 'You had no right to do that.'

'No.' He agreed with her. 'But you had left the keys in the ignition. Anyone could have done the same.'

She sniffed. 'You can't force me to stay here.'

'I have no intention of forcing you to do anything,' he declared dismissively. 'And very shortly I'll be leaving to pick up my daughter from school, so you'll have every opportunity to walk out if you wish.' He shrugged. 'It's your call.'

Matt covered the distance between Seadrift and St Winifred's Primary feeling a sense of incredulity. Had he really left Sara—if that really was her name—alone in his house? After spending the last few years isolating himself from everybody but his family and the people who worked for him, had he actually encouraged a complete stranger to spend the night in his home?

Was he mad? He knew practically nothing about her, and

what he did know was definitely suspect. She had no more decided on a change of life than he had. He'd bet his last cent that she was a runaway. But from whom? And from what?

Whatever it was, he knew that it made his own misgivings about leaving her in his house groundless. She wasn't a thief. He was sure of that. Nor was she anyone's idea of a nanny, although he was prepared to believe that she hadn't been lying when she'd said she'd been a teacher. That had been the only time when there'd been real conviction in her voice. So what was she? Who was she? And what was he going to do about her?

For the present, however, he had other things to think about. Not least the fact that he had to introduce her to Rosie. He had no idea what his daughter would think of him inviting a strange woman to spend the night. Rosie might only be seven, but she could be remarkably adult on occasion, and she was bound to wonder how Sara came to be there.

To his relief, he heard the bell that marked the end of the school day as he pulled up outside the gates. He wasn't late, thank goodness. But his early arrival did mean that he had to get out of the Range Rover and be civil to the other parents who were already gathered outside the school.

'Hello, Matt.'

Gloria Armstrong, whose husband farmed several hundred acres north of Saviour's Bay, gave him a winning smile. Like several of the mothers of children in Rosie's class, she was always eager to chat with him. Matt was by no means a conceited man, but he knew these women seemed to get a disproportionate delight in using his first name. It was a pity Hester wasn't still here to run interference for him.

'Gloria,' he responded now, nodding to her and to one or two of the other parents. Thankfully, there was a handful of fathers present, too, and he was able to ally himself with them as he waited for Rosie to emerge from the school buildings.

'I hear you've had no luck in finding someone to care for Rosemary,' Gloria added, not at all daunted by his offhand greeting. Her heavily mascaraed eyes moved over his tall figure with a certain avidity. 'I wish I could do something to help.'

Yeah, right. Matt schooled his features and gave a wry smile. 'I'm sure you've got enough to do looking after those three boys of yours,' he said pleasantly. 'Not to mention your husband. How is Ron, by the way?'

Gloria's mouth turned down. 'Oh, Ron's all right,' she said dismissively. 'So long as he has his golf and his beer and his cronies, he's as happy as a pig in muck!' She grimaced. 'I sometimes think he doesn't care about me and the boys at all.'

Remembering what Rosie had said about the three boys, two of whom were in her class, Matt reserved judgement. There was no doubt they were tearaways in the making, but who was he to condemn them? He'd probably been far worse in his youth. At least if half of what his mother maintained was true.

'I imagine the farm keeps him fairly busy,' he said neutrally, wishing he could move away from her. He noticed their conversation was being observed by more than one pair of interested eyes, and the last thing he needed was for someone to mention to Ron Armstrong that he'd been seen chatting up his wife at the school gates. Despite what he'd said to Gloria, he knew her husband was a hothead and a bully. He could imagine the headlines if the other man chose to take him to task for being a womaniser.

A womaniser! Him! Matt stifled a groan. Nothing could be further from the truth. These days he was virtually celibate. The last time he'd got laid had been before Hester retired. He'd had to spend a weekend in London, visiting his agent and doing some publicity, and one of the advertising execs had come on to him. She'd been exceptionally good-looking, he recalled, but their hasty coupling in her hotel room had hardly been memorable. He'd been glad he could honestly say he was leaving London the following morning, and he'd left strict instructions with his agent that he wasn't to give his phone number to anyone…

'I wish I had a job.'

He'd forgotten Gloria was still there, but her rueful remark forced him to acknowledge her again. 'You have a job,' he said, wishing Rosie would hurry. He glanced at his watch. 'I wonder what's holding them up?'

'Who?' Gloria looked up at him with heavy-lidded eyes.

'The kids,' said Matt quellingly. Then, with some relief, 'Ah—here they are.'

'You know, I could look after Rosemary.' Gloria grabbed his arm as he would have moved away. 'At least I've had plenty of experience.'

And not just in looking after children, thought Matt drily, shaking her hand off his sleeve. For the first time he felt a little sympathy for Ron Armstrong. Perhaps he had some justification for his temper, after all.

'It's okay,' he heard himself saying now. 'I'm hoping I've found someone. She just started today, as a matter of fact.'

Gloria's full mouth took on a sulky slant. 'Well, that's news,' she said, clearly not believing him. 'I was talking to Emma Proctor yesterday morning and she didn't say anything about you hiring a nanny.'

'She doesn't know yet,' said Matt, wondering how he could have been so reckless as to say such a thing. Now he would have to ring Emma and explain the situation to her.

'Obviously not.'

Gloria sniffed, but to Matt's relief Rosie had seen him and she came barrelling out of the gate towards them.

'Daddy! Daddy!' she squealed, flinging herself into his arms. 'You came! You came!'

'I said I would, didn't I?' said Matt, swinging her round. He grinned. 'Have you had a good day?'

'Quite good—'

'Your daddy's had a better one,' put in Gloria maliciously, before Matt could perceive her intent and deflect it. 'He's found someone to look after you, Rosemary. Isn't that nice? I expect she'll be coming to meet you tomorrow.'

Rosie's eyes grew round. 'Is that true, Daddy? Has the agency sent you someone else?'

'Not exactly.' Matt could have strangled Gloria as she stood there enjoying his discomfort. Clearly she thought he was making the whole thing up and she wanted him to have to admit it. Casting her a malevolent look, he ushered Rosie away towards the Range Rover. 'I'll tell you all about it as we go home,' he promised, flicking the key fob to unlock the vehicle. 'Okay?'

'But you have found a new nanny, haven't you, Daddy?' Rosie asked, clambering, with his assistance, into the front seat. 'You weren't just saying that?'

Matt reflected again how adult Rosie was at times. He had no idea what he was going to say to her. He couldn't lie to his daughter, but equally he had to come up with a reasonable explanation of who Sara was and why she was staying at the house.

If she was still there when he got back, he acknowledged. She could have taken the keys he'd left on the counter in the kitchen and made another attempt to start her car. Once she found it was operable, she was a free agent. Whatever he thought, she'd have no reason to stay.

He sighed, fitting his keys into the ignition, and Rosie gave him a troubled look. 'What's wrong, Daddy?' she asked shrewdly. She hesitated. 'Is it because you haven't found a nanny? Did you just say that because you don't like Mrs Armstrong? 'Cos that's all right. I don't like Rupert and Nigel either.'

Rupert and Nigel! Matt raised his eyes heavenward for a moment. Nobody but Gloria Armstrong would have called those two imps of Satan *Rupert* and *Nigel*. Rosie was always telling him some story or other about what they'd got up to in the classroom, about how Mrs Sanders was forever sending them to the head teacher for extra discipline.

But grumbling about the Armstrongs wasn't going to help him now. Choosing his words with care, he said, 'A young woman did come to see me today. Not from the agency,' he added quickly, holding up a hand to prevent Rosie from interrupting. 'She's a visitor. Her car broke down at the bottom of the road and she came to ask if she could use the phone.'

Rosie's face dropped. 'So she's not a nanny?'

'No.' Matt shook his head. 'But she is going to stay with us, at least until tomorrow. So I want you to be especially nice to her.'

Rosie sniffed. 'So who is she? Why is she staying with us?'

'I've just explained,' said Matt patiently. 'Her car broke down and—she can't get it fixed until tomorrow.' May God forgive him the lie. 'She's nice. I think you'll like her.'

'What's her name?'

'Sara. Sara Victor. What do you think?'

Rosie shrugged, and Matt thought at first that she was going to reserve her opinion until she'd met their visitor. But he was wrong. His daughter was simply considering her options.

'Perhaps she'll want to stay,' she said at last, with childish optimism. 'If she likes it here, she might want to take the job.'

Matt made no response to this. He was already regretting having to discuss Sara's arrival with her. But then, he'd known he'd have to give some explanation to his daughter. Unfortunately Gloria Armstrong had precipitated the event.

It seemed to take for ever to get back to Saviour's Bay. Now that she knew about Sara, Rosie wasn't interested in talking about her day at school. She just turned the conversation back to Sara, and he eventually gave up trying to talk about anything else.

She wanted to know Sara's age, what she looked like, where she came from. If she was on holiday, what was wrong with her car? The questions came thick and fast, and Matt dreaded getting back to Seadrift and finding that Sara had gone. He didn't know what he'd tell his daughter if that happened. And, however slight the association was, he knew Rosie would be very disappointed, too.

Would he be disappointed?

That was a question he chose not to ask himself. Yet he knew he was curious about Sara as well. From a professional point of view, he assured himself firmly. As a psychological case, she interested him greatly. But that was all it was, he told himself. He had no interest in her as a woman at all. The days when he'd allowed his hormones to govern his actions were long gone. Any relationships he had were short and rarely sweet. Which suited him.

It was something of a relief to find that the hired Ford was still parked where Sara had left it. If it wouldn't have caused complications that he chose not to get into right now he'd have shifted it inside his own gates. But towing it would require her assistance, and she might just be tempted to try and start it herself.

'Is that her car?' asked Rosie, peering over her shoulder as they drove up the private road to the house. 'What's wrong with it?'

'I've already told you. I don't know,' said Matt, disliking the untruth almost as much as his own behaviour. 'Can you sit still? We're almost there.'

'Where is she?'

Rosie was still full of questions, and Matt expelled a weary breath. 'I expect she's in the sitting room,' he said shortly, hoping Sara hadn't been invading the rest of the house. He didn't think it was likely. She'd seemed quite happy in the spacious sitting room, with its broad windows that overlooked the sweep of the bay.

Rosie had her door open as soon as he stopped the car, jumping down onto the paved forecourt, dragging her canvas bag behind her. Scurrying round the corner of the building, she briefly disappeared from view, but Matt could hear the dogs barking as she reached the back door.

Striding after her, he saw her stop outside the dogs' compound and open the gate. Then, after bending to fuss over the two animals, she turned to enter the house. 'Don't,' yelled Matt, but it was too late. Rosie had already opened the door, and the retrievers bounded boisterously after her.

By the time he reached the kitchen Rosie and the dogs had disappeared, but he could hear them rampaging into the sitting room, barking again. There was shouting, mostly from Rosie, and laughter, which he was amazed to identify as coming from his visitor, and when he arrived at the sitting room doorway he was confronted by a scene he'd never expected. Sara was down on her knees, fussing over the animals, and Rosie was standing watching her with a look of delighted anticipation on her small face.

It was a long time since he'd seen Rosie so animated with someone other than himself, and he felt a twinge of guilt for neglecting her, for making her a hostage to the life he chose to lead. It hadn't been so bad when they'd had Hester. She'd compensated for the extended family Rosie didn't have. But since Hester had retired Rosie had had only his parents to rely on. And, apart from the fact that they lived in Cumbria, they were enjoying their retirement too much for him to inflict a lively seven-year-old on them very often.

But Rosie was evidently enjoying herself now, and he suspected Sara was, too, though she sobered a little and scrambled to her feet when he appeared. He noticed she'd discarded the strappy shoes in favour of going barefoot, and he wondered why he was suddenly struck with the fact of how sexy bare feet could be.

'I'm sorry,' he said, distracting himself. Collecting his wayward thoughts, he indicated the dogs. 'I couldn't stop Rosie from letting them in.'

'That's okay.' Sara brushed her skirt, dispersing a fine cloud of dog hairs into the atmosphere. 'I had to meet them again sometime.'

'Sara, don't you like Hubble and Bubble?' demanded Rosie indignantly, and Matt gave an exasperated sigh. He could do without this.

'Not everyone's as mad about dogs as you are, Rosie,' he retorted, his tone sharper than it might have been because of his own reactions. He forced himself to look briefly in Sara's direction before adding, 'And I don't recall your being given permission to call our guest by her first name. I think you should apologise.'

Rosie flushed at the reproof, but before Matt could feel any remorse Sara intervened. 'I don't mind,' she said, smiling at the little girl. 'What was it you called the dogs? Hubble and Bubble?' And, at Rosie's nod, 'Well, I suppose they introduced us, didn't they?' She held out her hand towards the child. 'I'm very pleased to meet—all of you.'

Rosie was completely won over. Matt could see that. Any concerns she'd voiced on the way home from school were totally dispelled by the warmth of Sara's smile.

Conversely, Matt wasn't sure now that that was what he wanted. It was one thing feeling sorry for the woman, and quite another seeing his daughter responding to her undoubted charm. He knew absolutely nothing about her, he reminded himself irritably. He certainly didn't know why *he'd* invited her to stay.

'I'm pleased to meet you,' Rosie was saying delightedly, casting a triumphant glance up at her father. 'Daddy says you're going to stay with us. I hope you do.'

'Oh—well, it's just for one night,' Sara murmured a little awkwardly. 'It's very kind of your father to invite me.'

She didn't know the half of it, thought Matt, raking long fingers through his hair, but before he could respond Rosie jumped in again. 'But you do like it here, don't you?' she asked. 'Are you on holiday? Or are you looking for a job?'

Now Matt saw it was Sara's turn to look disconcerted. 'I— I haven't decided,' she said at last, a faint flush tingeing the skin of her throat. The unsuitable voile dress exposed a fair amount of her neck and throat, he noticed, and, as if conscious of this, she crossed her arms at her midriff, one hand seeking to protect herself from his eyes. 'This is a very—beautiful place.' She glanced towards the windows, the tip of her tongue touching her parted lips. 'I think you're very lucky to live here.'

Matt found to his annoyance that his eyes were following her tongue's sensual exploration. And he felt impatient with himself for being so immature. For God's sake, he was a grown man, not a schoolboy. What was there about this woman that affected him so?

'That's what Daddy always says,' exclaimed Rosie now, rather wistfully, and Matt wondered if he was depriving his daughter of a social life. Seadrift was remote. There was no getting away from it. But he resented the thought that a stranger should bring it to mind.

'I'm sure he's right,' Sara murmured, no doubt for her own reasons, he thought savagely. He didn't need her endorsement. In fact, he needed nothing from her, he thought irritably. She bent to pat the two retrievers, exposing the dusky hollow of her cleavage. 'You probably couldn't keep these two rascals if you lived in a town.'

'Do you live in a town?' asked Rosie. Then, without pausing, 'Would you like to live at the coast?'

Matt stiffened. 'Rosie!' he said warningly, half afraid he knew what was coming. But he couldn't stop her. It was too late.

''Cos Daddy's looking for someone to come and look after me,' she explained eagerly. 'You wouldn't have to do much. Just take me to school and stuff. You wouldn't really be a nanny,' she ran on, ''cos I'm too old for that. But you could live here—couldn't she, Daddy? And then I wouldn't be always getting in your way when you're working, like you said.'

CHAPTER FOUR

SARA didn't want to feel any sympathy for Matt Seton, but she couldn't help it. She saw the look of anguish that crossed his lean tanned features at the child's careless words. He obviously cared deeply about his daughter, and it hurt him to hear her describe the way she thought he thought about her. She sensed he was fostering all the remorse of a single father who was obliged to employ strangers to care for his child while he earned them both a living.

But she also glimpsed a thread of anger in the gaze he directed towards her, and she wondered if he thought she had engineered Rosie's innocent invitation.

'I—' She strove to find an explanation for not accepting the position that wouldn't offend the little girl. 'It's very kind of you, Rosie—'

'But Miss Victor is heading off tomorrow,' put in the child's father harshly, before Sara could finish, and, despite the fact that she'd been about to say something similar, Sara felt her hackles rise at his callous dismissal. 'Besides,' he went on, rather maliciously, she thought, 'I'm sure our visitor would find our way of life very dull.'

Rosie looked crestfallen now. 'Would you?' she asked, her dark eyes, so like her father's, gazing up at Sara in mute appeal. Sara thought it would have taken a harder heart than hers to resist her, but once again Matt Seton saved her the trouble.

'Of course she would,' he essayed flatly. 'Now—shall we get these animals out of here before they shed any more hair?'

Rosie's lip jutted. 'If you say so.'

'I do say so,' declared her father inflexibly, ushering the two retrievers into the hall. 'If you'll excuse us, Miss Victor?'

It was a perfunctory enquiry at best, and Sara expelled a breath before lifting her shoulders in a conciliatory gesture. 'Is there anything I can do?' she asked, deciding there was no point in pretending that she could go against his wishes, however enthusiastic Rosie might be.

Matt Seton paused in the doorway. 'You're a guest,' he said simply. 'If you'll excuse me, I'll go and see what my housekeeper has left for our evening meal.'

Sara took a couple of steps after him. 'It's early yet,' she protested. Then, with inspiration, 'Don't these dogs need exercising or something? I—Rosie and I could take them for a walk.'

'I don't think so.'

His cold denial came only seconds before Rosie's, 'Oh, why not, Daddy? We often take the dogs out after I get home from school.'

'*We* do,' he said, emphasising the personal pronoun. 'Besides—' he gave Sara another impatient look '—Miss Victor doesn't have any suitable footwear.'

'I don't need shoes on the beach,' she exclaimed, the idea growing on her. She found the prospect of running along the shoreline, paddling in the cool waters of this northerly sea, more and more appealing. She couldn't run away from her troubles. She knew that. But perhaps this was a way to escape from them for a while. 'We wouldn't go far. I promise.'

'I'm sorry.'

He was adamant, and her spirits plummeted. But how could she blame him really? She hadn't exactly behaved responsibly this far.

'You could come with us, Daddy.'

Clearly Rosie wasn't prepared to accept his refusal without an attempt to change his mind, and Sara sensed he was torn by the knowledge that he was on the point of disappointing her once again.

'Rosie,' he began, a little wearily, but she evidently sensed he was weakening.

'Please, Daddy,' she begged, clutching his hand. 'You need the exercise, too. You're always saying so. Come on. It'll be fun.'

Matt looked as if that was the last word he'd have used to

describe the proposed outing, and, judging by the look he cast in her direction, Sara guessed he blamed her entirely.

But this time he wasn't prepared to risk another rift with his daughter. 'Well,' he began slowly, 'perhaps for half an hour—'

He wasn't allowed to finish. Rosie squealed with delight, throwing her arms around his hips and hugging him tightly. Matt's hands were gentle on her shoulders, but over his daughter's head his eyes told Sara a different story. However, she wasn't prepared to deal with his resentment; not now. Glancing out of the window again, she saw that although the sun was still fighting with the clouds a stiff breeze was flattening the grass on the cliff top. She would wear her jacket, she thought, concentrating on the needs of the moment. There was no point in risking a chill, however bleak her future looked at present.

They left the house through the kitchen, but this time they turned away from the front of the house. Instead, they followed a grassy path through a walled plot where wallflowers grew in wild profusion and rambling roses covered a latticed trellis, their scent evocative on the afternoon air.

The dogs bounded ahead, their flowing tails wagging excitedly as they led the way across the cliffs to where a rocky path meandered down to the beach. They were obviously used to this walk, and although they occasionally turned back to ensure that their human companions were following they needed no encouragement.

'This is lovely, isn't it, Daddy?' exclaimed Rosie, who had thrown off her school blazer and was jumping up and down beside the adults. 'Aren't you glad you came now?'

Matt's mouth compressed for a moment, before the smile he reserved for his daughter appeared again. 'I guess,' he said drily. Then, with a disturbing look at Sara's feet, 'Are you sure you want to go down here without shoes?'

Sara had been wondering the same thing, but his sardonic words hardened her resolve. 'I'm sure,' she said, going ahead as if she was used to negotiating rocky paths in her bare feet every day. She started down with a confidence she didn't feel. 'No problem.'

In fact, her feet felt as if they'd encountered every sharp stone on the path by the time she reached the bottom. It was only by a supreme effort of will that she stopped herself from crying out at times. Still, the soft sand was balm to her bruised soles, and she strode off towards the water with real enthusiasm.

After a few moments Rosie joined her, and then, after assuring herself that Sara was all right, she raced off in pursuit of the dogs. With a feeling of inevitability Sara realised she was going to have to be content with Matt Seton's company, and she was hardly surprised when he said drily, 'Not as easy as it looked, was it?'

'I'm not as fragile as you seem to think,' she retorted, catching her breath when she inadvertently trod into a pool of cold water. Then, forcing her mind away from her own problems, she took a deep breath and said, 'I never realised there were still untouched beaches like this in England.' She looked about her. 'It's amazing!'

'Oh, Robinson Crusoe has nothing on us,' remarked Matt, matching her mood. 'Despite the isolation, it's a good place to live.'

'I can believe it.' She sighed, and then caught her breath again as an errant wave drenched her ankles. 'What made you choose it?'

'Its remoteness from London?' he suggested. And then, as if aware that his answer had raised more questions, he went on, 'No, I am from this area originally. I guess that's why it appeals to me.'

'But you used to live in London?'

Her audacity surprised her, and she was quite prepared for him to remain silent. But then he said, 'For my sins. When I left university it was the place to be.' He paused. 'How about you, Miss Victor? Are you a runaway from London, too?'

'You don't run away from places,' she retorted recklessly, and was instantly aware that she'd aroused his interest.

'No, you don't,' he agreed. 'Which begs the question, who are you running away from?' He waited a beat. 'Who—or what?'

That was too close for comfort, and, taking advantage of the fact that he was still wearing his shoes, she trod further into the water. It was cold, and her skin feathered instinctively, but anything was better than fencing words with a man who was proving far too perceptive for her peace of mind.

To her relief, Rosie provided a distraction. Seeing that Sara was in the water, albeit only up to her ankles, she came running back to join them, peeling off her own shoes and socks with obvious intent.

'No, Rosie.' Her father grabbed the little girl before she could scamper into the water. 'It's too cold yet,' he insisted, ignoring her protests. 'Miss Victor was just coming out—weren't you, Miss Victor?'

Sara didn't have a lot of choice. Besides, the water was proving much cooler than she'd anticipated. 'That's right,' she said, avoiding his eyes in favour of the child's. She stepped out onto the damp sand and smiled at Rosie. 'Look, I've got goosebumps.'

Rosie struggled to get over her disappointment. 'Have you?' she asked doubtfully, and Sara squatted down beside her to help her put her shoes on again.

'Everywhere,' she assured the little girl, indicating her wrists and bare legs, and knew the instant when Matt Seton joined his daughter in assessing her appearance.

She was immediately conscious of the fact that the hem of her skirt had fallen back to mid-thigh, exposing her knees and several inches of flesh above them. Matt's eyes seemed to touch her skin and, although she knew it was crazy, she felt that appraisal deep within her bones.

Heat, strong and totally inappropriate, flooded her chilled limbs, and she couldn't wait to get to her feet and put some distance between them. She wasn't attracted to this man, she told herself fiercely. She couldn't be. Not in her present situation. After the way Max had treated her, she'd always believed she'd never want to get involved with any man ever again, and for all she knew Matt Seton might be just like him. After all, he looked bigger and stronger, and therefore more dangerous.

When she tried to get to her feet again, however, her legs gave way under her. Her bruised hip screamed with pain when she tried to straighten it, and she sank down onto her knees in total humiliation.

But, the damp sand had barely had time to coat her skin before hands fastened about her upper arms and helped her up again. Favouring her uninjured leg, she managed to support her weight with an effort, and even managed a light tone as she said, 'Sorry about that. I must have lost my balance.'

Matt let her go with obvious reluctance. 'Are you sure that was all it was?' he asked, and she could tell from his expression that he distrusted her story. 'I think we'd better be getting back,' he added, whistling to the dogs, and she was grateful he was giving her time to pull herself together.

'I fall over all the time,' said Rosie comfortingly, trying to reassure her. 'Do you want to hold my hand?'

'Thanks.' Sara forced a smile, even though she knew her face must look pinched. 'I think I'm all right now.'

And it was true. She could put her weight on her injured hip again now. Not heavily, of course, and not with the freedom with which she'd come down the cliff path. But, as before, it got easier as she moved forward, and she faced the climb with only a small amount of trepidation.

Even so, going up the cliff was much different from coming down. Each step required an effort, and although Rosie surged ahead, Matt insisted on following behind. She didn't truly believe he was doing it because he got some pleasure out of watching her struggles, but she was very relieved when she reached the top.

She longed to sink down onto the grass then, and allow her aching limbs to relax, but she didn't dare. She had to keep going until she got back to the house at least. Even then she had to remain on her guard. Or Matt might get even more suspicious. She already knew he was not an easy man to deceive.

Back at the house, with the dogs corralled in their compound in the yard, Rosie was sent to change her clothes and Sara asked if it would be all right if she went to her room. 'I'd like to have a wash,' she said, picturing the bed where she had rested earlier with real longing. 'If you don't mind.'

Matt regarded her consideringly. 'Why don't you have a bath?' he suggested. 'I expect you're feeling quite stiff.'

Sara sucked in a breath. 'Why do you say that?' she demanded, and he lifted his shoulders in a careless gesture.

'Well, you have had a long drive,' he pointed out mildly, and she dipped her eyes to hide the relief that rose in her face.

'I—I see,' she said, glancing about her for the haversack which she'd left behind when they went out. She managed a slight smile. 'I suppose you're right.'

'Why else would your legs give out on you?' he queried, and she wondered just how innocent his remarks really were.

'I—they didn't give out,' she protested. 'I told you. I lost my balance.'

'I know what you told me,' he returned, taking off the cream sweater he'd pulled on over his black tee shirt when they'd left the house. He smoothed his ruffled hair with long-fingered hands. 'Okay. Have it your own way. But I'd still get in the bath if I were you.'

Sara straightened up. 'I might do that.'

'Be my guest.'

She was aware that he watched her as she left the kitchen. She didn't know what he was thinking, but she knew she hadn't done anything to improve his opinion of her by collapsing on the beach.

It was surprisingly easy to find the room where she'd rested earlier. She could hear Rosie clattering about in her room, which was apparently further along the galleried landing, but Sara went into her own room and closed the door behind her. Then, sinking down onto the side of the bed, she allowed her body to sag with relief. Exhaustion rounded her shoulders and she allowed her wrists to fall loosely between her knees.

Had he believed her? Or did he suspect that there was more to her conduct than a simple stiffness in her spine? No doubt he had a computer. He'd need one for his writing. Was he even now combing the Internet for any story that might match her unconvincing explanation?

She looked for her watch and then remembered that she'd taken it off before lunch. It was broken anyway, so it wouldn't have been any good to her. Besides, she knew it was nearly five o'clock. She'd seen a clock in the kitchen. Almost a whole day had passed since she'd left the apartment. She'd been a widow for almost twenty-four hours. She shivered. Oh, God, what was she going to do?

The effort required in taking a bath wasn't particularly appealing now, but she guessed the hot water might soothe her aches and pains. Somehow she had to get through the next fifteen hours without breaking down. When Matt left to take Rosie to school the following morning she'd ask him to give her a lift into Saviour's Bay. With a bit of luck her car might be repaired by lunchtime, and then she'd be free to move on.

But where?

And what if Matt wouldn't let her go?

But she wouldn't think like that, she told herself severely. He couldn't keep her here by force and, despite what he'd said before, she didn't think he'd report her to the authorities. Not without knowing who she was. He wasn't that kind of man. She didn't know how she knew that, but she did.

The corner bath filled quickly. She found some pine-scented bath gel in a glass cabinet over the sink and added a squeeze of fragrance to the water. Steam rose, warm and scented, into her nostrils, and she felt a twinge of anticipation at the prospect of feeling clean again. One day at a time, Sara, she told herself encouragingly. She had to believe that she'd get through this.

It was hard to hold on to that thought when she took off her clothes, however. With the removal of her dress it was impossible to avoid the many bruises and contusions colouring her pale skin. She looked as if she'd been in a fist fight, she mused bitterly, and of course she had. But there had only ever been one real contender.

Yet Max was dead and she was alive…

The incredible truth couldn't be denied and she sagged weakly against the basin. She hadn't meant for him to die, she insisted painfully. But who was going to believe her now?

For so long she'd accepted that her hands were tied, that there was nothing she could do to change things. Even without the threats Max had made against her mother, she'd known he would never let her go. He'd told her so many times. And she'd believed him. God knew, she'd had every reason to believe his threats before.

So what had happened last night? How had the victim suddenly become the hunted? She'd had no notion that anything different was about to happen. She'd been too busy defending herself to anticipate that help might come from a totally unexpected source.

She swallowed the sickly feeling that surged into her throat at the memory. She saw Max raising his hand towards her, saw herself falling against the corner table on the landing of their duplex apartment. Even now her hip throbbed in memory of the agonising pain that had stunned her at the impact. She remembered rolling herself into a ball, arms curled over her head in mute acceptance of the boot that would surely follow—but it hadn't happened. Instead, Max had lost his balance. He'd tripped, swearing as he'd stumbled over her crumpled body, and, unable to save himself, had fallen headlong down the stairs.

Another wave of nausea gripped her. It had been an accident, she assured herself now, as she'd assured herself then. If she'd rolled against his legs, if she'd caused him to lose his balance, it hadn't been deliberate. If he hadn't hit her, if he hadn't caused her to fall across the head of the stairs, she wouldn't have provided an obstacle. She'd never dreamt that he might trip over her; that he'd break his neck as he fell.

But it had happened. She could hear Max's voice in her ears, hear the frantic cries he'd made as he'd tried desperately to save himself. He hadn't given up without a struggle. She'd heard the scratching of his fingernails against the banister, the creaking of the wood beneath his weight. And then the awful thudding sound as his body pitched forward, no longer aggressive, out of his control.

An accident.

She sucked in a breath. That was what it had been. When she'd scurried down the stairs to where he was lying in the foyer of the apartment she'd had no other thought in her mind than to assure him she was sorry, so sorry, for what had happened.

But he'd been lying still, so very still, and she'd guessed at once that it was hopeless. She'd attempted to revive him. She'd even put her trembling mouth over his cold one and tried to breathe air into his lungs. He hadn't responded. That was when she'd called the emergency services. That was when she'd known she had to get away.

She'd realised how it would look to a stranger. Realised that she was virtually admitting her guilt. But it was no good. No one was going to believe it was just an accident. Men like Max, men who were fit and strong, didn't just fall down a flight of stairs without provocation. And if they arrested her, if they examined her and saw what he'd had done to her. Well, she was afraid her battered body would prove her guilt.

She expelled the breath she had hardly been aware she was holding, and then almost jumped out of her skin when someone knocked on the bathroom door.

Immediately she sprang to brace a shoulder against the panels, terrified that whoever it was out there was going to open the door and see her naked flesh. She suspected that Matt Seton was still curious about her. And if he glimpsed—

But she stifled the thought, saying instead, 'What do you want?' in a voice that sounded annoyingly tremulous even to her.

'You okay?'

It was Matt, and unreasonable irritation gripped her. 'Why shouldn't I be?'

'No reason, I guess. Except that you've been in there for over half an hour and I haven't heard a sound since the water stopped running,' he replied mildly. 'I wondered if you'd fallen asleep? That can be dangerous, you know.'

She gulped. 'Are you spying on me?'

'Hardly.' His tone had hardened, and she couldn't honestly blame him. He'd been concerned, that was all. Something she wasn't used to. 'Anyway,' he went on, 'supper will be ready in about an hour, so don't hurry. You've got plenty of time.'

Sara pressed her hot cheek against the wood. 'Thanks.'

'No sweat.' The harshness had left his voice. 'Just don't drown yourself, okay?'

Her lips quivered. 'Okay.'

'Good.'

She heard him leaving the bedroom, heard the outer door slam behind him, and breathed a little more easily again. But she couldn't help the frisson of pleasure she felt at the knowledge that he'd been worried about her. It was so long since anyone had cared about her in that way. Hugo had treated her with affection, it was true, but she'd always known that in any real confrontation he would always take Max's side. He was his brother, after all, and without Max's support his acting career would very likely have slid back into oblivion where it had begun.

But she had to stop thinking about Max, she thought fiercely, checking that the door was securely closed before crossing the room again and easing herself into the bath. There was no lock on the door, but she found she trusted Matt Seton not to come in without an invitation. As for Rosie: she seemed like the kind of little girl who would follow her father's example. Abandoning herself to anything but the reassuring embrace of the water, Sara sat down.

She winced as its heat probed the tender places of the hip and thigh she'd injured when she fell. Even sitting on the hard enamel was painful at first, but after a few minutes the warmth acted as an analgesic and she was able to relax. She leaned back against the side of the bath and closed her eyes.

Goodness, that felt good. She couldn't remember the last time she'd had a bath. These days taking a shower was so much quicker and easier. Besides, she avoided spending too much time in the bathroom. Without her clothes she felt that much more vulnerable, and it wasn't above Max to take advantage of it. She'd dreaded those occasions when he'd stepped into the shower with her and—

Her eyes jerked open. She must stop reliving the past. Eventually what had happened was going to catch up with her, but for now she had to think of something else. She had to think about herself, think of what she was going to do tomorrow. The future stretched ahead of her, uncharted. And, however shameful the admission, she was glad Max was never going to be able to hurt her again.

By the time she got out of the bath she was feeling infinitely more human. She dried herself on one of the large towels from the rack and then, after a moment's hesitation, wrapped herself in the cream towelling bathrobe she found hanging on the back of the door. She wondered if Matt would mind if she wore the robe for a couple of hours. Then she could wash and dry her bra and panties. The expensive scraps of silk and lace that Max had bought for her would need no artificial drying, and she'd feel infinitely fresher wearing clean underwear tomorrow.

When she opened the door into the bedroom, however, she discovered that, as well as checking on her well-being, Matt had also left a pile of clothes on the bed. Sara's eyes widened in amazement when she discovered a cellophane-wrapped package of bikini briefs beneath what were obviously his chambray shirt and sweat pants. The shirt and sweat pants were freshly laundered, but it was obvious that the package containing the briefs hadn't been opened. Where had they come from? she wondered. He hadn't mentioned a girlfriend. But a man like him was bound to have women friends. Hadn't he been speaking to one of them—Emma—earlier on?

Still, the idea that he might have contacted one of his girlfriends for help didn't sit well with her, and she caught her lower lip between her teeth as she turned the packet over in her hands. And discovered that the label indicated that they were suitable for a nine- to ten-year-old!

Rosie! she thought incredulously, a gulp of laughter escaping her. They had obviously been bought for Rosie, but just as obviously they were too big for her. Ripping open the cellophane, Sara pulled them out and examined them more closely. Made of white cotton, they looked plain and practical, and, although they'd probably be a tight fit, she thought they'd do very well.

A feeling of gratitude filled her, and with it a sense of shame at her own presumption. Matt was trying to help her; that was obvious. She had to stop believing that all men were like Max.

They weren't. He had been the exception. Was it evil to be glad he was finally out of her life?

The briefs were barely decent, but Sara didn't care. With Matt's sweat pants bulking around her thighs, and the ends of his shirt tied at her waist, she looked anything but provocative. He'd also left a pair of sports socks, which she found worked equally well as slippers. After she'd rinsed out her own bra and panties, and hung them on the radiator in the bathroom to dry, all that was left for her to do was brush out her hair and plait it again. She was sitting at the dressing table, securing it with an elasticated band, when there was another knock at her door.

She stiffened. She couldn't help it. Old habits die hard, she thought, taking a deep breath and calling, 'Who is it?'

'It's me. Rosie.' The little girl needed no further bidding before opening the door and putting her head round it. 'Can I come in?'

Sara found herself smiling. 'It looks as if you are in,' she remarked mildly. 'But, yes. Come in. What can I do for you?'

Rosie entered the room, revealing that she'd changed out of her school clothes into cut-off jeans and a pink tee shirt. She had evidently washed her face, too, though Sara could see the telltale smears of what appeared to be chocolate around her mouth. But she looked sweet and wholesome, and Sara wanted to hug her.

'Daddy says supper will be ready in ten minutes,' she declared, regarding her father's guest with interest. 'Are those Daddy's clothes?'

'Yes.' Sara nodded. 'He was kind enough to lend them to me.' She got up from the stool. 'How do I look?'

'We—ll.' Rosie was thoughtful. 'They look a bit big,' she confessed at last. Then, glancing about her, 'Don't you have any clothes of your own?'

'Not here,' replied Sara, determinedly suppressing thoughts of where the rest of her clothes were. 'Oh, and your father gave me these.' She held up the packet that had contained the bikini briefs. 'I hope you don't mind.'

'Oh, no!' Rosie giggled. 'Daddy's Aunt Margaret sent them

last Christmas. She's ever so old, and Daddy says her eyes aren't as good as they used to be.'

'Ah.' Sara screwed the packet into a ball, preparatory to taking it downstairs to throw away. 'Well, I'm very grateful for that.'

'Do they really fit you?' asked Rosie, staring at her critically, as if trying to imagine how they might look on an adult, and Sara grimaced.

'Just about,' she answered, a mischievous grin tugging at her lips. 'Shall we go down?'

Rosie hesitated. 'Have you changed your mind? About staying, I mean? I wish you would.'

Sara sighed. 'Rosie—'

''Cos Daddy really needs someone. We slept in this morning, and I was nearly late for school.'

Sara shook her head. 'I don't think we should be having this conversation, Rosie.'

'Why not?'

'Because—because, like your Daddy said, I've got to leave tomorrow.'

Rosie's lips pursed. 'Don't you like it here, either?'

'Of course I do.' Sara wished she didn't have to lie to the child. 'I think you're very lucky to live so close to the sea.'

'Most people don't.'

'Well, I do.'

'Then—'

'I think we should go down for supper,' Sara insisted firmly. She pulled a face at her reflection, knowing the little girl could see her. 'I just hope your father isn't expecting any visitors tonight.'

CHAPTER FIVE

MATT came awake slowly, staring up at the ceiling that was striped with bars of sunlight. He'd left the window open the night before, he remembered, and the slats of the blind were moving in the breeze.

He often left his window open. He liked to come awake to the muted roar of the sea. The constant movement of the tides gave him a feeling of constancy, a sense of knowing that in this world not everything was subject to change.

So why did he have such a feeling of unease this morning? he wondered, pushing the sheet back to his waist and running an exploratory hand over the rough pelt of hair that angled down to his navel and beyond. And then he remembered his uninvited visitor. Sara Victor, if that really was her name. And why should he care, anyway? She was leaving this morning. When he got back from taking Rosie to school he'd pretend to check her car and miraculously find that it was working. Then she'd have no excuse to hang about any longer, and he could get back to doing the job he loved.

Only it wasn't quite that simple. Rosie had taken an instant liking to her, which was unusual in itself. Since Hester had retired the little girl had been introduced to many of the would-be nannies who had turned up at his door, and she hadn't been impressed with any of them. Granted, most of the younger ones hadn't wanted to live in the area, but even those who had had left a lot to be desired so far as Rosie was concerned.

He'd agreed with her for the most part. He didn't want Rosie's life controlled by either a bimbo or a martinet. And, although he'd made it clear that he wasn't interested in any attachment, he'd always been aware of the dangers inherent in having a younger woman living in his house.

And now Rosie had formed an attachment of her own.

He'd seen it happening, of course. All last evening he'd been forced to watch his daughter falling more and more deeply under Sara's unconscious spell. And it was unconscious. He knew that. Sara hadn't set out to entrance the little girl; she just couldn't help doing so.

She had the knack of drawing Rosie out of herself. Without talking down to her, she was able to put herself on the child's level, and Rosie had responded in kind. Matt hadn't been aware that his daughter was missing anything until he'd heard her discussing her dolls' outfits with Sara. What did he know of women's fashions, or of the most attractive shades of lipstick and nail varnish? He hadn't even known Rosie knew about such things until she'd produced a bottle of some glittery substance, which had apparently come as a free gift with one of the pre-teen magazines he'd bought for her, and proceeded to paint Sara's nails with it.

When he'd protested that Miss Victor couldn't possibly want her nails painted that particular shade of pink, Sara had insisted she didn't mind.

'It's okay,' she'd assured him lightly. 'It washes off.' Then she'd given a wry smile. 'At least I hope it does.' She'd held up her hand and wiggled her fingers. 'Do you like it?'

Matt didn't remember what he'd said. Whatever it was, it had made no lasting impression on him. What he did remember was that she disturbed him; that he'd been far too aware of her as a woman ever since she'd appeared downstairs wearing his old chambray shirt and sweats.

When he'd left the clothes on her bed he'd never dreamt that he'd have such a powerful reaction to her wearing them. But the knowledge that she'd obviously not been wearing a bra had aroused the most unsettling images in his head. He'd found himself wondering whether she'd bothered to put on the briefs he'd found in Rosie's drawer. Or had they been too small for her? The possibility that she might be naked beneath the baggy trousers was all he'd needed to fuel his imagination.

He reluctantly recalled how he'd felt when Rosie had crept into his room after he'd retired, begging him to ask Sara to stay. 'Just for a few days, Daddy,' she'd entreated him appealingly, and, although Matt had told her no, he couldn't help the treacherous thought that employing Sara could be beneficial to both of them.

But that wasn't an option. Rolling onto his stomach, Matt was aware that his morning erection hadn't subsided. Hard and insistent, it throbbed against his stomach, and he was irritably aware that it was thinking about his house guest that had caused it. It was all too easy to imagine how delightful it would have been to strip the sweat pants from her and sate his burning flesh between her thighs. He could almost feel those long slim legs wrapped around his waist, her firm breasts crushed against his chest. When he brought them both to a shuddering climax she'd sob her gratitude in his ear, whispering how much she'd wanted him, how amazing their lovemaking had been...

'Are you awake, Daddy?'

The stage whisper sent Matt's senses reeling. And aroused an immediate feeling of self-disgust. Dammit, what was wrong with him? he asked himself irritably. What on earth was there about Sara Victor that aroused the kind of fantasies he hadn't had since he was a teenager? It wasn't as if she was incredibly beautiful. She was good-looking, yeah, but she was no super-model. Nor did she behave in a way designed to provoke such a reaction. If he was feeling in need of a woman it was his fault, not hers. He needed to get laid, and quick. Before he was tempted to do something they would all regret.

But right now Rosie took precedence, and, rolling onto his side to face her, he contrived a smile. 'Hey, sweetheart,' he said, with what he thought was admirable self-restraint. 'What are you doing up so early?'

Rosie was hovering by the door. In cropped Winnie the Pooh pyjamas, her cheeks pink, her hair tousled, she looked adorable, and Matt thought again how lucky he was to have her. 'Can I come in?' she asked, glancing over her shoulder half apprehensively. 'I want to talk to you.'

Matt compressed his lips. 'That sounds ominous,' he remarked drily, guessing the topic. 'Why do I get the feeling that I'm not going to like what you have to say?'

'Oh, Daddy!' Rosie took his response as an invitation to join him and came to climb onto the bottom of the bed. Then, realising she'd left the door open, she scrambled down again and went to close it. After she'd resumed her position against the footboard, she declared urgently, 'It's about Sara.'

Matt had assumed as much, but he didn't let on. Instead, he pushed himself up against his pillows and regarded his daughter enquiringly. 'Don't you mean Miss Victor?'

'She said I could call her Sara,' protested Rosie at once. 'Last night. When she came to say goodnight. She said that calling her Miss Victor made her feel as if she was back in school again.' She paused. 'Did you know she used to be a school-teacher, Daddy?'

Matt blew out a breath. So she'd told Rosie she used to teach, had she? He would like to think it had just been a casual admission, but he couldn't help wondering if she'd said it deliberately. To persuade him that she hadn't been lying about that, at least. Or to get the child to speak to him on her behalf.

'I believe she said something about it,' he admitted now. 'So—is that all you wanted to tell me?'

'Hardly,' said Rosie indignantly. 'I just wondered if you knew, that's all.'

'Well, I do.' Matt arched his dark brows. 'What else is new?'

'Daddy!' Rosie looked red-faced now. 'Give me a chance! I can't think of everything all at once.'

'Okay.' Matt contained his amusement. 'It must be something serious to get you out of bed before seven o'clock.'

'Oh, Daddy.' Rosie gazed at him impatiently. 'You know what I'm going to say.' She paused. 'Why can't you ask Sara to stay?'

Matt sighed. 'We talked about this last night, Rosie.'

'But you need a nanny. You said so yourself. Or I mean I do. Why can't it be Sara?'

'Rosie—'

'*Please!*'

'Look,' he said, trying to reason with her. 'We know nothing about Sara. We don't even know where she came from.'

'Then ask her,' said Rosie practically. 'I'm sure she'd tell you if you did. She told me I was very lucky to live by the seaside. She said that when she was just a little girl she had to live in the town.'

'Did she now?' Matt absorbed this information, wondering how true it was. He hesitated, loath to pump the child, but compelled to do so anyway, 'Did she tell you anything else?'

'Just that she never had a dog when she was little,' said Rosie thoughtfully. 'I'll ask her where she came from, if you like.'

'No.' Matt spoke sharply and the little girl's jaw quivered in response.

'All right,' she said, getting down from the bed. 'I won't say anything. But I think you're really—really mean.'

'Ah, Rosie—' Matt rolled to the side of the bed and grabbed his daughter's arm before she could get away. 'Honey, try to understand. You're very precious. How can I leave you with someone I hardly know?'

'You didn't know any of the other girls who came for the job,' replied Rosie tremulously, and Matt groaned.

'Baby, they came from an agency.'

'So?'

'So—' He pulled her towards the bed and swung his feet to the floor. Then, placing a hand on either side of her small waist, he gave her a gentle shake. 'Try to understand, sweetheart. I don't like disappointing you, but—'

'Then don't,' pleaded Rosie, seizing the opportunity. 'Give Sara a chance, please! I promise I'll be good. I won't play her up like I used to with Hester.'

'It's not you I'm worried about,' muttered Matt, but he was hesitating. His common sense was telling him to stick to his guns, to ignore the emotional demands his daughter was making on him, but his instincts were telling him something else.

All right, he knew nothing about Sara, but he'd bet his last cent that, whatever she was running away from, she was not a bad person. There was something innately honest about her, an integrity that was at odds with all he knew and suspected about her.

'Daddy…'

Rosie's wheedling voice made his decision for him. 'All

right,' he said, praying he wouldn't have cause to regret the impulse. 'We'll give her a few days' trial—'

'Hurray!' Rosie was excited.

'—but I'm making no promises beyond the weekend, right?'

'All right.' Rosie clasped her hands together. 'Can I go and ask her? Can I? Can I? I'm sure when she knows that you want her to stay she'll change her mind—'

'Hold on.' Matt held on to the little girl when she would have darted towards the door. 'What do you mean, you're sure she'll change her mind? What have you been saying to her, Rosie? Come on. I want to know.'

Rosie heaved a heavy sigh. 'Nothing much,' she mumbled, the sulkiness returning to her expression. 'I just said I wished she could stay, that's all.' She gave a jerky shrug. 'If you want to know, she said she couldn't.' And then, as her father gave her a stunned look, she added, 'But I know she wanted to, Daddy. Only she thought you didn't want her here.'

Matt stared. 'Did she say that?'

'No.' Rosie spoke crossly. 'I've told you what she said.'

'Are you sure?'

'Yes.' Rosie was indignant. 'Don't you believe me?'

Matt pulled a wry face. 'Do I have a choice?'

'So?' Rosie pulled her lower lip between her teeth. 'Can I go and ask her?'

Matt glanced at the clock on the cabinet beside the bed. 'Not yet,' he said heavily, already regretting his generosity. 'It's barely seven o'clock. We'll discuss it some more at breakfast.'

He let the little girl go, but now Rosie hesitated. 'You won't put her off, will you, Daddy?' she persisted. 'I mean, you will let her know that we—that we'd *both* like her to stay?'

Matt stifled an oath. 'Don't push your luck, Rosie,' he said, without making any promises. 'Go get your wash, and clean your teeth. As I say, we'll talk about this later. If that's not good enough for you we'd better forget the whole thing.'

Rosie's chin wobbled again, but she managed to control it. 'All right, Daddy,' she said huskily, and with a tearful smile she made good her escape before he changed his mind again.

*   *   *

Mrs Webb had arrived by the time Matt came downstairs.

The housekeeper, who was in her middle fifties, had worked at Seadrift for as long as Matt had owned the house, and there was usually an easy familiarity between them that wasn't much in evidence this morning.

However, there was a welcome pot of coffee simmering on the hob and, after giving her his usual greeting, Matt went to help himself to a cup. He hoped the caffeine would kick-start his brain, which seemed to have blanked during his conversation with Rosie. Why, in God's name, had he given in to her? What had possessed him to agree to asking Sara to stay?

'I understand you've got a new nanny,' said Mrs Webb suddenly, turning from the fridge and confronting him with accusing eyes. 'You didn't tell me you were interviewing anyone yesterday.'

Matt expelled a disbelieving breath. 'Who told you we had a new nanny?' he demanded, but he already knew. Gloria Armstrong would have lost no time in ringing his housekeeper to hear all the lurid details. He only hoped Mrs Webb hadn't said anything to expose the lie.

He was wrong, however. 'Rosie, actually,' she replied huffily, peeling the plastic wrap from a packet of bacon. 'She couldn't wait to tell me the woman had stayed the night.'

Matt gave an inward groan. 'Well—it's not settled yet,' he said lamely, silently berating his daughter for her big mouth. 'And—and the reason I didn't tell you I was interviewing anyone yesterday was because I didn't have any plans to do so.'

'Oh, right.' Mrs Webb regarded him sceptically. 'So she just turned up out of the blue?' She grimaced. 'How convenient.'

Matt's patience grew taut. 'Actually, it wasn't convenient at all,' he declared tersely. 'And, as I say, I'm not absolutely sure I'm going to employ her.'

'So where did she come from? The agency?'

'No.' Matt blew out a breath. 'As a matter of fact, her car broke down at the bottom of the road. Didn't you see it as you came by?'

Mrs Webb looked surprised. 'So that's *her* car. I assumed

some kids had stolen it and abandoned it when it ran out of petrol.'

'No.' But Matt was determined not to be drawn into telling the housekeeper the whole story. Not yet, anyway. 'She—she came to the house, wanting to use the phone, and when she discovered I was looking for a nanny she offered herself for the job.' He paused, and then went on doggedly, 'She used to be a primary school teacher.'

'Really?'

'Yes, really.' Matt wondered why it sounded so much more convincing the second time around. 'Now, where is Rosie? I want to speak to her.'

'Oh, I think she went upstairs again,' said Mrs Webb, obviously mollified by his explanation. 'She said something about waking—Sara, is it?'

Dammit! Matt suppressed another oath. What in hell's name did Rosie think she was up to? He'd told her he'd discuss Sara's employment at breakfast. He just hoped she hadn't jumped the gun.

Snatching up the morning newspaper that Mrs Webb always brought for him, he stalked out of the kitchen and into the library. Seating himself in the hide-covered chair beside the desk which he used for his research, he took another long swig of his coffee and then turned to stare broodingly out of the windows.

Beyond the cliffs, the sun had already spread its bounty across the dark blue waters of the bay. Whereas the day before it had been cloudy, this morning the sky was high and clear. Seagulls soared effortlessly on the thermals, their haunting cries mingling with the muted roar of the surf. In an ideal world he shouldn't have a care in the world, beyond the problems facing the protagonist in his current manuscript. Indeed, after taking Rosie to school he'd intended to spend the whole day finalising the book's denouement. Instead he had to deal with a situation that he very much suspected was far more complex than his uninvited guest was letting on.

Scowling, he flipped open the newspaper that he'd dropped on the desk. The latest images from a middle-eastern war he felt he had no part of dominated the front page. There'd been a derailment in southeast London, a well-known politician had been discovered in compromising circumstances, and someone who'd won the lottery six months ago was now broke again.

So what's new? thought Matt cynically, swallowing another mouthful of coffee. Why did journalists feel the need to fill their columns with negative news items? he wondered. Was it because stories about other people's problems, particularly the rich and famous, made the average reader feel better about their own lives?

Probably, he decided, flicking the pages. There was nothing like learning about someone else's misfortunes to make some people feel good.

He heard Rosie come scampering down the stairs and remembered he had his own problems to deal with. He'd half risen from his chair to go after her when a small picture towards the bottom of page four caught his eye. Sinking back into his seat, he stared at it disbelievingly. It was a picture of Sara, he saw incredulously. Only her name wasn't Sara; it was Victoria. Victoria Bradbury, actually. The wife of the entrepreneur Max Bradbury, and she was missing.

Victoria, he thought, acknowledging the connotation. Miss *Victor* hadn't wanted to stray too far from the truth. But no wonder she didn't want to tell him who she was. Although Matt had only heard Max Bradbury's name in passing, she didn't know that.

He read the article through, his brows drawing together as he assessed its content. According to the writer, Victoria Bradbury had disappeared two nights ago, and both her husband and her mother were frantic with worry. Mr Bradbury had apparently had a fall the same evening, which was why his wife's disappearance hadn't been noted until the following morning.

Luckily Mr Bradbury had been able to crawl to a phone and summon assistance before losing consciousness. His brother, the actor Hugo Bradbury, had said it was most unlike Victoria to leave the apartment without informing her husband where she was going. Fears were being expressed that she might have been kidnapped. Mr Bradbury had been detained in hospital overnight for tests, but had discharged himself the following morning to conduct the search for his wife personally. Max Bradbury was an extremely wealthy man and he intended to use all means at his disposal to find her.

The article ended with an appeal that anyone who might have seen Mrs Bradbury or knew of her whereabouts should contact the police and a London number was supplied.

Matt blew out a breath, slumping back in his chair and staring incredulously out of the window. Then, snatching up the newspaper again, he examined Sara's—*Victoria's*—picture more closely. It had to be her. He would swear it.

It was a more sophisticated Victoria than he was used to seeing, of course. For one thing she wasn't wearing her hair in a plait. Instead, it was coiled into a knot on top of her head. The carefully coaxed strands that framed her face and curved so confidingly beneath her jawline were familiar, and the wide-spaced eyes, the high cheekbones, the generous, yet curiously vulnerable mouth were unmistakable. Unless she had an identical twin, he was looking at a picture of the woman who had spent last night in his spare room. Dammit, what was she playing at?

Anger gripped him. It infuriated him that he'd been taken in by her air of vulnerability. Hell, he'd felt sorry for her. He hadn't believed her story, of course, and that was one thing in his favour, but he had felt a sense of responsibility for her which he realised now had been totally misplaced. She must have been laughing at him all along.

Max Bradbury's wife. He scowled. He wondered how long they'd been married. To his knowledge Bradbury was at least fifty, which must make him more than twenty years older than his wife. So what had gone wrong? Had she become bored with the old man? Hadn't he been giving her enough attention? Was this escapade intended to remind him how lucky he was to have such a young and attractive wife?

And, if so, what was the idea of asking for a job? Of pretending that she'd once been a primary school teacher. For God's sake, a man like Max Bradbury wouldn't have married a schoolteacher. No, she had to have been some kind of party girl or socialite. How else could she have met a man like him?

'Breakfast's ready, Daddy.'

Rosie's voice calling his name alerted him to the fact that it wasn't only his feelings Victoria Bradbury had insulted. It was his daughter's, too, and he dreaded having to tell the little girl that 'Sara' wouldn't be staying.

But he couldn't do that now. Before he made any decisions he might later regret he was going to have a frank discussion with his house guest and find out where the hell she got off, making a fool of him and his daughter. And after that he was going to ring the number they'd given in the newspaper. It would give him great satisfaction to send Victoria Bradbury back where she belonged.

Or would it?

His scowl deepened, and he quickly folded the newspaper and stuffed it into one of the drawers of the desk just as Rosie appeared in the doorway.

'Are you coming, Daddy?' she exclaimed, though there was a tentative note in her voice, and he remembered what he'd been going to do before the article in the newspaper had distracted him. 'Mrs Webb says breakfast is ready.'

'Is—Sara—up?' he asked, guessing his daughter would assume he was angry with her for disobeying him, and she gave a nervous shrug.

'She's in the dining room,' she said. And then added quickly, 'I haven't told her anything about what we were talking about, Daddy. Honestly. I just wanted to—to—'

'To see if she'd slept all right?' suggested Matt, helping her out, and Rosie gave a relieved nod.

'That's right,' she said. 'Are you coming?'

'I'm coming.' Matt paused only long enough to swallow the last dregs of coffee in his mug. 'You lead the way.'

Mrs Webb had laid the table in the dining room and was fussing about with a jug of freshly squeezed orange juice and a rack of toast. Matt guessed she was curious about their guest, too, and she was asking her what had gone wrong with her car when he entered the room.

Although she was answering the housekeeper's question at the time, Matt noticed the way Sara-Victoria's eyes darted to his face when he appeared. If he wasn't mistaken, there was a definite trace of trepidation in her gaze, and he wondered if she'd realised that her disappearance might have warranted media attention.

'Good morning,' he said, deliberately adopting an upbeat tone, and he saw the relieved hint of colour that entered her pale cheeks at his words.

She was wearing her own clothes again this morning, and Matt's eyes were irresistibly drawn to the taut breasts pushing at the semi-transparent fabric of her dress. Its shades of blue and green matched the luminescence of her eyes, which he was aware were watching him with wary intensity. Slim arms were wrapped protectively about her midriff, and he wondered if she realised what a giveaway that was.

'Um—good morning,' she responded at last, and Matt despised the sudden surge of blood that her husky voice caused to rush to his groin. All of a sudden he was remembering the sexual fantasies he'd been having about her earlier, and even the fact that he now knew she was another man's wife didn't make them any the easier to dismiss.

'Sit here, Daddy.'

Rosie pulled him to the seat beside hers, and Matt strove to act naturally. Hell, he thought, he was behaving as if he'd never been with a woman before. What was there about Victoria Bradbury that struck such a chord in his subconscious? What was there about her wary face that inspired thoughts of naked bodies and sweat-soaked sheets?

'Did you sleep well?' he asked at length, realising that, however much he might want to, he couldn't broach the subject of her identity while Rosie and Mrs Webb were present. In fact, he wouldn't be able to speak to her at all until Rosie had been delivered to school, and that might prove something of a problem. After all, he'd promised his daughter to discuss the subject of Sara's employment at breakfast.

'Very well,' she replied politely, evidently taking her cue from him, though he doubted she was being entirely honest.

Although she'd done her best to disguise them, there were still dark rings around her eyes, and, knowing what he knew now, he wasn't really surprised. 'It's so peaceful here.'

'Sara likes the seaside, Daddy,' put in Rosie eagerly, evidently hoping to prompt him into saying something positive, but it was Mrs Webb who spoke next.

'You're not from around here, are you, Miss Victor?' she observed, setting a bowl of cornflakes in front of Rosie. 'If I'm not mistaken, that's a southern accent.'

Matt saw the way the younger woman stiffened at these words, but she managed to produce a tight smile. 'I—yes. You're right. I'm from London,' she admitted, with obvious reluctance. Then, changing the subject, 'Just toast for me, please.'

'Are you sure?'

Mrs Webb was persistent and, taking pity on his guest, Matt intervened. 'I think we're all set here,' he said, regarding his own plate of bacon and eggs without enthusiasm. 'If we need anything else I'll come and find you. Okay?'

'Well—if you say so.' Mrs Webb wasn't giving up without a struggle. 'Couldn't I tempt you with an omelette, Miss Victor?'

Matt felt Sara's eyes dart to his again, and he guessed she was remembering the lunch he had made her the previous day. 'Toast is fine,' she insisted, and the housekeeper had to accept defeat.

'I'll leave you, then,' she said, giving Matt a speaking look. 'Remember, Rosie's got to leave for school in less than twenty minutes.'

'I haven't forgotten,' said Matt drily. 'Thank you.'

Mrs Webb pursed her lips and left the room, and as soon as the door had banged behind her Rosie made a face. 'She's cross because Daddy didn't ask her to sit with us and have her coffee,' she confided, with a giggle. 'We usually have breakfast in the kitchen, you see.'

'Oh.'

Sara looked to Matt for confirmation and he sighed. 'She does like to share all the village gossip,' he agreed, wishing

Rosie wasn't quite so candid. He pushed the toast rack towards Sara. 'Help yourself.'

'Thanks.'

She took a slice of toast and spread it thinly with butter, but once again Matt noticed that she barely touched it. At this rate she'd be just skin and bone in no time, he mused unwillingly. But it wasn't his concern. If she'd lost her appetite, it was doubtless because she was terrified he was going to find out what a liar she was. But why was she lying? Why had she run away? What the hell was she playing at?

'You don't have to leave today, do you, Sara?' Rosie asked now, nudging her father's ankle with her foot. And, although he gave her a warning look, she went on bravely, 'Sara could stay—' she faltered '—stay until tomorrow, couldn't she?'

'I don't think so,' Sara began, and although Matt was tempted to let her leave and be done with it, he saw his daughter's face and relented.

'Yes, stay,' he said flatly, deciding that she deserved the chance to explain why she'd been lying. And this way he could ensure that she'd still be here when he got back from taking Rosie to school. 'At least until tomorrow.'

He could see her indecision. She was probably weighing the advantages of staying here, where she believed no one knew who she was, against moving on and risking inevitable exposure. He was also aware that his own feelings were just as ambivalent. Dammit, he didn't owe her a thing, he told himself savagely. Yet he couldn't deny he felt sorry for her.

And how sensible was that?

CHAPTER SIX

SARA went back to her room after Matt had left to take Rosie
to school. She wanted to avoid giving Mrs Webb the chance to
ask any more questions. She was unpleasantly surprised to find
that the bed she'd slept in had already been made.

Which meant the housekeeper must have accomplished this
task while they were downstairs having breakfast. She didn't
for one minute think that Matt would have made her bed, and
she wondered uneasily what the woman had thought of the fact
that she didn't have any luggage.

For she had no doubt that Mrs Webb would have noticed.
She might not have actually interfered with any of her belongings, but in the course of her work she was bound to have
opened the bathroom door and seen that there was no toothbrush on the shelf.

Closing the door behind her, Sara leaned heavily back against
the panels. Why had she agreed to stay on for another day?
Why, when she'd realised what a gossip Mrs Webb was, hadn't
she made her excuses and left? Because her car was still not
fixed, she reminded herself impatiently. Perhaps she should contact the rental agency, which was a countrywide operation after
all, and ask them to supply her with a new car?

But, no. That would be foolish, she realised at once. At the
moment all anyone knew was that she'd left the apartment.
She'd deliberately not taken her own car because registration
plates were so easy to trace. In time they might get around to
checking with the rental agencies, but by then she intended to
have abandoned the car in favour of some other form of transport.

The trouble was, she needed money. She hadn't thought of
that when she'd left London, and although she'd used her credit
card to hire the car she hadn't considered using a cash machine
until she'd been forced to stop for petrol. Then she'd realised

that to do so would alert the authorities to her current where-abouts and she'd used most of her cash for the fill-up.

Working for Matt Seton would have solved all her problems, she thought regretfully. But she should have known that any legitimate employer would want the kind of personal details that she couldn't supply. Not to mention references, she remembered wearily. And who could blame him for that?

She knew the most sensible thing would be to leave now, before she said or did something to betray herself. Before she got in too deep, she acknowledged tensely. Last night there'd been times when she'd almost forgotten the events that had brought her here, when she'd begun to relax and enjoy herself. Did that make her a bad person? she wondered. Was the fact that for the first time in years she'd been able to be herself without fear of retribution a cause for self-disgust?

Max would have thought so. Max would have been incensed at her behaviour. He didn't like children and he'd have accused her of using Rosie to get to Matt. He'd have said that allowing the little girl to paint her nails had just been a way of attracting Matt's attention. Max had been insanely jealous, as she knew to her cost, and he'd have turned an innocent game into some-thing ugly.

Yet had it been so innocent? she fretted uneasily. Perhaps she was the provocative little tease that Max had always accused her of being. It was certainly true that she'd been acutely aware of Matt Seton ever since he'd emerged from his Range Rover the day before. In spite of her apprehension she'd recognised him at once for what he was: a disturbingly attractive man who she had soon realised was nothing like Max.

Thank God!

She didn't know how she had been so sure of that. It wasn't as if she was a terrifically good judge of character. She'd mar-ried Max Bradbury, hadn't she? Her lips twisted. She'd thought he was a good man. Because he was so much older than she was, she'd trusted him. She'd actually believed that his promise to take her away from what he'd convinced her was a boring existence had been inspired by love and not by an unnatural desire for possession. Instead, he'd turned her life into a nightmare, and even now he was still controlling her from the grave.

She shuddered. What was she doing, thinking about Matt Seton when it was because of her that her husband was lying cold on some mortuary slab? She could imagine how Matt would feel about her when he found out who she really was. However reluctant he'd been to offer her his hospitality up to this point would be as nothing compared to his revulsion when he discovered the truth. She was a murderess—well, she'd be convicted of manslaughter at the very least, she amended. He wouldn't want someone like her associating with his daughter.

And as for anything else... She gave a bitter smile. There were no men in a women's prison.

She moved away from the door, wincing as once again her hip reminded her of its presence. If only her car was operational, she thought fiercely. She really believed she might have made her getaway while Matt was out. It wasn't fair to involve him in her troubles. And if the police ever discovered that he'd allowed her to stay here he might be charged with harbouring a wanted criminal.

But he didn't know who she was, she assured herself, disliking that word 'criminal' again. Although she guessed it was only a matter of time before he found out. Max's death was bound to make news eventually. And, although she hadn't seen a television since she'd arrived, he was bound to have a set somewhere.

She walked restlessly to the windows. It was such a beautiful morning, she thought. She longed to get out of the house and escape her anxieties in the simple delight of feeling the wind in her hair and the sun on her face. Who knew how much longer she'd be free to enjoy such simple pleasures? Oughtn't she to make the most of it while she had the chance?

Despite being reluctant to meet Mrs Webb again, she opened her door and stepped out onto the landing. A railed gallery overlooked the main entrance and she saw to her relief that there was no sign of the housekeeper in the hall below.

Matt hadn't used this door the day before, but, having descended the stairs on tiptoe, Sara prayed it wouldn't present any problems now. She was unutterably relieved when the key turned and the handle yielded to her touch. Stepping outside, into the sunshine, she took a deep breath of the salt-laden air.

She heard the dogs barking as she walked across the forecourt. Their hearing was obviously sharper than Mrs Webb's, and Sara hoped the housekeeper would be too busy quieting them to notice her slipping out of the gates.

She wanted to go down to the beach if she could, but, remembering the steepness of the path they'd used the afternoon before, she guessed that was the only means of access. It meant circling the house again, but luckily the track beyond the gates led onto the cliffs without having to re-enter the property.

All the same, she was glad when she started down the path and the cliff face hid her descent from view. It wasn't that she was afraid of being seen, she assured herself. She wasn't a prisoner yet, for heaven's sake. She just needed a little time alone to think about what she was going to do next.

She must have walked at least a quarter of a mile along the beach when she heard someone calling her name.

She had been enjoying the unaccustomed freedom. The breeze was warmer today, and she could smell the sea. The damp sand had been totally untouched when she'd started along the shoreline, and she knew her footprints would soon be washed away by the incoming tide.

Hearing her name, however, she expelled a sigh and stopped. She didn't even have to turn to know who it was. Only Matt Seton knew she was staying here; only he was likely to come after her.

Stifling her resentment, she turned. As if he couldn't have allowed her to finish her walk in peace, she was thinking half irritably. For heaven's sake, he wasn't her keeper.

The sight that met her startled eyes caused her to quickly revise her opinion, however. Matt was still some distance away, but between them lapped a rapidly expanding stretch of water that successfully trapped her between the incoming tide and the cliffs. Fairly deep water, too, she saw, trying not to panic. It had already covered the rocks that formed a sort of breakwater at the foot of the headland.

As she watched, she saw Matt break into a run, splashing into the water that divided them with grim determination. 'Stay where you are,' he yelled, wading towards her, and Sara stood there, dry-mouthed, as he closed the space between them. The water came up to his thighs, she saw, soaking his jeans and plastering them to the powerful muscles of his legs. Despite the sunshine, she felt sure the water must be icy. It was far too early in the day for the sun to have gained any strength.

She watched his approach anxiously, wondering what she would have done if he hadn't appeared. She could keep herself afloat, but she wasn't a strong swimmer. If Max were here, he'd tell her how stupid she was.

Matt reached her without too much difficulty and she looked up at him with apologetic eyes. 'I should have told Mrs Webb where I was going, shouldn't I?' she began, before he could say a word. 'I'm sorry. I just wanted a walk. I had no idea—'

Her voice trailed away and Matt expelled a resigned sigh. 'Yeah, well, let's get you back before we start the inquest, shall we?' he suggested flatly. 'Here: there's no point in both of us getting soaked to the skin. I'll carry you.'

'Oh, that's not necess—' she started, but Matt wasn't listening to her. Before she knew what was happening, he'd swung her up into his arms. But she couldn't prevent the groan of agony that escaped her lips when his thoughtless handling brought her bruised hip into sharp contact with his pelvis. The pain was sharper than ever and it was difficult to get her breath.

Matt was instantly aware of her reaction. 'Did I hurt you?' he asked, frowning, and she guessed he'd seen the way the colour had drained out of her face.

'I—it's nothing,' she assured him quickly, not wanting to arouse his curiosity. 'You gave me a shock. I could have walked, you know.'

Matt looked as if that was open to discussion. But once again the precariousness of their situation forced him to put his own feelings on hold. 'Hang on,' was all he permitted himself, before plunging back into the water, heading for the dry sand further along the beach.

She put her arms around his neck, unafraid that they wouldn't make it. She trusted Matt implicitly, she realised, more aware of the strength of his arms supporting her than the chilly waters of the North Sea surging below. And, although every movement he made caused the fabric of her dress to chafe her sore skin, she bore it gratefully. The warmth of his body soothed her like nothing else she could remember.

Which was crazy, she chided herself impatiently, trying not to notice the length of his eyelashes or the darkening line of stubble on his jaw. Such a strong jawline, she mused, aware of him with every cell in her being. This close, she could see every pore and bristle, was only inches away from the sensual curve of his mouth.

His breath fanned her temple, warm and only slightly flavoured with the strong black coffee he'd drunk at breakfast. She could smell the soap he used, smell his sweat. And was helplessly aware of her own reactions to him.

She was instantly ashamed. She had no right to be speculating on what it would be like to be in his arms because he wanted her there. It was useless to wonder how she'd feel if he touched her, touched her intimately. But, if she allowed her slim frame to slide against him, would she find he was aroused?

She sucked in her breath. This had to stop, she told herself fiercely. She'd never had thoughts like this before. She'd certainly never considered herself a sexual woman. The only man she'd ever known intimately was Max.

Her husband's name acted like a douche of cold water. She shivered violently and Matt, misunderstanding, said sharply, 'Are you getting wet?'

'No.'

Her response was sharper than it might have been because of the way she was feeling, and Matt arched an ironic brow. 'Well, we're nearly there,' he said, nodding towards the dry sand directly ahead of them. 'I should have warned you about the tides around here. They can be dangerous.'

Sara shook her head. 'It wasn't your fault,' she said, turning to see the cliff path just a few yards away. 'You can put me down now.'

'Perhaps I don't want to,' remarked Matt, stepping out of the water onto the patch of sand that was still uncovered by the tide. He looked down into her startled face and she was uneasily aware of how emotionally vulnerable she was. 'I think you and I need to have a little talk, Mrs Bradbury.' He allowed her name to register with her. 'Don't you?'

Sara could scarcely breathe. 'How do you know who I am?' she asked, not bothering to try and deny it, and Matt hesitated only a moment before setting her on her feet.

'How do you think?' he asked, stepping away from her. 'I saw your picture in a newspaper, of course.' He paused, looking back at her. 'Look, do you mind if we continue this after I've got out of these wet clothes?'

Sara's mouth felt so dry she doubted her ability to speak. But she had to say something in her own defence. Swallowing, she whispered, 'It—it was an accident, you know. It wasn't my fault.' She drew a breath. 'I—I didn't mean to—'

'Deceive me?' Matt finished the sentence he thought she'd started in a dry, cynical voice. 'Yeah, right.' He glanced towards the path again. 'Well, like I say, I'd prefer to have this conversation when I'm not in danger of freezing my butt, okay?'

He attempted to pull the soaked jeans away from his legs, but only succeeded in drawing Sara's eyes to the way the denim was drawn taut over the swell of his sex. He intercepted her stare and gave a wry grimace. 'Sorry if I'm embarrassing you, Mrs Bradbury,' he added mockingly. 'I guess I'm not as cold as I thought.'

Sara's face flamed. 'You're not embarrassing me,' she exclaimed, even though her face was bright red. Now she looked anywhere but at his crotch. 'Would you prefer me to go first?'

Matt's lips twisted. 'Yes, I'd prefer you to go first,' he mimicked her prim tone. 'And when we get back to the house you're going to let Mrs Webb take a look at that hip. I know it's hurting you, and the old lady used to be a nursing auxiliary until she had a family and had to give it up.'

Sara pressed her lips together. This wasn't the time to argue with him, as he'd said, but she hoped he didn't think the fact that he'd discovered who she was gave him the right to order her about. She had no intention of letting Mrs Webb or anyone else examine her. If she was arrested— She licked her dry lips. Well, she'd face that problem when she came to it. Until then…

It was harder climbing the cliff path today than it had been the day before. She assumed fear—and the prospect of imminent exposure to the authorities—had stiffened her muscles, and it was difficult putting one foot in front of the other.

On top of that, her mind was buzzing with thoughts of what Matt intended to do with her. Had he already called the police? Or was he prepared to listen to her side of the story before turning her in? Although she knew there was no chance of her getting away, she couldn't help considering and discarding every option open to her.

Reaching the house, she had only Mrs Webb's ire to contend with, however. The housekeeper clicked her tongue when she saw Matt's wet clothes and said, 'Go and get into a hot shower before you catch your death.' Then she turned on Sara. 'You should have told me you were going out,' she exclaimed shortly. 'I would have warned you about the tides.'

'I know.'

Sara was contrite, but Matt chose to intervene. 'Give her a break,' he said, heading for the hall. 'She's had a shock. And, as far as getting wet is concerned, it is the middle of June, not November.'

'And that water's warm, is it?' Mrs Webb enquired, with some sarcasm, and he sighed.

'Warm enough,' he said, not to be outdone. 'Right. I'll see you in about fifteen minutes.'

Sara knew this remark was addressed to her, but she had no intention of staying in the kitchen until he returned. It was to avoid the housekeeper's questions that she'd sneaked out in the first place, and although she was fairly sure Matt hadn't told Mrs Webb who she was, she wasn't prepared to take that chance.

She waited until Matt had disappeared upstairs before saying casually, 'I'll be in my room, if anyone wants me.'

'Why don't you stay here?' The housekeeper sounded put out. 'Unless I'm not good enough for you, that is.'

Sara blew out a breath. 'I need to use the bathroom,' she said evenly. 'It has nothing to do with your company, I can assure you.'

Mrs Webb regarded her grudgingly. 'Matt says you're staying until tomorrow,' she remarked conversationally. 'Have you—er—have you known him long?'

Sara blinked. 'Matt?' She shook her head 'I only met him yesterday. I thought you knew.'

'I know what he said,' declared the housekeeper narrowly, looking sceptical. 'But he seems awfully concerned about someone he only met twenty-four hours ago.'

Sara wished she'd left when Matt had. Whatever she felt about it, Mrs Webb was determined to get her pound of flesh. 'I meant it,' she said, 'we barely know one another.'

But she couldn't help wondering what the housekeeper would say if she was honest. She and Matt might only have known one another for a short time, but their relationship couldn't be judged in terms of hours and minutes. Despite the shortness of their association, he probably knew her more intimately than anyone else.

Mrs Webb shrugged and returned to the casserole she'd been preparing before they came in, and Sara took the opportunity to get away. Favouring her uninjured leg, she left the kitchen, going as swiftly as she could up the stairs and along the gallery to her room.

It was amazing how quickly this room had become her refuge, she thought, sinking down onto the bed. It wasn't her room, and it certainly wasn't anything like the room she'd shared with Max. But it was bright and cheerful, and she felt at home there.

Which she had never done in the luxurious duplex apartment she shared with her husband. Situated in a fashionable part of the city, it had been decorated and furnished by a firm of interior designers that Max thought highly of. She'd had no say in any of it. The apartment was expensive and soulless, and she hated everything about it.

Or perhaps she'd simply hated the life she'd lived there, she acknowledged bitterly. Like his Rolex watch, his Armani suits

and his Bentley, she had been just another of Max's possessions. The only difference had been that he had treated his
watch, his clothes and his car rather better than his wife.

Her hip throbbed, reminding her that she ought to check and
see that it hadn't started bleeding. The skin had been seriously
scrubbed in places, and it wouldn't be the first time that she'd
had to repair the damage. But this time she didn't have a convenient wardrobe of clothes to change into, and she could imagine Matt's reaction if he saw blood on her dress.

Lifting the hem of her skirt, she examined the injury, noticing
that the skin was badly inflamed. But that was because of the
way Matt had carried her, and she could hardly blame him for
trying to save her life.

Nevertheless, there was a faint trace of blood oozing from
the point of her hip and she clicked her tongue in frustration.
Now what was she going to do? She didn't carry any adhesive
plasters in her haversack. Perhaps she'd find some in the bathroom cabinet. It was the kind of thing people did keep in case
of emergency.

Holding her skirt to her waist, she got up from the bed and
limped into the bathroom. Then, clutching her dress in one
hand, she reached up to the cabinet with the other.

'Sara?'

It was Matt's voice and she panicked. He mustn't see her
like this. All right, so he probably knew about Max's accident,
but there was no need for him to witness her humiliation. If he
chose to call the police she couldn't stop him. But she could
hold onto her dignity until then.

Pushing the bathroom door to with her uninjured hip, she
called weakly, 'What do you want?'

'Can I come in?'

Sara breathed a little more easily. She'd thought at first that
he was in. 'Why?' she asked, suddenly remembering what he'd
said about Mrs Webb. 'I don't need any assistance.'

'I'm not offering any,' he replied, his voice louder now. 'I've
brought you a gift.'

A gift!

Sara blinked. What kind of gift could he have brought her?

Some more of his old clothes? Or perhaps he wanted to show her the newspaper where he'd read about her? That seemed infinitely more likely.

'I—just leave it on the bed,' she called, deciding there was no point in expecting him to go away without achieving his objective. 'I'll be out in a minute.'

There was silence for a moment, and then she heard Matt's voice just outside the bathroom door. 'What are you doing?' he exclaimed. 'Is your hip all right?'

Sara trembled. 'It's fine,' she insisted. 'What do people usually do in the bathroom?' She closed the door of the cabinet, just in case he came to investigate, but that was a mistake. She had evidently dislodged the items inside and a tube of hair gel came clattering down into the basin in front of her.

'What the—?' Without more ado, the bathroom door was forced open, and Matt stood on the threshold staring at her with bleak horrified eyes. 'For God's sake,' he exclaimed, staring at her injury. 'Did I do that?'

'As if.' Sara managed the contemptuous rejoinder with amazing composure. But then, realising that her lacy briefs left very little to his imagination, she allowed her skirt to fall and sagged against the basin. 'I had a fall before I came away.'

Matt gave a disbelieving snort. 'You do a lot of falling in your house, don't you?'

'What do you mean?' Sara stared at him with confused eyes.

'Your husband,' he stated flatly, his eyes still fixed on the spot her skirt had now hidden from his gaze. 'He fell, too. What a coincidence!'

Sara's shoulders slumped. 'You don't know anything about it.'

'No.' Matt agreed. 'But I'm willing to listen if you want to tell me. I'm not jumping to conclusions here, but a simple fall wouldn't have caused that mess.'

'It did.' Sara was desperate. 'It was an accident. I didn't mean it to happen. And that's the truth.'

Matt's brows drew together. 'Hey, I'm not accusing you of anything,' he protested. His eyes darkened. 'I'd guess it had something to do with your running away, right?'

'If you say so.' Sara spoke wearily. 'So what now? Are you going to turn me in?'

Matt eyes sought hers. 'Turn you in?' he echoed blankly. 'You talk as if you're a criminal. The last I heard, running away isn't a capital offence.'

'Running away?' She repeated his words barely audibly. 'But you said you knew about—about Max having a fall.'

'So?'

'So—so what did it say about how they found him? Did it tell you the way he—he died?'

'He's not dead!' Matt spoke harshly now. He stared at her. 'Why would you think he was?' He shook his head. 'He apparently had the presence of mind to call the emergency services before he passed out. He spent the night in hospital and discharged himself yesterday morning. That's when you were reported missing. According to the article I read, your husband's afraid you might have been kidnapped.'

CHAPTER SEVEN

MATT wouldn't have believed Sara could get any paler, but she did. Every scrap of colour drained out of her face, leaving her unnaturally pallid. The circles around her eyes stood out in sharp relief and her mouth worked in silent consternation.

'You're—you're lying,' she got out at last, and he wondered why, if she'd believed her husband was dead, the news that he wasn't should have such a shattering effect.

'Why would I lie?' he reasoned, becoming anxious in spite of himself. 'Sara—'

'Max calls me Victoria,' she said dully. 'You must know that.' Then she slid to the floor in a dead faint.

It was the second time he'd had to pick her unconscious body off the floor. Not that she weighed much. She felt wholly insubstantial in his arms. How long was it since she'd eaten a decent meal? he wondered. In the last twenty-four hours she'd only picked at her food, and he suspected her weakness was due in part to hunger.

So, why? Why had she been starving herself? Why had she run away? And how had she sustained such an ugly bruise on her hip? As Matt carried her into the bedroom and laid her on the bed his mind buzzed with a jumble of questions. The most obvious explanation was fear. But what was she afraid of?

He straightened and stood looking down at her. He wished he could believe she was a spoiled wife who had grown bored with her pampered existence and decided to give her husband a wake-up call. Could she really have been that self-indulgent? Somehow he didn't buy it.

Her eyelids were fluttering and, realising that in a short time she was going to be wide awake and denying everything he was thinking, Matt came to an abrupt decision. Hoping she wouldn't object too much, he took the hem of her skirt and drew it up to her waist.

He was shocked again by the sight of the ugly lesions on her hip, but he knew he didn't have time to examine them more closely right now. Instead, he slipped his arm beneath her and eased her dress out of the way.

She began to protest now as consciousness returned, trying to push his hands away without any success. Matt wasn't listening to her. Horror had replaced his concern and he sank down onto the bed beside her in speechless disbelief.

There was barely an inch of her torso that didn't bear the scars of injuries old and new. Some bruises were obviously more recent than others, the colours ranging from stark black and blue to a jaundiced yellow or brown. She'd been beaten, and beaten badly, and Matt wanted to take the man who'd done this to her and wring his cowardly neck.

His hands trembled as he eased the dress away. Sara seemed to realise there was no point in trying to stop him. It was too late; too late for both of them. Matt closed his eyes for a moment against the murderous rage that was demanding revenge.

'Your husband did this to you?' he asked at last, when he had himself in control again, and she shrugged.

'Does it matter?' She sighed. His hands lingered at her waist. 'I think you'd better let me get up.'

'And I think you ought to have that hip treated,' said Matt flatly. 'From what I've seen, it needs medical attention.'

Her response was urgent. 'I don't need a doctor,' she exclaimed fiercely, and he didn't think this was the time to tell her that that was what he had been before he'd become a writer.

He expelled an unsteady breath, hoping she wouldn't mistake his concern for something less commendable. 'I've got some first aid stuff in my bathroom. I suggest you let me deal with your hip if you don't want me to involve anyone else.'

'I can do it,' she protested, but once again he prevented her from getting off the bed.

'I'm sure you can. I'm sure that's what you're used to,' he muttered harshly. 'But in this instance I'd prefer it if you'd let me make sure there's no infection.'

Sara made a weary sound. 'There is no infection,' she insisted. 'It's just bleeding a bit, that's all.'

'So I see,' he said grimly, unable to hide his reaction. And she suddenly seemed to realise that the lower half of her body was still exposed to his gaze.

'Mr Seton—'

'Don't call me that.' He was impatient. 'It's too late for us to behave as if we're just casual acquaintances. We're not. I know it and you know it. Whether you like it not, I feel responsible for you.'

'Don't patronise me!'

'I won't if you'll do as you're told.'

Her eyes flashed with sudden spirit. 'And I'm very good at doing as I'm told,' she told him bitterly, and he groaned at his own thoughtlessness.

'Sara—'

'Shouldn't that be Victoria?' she enquired painfully. And then, as if she'd just recalled why she was lying on the bed, 'Did I pass out?'

Matt nodded. 'Like a light.' He got up. 'Stay here. Please. I'll be back in a few seconds.'

Sara looked up at him. 'You did say—Max was alive?' she ventured.

'Yes.' Matt hesitated. 'Why would you think he wasn't? What happened before you ran away?'

Sara moved her head from side to side on the pillows. 'He was so still,' she whispered, obviously thinking about it. 'I couldn't find a pulse. I was sure—' She pressed her lips together. 'Oh, God, he's going to be so mad when he finds out what I did.'

Matt felt his anger surfacing again, and determinedly forced it back. 'I'll get my gear,' he said, heading for the door. 'Just—relax, okay? I won't be long.'

She didn't answer, and he could only hope that she'd be too distracted by what he'd told her to disobey him. It wasn't just an excuse to get his hands on her again, he assured himself. She was in such a frail state she might pick up some infection without her being aware of it. He didn't want to think what the ravages of blood poisoning might do to her fragile system. He'd seen too many tragic cases in the past.

Without taking the time to check what was in the bag he kept in his bathroom, he simply snatched it out of the cupboard and charged back along the landing. Only to encounter Mrs Webb at the top of the stairs.

'Something wrong?' she asked, her sharp eyes immediately noting the medical kit. 'Do you need my help?'

Matt gave her a resigned look. 'No help needed,' he said, aware that Sara's door was ajar and that she could probably hear everything that was being said. 'Miss Victor just needs an adhesive plaster, that's all.'

'Hurt her heel, has she?' Mrs Webb arched an enquiring brow. 'I could have told her that those shoes she wears aren't suitable for around here.'

'Something like that,' Matt agreed, his nerves screaming in frustration. 'If you'll excuse me…?'

'Very formal all of a sudden, aren't we?' remarked Mrs Webb with a sniff. 'Oh, well.' To his relief she turned towards his daughter's bedroom. 'I expect I'll hear all about it from Rosie. She seems to know what's going on.'

'Nothing's going on,' said Matt, gritting his teeth, but he was talking to himself. The housekeeper was already out of earshot.

Aware of the tension in his shoulders, Matt determinedly tried to relax before going back into Sara's room. He half expected to find her locked in the bathroom, but, although she was sitting up, she was still on the bed.

'I guess you heard that,' he said, hesitating only a moment before closing the door behind him. 'My housekeeper likes to feel she's in the know.'

'Yes.' Sara's tone was dry. 'Well, I suppose it's only a matter of time before she realises who I am.'

Matt shrugged. 'We'll deal with that when we have to,' he said, sitting down beside her and opening the leather bag. 'Now, let's see: what have we got? Gauze; adhesive plasters; bandages.' His fingers hesitated over the syringe and the advantages of injection. But, dismissing the idea, he added, 'And some antiseptic ointment. Good.'

'This really isn't necessary,' she murmured, and he saw she was embarrassed all over again. She'd pulled her dress down, too, even though she was running the risk of staining it. Her dignity still meant something to her, at least.

'We have to talk,' said Matt, opening the packet of plasters and examining its contents. 'Why don't you start by telling me why you thought your husband was dead?' He paused. 'Did you try to kill him?'

'No!' Her denial was instantaneous, and, looking into her horrified eyes, he couldn't help but believe her. 'I wouldn't do that,' she added, with a revealing tremor in her voice. 'Max fell. Down the stairs in our apartment. I tried to find a pulse but I couldn't.' She took a breath. 'It wasn't Max who called the emergency service. It was me.'

'So why didn't you stay and speak to them?' Matt asked, hoping that by getting her to talk to him he could divert her attention. He urged her back against the pillows again, avoiding her eyes as he lifted the hem of her skirt. 'I don't understand why you ran away.'

'Don't you?' The laugh she gave was without humour. 'No, well, perhaps it is hard for you to understand how I felt. I suppose the simple answer would be to say I panicked. I was afraid no one would believe my version of events.'

Matt frowned. 'Okay,' he said evenly. 'I'll buy that. Having seen what the bastard's done to you, you've got a point.' His jaw compressed as he cleaned the abrasion on her hip with a sterile wipe. 'But for goodness' sake, Sara, why did you stay with him?'

Sara caught her breath, and he guessed her hip was stinging. 'You don't know that Max did this to me,' she argued. 'If you met him, you'd think he was a charming man. Hugo thinks so, and so does my mother. As far as she's concerned I'm an ungrateful wife.'

The area around the abrasion was clean now, and Matt stared at it for a long time, trying to contain his anger. Who the hell was Hugo? he wondered, resenting the thought that some other man might be involved. He didn't like the idea that there was someone else she cared about.

'Who is Hugo?' he asked at last, when he had himself in

control again. But the question was too personal and he felt her eyes upon him.

'Hugo is Max's brother,' she replied at last, and Matt cursed his own stupidity. He remembered now seeing the man's name in the article he'd read about her disappearance. Her lips twisted as she added, 'He's harmless.'

'But he doesn't stop his brother from beating up his wife every chance he gets,' pointed out Matt harshly, and she sighed.

'I've told you,' she said, pressing a protective hand to her midriff. 'Hugo doesn't know anything about it. He—he thinks Max and I have the ideal marriage. He's a hopeless romantic at heart.'

Hopeless? Right. Matt shook his head. But touching her was becoming the finest form of torture, and the idea that some man felt he had the right to brutalise her infuriated him anew. 'What about your father?' he demanded roughly. 'Doesn't he care?'

'My father's dead and my mother wouldn't want to believe me. She has a very comfortable lifestyle, thanks to Max,' she said unsteadily. She looked down. 'Have you finished?'

'Not nearly,' retorted Matt, his tone savage. 'Dammit, Sara, women don't have to put up with this sort of thing today. Why don't you get a divorce?'

She stiffened then. Her muscles locked, and he felt the withdrawal of a confidence he'd hardly begun to explore. 'You don't understand,' she told him tersely, and he knew if he hadn't been applying a gauze coated with antiseptic ointment to her hip at that moment she'd have scrambled off the bed and left him. She licked her lips. 'Thank you for doing this, but please don't think it gives you the right to offer me advice. I know what I'm doing—what I *have* to do. And getting a divorce isn't an option!'

'Why the hell not?'

Matt was impatient, but she just regarded him with cool guarded eyes. 'Well, your knowing who I am solves one problem,' she declared, ignoring his outburst. 'I can't stay here now.' She hesitated. 'I'll have to go back.'

'No!'

The word was torn from him. She couldn't be serious. He

tried to concentrate on the two strips of adhesive he was smoothing over the gauze. To go back to a man who clearly had no respect—let alone any love—for her. For God's sake, after what she'd told him about the circumstances of her departure he had no doubt that Max Bradbury would have reserved some particularly unpleasant punishment for embarrassing him when she got back.

His hands trembled as he completed his task but he didn't immediately release her. Although he knew she was eager to end this awkward encounter, his hands lingered on her skin. He wasn't unaware of the impropriety of his actions. He was running the risk of her accusing him of God knew what! But at that moment it wasn't important. He simply didn't want to let her go.

His eyes drifted down, over the quivering muscles of her stomach. The dusky hollow of her navel tantalised him, made him catch his breath. Below her navel the lacy briefs offered little protection, the triangular shadow that marked the apex of her legs inviting his hungry gaze.

He wanted her, he realised, even as he rejected the thought as unworthy of him. This was no fantasy; this was real, this was honest—though he doubted she'd believe his feelings had no strings attached. She'd probably find any overture he made towards her, however innocent, utterly repulsive. He wasn't arrogant enough to think she felt any attraction to him.

Yet still he prolonged the moment. And, as if becoming aware that the atmosphere between them had changed, she struggled to get up. 'Please,' she said, and although there was no fear in her eyes there was withdrawal. And a mute appeal he found hard to resist.

'You do please—me,' he told her huskily. And despite herself, he was sure, she gave a helpless little moan.

'Oh, Matt,' she whispered, her voice breaking with emotion.

And, unable to prevent himself, he bent his head and kissed her, brushing the bruised skin with his lips.

She jerked beneath his caressing touch, her hands balling into fists at her sides. He would have liked to think it was to prevent herself from touching him, but he didn't believe that. Indeed, apart from one revealing twitch, she made no move either to encourage or stop him, and Matt knew it was up to him to show some sense here.

But it was hard to be sensible. Her skin was so tender, so delicate. She tasted good, too, the light film of perspiration that had beaded her skin when he'd cleansed her hip like nectar on his tongue. Even the faint scent of the ointment was not unpleasant. It certainly wasn't enough to deter his desire. He wanted to taste every inch of her. In spite of everything, he couldn't stop.

His breath dampened her flesh. His lips burned a circle of kisses around her navel before beating a sensual path over her flat stomach. His thumbs urged the folds of the dress aside, revealing the hem of her bra. The enticing hollow between her breasts was visible to his impassioned gaze. He caught his breath. He wanted to remove her bra, to expose the rounded swell of her small breasts. He could see her nipples were already straining at the delicate lace that confined them. He longed to feel those hard peaks against his palms.

Dear God!

His own reactions to what he was doing could no longer be ignored. Between his legs his arousal throbbed with a painful insistence, and the blood was pounding in his head.

But he had to stop. With considerable effort he lifted his head and looked at her, encountering an unexpected trace of regret in her gaze. He'd expected many things: indignation; disillusionment; anger, even. What he hadn't expected was that she might actually have welcomed his lovemaking, and his brows drew together in momentary disbelief.

But her first words didn't match the fleeting expression that had now disappeared entirely. 'Are you going to let me up now?' she asked, her voice as cold as her words. 'Or are you going to demand payment for your services? Max said all men were the same in that respect.'

Matt's face flamed. Jerking back, he moved to the foot of the bed, wondering how he could have fooled himself into believing that she might want anything from him. She'd merely tolerated his lovemaking, borne his maudlin sympathies. For

God's sake, she was married to someone else. What did he expect?

But then, as if she'd instantly regretted the harshness of her words, Sara gave a despairing little moan. 'I'm sorry,' she said, pulling down her skirt and scrambling across the bed towards him. She swung her feet to the floor beside him. 'I shouldn't have said that. I didn't mean it.'

'Didn't you?' Matt wasn't prepared to put his feelings on the line again. He was already deploring the impulse that had got him into this situation. Having her forgive him for being such an idiot was no compensation at all. Getting up from the bed, he thrust his hands into the hip pockets of his jeans, swayed back on his heels with what he hoped looked like cool indifference. 'Well, that's good. I'd hate you to think I'd planned to seduce you as well.'

'I don't.' She stood up, too, and although she was considerably smaller than he was without her high heels she was still too close for comfort. 'Matt, I—I know you meant well, but—'

'Spare me the lecture,' he said, his own voice harsh in his ears. 'I've obviously embarrassed you—embarrassed us both— and I apologise.' He stepped back a pace, to put some space between them. 'I'll leave you now. You can let me know what you intend to do when—'

'No!' She caught his arm then, her cool fingers slipping almost possessively about his wrist. 'Please, Matt. Don't go away mad at me.'

Matt expelled a heavy breath, trying not to consider what she wanted now. 'I'm not mad at you,' he said, after a few moments of self-denial. Forcing himself to concentrate on the reason why he'd come to her room in the first place, he nodded towards the loveseat. 'I bought you a couple of things in Ellsmoor. You may want to change before you leave.'

Sara's lips parted. She didn't even look at the jeans and tee shirt he'd found in the mini-market. 'You want me to leave?' she asked anxiously, her hands tightening on his arm, and he stared at her with guarded eyes.

'I understood that was what you wanted,' he said, stifling the sudden urge he had to beg her to stay.

Sara swallowed. 'It's what I ought to do,' she admitted. 'My staying here—well, it could put you in an awkward position.'

'Do I look like I'm worried?' Matt's lips twisted. 'It's your decision. I'm not sending you away.'

Sara gazed up at him. 'So—I can still stay until tomorrow?'

'You can stay as long as you like,' retorted Matt roughly, taking the hand resting on his arm and raising it to his lips. His mouth grazed her knuckles before seeking the network of veins at her wrist. 'I may not approve of what you're doing, but you're safe here. I can promise you that.'

'Oh, Matt.' She brought her free hand up to his face, cupping his jaw with unsteady fingers. 'I don't know how I'm ever going to be able to thank you.'

'No thanks are necessary,' Matt told her flatly. But when he would have turned away she reached up, and pressed her lips to the corner of his mouth.

'I'd like to stay,' she whispered at last, drawing back. 'For a few days at least, if you'll let me.' She moistened her lips. 'But I'm going to have to let—let Max know that I'm all right.'

'As opposed to being at his mercy?' suggested Matt, with some bitterness, but it was a reprieve and he was grateful for it. 'Why don't you leave that to me? You write a note and I'll get it to him without running the risk of his finding out where you are.'

Her eyes widened. 'You can do that?' She trembled. 'But how?'

'You don't want to know,' replied Matt, removing her hand from his face before temptation got the better of him. Then, at the anxious look she was wearing, 'Don't worry. I won't cause any trouble. Not until I know what kind of hold he has over you, at least.'

He walked to the door, eager now to withdraw and consider his options. 'Check out the gear. I'm going to speak to Mrs Webb. And don't fret that she's not trustworthy. She is. If it hadn't been for her this place would never have become the sanctuary it is.'

Sara looked painfully vulnerable as she stood watching him leave the room. But he wondered if he wasn't being the world's most gullible fool for taking her in. Or for being taken in by her? he mused, wanting to restore his sense of balance. He might be judging her husband without cause. But he didn't think he was. It might be foolish, but he trusted her.

But how the hell was he supposed to write fiction in his present frame of mind?

CHAPTER EIGHT

SARA spent the rest of the morning in her room, trying to come to terms with what Matt had told her.

Max wasn't dead, she repeated incredulously. He was alive. The fears she'd had on his behalf had been groundless. He'd been taken to hospital, sure, but he'd been well enough to discharge himself the following morning. And since then he'd been trying to cover himself by pretending that *she* had disappeared, that *she* might have been kidnapped.

She trembled. After Matt had left her, she'd taken up a position on the window seat, gazing out at the sun-drenched cliffs and the water beyond with a feeling of disbelief. She still found it hard to accept that she was here, hundreds of miles from London; that she'd escaped. However grateful she was that Max had survived, the manner of her departure remained a constant source of amazement. How had he let her get away?

Of course, he had been unconscious at the time. He must have hit his head when he fell and for a few minutes he'd been dead to the world. Dead to her, too, she thought bitterly. She should have known it would take more than a simple fall to kill a man like Max Bradbury.

Not that she wanted him dead, she assured herself. That was too high a price to pay, even for her freedom. But if only he had been a reasonable man, a man she could appeal to. When it had become obvious that their marriage was not what he had expected, that *she* was not what he had expected, why couldn't he have let her go? It was what any other man would have done; any normal man, that was. But it hadn't taken her long to find out that Max was anything but normal.

She supposed they must have been married for about six months when he'd struck her for the first time.

She'd already learned not to contradict him, particularly if he'd been drinking. He had said some incredibly cruel things to her, things he'd said he regretted bitterly when he was sober again, and she'd believed him. The crude words he'd used, deriding her for the smallest thing, belittling her intelligence, accusing her of being something she was not, had seemed so uncharacteristic of the man she'd believed she'd married. She'd been sure that it was the alcohol that was responsible for his ungovernable rage, and for a while he'd been able to hide his real nature from her.

But then everything had changed. It had only taken the discovery that she was on first-name terms with the commissionaire who worked in the lobby of their apartment building to invoke an almost insane fury. She'd been totally unprepared for the fist that had suddenly bored into her midriff and she'd been doubled over, gasping for air and sanity, when he'd stormed out of the duplex.

Of course, he'd apologised when he'd come back. He'd made the excuse of stress at the office, of being madly jealous of any man who spoke to her, of his own uncontrollable temper. He'd sworn it would never happen again, showered her with expensive presents until she'd been convinced of his regret.

Until the next time...

But she didn't want to think about that now; didn't want to consider what a naïve fool she had been, or how easily Max had managed to persuade her that she was actually to blame for his outbursts. In the beginning, desperate to make her marriage work—for her mother's sake as well as her own—she'd seized any excuse to explain his violence. The truth was, she hadn't been able to believe what was happening to her. She'd deluded herself that once Max realised she wasn't interested in any other man he'd come to his senses.

It hadn't happened. The violence had just got worse and there'd been nothing she could do. Max had made it very clear that he would never let her go, and she'd had the very real fear that if she did try to free herself he would turn his anger on her mother.

She was glad now that they'd had no children. Max would have had no compunction about using them in his unequal struggle for possession. Besides which, she realised now that his jealousy would never have allowed a third person to dilute the complete submission he demanded of her.

Thrusting these thoughts aside, she got to her feet and crossed to the small pile of clothes Matt had left on the loveseat. There were jeans, which she judged might fit her very well, a couple of tee shirts, two changes of cheap underwear, the kind that was available in supermarkets, and a pair of trainers.

She pressed her lips together after she had examined the clothes, her eyes filling with tears suddenly at his kindness. This presumably was the 'gift' he'd brought her, only to find her cowering behind the bathroom door. She'd been so afraid of him seeing her, of him finding out what Max had done to her, but now she was glad he knew. It was such a relief to have someone she could talk to, someone who wouldn't judge her. And, although she'd admitted nothing, she suspected Matt knew exactly what had been going on.

Sooner or later, she knew, she would have to go back, but please God not yet. Whatever excuse she gave, Max was never going to believe her version of events. Apart from anything else, she had shamed and humiliated him—or at least that was how he would see it. He was never going to forgive her for that.

Trying to ignore the inevitable, Sara carried the jeans and one of the tee shirts into the bathroom and took off her dress. The voile dress had been new, bought to go to the art exhibition Max had been planning to visit the evening when fate had overtaken both of them. It was strange to think it was the dress that had led to Max's accident. But then, it was on such simple things as these that her marriage had foundered.

As she hung the dress on the back of the bathroom door she thought how foolish she'd been to think that Max might like it. He hadn't chosen it, and for a long time now he had chosen all her clothes. But he had encouraged her to attend the fashion show with the wife of one of his colleagues, and, after seeing it modelled, Sara had fallen in love with its style and elegance.

Its style and elegance! Sara's lips curled in painful remembrance. Max hadn't thought it was either stylish or elegant. He'd said it was the kind of dress only a tart would wear, that she'd chosen it because she'd wanted to flaunt herself. She was quite sure that if he hadn't fallen down the stairs he'd have torn the garment off her, and she wished now that she'd taken the time to grab a change of clothes before fleeing from the apartment. She didn't like the dress now; she hated it. She took a breath. Hated *him*! God help her.

The jeans were a little big, but that didn't matter. At least they weren't tight on her hip. The tee shirt was cropped and ended a daring inch above her navel, which she worried about a little. But then she remembered Max wasn't going to see her. For now she could please herself what she wore.

The trainers fitted beautifully. Sara guessed Matt must have checked the size of her shoes before buying them. Whatever, she looked infinitely better. She felt almost her old self as she went downstairs at lunchtime.

The first person she encountered was Mrs Webb. The house-keeper was setting the table in the dining room again and Sara halted uncertainly, not sure she wanted to face another grilling.

But Mrs Webb had seen her and, straightening, she arched her brows appreciatively. 'You look nice,' she said, with none of the animosity that she'd exhibited earlier. 'Matt's got good taste.'

Sara gave a rueful smile, realising there was no point in pretending that she'd brought the garments with her. 'Where is— Matt?' she asked, for want of anything else to say, and the housekeeper returned to her task.

'He's in his office, study, whatever you want to call it.' She sounded indulgent. 'He said to tell you to go ahead and have lunch without him. I believe he's got a lot of work to catch up on, and he's got to pick Rosie up at three o'clock.'

Sara came a little further into the room. 'I didn't realise he was writing a book at the moment,' she said, feeling a familiar sense of inadequacy. 'I should apologise. I've taken up so much of his time.'

'Did I say he was complaining?' The older woman gave her a sideways glance. 'If you ask me, he's more than happy to have you here. Writing can be a lonely existence. And since Hester retired he's had to make do with Rosie's and my company.'

'Hester.' Sara remembered the little girl mentioning that name yesterday afternoon when she'd been trying to prove how grown up she was. 'Who—who is Hester?'

'She used to be Rosie's nanny,' explained Mrs Webb, straightening from the table again. 'She came north with Matt when he bought this place. She was from around here originally, just as he was.'

Sara nodded. 'But she left?'

'She retired,' replied the housekeeper, heading for the door. 'Now, you sit yourself down. I'll be back in a minute with your meal.'

Sara would have liked to ask if she could just have her meal in the kitchen, as she'd done the day before, but she was chary of getting too familiar with Mrs Webb. She didn't know what Matt had told her, if anything, and until she did it was probably safer to maintain a certain detachment.

The housekeeper returned with an appetising dish of lasagne and new bread, fresh out of the oven. She advised Sara to help herself and, although her appetite had been virtually non-existent since she left London, Sara found to her surprise that she was hungry.

She refused the glass of wine Mrs Webb offered, however. A diet cola was far more appealing, and by the time the housekeeper returned to see how she was doing she'd made a modest dent in the pasta.

'That was delicious,' she said, feeling pleased with herself. 'Did you make it?'

'Well, I didn't buy it,' remarked Mrs Webb drily. 'I don't hold with all those ready-made meals, although I suppose if you're a working girl you can't always spend half the day in the kitchen, can you?'

'No, I suppose not.'

Sara thought longingly of those occasions when she'd made a meal for her mother and herself. But that was in the days before Max came on the scene; before he'd come to the school to present a cheque to the governors to equip a new gymnasium and decided she was going to be the next Mrs Bradbury. Before Sara's mother had seen him as her last chance to escape from what she regarded as the near-poverty that had dogged her married life.

'So—can I get you anything else?' asked Mrs Webb, gathering the plates together. 'Some ice cream, perhaps?'

'Nothing else, thanks.' Sara took a deep breath, once again dispelling Max's image from her mind. 'Do you think Matt would mind if I took the dogs for a walk?'

The housekeeper looked surprised. 'I'd say he'd be delighted,' she replied drily. 'But are you sure you can manage them on your own? They're pretty wild.'

'I'm not as helpless as I look,' declared Sara with a smile. 'But I won't go down to the beach. I'm not that stupid.'

'Well, actually, you could now,' said the older woman thoughtfully. 'The tide's turned.'

Sara hoped so; she really did. But she wasn't thinking about the water that had trapped her earlier.

She accompanied Mrs Webb into the kitchen, helping her to load the lunch dishes into the dishwasher before going out into the garden. The two retrievers in their compound, sensing an outing, immediately set up a noisy greeting which completely masked the arrival of the young woman who suddenly appeared around the corner of the house.

Sara didn't know who was the most shocked: herself, because of her fear of being recognised, or the other woman, who clearly wasn't pleased to find her there. Sara didn't know how she knew the stranger didn't approve of her presence. She just sensed it. So who was she?

Mrs Webb supplied the answer. Following Sara out of the house, she saw the newcomer almost as soon as Sara did herself, and her lips parted in a pleasant smile.

'Mrs Proctor,' she said. 'What a surprise!'

The young woman came towards them. In a cream silk shirt tied stylishly at her waist and pleated linen trousers in a subtle shade of taupe she made Sara instantly aware of the limitations of her own attire. Mrs Proctor's hair was dark, a smooth silken cap that tucked confidingly beneath a most attractive chin. Sara guessed, too, that the hazel eyes set in a flawlessly oval face would miss little.

But for now the woman was obliged to acknowledge the housekeeper's greeting. Sara thought it was lucky that she hadn't let the dogs out. Mrs Proctor didn't look the type to appreciate having their paws on her clothes, and she ignored them as she produced an answering smile. 'Hello, Mrs Webb,' she said politely. 'Isn't it a perfect afternoon?'

And it was, thought Sara, glancing up at the clear blue sky above their heads. She just hoped the newcomer wasn't going to spoil it.

The realisation that she had no right to think things like that brought her up short. For heaven's sake, she chided herself, she probably had less right to be here than anyone else. In fact, scrub 'probably'. She had no right to be here at all.

'Is Matt working?'

Mrs Proctor's voice matched the rest of her: cool and cultivated, yet with an underlying note of arrogance. Sara had the impression she didn't care much for Mrs Webb either. But she was obliged to be civil.

'Yes, I'm afraid so.' Mrs Webb had brought the dogs' slip collars out with her, and now she handed them over to Sara. 'Is there anything I can do?'

In a pig's eye, thought Sara drily, guessing that the visitor would want nothing from the housekeeper. But it wasn't anything to do with her, and, dipping her head, she went to unbolt the compound gate.

'You're not going to let them out, are you?' Before Sara could open the gate, the woman stopped her. 'I mean—' She glanced down at her immaculate appearance. 'I really wish you wouldn't.'

Sara looked at Mrs Webb, and the older woman gestured resignedly towards the house. 'Perhaps you'd better come in then, Mrs Proctor,' she said, without enthusiasm. 'Maybe you'd like a cup of coffee before you leave.'

There was definite annoyance in the young woman's expression now, but she controlled it. 'That might be very nice,' she agreed, but her gaze had returned to linger curiously on Sara. 'I didn't realise Matt employed someone to exercise the dogs for him.' She wet her already glossy lips. 'Are you a local, Miss—Miss—?'

'She's from the agency.'

Matt's interjection caught them all unawares. Sara had assumed he was still closeted in his study and she was disturbed at how eagerly her eyes turned to him.

He was still wearing the black tee shirt and jeans he'd been wearing when he'd come into her bedroom, and, although she hadn't realised it at the time, his appearance had registered with her. The dark colour accentuated his raw masculinity, drew her unwilling attention to the impressive width of his chest, to the powerful muscles in his thighs. Looking at him, she could hardly believe how gentle he had been with her, how sensual his lips had felt against her skin...

But then what he'd said registered, too, and she dipped her head again, unable to meet his eyes. Dear God, was he offering her the job as Rosie's nanny? And, if so, what did she intend to do?

'I told you I was still looking for a nanny, didn't I, Emma?' Matt continued, addressing his remarks to the visitor. 'Meet Miss Sara Victor. We're giving each other a week's trial to see how it goes.'

Emma!

As Sara realised that this must be the woman who'd phoned Matt the day before, Emma Proctor looked decidedly put out. 'I thought you said that you hadn't seen any suitable applicants,' she exclaimed, giving Sara a disparaging look. 'This was rather sudden, wasn't it?'

'Isn't that always the way?' remarked Matt with amazing sanguinity. 'Sara just arrived yesterday.'

'She's very good with Rosie,' put in Mrs Webb, not to be outdone, and Sara wished they'd stop talking about her as if she wasn't there. Though she had no wish to draw attention to herself, she reminded herself firmly. And she could hardly object if Mrs Webb was sticking up for her.

'That's true,' Matt added now, but Sara noticed he raked a restless hand through his hair as he spoke. Perhaps he wasn't as relaxed about this as he appeared, she fretted anxiously. And was it fair to expect him to cover for her this way?

Meanwhile Emma Proctor was doing her best to hide her resentment and, ignoring Sara completely, she remarked, 'Mrs Webb told me you were working.' She treated the housekeeper to the kind of look she'd given Sara earlier. 'I was hoping you'd have time for a chat. I've been meaning to ask you about the books you said you'd sign for Darren's school fête.'

Matt's smile looked a little forced now. 'Well, I am working, Em—'

'But you're not working right now, are you?' she pointed out smoothly, with another impatient glance at Sara and Mrs Webb. 'It will only take a minute. And I have driven over specially.'

Matt took a deep breath. 'Okay,' he said, apparently accepting defeat. 'You'd better come in.'

Mrs Webb pulled a wry face at Sara as Emma went triumphantly up the steps and into the bootroom, and Sara felt an unexpected sense of camaraderie with the older woman. But when she started towards the dogs again Matt caught her arm.

'What are you doing?'

'Miss Victor asked if she could take the dogs for a walk,' said Mrs Webb, before Sara could respond. 'That's all right, isn't it?'

'No, it's not all right,' he retorted, and Sara, who had been momentarily struck dumb by the possessiveness of his strong fingers, shook herself free.

'Why not?' she demanded, aware that Emma Proctor had paused to listen to their exchange. Her eyes challenged his. 'I've got nothing to do until Rosie comes home.'

'Because you're not familiar with the area,' he said tersely, clearly aware of his audience. 'You can come with Rosie and me when we take them out later.'

'But—'

'I doubt if—Miss Victor, is it?—is likely to lose her bearings around here,' observed Emma Proctor, once again reminding him of her presence. 'This is the only house along this stretch of the coast.'

'Even so—'

Matt didn't say anything more, but his expression was compelling and Sara knew she couldn't go against him. He was sticking his neck out by allowing her to stay here, and the least she could do was respect his wishes.

'Okay,' she said, with a small shrug. Then, because she couldn't resist it, 'I suppose I'll have to go and pick Rosie up in a little while anyway.'

Matt's expression mirrored his impatience. 'We'll talk about that,' he stated flatly, and although his eyes promised a suitable retribution Sara wasn't alarmed. He followed Emma up the steps and into the house. 'I won't be long.'

Sara's lips twitched, and after Matt and Emma had disappeared she turned back to the dogs with a rueful smile. 'Sorry, guys,' she said, squatting down on her heels and pushing her fingers through the bars. 'You're going to have to wait. We all are.'

'You're staying on, then, are you?'

Mrs Webb's enquiry reminded Sara that there'd been a fourth witness to their exchange. 'For a short time,' she said, getting to her feet again. Then, because she had to know, 'What has he told you?'

'Me?' For the first time the housekeeper looked a little taken aback. 'Matt doesn't have to clear his arrangements with me.'

'I know, but—' Sara sought for words. 'He must have said something.'

Mrs Webb folded her hands together at her waist. 'As I say, he doesn't have to tell me anything. If he says you're going to be Rosie's nanny, then that's good enough for me.'

Sara sighed. 'Mrs Webb—'

'All right.' The housekeeper gave in. 'He asked me not to gossip about your arrival. I know you're in some kind of trouble, and he's trying to help you, but that's all. I trust Matt to know what he's doing. He is a trained psychologist, you know.'

Sara's eyes had widened. 'A trained psychologist?' she echoed. 'He didn't tell me that.'

'No, well, it's not something he likes me to gossip about either,' said Mrs Webb drily. 'Now, I must get on…'

'Why did he give it up?' asked Sara, unable to stop herself, and the housekeeper sighed.

'Can't you guess? To pursue his writing career, of course. Rosie was just a baby at the time.'

Sara bit her lip. 'Was that—was that when his wife left him?'

'Miss Victor—'

'Call me Sara, please!'

'Sara, then.' Mrs Webb folded her lips together for a moment before continuing, 'Don't you think you ought to ask Matt these questions, not me?'

Sara flushed, but she stood her ground. 'I'm sorry,' she said a little stiffly. 'I didn't mean to pry.'

'No—' Mrs Webb turned towards the house, only to pause with her foot on the bottom step. 'I don't suppose it will do any harm to tell you that Carol—that's his ex-wife—wasn't prepared to give up the comfortable existence she'd had as a doctor's wife. There was no certainty Matt would have any success as a writer.'

'But she left her baby behind,' protested Sara, unable to conceive of any woman doing such a thing, and the housekeeper nodded.

'Yes, well, she married one of Matt's partners in the practice just a week after their divorce became absolute,' she conceded with a grimace. 'Rosie would have been in the way.'

Then, as if she realising she had already said too much, Mrs Webb disappeared into the house.

CHAPTER NINE

MATT stared at the blank computer screen in front of him and scowled. For the first time in his writing career he was finding it almost impossible to concentrate on his work, and it irritated the hell out of him.

He knew what was wrong with him, of course. He was getting far too involved in Sara's life. Despite the fact that he'd promised her not to say or do anything to alert Max Bradbury to her whereabouts, the temptation to let the bastard know exactly what he thought of him was hard to resist. More than that, he itched to bury his fist in Bradbury's face, which was totally unlike him.

He'd always considered himself a reasonable man. Hell, when Carol had first left him and shacked up with Philip Arnold he'd never even thought of resorting to violence. Which probably said more about his relationship with his ex-wife than his own character, he conceded ruefully. In all honesty, if it hadn't been for Rosie they'd have probably split up long before they had.

So what did that say about the present situation? Why did he feel this overpowering need to protect Sara? And what had possessed him to tell Emma Proctor that she was Rosie's new nanny? By now the news was probably common knowledge throughout the county.

Yet, during the three days that had passed since Emma's visit, he had to admit that the demands on his time had been eased. Although he hadn't allowed Sara to pick Rosie up from school, there was no doubt that she had taken much of the responsibility for entertaining his daughter once she was home off his shoulders.

Of course, Sara wasn't a nanny. But he believed her story about being a teacher now. She was good with the little girl and Rosie liked her. In normal circumstances he'd have considered himself very lucky to have her, but these circumstances were anything but normal.

His scowl deepened. One of his main sources of discontent was the fact that Sara had resisted all his efforts to find out why she stayed with her husband. She insisted that in a few more days she would have to go back, and that was the real cause of his writer's block. Why did she feel any allegiance towards him? What twisted hold did the man have over her life?

Dammit! Leaving his desk, he walked to the windows, looking out on the scene that usually never failed to soothe his troubled psyche. The North Sea was grey today, reflecting the clouds that hovered over the headland. The mournful sound of a ship's foghorn seemed to echo his mood, and he lifted both hands to massage the taut muscles at the back of his neck.

He had to stop this, he told himself savagely. He had to stop behaving as if he had any role to play in Sara's future. Despite that emotional scene in her bedroom, when he'd made such a pathetic fool of himself, their association remained very much that of an employer and an employee. She'd accepted his excuse for staying on with obvious gratitude, but there'd been no further intimacy between them. Indeed, there were times when Matt wondered if he'd imagined the whole thing.

But then he'd remember the bruises he'd seen on her body and know he hadn't.

He swore again, balling a fist and pressing it hard against the windowframe. He increased the pressure until all the blood had left his fingers and his hand was numb. And then, with an angry exclamation, he withdrew it and thrust it into his pocket, finding a masochistic pleasure in the pain he'd inflicted upon himself.

At least he'd done as he'd promised and let Bradbury know that his wife was safe and well. Or as safe and well as a woman who'd been brutalised could be, he amended grimly. He had a friend at the *London Chronicle* and he'd merely called in a favour by getting him to deliver the note Sara had written. Of course he hadn't told her that he'd made the note public property, but there'd been no way he could have risked Max Bradbury burying it and continuing with his bogus concern.

As it was, there'd been a small item in yesterday's papers.

News of the letter had evidently circulated round the tabloid editors, as he'd hoped it would, and Bradbury had had to come up with a convincing explanation.

His story was that the blow he'd suffered to his head when he fell had temporarily robbed him of his memory. Thanks to Matt's friend, he was able to claim that he'd contacted the *Chronicle* himself, as soon as he'd remembered that Victoria had told him she was going to visit a schoolfriend in the north of England. He'd had a letter from her now, he said, and all was well.

Until she went back, thought Matt, feeling his muscles tighten again. He'd probably done her no favours by holding Bradbury's name up to possible ridicule, but it was too late now. It was just something else 'Victoria' would have to pay for.

Victoria!

His jaw clenched. One thing she had told him was that Victoria wasn't her real name. She'd been christened Sara, she said, and Matt could only assume that it hadn't been sophisticated enough for Max Bradbury's wife. Not that she'd complained about it to him. Despite the fear she obviously had of her husband, she was absurdly loyal. Even though she must know that by changing her name he had removed another of the props that had made her who she was.

Matt had decided not to show Sara the article in the newspaper. He hadn't wanted her to be concerned because Bradbury had implied that he knew where she was. The fact that he'd chosen to tell the media that she was in the north of England was just a coincidence. It had to be. But it was another example of how everything seemed to work to Bradbury's advantage.

Sara's rental car was no longer advertising her presence, at least. He'd had the garage in Saviour's Bay pick it up and return it to the local franchise in Ellsmoor, and, although he'd been forced to admit that there'd been nothing wrong with it in the first place, Sara hadn't complained. Whatever she chose to do after she left here, for the moment she seemed happy to be free of all obligations.

The phone rang before he could indulge in any further introspection, and, tamping down his resentment, he went to answer it.

'Yeah?'

'Matt?'

He recognised the voice at once. It was his agent, Rob Marco, and he pulled a wry face. He could guess what Rob wanted: some kind of timeframe for the completion of the new manuscript. The fact that he should have been in the final stages by now was just another cause for his tension.

'Hi, Rob,' he answered now, dropping down into his leather chair and propping his feet on the edge of his desk. He glanced at his watch. 'How are things with you?'

'They could be better,' replied Rob, with just the trace of an edge to his voice. 'How are things with you, Matt? When can I expect the new manuscript?'

Matt gave a sardonic snort. 'I should have guessed this wasn't a social call,' he said, hooking the phone between his ear and his shoulder and pulling open the bottom drawer of the desk. 'I don't work well with deadlines, Rob. You know that.'

There was a moment's silence while the other man considered his response and Matt used it to lift the half-empty bottle of whisky from the drawer. Unscrewing the cap, he treated himself to a healthy swig before setting it down beside the computer. He deserved some consolation, he told himself defensively. It was lunchtime, after all, and problems were assaulting him on all sides.

'I'm not giving you a deadline,' said Rob at last, his tone infinitely more conciliatory. 'But, as you know, your next book is due for publication in the spring. Your publishers would just like to be able to announce the date of publication of the new novel on the flyleaf.'

'What you mean is, they're hoping I'll sign a new contract,' remarked Matt drily. 'Have they come to you with any figures? I assume they've got an offer in mind?'

Rob sighed. 'We haven't gone into specifics, Matt. I wouldn't do that without your say-so. But Nash is a good publisher. They've done pretty well by you in the past.'

'In other words, you're interested,' said Matt, studying the toes of his loafers. Rob was a good agent, and if he was recommending another deal it meant Nash had come up with a pretty spectacular sum. Of course, the book Nash was hoping to negotiate for wasn't his current work in progress. Their interest had been prompted by his next project, an outline of which had been with his publishers for the past three weeks.

'It's inviting,' affirmed Rob. 'I doubt if you'd get a better offer.' He paused. 'They're hoping they can persuade you to sign a three-book deal this time. They're talking seven figures. That's as much as I'm going to say.'

Matt shook his head. 'Seven figures,' he echoed wryly, wishing he felt more enthusiasm for Rob's news. But right now getting his current manuscript finished and ready for despatch seemed an insurmountable task. The idea of committing himself to writing three more books, even with a seven-figure advance, sounded almost impossible to achieve.

'What's wrong?' Rob was nothing if not intuitive. 'Isn't it enough?'

'More than enough,' responded Matt, blowing out a breath. 'Thanks, Rob. As I've said before, you're the best agent in the business.'

'But you're not happy.' Rob wasn't deceived. 'Come on, Matt. What's your problem? Is it Rosie?'

'Rosie's fine.' Matt chose to answer his last question first.

'You got her a nanny, right?'

Matt hesitated. 'Not exactly.'

'Not exactly?' Rob was curious. 'What's that supposed to mean? Either you got her a nanny or you didn't.'

Matt wished he'd just answered in the negative and been done with it. 'I've got a temporary nanny,' he said at last. Then, hoping Rob would take the hint, 'Thanks for calling, Rob. I'll be in touch as soon as I have some definite news.'

Rob sounded put out. 'Is that all you're going to say?' he exclaimed. 'You haven't even told me how the new manuscript is coming along.'

'It's getting there,' said Matt evasively. 'I'm sorry if you think I'm ungrateful. I've got a lot on my plate at the moment.'

'Including the temporary nanny?' suggested Rob shrewdly.

'Who is she, Matt? A girlfriend? I tell you, pal, that's not a good idea. You should never mix business with pleasure.'

If only he could, thought Matt bitterly, and then chided himself for the thought. Just because Sara was grateful for his protection it did not mean she spent her time fantasising about what *he'd* be like in bed. After her experiences, sex would be the last thing on her mind. Besides, however unhappily, she was married. And at no time had she let him think that anything else was on the cards.

It was pathetic. *He* was pathetic, he thought irritably. At the first opportunity he should find himself another woman and get a life. There was always Emma. Since her husband had died she'd made no secret of the fact that she'd be willing to advance their relationship. But he wasn't attracted to Emma; he hadn't been attracted to anyone for a long time. So why the hell was Sara Bradbury playing havoc with his hormones?

'It's nothing like that,' he told Rob shortly. 'She's just someone I met recently who was looking for a job. But she's not staying. As I said before, it's just a temporary arrangement. But Rosie likes her. And that's what matters.'

'So what's she like?' Rob was trying to sound casual and failing abysmally. He'd probably made the connection between his evasion and Sara's arrival, thought Matt grimly. 'Is she young? Attractive? Married?'

A knock at the study door interrupted Matt's concentration. 'Come in,' he called impatiently, guessing it was Mrs Webb with a sandwich for his lunch. Then, to Rob. 'I'm not getting into what she looks like. She's—passable, okay? But in any case she doesn't interest me.'

It was only as he was completing this sentence that he looked up and realised it wasn't the housekeeper who was hovering in the doorway. With an inward groan, he let his eyes meet Sara's across the width of the room. She had evidently heard what he was saying to Rob and taken exception to it. He was devastated by the injured look that crossed her face.

'Ah. Damn—' His exclamation was audible to both Sara and Rob, but he didn't have time to spare his agent's feelings right now. 'Speak to you later, Rob,' he said quickly. 'Something's come up.' And, slamming down the phone, he got to his feet. 'Sara—'

'You didn't have to do that,' she said, the stiffness of her words only equalled by the rigidity of her stance. Matt closed his eyes for a moment against the almost irresistible impulse he had to leap across his desk and take her in his arms. 'I could have come back.'

She looked so delicate standing there, so fragile. Only yesterday he'd thought she was losing that look of vulnerability; that the time she'd spent outdoors with Rosie and the dogs had added a glow of health to her pale skin. She was still far too thin, of course, but her appetite was definitely improving. She'd been gaining in confidence, too. He could have sworn it.

Now his careless words had spoiled everything. And he could hardly tell her he'd only said what he had to put Rob off the scent. She wouldn't want to know why he'd said it. It wasn't her fault that she was having such a stressful effect on his life.

'Sara—' he began again, but she wouldn't let him finish.

'I only came to ask if you'd like your lunch now,' she continued, in the same unyielding tone. 'I heard the phone and it seemed a good opportunity to interrupt you.'

'I don't mind—'

'That's all right, then, isn't it?' She took a breath. 'I'll get your tray. Mrs Webb left it ready.'

'Dammit!' Matt swore. He'd forgotten that the housekeeper had told him she had a dental appointment at twelve o'clock. 'There's no need for you to run around after me. I don't expect it. I'm not your husband.'

'No, you're not.'

Sara was already retreating through the door when Matt went after her. He didn't know what had made him say what he had, but it was obvious she'd been hurt by his words. The trouble was, it was becoming more and more difficult not to show how he was feeling, and he wished he could explain it to her.

He caught her in the hall outside his study, his hand closing round her arm and bringing her to a halt. 'Sara,' he started again. 'I'm sorry if I was short with you. When Rob gets on the phone it's usually because he wants something that I can't give him.'

'I'm really not interested,' she said, making an effort to release herself from his hold, and Matt gave an impatient sigh.

'Listen to me,' he said. 'Rob Marco is my agent. He was ringing to ask why he hasn't had the new manuscript. I was making the excuse that I still didn't have a permanent nanny for Rosie.'

Sara's brows arched scornfully. 'So?'

'So that's why I said what I did,' exclaimed Matt doggedly. 'You probably thought I was criticising you. I wasn't, whatever it sounded like. I was just trying to distract Rob from his impression that you're really my girlfriend.'

'Look, I really don't care—'

'No, but I do,' muttered Matt, his patience wearing thin. 'I'm telling you the truth, dammit. If I'd finished the damn manuscript we wouldn't be having this conversation.'

'I hope you're not implying that I'm to blame for that,' she countered coldly, stiffening her back, and Matt expelled a long breath.

He was trying hard not to be aware of her small breasts rising and falling in tempo with her increasing indignation, the widening gap between her tee shirt and jeans exposing the intriguing hollow of her navel. She was so incredibly sexy, with her face flushed, her eyes sparkling with aggravated fire. He could feel a sensuous warmth spreading from his fingers to every erogenous nerve in his body, and he knew he was getting dangerously close to combustion.

'I didn't say that,' he said now, struggling to contain his frustration, and she uttered a triumphant snort.

'Good,' she said fiercely, and he had the sudden suspicion that she was using her anger to put a barrier between them. 'Because I suggest that bottle of whisky on your desk is far more culpable than me!'

Matt choked on an oath. 'Are you kidding?' he gasped. 'I've had one mouthful of Scotch and that's all.'

'So you say.'

'It's the truth.' He was aware of a growing sense of outrage. 'I'm not an alcoholic.'

'Well, it isn't even lunchtime yet,' she persisted, and he shook his head in angry disbelief.

'Where do you get off telling me what to do?' he demanded, using his free hand to pull her round to face him, and then could have died with mortification when he saw her flinch.

It was obvious that she had encountered this kind of situation before and she expected the worst. The look in her eyes damned and humiliated him, and with a groan of anguish he hauled her into his arms.

'God, I'm sorry,' he muttered, one hand cradling the back of her neck while the other circled her waist. Silky hair brushed his fingers and her skin was incredibly soft beneath his hands. 'Hell, Sara, don't you know I would never hurt you?'

Her response was muffled, but he could feel the sudden wetness that was dampening his shirt. She was crying, and her distress assaulted him like acid on an open wound. He felt so powerless; so useless. He wanted to help her, but all he was doing was turning her against him, too.

'Sara, Sara,' he breathed, his fingers caressing her nape, and she did the unforgivable and turned her face up to his.

Her eyes were flooded with tears, but her expression was more forgiving than accusatory. Lashes, several shades darker than her hair, sparkled with jewelled drops, and Matt's tongue itched to lick them away. She was so beautiful, so vulnerable, and the knowledge that he had no right to hold her like this was tearing him to pieces. Did she know what she was doing? he wondered. What she was doing to him? Of course she did, he assured himself. He was holding her too close for the swelling in his pants to be ignored.

Then, 'Matt,' she said huskily, and it was more than he could bear.

When her hand lifted to his face he caught it and brought her palm to his lips. But even that wasn't enough. He wanted her so much, wanted more than he had any right to expect, and he might never have another chance like this.

Her eyes were wide now, her lips parted and unknowingly

sensual. There was a moment when he might have drawn back, when he might have fought the demons that were riding him, but the sight of her tongue defeated him. When the pink tip appeared to circle her lips, he knew he had to taste it, and, cupping her face between his hands, he bent his head and kissed her.

'Forgive me,' he groaned, his tongue slipping into her mouth, and after only a momentary hesitation she yielded to his intimate caress.

He'd intended to be gentle with her. He was fairly sure that any relationship she'd had with her husband would not have been gentle, and he'd wanted there to be no confusion between who was holding her, who was kissing her now.

But the moment his mouth covered hers all reason deserted him. He was like a man in the desert who was suddenly presented with a flask of cool clear water and didn't realise until that moment that he was dying of thirst. Maybe it was the way her lips opened to his, or the sensuous brush of her tongue. Or perhaps the devastating realisation he had that she was kissing him back.

Whatever, at that moment all bets were off. The heat that flared between them was automatic and uncontrollable, and Matt's mind swam with the emotions she so easily aroused inside him. He was like a man possessed, and when she wound her arms around his waist and hooked her thumbs into his belt he swayed back against the wall behind him, taking her with him.

The blood was pounding in his head, thundering through his veins, making any kind of coherent thought impossible. She burrowed against him, making him overwhelmingly aware of the layers of fabric that divided them. His skin felt raw, sensitised. He had to fight the urge to peel her tee shirt from her and bury his face between her breasts.

His hands slid down her back as he continued to kiss her, lingering on the bare skin of her midriff that was so tantalisingly warm to his touch. The temptation to slide his hands beneath the tee shirt and caress the erect nipples that were straining the soft material was almost irresistible, but he dammed the impulse and cupped her rounded bottom instead.

Urging her against him was the purest form of torture, but it was worth it. Spreading his legs, he cradled her against the erection throbbing between his thighs. She rubbed herself against him and he wondered if she had any idea what she was inviting. How much more of this could he take without losing it completely?

And then she moaned.

It was a plaintive little sound, barely audible, in fact, but he heard it. For a moment he thought he'd hurt her. He was half afraid that his urgent hands had been too rough for her delicate skin. But then, with a shocking sense of his own insanity, he suddenly realised what was wrong.

With unsteady hands he managed to put some space between them, avoiding her eyes as he made some inane apology for touching her as he had. And all the while he chided himself for being a fool, for imagining that she had been as caught up in her emotions as he was. It wasn't true. That grotesque little moan had proved it. He'd been making love to a woman who had undoubtedly been conditioned never to say no…

CHAPTER TEN

'BUT why can't you stay?' Rosie gazed up at Sara with tear-filled eyes. 'I don't want you to go.'

'And I don't want to go,' said Sara, wondering if she was being entirely wise in admitting as much. But she hated lying to the child. 'I'm sorry, sweetheart. But this was just a temporary arrangement.'

'But why?' Rosie wouldn't let it go. 'You like it here. You said so. And I like you. Mrs Webb likes you. Even Daddy likes you.'

Does he?

Sara reserved judgement on that. Since that morning a couple of days ago, when Mrs Webb had gone to the dentist, Matt had barely spoken two words to her, and she was left with the unhappy conclusion that he regretted what had happened.

She regretted it, too, she reflected painfully, but for totally different reasons. Which was quite an admission to make, she conceded with a twinge of shame. Was she wicked for regretting that Matt hadn't gone on and finished what he'd started? Was it completely unforgivable to wish that for once in her miserable life she might have known the joy of a real man's love?

Only Matt didn't love her, she reminded herself swiftly. Once again she was deluding herself about the reason for his actions, just as she had deluded herself that Max had ever really cared about her. She was a pathetic creature, so desperate for affection that she was willing to do almost anything to prove that Max's estimation of her wasn't true.

And, until Matt had pushed her away from him and taken refuge in his study, she had believed that she might be happy here. For the first time in years she'd felt secure; wanted; almost content. It was only later that she'd wondered if she hadn't been deceiving herself all along. It wasn't the house or the circum-

118

stances of her employment that had made her feel secure. It was Matt. Only Matt. And how sad was that?

'When are you leaving?'

Until Rosie spoke again Sara had been staring blindly out of the window, but now she turned to the child with rueful eyes. And felt even worse when she saw the tragic look on the little girl's face.

'Well, not today,' she said with determined cheerfulness, picking up a velour skirt and jacket that belonged to one of Rosie's dolls and exhibiting it for her approval. 'What do you think of this? Smart, or what?'

They were sitting on the floor of the family room, and until Rosie had brought up the subject of Sara's employment again they'd been sorting through the toy cupboard for things Rosie could donate to the school fair.

Matt had collected his daughter from school a couple of hours ago. Sara had been having a cup of tea with Mrs Webb in the kitchen when they'd got back and Matt had merely deposited the little girl with them before heading back to his study.

'That man's overdoing it,' the housekeeper had remarked sagely as Rosie helped herself to a biscuit from the tin. 'He's looking tired, don't you think? I suppose it's because he's trying to get as much done as he can before you have to go back to London. He's going to miss you and that's a fact.'

Sara had made some non-committal comment, not wanting to get into a discussion about Matt in front of the child. It was only now she realised that, however distracted she'd seemed at the time, Rosie missed very little.

As if to underline this thought, she scrambled to her feet now and climbed onto the window seat. 'Shall we go for a walk?'

'A walk?' Sara looked up at her. 'But it will be supper time soon.' She paused. 'Besides, I thought you wanted to tidy the toy cupboard.'

'I can do that any time,' said Rosie, her small fingers making damp circles on the glass. She glanced back with accusing eyes. 'When you're not here.'

Sara sighed. 'Oh, Rosie—'

'Well, can we? Go for a walk, I mean? We don't have to

take the dogs. Daddy took them out before I went to school this morning.'

'Did he?'

Sara hadn't known that. He must have taken them out incredibly early, she thought. She'd been up herself at seven o'clock.

'Daddy's always up early,' continued Rosie, getting down again and standing with her feet apart and her hands on her hips, staring at Sara. 'I'm never late for school these days.'

'Well, that's good,' said Sara, getting to her feet and smiling at the little girl. 'You don't want to be late, do you?'

'I don't care.' Rosie was deliberately offhand. 'I'll be going away to school soon, and then it won't matter.'

Sara blinked. 'Going away to school?' she echoed. 'Who told you that?'

Rosie shrugged, bundling all the toys and games they'd taken out back into the cupboard and closing the door. 'Are we going for a walk?'

'In a minute.' Sara wanted to know what Rosie had heard. 'Is that what your daddy says?'

Rosie was still offhand. 'Maybe.'

'What do you mean, maybe? Either he did or he didn't.'

Rosie pursed her lips. 'I heard him talking to Mrs Armstrong.'

Sara frowned. 'Mrs Armstrong? Is that your teacher?'

'No. My teacher's Mrs Sanders,' said Rosie scornfully. 'Mrs Armstrong is Rupert and Nigel's mother.'

'Oh, I see.' Sara assumed they must be children in her class. 'And—you heard your daddy telling Mrs Armstrong that you'd be going away to school soon? Is that right?'

'No.' Rosie started for the door. 'Can we go?'

Sara heaved a sigh. She had no right to question the child, but she wanted to know what Matt had been saying. It was obvious it was on Rosie's mind, and perhaps he ought to be told that it wasn't wise to discuss his daughter's future with—with whom? Who was this Mrs Armstrong? Apart from being Rupert and Nigel's mother, of course. Was she another woman, like Emma Proctor, who considered herself more than just a friend?

'We'll go when you tell me what you heard,' she declared firmly, and Rosie sniffed.

'Does it matter?'

'I think it might.'

Sara gazed at her solemnly, wishing she didn't have to be stern with her. Rosie looked so adorable in her white canvas shorts and striped tee shirt, and Sara was tempted to take her in her arms and hug her and tell her that Matt wouldn't dream of sending her away to school. But until she knew what had been said she had to tamp down her emotions, even if the little girl had found a special place in her heart.

'Oh—well…' Rosie was reluctant to go on. 'It was something Mrs Armstrong said, that's all.'

'Which was?'

'Well, she said Daddy hadn't been very lucky with nannies,' mumbled Rosie unwillingly. 'That when you left he'd likely have to send me away.'

'She said that!' Sara was appalled.

'Not 'xactly.'

'Well, what *exactly* did she say?' demanded Sara, and then felt her face flood with hot colour when she suddenly realised that Matt was standing in the open doorway.

He must have heard what they were saying, she thought, a sinking feeling in her stomach. Oh, God, he was going to think she'd been pumping the child for information. He might even think she was curious about this Mrs Armstrong, whoever she was. And just because he might be right that was no excuse.

'What's going on?' he asked, his gaze moving between them, and Sara and Rosie exchanged an embarrassed look.

The little girl recovered herself first. 'We were just talking about school, Daddy,' she said, with remarkable aplomb. 'Now we're going for a walk.'

'Wait a minute.' Sara thought she should have known that Matt wouldn't swallow that. 'I think you should go and check with Mrs Webb first. She may have something she wants you to do.'

'Like what?'

Rosie was indignant, but her father's expression warned her not to argue. With a hunching of her shoulders she marched out of the door, leaving Sara to face the music alone.

Matt waited until his daughter was out of earshot and then arched an enquiring brow. 'School?' he said, without inflection. 'What have you been telling her?'

'Me?' Despite the quickening of her heartbeat, Sara managed to sound reasonably calm. 'I haven't been telling her anything. Well, not about school anyway.'

Matt came further into the room. He was wearing shorts today, khaki shorts that exposed his long muscled legs. Like hers, his black tee shirt barely skimmed his waistband, and her eyes were unwillingly drawn to the wedge of brown skin that appeared every time he moved.

Why was it that when she looked at him she was so acutely aware of her own sexuality? she wondered. Why, when for years she'd believed herself immune from any man's attraction, was she so irresistibly drawn to Matt's masculine grace? It was pointless, when all was said and done, and foolish. But she couldn't help herself. And if Max ever found out...

Well, he'd make her suffer for it, she reflected bitterly. But then, he'd make her suffer anyway. And perhaps she deserved his contempt. She was his wife, after all. She shouldn't be having these kinds of feelings for a man who wasn't her husband. Yet it was such a long time since Max had engendered anything inside her but fear and revulsion.

Even thinking about what was facing her when she returned to London was terrifying. Max was never going to forgive her for leaving him as she had. She mustn't forget that he knew that she was to blame for his fall. However accidental it might have been, she would bear the brunt of his wrath.

'So what were you talking about?'

Matt's words broke into her pained reverie and she forced herself to meet his dark gaze. Was that an accusation she could see in the depths of his eyes? Or was it just, as Mrs Webb had said, that he did look excessively weary?

She hesitated now, and then, deciding she had nothing to

lose, she said quietly, 'Are you thinking of sending Rosie away to school?'

'What?'

He looked stunned, and Sara felt somewhat reassured. 'You're not?'

'What the hell are you talking about?' he demanded, and then, as if noting how his angry words affected her, he calmed down. 'Where did you get that idea?'

'Would you believe from Rosie?' Sara dug her fingers into the back pockets of her jeans, aware that her hands were sweating. She wished she had shorts to wear, she thought ruefully. The jeans were far too warm for the humid weather they were having at present. But beggars couldn't be choosers. 'I think she's worried about what you're planning to do when I leave.'

'Rosie?' Matt shook his head. 'But I've never—'

'Not even to Mrs Armstrong?' asked Sara, before she lost her nerve, and Matt's eyes narrowed.

'Gloria?' he said, apparently confirming that he knew the woman far better than Sara could have wished.

'If that's her name,' she agreed, annoyed to hear the note of censure in her voice. 'I believe you were discussing the problems you were having in keeping a nanny with her.'

'Blast!' Matt raised a hand and raked long fingers over his scalp. His action widened the gap between his shirt and his shorts and once again Sara's eyes were drawn to his flat stomach. 'What did Rosie say?'

'What? Oh—' Sara swallowed, finding it difficult to drag her gaze away from his taut body. Trying to concentrate on what she was saying, she mumbled, 'I don't remember exactly what she said now.'

'No?' Matt didn't sound convinced, and, as if becoming aware of her distraction, he uttered a rough oath. Turning away from her, he added in a strangled voice, 'Dammit, Sara, will you stop looking at me that way? It's difficult enough keeping my hands off you as it is.'

Sara sucked in her breath. She'd never expected that. 'I'm sorry,' she said huskily. She turned towards the door. 'Would you like me to go?'

Matt gave an incredulous snort. 'No, I wouldn't like you to go,' he retorted harshly. 'I think you know what I'd really like you to do, so don't let's pretend we're fooling anybody here. You're married, and for some crazy reason you insist on going back to your husband. I can't say I'm happy about it, but my feelings don't count for much, do they?'

'Matt—'

'Don't,' he advised her grimly, putting the width of the room between them. Then, squaring his shoulders, he turned back to face her. 'Now, tell me what you know about my conversation with Gloria.'

Sara licked her dry lips. She didn't want to talk about Gloria Armstrong, she thought impatiently. What she really wanted was for Matt to tell her how he really felt about her being here. Yet, as he'd said, she had no right to expect anything more from him. He'd done what he could to help her and that ought to be enough.

But it wasn't. She wanted so much more.

He was waiting for her answer, and her heart gave an odd little flutter at the strangely vulnerable look on his face. He was a tall man, strong and virile, his dark hair tumbled by the restless invasion of his hands. Even with the shadow of stubble on his jawline and his mouth set in a grim line he set her pulses racing. She had no fear of him. He'd taught her that strength could be tempered not with violence, but love.

But she couldn't tell him that. Shaking her head, she struggled to remember what they'd been talking about before she'd been distracted. 'I—I've told you all I know,' she submitted at last. And then, to assuage her own frustration, she added, 'Is Mrs Armstrong another of your admirers?'

'Another of my—' Matt's eyes darkened. 'I don't have admirers, Sara. Gloria Armstrong's husband farms the land north of here. They have two boys who are in Rosie's class.'

Sara lifted her shoulders. 'I see.'

'Do you?' Matt turned away from her again and stared broodingly out of the window. 'What did you think? That I have a covey of women I can call on when I want to get laid?'

Sara couldn't prevent herself. 'And do you?'

'Oh, sure.' Matt scowled at her over his shoulder. 'I'm a regular stud!'

Sara pressed her lips together, not sure how to take him now. 'Why doesn't that surprise me?' she muttered, and he made an exasperated sound.

'I won't dignify that comment with a response,' he stated harshly. 'Dammit, Sara, don't you know me better than that? And before you start on Emma, I'll tell you that she and I are just good friends.'

'Her husband, too?'

'What's it to you?' Matt swung round. Then, as if taking pity on her, he made an impatient gesture. 'She's a widow,' he said. 'Her husband was killed in a car crash about two years ago, leaving her with a ten-year-old son to raise on her own.'

Sara frowned. 'This would be—Darren, yes?'

'You don't miss much, do you?' Matt was ironic. 'But, yeah. Darren's her son.'

'I suppose—I suppose she depends on you,' ventured Sara cautiously, not quite sure where she was going with this. 'Are you—very close?'

'I told you—'

'I know what you said,' said Sara quickly, 'but you have to admit Mrs Proctor doesn't behave like a—a casual acquaintance.'

Matt groaned. 'What does it matter to you?'

Sara stared at him. 'It matters,' she said huskily, and then, shaking her head, she started towards the door. 'I—I'll see what Rosie's doing.'

'Don't!'

His hoarse command resonated through every nerve in her body, but before she could do anything more than register the fact that Matt was as aroused by their exchange as she was they heard the sound of Rosie's footsteps scampering along the hall towards them.

At once, Matt turned back to the window, adjusting the fit of his shorts with an unsteady hand. By the time Rosie appeared in the doorway he had control of himself again, but Sara couldn't forget the smouldering look he had cast in her direction in the seconds before Rosie burst into the room.

'Daddy, Daddy!'

Rosie's excitement was palpable and, however he was really feeling, Matt managed a tolerant smile for his daughter. 'Hey, sweetheart,' he said, 'what on earth's going on? What did Mrs Webb say?'

Rosie shook her head, her sooty bob bouncing about her face. 'Mrs Webb didn't say anything,' she exclaimed, wrapping her arms about his waist. 'Uncle Rob is here. He came in a taxi. Didn't you hear it?'

'Rob?' Matt was clearly shocked. 'Rob's here?'

'That's what the lady said,' remarked a drawling voice behind them, and Sara swung round to find a tall fair-haired man standing in the doorway. 'Hey, Matt! Long time, no see.'

Sara saw Matt register the complications that the other man's arrival might represent before he could control his features. Already the man's eyes were turning in her direction, and there was speculation as well as admiration in his gaze.

'And you must be the temporary nanny,' he declared lightly. 'I should have known Seton would fall on his feet.'

'That's Sara,' said Rosie at once, letting go of her father to skip across the room to take her hand. But Matt had recovered now, and his harsh voice overrode the little girl's introduction.

'What are you doing here, Rob?' he asked with obvious exasperation. 'I said I'd be in touch.'

'And you know what they said about the mountain and Mohammed?' Rob was sardonic. 'I thought you might be pleased to see me.' He held up the leather attaché case in his hand. 'I come bearing gifts.'

'I don't care what the hell you come bearing,' retorted Matt flatly. 'You should have let me know you were coming.'

'Yeah.' Rob pulled a face. 'Well, I can see you're pretty tied up at the moment.' He looked at Sara again. 'Nice to meet you, Sara. Nannies are getting better-looking all the time. I'm Rob Marco, by the way. Matt's agent, in case he hasn't mentioned me. I must say, you must have some patience to deal with this bad-tempered bast—guy!'

'Oh—' Sara exchanged an awkward look with Matt. 'We get along,' she said. Then, nervously, 'If you'll excuse me—'

'Me and Sara are going for a walk,' declared Rosie, who hadn't forgotten anything. 'You don't mind, Daddy, do you? Not now you've got Uncle Rob to talk to.'

Sara thought there was a lot Matt would have liked to say but his daughter had effectively silenced him. Instead, it was left to Rob Marco to remark drily, 'Shouldn't that be *Sara and I*, Rosie?' He gave Sara a mocking grin. 'Aren't *nannies* supposed to notice stuff like that?'

'Cut it out, Rob.' Matt spoke before Sara could attempt to defend herself. Then, to his daughter, 'You can go for a walk. But only as far as the cliff path, okay?'

Rosie pursed her lips. 'But, Daddy—'

'Take it or leave it.'

Matt was unyielding, but Sara's attention was suddenly riveted by the speculative expression on Rob Marco's face. 'Hey,' he exclaimed, staring at her, 'I know you.' His brows drew together consideringly. 'You're Victoria Bradbury, aren't you? Max Bradbury's wife. I'd recognise those classy features anywhere.'

Sara's face drained of colour. 'No, I—'

'Sure you are.' Rob was adamant. 'Hell, I saw your picture in the paper just a few days ago.' He snorted. 'Your husband was insisting you'd been kidnapped. I might have known the guy was just covering his backside.'

'Please—'

Sara didn't realise she was begging him not to go on, but it did no good.

'Of course, that wasn't the end of it. Not this time,' Rob continued, apparently indifferent to the dismay on her face. 'Bradbury had apparently had a fall and banged his head, and a couple of days later he claimed it was all a mistake. He said he'd now had a letter from you and that you were staying with a schoolfriend. He reckoned he'd forgotten all about it, but it got people talking, I can tell you. I mean, after what happened to his first wife, it would have been quite a coincidence if you'd disappeared, too.'

Sara's lips parted. 'Max's first wife drowned,' she said, hardly realising she was confirming his suspicions by admitting as much, and Rob pulled a wry face.

'Well, that's the story, anyway,' he agreed drily. 'But there have always been doubts that that was the truth.' Then, as if belatedly acknowledging the upheaval he was causing, he added, 'Well, no worries. I can see you're okay. But—' his eyes switched to Matt '—don't tell me you're the old school-friend, pal, 'cos I won't believe it.'

CHAPTER ELEVEN

MOONLIGHT streamed into the bedroom. Sara hadn't drawn her curtains deliberately. She'd left the window ajar, too, so that she could hear the ceaseless boom of the sea. It might be the last time she could indulge herself in this way, and, although she was tired, she was too unsettled to sleep.

Rob Marco's presence weighed heavily on her mind. Matt's agent was going back to London the next day, and although she had no doubt that Matt would impress on him the need to keep her whereabouts a secret she didn't altogether trust him. She guessed he resented her just as much as she resented his intrusion into their lives. As far as he was concerned she was the reason Matt hadn't finished his new manuscript, and was it that unreasonable to wonder if he might not drop a hint in certain circles, enabling Max to find her?

He had the right connections, after all. He'd admitted that he and Max's brother belonged to the same club, and it would be so easy for him to mention to Hugo that she was staying with a client of his. She could hardly blame him. Matt's sales provided a large part of his income and, if what he'd been saying at supper was true, there was a rather impressive contract in the offing, only awaiting Matt's signature.

So what was she thinking? That she'd have to go back to London, too? The very idea terrified her, but she knew that the longer she put it off, the harder it was going to be.

The news that Max had made her letter public was daunting. She wondered if that had been Hugo's idea. It simply wasn't like her husband to admit that he'd made a mistake. Of course, it was possible that he was still suffering concussion from the fall, and perhaps if she could get back before Max had totally recovered from his injuries he might be persuaded that she'd meant no harm.

Yeah, right.

A shudder racked her slim body, and even though it wasn't a cold night she pulled the sheet more closely about her. Since she had no nightwear, she was obliged to sleep in the nude, and tonight, for the first time since she'd come here, she felt exposed and vulnerable.

Dear Lord, Max was going to be so angry with her. He'd been angry in the past, frequently, but he'd never had such an excuse for punishing her before. She should never have run away as she had; she should have stayed and faced the consequences. The excuse she'd given Matt for her flight seemed such a pitiable thing now that she knew Max was alive and well. Who would believe her story? Her mother? Unlikely. Max? No chance.

Besides, it had been an unforgivable thing to do and she knew it. What kind of a woman was she that she should leave her husband's unconscious body lying unattended at the foot of the stairs? What kind of wife didn't care if her husband was alive or dead?

An abused one, she answered herself bitterly. Only an abused woman would have run as she had. Only an abused wife would have believed that her word would mean less than nothing to the people who mattered. Only someone who was used to being tortured for the mildest transgression would have expected to be punished for a simple accident.

And she hadn't left him completely alone. She'd called the emergency services and left the apartment unlocked so that they could get in and attend to him.

Yet, with hindsight, she realised that that was just another rod for Max to beat her with. He was a wealthy man. A connoisseur of beautiful things. The apartment was full of porcelain and artwork that was totally irreplaceable. He'd accuse her of caring so little for his possessions that she'd been prepared to invite a thief into their home.

Sara expelled a long shuddering sigh. It seemed that everything she'd done since Max's accident had been designed to condemn her. She wondered now what he'd told her mother. If past experience was anything to go by he'd have aroused her sympathy for the mistake he was supposed to have made, at the same time leaving her with the distinct impression that Sara was to blame. Perhaps he'd also implied that she'd left without giving him any warning—which was true!—and in his confused state, he'd naturally jumped to the wrong conclusion.

Oh, yes, she was sure Max's story would exonerate him. And, because her mother thought the sun shone out of his eyes, she'd have swallowed it hook, line and sinker.

Sara sniffed, feeling the hot tears behind her eyes. She despised people who felt sorry for themselves, but right now she couldn't help it. Her mother had always taken Max's side against her, had never been willing to listen to any complaint her daughter attempted to make. Right now, Sara knew, it would be incredibly easy to convince herself that without her mother's encouragement she would never have married Max in the first place, even if that wasn't entirely fair.

Nevertheless, it was true that since her father's death some fifteen years ago her mother had depended on her daughter more and more. The fact that Mr Fielding had died in the course of his work as a police constable had caused her mother both bitterness and grief. She'd been sorry he was dead, but she'd resented the fact that he'd left her with only his police pension to live on. Sara could do nothing to change her mother's belief that she'd been badly let down.

She could never remember her mother speaking of her father without that thread of bitterness running through her words. And although another woman might have gone out and made an alternative life for herself, Mrs Fielding had chosen to stay at home feeling sorry for herself.

Sara had worked to support herself through college. She'd gained admission to a local university, which had enabled her to continue to live at home. She'd done her best to make life comfortable for her mother. But it had never been enough. She had never done enough. Until Max Bradbury came on the scene.

Sara still didn't know why he'd taken such a fancy to her. She was totally unaware that her pale oval features possessed a subtle beauty that Max had insisted was only evident to the discerning eye. She had been flattered by his attentions; she admitted it. And the idea that her mother would never have to worry about money again had been appealing.

Oh, she'd been attracted by his money, too, she conceded wearily. In the weeks before their marriage she'd only had to mention that she needed something and it had been hers. Gifts of cosmetics and lingerie had arrived daily, and she'd learned not to confide her wishes to him. It wasn't that she hadn't appreciated what he was doing for her. It was just that she hadn't liked the feelings of obligation she'd started to have.

Her mother had been in seventh heaven, of course. Max owned property in Bloomsbury, and he'd suggested that Mrs Fielding might prefer to live in a comfortable apartment, free of rent, after they were married, instead of staying on alone in the small townhouse she and Sara had shared.

Max had known what he was doing, Sara thought now. With Mrs Fielding ensconced in her new home there'd been no way she could back out. Besides, she hadn't wanted to. She'd convinced herself she was a very lucky woman, indeed.

Max was older, of course, and he'd told her his first wife had died in tragic circumstances. But that had only aroused her sympathy. She'd believed him when he'd said he'd never expected to fall in love again.

It hadn't been until after the wedding was over that she'd come to realise that Max's interest in her had been inspired by other, less flattering motives. He had seen her as a woman without any protection. A possession he could use in any way he chose.

From the very beginning he'd known she was at his mercy. Even when he'd told her he was sorry for hurting her he hadn't meant it. He'd enjoyed brutalising her too much to abandon his cruelty. There had seemed no way she could escape the hell her life had become.

She shivered now, in spite of the warm summer air drifting in through the open window. Not for the first time she wondered if Max's first wife's death had been the accident he claimed. Perhaps the poor woman had killed herself. If he had hurt her, too, why not?

She so much didn't want to go back to London. But God

help her, what else could she do? She was Max's wife; Max's possession. And he was never going to let her go.

Realising she wouldn't sleep in her present state of mind, Sara pushed back the covers and got out of bed. Not bothering with underwear, she pulled on one of her tee shirts and Matt's old sweat pants. The fleecy lining of the pants was warm against her bare legs and she was comforted by the knowledge that they belonged to Matt, that they'd clung to his long legs as they were clinging to hers.

Then, opening her bedroom door, she went out onto the landing. The house appeared to be in darkness. Mrs Webb was long gone and Rosie would be fast asleep, clutching the furry bunny that always shared her bed.

Sara's lips twitched at the thought of the little girl. She would have so much liked a little girl like Rosie herself. But even if Max had wanted a child she would have done her best to avoid giving him that hold over her. It was bad enough knowing that her mother was at his mercy. She would never have forgiven herself if she'd caused a child to suffer because of her.

She was barefoot and her feet made no sound on the stairs. She didn't know which room Rob Marco was occupying, but she guessed he would be fast asleep, too. He'd delivered his small bombshell and she doubted he had any feelings of remorse to keep him awake.

She was crossing the hall to the library when she became aware that someone was standing in the passageway that led to the kitchen. Her heart leapt into her throat and she was half afraid that Rob Marco had had the same problem as herself. But then Matt said roughly, 'What the hell are you doing?' and the breath gushed out of her lungs in a rush.

'I—I can't sleep,' she replied in a strained voice. 'I came to get something to read.' Then, more defensively, 'What are you doing?'

Matt's shoulders lifted. He was just a shadow in the darkness, but, as if wanting to reassure her, he moved into the shaft of moonlight that speared through the fan-shaped window above the door.

'Would you believe getting a drink?' he asked, pushing his

hands into the pockets of the black jeans he'd worn at supper. His action drew her attention to the fact that the jeans weren't fastened. They looked as if, like hers, they'd been pulled on for decency's sake and little else. He wasn't wearing a shirt either, and his chest gleamed like copper in the pale light.

Sara made a helpless little sound. 'Isn't it the truth?' she asked, and heard his sudden intake of breath.

'No.'

She frowned. 'Are you worried about finishing your book?'

'Oh, yeah.' Matt was sardonic. 'I'm always worrying about stuff like that.'

'You are?' She stared at him and he scowled.

'No, dammit,' he muttered. Then, with a speculative glance up the stairs, he walked past her and opened his study door. 'Let's go in here. I prefer not to risk having my conversations overheard.'

Sara followed his gaze. 'But who—?'

'Walls have ears,' he remarked drily, switching on the lamp beside his desk and holding open the door. 'Are you coming in?'

Sara knew she ought to say no. She insisted to herself that had she known she was going to run into Matt she'd never have come down here. Borrowing a book was such a pathetic excuse, after all. Hadn't she really been hoping to find the decanter of Scotch that was kept on the table just inside the library door? She wasn't in the habit of using alcohol as a sedative, but she had wondered if it might improve her chances of getting to sleep.

Now, faced with temptation, she crumbled. This might be the last opportunity she'd have to be alone with Matt, when all was said and done. With a nervous twitch of her braid, she didn't hesitate before following him into the room.

She'd never been in Matt's study before, not with the door closed and the glow of lamplight to add to the illusion of enchantment. The only other occasion she'd ventured into his domain had been when she'd come to ask him if he wanted lunch, and she remembered only too well how that had turned out.

And he'd been fully dressed then, she reminded herself

tensely, turning her head away from the intimacy he represented. With his hair rumpled and the shadow of stubble on his jawline he made her think of all the things she'd forfeited when she'd married Max. And she was suddenly acutely aware of the seam of the sweat pants abrading the sensitive place between her legs.

To distract herself, she looked about the room, noticing the sophisticated computer on his desk, the laser printer and the stacks of printed sheets, the modem that enabled him to send his finished manuscript over the phone lines. There was a leather office chair behind his desk and a matching easy chair in the corner, and shelves of reference videos and CDs to play on the comprehensive digital system that occupied a space beneath the window.

It was a working environment, yet it possessed a warmth and charm that Sara hadn't noticed on her first visit. Perhaps it had something to do with the huge potted fern that filled another corner, or the many pictures on the walls that reflected his love of this part of the country. Castles and the wilderness of Coquetdale, ruined peel towers and rugged coasts, the impressive bulk of Holy Island, with the magnificent arches of Lindisfarne Priory still standing after years of Viking attacks.

'Isn't that where St Cuthbert is supposed to have translated the gospels?' she asked in a tight voice, desperate for something to say. She was instinctively aware that Matt was watching her and she sensed him shake his head.

'That's Lindisfarne Castle,' he said tolerantly. 'Nothing remains of the old monastery. But it's said that they used the stones from its ruins to build the castle.'

Sara managed a fleeting glance in his direction. 'How interesting.'

'Yes, isn't it,' he agreed without conviction. 'Is there anything else you want to know?'

Sara's shoulders sagged. It was obvious he knew exactly what she was doing; why she was finding it so hard to behave naturally. But what was she supposed to say, for heaven's sake? She could hardly come right out and tell him how she was feeling. He wouldn't want to know that.

'Are there ghosts?' she enquired at last, and Matt's nostrils flared.

'Where?' he countered. 'On Holy Island? Or in this room?'

Sara had to look at him then. 'I don't know what you mean.'

'Yes, you do.' He wasn't having that. 'Personally, I don't give a damn about ghosts, dead or alive. And I don't believe you came down here just to indulge in a discussion about the supernatural.' He impaled her with his dark gaze. 'Did you?'

Sara was defensive. 'You know why I came—'

'To get a book,' interrupted Matt. 'Yeah, you said. I just don't happen to believe it, that's all.'

Sara held up her head. 'Well, you're flattering yourself if you think that I hoped I'd run into you,' she retorted indignantly, and Matt sagged back against his desk and folded his arms across his broad chest.

'Did I say I thought you'd hoped you'd run into me?' he enquired, regarding her steadily. 'Could be you were planning to run away again.'

Sara caught her breath. 'In my bare feet?' she exclaimed. 'I don't think so.'

Matt surveyed her bare toes with a critical eye and Sara had to resist the urge to curl them into the carpet. 'Okay,' he conceded, acknowledging her point. 'So what are you doing, wandering about my house in the dead of night?'

Sara sighed. 'I couldn't sleep.'

'Yeah, you said that.'

'Well—' She gave a nervous little shrug of her shoulders. 'I thought I might get myself a—a nightcap.'

Matt's brows ascended. 'A nightcap? As in cocoa, Ovaltine, or what?'

'As in whisky,' admitted Sara reluctantly. 'I noticed you have a decanter of Scotch in—in the library.'

'Whisky?' His tone was deliberately mocking now. 'You were thinking of using whisky as a sedative? Why, Sara, have I corrupted you?'

Sara looked annoyed. 'There's no need to be sarcastic,' she said shortly. 'There's a great deal of difference between taking a drop at bedtime and swigging alcohol in the middle of the day!'

Matt gave a snort. 'I was not swigging alcohol,' he exclaimed. 'Hey, I was stressed, okay?' He gave her a dark look. 'And, before you jump down my throat again, I'm not blaming you. This is my problem. I'll get over it.'

Sara felt ashamed. 'Is—is the book going badly?' she ventured, desperate to avoid the growing intimacy between them, and Matt gave a dismissive shrug.

'What's that expression? It's going as well as can be expected?' Then, tucking his hands beneath his arms, he gave her a cynical smile before commenting, 'Well, isn't this cosy? I haven't been to a pyjama party since I was in short trousers.'

Sara hunched her shoulders. 'I'm not wearing pyjamas.'

'Don't remind me.' His eyes were narrowed and intent. 'You're wearing my old sweat pants, which is a lot less easy to deal with.' His gaze lowered to the tied waistline. 'Humour me. Are you wearing anything underneath?'

Sara was taken aback. 'Are you?' she countered before she could prevent herself, gesturing towards his jeans, and Matt uttered a colourful oath.

'Don't ask,' he advised her harshly. 'Not unless you want to find out.'

Sara's throat was dry. 'Perhaps I do,' she ventured, staring at him, and Matt closed his eyes to avoid her disturbing gaze.

'Sara,' he said heavily. 'This is—not wise.'

Sara sighed. 'I know,' she agreed huskily. 'But—I'm leaving tomorrow.'

Matt's looked stunned. 'You don't mean that.'

'I do.' Sara swallowed. 'You knew I'd have to leave sooner or later. Now that—now that Rob knows I'm here, I think it's the wisest thing to do.'

'No!' Matt's denial was heartfelt. 'For God's sake, Sara, you know how I feel about you going back to that bastard!' He straightened from the desk. 'Dammit, I don't want you to go.'

Sara stepped backward. It wasn't that she was afraid of him. Afraid of herself, perhaps. Afraid of what she'd do if he touched her.

'Matt—'

'No, don't say anything,' he implored her unsteadily. 'I don't want to hear you tell me again that you're his wife—'

'I am.'

'But he doesn't love you!' exclaimed Matt angrily, coming towards her, and this time when she retreated from him she felt the panels of the door at her back. 'He wouldn't treat you as he does if he cared about you. You're kidding yourself if you think he's ever going to change.'

Her breathing suspended. What was she doing? she asked herself wildly. Why didn't she get out of there while she still could? However Matt felt about her, there was no doubt that she was the one who'd provoked him, and, while the knowledge excited her, it wasn't something to be proud of.

There was a hunger in the way he looked at her, a deep primitive hunger that shredded her nerves and melted her flesh. She wanted him, she thought incredulously. She really wanted him. She wanted to know what it was like to be loved by a man whose prime objective wasn't to subjugate her to his needs.

She longed to feel Matt's arms about her, Matt's body pressed in intimate association with her own. She longed for him to kiss her; to show his need for her; to validate her feelings with his mouth.

But all Matt did was place one hand on either side of her head and stand looking down at her with guarded eyes. Although she ached for him to touch her, he seemed quite content to look and not touch. His skin seemed very dark in the shadowy light behind him, the glow of the lamplight creating an aura of brightness around his powerful frame.

There was a faint covering of dark hair on his chest that arrowed down to his navel. A film of perspiration at his nape caused his hair to cling to the side of his neck. She wanted to touch him so badly she was trembling. Did he have any idea what his prolonged scrutiny was doing to her?

'Do you love him?' he asked at last, when Sara was beginning to feel faint from the power of her emotions.

'M—Max?' she stammered, and Matt's jaw compressed.

'Do you?' he demanded, and her mouth quivered.

'You must know I don't,' she said unsteadily. 'I sometimes wonder if I ever did.'

'So you married him for his money, right?' Matt was matter-of-fact. 'And now you wish you hadn't.'

Sara was hurt. 'Is that what you think? My God, you don't have a very high opinion of me.'

Matt's eyes bored into hers. She had the feeling he could see into her very soul, and it wasn't a pleasant feeling. What was he thinking? she wondered. What kind of a woman did he think she was?

Then, just when she was sure he was going to push himself off the door and move away from her, he lifted his hand and cupped her throat. His thumb probed the curve of her jawline before rubbing roughly across her bottom lip. A plaintive sigh escaped her at the intimacy he was evoking. She felt herself leaning towards him and forced herself to draw back.

'I think you're a very brave woman,' he told her, surprisingly, his hand moving down her throat and over the quivering rise and fall of her chest. 'But you're also a very foolish one,' he added roughly. He paused. 'And that makes me angry.'

Sara took a breath. 'You don't understand—'

'I don't want to understand,' he told her harshly, lowering his head and brushing his mouth against the soft curve of her neck. He parted his teeth and bit her in the hollow of her shoulder, very gently. 'Or I might feel some compunction about doing this.'

Sara lifted her shoulder helplessly to his mouth. But Matt was still supporting himself on his hands. And, although his mouth was doing devastating things to her emotional stability, he was deliberately keeping a safe distance between them.

'Matt—'

'Don't tell me no,' he groaned, his mouth trailing hotly up her throat to her cheek. The heat of his breathing moistened her skin, mesmerising her. And when his mouth slanted over hers she closed her eyes in sensual delight.

'I wouldn't stop you,' she managed breathlessly against his lips, and his tongue slid possessively into her mouth.

Her limbs went weak with longing. Her heart was beating so

loudly in her ears that she couldn't think straight. She wanted nothing more than to sink down onto the floor and let Matt do whatever he wanted with her. For the first time in her life she was totally at the mercy of her emotions. The idea of getting naked with him was just the start.

She put out a trembling hand. 'May I touch you?' she whispered, and he sucked in his breath.

'Can I stop you?' he countered hoarsely, revealing his own weakness. And with a shiver of anticipation she allowed her fingers to stroke over the soft hair on his chest.

He shuddered beneath her caress. When her hand strayed lower, over the flat planes of his stomach to the open waistband of his jeans, he jerked uncontrollably. The hair coarsened as it disappeared below the vee and, unable to stop herself, Sara slipped her hand inside his zip.

He wasn't wearing anything else, she discovered breathlessly. But he was hot and aroused, and when her fingers closed about him he uttered a low moan. 'God, Sara,' he muttered, his voice thick with emotion. And, as if he could no longer support himself, his arms gave way.

His weight crushed her against the door. But she loved it. It was what she wanted, and there was a palpable delight in feeling his erection pressing into her mound. She desperately wanted to push down her pants and his, let the silken length of his hot flesh sink into hers. She was certainly ready for him. In the pit of her stomach a pulse was beating, and she could feel her own arousal pooling between her thighs.

His hands sought her buttocks, finding her soft cleft and hauling her against him. All sanity was suspended. The rights and wrongs of what she was doing didn't apply.

Lifting her arms, she wound them round his neck. Her fingers slid into his hair, scraped possessively across his scalp. Her mouth opened wide beneath the hungry penetration of his invasion. She shared his tongue's sensual dance, returning his kiss with all the heat and urgency of her generous nature.

It wasn't enough. Even when his hand pushed her shirt out of the way and he caressed the swollen fullness of her breasts she wanted more. Then he took one throbbing nipple between his teeth and suckled eagerly, and she knew what she had to do.

Dragging a hand from his shoulder, she fumbled at the waist-band of the baggy pants. She felt a quiver of satisfaction when they slipped obediently down to her ankles. She kicked them off, going up on her tiptoes to try and assuage the ache between her legs. She rubbed herself against him, loving the intimacy it evoked, and Matt knew immediately what she'd done.

'Sara,' he said thickly, and she shivered pleasurably when his hand found its way between her legs and found the throbbing nub within its folds of flesh. 'God, Sara, you are beautiful.' His breath shivered from his lungs. 'I want—'

He broke off then, and without saying another word he pushed himself away from her. Her moan of protest had barely left her lips before he took her hand and pulled her across the room.

She had no idea what he was going to do. But she was very much afraid he was going to sit her down and tell her this couldn't go on. That, however much he might desire her phys-ically, he was not prepared to perjure his soul for her sake.

Yet his hand was gripping hers tightly. And when he paused to peel her tee shirt over her head her fears were overtaken by pure excitement. Would he have done that if he was going to send her away? she wondered unsteadily. And why didn't she feel any shame at her nakedness with him?

When he pushed her down into the armchair she gazed up at him uncomprehendingly. The leather was cool against her bottom, but she hardly noticed. Her eyes were wide, enquiring, anxious even now that she might have mistaken his intentions.

But Matt's gaze was dark and passionate, and when he pressed her back against the velvet cushion behind her and knelt between her parted knees, her breath caught helplessly in her throat.

Then his mouth was on hers, his bare chest crushing her swollen breasts. Her nipples pressed, hard and pointed, against his hair-roughened skin. Her fingers sought the front of his trou-sers, eager to please him as he was pleasing her.

Matt brushed her hands aside, however, and, drawing back,

cradled her breasts in his hands. His thumbs abraded the sensitive nipples, arousing another moan of pleasure from her.

Then, bending his head, he suckled from first one, then the other, causing her to quiver with sheer delight. She shifted restlessly beneath him, striving towards a fulfilment that had always been beyond her. Even now she doubted her capacity to please either of them. Max had always said she was a sexless bitch.

When Matt parted her legs and began depositing soft sensual kisses along her inner thigh, she groaned in protest. She hadn't known she had so many erogenous zones, but it seemed as if everywhere Matt touched her body turned to flame. Her skin felt thin, sensitised. Every nerve leapt eagerly towards his touch.

Then he reached the apex of her legs, but he didn't stop. 'You're wet,' he said, with obvious satisfaction, and when his tongue probed the damp curls that hid her womanhood she caught her breath. She was helpless to stop what was happening and she gasped as she lost all control.

Her climax was shattering. She'd never had such an experience, and when Matt pulled her into his arms she was crying uncontrollably.

'Hey, baby,' he whispered, his hand cradling her head, comforting her. 'It's okay. I'm still here.'

Sara gulped. 'But you—you didn't—'

'Not this time,' he agreed gently. 'This was for you. Only you. Was it good?'

Sara groaned. 'You know it was,' she said, holding his face between her hands and drawing back to look at him. 'But why? Why didn't you—?'

'It's not what you want right now,' he said, getting to his feet and leaving her feeling strangely bereft. 'You'd better get dressed,' he added, picking up her clothes from the floor and dropping them in her lap. 'It will be light soon.'

'Matt!'

But he had turned away and, suddenly intensely aware of her nakedness, Sara hurriedly dressed again. Then, when the cord on the sweat pants was securely tied, she said tightly, 'Am I supposed to thank you, or what?'

'No!' He swung round, his face contorted with an emotion

she couldn't understand. Then, harshly, 'You are still planning on going back to London, aren't you?'

Sara was shocked. 'I—I have to—'

'That's what I thought.' Matt was laconic. And then, almost defiantly, 'I should tell you that it was I who arranged for your letter to be made public. I'd hate you to find out some other way.'

Her brows drew together. 'You?' She was confused.

'Yes, me,' he said flatly. 'I couldn't risk Bradbury keeping it quiet and maybe setting the police to search for you. I got a friend of mine at the *Chronicle* to deliver your letter himself.'

Sara tried to think. She remembered being surprised at Max's generosity, but now she realised that he'd had no choice.

'You were probably right,' she said at last, hardly capable of thinking at all at the moment. 'Well, at least I'm forearmed.'

Matt stared at her. 'You don't have to go back to him,' he stated harshly.

'I do,' she said. 'I'm sorry.'

'Not half as sorry as me,' he told her contemptuously. 'You're a fool, Sara, but not as big a fool as me for getting involved with you.'

CHAPTER TWELVE

IT WAS after eight o'clock in the evening when Matt heard someone at the door.

It was the dogs who warned him first. They'd started barking as soon as the car had turned into the private road that led up to the house, and by the time it pulled into the driveway they were frantic. Matt was torn between the desire to go and quieten them—before they woke Rosie—and seeing who it was.

He had no idea who might be calling at this time of the evening. He didn't get too many visitors at all, and his parents were away in Italy at the moment, enjoying a tour of the wine country.

It could be Emma, of course. Since Sara had left, she'd become almost too friendly for his liking. She seemed to see the other woman's departure as an opportunity for her to prove how helpful she could be, and, despite his protests, she'd insisted on collecting Rosie from school at least three times this week. But he didn't think it was Emma. He'd been distinctly short with her on the phone that afternoon.

His own moods swung from enforced cheerfulness, for Rosie's sake, to total despair when he was on his own. It was a week since Rob Marco had returned to London, taking Sara with him, and nothing seemed to make any sense any more.

The morning she'd left was engraved in his memory. She hadn't come downstairs at all until after he'd taken Rosie to school. When he'd returned she'd been sitting in the kitchen with Rob and the housekeeper, already wearing the voile dress and high heels she'd arrived in.

It was obvious she'd wanted to save his daughter any more distress than necessary. But that hadn't prevented him from feeling sick to his stomach that she'd meant what she'd said when she'd insisted she had to leave.

However, Rob's presence had prevented him from saying

anything stupid. Besides, he'd had the feeling that he'd already burnt his boats as far as she was concerned. She had no idea how he really felt about her leaving. And even thinking about what she might have to deal with when she got back to her husband had torn him apart.

He'd managed to hide his feelings until after the taxi taking her and Rob to Newcastle Airport had departed. Then, shunning even Mrs Webb's company, he'd locked himself in the study and spent the rest of the day in a morass of self-pity.

Despite its attraction, getting drunk had not been an option. Rosie had still had to be picked up from school that afternoon, and he'd had no desire to ask for Emma's help again.

He'd wanted to keep Sara's leaving to himself. But Emma had turned up at the house a couple of days later on some trumped-up mission and he'd had to tell her. Since then he'd had to fend her off with grim determination.

He supposed he was an ungrateful bastard. Emma meant well, goodness knew, and until Sara had come on the scene their relationship had been moving along quite nicely. Now, however, she seemed to think he was ripe for an affair, and he wondered what she'd seen in his and Sara's association to merit that conclusion.

Rosie had taken a good deal of his patience. She'd been terribly upset when she'd discovered that Sara had left without even saying goodbye. She couldn't understand why someone who'd obviously liked staying there had to leave, and Matt had eventually explained that Sara had a husband and family back in London.

The trouble was, Rosie kept asking about Sara's husband. She'd wanted to know if they had any children and why she couldn't write to her from time to time and tell her how she was getting on.

'I'm sure she'd like to know, Daddy,' she'd said, just the day before, and, although Matt was fairly sure that was an accurate assessment, there was no way Sara would be able to justify any communication from them.

It was thinking of her, living with her husband again, that was a constant torment. He'd scoured the newspapers daily, expecting to find some item detailing Sara's return. He'd been sure Max Bradbury would miss no chance to gain a bit of publicity, particularly of a positive nature. And he'd want the world to know that his second wife was safely home again.

Now, however, the dogs' barking was getting the better of him. Deciding that whoever was at the door would have to wait, he strode out of the sitting room and into the kitchen. Opening the back door, he made straight for the dogs' compound. They were instantly reassured by his arrival and, bending, he unlocked the gate and let them out.

He was trying to prevent them from jumping all over him when a man came around the side of the house. He was a large man, with a protruding stomach and an extravagant moustache. Matt wasn't alarmed. He was a big man himself, well able to take care of himself. And, although the other man's appearance was unexpected, he looked more flustered than aggressive.

'Mr Seton?'

'Yes.'

Matt had barely given his response when the dogs saw the visitor. Barking joyfully now, they flung themselves upon the newcomer, almost knocking him off his feet.

The man was attempting to push them off when another man appeared. 'Hugo,' the second man was saying impatiently, 'what the hell is going on?' Then he saw Matt and his eyes narrowed speculatively for a moment before a disarming smile lifted the corners of his full mouth. 'I'm so sorry,' he exclaimed, in an entirely different tone. 'We seem to be causing something of a disturbance.'

Matt faced the two men warily. Even without hearing his brother's name he'd have known Max Bradbury anywhere. Apart from the fact that he'd seen his face on the covers of a dozen magazines and periodicals, the man exhibited a smug self-satisfaction that Matt found both provoking and unpleasant. Visions of Sara's bruised and battered body kept flashing in front of his eyes and he longed to grab Bradbury by the throat and knock that complacent smile off his well-fed face.

It was lucky the dogs chose that moment to transfer their attentions to Max. Barking excitedly, they lunged towards him, and Matt had to grab them by the scruffs of their necks to hold them back. He was tempted to let them do their worst, but that would achieve nothing, Instead, he bundled them back into their pen, and by the time he straightened he had himself in control again.

'Can I help you?'

Max Bradbury came forward, bypassing his brother without even a backward glance. 'Oh, I hope so,' he said warmly, holding out a fleshy hand for Matt to take. 'I do hope so, Mr Seton. It is Mr Seton—the famous *Matt Seton*—isn't it?' he inserted ingratiatingly before going on. 'Allow me to introduce myself: I'm Max Bradbury. And this is my brother, Hugo.' He gave a dismissive little shrug. 'You may have heard the name, but that's not important now. What is important—imperative, in fact—is that I get in touch with my wife. I'm given to understand that Victoria may have been staying with you in the past two weeks.'

Whatever Matt had expected, it wasn't this. Compelled to shake the other man's hand or risk offending him before he knew why he was here, Matt took a second to consider his words. But his mind was buzzing with the apparent news that, as far as Max Bradbury was concerned, Sara was still missing. Had she changed her mind about going back? he wondered, trying to contain his own agitation. Or, dear God, had Bradbury done something to her and coming here was just a ploy to cover his actions.

'Your wife?' Matt echoed at last, surreptitiously wiping Max Bradbury's sweat from his palm. Then, hoping he didn't sound too concerned, 'I'm sorry. I don't know any Victoria Bradbury, I'm afraid.'

Max's eyes briefly flashed with an anger he couldn't conceal and Matt was slightly reassured. Sara's husband wasn't acting like a man in control of the situation. But then Max's smile returned as he continued, 'Perhaps I should have said Sara, Mr Seton. Sara Fielding. Victoria—that is to say, my wife—may be using an alias.' He gave an amazingly convincing chuckle. 'I'm sure you appreciate the advantages of travelling incognito yourself.'

Matt was hardly listening to him. He was wondering how the hell Bradbury had traced his wife here. He had to have been given some clue to turn up on his doorstep. But who was likely to have helped him? Dammit, he needed time to think.

Rob? He frowned. He couldn't believe his agent would have done it. Rob was many things, but he wasn't a grass. He knew what Matt had said about keeping Sara's whereabouts to himself.

He saw Hugo Bradbury watching him over his brother's shoulder and wondered what he was thinking. He was clearly younger than Max and, if Matt wasn't mistaken, he was also rather obviously gay. He looked as if he wasn't happy with the situation either, and Matt guessed he had come here under duress. Sara had said that her brother-in-law was harmless, but Matt reserved judgement. He'd done little to help her when all was said and done.

'I'm afraid I can't help you, Mr Bradbury,' Matt said shortly, eager to get on the phone to Rob and clear him of any involvement. He also wanted to know where Sara had gone after they'd reached Heathrow. He hadn't spoken to his agent since he'd put off signing the new contract. He guessed Rob would still be fuming over what he saw as a deliberate endangerment of Matt's career. But the man wasn't vindictive. 'I'm sorry, Mr Bradbury,' he added. 'There's no Sara Fielding here either.'

Max's smile thinned. 'But she has been here, hasn't she?' he persisted, glancing towards the house as if he suspected Sara might be hiding inside. 'My information was quite specific, Mr Seton. There has been a young woman called Sara staying here, acting as a temporary nanny for your daughter, I believe?'

Matt stifled a curse. 'Well, yes. That's right,' he agreed at last, knowing there was no point in denying something that seemed to be public knowledge. 'But her surname wasn't Fielding, Mr Bradbury. It was something else entirely. In any case, she left a week ago.'

Max's nostrils flared. 'Nevertheless, I would like to speak to her,' he said, his control slipping a little. 'I've travelled a long way, Mr Seton. Surely you can understand my concern.'

Matt was tempted to tell him exactly what he thought of his

so-called concern. That it was his behaviour that had driven
Sara to run away. But then he remembered: as far as the public
at large was concerned Sara was staying with a schoolfriend.
Wasn't Bradbury being rather reckless in risking exposing that
story for a lie?

'I'd be interested to know why you thought you might find
your wife here,' Matt ventured at last, holding the other man's
gaze with innocent speculation. 'Is she missing?'

Max took what Matt realised was a calming breath, and his
own anger swelled at the knowledge of how often the man must
have used his anger against his wife. He could see the fury in
Max's eyes, glistening below the surface of congeniality. Was
he wondering how much he needed to say to persuade Matt to
tell him what he needed to know?

'I haven't seen my wife for a couple of weeks,' he conceded
at last, ignoring his brother's sudden murmur of disapproval.
'She's perfectly all right. I had a letter from her assuring me
that all was well. But I'm afraid she didn't tell me where exactly
she was staying, and in the circumstances I've been left with
no choice but to try and find her.'

Matt's brows drew together. 'In the circumstances?' he
prompted. He knew he was pushing his luck, but he needed to
know. 'Is there some—emergency?'

Max scowled. 'You could say that,' he said, without giving
anything away. 'But it's family business.' He arched an impe-
rious brow. 'You understand?'

Matt didn't understand, but he didn't see how he could pursue this without arousing Bradbury's suspicions any more than
they were aroused already.

'I admire your persistence,' he lied. There was nothing about
Max Bradbury he admired. 'I can imagine how daunting it must
be, combing the whole country for your wife's whereabouts.
What made you think she might be in this neck of the woods?
Is Northumberland a favourite haunt of hers?'

'We haven't been combing the country,' put in Hugo unexpectedly, and Matt saw Max Bradbury turn to give his brother
a killing look.

But then, as if realising that the statement couldn't be left in isolation, he muttered, 'My brother's right. My wife hired a car from a nationwide franchise. It was handed back to an agency in Ellsmoor nearly two weeks ago. Ellsmoor is, as you know, just a short distance from Saviour's Bay.'

Matt blew out a breath. He should have guessed that Bradbury would get around to checking out the car hire firms eventually. All the same, that still didn't explain how he'd found out that Sara had been here. He'd impressed upon the garage in Saviour's Bay, who had returned the car for him, that his name wasn't to be mentioned.

But Bradbury didn't know that.

'You say the car was handed back to an agency in Ellsmoor?' Matt mused, as if considering the situation. 'I do hope whoever handed it in hadn't found it abandoned. The tides around here can be treacherous. I've almost been trapped myself a couple of times.'

Max's mouth thinned. 'I hope you're not implying what I think you're implying, Mr Seton,' he said harshly, and Matt knew he'd caught him on the raw.

'Oh,' he murmured artlessly, 'you mean because your first wife drowned in the Solent? I suppose it must be very worrying for you not knowing where—Sara, is it?—is.'

Max looked murderous. 'If you know where she is, I'd advise you to tell me,' he snapped. 'I can be a good friend, Mr Seton. But a very bad enemy.'

'I hope you're not threatening me, Mr Bradbury.' If Matt hadn't been so concerned about Sara he'd almost have said he was enjoying this. 'As I say, the young lady who was staying here has left, and without leaving a forwarding address. Even if she was who you think she was, I have no idea where she is now.'

Which was nothing but the truth.

Max sucked in his breath. 'But you must know something,' he exclaimed sharply. 'Was this woman driving a car? Where did she come from? How did she get about?'

Matt shrugged his broad shoulders. 'I'm not on the witness stand, Mr Bradbury,' he replied coldly. 'As you prefer to keep your reasons for wanting to find your wife to yourself, surely I can claim the same privilege for my—temporary nanny.'

Max's cheeks were red with rage. Like his brother, he, too, was a large man, but without the gentling effects of Hugo's moustache. In fact, there was something almost bestial about Max's features, contorted as they were now. The man was a monster, Matt thought starkly. Thank God he hadn't had to invite him into his house.

Max, however, seemed to have realised he was not going to get anywhere by being aggressive. Changing tack, he lifted a hand in mock defeat. 'I can see you are a loyal friend, Mr Seton,' he said, glancing round at his brother. 'This young woman, whoever she is, is lucky to have found such a gallant protector in you. I have to say my own wife does not deserve such blind devotion. Her mother is very ill, you see, and Sara has disappeared without even contacting the hospital once to see how the old lady is faring.'

Matt managed not to show his surprise at this news. Surely Sara wouldn't have run away if she'd known her mother was ill.

'I'm sorry,' he said again. And he was. If Sara's mother was ill, he was fairly sure she'd want to know about it. Max would know that too, of course. Matt suspected Max would say anything to get his own way.

'I am sorry, too,' said Sara's husband now, casting another look over his shoulder at Hugo. 'I am very fond of Alicia; that's my wife's mother, you know. She's a widow, and life hasn't always been kind to her. I've done what I can, but...' He lifted his shoulders, bulky beneath the jacket of his dark blue suit. 'I'm not her daughter. What can I say?'

Matt wondered. Max sounded sincere, but, knowing what he did about the man's character, Matt wasn't convinced. He looked at Hugo, trying to gauge his reactions. The younger man's smile was rueful. A silent endorsement of his brother's comments? Or an acknowledgement that he had already said too much?

'I wish I could help you,' Matt said finally, not meaning a word of it. But right now he'd say anything to get rid of them.

Where the hell was Sara? Why hadn't she contacted her mother? If Max was lying, Matt promised himself he'd pay for it.

A few minutes later Matt was back in the study, jerking up the phone. The Bradburys had departed just a couple of minutes ago, and Matt had watched the car until it was out of sight. Max Bradbury had insisted on giving him his card, which listed all his phone numbers, but Matt had already dropped that into his wastebin. There was no way he'd give Sara's husband the time of day, let alone anything else.

Rob answered on the second ring. 'Marco,' he said flatly, and Matt wondered if he was responsible for the lacklustre tone of his voice.

'Rob?' he said quickly. 'It's Matt. Have you got a minute?'

'Well, well.' Rob didn't sound like a man who was expecting good news. 'If it isn't the incredible shrinking career man!'

'Yeah, yeah.' Matt allowed him his moment of sarcasm. 'I know I was a big disappointment to you when you turned up last week. But I've been thinking things over, and if you express-mail the new contract to me I'll sign it.'

Rob gave a stunned cough. 'You will?' Then he was silent for a moment before saying, 'Okay. What do you want? Your signature never comes without strings attached.'

'You wound me.' Matt tried to sound hurt, and failed miserably.

'That's my line.' Rob was laconic. Then, 'Let me guess: this has something to do with the delectable Mrs Bradbury, doesn't it?'

Matt sighed. 'All right. Yes, it does.' He paused. 'She did get on the plane with you, didn't she?'

'And hardly spoke the whole way,' agreed Rob drily. 'That is one close-mouthed lady, Matt. I'm not used to women blanking me for the best part of three hours. You know that.'

'My heart bleeds.' Matt gnawed at his lower lip. 'So what happened when you got to Heathrow?'

Rob hesitated. 'What is this, Matt? An inquisition? Do I take it she hasn't written and thanked you for taking her in. You did take her in, didn't you, pal? That nanny business was just so much hot air.'

Matt expelled a wry breath. 'Just answer the question, Rob. Did you give her a lift into town?'

Rob sighed. 'No way, man. I didn't even get the chance to offer. As soon as we cleared the Arrivals hall she took off running. I didn't see her again. I guess she got a cab into town.'

Matt swore. He'd more or less expected that. 'And you didn't tell anyone who she was or where she'd been?'

'No.' Rob sounded put out. 'I said I wouldn't and I haven't. Why? Have you had a visit from her husband? From what I hear, that sounds like the way he works.'

CHAPTER THIRTEEN

SARA stood at the window of the bed and breakfast where she was staying in Paddington and wondered for the umpteenth time what she was going to do.

It was a week since she'd left Saviour's Bay—since she'd left Matt—and her decision was getting harder to make, not easier.

At first she'd checked into the small lodging house because the idea of going back to Max immediately after what she'd shared with Matt had been too painful to consider. She'd felt no shame. She might have been unfaithful to Max in word and deed, but Matt had made sure that she returned to her husband as unsullied as when she'd left him.

Which was a contradiction in itself, she thought bitterly. But Max couldn't actually accuse her of sleeping with another man. Well, he could accuse her of it, if that was what he believed, but she could answer honestly that she hadn't.

So why did she have such a feeling of loss because Matt hadn't made love to her with his body? Why was she becoming more and more depressed because she knew she might never see Matt again? She'd always known that they had no future. She'd left him in no doubt of what she ultimately intended to do. So why was she regretting it now, when it was over? When it was far too late to have a change of heart?

Of course, where her heart was concerned there'd been no change. Almost from the first moment she'd set eyes on Matt she'd known he was going to mean something in her life. She had no logical explanation. She'd just known he was a man she could trust.

She supposed she wasn't typical of most women in her situation. After years of being abused by one man, how could she instantly have feelings for another? And, if she did have feelings, how did she know they were genuine? She had so little experience to draw on. So much in her life she wanted to forget.

She didn't know why she was so certain she loved him, but she was. It certainly wasn't because Matt had encouraged her to feel that way. On the contrary, most of the time he'd kept a safe distance between them. What affection she'd had had mostly been from Rosie.

Yet, for all that, she'd known he wasn't indifferent to her. The awareness between them, that had begun that first morning, had grown almost without any encouragement from them. It had started even before he'd seen what Max had done to her. And when he'd tended her bruises and touched her with his lips…

Sara trembled. Was she exaggerating what had happened between them? She didn't think so, but it was too late now. Matt had been attracted to her; he had wanted her to leave Max. But that didn't add up to a lasting commitment. He'd been thinking of her, not himself. He'd wanted her to take control of her life.

If she dared.

She frowned now. She knew she'd changed during those days at Seadrift. For the first time in years she'd had the chance to look objectively at her marriage. Without Max's oppressive presence she'd been able to think for herself again. And what she'd discovered had not been a pretty sight.

She saw now that it was Max who had robbed her of her confidence. Slowly but surely he'd convinced her that she was to blame for the punishment he'd subjected her to. And, although she'd been weak to believe him, she'd been living under so much pressure she'd had no strength left to fight his cruelty.

The guilt was his, not hers, she'd realised. Being with Matt had shown her that there was another way. All she'd needed was time to rest, to relax, to find the woman she'd used to be. And being with Matt and Rosie had been the happiest time of her life.

That was the real reason why she hadn't returned to the apartment in Knightsbridge. She'd needed time alone, to think about the future, to decide what she was going to do. Max still frightened her, of course. She couldn't dismiss three years of abuse in only two weeks. But she was prepared to face him again, to show him that the chains he'd bound her with were broken, to make another bid for freedom.

There was still her mother to think about, of course, and she knew a fleeting sense of despair at the knowledge that she'd get no support from her. But surely if she could show her what Max had done, if she could explain to her why she'd run away…

She wasn't hopeful. However determined she'd been in the past, her mother had always been able to get under her defences, to persuade her she was exaggerating Max's behaviour. She really believed her life would have to be in imminent danger for Mrs Fielding to forfeit her comfortable lifestyle. As far as her mother was concerned she was lucky to live in such luxury.

Still, she had to try. This was her last chance, and if she let Max take control of her again she very likely would die—of heartbreak, if nothing else…

St Jude's Hospital was in Euston Road.

If Sara hadn't been so concerned, the incongruity of its title might have amused her. But when she burst through the doors she was already running on adrenalin and little else.

The idea that she'd been hiding out in Paddington while her mother had been fighting for her life just a comparatively short distance away had horrified her. But until she'd gone to her apartment to speak to her she hadn't even known her mother was ill.

It was a neighbour who'd put Sara in the picture.

'Mrs Fielding had a heart attack a few nights ago,' she'd told the stunned young woman sympathetically. 'Didn't you know?'

'I—I've been away,' Sara had answered abstractedly, and the woman's expression had revealed that she'd read the newspapers, too.

'Of course,' she'd said understandingly, but Sara had had the feeling that she'd put her own interpretation on recent events, as everyone else would have done.

'Anyway,' she went on, 'it was lucky your husband was here

when it happened, wasn't it? It was he who called the ambulance, you know.'

That was when Sara's blood had chilled. Max had been visiting her mother? Max never visited her mother. Indeed, Mrs Fielding had often claimed that it was Sara who stopped him from going to see her. But in fact Max himself had nothing but contempt for the older woman. Though it suited him to keep that from her.

He'd always been repulsively flattering whenever Mrs Fielding had visited her daughter, however. He wasn't a fool. He'd known that she was an invaluable—if unwitting—ally in his bid to control his wife. And, despite her fears for her mother's safety, Sara couldn't believe he'd have hurt her now.

Even so, her heart was beating unpleasantly fast as she approached the reception desk. Stammering a little, she explained that she was Alicia Fielding's daughter. She added that she'd been away and had only just discovered that her mother was in the hospital.

'What ward?' asked the woman dispassionately, and Sara realised belatedly that she had no idea.

'She had a heart attack,' she said, by way of an answer. 'I don't know what ward she's in.'

The woman heaved a resigned sigh and turned to the computer screen beside her. 'What name did you say?' she asked, and Sara knew a moment's panic that her mother's name might not appear on the screen.

'Fielding,' she said hastily. 'Alicia Fielding. She—she had a heart attack.'

'So you said.' The receptionist was hardly sympathetic. 'Ah, yes. Here it is.' She paused. 'Ward 32. Intensive Care.'

'Intensive Care!' Sara fairly squeaked the words. 'Where do I find that?'

'Third floor,' said the woman. 'You'll find the lifts along there.' She pointed an indifferent finger along the corridor to her right. 'They'll probably let you in. The ICU don't keep regular visiting hours, for obvious reasons.'

'Thanks.'

Swallowing convulsively, Sara fairly ran along the corridor

the woman had indicated. She was glad now that since returning to London she'd invested her last few pounds in a cheap summer dress and deck shoes. Although she expected her mother to object, she was glad of the flat heels now.

The lifts were huge things, big enough to take the patient trolleys she'd seen in the A and E department as she'd passed. They moved ponderously, too, and she was biting her lip with impatience by the time she reached the third floor.

She found the Intensive Care Unit without difficulty. There were only two departments on this floor. The other appeared to be a recovery ward for patients from the ICU. But the receptionist had said her mother was in the former.

There was a senior nurse on duty, and she looked at Sara curiously when she gave her name. Of course, Sara thought wearily, she'd probably recognised her. And, even if she hadn't, the name would have given her away.

'Mrs Fielding is holding her own,' she said, in answer to Sara's initial enquiry. If she was wondering why Sara hadn't known about her mother's illness until now she was professional enough to keep it to herself. 'She's in there,' she added, pointing towards a glass-framed cubicle. 'You can go in, but please don't excite her. She's had a really tough time.'

Sara hesitated. 'It was a heart attack?' she asked awkwardly, and the nurse nodded.

'But you'll find her face is rather bruised, too, I'm afraid.' She touched Sara's arm. 'It looks much worse than it really is. That's why I'm warning you. According to her son-in-law— But, of course you must know this,' she exclaimed, with some embarrassment, breaking off.

'I don't know anything,' said Sara fiercely, uncaring what Max would think when he found out. 'As I said before, I didn't even know my mother was ill.' She took a breath. 'Please, do go on with what you were saying. What did my husband tell you?'

'Well…' The nurse was clearly reluctant to be the bearer of bad news, but she evidently reasoned that Sara was a close relative and deserved to know the truth. 'According to Mr Bradbury, Mrs Fielding was in the kitchen of her apartment, making a pot of tea, when she collapsed. She hit her face on the sink, I believe. He was most distressed. I tried to tell him that these things happen all the time, but I think he was worried we'd believe he'd done it.'

The nurse gave an embarrassed little chuckle, but Sara wasn't laughing. The explanation Max had given sounded so horribly familiar to her. On one occasion—just once—he'd given her a black eye. And spent the next few days telling everyone she'd walked into a door.

He'd been careful after that. The injuries she'd suffered at his hands had never embarrassed him again. But the idea that he might have attacked her mother was still incredible. Surely even he would never have sunk so low.

Thanking the nurse, Sara hurried towards the cubicle she'd indicated. Pausing outside, she looked in, her heart beating uncomfortably fast in her chest.

Her mother was lying amid an impressive array of tubes and computer screens, an IVF bottle suspended beside the railed hospital bed. She looked older than Sara had ever seen her, and the bruises on her face stood out in stark relief against her pallid skin.

Oh, Mum, she thought achingly, what really happened? As far as she knew, her mother had never had any heart problems in the past. Was it something Max had said that had caused this? Something he had done? Or was she damning the man without a shred of evidence to support her fears?

Taking a deep breath, she pushed against the swing doors and entered the cubicle. The smell of antiseptic was strong, mingling with the usual odours associated with a hospital ward. The room was warm, too, but not unpleasantly so. The hum of the air-conditioning unit was just one of the many systems running in the room.

Her mother's eyes were closed when she entered the cubicle. But as she approached the bed there were definite signs of awareness. The old lady's lids flickered, before lifting warily, as if she wasn't entirely sure she wanted to see who her visitor was.

Then she saw her daughter and her eyes filled with tears. 'Sara?' she said disbelievingly. 'Oh, Sara, is it really you?'

'It's me,' said Sara, sniffing back her own tears and bending to take her mother's limp hand. 'How—how are you, Mum? I'm so sorry I wasn't here when you needed me.'

Mrs Fielding gazed up at her as if she still couldn't quite believe her eyes. 'Where have you been?' she asked, her voice hoarse and unsteady. 'I—I was so afraid—'

Sara's stomach clenched. 'Mum—'

'I thought you must be dead,' went on her mother urgently, gripping Sara's hand. 'You were missing and I had no idea where you were.'

'But Max had a letter—'

'From you? Yes, so he said. But I've never seen any letter, and I had only his word that you'd written it.'

'But it was in the newspaper, too,' said Sara, wishing she'd been able to tell her mother where she was. 'I'm sorry you've been worried. There was no need.'

'But why did you run away?' protested Mrs Fielding. 'What happened that night? I never believed Max's story. Not when he didn't appear to know where you were.'

The old lady was getting agitated, and, bearing in mind what the nurse had said, Sara endeavoured to calm her down. 'We'd had a row,' she said gently. 'One of many, as I've said before. I—Max fell down the stairs, and I thought he was badly injured. I called the emergency services, but I was afraid they'd blame me, and I—well, I ran away. Cowardly, huh?'

'Oh, Sara—'

'Never mind that. I'm here now, and the nurse says you're making good progress,' Sara added soothingly. She forced a smile. 'How do you really feel?'

'Forget about me,' exclaimed her mother dismissively. 'Sara, why didn't you tell me? Why didn't you talk to me? Why couldn't you have shown me what that monster had done to you?'

'Mum, Mum!' Sara didn't know where all this was coming from. 'It doesn't matter now—'

'It does matter.' Her mother was looking up at her with tears streaming down her cheeks. 'Thank God you're here. Thank God you're alive. I've been so—so worried.'

Sara squeezed her hand. 'I'm all right, honestly,' she said, though she was becoming more and more convinced that Max must have played a part in her mother's collapse. 'It's you I'm worried about. Why didn't you tell me you'd been feeling unwell?'

Her mother moved her head from side to side on the pillow. 'Because I hadn't been,' she said simply. 'When you—when you disappeared that evening I was worried, of course. But then Max said you were staying with a schoolfriend, and I suppose I accepted that. He—he had always been so—so kind to me, as you know, and I actually felt sorry for him because he seemed so—so alone.'

Sara nodded, sure she knew what was coming next. She had been the victim of Max's frustrations too many times not to see a pattern here.

'Did—did he do this?' she asked huskily, her free hand brushing her mother's cheek, but Mrs Fielding only grasped both her hands in a surprisingly strong grip and held on.

'Listen to me,' she said fiercely, her eyes glancing towards the door, as if she was half afraid they were going to be interrupted before she could finish what she had to say. 'Sophie Bradbury came to see me, Sara. Sophie Bradbury. What do you think about that?'

Sara blinked. 'Who?'

'Sophie Bradbury,' said her mother again. 'Well, I don't know what she calls herself these days. But that doesn't matter. You know who she is, don't you?'

'Do I?' Sara was taken aback. 'I don't think so.' She frowned, thinking. 'The only Sophie Bradbury I've heard of is Max's first wife. But she's dead.'

'She's not.' Mrs Fielding delivered her news triumphantly. 'She's alive. That's what I'm saying. She came to see me last week.'

Sara's legs gave way, and she grabbed the nearby chair and sank weakly into it. 'Sophie?' She said the name again, as if she couldn't quite believe it. 'Sophie's alive?'

'Very much so.' Her mother nodded vigorously, making the IVF bottle attached to her arm shake alarmingly. 'She lives in the United States these days, but she's been staying with her mother in Bournemouth for the past three weeks.'

Sara was stunned. 'But Max thinks she's dead,' she protested.

'Does he?' The old lady was beginning to look weary now. The excitement of seeing her daughter again was taking its toll, and Sara wondered if she should allow her to go on. 'It may have suited him to believe it. Anyway, when Sophie learned you were missing she was afraid he might have done something terrible to you.'

Sara felt slightly sick. 'Oh, Mum—' She was finding it difficult to take all this in. 'But Max had my letter—'

'Never mind the letter,' said Mrs Fielding weakly. 'What matters is Sophie told me what he was like, what he'd done to her. She was frightened of him, as I'm sure you are. Why, she even had to fake her own death to get away from him.'

Sara could hardly believe it. And now was not the time to remind her mother that she had never believed her before. 'So where is she?' she asked. 'How can we get in touch with her?'

Her mother made a careless gesture. 'I don't know,' she said, and Sara's spirits took a dive.

'You don't know?' she exclaimed. 'Then how do you know she wasn't lying? She could have made the whole thing up. She could be anyone. Some people will do anything to draw attention to themselves.'

'She had photographs.' Mrs Fielding seemed curiously unfazed by her reaction. 'They were of their wedding. Hers and Max's. She got them from her mother to show me, to prove she was telling the truth.'

Sara shook her head. 'I don't know, Mum…'

'Well, I believe her,' replied her mother staunchly. 'I believe she has no reason to lie. I also think she'd be prepared to make a statement confirming Max's cruelty. Particularly now you've turned up safe and well.'

She paused then, looking somewhat anxiously at her daughter. 'You are safe and well, aren't you, my dear? I must say, you do look better than you did before you went away. What did Max say when he saw you? I'm surprised he let you come and see me on your own.'

'Max doesn't know I'm here,' said Sara flatly. 'It was Mrs Taylor—your neighbour—who told me you'd been ill. She also told me Max was with you when you had your attack. Are you too tired to tell me what he was doing at your apartment?'

The old lady sighed. 'He was hoping I'd heard from you, of course,' she said. Then, 'But that doesn't matter. Let's just say I realise now what a blind fool I've been all these years.'

Sara groaned. 'Max hit you?' she asked, appalled, but Mrs Fielding was shaking her head again.

'No, he didn't go as far as that, but he did threaten me.' She gave a rueful little smile. 'It was when I told him that I knew Sophie was alive that he became quite unpleasant. He accused me of being a parasite, of living on his charity all these years. I'll admit he frightened me a little. But I don't know if I can honestly blame him for my attack.'

Sara was horrified. 'Oh, Mum,' she said helplessly, wishing she'd been there to defend the old lady herself. But then another thought struck her. 'Do you really think he knew Sophie was alive?'

'I think it's possible,' said her mother slowly. 'He didn't seem as shocked as I expected he would be at the news. But I don't think he found out until after he'd married you. The fact that he was already married again must have been a strong deterrent to exposing the truth.'

'Yes.' Sara was still incredulous.

'Sophie is here because she wants a divorce, and after all this time, she knows she can get one fairly easily. It may not be necessary, of course. I'm not sure what happens in these circumstances.'

'Lucky Sophie.' Sara couldn't help feeling envious. She wished Max was out of her life, too. She wished she was free to be with Matt again.

But her mother wasn't finished.

'You know what this means,' she persisted, tiring rapidly now, but determined to finish what she had to say. 'When Max married you he was still married to Sophie. Maybe your marriage isn't legal. You could be a free woman, Sara. And no one would be more relieved about that than me.'

It was early evening when Sara arrived at the apartment in Knightsbridge that she and Max had shared for the past three years.

She hadn't left the hospital until about half an hour ago. Although her mother had been exhausted after her revelations, and had slept for most of the afternoon, Sara had wanted to stay until she woke up again.

The nurse had suggested she should go home and come back again later, when her mother was rested, but Sara had declined. She'd wanted to be there when her mother opened her eyes again. She'd wanted to reassure her that she was there and all was well.

Perhaps part of it was that Sara had wanted to put off returning to the apartment. Despite what her mother had told her, she couldn't believe Max would let her go without a fight. If he threatened her or her mother she would tell him she'd use what she knew against him, she told herself firmly. But Max was an unknown quantity. How far would he go to protect his reputation?

She wondered if Hugo knew about Sophie. She didn't think so. Max's brother might be many things—weak being one of them—but she didn't believe he was a liar. Yet, as far as his brother's character was concerned, he did have a blind spot. Without it, surely he'd have seen what was going on.

There were no lights showing in the apartment, but that didn't mean anything. It was still daylight and Sara glanced at her wrist, realised she didn't have a watch, and shuddered in spite of herself. She couldn't help remembering how her watch had come to be broken. The idea that Max might be reasonable was just too unbelievable to be true.

Perhaps she should wait until tomorrow morning, she thought doubtfully. Although it was still fairly early, night was coming, and everything seemed different after dark. But she recognised it for what it was: a pathetic attempt to put off the inevitable. She had to speak to Max; she had to collect her belongings.

She had to prove to herself, and him, that she was not going to be bullied any more.

Yeah, right.

The trouble was, she didn't believe it.

Oh, she believed what Sophie had told her mother. But what of it? The idea that Max might allow her to live her own life again seemed just as remote as ever.

It would never happen, she thought dully. He was never going to let her go. Already she could feel the chains of his possession closing about her.

She had to make it happen, she told herself desperately. She'd been afraid of him for far too long. Whatever it took, whatever he did to her, she had to stand up to him. She had to break the chains once and for all.

The doorman looked taken aback when he admitted her. 'Mrs Bradbury,' he said, politely enough, but she knew he was assessing her appearance with a critical eye. She knew she looked pale and harassed, and his attitude didn't help things. The man gave a smirk. 'What a pleasure it is to see you again.'

'Thank you, Patrick.'

Sara determined not to let him intimidate her. This was not the man she had once been friendly with. He was long gone, despatched by Max, she was sure, and this man had taken his place. He was always polite, but Sara had always had the feeling that he was Max's ally. She was certain she could expect no sympathy from him.

Now, tugging on her braid, she asked, 'Is Mr Bradbury in?'

'I believe so, Mrs Bradbury,' Patrick replied, pressing the button to summon the lift for her. 'He'll be delighted to see you, I'm sure.'

'I'm sure.' Sara's voice was tight. She walked into the lift. 'Thanks.'

Patrick drew back as the doors closed, and as if that was the signal for Sara's nerve to give out on her she sank against the panelled wall of the lift in mute panic. Weakness, like a debilitating blanket, enveloped her, and she had to steel herself not to stop the lift and send it down again.

Only the thought of facing the doorman's smug expression

kept her from doing so. She was committed now. Forcing her legs to support her, she straightened, watching the indicator light moving through the floors. Three, four, five, six... At seven, it stopped, and she stepped out onto royal-blue broadloom that was inches thick. She was here. Back in the place she had never wanted to see again.

Max's was the only apartment on this floor and the one above. Sara would have preferred a house, with a garden, but her opinion hadn't been invited. Max had said he preferred the privacy afforded by having no immediate neighbours, and in the beginning she'd assumed it was only a temporary arrangement anyway.

How wrong she'd been.

She was approaching the double panelled doors when they opened. She should have known that Patrick wouldn't have been able to resist warning Max of her arrival. His excuse, had he needed one, would be that he'd known Mr Bradbury was anxious to know she was safe and well. He'd primed her welcoming committee, even if it was a committee of only one.

Panic flared again as Max stepped into the hallway and the concealed lighting that ran along the tops of the walls illuminated his smiling face. She wasn't fooled by his apparent pleasure at seeing her. She knew, as he did, that the doorman would be watching their reunion avidly on the CCTV cameras.

'Victoria,' he exclaimed, as she paused to gather her composure, and before she could guess his intentions he had covered the space between them and was enfolding her in his arms. 'My dear Victoria, you have no idea how glad I am to see you.'

Sara's first reaction was to try and get away from him, but experience had taught her it was wiser not to fight. Even so, she was aware that he was squeezing her far more tightly than was necessary. Crushing her ribs, making it difficult for her to drag any air into her lungs.

'Please...' she got out at last, and, as if he hadn't been aware of her discomfort, Max released her to lay a possessive arm across her shoulders.

'I'm sorry,' he said, his eyes glinting with cold malevolence. 'Was I hurting you? Well—' he urged her towards the door and into the apartment '—put it down to my delight at seeing you again, Victoria.'

As soon as they were through the door Sara struggled free of him, however. Without Patrick's unseen eyes monitoring her every move she felt more prepared to defend herself. She had to defend herself, she told herself grimly. If Max hurt her, this would be the last time he had the chance.

So why did that sound so hollow?

Max closed the doors behind him. The click they made caused a shiver of apprehension to feather her spine but she tried not to show her fear.

Max was looking at her with an expression of satisfaction he didn't try to disguise. 'Victoria,' he said at last, the breath he took expanding the buttonholes on his waistcoat. 'How good of you to grace me with your presence. I must admit, I was beginning to have my doubts about you. But whatever are you wearing? And your hair... My dear, you look like a refugee. Still, I'm happy to see you've come to your senses at last.'

'I haven't—' Sara broke off, licking her dry lips. Then, stepping back into the elegant drawing room behind her, she added, 'I haven't come to my senses, Max. Or at least, I have. That is, I'm not staying. I'm leaving you, Max. I've seen my mother and I know about Sophie. About how she faked her own death to get away from you. You can't stop me—'

'Hey...' Max came away from the door, spreading his hands in a gesture that on anyone else would have looked conciliatory. Following her into the drawing room, he assumed an expression of mild indignation. 'Have I said I'm going to try and stop you, Victoria? Just because your mother's been filling your head with lies doesn't mean we can't sort things out. The woman's senile, for heaven's sake. You must know that. I was half afraid she was going to accuse me of assaulting her!'

'I bet you were.' Sara moved, putting the width of a Regency striped sofa between them. 'You must have got quite a shock when she collapsed.'

'I did. Of course I did.' Max was defensive now. 'I had no idea what the crazy old bat was likely to say next.'

'That you threatened her, perhaps?' suggested Sara, before

she could lose her nerve. 'You didn't like what she was saying so you lost your temper, didn't you? That was a mistake, Max. You've lost your strongest ally.'

Max's broad face hardened. 'I don't need allies,' he said indifferently. 'I have you.'

'You don't.' Sara knew her voice wasn't as strong as she'd have liked, but that couldn't be helped. 'Didn't you hear what I said, Max? I'm leaving you. I—I only came back to tell you goodbye.'

Max sighed. 'My dear Victoria, you know you don't mean that. If you'd really wanted to leave me you'd have sent me another letter.' He paused. 'Where have you been, by the way? I think I deserve an explanation.'

'You don't deserve anything.' Sara quivered with indignation. 'You've been lying to me for years.' She took a breath. 'How long have you known Sophie is still alive?'

Max shrugged. 'Sophie?' He made a careless gesture. 'My first wife is dead, Victoria. She was drowned in the Solent ten years ago.'

'That's not true.' Sara was amazed he would think she'd still believe it. 'She only pretended to drown. With her mother's help she escaped to the States. She's been living there ever since. You know that.'

Max shook his head. 'I know that's what your mother says,' he said patiently, almost as if he was speaking to a child. 'But it's not true. And, even if it was, it has nothing to do with us.'

'It does.' Sara was desperate. 'If Sophie is alive, you were not free to marry me.'

'You're wrong.' He was smug. 'Sophie was legally declared dead before our marriage could take place.'

'Even so—'

'Face it, Victoria. We are married. Do you think I'd make a mistake like that?'

'But our marriage is a mockery,' protested Sara, her hopes for the future fading before her eyes. 'I—I want a divorce.'

'I don't.' Max was infuriatingly casual. 'And if there's the slightest chance that I may have overlooked something, we can easily rectify it. I'll arrange for us to—how shall I put it?—

restate our wedding vows. Yes, that sounds good. No one but ourselves need know why we're doing so.'

'No!' Sara's jaw dropped. 'Do you honestly think I'd do something like that?' she gasped. 'You are crazy.'

'Like a fox,' said Max drily, but his mouth had tightened ominously even so. Then, obviously making an effort to control himself again, he said, 'You still haven't told me where you've been, my dear.' He arched a quizzical brow. 'Or would you like me to tell you?'

Sara was taken aback, and showed it. 'You don't know where I've been,' she said quickly, but Max merely bared his teeth in a mocking smile.

'I'm afraid I do,' he said. 'I know exactly where you've been hiding yourself. And who with. A charming young lady in Ellsmoor heard me asking about you and kindly volunteered the information I needed. I think her name was Proctor. Is that right? Emma Proctor? She was very kind.' Then his features hardened again. 'So, how long have you known Matt Seton?'

Sara's fingers gripped the back of the sofa. She wanted to tell him she didn't know what he was talking about, but she was very much afraid her face had given her away.

'I—I told you in my letter,' she insisted. 'I've been staying with friends—'

'Not *friends*,' Max contradicted her harshly, leaning across the sofa and imprisoning her white-knuckled hands beneath his. 'One friend, Victoria.' His face contorted. 'I repeat, how long have you known Seton? How long has he been your lover?'

'My lover!' Sara could feel all the blood draining out of her fingers as Max's grip tightened. But it wasn't that that caused her breath to strangle in her throat. 'Matt Seton's not my lover!'

'Isn't he?' Max knelt on the sofa to increase his hold on her. He stared at her intently. 'So why are you looking so guilty?'

'I'm not looking guilty.' But she was, and she knew it. 'You're hurting me.'

'I can hurt you a whole lot more than this,' snarled Max savagely. His lips curled. 'Who would have thought it? My frigid little wife has the hots for a famous author. I wonder how long his sales will hold up when my publicity people are through with him? Dare you risk that?'

'Oh, I think my public has more sense than to believe an abusive bastard like you,' remarked a casual voice from the doorway, and Sara looked beyond Max to see Matt and Hugo standing watching them. 'And I suggest you let go of Sara. At once, if you don't mind. We don't want any more visible signs of your cruelty on her when she files for her divorce.'

CHAPTER FOURTEEN

SARA took the train to Newcastle, spent the night at the Station Hotel, and hired a car to drive north the following morning.

Needless to say, she hadn't slept. Although she was excited at the prospect of seeing Matt again, she couldn't help wondering if she wasn't being too presumptive. After all, Matt was a famous man. He could pick and choose his friends, male as well as female. The very fact that he hadn't been in touch with her since he returned to Northumberland three months ago should have been enough to give her pause.

Maybe she should have waited for him to contact her. He was bound to visit London some time. Or should she have phoned him before recklessly boarding the train? Just because he hadn't wanted her to go back to Max that didn't mean he wanted her himself.

The truth, which was always the hardest to stomach, was that she wanted to see him. She was desperate to see him, actually, she thought ruefully. She had to know if they had a future together. She had to know if his kindness to her had been motivated by pity—or love.

Judging by the weeks and months that had gone by since he'd left London, the former seemed infinitely more probable. She'd known he felt sorry for her, that he'd wanted to protect her. Why couldn't she get her head round the fact that that was all he wanted? Why did a little voice inside her keep insisting that they deserved another chance?

If they'd had the opportunity to talk three months ago things might have been different. Clearer, certainly. As it was, all she had to go on was the stand he'd taken on her behalf when Max had been threatening her; his support when she'd explained that she'd been protecting her mother. And his efforts to ensure that until she got her divorce she had a place to live.

The scene Matt and Hugo had interrupted in Max's drawing

171

room was indelibly printed on her mind. Despite what had happened since then, subconsciously she kept replaying it in all its awful detail, reliving the moment when Max had realised he had underestimated his enemy.

Underestimated his brother, too, she remembered. It was Hugo who had let Matt into his brother's apartment; Hugo who had told him about Mrs Fielding's heart attack and his fears that Max might have had something to do with it.

To begin with Max had tried to bluff it out. He'd tried to convince Matt that he'd only been teasing his wife by threatening him; that he was jealous.

Of course, he hadn't known how intimately Matt had come to know her, that anything he said would be suspect to a man who'd seen what he'd already done to her in the past. He'd probably hoped that he could deceive Matt as he had deceived her mother. Certainly when he'd released her and got up from the couch there'd been nothing but bland geniality in his face.

Matt, however, had had a different agenda.

'Pack an overnight bag, Sara,' he'd said, ignoring Max's protestations as if he wasn't there. 'You can collect the rest of your clothes later.'

And, because that had been exactly what she'd wanted to do, Sara had obeyed him. She didn't know what had happened after she'd left the room. She'd closed the doors of the drawing room behind her, running up the stairs to the first floor as if the devil himself was at her heels.

It had taken only a few minutes to throw some trousers and shirts into a bag. She'd added underwear, shoes and stockings to the leather tote, sweeping her toothbrush, moisturiser and lipstick into a make-up case.

Then, cramming the bag shut, she'd picked it up and taken a last look around the bedroom she had shared with her husband. Even looking at the bed had caused a sick feeling in her stomach, and, with the bag banging against her legs, she'd hurried down the stairs again, eager to be gone.

She'd half expected to hear angry voices as she'd descended the stairs. She'd been apprehensive of what Max might do if he was cornered. But when she'd opened the drawing room doors again she'd found her husband and Hugo seated together on the couch while Matt had been standing by the window.

Matt had looked relieved when she'd reappeared again. She guessed he'd wondered if she might change her mind about leaving. After all, only days before she'd told him that she had no choice but to return to her husband. Despite Hugo's revelations, he was still unaware that Max's first wife was alive, that her mother's eyes had finally been opened.

Right then, however, it had been Max's face that had drawn her attention. Scarlet with rage, he'd been forced to watch their departure with furious eyes. He'd said nothing, but his eyes had promised retribution, and she was sure it was only Hugo's hand on his sleeve that had stopped him from saying how he felt.

She didn't know what Matt had said to him even now—what he'd done—but clearly it had been enough to prevent any immediate retaliation. Nevertheless, Sara had worried that Max's desire for revenge would overcome Hugo's common sense.

It hadn't happened.

Max himself had suffered a stroke a few days later that had left him severely paralysed and barely able to speak. Hugo had had to abandon the play he'd been appearing in to take charge of his brother's affairs, and he had been more than willing to co-operate with Sara in any way he could.

It had been a difficult time for all of them. And, although Sara hadn't wanted to accept anything from the Bradburys, Hugo had insisted on organising convalescent treatment for her mother when she'd left the hospital. He'd also arranged for the deeds of Mrs Fielding's apartment to be made over to her, ensuring that she would keep her home whatever happened.

He'd wanted to provide an apartment for Sara, too, but, although she'd thanked him, she'd turned him down. Matt had found her somewhere to live until her affairs were settled. A friend of his, another doctor, was planning to spend six months working in the United States and he was quite happy for her to look after his house in Putney while he was away. It had two bedrooms and a garden, and Sara had spent much of the past three months sitting on the patio, trying to make some sense of her life.

Of course, to begin with, she'd spent quite a bit of time at the hospital with her mother. Matt had respected this, but it had meant they'd had little time to talk. Although he'd told her about Max's visit, and his own concern for her whereabouts which had culminated in Rob Marco's supplying him with Max's address, they hadn't discussed personal matters.

She'd been so grateful that he'd run into Hugo outside the apartment building. She doubted he'd have been admitted on his own. And if he hadn't…

But they hadn't talked about that either. Although he'd stayed on for a while she'd known that Matt was eager to get back to his daughter. He'd left her with Mrs Webb and her family while he'd made the trip, but he couldn't stay away indefinitely.

Nevertheless, he had been a tower of strength when Max had had his attack. And when Sara had tried to blame herself for being the cause of it he'd put her straight.

'You have to stop feeling guilty for being a victim,' he'd said, just a couple of days before he'd returned to Northumberland. 'Max had been living on the edge for far too long. His blood pressure must have been sky-high. It was only a matter of time before he snapped.'

Sara suspected he was right, but it had put another obstacle between them. There was no way they could talk about their future with Max lying paralysed in a hospital bed. It was only now, with her initial decree for divorce in her bag, that she felt able to come here and find out if she meant anything to him. Or whether circumstances had blinded her to the obvious: that she was merely another patient to add to his casebook.

She'd read most of Matt's books now. Although his kind of hard-edged crime novel wasn't usually her choice of fiction, she'd found his style of writing fascinating. The main character in all his books was a criminal psychologist, and she'd seen Matt himself in the intelligent caring man he wrote about.

She'd seen, too, that apart from his special treatment of her she had no real reason for believing she was any different from any of the women in his novels. Some of them became attracted to the character he wrote about, but at the end of every book the man was on his own again.

Was that how Matt wanted to live his life? she wondered anxiously, as the signs for Ellsmoor began to appear on her right. Was she only asking for more pain by coming here? Pain of a different sort, and far more devastating?

She had to find out. She couldn't go on not knowing. It was killing her. Living every day as if it was her last.

She passed Rosie's school just as the children were streaming out of the classroom for the morning break. She was tempted to stop and speak to the child, but she knew that was just a delaying tactic. But it did make her think.

Although Rosie had been keen enough for her to be her nanny, Sara didn't know how she'd feel about anything else. Would she want to share her father's affections with another woman? Sara's experience, limited as it was, didn't condition her to expect any happy endings.

It was nearly eleven o'clock when she turned into the private road that led up to Matt's home. Her hands were slippery on the wheel of the hired car, but she succeeded in turning into the gates of Seadrift and drawing the car to a halt in front of the house.

It was amazing how familiar everything looked. It was a warm sunny morning, and the walls of the house were bathed in a mellow light. Her eyes moved beyond the house to the cliffs and the ever-changing sea beyond, and she took a deep breath. She had the most ridiculous feeling that she'd come home.

Although she'd have liked to go round to the back of the house, she rang the front doorbell instead, stepping back a little apprehensively when she heard footsteps in the hall.

Mrs Webb opened the door, her eyes widening in surprise. 'Why Miss Victor,' she began, and then corrected herself. 'I mean, Mrs Bradbury. What are you doing here?'

It was hardly the greeting Sara could have hoped for. 'I— I've come to see Matt,' she said firmly, wishing she felt more confident. 'Could you tell him I'm here?'

Mrs Webb shook her head, and Sara's spirits sank. But the housekeeper only said, 'You've changed your hair, haven't you? It suits you.'

'Thank you.' Sara had had the long hair Max had always coveted cut to a length that barely touched her shoulders. Then, trying to be patient, 'Is Matt in?'

Once again Mrs Webb shook her head. 'I'm afraid he's not,' she said, briefly dashing Sara's spirits for a second time. 'He's taken the dogs out, Mrs Bradbury. I believe he's gone down to the beach. Do you want to come in and wait?'

Sara's head turned towards the cliffs and her stomach fluttered in anticipation. 'I—no,' she said, realising there was no way she could go into the house and sit and wait for Matt to come back. 'I—er—I'll go and meet him.'

'Are you sure?'

The housekeeper looked disappointed, and Sara guessed she'd been hoping to hear what was going on. But it seemed fitting somehow that she should meet Matt on the beach. After all, that was where their relationship had changed so dramatically.

'I expect I'll see you later,' Sara murmured, hoping she wasn't being too presumptuous, and, leaving the woman to gaze consideringly after her, she walked away.

She was glad her shoes had only modest heels as she crossed the grassy stretch to the cliff path. Although it was a beautiful morning, dew had soaked the grass and her heels sank into the soft earth. She was wearing a cream silk blouse, and a brown suede skirt, and the breeze blew the lapels against her cheek.

She paused at the top of the path and looked for Matt. And saw him. He was standing with his back to her, at the edge of the water, throwing spars of driftwood for the dogs to rescue. The two retrievers were charging excitedly into the surf, fetching the wood back to him and waiting with wagging tails for him to repeat the procedure.

Sara's heart leapt into her throat at the sight of him. She hadn't realised until then just how much she'd needed to see him, and her knees shook a little as she started down the path.

She didn't know what alerted him to her presence. It wasn't the dogs. They were too busy playing to pay any attention to someone who was still so far away. But Matt glanced around and saw her, and, leaving the animals, he strode across the sand to meet her.

Sara reached the bottom of the path at the same time he did. They both halted, as if now that they were face to face they had nothing to say to one another. Then, feeling it was incumbent upon her to break the silence, Sara said breathily, 'You're wet!'

Matt glanced down. The legs of his jeans were soaked. 'I know,' he said ruefully, but he didn't sound as if he cared. 'You're not,' he added, after a moment. 'In fact, you're looking great. Life must be agreeing with you.'

Sara didn't know how to answer that. But as she continued to look at him she saw that he had lost weight. Although he still looked good to her, she saw that his cheeks had hollowed, there were pouches beneath his eyes, and his mouth had a distinctly cynical curve.

But she couldn't say that either. Instead, she chose to gesture at her own clothes, saying lightly, 'It must be quite a change for you to see me in something decent at last.' And when that didn't provoke any response she went on, 'Do you like my hair?'

'I liked it before,' said Matt indifferently. Then, as Mrs Webb had done before him, 'What are you doing here, Sara?'

Sara took a deep breath and decided she had to be forthright about this. 'I—thought you might be glad to see me,' she said, lifting her shoulders in an embarrassed gesture. 'Was I wrong?'

Matt swayed back on his heels. He was barefoot, she noticed, the cuffs of his jeans rolled to his knees.

'I'm always pleased to see a friend,' he replied at last, which wasn't at all what she wanted to hear. 'How's your mother?'

'Oh—' Sara was taken aback. 'She's much better, thanks. She's home again now, of course, but a friend of hers is staying with her.' She paused. 'If it works out, it may become a permanent arrangement.' She paused. 'Her friend is a widow, too.'

'Sounds like a good idea,' said Matt evenly. 'And Max?'

'Max?' She swallowed. 'I believe he's making good progress. He's still paralysed. I don't think that will change. But his speech is improving.'

'That's good.'

'Yes.' Sara didn't know what else to say, so she took the easy way out. 'My mother asked me to thank you for what you did. She's very grateful. We both are.'

Matt's nostrils flared for a moment. 'It was my pleasure,' he said politely. Then, carelessly, 'I expect you've been busy. Dave says you've kept him up to speed on the house. Do you think you'll stay there the full six months?'

I hope not, thought Sara anxiously. Dave Sloan was the doctor whose house Sara was living in. But it was another opening. 'Has he been in touch with you? He didn't mention it.'

'Why would he?' Matt's tone was cooler now. 'As far as Dave is concerned we're just acquaintances. He probably assumes you used to be a patient of mine.'

'And was I?' asked Sara, desperate to break through the wall Matt was steadily erecting between them. 'Was that all I was to you? Just another specimen for your casebook?'

'Don't be so bloody stupid!'

Matt turned away from her now, whistling for the dogs that had strayed further along the beach. He seemed as far away from her as ever, and in spite of what he'd said she sensed he wished she'd never come here.

Moving until she could see his face again, she touched his arm and was startled when he pulled away from her. He was wearing a sleeveless tee shirt and his skin was chilled beneath her fingers.

'You're cold,' she said, without thinking, and he looked at her with eyes that were as dark and bruised as hers used to be.

'Look,' he said grimly, 'there was no need for you to come all this way just to thank me for helping you. A phone call would have sufficed.'

'Not for me,' said Sara fiercely. 'I wanted to see you again.' She waited a beat. 'I thought—I hoped you might want to see me, too.'

'I am pleased to see you,' said Matt, but there was no warmth in his voice. 'It's good to know that you've taken control of your life again.'

'Is it?' Sara pressed her lips together. 'Why do I get the

feeling that you don't mean that? What's wrong, Matt? We used to be so—so close. Now—now you're acting like we're strangers.'

'We are strangers, Sara,' he said quellingly. 'I was there when you needed someone. Don't try and make it into something different. It doesn't work.'

Sara stared at him. 'Is that what you think?'

'It's what I know,' he told her flatly. The dogs were racing towards them now, and he moved to deflect their noisy excitement. 'Go find someone else to play with. I'm too old for these games.'

'What games?' Sara was trembling. 'I think you're mixing me up with someone else.'

Matt glanced over his shoulder. 'It's not me who's doing the mixing,' he said coldly. Then, as the dogs reached him and he grabbed for them, 'I just hope you know what you're doing, Sara. Because, God help me, I don't.'

'Obviously not.' Sara gulped. 'You clearly have no idea how much courage it took for me to come here.' Turning, she looked up the cliff path through eyes that were virtually blinded with tears. 'Don't tell me you don't know why I came,' she added in a muffled voice, 'when what you really mean is that you hoped you'd seen the last of me!'

She heard his sudden intake of breath a moment before the dogs reached her. Her words had evidently surprised Matt, perhaps causing him to momentarily relax his hold on the animals. Whatever, Sara was suddenly assaulted by two damp squirming bodies whose wet noses and sandy paws showed no respect at all for her or her clothes.

She gasped, staggering back under their exuberance, helpless laughter mingling with her tears. They were so excited, so welcoming, that she wanted to wrap her arms about them and bury her tear-stained face in their soft fur.

Her heel turning on a pebble gave her her wish. Without anything to save her she lost her balance, and the weight of the dogs bore her back onto the sand.

For a moment she was overwhelmed by doggy breath and

licking tongues, and then Matt was hauling them off her, his anger causing even the retrievers to cower away from him.

'God, I'm sorry,' he apologised, helping her to sit up. 'Crazy beasts!' Then he saw the tears on her face. 'Did they hurt you?'

Sara shook her head. 'No more than you did,' she said unsteadily, but when she would have got to her feet Matt stopped her.

'Don't say things like that,' he muttered. 'How did I hurt you? All I did was give you time to come to terms with what had happened. And you have.'

Sara looked up at him. 'And that means—what?'

An expression of weariness crossed Matt's lean face. 'You know what it means.' His tone was bleak. 'I asked you how Max was and you told me. You've been to see him, haven't you? Several times. You're thinking of going back to him.'

'No!' Sara was horrified that he should even think such a thing. 'I've been to see him, yes. But that was only a—a courtesy. I don't want to live with him again.' She shivered. 'I couldn't.'

Matt's eyes narrowed. 'You don't have to spare my feelings, you know,' he said harshly. 'I know how much he thinks of you; how much he wants you back. And it's not as if he's a danger to you any more. You could call the shots any way you chose to play it.'

Sara stared blankly at him. 'Where is all this coming from?' she demanded. 'Surely you know, better than anyone, that I'd never go back to Max, however sorry I felt for him? I don't hate him any more, that's true, but I don't have any intention of—of staying with him. I've got my first set of divorce papers in my bag if you don't believe me.'

Matt sat back on his heels. 'But Rob said—'

'Yes?' Sara quivered. 'What did Rob say?'

Matt raked an unsteady hand through his hair. 'He said—hell, don't blame Rob. He got it from your husband's brother. Hugo—Hugo told Rob that he's optimistic that you and Max—'

'I don't care what Hugo said. There is no me and Max,' declared Sara, uncaring if her words were ungrammatical. She couldn't take her eyes off Matt. 'Is that what you thought? That Max and I were getting back together?'

'It seemed possible,' said Matt, heaving a sigh. 'After all, you married him. You must have cared for him once.'

'You accused me of marrying him for his money,' retorted Sara, blinking back her tears, and Matt shook his head.

'I know you better than that now,' he told her heavily. 'Dear God, Sara, a man will say anything to protect himself.'

Sara licked a tear from the corner of her mouth. 'Did you need protection?' she asked huskily, and Matt's lips took on a rueful curve.

'You better believe it,' he said, cupping her jaw with one cold hand. His thumb brushed over her lower lip and he bent his head to rescue another tear from her cheek with his tongue. 'I think you'd better tell me again why you came here. I don't want to make any more mistakes.'

Sara shivered again, but this time with anticipation, not from fear. 'You know why I came,' she breathed, and Matt blew softly in her ear.

'Indulge me,' he said, his free hand coming to slide the collar of her silk shirt aside so that he could touch her bare shoulder with his lips. 'My confidence is at a pretty low ebb at the moment.'

Sara turned her face against his rough cheek. 'Didn't you finish your book?' she asked innocently, and he growled his indignation.

'You'll have to get it through your head that there are more important things in my life than my writing,' he told her thickly.

'Rosie. I know.'

'Not just Rosie,' he said, tilting her face up to his. His fingers caressed the skin below her ears. 'Why did you take so long to come to a decision about us?'

'So there is an "us"?' Sara whispered, and once again he made a sound of impatience.

'If you want there to be,' he said at last. 'Do you?'

'Need you ask? And I didn't know if I was doing the right thing by coming here. I've never done anything like this before.' Sara's hands came up to grip his wrists. And when he continued to just look at her she said unsteadily, 'Can't you kiss me? Please! I'm shaking.'

'That's the cold,' said Matt, but something in her expression seemed to wither whatever control he'd been putting on himself. With a groan of submission he linked his hands behind her neck and pulled her towards him and her wishes were fulfilled when his mouth slanted over hers.

Sara groped for him, her fingers encountering the tight fabric of his tee shirt before tearing it free of his pants and burrowing beneath. His skin was warm and masculine, the muscles taut beneath her hands. As her mouth opened wide beneath the hungry penetration of his tongue her breasts peaked against his chest, and between her legs she felt the liquid proof of her arousal.

Oh, God, she loved him, she thought achingly, lying back and drawing him down on top of her. And although Matt protested that she was going to get sand in her hair, too, she didn't care. This was her moment, this was where she wanted to be, and it was just so heavenly to feel his powerful body crushing hers into the sand.

He kissed her many times, kisses that grew more and more passionate, more and more devastating. She felt drugged with emotion, drugged with the sensual urgency of his mouth. And so weak with longing she didn't think she would ever have the strength to get up.

Matt peeled her shirt away from her breasts and she trembled when he said, 'No bra?'

'I didn't think I needed one,' she whispered in answer, shifting uncontrollably when he took one of the sensitive peaks into his mouth.

'You didn't,' he said, rolling the taut areola against his tongue before beginning to suck on it strongly. So strongly that she could feel its pull deep down in the pit of her stomach.

When she felt his hand between her legs, her knees trembled. She shouldn't have worn any pants either, she thought dizzily, as his fingers slid beneath the scrap of silk and lace and found the moist core of her. She arched up against his hand, already aching for a fulfilment only he could give her. But she wanted him, not a replacement, and somehow she managed to push his hand aside.

'Matt—'

But Matt had misunderstood. Bracing himself with his elbows, he lifted himself away from her. 'I know,' he said. 'I'm going too fast. I'm sorry.'

He would have sunk back onto his knees then, but Sara wouldn't let him. With a groan of frustration she grasped the waistband of his jeans, and before he could stop her she'd released the buckle.

'You're not leaving me again,' she said tremulously. 'I want you, Matt. All of you. Not just—not just an imitation.'

'Dammit, Sara—'

He tried to hold the two sides of his pants together, but Sara had already opened his zip, and she stared at him as she slipped her hand inside and caressed him.

'Tell me you don't want me,' she exclaimed, the engorged length of him throbbing in her hand, and Matt was forced to admit defeat.

'Of course I want you,' he admitted, his voice hoarse with emotion. 'Dear God, Sara, I've wanted you since the first time I touched you. You know that.'

'I do now,' she whispered, her fingers going to the button on her skirt. 'Help me, darling. I want there to be no barriers when you make love to me.'

Matt groaned. 'Sara—'

'You're not going to refuse me, are you?' she breathed unsteadily, and he closed his eyes against the unconscious provocation she represented.

'We should go back to the house,' he offered half-heartedly, but she was already easing his jeans over his tight buttocks.

'And have Mrs Webb speculating on what we're doing,' murmured Sara softly. 'I don't think so. Do you?'

'I can't think any more,' admitted Matt, kicking off his jeans without further protest. He tore his tee shirt over his head as she dispensed with her shirt and used it to make a soft bed for them to lie on. 'Here…' He nuzzled her bare shoulder as she attempted to slip out of her skirt and briefs. 'Let me.'

When Sara lay back on the sand Matt went with her, and she was tantalised by the roughness of the hair that surrounded his swollen shaft. She wanted to touch him again, but he wouldn't let her.

'I don't want any substitutes either,' he told her, making her blush. He parted her legs to kneel between her thighs. 'I just want you. The woman I love.'

He entered her in one sleek sure movement. Sara's muscles expanded and then closed tightly around him, so that he moaned a little at the knowledge that this would not last long.

They were hungry for one another, and in a few regrettably short strokes Sara felt her senses spinning away from her. Seconds later Matt joined her, his release pumping hotly inside her. Matt's seed, she thought dreamily. She hoped that one day she would have Matt's baby. A new life to make her life complete…

EPILOGUE

THEY didn't get another chance to be alone together until after Rosie had gone to bed that evening.

The little girl had been delighted to see Sara again. She'd spent most of the time since her father and Sara had collected her from school asking how long she was going to stay, whether she had decided to be Rosie's nanny, after all.

'Sara's going to live with us,' Matt had told her at last, after he and Sara had decided it was the easiest way of breaking the news of their relationship to the little girl. 'She's not going to be your nanny exactly. She's just going to live here.'

'Like a mummy?' Rosie had asked excitedly, and although Matt had been tempted to say *Exactly like a mummy*, he was afraid of jumping the gun.

But Sara hadn't had any such inhibitions. 'Would you mind if I married your father?' she'd enquired softly, and Rosie had hardly hesitated.

'I don't think so.' She'd paused. 'Could I call you Mummy?' she'd added. 'I've never had a mummy, you see. I think I'd like that.'

'You can call me anything you like,' Sara had told her gratefully, giving her a hug. 'We're going to be a real family. Would you like that?'

This time Rosie had had no reservations. 'Yes, please,' she'd said eagerly. 'Will you be getting married soon? Can I be your bridesmaid?'

Sara had looked at Matt then, and he hadn't been able to hide his amusement. 'Why not?' he'd answered blandly, and he and his wife-to-be had exchanged a look of complete understanding over his daughter's head.

Mrs Webb hadn't been at all surprised at the outcome, or so she'd said anyway. 'I always knew you were sweet on her,' she'd said to Matt, causing him to get a little red-faced at the

185

backhanded compliment. 'I'm very happy for you. I'm sure you'll have a great life together.'

But now Mrs Webb had gone home, Rosie was safely asleep in her own bed, and Sara was getting her first real look at Matt's bedroom.

It was a very masculine room, she thought, but it suited him. It suited her, too, she thought languidly some time later, after Matt had made love to her again. The hangings of rust and gold gave the room a warm ambience, and she was anticipating lots of evenings spent here, either listening to music or watching the television that occupied a carved cabinet at the foot of the bed.

Or making love, she reminded herself, with a delicious sense of completeness. Matt had told her he loved her in so many different ways, and it was difficult now to imagine how empty her life would have been if they'd never met.

But perhaps they would have met one day, she reflected. Hugo did know Rob Marco, after all. It was possible that with one of those quirks of fate they might have met, and fallen in love.

But Max would never have let her go, she remembered, the thought causing her to nestle even closer to Matt's drowsing form. And Matt would never have known what Max had done to her if he hadn't rescued her from the sea. She owed him her life as well as her happiness, she thought fancifully. And that was as it should be.

'Are you happy?' Matt asked suddenly, and she realised his eyes had opened and he was studying her grave expression rather thoughtfully. 'You're not regretting anything, are you?'

'As if I would,' she breathed, her lips closing on one of his taut nipples. 'I love you, Matt. I was just thinking how fate plays tricks on all of us. When Max fell down the stairs I thought my life was over. Little did I know it was just beginning.'

Matt rolled over onto his side so that he could look at her. 'I like that analogy,' he said. 'I feel the same. Little did I know when you walked round the corner of the barn that I'd found my destiny.'

'Your destiny?' Sara dimpled. 'That's very poetic.'

'I can write poetry, too,' said Matt drily. 'It's just not fit for public consumption, that's all.'

'I bet it is.' Sara's eyes sparkled. 'You don't do anything by halves. Look at the way you handled Max. I was full of admiration.'

Matt gave her an old-fashioned look. 'Yeah, right.'

'I mean it,' she insisted. 'I've never known Max to back down over anything. What did you say to him? Did you psychoanalyse him or something?'

'Nothing so dramatic.'

'Matt!'

'Oh—well, I guess I reminded him that I had friends in the media, too. And—I also told him that I had pictures of you that would look pretty damning on the front pages of the tabloids.'

Sara gasped. 'But you don't. Have pictures of me, I mean.' She paused. 'Do you?'

Matt pulled a wry face. 'What do you think? That I crept into your room at night and took photographs of your naked body?'

'Well, no, but—'

'He didn't know it wasn't true,' said Matt flatly. 'And once you told me about his first wife I realised why my words must have struck home.'

Sara shook her head. 'Amazing.'

'You don't mind?'

'Mind?' Sara gazed at him incredulously. 'My darling, I was in bondage and you set me free.'

'Now who's the poet?' he asked, his lips caressing her shoulder, and she gurgled with laughter.

'Not me,' she said firmly. 'I'm just a primary school teacher and part-time nanny!'

'And the love of my life,' added Matt, his hand suddenly busy elsewhere. 'Hmm, what was that you said? That I set you free? Well, my darling, do you feel like showing me some gratitude?'

And she did.

THE BEDROOM BARTER

BY
SARA CRAVEN

Sara Craven was born in South Devon and grew up in a house full of books. She worked as a local journalist, covering everything from flower shows to murders, and started writing for Mills & Boon in 1975. When not writing, she enjoys films, music, theatre, cooking, and eating in good restaurants. She now lives near her family in Warwickshire. Sara has appeared as a contestant on the former Channel Four game show *Fifteen to One*, and in 1997 was the UK television *Mastermind* champion. In 2005 she was a member of the Romantic Novelists' team on *University Challenge – the Professionals*.

CHAPTER ONE

THE waterfront was crowded, the air full of the reek of alcohol, greasy food, and the sultry rhythms of local music. People had spilled out of the crowded bars and sleazy clubs, forming shifting and edgy groups in the stifling humidity of the South American night.

Like a powder keg that only needed a spark was Ash Brennan's wry assessment.

He moved easily but with purpose, at a pace barely above a saunter, over the uneven flagstones, his cool blue glance flicking over the gaudy neon signs advertising booze and women, ignoring the glances that came his way, some measuring, some inviting. All the time maintaining his own space.

Logistically it was only about a mile from the Santo Martino marina, where millionaires moored their yachts and where all the nightspots and casinos which catered for well-heeled tourists were sited. In reality it was light years away, and any tourist foolhardy enough to venture down here would need to take to his expensive heels or risk being mugged or worse.

Ash reckoned that he blended sufficiently well. The sun-bleached tips of his dark blond hair brushed the collar of the elderly blue shirt, which lay open at the throat to reveal a tanned muscular chest. Faded khaki pants clung to lean hips and long legs. His feet were thrust into ancient canvas shoes, and a cheap watch encircled his wrist.

His height and the width of his shoulders, as well as his air of self-possession, suggested a man who could take care of himself and, if provoked, would do so.

5

He looked like a deckhand in need of rest and recreation, but selective about where he found them.

And tonight his choice had apparently fallen on Mama Rita's. He went past the display boards studded with photographs of girls in various stages of undress and down two steps into the club, where he paused, looking round him.

It was the usual sort of place, with a long bar and, closely surrounded by tables with solely male occupants, a small stage lit by powerful spots, with a central pole where the dancers performed.

The air was thick with tobacco smoke and the stink of cheap spirit. And, apart from the sound of the piano being played by a small sad-faced man with a heavy moustache, there was little noise. For the main part, the clientele sat brooding over their drinks.

Waiting for the girls to come on, Ash surmised.

Just inside the door, an enormous woman sat behind a table. Her low-cut sequinned dress in lime-green billowed over her spectacular rolls of fat as if it had been poured there, and her curly hair was dyed a rich mahogany. Her lips were stretched in a crimson-painted smile which never reached eyes that resembled small dark currants sunk into folds of pastry.

Mama Rita, I presume, Ash thought with an inward grimace.

She beckoned to him. 'You pay the cover charge, *querido*.' It was an instruction rather than a question, and Ash complied, his brows lifting faintly at the amount demanded.

'I only want a drink, Mama. I'm not putting in an offer for your club.'

The smile widened. 'You get a drink, my man. My best champagne, and a pretty girl to drink it with you.'

'Just a beer.' Ash met her gaze. 'And I'll decide if I want company.'

For a moment their glances clashed, then she shrugged, sending the sequins rippling and sparkling. 'Anything you say, *querido*.' She snapped her fingers. 'Manuel—find a good table for this beautiful man.'

Manuel, tall, handsome and sullen, set off towards the front row of tables clustering round the stage, but Ash detained him curtly.

'This will do,' he said, taking a seat at the back of the room. Manuel shrugged and went off to the bar while Ash, leaning back in his chair, took more careful stock of his surroundings.

He'd been told that Mama Rita had the pick of all the girls who came to Santo Martino, and it seemed to be true. A few of them were already sitting with customers, encouraging them to run up bar bills of cosmic proportions, but there were several lined up at the bar and Ash surveyed them casually as he took out a pack of thin cheroots and lit one, dropping the empty book of matches into the ashtray.

They were a fairly cosmopolitan mix, he thought. All of them young and most of them pretty.

He spotted a couple of North Americans and a few Europeans, as well as the local *chicas* who'd strayed into port from farms and plantations of looking for an alternative to early marriage and endless childbirth. Well, they'd found that all right, he thought cynically, stifling a brief pang of regret. Because he wasn't there to feel compassion. He couldn't afford it.

'You see something you like, *señor*?' Manuel was back with his beer, his smile knowing.

'Not yet,' Ash returned coolly, tapping the ash from his cheroot. 'When I do, I'll let you know.'

Manuel shrugged. 'As you wish, *señor*. You have only to speak.' He nodded towards an archway with a beaded curtain behind the stage. 'We have rooms—very private rooms—where the girls would dance for you alone,' he added with blatant insinuation. 'I can arrange. At a price, *naturalemente*.'

'You amaze me,' said Ash. 'I'll bear it in mind.'

The beer was surprisingly good, and wonderfully cold,

and he took several long deep swallows, turning his attention away from the flashing smiles of the hopeful girls and focussing instead on the piano player who was still doggedly persisting with a range of old standards in spite of the indifference of his audience.

I hope the old witch at the door pays you well, brother, Ash told him silently as he stubbed out the cheroot. You deserve it.

The pianist reached the end of his set and half-rose to acknowledge the non-existent applause. He seated himself again, and struck a chord loudly.

The bead curtain shivered and admitted a girl.

At her entrance a strange sound like a low growl went through the room. The predators scenting their prey, Ash thought with distaste, then paused, eyes narrowing as he saw her properly.

She was blonde, and slightly less than medium height in spite of her high heels, her slim, taut body complemented by the fluid lines of the brief black dress she was wearing. The strapless bodice was cut straight across the swell of her high rounded breasts, making her skin glow like ivory. The silky fabric clung to her slender hips, ending just below mid-thigh, giving the troubling impression that beneath it she was naked.

But she did not climb up on the stage and begin her routine. Instead, head slightly bent, looking at no one and ignoring the whistles and ribald shouts, she skirted the edge of the platform until she reached the piano. She leaned back against it, as if glad of its support, while the pianist played the introduction to 'Killing Me Softly'.

She had an incredible face, Ash thought frowningly, his attention completely caught. In contrast to the tumble of fair hair on her shoulders her brows and lashes were startlingly dark, fringing eyes as green and wary as a cat's. She had exquisite cheekbones, and her mouth was painted a hot, sexy pink.

And she was scared witless.

He'd known it from the moment of her entrance. Even across the crowd of waiting men he'd felt the force of her fear like a cold hand laid on his shoulder. Now he noticed the small hands balled into fists among the folds of her skirt, the blank, tense smile on her lips.

She was like a small animal, he thought, caught in the headlights of a car and powerless to move.

But there was no problem with her voice when she began to sing. It was low-pitched, powerful and faintly husky. The kind of voice a man would want to hear moaning his name at the moment of climax, Ash thought, his mouth curving in self-contempt.

Her audience was listening while she sang, but with a faint restiveness. However appealing her voice might be, it was the promise offered by the skimpy dress that mattered to them. They couldn't believe it was just a song that was on offer. All the other girls took off their clothes, so why shouldn't she?

She moved effortlessly into the next song—'Someone to Watch Over Me'. She was no longer staring at the floor. Her head was up, and she seemed to be looking far beyond the confines of the club with a wistfulness and undisguised yearning that matched the words of the song.

And in that moment, as her voice trembled into silence, Ash's gaze met hers over the heads of the crowd. Met— and held it for one endless, breathless moment.

Now, he thought, I know why I came here tonight.

The number over, she ducked her head swiftly and shyly in response to the sprinkling of applause, and went back the way she had come. Ash waited to see if she would glance back at him, but she did not, simply vanishing behind the curtain, followed by catcalls and shouts of disappointment.

Ash drained his beer and got to his feet. Mama Rita looked up at his approach, her eyes sharp and shrewd.

'You want something, *querido*?'

'I want the songbird,' Ash said levelly.

She considered that. 'To sit with you—have a few drinks—be nice?'

'Nice, yes,' Ash told her. 'But in one of your private rooms, Mama. I want her to dance for me. Alone.'

Her brows lifted and she began to laugh, the sequins shaking and flashing. 'She's my newest girl. She still learning, *mi corazón*. And maybe I'm saving her for a rich customer, anyway. You couldn't afford her.'

He said softly, 'Try me.'

'Crazy man,' she said. 'Why spend all your money? Choose another girl. One who dances good.'

'No,' he said. 'The songbird. I'll pay the price for her.'

She looked him over. 'You got that sort of money?' There was frank disbelief in her voice.

'You know that I have.' Ash took a billfold from his back pocket, peeled off some notes, and tossed them on to the table in front of her. 'And I know what I want.'

She picked them up swiftly. 'That for me,' she said. 'Commission. You pay her too. Whatever she worth. Whatever you get her to do. Should be easy,' she added. 'Beautiful man like you, *querido*.' She chuckled again. 'Teach her some lessons, *Sí?*'

'*Sí,*' Ash said softly. 'The lessons of a lifetime.' He paused. 'Does she have a name?'

She tucked the money he'd given her into her cleavage and surged to her feet. 'She called Micaela.' She leered triumphantly at him. 'You have another beer—on the house. I go tell your songbird that she's lucky girl.'

I only hope, Ash said silently, watching Mama Rita's departure, that she thinks so too.

But that, he thought as he went back to his table, was in the lap of the gods—like so much else. And he ordered his beer and settled down to wait.

Chellie sank on to the stool in front of the mirror, gripping the edge of the dressing table until the shaking stopped. It was nearly a month since she'd started singing in the club, and she ought to be used to it by now. But she wasn't, and maybe she never would be.

It was the men's faces—the hot, hungry eyes devouring her—that she couldn't handle, the things they called out to her that she was thankful she couldn't understand properly.

'How do you bear it?' she'd asked Jacinta, one of the pole dancers and the only girl working at Mama Rita's to be even marginally friendly.

Jacinta had shrugged. 'I don't see,' she'd replied brusquely. 'I smile, but I don't look at them. I look past— think my own thoughts. Is better that way.'

It seemed wise advice, and Chellie had followed it. Until tonight, that was, when, totally against her will, she'd found herself being drawn almost inexorably to a man's gaze. True, he'd been sitting by himself at one of the rear tables, in itself unusual, as most of the male clientele liked to bunch at the front, baying like wolves for every inch of exposed flesh. But that wasn't the only thing that had seemed to set him apart.

For one thing, he was clearly a European, and they didn't get many at the club.

For another, he was strikingly—almost dangerously attractive, his surface good looks masking a toughness as potent as a clenched fist.

Even across the crowded club he'd made her aware of that.

She thought in bewilderment, Somehow he made me look at him…

So, what could have brought him to seek the tawdry erotic stimulus of a place like Mama Rita's?

Chellie's experience of men was frankly limited, but instinct told her that this was the last man on earth who would need to buy his pleasures.

Oh, God, she thought impatiently, things must be bad if you're starting to fantasise about a customer.

And things were indeed about as bad as they could get. Her life had become a nightmare without end, she realised as she peeled off the loathsome blonde wig, and ran her fingers thankfully through the short feathery spikes of raven hair that it concealed.

Mama Rita had been adamant about that. Brunettes were no novelty in this part of the world. The men who came to her club wanted blondes, and pale-skinned blondes at that.

It had seemed such a small concession at the time, and she'd been so desperate—so grateful for a place to stay and the chance to earn some money—that she'd probably have agreed to anything. Especially as she was being given the chance to sing. She'd thought it was the end of the disasters that had befallen her. Instead, it had only been the beginning.

She wouldn't need to stay at the club long, she'd told herself with supreme confidence. She'd soon save enough for an air ticket out of here.

Only it hadn't worked out like that. The money she received had seemed reasonable when it was first offered, but once Mama Rita had exacted rent for that tiny cockroach-ridden room on the top floor of the club, money for the hire of the tacky dresses she insisted that Chellie wore, and payment for the services of Gomez the piano player—which she was convinced he never saw—Chellie barely had enough left to feed herself.

And, worst of all, Mama Rita had taken her passport, which was about all she had left in the world, and locked it away in her desk, making her a virtual prisoner.

The trap had opened and she'd walked straight into it, she realised bitterly.

There was always the option of earning more, of course, as Mama Rita had made clear from the start. Chellie could be friendly, and sit with the customers, encourage them to buy bogus and very expensive champagne. But even if the thought of it hadn't made her flesh crawl she'd been warned off by Jacinta.

'You earn more—she takes more,' the other girl had said with a shrug.

'You sit with a customer one day; you take your clothes off next. Because you don't get out of here unless Mama Rita says so. And she chooses when and where you go. And you ain't served your time yet.'

She'd paused, giving Chellie a level look. 'There are worse places than this, believe it. And don't try running away, because she always finds you, and then you will be sorrier than you ever dreamed.'

I think I've already reached that point, Chellie thought bleakly. And who ever said blondes had more fun?

She sighed, then got up and began to root along the dress rail in the corner. She performed two sets each evening and had to wear something different for every appearance, which presented its own problems. When she'd begun, she'd worn evening dresses, but these had gradually been taken away and replaced by the kind of revealing costumes the dancers and hostesses wore. Which severely restricted her choice.

She bit her lip hard when she came to the latest addition, a micro-skirt in shiny black leather topped by a bodice that was simply a network of small black beads. She might as well wear nothing at all, but she supposed that was the point Mama Rita was making.

But that's never going to happen, she told herself with grim determination. I'm going to get away from here somehow, whatever the risk. And from now on I'm trusting no one. Especially men...

Her whole body winced as she thought of Ramon. She tried very hard not to think of him, but that wasn't always possible, although the physical memory of him was mercifully fading with every day that passed. She could barely recall what he looked like, or the sound of his voice. One day she might forget his touch, she thought with a shiver, or even the painful delusion that she'd been in love with him.

In a way, she acknowledged, everything that had occurred between them seemed remote—as if it had happened to two other people in some separate lifetime.

Only it hadn't, of course. And that was why she found herself here, duped, robbed and dumped, in this appalling mess.

It might be humiliating to retrace the steps that had brought her here, but it was also salutary.

After all, she'd needed to escape from her life in England and the future that was being so inexorably planned for her. In spite of everything, she still believed that. It was just unfortunate that, through Ramon, all she'd done was jump out of the frying pan into a fire like the flames of hell.

But somehow she was going to wrench her life back into her own control.

I'll survive, she told herself with renewed determination.

As she hung the black dress back on the rail the flimsy curtain over the dressing room entrance was pushed aside and Lina, one of the lap dancers, came in.

'Mama Rita wants to see you, girl, in her office—now.'

Chellie's brows snapped together. It was the first time she'd been summoned like this. Usually a girl was called up because of some misdemeanour, she thought, tensing in spite of herself. She'd seen several of the girls with scratched faces and bruised and bleeding mouths after an encounter with Mama Rita's plump ring-laden hands.

Aware that the dancers operated a grapevine second to none, she strove to keep her voice level. 'Do you know why?'

Lina's eyes glinted with malice. 'Maybe you're going to start working for your living, honey, like the rest of us.'

Chellie faced her, lifting her chin. 'I do work—as a singer.'

'Yeah?' Lina's tone was derisive. 'Well, all that may be about to change. The word is that some guy wants to know you better.'

Chellie felt the colour drain from her face. 'No,' she said hoarsely. 'That's not possible.'

'Take it up with Mama Rita.' Lina shrugged indifferently. 'And don't keep her waiting.'

The office was one floor up, via a rickety iron staircase. Chellie approached it slowly, the beat of her heart like a trip-hammer. Surely—*surely* this couldn't be happening, she thought. Surely Lina was just being malicious. Because Mama Rita had told her at the beginning that there were plenty of willing girls at the club, and that she would never be pressured into anything she did not want.

And Chellie had believed that. In fact, she'd counted on it.

There was a clatter of feet on the stairs and Manuel came into view.

Chellie stepped back to allow him to pass, trying not to shrink too visibly. From the moment she'd started working at the club she'd found him a problem. If she hadn't already been repelled by his coarse good looks, then his constant attempts to get her into corners and fondle her would have aroused her disgust.

The first night in her cramped and musty room, some instinct had prompted her to wedge a chair under the handle of her door. And some time in the small hours she'd woken from an uneasy sleep to hear a stealthy noise outside, and the sound of the handle being tried in vain. She'd observed the same precaution ever since.

There was no point in complaining to Mama Rita either, because the other girls reckoned Manuel was her nephew—some even said her son.

Now, he favoured her with his usual leer. '*Hola*, honey girl.'

'Good evening.' Chellie kept her tone curt, and his unpleasant grin widened.

'Oh, you're so high—so proud, *chica*. Too good for poor Manuel. Maybe tomorrow you sing a different tune.' He licked his lips. 'And you'll sing it for me.'

She controlled her shiver of revulsion. 'Don't hold your breath.'

The office door was open and Mama Rita was sitting at her desk, using her laptop. She greeted Chellie with a genial smile. 'You were a big hit tonight, *hija*. One of the customers liked you so much he wants a private performance.'

Chellie's heart skipped a beat. 'Any particular song?' She sounded more cool than she felt.

'You making a joke with me, *querida*?' The geniality was suddenly in short supply. 'He wants that you dance for him.' The mountainous body mimed grotesquely what was required.

Chellie shook her head. 'I don't dance,' she said, her mouth suddenly dry. 'I—I never have. I don't know how…'

'You have watched the others.' Mama Rita shrugged. 'And he don't want some high-tone ballerina. You have a good body. Use it.'

Yes, Chellie thought, but I've only watched the girls table dancing in the club itself. That has limits. The private room thing is totally different…

She said desperately, 'But you employ me as a singer. That was the deal. We have a contract…'

Mama Rita laughed contemptuously. '*Sí*, but the terms just changed.'

'Then you're in breach, and that cancels any agreement between us.' Chellie kept her hands bunched in the folds of her skirt to conceal the fact that they were trembling. 'So, if you'll return my passport, I'll leave at once,' she added with attempted insouciance.

'You think it that simple?' The older woman shook her head almost sorrowfully. 'You dream, *hija*.'

'I fail to see what's so complicated.' Chellie lifted her chin. 'Legally, you've broken the association between us. End of story.'

'This my club. I make the law here.' Mama Rita leaned forward, her eyes glittering like her sequins. 'And you go nowhere. Because I keep your passport as security until you pay your debts here.'

Chellie was suddenly very still. 'But the rent—everything is paid in advance.'

Mama Rita sighed gustily. 'Not everything, *chica*. There is your medical bill.'

'Medical bill?' Chellie repeated in total bewilderment. 'What are you talking about?'

There was a tut of reproof. 'You have a short memory. When you first come here I call a doctor to examine you. To check whether you sick with pneumonia.'

Chellie recalled with an inward grimace a small fat man with watery, bloodshot eyes and unpleasantly moist hands, who'd breathed raw alcohol into her face as he bent unsteadily over her.

She said, 'I remember. What of it?'

Mama Rita handed her a sheet of paper. 'See—this is what you owe him.'

Chellie took it numbly, her lips parting in shock as she read the total.

She said hoarsely, 'But he can't ask this. He was only with me for about two minutes—he prescribed none of the stuff listed here—and he was drunk. You know that.'

'I know that you were sick, girl, needing a doctor. And Pedro Alvarez is good man.' She nodded, as if enjoying a private joke. 'Plenty discreet. You may be glad of that one day.'

She paused, studying Chellie with quiet satisfaction. 'But you don't leave owing all this money, *chica*. So, you have to earn to pay it. And this man who wants you has cash to spend. Good-looking *hombre* too.' A laugh shook her, sending the rolls of fat wobbling. 'Be nice—you could make all you need in one night.'

'No.' Chellie shook her head almost violently, her arms crossing over her body in an unconsciously defensive gesture. 'I can't. I *won't*. And you can't make me.'

'No?' The small eyes glared at her with sudden malevolence. Mama Rita brought the flat of her hand down hard on the desk. 'I patient with you, *chica*, but no more. You do what you're told—understand?' She sat back, breathing heavily. 'Maybe I give you to Manuel first—let him teach you to be grateful. You want that?'

'No,' Chellie said, her voice barely audible. 'I don't.'

Mama paused. 'Or I send you to my friend Consuela.' She gave a grating laugh. 'She don't ask you to sing or dance.'

Oh, God, Chellie thought, her throat closing in panic as she remembered overheard dressing room gossip. *Not that—anything but that.*

She bent her head defeatedly. 'No,' she said. Then, with difficulty, 'Please…'

'Now you begin think sense.' Mama nodded with satisfaction. 'Lina will take you to room. Then I send him to you.'

Lina was waiting in the passage outside. She gave Chellie a contemptuous grin. 'Joining the real world, honey? After tonight, maybe you won't be looking down your nose at the rest of us.'

'Is that what I did?' Chellie asked numbly. 'I—I'm sorry. I didn't realise.'

Lina looked at her sharply. 'Hey, you're not going to pass out on me, are you? Because Mama would not find that funny.'

'No,' Chellie said, with an effort. 'I'll try and stay conscious.'

'What's the big problem, anyway?' Lina threw open a door at the end of the passage. 'You must've known Mama wasn't running no charity. So, why come here?'

Chellie looked around her, an icy finger tracing her spine. The room, with its heavily shaded lamps, wasn't large, and was totally dominated by a wide crimson couch with heaped cushions that stood against one wall. Music with a slow Latin beat was playing softly, and a bottle of champagne on ice with two glasses waited on a small side table.

She said wearily, 'It wasn't exactly my choice. I was robbed, and I went to the police. One of them said he'd find me a safe place to stay while they traced my money. And this was it.'

'That figures.' Lina shrugged. 'It's how Mama gets a lot of her girls—she pays the police to send her the debris that washes up on the beach.'

Chellie bit her lip. 'Thanks.'

'De nada.' Lina walked to the door, then hesitated. 'Look, honey, it's no big deal. Just smile and make like you're enjoying yourself. It's not your first time—right?'

'No.' Chellie tried not think about those few humiliating, uncomfortable nights with Ramon. At the time she'd thought nothing worse could happen to her. How wrong could anyone be? she asked herself with bitter irony.

'If things get heavy there's a panic button under the table,' Lina added. 'But don't press unless you actually need to, or Manuel won't like it. And you really don't want to upset him. He's one of the bad guys.' She fluttered her fingers in mocking farewell. 'So—good luck.'

All the walls were hung with floor-length drapes, so it was impossible to tell where the window was—if it existed at all. And past experience suggested it would be locked and barred even if Chellie could find it—before the client found her.

But she could really do with some fresh air. The atmosphere in the room was heavy, and thick with some musky scent. She began to walk round the edge of the room, her heels sinking into the soft thick carpet, lifting the curtains and finding only blank wall to her increasing frustration.

She wasn't sure of the exact moment when she realised she wasn't alone any longer.

She hadn't heard the door, and the carpet must have muffled the sound of his footsteps. Yet he was there—behind her. Waiting. She knew it as surely as if he'd come across the room and put a hand on her shoulder.

For a moment she felt the breath catch in her throat, then she allowed the curtain she was holding to drop back into place and turned slowly and reluctantly to face him.

And paused, her eyes widening in total incredulity as she recognised him. As she registered all over again, but this time at much closer quarters, the cool, uncompromising good looks—the high-bridged nose, the strong lines of jaw and cheekbones. The face of a man who did not take no for an answer.

He was lounging on the sofa, totally at his ease. There was even a faint smile playing round his firmly sculpted mouth.

She was more frightened than she'd ever been in her life—her whole body shaking—embarrassed to the point of nausea—yet for one moment her overriding emotion was disappointment.

She'd thought he'd strayed into the club by mistake, but she was wrong. He was no better than the whooping, slavering crowd bunched round the stage. And regret sliced at her.

He said softly, '*Buenas noches*, Micaela.'

Her throat muscles were too taut for words, so she ducked her head in a brief, awkward nod of response.

Micaela, she thought. That was her name in this place— her identity. And her shield. If she could just hide behind it, she could perhaps make herself believe that none of this was happening to her. That she was someone altogether different, in another place, just as she did when she sang. And somehow she would be able to—endure...

He was silent for a moment, the cool blue gaze travelling over her so slowly and thoroughly that it made removing her clothes seem almost unnecessary.

Beneath the fragile covering of the black dress Chellie felt her skin tingle and burn under his absorbed scrutiny. She knew she should begin the pretence. Micaela would force her mouth into a smile, but Chellie found it impossible.

Although this was not the worst that could happen to her, and she knew it. Outside this room, in the real world, was the threat of Manuel and the woman Consuela, and all the other unnamed horrors they implied.

She thought, *I must do this. I have no choice…*

His own smile widened a little. He said, 'Aren't you supposed to offer me a drink?'

'Oh—yes.' She moved to the table, stumbling a little in her haste. Glad of a momentary reprieve. 'Would you like some champagne?'

And in her head she heard the echo of another girl—her father's hostess, making sure his guests had all they needed. A girl she had wanted to leave behind.

Beware what you wish for, someone had once told her. Because it might come true.

'Not in the least,' he said. 'But don't let me stop you. You look as if you need it.'

Chellie paused uncertainly. One of the club rules, she knew, was that the champagne was for the client. The girl did not drink alone, if at all.

She slid the bottle back into the melting ice. She said huskily, 'I—I'm not thirsty.'

'That makes two of us,' he said. 'See how much we have in common already?' There was faint mockery in his voice. He looked her over again, almost meditatively, his eyes half closed.

'I know you can sing,' he said. 'So, shall we discover what other talents you possess?' He leaned back against the cushions—a man preparing himself for enjoyment. 'Starting now?' he added gently.

It was not a request, but a demand. She bent her head in acquiescence and came to stand in front of him, just out of reach but no more than that. Then, slowly, she began to move to the beat of the music.

CHAPTER TWO

SHE had not told Mama Rita the truth when she'd said she couldn't dance. Because dancing had been one of her passions in that other, seemingly far-off lifetime.

Then, she'd turned herself deliberately into a party animal, going whenever she could to clubs and discos, losing herself totally in the pounding noise and frenetic rhythms of the music. Using the fevered momentum of her body to exorcise her teeming frustrations over her abortive singing career—as well as all the other limitations that being her father's daughter had imposed on her life.

But this was not the same kind of music at all. This was slow and swaying, and deliberately, infinitely seductive. It wasn't meant to induce forgetfulness. It had the opposite purpose—to entice the man watching her into opening his wallet to pay for each further revelation.

And that was what she had to do in order to survive.

She tried desperately to remember what Jacinta had told her. Smile, but don't look. Raise a mental barricade and keep the greedy, leering eyes at bay. Close yourself off emotionally from all that follows.

Because this is not you, she reminded herself. This is Micaela, and she does not even exist, so that nothing that happens to her can harm you.

Not that the client's meditative blue gaze held any real hint of incipient lust, or even particular interest in her performance so far. He, too, seemed to be thinking about something else.

He asked for me, Chellie thought, bewildered. So why isn't he looking at me? Am I boring him? Oh, God, I need—

I really need to get this right, or Mama Rita will make me suffer.

She began to move her hips with deliberate sinuousness, her hand smoothing the brief silky skirt against her slender thighs, even pulling it up slightly, then letting it drift back. And saw his brows lift in almost mocking acknowledgement of the teasing promise that her actions implied.

'Why not come a little closer?' he invited softly. 'Or does that cost extra?'

Chellie shook her head, not trusting her voice.

'There's nothing to be scared of,' he went on. 'I don't bite, unless specifically requested to do so. And, anyway, I believe the rules state that I'm only allowed to watch—not touch.'

Rules? Chellie thought wildly. In a place like this? What rules could possibly apply? Was he crazy or just naïve?

'Or not without your permission, at least,' he added almost idly. 'Which I admit doesn't seem likely at the moment.' He took out his billfold. 'Perhaps this might soften your heart—hmm?'

He extracted some notes and placed them on the table beside the ice bucket. 'So, maybe we could—move the performance on a little? Just so that my evening isn't completely wasted.'

In other words, he was telling her to take off her dress.

Chellie's stomach lurched in swift panic as she remembered how little she was wearing beneath it. She was braless, and the rest of her underwear was little more than a glorified G-string. Which he would undoubtedly want her to remove as well.

It occurred to her that this stranger would be only the second man to see her naked. The first, of course, had been Ramon, but he'd been in too great a hurry to pay much attention.

Her whole body shivered as she recalled how he'd pushed her back on the bed, the weight of his body crushing her into the mattress, the painful, grunting thrusts which she'd thought would never end.

Which she was going to have to endure again…

He said, 'I'm waiting for you—Micaela.'

If he'd seemed uninterested before, he was certainly giving her his undivided attention now, his mouth oddly hard, the blue eyes implacable, almost analytical—as if he was observing her through a microscope and did not much care for what he saw.

She pivoted slowly in front of him, letting the skirt swing out away from her slim legs. Going blindly, automatically through the motions, while her mind shivered on the edge of chaos.

Oh, God, she thought imploringly. Let this not be happening to me. Let me wake up soon—please…

The zip that fastened her dress was at the side, reaching from breast to hip. Once she began to lower it the dress would simply fall away from her body. And after that there could be no retreat.

Her shaking fingers undid the tiny hook first, then fumbled for the metal tongue of the zip.

And halted as her entire being froze in outrage and rebellion over what she was being made to do. Her eyes met his in a glance that mingled pleading with outright defiance.

She said hoarsely, 'I can't. I'm sorry, but I just—can't…'

She sank down on to the carpet, because her legs would no longer support her, and covered her face with her hands.

She was expecting an angry reaction and knew that it would be perfectly justified. He might even be violent. Or he could just walk to the door and summon Mama Rita— or even Manuel. Her teeth bruised her lower lip as she recognised the kind of retribution she was inviting.

Yet, strangely, it made no difference to her decision, she realised with an odd calm. Whatever kind of aftershock it might create, she knew she could not strip in front of this man or any other.

Nor could she—or would she—allow him any of the intimacies his money gave him the right to demand.

She thought, I'd rather die...

Although death might not be the worst thing that could happen to her.

The silence in the room seemed endless. Perhaps he'd simply walked out already, leaving as quietly as he'd arrived, she thought, venturing to look up. Gone to make his complaint and demand his refund.

But he was still there, lounging on the sofa, apparently unmoved by her outburst. And if he was furious with disappointment and thwarted desire then he was masking it well.

When at last he did speak, he had the gall to sound faintly amused.

'Have you ever considered changing your job?' he asked. 'Because you seem to lack total commitment to your current career.'

Somehow she managed to scramble to her feet, glaring at him as she did so.

She said thickly, 'Don't you laugh. Don't you dare laugh at me—you bastard.'

He stood too. He was tall. Even in her heels Chellie found she had to look up at him, and resented it.

He said with sudden harshness, 'You're right. This is no laughing matter. And it might be better not to call me names.' He gestured at the sofa. 'Sit down.'

'No.' She took a step backwards, hugging herself defensively.

'Do as you're told,' he said curtly. 'Before you fall down again.' He reached into a back pocket and produced a slender hip flask. 'Here.' He removed the stopper. 'Drink this.'

Chellie stayed where she was. 'What is it?'

'Brandy,' he said. 'And a damned sight safer than your boss's inferior and possibly drugged champagne.' He paused, surveying her pale face and shocked emerald eyes. 'Go on—have some. You need it.'

She shook her head. 'My troubles are just beginning,' she said in a muffled voice. 'Brandy won't cure them.' She swallowed. 'I—I'd better go. Do you want me to send you one of the other girls?'

'If so, I'd have asked for them in the first place,' he returned brusquely. 'But I picked you.'

'I know.' Chellie caught her trembling lower lip in her teeth. 'And I'm sorry. I thought I could do this—I—I really meant to—but…'

'For a moment there, I thought so too.' He slanted a wry smile. 'You almost had me fooled. However, I'm trying to live with the disappointment.'

She stared at him. 'You're saying that you *knew* I wouldn't go through with it?' Her voice shook.

'Of course.' He shrugged. 'Now, sit down and drink some brandy.'

Chellie obeyed reluctantly, her gaze mutinous and suspicious. What was going on here? she asked herself. She'd been bought and paid for. Why didn't he insist that she kept the bargain? And how could be possibly have known that she'd fall at the first hurdle?

The brandy was powerful stuff, and she nearly choked as she swallowed it, but she felt it warming her, thawing the icy core lodged deep inside her.

'Thank you,' she said stiltedly, as she handed back the flask.

He shrugged again. *'De nada.'* He sat down too, but at the opposite end of the sofa, deliberately creating a distance between there. It should have reassured her, but it didn't— because he was still there in her sightline—in her space.

'Tell me something,' he said, after a moment, 'do you suppose this room is bugged in any way?'

She gasped. 'What are you talking about?'

'It surely isn't that hard to comprehend.' He spoke with an edge. 'Does Mama Rita use hidden cameras—microphones? Check what's happening?'

Slowly, Chellie shook her head. 'I don't think so. The other girls would have mentioned it, if so.'

He nodded. 'Good.'

Tinglingly aware of his continuing scrutiny, Chellie tugged ineffectually at her skirt, trying to pull it down over her knees.

She said uncertainly. 'Why are you staring at me?'

'Because I've paid for the privilege,' he said. 'So I may as well take advantage of the time I have left.'

Her lips parted in sheer astonishment. 'That's all you want?' she queried huskily.

'It will do,' he said. 'Unless, of course, you'd like to take something off for me?'

There was a silence, then she said in a small, stifled voice, 'I should have known that—all this was too good to be true. Was the brandy meant to give me Dutch courage?'

He said coolly, 'I was actually hoping that you'd remove that ghastly wig. Or are you going to pretend that it's your natural hair?'

She was startled into a faint giggle. 'No—no, of course it isn't. But Mama Rita insists I wear it.' She pulled the wig off and tossed it on to the floor, running awkward fingers through her dark hair.

'Good,' he approved softly. 'That's an amazing improvement.'

Her face warmed, but she said nothing.

She still didn't understand or trust this *volte face*. And even now her reprieve might only be temporary, she reminded herself. He was only at arm's length. Perhaps he was just lulling her into a false sense of security. Whatever, she could not afford to relax.

A fact apparently not lost on him. He said softly, 'You're like a wire stretched to snapping point.'

Chellie sent him a fulminating glance. 'Does that really surprise you?'

'No,' he said. 'What does puzzle me is how you come to be in this hellhole. I'm sure you'll tell me it's none of my business, but, as a life-choice, it seems a seriously bad move.'

'Choice?' she repeated with stunned disbelief. 'Are you mad?' Her voice rose. 'Do you honestly think that if it had been down to me I'd ever have set foot in a place like this?'

'If that's truly the case,' he drawled, 'why do you stay?'

Her hands gripped each other until they ached. 'Because I can't leave,' she said in a low voice. 'I have no money, no passport, and no other option.'

His brows lifted. 'Were you robbed?'

'Mama Rita took my passport.' Chellie bent her head. 'Someone—someone else had my money. As a result I was turned out of my hotel room, and they kept my luggage.'

She paused. 'I'd been suffering from a virus, anyway, so I wasn't exactly thinking straight.' *Quite apart,* she thought, *from realising that Ramon had walked out on me. Left me broke and stranded.*

But she couldn't afford to think about that—about her sheer criminal stupidity. Or she might break down—lose it completely in front of this stranger.

Instead, she straightened her shoulders. 'I knew I needed to find the British consul pretty urgently,' she went on. 'So I stopped this police car to ask the way.'

'Not very wise,' he said.

'So I found out.' She shivered. 'At first the policeman threatened to jail me for vagrancy. Then he seemed to relent. He said the consul's office was closed for the day, but he'd take me somewhere safe in the meantime.'

She tried to smile. 'I can even remember feeling grateful to him. Only he brought me here, where I've been ever since.'

'Hardly your lucky day.' His voice was expressionless.

'No,' Chellie admitted tautly. 'But I know there are worse places than this, because Mama Rita has already threatened me with them if I don't do as she says. I could have ended up in one of them instead.' *And it could still happen…*

Her voice broke slightly. 'You know—I—I really believed she was going to let me sing my way out of here. We had this deal—in writing.' She attempted a laugh. 'How naïve can you get?'

His tone was dry. 'Mama Rita is a woman who believes in exploiting all the assets at her disposal.' He paused. 'The only question is—do you intend to stay here as one of those assets?'

'You mean—why don't I run away?' Chellie shook her head. 'With no passport I wouldn't get very far. And she'd simply find me and bring me back—or hand me over to her friend Consuela,' she added, shuddering.

He said softly, 'In an ideal world, how far would you like to run?'

She lifted her chin. 'For preference—to the other side of the universe.'

He said, 'I can't promise that—but there's always St Hilaire, instead.'

Her brow creased. 'Where is that? I've never heard of it.'

'Hardly surprising,' he returned. 'It's in the Windward Islands, and not terribly big. I'm taking a boat there for its owner.' He paused, giving her a level look. 'You could always go with me.'

Chellie stared at him. She said uncertainly 'Go—with you?' She shook her head. 'I—I don't think so.'

'Listen,' he said. 'And listen well. I may be the first man to pay for your company, but I certainly won't be the last. And the next guy along may not respect your delicate shrinkings. In fact, he could even find them a turn-on,' he added laconically. 'And expect a damned sight more pleasure from you than I've had. Are you prepared for that?'

Colour flooded into her face. 'You don't mince your words.'

'Actually,' he said, 'I'm letting you down lightly.'

She was quiet for a moment. 'Why should I trust you?'

'Because you can.' The blue eyes met hers in a single, arrogant clash, and Chellie found herself looking away hurriedly, aware of the sudden thud of her heart against her ribcage. Even if he wasn't here alone with her, she thought, he would still be one of the most disturbing men she had ever encountered.

She lifted her chin. 'I've trusted other people recently. It's been a disaster every time.'

He shrugged. 'Your luck has to change some time,' he said. 'Why not now?'

She hesitated again. 'When you say—go with you…' She paused, her colour deepening. 'What exactly do you mean?'

His mouth curled. 'Listen, songbird, if I really wanted you, I'd have had you by now.' He paused, allowing her to assimilate that. 'The boat has more than one cabin, so you can have all the privacy you want. I'm offering you safe passage to St Hilaire and that's all. There's nothing more. So—take it or leave it.'

She should have been relieved at his reassurance. Instead she was aware of an odd feeling closely resembling pique.

She was angry with herself because of it, which in turn sparked a sudden sharpness in her voice. 'You don't look much like a philanthropist to me.'

'Well, sweetheart,' he said, 'your own appearance is open to misinterpretation—wouldn't you say?'

He seemed to have an answer for everything, she thought with growing resentment.

She said, 'It's just that—I can't pay you—as you must know.'

'Don't worry about it,' he directed lazily. 'I'm sure we can reach some mutually agreeable arrangement.' And, as her lips parted indignantly, he added, 'Can you cook?'

'Yes,' she said swiftly, and on the whole, untruthfully.

'Problem solved, then. You provide three meals a day for Laurent and myself, and you'll have paid for your trip several times over.'

'Laurent?'

'The other crew member. Great bloke, but not gifted in the galley.' He paused. 'Well?'

No, she thought, that's not the word at all. 'Dangerous' comes to mind. But so does 'tempting' at the same time.

She said slowly, 'I—I don't understand. Why should you want to help me? We're total strangers to each other.'

'We share a nationality,' he said. 'We're both a long way from home. And one look tonight told me you were in deep trouble. I thought maybe you might need a helping hand.'

She stared at him. 'Your name isn't Galahad, by any chance?'

'No,' he said. 'Any more than yours is Micaela.'

Chellie bit her lip, once again at a loss. 'I'm still not sure about this…' she began.

He gave a quick, impatient sigh. 'Understand this, darling.' His tone bit. 'I'm not about to force you on board *La Belle Rêve*. And I'm not going to beg you on my knees either. It all depends on how badly you want to get out of your current situation. But I'm sailing tonight, whether you're with me or not.'

He paused. 'So—no more discussion. We're wasting valuable time. I'm the rock. This is the hard place. You have to make the decision, and make it now.'

'And when we get to St Hilaire?' she asked jerkily. 'What then?'

'There'll be other choices to consider,' he said. 'There always are.'

'You forget,' Chellie said. 'I still have no passport, which reduces my options to zero. Unless, of course, St Hilaire has openings for singers,' she added wryly.

He was silent for a moment. 'You say Mama Rita took it from you. Do you know where she keeps it?'

'In her desk—locked in the top right-hand drawer. She showed it to me once.' Chellie bit her lip. 'To convince me she still had it, and therefore still had me. Playing cat and mouse.'

'And the key to her desk? Where's that?'

Chellie grimaced. 'On a long chain round her neck.'

He shuddered. 'Which is where it can definitely remain.'
He paused, frowning. 'Where will Mama Rita be now?'

'Down in the club. She'll come up at the end of the night
to count the takings, but that's usually the only time. She
considers she's one of the features of the place. That people
come just to see her.'

'Well,' he said softly, 'she could be right. After all, something brought me here this evening. So let's hope that her
ego keeps her right there in front of her admiring public.'

'Why? What are you going to do?' she asked.

'Break into that desk, of course.' His tone was almost
casual.

Her jaw dropped. 'Are you crazy?'

'Well, we can hardly take the damned thing with us.
People might notice.' He gave her a dispassionate look. 'I'm
surprised you haven't tried to get into it yourself.'

His faint note of criticism needled her. 'Because I
wouldn't know how,' she said tautly. 'Unlike you, it seems.'

'Merely one of the skills I've acquired along the way.'
He shrugged, apparently unfazed. 'For which you should be
grateful.' He gave her a questioning look. 'I hope there's a
back way out of here?'

'Yes, but that's always locked too, and Manuel has the
key.'

'Well, that shouldn't be a serious problem.' He got to his
feet, and Chellie rose too.

She said breathlessly, 'You don't know him. He's always
hanging round—and he has a knife.'

'I'm sure he has,' he returned with indifference. 'I
thought when I saw him that serving drinks couldn't be the
entire sum of his talents.'

She said in a low voice, 'It's not funny. He's really dangerous—worse than Mama Rita.'

He said softly, 'But I could be dangerous too, songbird.'
He paused. 'And don't say that hasn't already crossed your
mind.'

She stared at him, the silence between them crackling like

electricity. He knew how to break open a desk, she thought, and he wasn't scared of knives. Just who was this man—and how soon would she be able to get away from him? And, most of all, how much was it going to cost her? Her throat closed.

She said huskily, 'Perhaps you just seem—the lesser of two evils.'

'Thank you,' he said, his mouth twisting. 'I think. Is Mama Rita's office on this floor, by any chance?'

She nodded. 'Just along the passage. You—you want me to show you?'

'It could save time,' he said. 'Also it might stop me intruding on anyone else's intimate moments. I presume this isn't the only private room?'

'No,' Chellie said. 'But this is reckoned to be the best one. It must have cost you plenty to hire it.'

'Well, don't worry about it,' he said. 'I expect to get my money's worth in due course.' He looked into her startled eyes and grinned. 'All that home cooking,' he explained softly.

He kicked the blonde wig out of sight under the sofa. 'You won't need that again.' He looked her over. 'Do you have other clothes? Because you could change into them while I'm breaking and entering.'

'I haven't very much.' It was humiliating to have to make the admission.

'Then grab a coat from somewhere,' he said. 'We need to make an unobtrusive exit, and you're far too spectacular like that.'

As Chellie went to the door she was crossly aware that her face had warmed.

The passage outside was thankfully deserted, but there was a lot of noise drifting up from the floor below—music with a strident beat, and male voices laughing and cheering.

He said softly, 'Let the good times roll—at least until we're out of here.'

The door of Mama Rita's office was slightly ajar, and the

desk lamp was lit although the room was empty. Apart from the desk there was little other furniture, and most of that, he saw, was junk, with the exception of a nice pair of ornately carved wooden candlesticks standing on a chest against the wall. The air was stale with some cheap incense, and he grimaced faintly.

He said, 'She doesn't seem to worry about being robbed.'

'She doesn't think anyone would dare. Besides, she has a safe for the money.' Chellie pointed to the desk. 'That's the drawer.'

'Then I suggest you leave me to it while you go and change. I'll see you back here in a couple of minutes. And bring the stuff you have on with you,' he added. 'If they believe you're still somewhere on the premises, it will give us extra minutes.'

'Yes, I suppose so.' Chellie hesitated. 'Be—be careful.' Her tone was stilted.

He said softly, 'Why, darling, I didn't know you cared.'

'I don't,' she said with a snap. 'You're my way out of here, that's all. So I don't want anything to go wrong.'

He grinned at her. 'You're all heart.'

She looked back at him icily. 'You said it yourself. The rock and the hard place. That's the choice, but I don't have to like it.'

He shrugged. 'I'm not that keen myself, but there's no time to debate the situation now. We'll talk once the boat has sailed.'

Biting her lip, Chellie left him to it.

Once alone, Ash crossed to the door and listened for a moment before pushing it almost shut. Then he went back to the desk, swiftly unbuttoning his shirt and extracting the flat pouch he had taped to his waist. He chose one of the skeleton keys it contained and opened the drawer that Chellie had indicated.

Inside, lying on the untidy jumble of papers, was a large-bladed knife, businesslike and menacing at the same time.

Ash's lips pursed in a silent whistle. 'Songbird,' he said softly, 'I think you may have underestimated Mama Rita.'

There were several passports in the drawer but only one with the distinctive maroon cover. He opened it, swiftly checking the details with a nod of satisfaction.

So far, so good, he told himself.

He gave the photograph a cursory glance, then paused, studying it more closely. The girl in the picture looked back at him, a faint, almost defiant smile playing about the corners of her mouth, the green eyes cool and candid. And totally unafraid.

His mouth curled cynically. 'But that was then, darling,' he told the photograph. 'How things can change.'

He closed the passport, slipping it into his back pocket, then replaced his keys in their pouch, retaping it to his skin.

He took the knife and used it to force open the other drawers in the desk, scattering their contents all over the floor to give the impression of opportunist theft. Then he closed the top drawer and forced that too, using the tip of the knife to damage the lock.

He felt brief sympathy for the other girls whose passports had been stolen and held against their good behaviour, but there was nothing he could do about that.

Besides, none of them were rich men's daughters.

Only you, songbird, he thought. And you're coming with me, whether you like it or not.

Chellie's heart was racing as she went up to her room, and she made herself breathe deeply and evenly, trying to calm down and be sensible. As she opened the door she braced herself against the usual scuttling noises, her skin crawling with revulsion.

At least on the boat she'd be spared that particular nightmare, she thought, switching on the naked lightbulb which dangled from the ceiling. But vulnerable to plenty of others in its place, an unwanted voice in her head reminded her.

She knew nothing about her rescuer—not even his name.

There was no guarantee that he'd keep any of his side of the bargain. In fact, by trusting him even marginally, she could find herself in a far worse mess.

He looked tough enough, she admitted unwillingly. His body was lean and muscular, with wide shoulders and a strong chest. But then the life he'd chosen—delivering other people's boats, with some petty thieving on the side—was a pretty chancy existence.

Under normal circumstances he was the last man in the world she would ever have turned to for help.

But she couldn't let herself worry about that now. Desperate situations required desperate measures, and she had to get away from this place, whatever the means.

Once I'm out of here, and I have my passport back, I can think again, she told herself with a touch of grimness.

It was amazing the effect that even a whisper of hope could have. After these weeks of fear she was beginning to feel a resurgence of her old spirit. The conviction that her life belonged to her again, and she was back in control.

Swiftly, she stripped off what little she was wearing and put on the underwear—white cotton bra and pants—she'd washed earlier in the day. They still felt damp, but that couldn't be helped. She dragged her one and only tee shirt over her head, and pulled on a brief denim skirt. She stowed the black dress and G string in her canvas shoulder bag, along with her few toiletries and what little money she had left.

Then she took her sandals from the cupboard, banging them together
to dislodge any lurking cockroaches, and slipped them on to her feet.

'Ready to go,' she said, half under her breath.

On her way to the door she caught sight of herself in the piece of broken mirror which hung from a hook on the wall. Once more her hand went involuntarily to her shorn head as she experienced a pang of real pain at the loss.

Her hair, dark and glossy as a raven's wing, had been cut

in a sleek chin-length bob when she'd arrived here, but Mama Rita had ordered it to be chopped off to make more room for the wig. Lina had been given the scissors and had enjoyed her task, while the others laughed and jeered.

I'm barely recognisable, she thought.

But maybe that would be an advantage when the time came to continue her journey—alone.

Think positive, she adjured herself.

After all, that was what she had to aim for—to focus on— to the exclusion of everything else. Taking charge of her own destiny once more.

What had happened with Ramon was a glitch, but no more than that. And she would make damned sure that no other man ever made a fool of her again. Including Sir Galahad downstairs.

Him, perhaps, most of all.

She extinguished the light and went quietly down the rickety steps.

She was halfway along the passage to Mama Rita's room when Manuel came round the corner.

Chellie checked instantly at the sight of him, and he stopped too, his eyes narrowing in suspicion.

'*Hola, chica*,' he said. 'What you doing, huh?'

From some undiscovered depth Chellie found the strength to smile at him. 'I thought I'd go down to the bar for a drink.'

'Where's that *hombre* who hired you?' He was frowning.

'Asleep.' Chellie gave him a long, meaningful look from under her lashes. 'And not much fun any more.'

He looked her over. 'Why you in those clothes? And where your wig? You supposed to be blonde.'

'My dress got torn.' She shrugged casually. 'And that wig is so hot. Surely I don't need it just to buy a beer?'

A slow, unpleasant grin curled his mouth. 'I have beer in my room, *chica*. You want more fun? You have it with me.'

'No.' Chellie took a step backwards, her hand closing on the strap of her bag in an unconsciously defensive gesture.

He noticed at once, his gaze speculative. 'What you got there, *hija*?'

'Nothing,' she denied, lifting her chin. 'And I'm going to have my drink in the bar—without company.'

For a moment he stared at her, then, to her astonishment, she saw him nod in apparent agreement. It was only when he slid to his knees, eyes glazing, then measured his length completely on the wooden floor that she realised who was standing behind him, grasping one of Mama Rita's wooden candlesticks and looking down at his victim with grim pleasure.

She said shakily, 'My God—is he dead?'

'Not him.' Ash stirred the recumbent body with a contemptuous foot. 'I knew what I was doing. He'll have a bad headache when he wakes up, that's all.'

'All?' Her laugh cracked in the middle. 'Breaking and entering, and now GBH. What next, I wonder?'

'Well, I can't speak for you.' He went down on one knee, and rifled through the unconscious man's pockets, producing his keyring with a grunt of satisfaction. 'But I plan to get out of here before he's missed.' He got to his feet, his glance challenging. 'I have your passport, so are you coming with me? Or would you rather stay here and accept his next invitation? It may not be as cordial as the last,' he added drily. 'But perhaps you don't care.'

Not just the rock and the hard place, Chellie thought. This was the devil and the deep blue sea, and she was caught between them, as trapped as she'd always been.

And, it seemed, she had to choose the devil…

For now, she told herself, but not for ever. That was the thought she had to cling to. The resolution she had to make.

She felt a small quiver of fear, mixed with a strange excitement, uncurl in the pit of her stomach as she looked back at him, meeting the blue ice of his gaze.

She said lightly, 'What are we waiting for, Galahad? Let's go.'

CHAPTER THREE

THE air outside was warm and so thick she could almost chew it, but Chellie drew it into her lungs as if it was pure oxygen.

She thought, I'm free. And that's the way I'm going to stay. For a moment, she felt tears of sheer relief prick at her eyes, but she fought them back. Because there was no time to cry. Instead she had to make good her escape. Or the first part of it, anyway.

Getting out of the club had been just as nerve-racking as everything that had gone before it. They had dragged Manuel, who had already begun to stir and mutter incoherently, into the office and locked him there with his own keys.

The way to the back door led past the girls' dressing room, so they'd had to waste precious seconds waiting for the coast to be clear. He'd gone first, to unlock the rear door, and had slipped past unseen. But when it had been Chellie's turn she'd found herself catching Jacinta's startled gaze.

She'd made herself smile, and even give a little wave, as if she didn't have a care in the world, but there was no certainty that the other girl wouldn't mention what she'd seen once Chellie's absence had been discovered. In fact, she might not be given a choice, Chellie told herself with a pang.

However, she needed to put space between Mama Rita's and herself and waste no time about it, she thought, breaking into a run.

'Take it easy.' The command was low-voiced but crisp,

39

and her companion's hand clamped her wrist, bringing her to a breathless halt.

'What are you doing? We need to get out of here. They'll be coming after us...'

'Probably,' he returned. 'So the last thing we want is to draw attention to ourselves. If we run in this heat, we'll be remembered. If we walk, we're just another anonymous couple among hundreds of others. So slow down and try and look as if you want to be with me. And for God's sake stop peering back over your shoulder. Your whole body language is shouting "They're after me",' he added, his tone faintly caustic.

'Oh, please excuse me,' Chellie hit back, heavily sarcastic. 'But the role of fugitive is still rather new to me.'

'Just as well,' he returned, unmoved. 'Hopefully you won't have to play it for long.'

He released his grip on her wrist and clasped her fingers instead, drawing her closer to him, adapting his long stride to her shorter pace. Making it seem, she realised unwillingly, as if they were indeed a pair of lovers with the rest of the night to spend together.

On balance, Chellie thought she preferred a bruised wrist to this implied intimacy. The touch of his hand, the brush of his bare arm against hers was sending a tantalising ripple of awareness through her senses, which, frankly, she didn't need or understand.

Life had taught her to be wary of strangers—to maintain her cool in unfamiliar situations. After all, it had taken a long time for Ramon to get under her guard, until, unluckily, she'd taken his persistence for devotion rather than greed.

But now she'd been thrown into the company of this stranger. Condemned, it seemed, to endure the proximity of a man who had no apparent compunction about committing burglary or hitting over the head anyone who got in his way. And knowing it had been done for her benefit hardly seemed an adequate excuse.

Someone who'd just walked in off the street and apparently felt sufficient compassion to take up her cause, she thought uneasily. And, on the face of it, how likely was that?

Sure, he'd offered her a way out, and she'd taken it. Yet she was risking a hell of a lot to accept his help, and she knew it. Which made her undeniable physical reaction to him all the more inexplicable. But if she was honest she'd been conscious of it—of him—since that first moment in the club when their eyes had met. And she'd found herself unable to look away.

When she was a small child, someone had warned her about wishing for things, in case her wish was granted in a way she did not expect. And Nanny had been quite right, she thought ruefully.

Because only a couple of hours ago Chellie had sung about wanting 'someone to watch over her', and that was precisely what she'd got. And every instinct was warning her that, among so many others, this could be her worst mistake so far.

The sooner I get away from him, the better, she thought, her throat muscles tightening. But that's not going to be so easy. Because I seem to have passed seamlessly from Mama Rita's clutches into his.

Oh, God, how could I have been such a fool? And is it too late to redress the situation somehow?

She drew a breath. 'What did you do with Manuel's keys?'

'Threw them into an open drain.'

'Oh.' She moistened dry lips with the tip of her tongue. 'That's—good.'

'I thought so,' he returned with a touch of dryness.

She looked down at the cobbles. 'This boat we're leaving on—where is it exactly?'

'It's moored at the marina,' he said.

'Isn't that the first place they'll look?'

'I doubt it.'

'Why?'

He shrugged. 'Because they have no reason to connect me with boats.'

'You don't seem very concerned.'

'And you're tying yourself into knots over possibilities,' he retorted.

Chellie subsided into silence again, biting her lip. Then she said, 'My passport—you did find it?'

He sighed. 'I told you so.'

'Then—could I have it, please?'

He gave her a swift sideways glance. 'Thinking of making an independent bid for freedom, songbird?' He shook his head. 'You wouldn't get half a mile.'

Knowing he was right did nothing to improve her temper. Or alleviate the feeling that she was cornered.

'Besides,' he went on, 'like Mama Rita, I feel I need something to guarantee your good behaviour.'

She gasped. 'Are you saying you don't trust me?' she demanded huskily.

'Not as far as I could throw you with one hand, sweetheart.' He paused. 'Any more than you trust me.' He slanted a grin at her. 'Grind your teeth if you like, but I'm still your best bet for getting out of here unscathed, and you know it. And what's a little mutual suspicion between friends?'

'I,' Chellie stated with cool clarity, 'am not your friend.'

He shrugged again. 'Well, my Christmas card list is full anyway.'

'However,' she went on, as if he hadn't spoken, 'I'd still like my passport back.' She paused. 'Please.'

'My God,' he said softly. 'The authentic note of the autocrat. That didn't take long to emerge. From downtrodden victim to ''she who must be obeyed'' in one easy step.' His voice hardened. 'And what am I supposed to do now, darling? Turn pale and grovel? You should have tried it with Manuel. He'd have been most impressed.'

'How dare you.' Her voice shook.

They had stopped walking. Suddenly Chellie found herself being propelled across the quayside and into the shadows between two wooden buildings, where he faced her, his eyes glittering, his hands gripping her shoulders, immobilising her completely. Making her look back at him.

'Oh, I dare quite easily,' he said. 'Because someone should have stopped you in your tracks a long time ago. And then perhaps you wouldn't need me to get you out of this mess now.'

'I don't need you,' Chellie flung back at him recklessly. 'There'll be other boats. I can find a passage out of here without your questionable assistance.'

'Yes,' he said, grimly. 'But probably not tonight. And that's only one of your problems. Because how long can you afford to wait? How long before word gets round that a girl with eyes like a cat and a bad haircut is trying to leave port and Mama Rita tracks you down?'

He paused. 'And there's the small question of cost,' he went on remorselessly. 'You've no real cash, so are you really prepared to pay the alternative price you might be charged? If so, you could find it a very long voyage.'

'You're vile.' She choked out the words.

'I'm a realist,' he returned implacably. 'Whereas you...' He gave a derisive laugh. 'In spite of everything that's happened, you still haven't learned a bloody thing, have you, sweetheart?'

She said in a stifled voice, 'Please—please let go of me.'

'Afraid I might want to teach you a valuable lesson?' He shook his head derisively. 'Not a chance, sweetheart. You're not my type.'

But he made no attempt to release her, and Chellie, trapped between the hard male warmth of his body and the wall of rough planking behind her, felt herself begin to tremble inside.

Suddenly the world had shrunk to this dark corner, and the paler oval of his face looking down at her. The sheer physical nearness of him.

She was dimly aware of other things too. Men's voices shouting angrily and the loud blare of a vehicle horn. But all that seemed to be happening in another world—another universe that had no relevance to her or the quiver of need that was growing and intensifying within her.

She saw his head turn sharply, heard him swear quietly and succinctly under his breath, then, before she could even contemplate resistance, he swooped down on her, and for one startled, breathless moment her mouth was crushed under his.

But not in anything that could be recognised as a kiss. That was the real shock of it all. Because the tight-lipped pressure of his mouth on hers was simply that—physical contact without an atom of desire or sensuality.

A harsh, untender parody of a caress.

And one that was over almost as soon as it had begun.

Chellie leaned back against the wall, her legs barely able to support

her, looking up at him, trying and failing to read his face.

She said in a voice she barely recognised, 'What was—*that* about?'

He said, '*That* was Manuel in a Jeep, with another guy driving him.' He paused. 'Bald, built like a bull. Do you know him?'

'Rico. He's a bouncer at the club.' Chellie spoke numbly, trying to drag together the remnants of her composure without success. 'Did they see us?'

'I think they might have stopped if so,' he said drily. 'Besides, I made sure you were well hidden.'

'Yes,' she said. And, again, 'Yes.' *So that was why...* She shivered.

He took her hand again. 'Come on.'

She hung back, staring up at him, her eyes blank with fright. 'What are we going to do now?' Her voice was barely more than a whisper.

He shrugged. 'We go down to the marina and get aboard the boat, as planned. What else?'

'But—everything's changed.' Her voice was a little wail of protest. 'They'll be there first—waiting for us.'

'Then we'll make damned sure they don't see us.' He sounded appallingly calm. 'But I'd bet any money that they're not going anywhere near the marina. Trust me on that, if nothing else.'

He put his arm round her and set off down the quay again at a brisker pace. 'On the other hand, I'd prefer us not to be loitering around on their return journey. Going on a wild goose chase often brings out the worst in people,' he added wryly.

Chellie went with him mechanically, her thoughts in turmoil. But it wasn't simply the threat of discovery that plagued her. Because, to her own amazement, that no longer seemed to be her first priority.

Instead, she found she was reliving the moment when she'd stood with him in the darkness with his mouth on hers. Examining—analysing every trembling second of it.

And realising, to her horror, that she'd wanted more. That she'd needed him to recognise that she was female to his male. That she—wanted him.

The breath caught in her throat.

My God, she thought, with a touch of hysteria. It's completely crazy. How can I be feeling like this? I—I don't even know his name.

Nevertheless, that was the shaming truth she had to face—to endure. That there'd been more than a moment when she'd actually wanted her lips to part under his, inviting—imploring his deeper and more intimate invasion. When she'd longed to feel his hands on her body—the sting of his thighs against hers.

A soft, aching instant when she'd been ready to go wherever he might lead.

A small sound escaped her, halfway between a laugh and a sob.

He noticed instantly. 'What is it?'

'Nothing,' Chellie disclaimed instantly. 'At least—I—don't think I'm handling this situation very well.'

He was silent for a moment, and when he spoke his voice was abrupt. 'You're doing all right.'

It wasn't what she'd wanted to hear. She'd hardly expected praise of the highest order, but she'd hoped, at least, for a little warmth and reassurance.

She thought, I wanted him to smile at me as if he meant it…

But I mustn't think like that, she told herself in sudden anguish. It isn't right. And it certainly isn't safe.

Although his arm round her felt safe. Safe—but oddly impersonal. Just as his kiss had been.

Well, now she knew the reason for that totally sexless performance. *I made sure you were well hidden.*

Someone to watch over me, she thought wearily. That's what I wanted, so I can hardly complain about the way he does it. And it was only a minute ago, anyway, that he told me I wasn't his type.

She felt her face warm at the memory. She could only be thankful that she hadn't yielded to that swift, burning temptation and responded to the taste of his mouth. Oh, it would have been so frighteningly easy—and such a disaster.

Because he wasn't her type either, she reminded herself forcefully. He was more than merely attractive, and he might have an educated voice, but that was only a veneer. Underneath there was a darkness—a danger.

And certainly no Galahad either, she thought. He was just a buccaneer, like all the others who'd once pursued their predatory trade up and down the Caribbean sea.

If she'd met him in London, or down at Aynsbridge, she wouldn't have given him a second glance.

Unless he'd looked at you first, said a sly voice in her brain. And you'd suddenly found you couldn't tear yourself away…

Her problem was that she wasn't accustomed to instant sexual attraction. Had always written off that kind of emotion as cheap. Told herself that passing attractions could have no place in her life.

Liking should come first, she'd always believed. A mental attunement that could blossom into real love—Shakespeare's 'marriage of true minds' that 'looks on tempests and is never shaken'.

So how, then, did she explain Ramon?

A chapter of accidents, she supposed wearily. She'd been searching desperately for a way to break her father's yoke and release herself from the stultifying boredom of her life. Something that would take her further than non-stop partying.

She had also been rebelling over his persistence in pushing Jeffrey Chilham at her as a future husband. It was to have been a purely dynastic marriage—Jeffrey, a widower at least twenty years her senior, was poised to take over the running of the corporation when Sir Clive retired—and there was nothing the matter with him that a complete personality transplant could not have cured.

He was correct, worthy, and so ponderously indulgent in his attitude to her that she'd often longed to fling herself at him, screaming, and sink her teeth into his jugular vein.

As a result, she'd been driven to parading a succession of totally unsuitable young men in front of her father. She'd had no intention of marrying any of them. She had just wanted to convince Sir Clive that she was a person in her own right, and not for sale. That she was capable of finding her own husband.

Nevertheless, it had been painful to see them fade away, one after the other, after being exposed by him to the social equivalent of an Arctic winter.

The gossip columns had enjoyed a field-day with her, their comments becoming increasingly snide as one relationship after another had withered and died. Chellie had loathed finding herself portrayed as some heartless rich bitch who chewed men up and spat them out, treating love and marriage as a game for her ego.

Ramon had been so different—or was that just what she'd persuaded herself to believe? He was certainly unlike the suits who hung round her, trying to curry favour with her father and failing.

And he'd braved the full force of Sir Clive's icy disapproval to be with her, which had earned him mega-points in her regard at an early stage in their acquaintance.

She'd never dreamed, of course, that she was simply being carefully and ruthlessly targeted.

He'd talked to her, too, in that deep, softly accented voice that seemed to caress her like dark velvet. Shown her for the first time the possibility of another kind of life outside her father's aegis.

He'd spoken to her of rainforests, and rivers as wide as oceans. Of remote *estancias* where herds of cattle grazed on thousands of acres. Of the house that he'd inherited as his father's only son and the fruit and coffee plantations that surrounded it.

And, of course, of the wife he needed to live beside him there. The girl who, miraculously, seemed to be her.

He'd wooed her so delicately, offering her what she'd believed was adoring respect, keeping her newly awakened senses in ferment. She was his angel on a pedestal, to be worshipped always.

He'd sold her a dream, Chellie thought with self-derision, and she'd bought into it completely. She hadn't even thought to ask who was running those vast plantations while he was away. All she could see was herself, riding beside Ramon through an endless sun-drenched landscape. She'd been lost in the glamour of it all.

The question of money had never really been addressed, of course. Ramon was well dressed, had a flat in the right part of town, was seen in the best places and drove a fast car. Naïvely she'd supposed that that, and all his talk of family estates, added up to solvency. And that her own financial standing was immaterial to him.

Boy, was that the mistake of the century, she thought, grimacing inwardly. A little plain speaking on both sides would have saved a multitude of troubles.

And her father's stony opposition had simply fuelled her resolve—her certainty that Ramon, and the life he described so lyrically, was all she would ever want.

And when Sir Clive, working himself into one of his furious rages, had forbidden her to marry Ramon, or even to see him again, the decision to run away with him had almost been made for her.

Perhaps if it hadn't been for his totally unreasonable blanket condemnation of every other man but Jeffrey, she might, in turn, have dealt more rationally with his opposition. Might even have listened to the dossier he'd no doubt had prepared on Ramon and taken his warnings seriously.

Instead, she'd closed her eyes and ears to his outbursts. Ignored his threat to cut her out of his life and render her penniless if she disobeyed him.

Maybe she'd even thought that if he saw her happily married and living a useful, contented life—if there were grandchildren to soften his heart—he would relent and admit he'd been wrong.

In fact, it was supposed to be roses all the way, Chellie thought. But how wrong could anyone be? She sighed faintly.

'Are you all right?' His question sounded abrupt, but the arm around her tightened fractionally.

'Fine.' Chellie forced a smile to reinforce the fib. Remembering how completely Ramon had fooled her had been a painful procedure, but valuable in its way. There was nothing she could do to redeem the past, but the future was a very different matter.

During her time at Mama Rita's she'd found it almost impossible to think beyond one bitter day at a time. Now she had to make serious plans about her life. And, naturally, those did not and could not feature the man walking at her side.

I'll always be grateful to him, she told herself restively. But gratitude is all there can ever be. I don't intend to make an abject fool of myself a second time, however attractive he may be.

She saw with surprise that they'd reached the marina already, and tensed as she looked around her.

Ramon had brought her here, she thought. They'd had dinner at the Casino, then Ramon had played blackjack and lost. She'd ascribed his subsequent moodiness to his bad luck, but she realised now he had been planning his escape—working out how to ditch her and vanish.

Having first given the condemned woman a hearty meal, she thought wryly.

And his scheme had been entirely successful.

She wondered if he'd ever given her a second thought since—concerned himself even marginally with how she might be surviving, alone and penniless, in an alien, dangerous environment. But she doubted it. He probably hoped that she'd simply disappear for good too. And she nearly had.

Her fate had been sealed from the moment he'd discovered that if she married against her father's wishes her trust fund would only become available on her thirty-fifth birthday.

She'd seen the shock on his face when she told him—the total disbelief masking what she now realised had been anger.

But he'd had every right to be angry, she thought with irony. He'd spent a lot of time and effort pursuing a rich heiress only to find, when he caught her, that she didn't have a bean.

That her father had used his money to control her life, refusing to allow her to train for anything which would have allowed her to earn her own living and conceding her only a small allowance.

Pin money, she thought. Isn't that the old-fashioned term? It sounds sufficiently derogatory. Because the only career I was being groomed for was 'rich man's wife'.

And there were plenty of potential bridegrooms right here

in the marina's basin, she realised, with a wry twist of her mouth. There were a lot of glamorous yachts moored there, with some serious partying going on too.

Her ears were assailed by a non-stop barrage of laughter, talk and the chinking of glasses from the floodlit decks. She was dazzled by designer wear and jewellery.

A couple of months ago, if she'd been in Santo Martino, she'd probably have been a guest on one of these boats, working on her tan by day and parading her own wardrobe each evening.

She suddenly wondered what would happen if she walked up one of the gangways and introduced herself. *I'm Clive Greer's daughter, and I need help.*

For a moment the temptation to pull free of her companion's confining arm and make the attempt was almost overwhelming. Almost, but not quite.

My bloody passport, she groaned inwardly. Without it I'm going nowhere, even if they were prepared to lend me a hand. And looking like this, with my hair like a badly mown lawn, would anyone believe me?

She'd already noted and resented some of the disdainful looks being aimed in their direction.

'Come on, songbird. No time for cocktails tonight.' There was a note of amusement in his voice as he urged her forward.

So now he's a mind-reader, she thought crossly.

'People are staring at us,' she muttered.

'Not for much longer,' he returned. 'We'll soon be out of here.'

She bit her lip. 'You haven't seen the Jeep?'

'Relax,' he advised lazily. 'If *we're* getting the beady eye, can you imagine the effect that Manuel and Rico would have on this select gathering? They'd suffer the death of a thousand ice-picks before they'd gone twenty yards.' He paused. 'And there's *La Belle Rêve* at last.'

Chellie's eyes widened incredulously. The motor yacht

was twice as large as she'd imagined, its sleek lines comparing favourably with any of the other boats in the basin.

She said faintly, '*That's* what you're taking to St Hilaire?'

'You don't think I'm capable?' He sounded amused.

'Far from it.' She offered him a swift, glittering smile. 'I suspect you're capable of anything.'

An olive-skinned man with thick curly dark hair, wearing cut-off jeans and a denim waistcoat, was waiting at the top of the gangplank. He watched them come aboard, then looked at her companion, his brows raised, smiling a little.

'*Mon ami*, I was becoming anxious about you, but now I fully understand the reason for your delay.'

He stepped forward, took Chellie's hand, and made a slight bow over it. '*Mademoiselle*, I am Laurent Massim. *Enchanté*. May I know your name?'

Chellie's hesitation was fractional, but it was noticed by the man beside her.

He said with faint amusement, 'According to her passport, she's Michelle Greer, and she's the new ship's cook.'

Chellie bit her lip. Hiding her identity had never been an option, of course, but fortunately he didn't seem to have made any inconvenient connections. But then who would expect the daughter of a major industrialist to be working in a strip club in South America?

Well, she thought, long may he remain in ignorance.

She faced him, chin up. 'And you?' she queried. 'Do you also have a name, or is it a deadly secret?'

'Not at all,' he said. 'I'm Ash Brennan.'

For a moment Chellie thought she detected an odd note in his voice, almost like a challenge. But maybe he was simply responding to her in kind.

He turned to Laurent. 'If we're cleared for departure, I suggest we get going.' He glanced at Chellie. 'And it might be better if you went below before someone realises we're carrying an extra passenger.'

'Thank you.' The adrenalin that had carried her on that

long trek along the quayside had evaporated, leaving her drained and apprehensive.

She negotiated the companionway with care, clinging to the rail because her legs were shaking under her.

She found herself in a large saloon, luxuriously furnished with slate-blue leather seating, expensive rugs on the wooden floor. At one end was a fully stocked bar, and beyond it the galley, streamlined and gleaming like the interior of a spaceship. Chellie regarded it with foreboding.

While she was looking around, Ash joined her.

'We'll be underway very soon.' He studied her with narrowed eyes. 'Are you all right? You don't get seasick, do you?'

She summoned a pallid smile. 'Not as far as I know. And certainly not while I'm still in harbour.'

'The weather report is good,' he said. 'It should be plain sailing to St Hilaire.'

Plain sailing? Chellie controlled the bubble of hysteria threatening to well up inside her. How could it possibly be any such thing?

She shook her head. 'I can't really believe this is happening,' she said huskily. 'At any moment I'm going to wake up and find I'm back in cockroach alley.'

He said quietly, 'It's over, Michelle. Don't you know what this boat is called? *La Belle Rêve*—the beautiful dream. So there'll be no more nightmares.'

She didn't look at him. 'I—I'll try and remember that.'

'You're out on your feet,' he added curtly. 'I'll show you where you're going to sleep.'

She'd half expected to find herself in some tiny cupboard with a bunk, so the spacious stateroom took her breath away. A queen-sized bed, with storage underneath, had been built against one wall, with windows above it. Another wall held fitted cupboards, and there was even her own shower room, compact but beautifully fitted.

She said uncertainly, 'You're sure about this? The owner won't mind?'

Ash shrugged. 'Why should he care? As long as I bring the *Dream* to St Hilaire in one piece.'

He opened the door of one of the cupboards. 'The owner's daughter uses this stateroom when she's aboard. She's left a few of her clothes. Shorts, swimwear—that kind of thing. Feel free to borrow anything you need.'

Chellie gasped. 'I couldn't possibly do that.'

'She's a terrific girl,' he returned. 'She'd want to help, I promise.' He looked her over critically. 'And you're pretty much the same size. Besides, you can't manage with just what you're wearing.'

Chellie looked down at the floor. 'I seem to be beholden to a growing number of people,' she said stiffly.

'Worry about that in the morning,' he returned indifferently. He paused. 'There'll be coffee and sandwiches later, if you're interested.'

'I don't think I can eat a thing.'

'Then I'll leave you in peace.' He gave her a brief, hard smile and turned away. 'Goodnight.'

As the door closed behind him Chellie sat down limply on the edge of the bed. Her heart was beating fast, and she found it hard to collect her thoughts.

Ash Brennan, she said silently. So I know his name at last. But that's all I know. The rest of him is still an enigma. And I mustn't forget that.

However, it seemed that he'd meant what he said. She was just another member of the crew. So maybe her suspicion that she'd merely exchanged one trap for another was completely unfair.

But she couldn't deny that she was in his power, she thought, pressing her fingertips to her aching forehead. Or that she had no real control over how he exercised that power.

His attitude towards her on the way here had been brisk and businesslike, yet she couldn't forget the way he'd watched her in the club when she was singing—or the glittering, unashamed flare of desire in his eyes when she'd danced for him.

But even then he seemed to be wanting me against his will, she acknowledged with bewilderment. And isn't that exactly how I feel myself?

But she was too tired to think straight. Sighing, she rose and went over to the cupboard, examining the clothing that hung on its rail—smart cotton pants and tops, crisp shorts and shirts, and slips of dresses with floating skirts and shoe-string straps, most of them with designer labels. She handled them appreciatively, realising that she and their absent owner were the same size.

In the top drawer she found bikinis and pareus. The second held undies, and nightwear filled the third.

Kneeling, Chellie took out one of the nightdresses, letting the filmy white material drift through her fingers like gossamer. It was enchantingly pretty and unequivocally transparent—d the others were equally revealing.

So this was what the owner's daughter wore during the long, moonlit Caribbean nights, she thought, her mouth twisting a little. But did she wear them for herself alone?

A terrific girl. That was what Ash Brennan had said. And there'd been warmth in his voice—maybe even a hint of tenderness. He must know her very well, perhaps intimately, to make this offer on her behalf. To be so sure she wouldn't mind.

She looked back at the wide bed, wondering if they had ever lain there together, and, if so, why she should care? Especially when she would part from him on St Hilaire, never to meet again.

At the same time she suddenly heard the soft throb of the engine, and realised the boat was moving.

She got to her feet, still holding the nightdress against her.

She said aloud, 'We're on our way. And I'm committed now, whether I wish it or not. There's no turning back.'

And found herself shivering at the stark finality of her own words.

CHAPTER FOUR

HALF an hour later, Ash came down the passageway and paused outside the stateroom door. He knocked lightly, and waited, but there was no reply, and after a moment he opened the door and went quietly in.

He trod silently over to the bed and stood looking down at its occupant, his brows drawn together in a frown. The bedside lamp was still on, so she must have fallen asleep as soon as her head touched the pillow.

She was lying motionless, her breathing soft and regular. Her cheek was cradled on her hand, and the strap of one of Julie's excuses for a nightgown had slipped down from her shoulder, giving her an air of curious vulnerability. Something glistened on her face and, as he bent closer to extinguish the lamp he realised that it was a solitary tear.

His hand lifted, obeying an involuntary impulse to wipe it away, but he managed to control it just in time.

He needed to get a grip, he adjured himself. Next thing he'd be hitching up that errant strap and smoothing those absurd spikes of black hair. Tucking her in for the night, for God's sake. And there was no room for that because, as they said, this was business—not personal.

He switched off the lamp and straightened, leaving just the moonlight flooding through the undrawn curtains.

Chellie stirred suddenly in her sleep, murmuring something, and Ash backed hastily away from the bed, feeling his foot catch against an object on the floor as he did so.

He glanced down and saw that it was her bag, and that the black dress she'd worn at the club was spilling out of it.

He paused, jolted by the sudden memory of how pale her

skin had looked against it, and the smooth, supple movement of her body as she danced for him.

Remembered too that there'd been a moment when he'd
let himself forget why he was there. When he'd longed, with
an intensity of emotion that had twisted his guts into knots,
to see her take it off. When every drop of blood had sung
in his veins in anticipation of seeing her naked.

God, he thought with bitter self-derision, just like some
adolescent, peeking at top-shelf magazines.

She wasn't the first girl he'd watched take off her clothes,
for heaven's sake, but she was certainly the first not to go
through with it, he thought, his mouth curling cynically.

And he wasn't the first man she'd stripped for either. He
needed to remember that too.

It was no big deal for her, he told himself. It couldn't be,
after the way she'd lived her life, so why, suddenly, the
maidenly shrinking? Unless she'd balked at being paid to
do it.

Whatever the reason, his instinct had told him with total
certainty that it wasn't going to happen. And that the desire
that pierced him would not be satisfied.

He drew a deep, sharp breath. That, he told himself, had
been a moment of weakness that would not be repeated.

He had to ditch those memories—bury them deeply and
permanently. Along with the moment when he'd pretended
to kiss her, shielding her with his body, and felt her lips
tremble under his.

She may be anybody's, he told himself, but she isn't
yours. Don't lose sight of that ever again.

He went to the door and left as quietly as he had come.

Laurent was in the pilot house, humming quietly to himself.
He looked round as Ash arrived, carrying a plate stacked
with chicken sandwiches and two steaming mugs of coffee.

'She is asleep?'

'Out for the count,' Ash confirmed briefly, putting the
food down.

'*La pauvre petite*. What an ordeal for her.'

Ash shrugged. 'A self-inflicted wound, but unlikely to leave permanent scarring. She's already showing signs of recovery.'

'You are hard on her, I think.' Laurent took a sandwich and bit into it appreciatively. 'Did you have many problems persuading her to go with you?'

'She was just about to be launched on a career as a lap dancer, and worse. Any alternative would have seemed good.'

'And they just let her go?'

'Not exactly.' Ash smiled thinly. 'There was one hitch, but it was dealt with.'

'I can imagine.' Laurent gave him a wry look. 'They came after you?'

'Oh, they were on our trail. But sadly it was the wrong one. I left an empty matchbook from the Hotel Margarita on the table for them to find, and they went scorching off to the other side of town to browbeat some unfortunate desk clerk.'

'So all is well.' Laurent nodded. 'Victor will be relieved. His faxes are becoming increasingly agitated.'

'Then I'd better put him out of his misery and tell him to keep quiet from now on. As far as the target's concerned, she's just getting a lift to St Hilaire. I don't want anything to arouse her suspicions that there could be more to it than that.'

Laurent tutted in reproof. 'Target! Such a cold word to use about such a beautiful girl.'

Ash's mouth tightened. 'I just want it finished with. I need Daddy to hand over the money for his spoiled princess. One last smooth operation before I retire, and no hiccups.'

'The girl—you think she could make difficulties?'

'Tonight she was so terrified she'd have grasped at any straw she was offered,' Ash said slowly. 'But tomorrow morning she's going to wake up rested and no longer scared stiff. And sooner or later she's going to start thinking, and wondering about things—like how I happened to turn up so conveniently to rescue her. She's going to ask questions.'

'Then let us hope we reach St Hilaire before you have to provide any of the answers,' Laurent said cheerfully. 'Now, go and fax Victor. Reassure him that all has gone according to plan, and tell him to stay off your back.' He shot Ash a shrewd look. 'Then you should also get some sleep, *mon vieux*. Because, if you are right, you could need all your wits about you tomorrow.'

'Later. I'm not tired yet.' Ash took his coffee over to the leather bench and sat down, watching the silvery water rippling past the bows.

Although that wasn't strictly true, he thought. Now that the mission had been accomplished the tension was seeping out of him, leaving him almost boneless with weariness.

But he wasn't going to bed yet, he decided grimly. Not while there was a chance that he was going to lie awake in the moonlight, seeing a girl's dark head on a pillow and the trace of a tear on her cheek. Remembering the fragrance of her skin, and the sweetness of her mouth when he'd held her for that brief time.

He swore under his breath.

It's time you gave up this game, Brennan, he told himself. You're getting soft in your old age. And that won't do. Because it's not over yet, and the stakes are far too high.

And he sighed soundlessly.

Chellie opened heavy eyelids, blinking at the sunlight pouring into the stateroom. For a moment she felt totally disorientated, then as recollection slowly returned she sat up, stretching and running her fingers through her hair.

She was on *La Belle Rêve*, and Santo Martino with all its horrors was far behind her. And for that she was so thankful.

But it was the immediate future that had to concern her now. What would happen when they arrived at St Hilaire? Her options seemed few, and all equally unattractive.

And the last thing she wanted was to find herself stranded and broke all over again in some other remote spot.

She knelt up on the bed and looked out of the window. There was nothing outside but the vivid unbroken blue of the Caribbean as far as the eye could see.

She had no idea what time it was. Ramon had helped himself to her platinum watch along with everything else, and at the club day and night had seemed to merge into a blur. But the position of the sun told her that she had been asleep for a long time, and it was probably time she put in an appearance on deck.

It was so wonderful to have a proper shower again, she discovered gratefully. To feel the sheer bliss of warm water streaming over her hair and body, and to be able to cherish her skin with scented soap and lotions.

If she only had her own clothes to wear life would be almost perfect. As it was, she had no choice but to borrow once more from the owner's daughter.

I'll use the absolute minimum, she thought. And replace every single item as soon as I get the opportunity.

Whenever that will be, she added, biting her lip.

She put on a pair of white cut-offs and a sleeveless jade-green top, thrusting her feet into her own sandals, then, with a certain reluctance, left the stateroom and climbed up the companionway.

She felt frankly awkward about confronting her saviour in the unrelenting light of day. However grateful she might feel, there were inherent difficulties in being under an obligation to a man about whom she knew so little. And to whom she'd found herself so instantly and unwillingly attracted.

Although why she should feel drawn to him she really didn't know. He might have come to her aid when she was in deep trouble, but he hadn't shown her any real sympathy or concern.

In fact, he'd hustled her almost curtly through the streets

and on board this boat, as if he was already regretting the impulse which had led to her rescue.

If impulse was what it had been, she thought, and paused, frowning, at the top of the companionway, aware of a sudden uneasiness.

'So there you are,' said Ash, appearing from nowhere. He was wearing a pair of elderly navy shorts and the rest of him was tanned skin, she realised with a totally unwelcome flicker of excitement.

'Good morning,' Chellie returned coolly. Excitement notwithstanding, he could do with a lesson in politeness.

'Only just.' Unsmilingly he consulted his watch. 'And breakfast is well overdue.'

'I—lost my watch,' she said. 'And I overslept.'

'I'll give you an alarm clock.' He paused. 'You'll find ham in the fridge. We'll have it with scrambled eggs, toast and strong coffee. And sooner rather than later, if that's all right,' he added pointedly.

Oh, God, Chellie thought, her heart sinking. She'd forgotten this particular detail.

She said, 'Scrambled eggs?'

'That's what I said. Is there some problem?'

'Not at all.' Chellie lied in her teeth. She gave him a bright smile. 'Just checking.'

'There's a bell in the galley. Ring it when the food's ready.'

For whom the bell tolls, Chellie thought glumly as she made her way down to the galley and looked around her. There was an electric oven, with a hob, and—oh, joy—a toaster and a cafetière waiting on the counter beside it. So far, so good, she thought, opening cupboards and drawers and finding crockery and cutlery. At least that bit would be easy-peasy.

She knew the theory of scrambled eggs, of course. Butter and milk, she told herself, and a lot of stirring. And, in her experience, someone else to do it.

She laid one of the tables in the saloon, then spooned

coffee into the pot, added boiling water, and carved some uneven slices off a loaf, slotting them with difficulty into the toaster.

She arranged the ham on plates, and began to beat up the eggs in a basin. The butter was beginning to turn brown in the pan as she added her mixture quickly and began to scrape at it with a fork, watching with dismay as it separated into long leathery strands.

At the same time a strong smell of scorching signalled that the bread was stuck in the toaster and needed to be poked out with a knife.

She felt like a wet rag as she finally rang the bell.

When Ash and Laurent arrived, she saw their brows lift as they inspected the plates she set in front of them. The ham, fortunately, was excellent, but no one lingered over their meal.

'This coffee's so weak I'm surprised it could crawl out of the pot,' Ash told her crushingly. 'You've cremated the toast. And as for this…' He stabbed at the rubbery mixture on his plate. 'I could use it to mend the tyres on a four-wheel drive. You said you could cook.'

'Or did you just make assumptions because of my gender?' Chellie shot back, furious at this condemnation of her efforts.

'Don't start that,' he advised brusquely. 'Preparing food is your job as part of the crew. The sole justification for your existence on this boat, as it happens, and gender doesn't feature in the equation. So make sure dinner is better.'

My God, did I really ever find him even remotely attractive? Chellie asked herself incredulously as he stalked out of the saloon and back up to the pilot house. *It must have been temporary insanity brought on by stress.*

Laurent accorded her a sympathetic smile. 'I bought some fresh beef in Santo Martino,' he told her. 'You can make a stew with it, *hein*?'

'No,' Chellie said in a hollow voice. 'I don't think I can, actually.'

Laurent sighed. 'I think maybe I should help, *cherie*, before Ash makes you walk the plank.'

Chellie stared at him. 'But he said you couldn't cook either.'

He shrugged. 'Maybe that was to arouse your sympathy, *cherie*, and make sure you sailed with us.' His eyes danced. 'After all, you are a very beautiful girl, and better to look at than the horizon all the time.'

She bit her lip, putting a self-conscious hand up to her hair. 'I'm a scarecrow.'

He patted her on the shoulder. 'It will grow,' he said gently.

He was brisk and competent as he supervised her cutting the meat into cubes and browning it in oil with garlic and onions. She cooked chopped vegetables in the oil too, then placed the whole concoction with red wine and vegetables, herbs and seasoning in a large electric crockpot which he produced from a cupboard.

'C'est tout.' Laurent switched on the pot and adjusted the setting. 'Now it cooks slowly until we are ready for it this evening.' He grinned at her. 'And you have learned how to feed a hungry man.'

Most of the hungry men I know feed themselves, Chellie returned silently. Using their platinum cards.

'Any more little jobs our gallant captain would like me to do?' she asked with spurious sweetness. 'Like swabbing the decks with my toothbrush?'

Laurent's smile faded, and he gave her an old-fashioned look. 'You might be wiser not to suggest it, *mademoiselle*.' He paused. 'You would prefer, perhaps, to have remained in Santo Martino?'

There was a silence, and Chellie swallowed. She said in a low voice,

'Did he tell you—where he found me—and why?'

'Yes, he told me.' Laurent nodded. 'It was a very bad time for you.'

'And it also makes me an ungrateful bitch,' she said bitterly.

He shrugged. 'Ash is no saint, *mademoiselle*. But which of us is?'

'I should have told him I couldn't cook.' Chellie sighed. 'But it would have made me sound so stupid—so useless.' She shook her head. 'I thought— Everyone cooks, so how hard can it be?'

He gave her a consoling pat on the shoulder. 'Well, you have discovered the answer to that, *ma petite*. But there are not many meals before St Hilaire,' he added encouragingly. 'Your present ordeal will soon be over.'

Maybe, Chellie thought when she was alone. But that doesn't mean I'm going to be able to forget in a hurry. And putting Ash Brennan out of my mind could be one of the hardest things I've ever done.

She felt the sudden pressure of tears, hot and heavy in her throat.

What's happening to me? she asked herself passionately. And how can I please make it stop? Because I don't want this. I don't need it. And, what's more to the point, neither does he.

It was useless telling herself that she was being a pathetic fool. That in reality she knew next to nothing about him. And that after they reached St Hilaire in all probability she would never set eyes on him again.

It's all true, she thought sadly. And it makes no difference—no difference at all. It's too late for that.

And she felt the knowledge—the sheer hurt of that bleak realisation—harden inside her like a stone.

She worked steadily, with just a suspicion of gritted teeth, clearing the washing up and tidying the galley, determined that Ash should have nothing else to criticise. But once that was finished she found herself at something of a loss.

Her position on board was frankly equivocal, she thought, grimacing. Stuck somewhere between non-paying passenger and failed cook. And popular on neither front.

She wondered if she should spend the day in her stateroom, out of sight and out of mind, with the handful of paperback books and magazines which she'd found in a cupboard in the saloon.

Except that was the coward's way out. And she didn't want Ash to gain the impression that she was deliberately avoiding him, in case he asked himself why.

So she would go and spend some time on the sundeck—and if he wanted to clap her in irons, good luck to him.

In her stateroom, she picked the least revealing of the bikinis on offer—plain black with a pretty voile overshirt patterned in black and white—but she still felt thoroughly self-conscious and a little daunted as she emerged into the brilliance of the sunshine.

As if I'm coming out of hibernation after a long winter, she thought wryly as she climbed to the sundeck. Or out of jail after a reprieve.

At the club, she'd almost become a creature of the night, spending most of the day asleep in an exhausted attempt to forget her fetid surroundings. Only aware of the weather outside when rain heavy as pebbles began drumming on the roof, or tropical lightning lit up the room like a laser show.

I'll never take fresh air and sunshine for granted again, she swore fervently.

Ash was there before her, sitting at the table, going through a sheaf of paperwork. He acknowledged her presence with a brief nod, but she felt he was simply preoccupied rather than unwelcoming.

Well, it was a start, she thought. She slipped off her shirt and stretched out on one of the cushioned loungers, closing her eyes, feeling the heat penetrating down to her bones, dispelling the last, lingering chill of fear.

She realised now that being afraid had become a way of life. That she'd begun waiting from hour to hour for the next blow to fall. And that was insidious, because it withered hope and sapped the will to resist.

If Ash hadn't come, she thought, how long before she'd have stopped caring what happened to her? Before she'd yielded listlessly to whatever plans Mama Rita had for her?

In many ways it had been the same with her father, she realised. What had been the point of fighting him when she always lost? Maybe this was why Ramon had found her such an easy victim. Because rebelling against her father in such a basic way was her only chance of victory in their war of attrition.

'Here.' Ash's voice broke curtly into her reverie, and she looked up with a start to see him holding out a large tube of cream to her.

'I'm sorry,' she said. 'I—I was miles away.'

'You'll be miles away in hospital if you're not careful.' He uncapped the tube. 'Sunblock,' he said. 'Use plenty.'

'Oh,' Chellie said. 'Well—thank you.'

'Think nothing of it,' he returned politely. 'I didn't want you to suffer the same fate as the toast, that's all.' And he went back to the table and his papers.

Beast, thought Chellie, sending a muted glare to join him. But maybe it was better this way. Because if he ever started being nice to her then she would really be in trouble.

She applied the sunblock with conscientious care, then settled back and opened one of the magazines she'd brought with her and began glancing in a desultory way through its glossy pages.

On the face of it, everything back to normal, she thought. Only she knew, deep in her heart, that nothing would ever be the same again.

She was disturbingly aware of him, seated only a few yards away. She found she was registering every slight movement, even the rustle of the papers as he turned them over.

Before long I'll be counting the hours again, she thought bitterly. Panicking about the length of the trip to St Hilaire.

Ash shuffled the papers together and rose. He said, 'I'm going to get Laurent a beer. Do you want anything?'

'A Coke, maybe.' Chellie reached for her shirt. 'Shall I get them?'

'Relax,' he advised lazily. 'You're like a cat on hot bricks.' He gave her a long look. 'What's the matter? Scared that Manuel is going to come over the horizon, flying the skull and crossbones and singing ''Yo-ho-ho and a bottle of rum''?' He shook his head. 'Unlikely.'

She smiled tautly. 'But not impossible.'

'Roughly on the same level as being abducted by aliens.' He paused. 'Rats like Manuel don't stray far from their sewers.'

She said in a low voice, 'There was a time, not so long ago, when I wouldn't have believed that people like him— like Mama Rita—even existed. I know better now. And I never believed in miracles either,' she added. 'I'm having to rethink my position on them too, thanks to you.'

She hesitated. 'And I haven't thanked you, have I? Not really. Not as I should have done.' She bit her lip. 'Maybe now would be an appropriate time.'

'Did you sleep well last night?' Ash's tone was quizzical, and when she nodded he smiled at her swiftly, with a charm that made her heart lurch. 'Then that's all the thanks I need,' he said, and went.

Chellie subsided limply against her cushions. She'd felt that smile like the brush of his fingers across her skin.

She thought, Oh, God, I'll have to be careful. So very careful.

She could hear him talking to Laurent. Heard the sound of their laughter. Men comfortable in their skins, at ease together.

I wish I could be like that with him, she thought. Relaxed. No edge.

Able to meet and part as friends.

But we're barely acquaintances. He walked into my life, and saved it, and soon he'll walk away again. In a few months, or even weeks, I'll be a vague memory. A half-forgotten incident. And to pretend anything else would be ludicrous.

Ash came back a few minutes later and put a bottle of Coke with a straw down beside her. He moved over to the rail and stood watching the boat's wake, apparently lost in thought as he drank his beer.

Chellie took a long swallow of her ice-cold drink to ease her dry throat, then she rose and went to stand beside him.

She said constrictedly, 'I—I'm really sorry about breakfast.' She took a deep breath. 'I—lied because I was afraid you'd leave me behind if I said I couldn't cook.'

'No,' he said, after a pause, 'I wouldn't have done that.' His mouth twisted. 'But I might have asked you to display one of your other talents instead.'

Chellie tensed, giving him a wary sideways glance. 'What do you mean?' She hoped he hadn't detected the faint tremor in her tone.

He said quietly, 'You have the most beautiful singing voice. I might have asked for an after-dinner serenade.'

She flushed, surprised. 'Thank you.'

'Did you sing professionally back in Britain?' The question sounded casual, but the blue eyes were curious.

Chellie shook her head. 'No. I was never able to have proper training.'

'Was that what you wanted?'

'Yes, at one time I wanted it very much.'

For a brief, painful moment she could remember how she'd begged to be allowed to enter for a scholarship to a leading academy, and how she'd been brusquely refused. What was more, her father had given instructions at her school that her musical studies were to cease with immediate effect. How many times had she cried herself to sleep in the weeks that followed? She'd lost count.

She said flatly, 'It just wasn't considered a viable career. And they were probably right.' She forced a determined smile. 'After all, I hardly wowed them at Mama Rita's.'

'Choose another audience,' he said. 'And, training or not, it might be a different story.' He slanted a faint grin at her. 'Besides, you made a profound impression on me. Or had you forgotten?'

Her flush deepened. 'No. But you aren't exactly the typical Mama Rita customer.' She paused. 'Whatever made you pick that particular bar?'

He shrugged. 'It sold alcohol.'

'Yes, but so did a dozen others. And that wasn't its main commodity, as you must have realised.'

'Yes, I knew.' He gave her a mocking glance. 'Never underestimate the depravity of the male sex, songbird.'

Chellie looked away. She said quietly, 'You don't look like someone who needs to pay for cheap thrills.'

'The thrills were certainly questionable.' Ash's voice was dry. 'Cheap they were not.'

She winced. 'I'd forgotten that.' She lifted her chin. 'And I've caused you enough problems already, so I don't intend you to be out of pocket as well. I—I will repay you somehow—some day.'

'Oh, forget it,' he said with a touch of impatience. 'God knows, I could do with a few credits on my moral balance sheet.'

There seemed to be no answer to that. Chellie was silent for a moment while she searched for a neutral subject. Eventually she said, 'This is a fabulous boat.'

'Thank you. I'll tell the owner you said so.'

'You said you were delivering it for him?' Her brow creased. 'From Santo Martino?'

'No, from La Tortuga. He'd just put in there when he was suddenly called away on business. So he needed someone to sail 'La Belle Rêve' back to St Hilaire.'

'Is that where he lives?'

'Some of the time. But he's not there at the moment.'

'Oh,' she said. 'So, what were you doing in Santo Martino?'

'Fuel,' he said. 'Supplies. It's a good marina.'

'You must be great friends with this man,' she said. 'If he's prepared to trust you with his boat.'

'Ah,' he said lightly, 'but I'm eminently trustworthy.'

And his daughter, she thought. *Does he trust you with her too?* Thought it, but did not dare ask it aloud. Because it was too personal—and too revealing a question. Besides, it was none of her business.

He'd done her the greatest favour of her life, but that didn't compel him to reveal every detail of his private affairs to her.

Not that he ever would, she thought slowly. There was something about Ash Brennan—something closed and separate. You could probably know him for a dozen years and never do more than scratch the outer shell.

He seemed—totally self-sufficient. Complete in himself. So, even if he met a woman he wanted, would he be prepared to allow her into his heart and mind? Make the necessary emotional commitment? It seemed less than likely.

Maybe it's as well we're going different ways, she thought, before I wreck my heart on his indifference.

She hurried into speech again. 'Will you stay on St Hilaire for long?'

He shrugged. 'Possibly. My plans are flexible.'

'Is this what you do for a living? Skipper other people's boats?'

'I can turn my hand to all kinds of things,' he said. 'And you ask a lot of questions, songbird.'

She flushed again. 'I'm sorry. I'm just envious, I suppose, of all the freedom you seem to have.'

'No one is ever completely free,' he said. 'But I'm working on it.' He paused. 'And what about you, Michelle Greer? What are your plans for the next fifty years?'

She stared down at the sea. 'I'm not making any immediate plans,' she said in a low voice. 'I don't seem to be very good at it.'

'I'd quite like to ask a few questions of my own.' He drank some of his beer. 'Are you up for it?'

'Why not?' Chellie returned with a touch of defensiveness.

'Oh, I can think of several reasons.' Leaning on the rail, he sent her a fleeting grin. 'You're a bit of a mystery, Michelle.'

'Really?' She raised her eyebrows. 'You, of course, are an open book.'

'I do hope not,' he said softly. 'How dull it would be if everyone I met could guess how things would end.'

'You don't have to worry about that,' she said. 'Ask away. I have nothing to hide,' she added, mentally crossing her fingers.

'Is that a fact?' His drawl was amused. 'Then that probably makes you unique. But we won't pursue that—or not at the moment, anyway.' He paused. 'How did you come to be in South America?'

'I went there to be married.'

If she'd expected a reaction she was disappointed. He simply nodded thoughtfully.

'So,' he said. 'What happened to the happy bridegroom?'

'He—changed his mind. Perhaps, like you, he preferred his freedom.'

'Why come all this way for a wedding?'

Chellie shrugged defensively. 'Lots of people get married in exotic locations. As it happens, Caribbean islands are immensely popular.'

He nodded. 'Santo Martino less so, I'd have thought.'

'The actual ceremony was going to be held on Ramon's estate up country. He said the easiest way to reach it was by river, so we came here to catch a boat.

She attempted a laugh, trying to make a joke of it. 'Instead, I caught a virus.'

'So you said. And Ramon?'

'Perhaps he took the boat home. He didn't wait around to tell me.'

'And of course the boat wasn't the only thing he took.' He sounded almost matter-of-fact.

Her mouth tightened. 'No. Do we really have to go through all this? It's hardly one of my favourite memories.'

'Are you still in love with him?'

'*What?*' She stared at him.

'It's a simple enough question. If he suddenly appeared here on deck now—would you forgive him—take him back?'

'Certainly,' she said. 'When all hell freezes over.'

'Yet once you cared enough to come halfway across the world with him.'

'I thought I did,' Chellie said tightly. 'I also believed that he cared for me. I was wrong on both counts.'

'So,' he said, 'when did you realise you weren't in love?'

She thought, *When we were in bed together. When I felt his hands on me—and he pushed himself into me. When he was hurting me, and he wouldn't stop...*

She said, keeping her tone deliberately light, 'I think I've told you quite enough. All other information is on a "need to know" basis.'

He moved swiftly, sharply. Came to her, taking her face between his hands and looking deeply into her startled green eyes.

He said softly, 'And just how the hell, songbird, would you know *what* I need?'

He let her go just as suddenly and walked away, leaving her leaning against the rail as if it was her sole support in the whole world. And staring after him with one shaking hand pressed to her parted lips.

CHAPTER FIVE

SHE almost called to him. Almost asked him to come back. She wanted him to explain what he'd said—and the note of suppressed anger that she'd detected beneath the words.

But some providence—or maybe it was simple self-preservation—kept her silent. Because it was not just words that she wanted from him, and she knew it. Nor was it anger. No, although she was ashamed to admit it, her needs were very different.

She went numbly back to her lounger and lay down, struggling to regain her composure. Her face still burned where he had touched her. His touch had been light, but she felt as if she would bear the marks of his fingers through all eternity.

'Oh, God,' she whispered to herself, 'why did he have to do that? Why did he have to put his hands on me?'

And that was not the worst of it. He'd been so near to her that she'd found herself breathing the erotic male scent of his skin. She'd been aware that her nipples were hardening urgently against the flimsy cups of the bikini, felt the first scalding rush of arousal between her thighs.

The desperation of her own need had scared her. Had almost overwhelmed her.

If he had taken her in his arms she would have yielded completely. And he must have known that. He could not have been oblivious to the sheer physicality of her response. To that shock of trembling desire.

He had been as aware of her as she'd been of him—hadn't he?

But—he hadn't followed through. Instead he'd walked away. And perhaps, she thought painfully, his words could

73

be interpreted as a warning to her not to expect more than he was prepared to give. He'd rescued her, given her temporary sanctuary, but that was as far as it went.

He'd probably decided she was more trouble than she was worth, and wanted no further involvement. And once they reached St Hilaire all contact between them would be severed.

She supposed she should be grateful to him for not taking advantage of her vulnerability, but she couldn't feel thankful. Or not yet, at least.

She closed her eyes, forbidding herself to cry, ashamed of her own reactions—her own weakness. Her experiences in Santo Martino must have affected her more deeply than she'd realised. That was the only explanation.

I don't seem to be the same person any more, she told herself. I don't think or feel as I did. I don't know myself. It's ludicrous—and it can't be allowed to go on. I've got to build up my immune system again—particularly against men like Ash Brennan.

She would certainly need to pull herself together before they arrived at St Hilaire. She couldn't afford to give the impression that she was still dependent on Ash in any way—that she was in want of his continued help. She had to show by her attitude that she'd recovered and was ready to take charge of her life.

And she would manage alone, she added grimly. She would have to, because she had no intention of asking her father for assistance.

Not when she'd put herself in terrible danger and come within a whisker of wrecking her entire life in order to escape his control in the first place.

Because that was what had happened. She could see that so clearly now. See that Ramon had simply seemed a lifeline—a way of resolving her frustration and unhappiness with her existence. Drastic but effective.

I wished myself into love with him, she thought, her mouth twisting wryly. He seemed to be offering me a lifestyle that was the opposite to everything I'd ever known. Something that had a surface glamour all its own.

But getting away from my father was always the main attraction, even if I didn't realise it at the time.

I had to learn it the hard way, she thought, shivering.

But there was no substance to my relationship with Ramon, and even if he'd turned out to be a thoroughly decent guy it couldn't have lasted.

Looking back, she realised she'd had doubts even before they'd left England. There had been details about his background that didn't jell. Vague contradictions in the stories he'd told her that should have alerted her.

If I'd given myself time to stop and think, she told herself with sudden energy, I wouldn't have gone to the end of the street with him. And I'd have saved myself a hell of a lot of misery—and sheer terror.

Above all, I would not have met Ash, and that, in itself, would have been a kind of safety. A security I've lost for ever now. Because he's under my skin—in my blood.

And the first thing I need to do on St Hilaire is get away from him, as far and as fast as I can. And start to forget. Or try to, at least.

She found herself shivering.

Ash strode into the pilot house, his body taut, his mouth set.

Laurent swung round in his leather chair, giving him a quizzical look. *'Ça va?'*

'Not particularly.' Ash flung himself into the adjoining seat, his expression brooding.

'Then I regret I must add to your troubles. Another fax from Victor. There has been a change of plan.' He paused. 'The girl is now to be taken directly to England, and handed over there.'

'Not by me,' Ash returned curtly. 'The deal was St Hilaire—nowhere else—and that's how it's going to stand.' He shook his head. 'Oh, God, I knew I should never have got involved in this.'

Laurent grinned wickedly. 'But you were ideal—the only choice, *mon vieux*. Your irresistible charm was essential to entice *la petite* Michelle away from her lover. How were we to know that the *affaire* had already ended in tears?'

A muscle moved beside Ash's mouth. 'He told her he had a country estate.' He gave a short laugh. 'A shanty in a clearing, I don't doubt.'

Laurent gave a philosophical shrug. 'Then it is as well, perhaps, that it ended while she still had some of her illusions.'

Ash sighed harshly. 'I don't think she had many to start with. And she'll be left with even fewer when she realises she's just swapped one cage for another. That she's been bought and sold. What price her illusions then?'

'You are in danger of breaking your own rules, my friend,' Laurent warned quietly. 'Do the job—earn the money—don't get involved. Isn't that you've always said? How you have survived?'

'I haven't forgotten,' Ash said shortly. 'And the rules still apply.' He sighed again. 'And now I'd better fax Victor and tell him to give Clive Greer a message—that I'll keep his daughter under wraps on St Hilaire until he hands over the money and comes to fetch her. In person. As agreed.'

'He will not like that.'

Ash shrugged. 'Victor and I stopped agreeing about a lot of things some time ago. That's one of the reasons I decided to make this my last assignment and move on.'

'I know that, *mon ami*. But I did not, in fact, refer to Victor. I meant Clive Greer—a very different opponent, I think. Maybe you should be careful.'

'I intend to be.' Ash sent him a swift bleak smile.

And thought, as he bent forward on the pretext of studying the instruments, I have to be—for all kinds of reasons…

Chellie had every intention of thinking positively, but it wasn't easy when her unhappy thoughts insisted on marching round and round in her head as if they were on a treadmill.

Instead of asking Ash a lot of questions he didn't wish to answer, she'd have done better to find out more about St Hilaire, she thought ruefully, applying more sunblock to her exposed skin. And that way she might have avoided undergoing an interrogation herself—and its aftermath.

But the plan she'd formulated in Santo Martino, to find the local consular office and ask for assistance, still seemed good to her, although she would certainly need to conceal her father's identity if she wanted them to help her in any practical sense.

Because they would feel Sir Clive was the obvious person for her to approach, particularly if a financial loan was involved, and she was certainly going to need money to get herself out of the Caribbean.

But she would not ask her father for assistance under any circumstances. For one thing it would put her under a crushing psychological disadvantage to present herself to him as a loser, although she didn't doubt that was how he thought of her anyway.

But I don't need my nose rubbed in it, she told herself.

And now that she'd managed to win herself a 'Get Out of Jail Free' card, she was determined not to relinquish it, however hard the going might become. And no job, no home and no prospects was about as hard as it could get.

By the time she faced her father again she had to hold some kind of winning hand.

Somehow I have to be in a position to dictate my own terms, she thought with resolution.

What she did need, however, in the short term, was her passport. She'd assumed that once they were safely out of Santo Martino Ash would simply hand it over, yet it hadn't been mentioned since she came on board, and this made her uneasy.

It might just have slipped his mind, of course, but somehow she did not think so. There didn't seem to be much the matter with his mental processes.

In fact, she had the distinct impression that he was invariably several steps ahead of her, and maybe it was time she redressed the balance a little.

After all, she argued, her passport was a valuable piece of her personal property. Certainly the local consul would want to see it as proof of her identity, so she had every right to retrieve it without further reference to anyone.

And how hard could that be? *La Belle Rêve* was pretty sumptuous, but it was just a boat with all the limitations that implied. And there could only be so many hiding places.

The obvious place to look, of course, was in Ash's sleeping quarters, she realised, chewing her lip. And there couldn't be too many cabins to search before she found the right one.

She left her magazine open beside the sun cream on her lounger, to indicate to all interested parties that her absence was only temporary, and, slipping her shirt over her bikini, went below, sauntering casually while she was in the view of the pilot house, then moving in swift and silent caution on bare feet once she was out of sight.

Now, she told herself, it was just a question of opening doors. She discovered the crew quarters first, but only one of the bunks was being used there and that, to judge from the clothing and personal items scattered around, belonged to Laurent.

Next she tried the stateroom next to her own, her pulses flickering oddly at the idea that Ash might be sleeping just on the other side of a thin wooden partition, but the neat twin berths were clearly unoccupied.

Which meant that he must be using the master suite in the stern.

Establishing himself as the man in charge in every possible way, Chellie thought caustically. I should have realised—and gone there first.

She opened the door and looked in. It had been furnished to impress, there was little doubt of that. The wide bed, piled with pillows, occupied the centre of the room like an ivory satin island, and the fitted wardrobes and dressing chests had been made from some expensive pale wood. Her feet sank into the thick carpet as she made her way across the stateroom.

The khaki pants he'd been wearing yesterday were lying across the laundry bin in the luxurious shower room, but a swift search soon revealed that their pockets had been emptied.

She swore softly, and turned her attention to the night tables that flanked the bed, but all she found were a few coins, a clean handkerchief, and a paperback copy of the new John Grisham.

And one other item that stopped her in her tracks: a framed photograph of a girl—blonde, slim and pretty in vest top and shorts—smiling with total confidence into the camera.

Chellie picked it up and studied it, aware that her heartbeat had altered. That it was now thrumming slowly and painfully against her ribcage.

The owner's daughter? she wondered. Or someone completely different? The current top of a long and varied list?

And right there beside the bed, where it would undoubtedly be the last thing he saw at night and the first in the morning.

She replaced it, swallowing past the sudden ache in her throat.

Well, what had she expected? she asked in self-derision. He was A list attractive and seriously footloose. Not at all the type to lead a celibate life. She'd known that from the first moment.

Maybe she was just surprised that he cared enough to keep such a personal memento. He must really consider himself spoken for, she thought. Which explained a good deal.

Suddenly she didn't want to continue the search any longer. She needed quite seriously to get out of the room and close the door firmly behind her—in more ways than one, she thought, biting her lip.

She had to think, and for that she needed solitude—and privacy.

She'd just reached her own stateroom, had her fingers on the doorhandle, when Ash said, 'So here you are.'

She swung round, gasping. She'd been so lost in thought that she'd been quite oblivious to his approach.

She thought, *A moment earlier and he'd have caught me. I need to keep my wits about me.*

She managed to keep her voice reasonably level. 'You— startled me.'

'Evidently.' His tone was sardonic. 'I must learn to cough discreetly.' He studied her, frowning a little. 'What are you doing?'

'Looking for a little peace,' she returned, lifting her chin in challenge. 'I wasn't aware I required your permission.'

His mouth tightened. 'You don't. I was simply—concerned. I thought maybe you'd had too much sun.' He studied her. 'You look—flushed.'

Perhaps I do, she thought, but that has nothing to do with the heat of the day.

She shrugged. 'I'm not aware of it,' she said, deliberately casual, trying to ignore the fact that they were facing each other in a confined space. 'Was there anything else?'

'Actually, some lunch would be good.' He paused. 'Nothing too onerous. Just some soup and a few sandwiches, perhaps.'

'Fine,' she said. 'I'll ring when it's ready.'

He gave her another searching look. 'Are you really all right?' he asked abruptly.

'Never better.' She flashed him a meaningless smile. 'Now, if you'll excuse me, I'll get back to my duties.'

Ash propped a shoulder against the wall, effectively

blocking her retreat. 'I'm beginning to realise how those old Roman slavedrivers must have felt,' he remarked.

'Well, don't worry about it,' Chellie said crisply. 'I'm sure any stirrings of compunction will soon wear off. At least by the time we get to St Hilaire, anyway.' She paused. 'When will that be, exactly?'

'Exactitude isn't a particular virtue in the Caribbean,' he said. 'But we're aiming for tomorrow afternoon.' His mouth twisted wryly. 'So my opportunities to crack the whip are therefore numbered.'

'My,' she said. 'Things are getting better all the time.'

He said courteously, 'I'm glad you think so.' He studied her for a moment, brows lifted. 'Do I take it you're not enjoying the voyage?'

'Was enjoyment the intention?' Her laugh was brief and deliberately artificial. 'I hadn't realised.'

He said slowly, 'It's also escaped your notice, apparently, that I've been fighting quite hard not to make a bad situation worse.'

'How could you possibly manage that?' She sent him a mutinous glance.

He said quietly, 'Like this.' And pulled her forward into his arms. His hands slid round her body under the loose shirt, pinning her against him, making her wholly aware that they were both almost naked. Forcing her to recognise that he was unashamedly aroused.

She had raised her hands instinctively to push him away. Instead her palms encountered the naked muscularity of his chest and lingered there of their own volition, savouring the smooth heat of his skin and the harsh thud of his heartbeat.

Ash bent his head, the blue eyes glinting down at her like sun-drenched azure, and Chellie's lips parted in a gasp of shock. She tried to say something—to find words of pro-test—of denial, even—but then his mouth closed on hers, warm and totally possessive, and the chance was lost—if it had ever truly existed.

His lips were moving on hers, softly but with purpose,

sending messages of deliberate sensual demand to her reeling brain. He was teasing her tongue with his, coaxing her to respond. To grant him the total access to her surprised mouth that he was seeking.

Her head fell back and her lashes drifted down, preparing her for this initial surrender. Presaging what might follow.

She found she was lifting her arms and winding them round his neck, pressing even closer to him, so that her breasts in their fragile covering grazed the wall of his chest.

His kiss deepened instantly, passionately, and she tasted hunger on his mouth. Recognised it because she shared it. And because she needed so desperately for it to be assuaged.

Ash pushed the shirt from her shoulders, letting it drop to the floor. His hands were stroking her skin, tracing the vulnerable line of her backbone, brushing the sensitive nerve-endings, making her sigh and quiver in mounting excitement.

She felt him unsnap the clip that held her bikini top and slide down the straps. The flimsy cups fell away, releasing her bare breasts to the caress of his fingers.

His touch was gentle, but very sure, circling her hardening nipples, encouraging them to some peak of sweet intensity she had never known before or even dreamed was possible. Making her glory in this new intimacy.

Her legs were shaking under her and she leaned back, seeking the support of the stateroom door.

The note of her breathing had changed, and her pulses were going crazy. She could feel the fiery strength of his erection against her thighs, and knew that neither of them could wait much longer.

All she had to do was open the door behind her, she realised with a swift intake of breath—and the bed would be there waiting for them.

And this time, her frantic body told her, consummation would be very different.

This time.

Suddenly, unwillingly, she was back in that first hotel

room, spreadeagled across the awful bed and its creaking mattress, with Ramon on top of her, his face contorted as he drove for his own satisfaction. Ramon—hurting her and not caring. Ramon—using her without love.

Just as Ash would do—if she allowed it.

She heard herself make a small hoarse sound of negation. Found that she was pushing at Ash with new-found strength, struggling to free herself, the image of the photograph on his night table forcing its way into her reluctant memory. Reminding her that they were still virtual strangers and that he had a life about which she knew nothing.

At the same time, to him she was nothing more than a body he had briefly coveted in Mama Rita's club, but not enjoyed. Or not then, at least.

She could see now that he'd simply been—biding his time. Waiting for the moment when she would simply fall into his hand.

Well, she owed him, and she knew it, but she could not repay the debt with sex. He would take her with more finesse than Ramon, she had no doubt of that, but his purpose would be the same—to satisfy a transient desire. And she would not allow herself to be used like that again, only to be discarded when he chose to walk away.

Ramon had ignored her reluctance, and her protests. He'd imposed himself on her with almost casual brutality.

Ash, however, released her at once, staring down at her, his brows snapping together. 'What's the matter?'

She stared down at the boards under her feet. 'I—I can't.' Her voice trembled. 'I—I just remembered something. Someone.'

Her words seemed to fall into a long and terrible silence. When at last she ventured to look up at him, she saw his face cold as a stone mask.

'Ash,' she said. And again, 'Ash—I'm sorry.'

She wanted to explain to him, but thoughts were churning in her head and she couldn't form a coherent sentence.

'No,' he said. 'Don't be sorry.' The words were curt and

clipped. His smile glittered without warmth. 'I also have things I need to remember.'

He paused. 'I suppose I should thank you for reminding me. But I don't feel particularly grateful right now. So let's agree we've both been saved from a really bad mistake and leave it there.' He gave a slight shrug. 'After all, nothing really happened.'

From some far distance she heard herself say huskily, 'Didn't it?'

'It was a kiss, songbird.' His voice was quiet, but it bit. 'And you've been kissed before, and far more than that, so don't treat me to any virginal vapours. Just forget it ever took place. As I shall.'

He stood aside, pushing sweat-dampened hair back from his forehead. 'And now, please don't let me keep you from your real duties any longer.'

She had to reach down to retrieve her shirt and bikini top. When she straightened, her face was burning. She hoped without much conviction that he would think it was down to the exertion of bending, rather than the confusion of embarrassment and frustration that was consuming her entire body.

She put on the shirt, dragging its edges together to conceal her exposed skin as she eased her way past him.

Once clear, she risked a swift glance over her shoulder to see if he was still there—if he was watching her go with any kind of regret. But he'd disappeared, presumably to his cabin, and she realised she could make her escape in relative peace.

She went quickly up the companionway, only to find when she reached the galley that she was panting as if she'd just taken part in a marathon.

Her first action was to fumble her way back into her bikini top and fasten the shirt over it. She was only sorry the buttons didn't reach to her throat.

The rasp of the cloth against her awakened flesh was a torment she could do without.

She ran cold water from the tap over the tumultuous pulses in her wrists, and splashed cool droplets on to her face in an attempt to calm her hectic flush.

He'd said forget it, she thought with a kind of desperation, but how could she? Especially when all she wanted was to hide away somewhere in a dark corner where she would never have to set eyes on him again.

But there was small chance of that in the confines of *La Belle Rêve*. And in practical terms she was going to have to face him pretty soon, anyway, because she had lunch to prepare and serve.

Oh, God, she groaned inwardly, scanning the cupboards for tinned soup. How much worse can it all get?

It made her squirm to remember how easily she'd melted into his embrace, as if it had been invented for her alone, when what she should really have done was fight him off at once.

In fact, she should never have allowed the situation to develop in the first place, she thought gloomily. She should have remembered why she was there and kept her dealings with him on a strictly businesslike basis.

Even when he mentioned St Hilaire you never asked him for your passport, although it was the perfect opportunity, she castigated herself bitterly. Even if you'd made him mad, at least it would have kept him at arm's length.

She heard footsteps crossing the saloon and tensed. Had Ash noticed that she'd been in his cabin? she thought frantically. Had she moved something, or left a drawer open? And what excuse could she offer if he accused her of prying?

Except I don't need an excuse, she told herself swiftly. He has my property. I want it back. End of story.

But when she turned, prepared to give battle, she saw with relief that it was Laurent.

'May I offer any help?'

'I think I can manage.' She grimaced. 'Even I ought to be able to open a can of soup.'

'Are you sure? You seem a little flushed—out of sorts.'

She shrugged a shoulder. 'Too much sun,' she said lightly. 'I'm still not used to it.'

'Ah,' he said, his eyes considering her shrewdly. 'That might account for it.' He paused. 'I took some savoury pastries from the freezer earlier. Would you like me to heat them?'

'Yes, please,' Chellie said gratefully.

She poured the creamy vegetable soup into a pan, and began to warm it gently while Laurent busied himself at the oven.

She said, 'I just hope we get to St Hilaire before I poison everyone.'

He clicked his tongue. 'That is not fair. You should not put yourself down in such a way, *mademoiselle*.'

'Please,' she said. 'My other friends call me Chellie.'

His brows lifted, 'You flatter me—Chellie. *Merci du compliment.*'

'So, tell me something about St Hilaire?' She kept her voice bright, interested. 'I gather it's not very big?'

'No,' he said. 'But my home is there, so I think it very beautiful.'

'Are you married?'

'Yes.' His face relaxed into a smile. 'And I have a son and a daughter.'

Chellie remembered there had been family photos in his cabin, but could not say so, of course. She said, 'They must miss you—when you're away like this.'

He shrugged. 'It does not happen so often.'

'Oh,' she said. 'Then this isn't how you earn your living—sailing other people's boats?'

'No,' he said. 'On St Hilaire I manage a banana plantation. And I have a boat of my own,' he added with a touch of dryness. 'I like to fish.'

Chellie hesitated, fighting with herself and losing. She said, trying to sound casual, 'And Ash—does he live on the island too?'

'There—and in other places.' He paused, giving a slight shrug. 'Unlike myself, he is a single man. So—he enjoys his freedom.'

'Yes,' she said. 'I'm sure he does.' *But for how much longer?* she asked herself, remembering the photograph beside his bed.

She concentrated her attention fiercely on the soup. After a moment or two, she said, 'Laurent—will you tell me something?'

'If I can.' He sounded faintly wary.

She drew a breath. 'Is Ash sorry that he rescued me? That he brought me out of that awful place?'

Laurent hesitated. 'I think, *cherie*, he regrets there was ever a necessity to do so.'

Her smile was wry. 'I'm sorry too.' She swirled a spoon in the soup, watching tiny bubbles begin to form. She said, 'But with Ash there's more to it than that—isn't there?'

He spread his hands. 'In life there are always—complications.'

She gave a wintry smile. 'And I'm one of those complications?'

He shook his head. 'I think I have already said too much.' He became businesslike. 'The pastries require five more minutes. There is salad in the refrigerator, also vinaigrette dressing in a small jar. Ash suggested that we eat on deck.'

'Fine,' she said, over-brightly. 'But I'll have my meal here. Less—complicated, you understand.'

Laurent gave her a quizzical look as he prepared to depart. 'I think that I begin to,' he murmured. 'Perhaps it may be better for you to—stay out of the sun, *cherie*.' And he went off, whistling under his breath.

Lunch was not as difficult as she'd feared, after all. Ash barely looked at her as he thanked her with cool politeness for the tray of food she set in front of them. Nor did he query her failure to join them.

Perhaps he was glad not to have to face her, Chellie thought as she ate her solitary meal.

Once it was all finished, and cleared away, Chellie went to her stateroom and took a long cool shower, changing back into the clothes she'd worn earlier.

No more chasing a tan, she told herself. In future it would be safer to cover up.

Now she needed something to occupy her—something that would stop her thinking again, because there was no guarantee that she could keep her thoughts under sufficient control for her own peace of mind.

She'd noticed there were cleaning materials in a locker near the crews' quarters, and she decided to turn her attention to the saloon.

If her father were here now, he wouldn't believe his eyes, she thought, applying polish to a table surface and rubbing vigorously, but for the first time in her life, she actually felt useful.

The scent of the casserole was beginning to permeate through from the galley, and she sniffed with real appreciation as she worked.

The events of the past twenty-four hours notwithstanding, she was beginning to see the attraction of life on board. Maybe she could seriously learn to cook and become part of the crew on another boat—preferably in a different ocean on the other side of the world.

Although she could well imagine her father's reaction to the news that she'd opted to become a sea-going skivvy. His cold displeasure.

She paused, wiping a few beads of perspiration from her forehead, aware of a faint shiver of uneasiness, as if she'd conjured up his actual presence.

Which was ridiculous, she told herself, resuming her vigorous rubbing, because Sir Clive was hundreds of miles away and the Caribbean was the last place he'd look for her. If, of course, he bothered to look at all, she conceded wryly.

Her elopement with Ramon would have made him very angry. So angry, probably, that he'd written off his unsatisfactory daughter with the same icy finality he'd show a bad debt. A line drawn and no further reference made.

My God, she thought. How many times have I seen him do it? So why should he treat me any differently?

Besides, Ramon had covered their tracks with extreme care. She could remember how impressed she'd been with his caution, the deliberate false trails that he'd laid. His insistence that they should not be followed. And how she'd naïvely interpreted it as his genuine wish to shield her from her father's wrath by putting themselves beyond his reach and winning their freedom.

Nice plan, she acknowledged ruefully. Yet its only achievement had been to enmesh her in a different kind of slavery.

And one that, in her heart, she had no real wish to escape.

It was an acknowledgement that struck her with all the force of a hammer-blow.

Chellie straightened slowly, feeling pain stir inside her with icy and corroding bitterness as she suddenly found herself reliving those all too short moments in Ash's arms. As she tasted once more the drugging sweetness of his kiss on her lips.

And stopped there, gasping, shaking her head in a despairing attempt to bring herself back to reality.

She said aloud, 'Don't do this to yourself, Michelle. Wake up and smell the coffee. Start repeating ten times a day, ''There is no future with Ash Brennan'' until you learn some sense at last.'

And tried to ignore the tiny warning voice in her brain which whispered that it might already be much too late. That she could be lost for ever.

CHAPTER SIX

ASH, of course, must never know how she felt.

That was what she kept repeating to herself, over and over again, as this seemingly endless day drew towards its close.

He must never be allowed to suspect, even for a moment, the riot of emotional confusion churning inside her.

I'd rather be back at Mama Rita's than have him guess how I'm feeling right now, she thought, wincing, as she went down to her stateroom to change for dinner.

She needed somehow to practise his own brand of cool indifference if she was to survive the remainder of this short voyage with her pride undamaged.

And when they reached St Hilaire she had to walk away without looking back. Grateful, but casual. Drawing a line under the whole affair.

No regrets, she thought, swallowing past a sudden tightness in her throat, and no recriminations—no matter how difficult that might be.

Because, although she might be able to keep her pride intact, she could not make any similar guarantees about her heart.

She groaned inwardly. Oh, God, she thought wretchedly, what am I doing to myself?

First Ramon—and now this—this disaster.

Did she never learn? she demanded of herself with savage intensity. Was she really planning to be a loser all her life, sighing for a whole series of Mr Wrongs?

And wasn't she making far too much of it all anyway? After all, as Ash had said himself, nothing had really happened. He'd made his play, been turned down, and shrugged it off.

Which indicated fairly bruisingly the relative unimportance of the encounter in his scheme of things, she thought unhappily. As far as he was concerned the point of no return had by no means been reached. Whereas as soon as his mouth had touched hers she'd gone up in flames—ready to give him anything he asked for.

And it was small consolation to tell herself that, in fact, she'd been the first one to draw back. Because it should never have been allowed to happen at all. And belated second thoughts didn't change a thing.

For God's sake, she castigated herself, I hardly know him. It may seem an eternity, but the truth is that he walked into my life less than forty-eight hours ago. And that is no basis for any kind of relationship—and certainly not a one-night stand. I'm worth more than that.

Besides, it went across every principle she had ever possessed. She'd believed that she was being seriously courted by Ramon, yet she'd held out against him for weeks on end, telling herself it would make their eventual union on their wedding night doubly precious.

She looked at herself in the mirror, running her fingers regretfully through the short, feathery spikes of black hair.

She seemed to have become a stranger to herself in all kinds of ways, she thought, sighing. But then for the last few weeks of her life survival had been the name of the game. She could afford nothing else.

And that was the situation she'd be forced to battle with for the foreseeable future.

Meanwhile, there was tonight to get through. And it was even more important not to lurk out of the way in the saloon or her own stateroom, as if she was too scared to face him. That would be instant self-betrayal.

She needed to be smiling and totally insouciant—as if she didn't have a care in the world and those few devastating moments in his arms had been shrugged aside as trivial. That was the way to play it—the only way.

She'd taken something quiet and unobtrusive from the

wardrobe, but now she thought, To hell with it, selecting instead with a certain defiance an ankle-length wraparound skirt, with crimson tropical flowers on a creamy background, topped by a square-necked, short-sleeved blouse in the same vibrant colour as the flowers.

Go out in style, she told herself, smoothing the silky fabric over her slim hips and crushing down the wayward thought that maybe Ash might also be left with something to regret.

Because the words 'if only' would feature rarely, if ever, in his vocabulary, and she knew it. And she'd be an even bigger fool if she hoped for anything else.

So—I'm a fool, she thought, and sighed soundlessly.

The casserole was delicious, served with a mound of fluffy rice and some tiny green beans which Laurent had shown her how to turn lightly in butter.

'Amazing,' Ash commented when he put down his fork. He gave her a brief smile across the table, which she'd set with small candles in pretty glass shades. 'You seem to have widened your repertoire since this morning.'

Chellie murmured something, then concentrated her attention on the remaining grains of rice on her own plate.

In spite of all her good resolutions, she was still finding Ash a disturbing dinner companion. He too had apparently decided to make an effort for their last night at sea, and was wearing well-cut dark pants with an open-necked white shirt that set off his tan. His blond hair was still darkened by damp from the shower, and she was tinglingly aware of the faint muskiness of some expensive cologne lingering on his skin.

He and Laurent had been involved in some low-voiced, forceful conversation when she'd first entered the wheelhouse, trying to hide her feeling of self-consciousness. He'd paused instantly, his brows lifting sharply, his attention completely arrested as he looked at her.

It had been only momentary. A breath later and he'd

turned back to Laurent. But for those few seconds Chellie knew that he'd been looking at her. Seeing no one but her. And she'd seen the sudden flare in his eyes.

Now, she drew a steadying breath and made herself meet his gaze again across the table.

'I can't claim the credit,' she denied stiltedly. 'I was coached by an expert.' She turned to the man beside her. 'Thank you, Laurent.'

He shrugged in self-deprecation. 'I had an apt pupil.' He paused. 'I have been saying to Ash that he should make you a permanent member of the crew.'

There was a silence, then from somewhere Chellie managed to produce a laugh that sounded genuinely amused.

'I don't think that would appeal to either of us,' she said cheerfully.

'Besides, I have a life to get on with.' She looked back at Ash. 'And *apropos* of that—may I have my passport back, please?'

'Right now?' He drank some of the red wine in his glass, leaning back in his chair. 'Why—are you planning to swim for it?'

'Not unless I have to.' *Be cool, be casual. Keep the joke going.* 'But I'm going to need it as soon as we get to the island, as proof of identity for the local consul.'

'Then there's no great hurry.' He was watching her from under lowered lids. 'Because tomorrow is Saturday and the office will be shut until Monday.'

'Shut?' Chellie could not conceal her dismay. 'Oh, no, not again, surely?' Being at Mama Rita's had made her lose all track of time, it seemed. 'But what if there's an emergency?'

Ash shrugged. 'We tend not to have them.' He paused. 'And I don't think your problems would be considered in that light anyway,' he added flatly.

She stiffened. 'You mean it's all right for me to be stranded as long as the consul gets his round of golf?'

'Set of tennis, I think,' he corrected blandly. 'And don't worry—you won't be sleeping on the beach.'

She lifted her chin. 'Says who?'

His mouth twisted mockingly. 'Well, the local police, for a start. They take a dim view of vagrancy.'

She bit her lip. 'Then would it be possible for me to remain on the boat—just until Monday morning?' She hated having to ask him for another favour—detested the faint note of entreaty she detected in her own voice.

Ash shook his head. 'I'm afraid the owner wouldn't permit that.'

Swallowing, Chellie made herself turn to Laurent. 'I don't suppose…?'

He spread his hands regretfully. 'My house is not large, *cherie*. And my wife, although the delight of my heart, is convinced all other women find me irresistible. I think your presence would make her—uneasy. You see the problem?'

'Yes,' she said, smiling resolutely. 'Of course. In that case I'd better head for the local Mama Rita's. I suppose there is one?'

'I doubt it.' Ash lit a cheroot. 'But isn't that a pretty drastic course to take, anyway?'

'Desperate situations,' she said, 'call for desperate measures.'

'Nevertheless,' he said slowly, 'there are a number of perfectly respectable places to stay on St Hilaire.'

'I'm sure there are,' she said. 'Places where they prefer their bills to be paid.'

'Naturally,' he said. 'So why don't you let me stake you to a room while you're on St Hilaire?'

Chellie's hands clenched together unseen in her lap. She said evenly, 'I don't think that's a very good idea.'

'No?' A slow smile curved his mouth. 'Would you care to elaborate?'

He was daring her to accuse him of wanting to share the room with her, she thought furiously. But she wasn't going to fall into that trap—particularly with Laurent as an interested audience.

Her mouth tightened, but she managed to keep her voice even. 'Because you've done quite enough to help already. It's time I started shouldering my own responsibilities.'

'Well, no-one would argue with that.' Ash shrugged a casual shoulder.

'But maybe you should wait until the odds aren't so heavily stacked against you.'

He made himself sound like the voice of sweet reason, Chellie realised, the gall and wormwood of thwarted rebellion stirring inside her. And as if butter wouldn't melt in his mouth...

'Come on, songbird.' His smile widened, suggesting that he'd accurately discerned her inner struggles and was amused by them. 'Let me lend a hand one last time. You can always pay me back.'

She swallowed. 'Please treat that as an absolute. Although I'm not sure when it will be possible,' candour forced her to add.

Ash tapped the ash from his cheroot.

'You could always pay me something on account tonight,' he suggested softly. 'After all, you know what I really want.'

Chellie found herself going rigid, then caught the wicked glint in his eyes and relaxed again.

She said lightly, 'Why not? After all, I didn't really cook the dinner, so I owe you already.' She paused. 'Any special requests?' she added, sending him a challenging look.

'Oh, Laurent's the musician round here.' Ash turned to him. 'Why don't you get your guitar, *mon vieux*? Michelle is going to sing to us.'

Laurent's brows lifted. '*Vraiment?* Then I should be honoured.'

Left alone with Ash, Chellie found tension seeping back as reason and desire fought a secret battle inside her.

She looked out at the moonlight streaming across the water. She said with a touch of uncertainty, 'It's—beautiful tonight.'

'Yes.' She realised that he was looking straight at her, not following the direction of her gaze at all. 'Very lovely.' His blue gaze rested meditatively on her parted lips, then moved downward to the swell of her breasts under the brief top and lingered, as if he was indulging a cherished memory.

In spite of herself, she felt her skin warm under his scrutiny. She could also remember, all too well, the arousing play of his fingers on her naked flesh, and how she'd longed to feel the caress of his lips against her heated nipples.

She thought achingly, Don't—don't do this to me—please...

She had to break the spell somehow. She began to reach for the used dishes. 'I—I ought to clear the table.'

'Laurent and I will do it,' he said, adding laconically, 'Save your strength for later.'

'Later?' She could have bitten her tongue. The query had been far too sharp—too pointed. It had sounded nervous. But then why shouldn't it—after the way he'd just been looking at her?

'For your singing,' he said. 'I understand it takes a lot of breath control?'

'Oh,' Chellie said, feeling foolish. 'Well—yes.'

He drew on the cheroot, watching her reflectively, his eyes shadowed by the sweep of his lashes—unreadable. 'That colour really suits you,' he said eventually. 'But I'm sure you know that already.'

'My first and last dinner on the boat,' she said, speaking a little too quickly. 'I thought I should dress up a little.' She hesitated. 'It's lucky that—these things—her clothes—fit me.'

He smiled faintly. 'Very lucky.'

There was another silence. Ash reached across and stubbed out the remains of the cheroot.

She said, 'I—I didn't know that you smoked.'

'Why should you?' he said. 'I do it very rarely—mainly when I'm under pressure. But I'm well aware it's a bad habit which I shall have to break quite soon.'

She bit her lip. 'And—do you feel—pressured now?'

'Of course,' he said. 'I have an expensive boat to take to St Hilaire.' He paused. 'Among other considerations.'

This time, Chellie thought, she was not taking the bait.

She was thankful to hear Laurent returning. As well as his guitar, he'd brought a tray with coffee and brandies.

'We should drink,' he announced, 'to our smooth passage so far, and our safe haven tomorrow.'

Smooth? Chellie thought bitterly, as she obediently echoed the toast. I feel as if I've been tossed from one storm to another. And it's not over yet. I still have to get away from St Hilaire, which is becoming less of a sanctuary by the minute.

'So.' Laurent sat back in his chair and applied some fine tuning to his guitar. 'What would you like to sing?'

Chellie shook her head. 'You play something,' she said. 'And if I know the words, I'll join in.'

He thought for a moment, then played a few soft chords, quite different from any of the lilting West Indian or Creole numbers she'd expected.

He said, 'You will know this, I think? "Plaisir d'Amour"?'

She knew it all right, with its echoing lament for betrayal and lost love, and for a moment she was tempted to ask him to choose another less potent melody. But that, she knew immediately, would be unwise. It would simply cause unnecessary fuss, might even turn an unwanted spotlight on her fragile emotional state. And that she could not risk—in case Ash looked again, and saw too much.

So, she thought reluctantly, it was far better to sing with good grace and have done with it.

She let him play the melody, then came in with the reprise, her voice warm and strong. '"*Plaisir d'amour ne dure qu'un moment, Chagrin d'amour dure toute la vie*".'

She sang the whole thing through in French, her own inner sadness and regret lending a whole new depth of emotion to her performance, then repeated the plangent melancholy refrain one last time in English. '"The joys of love are but a moment long, The pain of love endures the whole life long".'

It was, she thought, as she allowed the final syllables to linger on the night air, a reminder worth repeating.

When she'd finished there was a silence, then Laurent said, 'That was wonderful.' He turned to Ash. 'Didn't you think so, *mon ami*?'

'Beautiful.' He looked at Chellie, his mouth twisting faintly. 'Although it wasn't quite what I had in mind. Those are fairly negative sentiments.'

'Negative,' she said. 'Or realistic, perhaps.' She gave a slight shrug. 'Everyone has to make their own interpretation—choose for themselves.'

'So, what side of the fence do you come down on, Michelle?' The question was put lightly but his eyes were intense, fixed on hers. A hungry gaze, she realised. Warning her that he was asking far more than his words suggested at face value.

Telling her without equivocation that her answer would decide whether or not she would spend the night in his arms.

The joys of love are but a moment long. The line still sang in her mind, with its chilling emphasis that, however passionate or miraculous that moment might be, it could not last. And that, if she surrendered to it, an eternity of loneliness might follow. Something she could not afford to forget.

Chellie lifted her chin. She said, quietly and clearly, 'That's quite simple. I choose not to be unhappy for the rest of my life.'

She forced her mouth into the semblance of a smile. 'And now, if you'll excuse me, I'll wish you both goodnight.'

She walked away with her head held high, and without hurrying or glancing back. But at the bottom of the companionway she stopped, leaning shakily against the wall, pressing a hand to her trembling mouth.

'Oh, God,' she whispered. 'How long am I going to be able to carry on pretending?'

Up in the wheelhouse there was a heavy silence which Laurent eventually broke, his voice quiet. 'You have a real problem, *mon ami.*'

Dull colour spread across Ash's cheekbones. He reached for another cheroot. Lit it. 'Nothing I can't handle.'

'First handle Victor,' Laurent said shortly. 'Explain to him why you have decided to keep the girl on St Hilaire instead of taking her back to England, as instructed. And see how near you come to the truth, *hein*?' he added with dry emphasis.

Ash dealt with Victor and his concerns in one succinct phrase.

'I made it clear from the start that the final negotiations would be conducted on my own territory,' he added curtly.

Laurent gave him a level look. 'Unfortunately Sir Clive Greer does not wish to come halfway across the world to make the payment and collect his daughter—and he is not a man used to having his wishes disregarded.'

Ash shrugged. 'He can take it or leave it. Just as long as he pays us the agreed amount.'

Laurent stared at him. 'You are still saying this is just about money?'

Ash drew deeply on the cheroot. 'Of course,' he said. 'What else?'

'Then why keep her with you instead of taking the next flight from St Vincent or Barbados?'

'Because in a situation like this, he's the obvious one for her to turn to,' Ash said. 'Yet she's never even mentioned him. Admitted he's her father.' His mouth tightened. 'Don't you find that strange?'

Laurent gave him a cynical look. 'He is buying her back. That is all you need to know. And it is clear that he already regards her as damaged goods,' he added, his mouth twisting in distaste. 'So beware of making a bad situation worse.'

'Why?' Ash stubbed out the cheroot with sudden violence. 'Because he may reduce the price?'

'And you said it was just the money.' Laurent shook his head as he began to collect the used crockery together. 'I think you are fooling yourself, *mon vieux*.'

Ash glared at him. 'When I need your advice, I'll ask for it.'

Laurent grinned back. 'Life is too short, I think,' he said, and began to hum *'Plaisir d'Amour'* softly under his breath.

Chellie sat on the edge of the bed, head bent, fingers almost convulsively gripping the edge of the mattress.

She'd done the right thing, she told herself with harsh vehemence. The sensible thing. The *only* thing.

She'd made it crystal-clear to Ash that she intended to hold him at arm's length for the remainder of their acquaintance. However long that might be.

Two days, she thought, if she was lucky. If the consul turned out to be co-operative and helpful, and actually believed her unlikely story. And then she would be on her way out of Ash's life for ever.

But going where?

That was something she hadn't yet thought through with any clarity. The present had been occupying her mind too fully to spare much time for the future.

But she'd made a start by accepting that Ash could never be part of it, for so many reasons.

He was very much an enigma, she thought, and that in itself carried its own kind of glamour. And he'd saved her, and she would always be grateful for that. So maybe that was all there was to it—and one day she would only remember the gratitude and dismiss the rest as a passing fancy.

But now she had to concentrate on the rest of her life. Galling as it was, it was clear she had little choice but to return to England. She needed access to money, and although the money from her late mother's legacy only brought in a modest income, it would support her until she could find work of some kind. And a bedsit, too. She could no longer afford her old flat.

Besides, by this time Ramon would probably have run up astronomical bills on her credit cards, and she would have to deal with that.

She would also need to get some qualifications. Becoming a professional singer was beyond her reach, but a catering course would be useful, she thought slowly, although she was cancelling her original wild idea of working on boats. Dry land would be much safer. Or maybe she would learn computing skills.

She sighed soundlessly. The outlook seemed pretty bleak. She'd been taught a very costly lesson in the past weeks— but the financial implications were the least of it. And somehow she would have to deal with that. Somehow.

But first and foremost she had to tackle the consul—get him on her side. Because she didn't want to contemplate what might happen if he refused to help. And they were not always sympathetic to people turning up on their doorstep without means.

I should have to turn to Ash again, she thought, her heart missing a painful beat. I'd have no choice. I can't count on some other saviour coming to my rescue.

She slid off the bed and began to undress, her mind still going in weary circles.

She would have to borrow some more clothes, of course. That was unavoidable. She couldn't visit the consul wearing a crumpled denim skirt or Mama Rita's black dress, not if she wanted to be taken seriously.

Some underwear, a pair of cotton trousers and a couple of tops should be enough, she thought, replacing the crimson blouse and skirt on their hanger and touching their silky folds with a rueful hand. Emergency rations from now on.

And she would have to find some way of compensating

her unknown benefactress, too, for the unrestricted access to her wardrobe.

Although she probably won't miss any of the stuff I've used, Chellie thought with a faint shrug. Most of it seems to be brand-new. I expect she has a new selection in every port.

But she'd return what she could, she decided—washed, ironed and pristine.

She took another quick shower, then cleansed and toned her face, and ran a brush through her hair before reaching for her nightgown.

And paused, looking at her naked reflection in the mirror, seeing herself for the first time as an object of desire in a man's eyes. Remembering, with a sharp indrawn breath, how Ash had stared at her, his gaze urgent—demanding. Wanting her.

No one, she thought, had ever looked at her in quite that way before. And maybe no one would ever again.

And she'd rejected him. She closed her eyes, pressing her clenched fist against her mouth. She'd gone for the wise, brave option. Obeyed her mind and not the unbidden, uncontrollable clamour in her flesh.

But would Ash accept her no for an answer? Or would he choose instead to come and find her—and take—because he knew that was what she really wanted…?

She could not be dishonest with herself any longer.

There was a flask of her favourite scent among the toiletries in the bathroom. Chellie found herself almost dreamily touching the crystal stopper to her throat, her breasts, the curve of her elbows and her thighs.

She picked up the lip-lustre she'd used earlier and softened the lines of her mouth with colour.

The girl looking back at her from the mirror seemed totally alien, her bare skin faintly flushed, her eyes wide and drowsy with expectancy and her mouth curving into a slow smile.

She breathed the cloud of fragrance rising from her warm

flesh, and the older, muskier scent that she realised was intermingled with it. A scent that was totally wanton—and wholly female.

There was an ache in her breasts, their rosy peaks already jutting in excitement. A soft, sensual throb that was echoed deep inside her and yearned to be assuaged.

She was a woman at last—ready and eager for her lover.

He will come to me, she thought. He must...

She went softly to the door and drew back the little bolt she had fastened earlier. She extinguished all the lights except the small shaded lamp beside the bed.

Then she slid under the covers, drawing the sheet loosely up to her hips, and settled back against the pillows to wait for him.

It was his own choice now, she thought. All he had to do was tap at the door, and she would say his name and open her arms to welcome him.

She measured out the time by the pace of her own heartbeat. Was it really so agonisingly slow?

And when at last she heard his footsteps, descending the companionway and approaching down the passage, her heart seemed to stop beating altogether.

She swallowed, her eyes fixed on the door, listening—hoping for his knock.

She heard him slow—come to a halt outside her door. There was a silence—endless—brooding—and she wanted to call out to him, but her taut throat muscles refused to obey her.

She heard a faint noise, saw the doorhandle turn slightly. Her entire body tensed in a mixture of nervousness and longing as she waited for the door to open.

But it remained where it was, and a moment later she realised the handle had been gently released again.

Then she heard him going away from her, his footsteps fading, and presently the sound of his own door shutting with an awful finality.

She knew then that he would not return. That she would spend the night alone. And she turned over, burying her face in the pillow, her body as rigid and as cold as a stone.

And, presently, she wept.

CHAPTER SEVEN

CHELLIE awoke early the following morning and lay for a while, looking out at the cloudless sky. The storm of tears that had assailed her the previous night had left her feeling drained of all emotion. At one point she had even been forced to stuff the corner of the pillow into her mouth to muffle the harsh sobs that were tearing through her, terrified that they might be heard. And eventually, she supposed, she must have fallen into an exhausted sleep.

She could remember brief, uneasy dreams, but none of them had left any lasting trace.

And now it was the next day, reality once more. All dreams must be forgotten. She had to get up and repair the ravages, and pretend that everything was fine.

Maybe I should take up acting as a career, she thought with a grimace as she pushed back the sheet and got out of bed.

The scent she had applied with such hope last night still lingered on her skin, making her feel vaguely nauseated. She knew she would never wear it again.

She looked pale, she thought critically, catching sight of herself in the mirror, and her eyes felt bruised, but apart from that she appeared relatively together. Her face would not give away any secrets.

She showered rapidly, and dressed in pale pink linen shorts and a matching camisole top. Then she made her way straight to the galley, reviewing all the information that Laurent had passed on yesterday.

Today, the bread was cut precisely, and toasted evenly, the coffee was strong and aromatic, and the eggs boiled for four minutes only. She gave a nod of satisfaction as she rang the bell.

She was setting the food on the table in the saloon when Ash appeared, wearing a pair of frayed denim shorts. He halted in the doorway, the blue eyes narrowed slightly as he studied her.

Chellie met his gaze, her smile deliberately cool and non-committal.

He said slowly, 'You're an early riser.' He paused. 'Couldn't you sleep?'

'Just as soon as my head hit the pillow,' Chellie lied. 'But after the trouble I got into yesterday I thought I'd better make a prompt start today.' She gave a light laugh. 'After all, I don't want to be keel-hauled at this stage of the voyage.'

Ash's brows lifted as he surveyed the table. 'It all looks—wonderful. You amaze me.'

'It's not really very astonishing.' Chellie poured coffee with a steady hand and handed him the cup. She added quietly, 'I try never to make the same stupid mistake twice, that's all.' She let that sink into the silence, then picked up the waiting tray. 'I'll take Laurent's food up to him.'

'No,' he said. 'I'll do that. You stay here and have your breakfast. I'll be straight back.' He paused. 'I think we need to talk.'

Alone, Chellie sank down on to a chair, aware that her mouth was dry and her legs were trembling under her. She took a gulp of chilled pineapple juice.

Talk? she thought desperately. What could he possibly want to talk about? Especially when she was so anxious to avoid any kind of *tête-à-tête*?

She wondered with sudden dread if he had come back to her door after all the previous night, and heard her weeping.

What am I going to say to him if so? she asked herself frantically. How can I possibly explain?

The worst-case scenario was that he intended to tell her

why he'd had second thoughts and walked away from her last night.

Because, however reasoned his explanation, she wasn't sure that she could bear to hear it. Knowing there was no place for her in his life was one thing. Hearing it from his own lips quite another.

Supposing her emotions got the better of her all over again?

'Oh, God,' she whispered to herself. That would be the ultimate humiliation. To weep for his favours in front of him.

And she couldn't let him arrive back and find her sitting like a bump on a log, staring at the food, either, she told herself with renewed determination. Somehow she had to make herself eat something, and do it with every sign of appetite and enjoyment. Everything normal in this best of all possible worlds.

She poured herself coffee, took a heartening swig, then cut the top off her egg and reached for a slice of toast.

'I started without you,' she said brightly as Ash returned and took a seat opposite her. 'I hope you don't mind?'

'Not at all,' he said politely. 'You may find this hard to believe, but I'm really quite tolerant.'

'I'll try to remember.' She forced down another spoonful of egg.

There was a pause, then he said, 'Laurent has been very complimentary about your French accent'

'Oh.' She flushed. 'That's—kind of him.'

'It's a pity we'll be at St Hilaire so soon,' he went on. 'Or you might have revealed even more hidden talents.'

'I doubt that,' Chellie returned shortly. 'I can sing and speak French. That doesn't amount to much.'

'And you can dance, too,' he said. 'We mustn't forget that,' he added silkily, a disturbing glint in his eyes. 'Even if the performance was a little—curtailed.'

Her face warmed. 'I'd prefer not to be reminded of that— any of it.'

'Well, there we differ,' he said, shrugging. 'Because it will always remain one of my most cherished memories.' He paused. 'So, where did you learn to speak French so well?'

Chellie hesitated. 'My mother was French,' she revealed reluctantly.

'Ah,' he said. 'Then that would explain "Michelle".'

She shook her head. 'Not exactly. I was named for my grandfather. He died just before I was born. Otherwise…'

Her voice faltered into silence, and Ash sent her a keen glance.

'Yes?' he prompted.

She stared down at her plate. 'Otherwise my father would never have agreed,' she said slowly, angry with herself for revealing so much. 'He always hated the name and had wanted me to be christened Elizabeth. In fact, that's what he started calling me after my mother died, until he was eventually persuaded it wasn't a good idea.'

He said lightly, 'A man of strong will. Who managed to talk him round?'

'My nanny,' she said. 'Our family doctor. My aunt Margaret.' She shrugged. 'Anyway, it doesn't really matter. It was all a long time ago.'

'Yet you've remembered it?'

She thought, *Oh, I remember more than that. The way he tried to remove every trace of my mother from the house, as if she'd never existed, or as if he'd demeaned himself by marrying a girl who was a foreigner and who'd worked as a cabaret singer. The way he tried to stifle my own interest in music.*

'Some things tend to stick.' She made her voice dismissive. 'Is that all you wanted to know?'

'It's not even a fraction of it,' Ash drawled, pouring himself more coffee.

'However, it's all I'm prepared to say on the subject.' She drew a breath. 'Now, may I ask a question? What time will we reach St Hilaire?'

'Early afternoon.'

'I see.' Chellie bit her lip. 'And you're quite sure I can't reach the consul over the weekend?'

'Don't even try,' he advised lazily. 'Not if you want him on your side. Anyway, what's the hurry?'

'It clearly hasn't occurred to you,' Chellie said tautly, 'that I might want to get on with the rest of my life.'

'No,' he admitted. 'I wasn't even aware you knew what form it was going to take.' He leaned back in his seat, eyelids drooping as he studied her. 'So, what do you have in mind?'

'That,' she said, 'is none of your damned business.'

'Wrong,' he said. 'According to the old saying, if you save someone's skin, then they belong to you for evermore. So I have a vested interest in your future, songbird. Not to mention that pretty hide of yours,' he added mockingly.

Chellie set her jaw. 'Until you get tired of playing Galahad, anyway,' she said stonily.

'I am not playing anything, Michelle.' Ash sounded weary. 'In fact, I'm bloody serious. So may we please stop fencing and start talking some sense?'

She flushed. 'Very well,' she said constrictedly. 'If we must.'

'Where do you intend to go after St Hilaire? Home?'

She hesitated. 'I have no home—in that sense. But I'll head for London, I suppose. I—know people there. There'll be someone I can stay with while I sort myself out.'

'My God,' he said.

'You don't approve?' She tilted her chin in challenge.

'I've had nightmares I've enjoyed more,' he said shortly.

'I've been staying with you,' Chellie objected. 'And you're a complete stranger.'

'How odd you should think that,' he said softly. 'When I feel as if I've known you all my life.'

Her throat tightened, making breathing difficult. The words seemed to hover in the air between them, but she couldn't think of a single comeback, or even meet his gaze.

So she busied herself instead with collecting up the used crockery.

Eventually he spoke again. 'Is someone else's sofa your only scheme?'

'At the moment. But please don't concern yourself. I'd be going to friends, you know.'

His brows lifted. 'Are these the same friends that allowed you to run away with your con-man boyfriend?'

She piled the dishes on to a tray. 'I didn't really tell them about Ramon. Certainly not what we were planning. I didn't mention that to anyone.'

'Why all the secrecy?'

She thought, *Because I was scared that word would somehow get back to my father and he'd find a way of stopping me. After all, he always had before…*

She shrugged. 'Up to then my life had been an open book,' she countered. 'I enjoyed having something to hide for once.' She paused. 'Besides, Ramon never really wanted to meet my friends.' She pulled a face. 'He said that he only wanted to be with me, not other people.'

'How sweet and caring of him,' Ash drawled.

'I thought so then,' Chellie returned, carrying the tray into the galley. 'But I won't be so naïve in future. I'll keep reminding myself that everyone has a hidden agenda.'

'That doesn't bode well for future relationships.'

Chellie was uneasily aware that he'd followed her and was standing only a couple of feet away, arms folded, leaning against the worktop.

'I'm not planning to have any.' She shrugged a casual shoulder. 'I intend to savour my independence.'

'I hear the words, songbird,' he said softly. 'But I'm not convinced. That beautiful bottom lip of yours is much too soft and generous for such a hardline attitude. One day you'll want to share your kisses—and your life.'

'And set myself up for another disappointment?' Her tone was suddenly ragged as she remembered last night—how she'd stared across at the door, her whole body aching with the consciousness of his presence on the other side of it. How she'd yearned—prayed for it to open. And how he'd left her, torn apart with longing and frustration and totally bereft.

She shook her head. 'I don't think so.'

There was an odd silence, then he said, 'I didn't realise that he'd got to you quite so deeply. I'm—sorry. But not all men are like Ramon. You'll learn to trust again, Michelle. I promise you will.'

'You should write a magazine column.' She kept her tone light and mocking. '"Advice for the dumped-on". As for promises,' she added casually. 'Just guarantee to get me to the consul on St Hilaire first thing on Monday morning and I'll be completely happy.'

'You think so?' he asked with sudden harshness. 'I say you're wrong, Michelle. In fact, right now, I doubt if you'll ever discover the true meaning of the word as long as you live.'

And he walked away, leaving her standing there, staring after him in shocked silence.

The road ran dizzyingly along the coast, allowing Chellie tantalising glimpses, through the clustering palm trees which fringed it, of silver beaches below and a sea shifting endlessly from shades of emerald to turquoise, through all the colours in between.

Not that she had much opportunity to be entranced. She was more preoccupied with retaining her seat in the Jeep that was taking her—somewhere.

The driver, Alphonse, was a cheerful soul with a wide grin, who whistled and hummed snatches of song while he drove.

She'd asked him in English and French where exactly they were heading, but had been answered with only a smiling shrug and a 'Not far,' which told her nothing.

She supposed the sensible course would have been to find out her eventual destination before getting into this bone-shaking vehicle and being jolted over roads little better than cart tracks in places, while she clung, white-knuckled, to the side of the Jeep.

But then, from what she'd seen so far, carts seemed to be the preferred form of transport.

Besides, she'd been so relieved to find that Ash was not coming with her that all other considerations had paled into insignificance.

Her last hours on board *La Belle Rêve* had not been easy. She had been at pains to keep out of Ash's way. She'd felt too raw and confused to risk another confrontation so soon. And he had seemed equally keen to avoid her.

Fortunately the approach to St Hilaire had provided a new focus, and she'd hung over the rail, scanning its high and rocky hinterland with genuine interest.

Laurent had come to lean beside her with a sigh of quiet satisfaction. 'Home at last.' He pointed to the tallest peak. 'That is L'Aiguille,' he told her. 'The Needle—our volcano. It is thanks to her and her little sisters around her, Les Epingles, that our island is so fertile and our crops grow so well.'

'Volcano?' Chellie repeated in a hollow voice. 'Is it dangerous?'

Laurent gave her a teasing glance. 'It is not considered in a fatal phase,' he said solemnly. 'You may climb up to the crater and inspect it for yourself, if you wish.'

She forced a smile. 'I think I'll pass. Besides, I won't really be around long enough for any sightseeing. I want to be on my way as soon as possible.'

'As soon as possible?' Laurent mused, and shook his head. 'I don't think we have a phrase for that in these islands.'

She laughed, then became aware that Ash was watching and moved away, going down to her stateroom. She packed a few judiciously chosen items from the closet and drawers into her bag, then changed into a cream linen dress, ornamented down the front by large black buttons, and slid her feet into low-heeled black pumps.

When she met the consul she needed to look like someone merely suffering from temporary financial embarrassment, she thought, rather than some pathetic waif or stray. And this outfit, by one of her own favourite designers, should do the trick.

They anchored in the middle of St Hilaire's surprisingly large harbour, and a launch arrived with promptitude to take them to shore.

Chellie couldn't help noticing that while Laurent was greeted with laughter and uproarious slaps on the back, Ash was treated with smiling respect, triggering all sorts of questions in her mind.

Questions, as she reminded herself, which were never likely to be answered.

As she stood hesitantly on the quayside, Laurent came over to her. 'Mam'selle Chellie.' He took her hand. 'I wish you *au revoir*. I look forward to hearing that you have become a great singer when we meet again.'

Unlikely on both counts, Chellie thought, as she smiled and murmured something non-committal.

She looked around, noting how the low red-roofed houses clung to the steep hillside above her in charmingly haphazard fashion. Confronting her was a row of warehouses, brightly painted, and there were a number of stalls offering fruit, vegetables, pottery and woven baskets.

'Your room's all arranged.' Ash appeared suddenly beside her, making her jump. 'I'm sorry I can't accompany you,' he added, without the least sign of regret. 'But I have things to do. Alphonse, here, will deliver you in perfect safety.' He signalled, and a tall, rangy man climbed down from the Jeep and took Chellie's bag for her.

Ash added no further explanation, wished her a perfunctory goodbye, and turned away.

And that, she told herself with a certain defiance as she got in the Jeep, was exactly—absolutely—what she wanted.

I have to stop thinking about him, she told herself force-fully as they drove off. Or I'm going to go mad. We've said goodbye, and now I'm on my own, in charge of my own destiny. I need to concentrate on that. Focus on the rest of my life—and taking the next step towards it.

She'd expected to be driven straight to some small hotel in St Hilaire itself, but the capital was long behind them now, and still the Jeep lurched on its precarious way.

In spite of her attempt at positive thinking, there was a rawness deep inside her, and an odd sense of disorientation, not lessened by this unexpected journey.

She could only imagine they were destined for some se-cluded tourist resort in an exclusive corner of the island, and while the idea of some rest and relaxation beckoned seductively, it wasn't really convenient to be marooned so far from the hub of the capital. Especially, she thought broodingly, when she needed to present herself at the con-sular office first thing on Monday morning.

Perhaps that consideration had slipped Ash's mind, but she didn't think so. He didn't strike her as someone who forgot much. Or nothing, anyway, that he wanted to remem-ber…

But then what did she know? He'd revealed so little of himself during their brief time together that he was still a cross between an enigma and a chameleon. Always chang-ing, she thought with a stifled sigh, like the restless sea beneath the cliffs.

And paused, her hand flying in shock to her mouth as she too remembered something.

My passport, she thought, horrified. Oh, God, he still has it.

She turned to Alphonse. She said in French, 'We must go back to the town. Find Monsieur Brennan. It is very important. A matter of life and death.'

But Alphonse merely grinned at her, said something that was apparently meant to be soothing in some incomprehen-sible local *patois*, and drove on.

She tried again. 'No, you must turn round. I really need to go back.'

For a moment she thought he was going to do as he asked, because he turned the wheel suddenly, swinging the Jeep across the road almost at a right angle and startling a small yelp from her.

But, instead of completing the expected U-turn, he left the coast road altogether, taking a narrow dusty track that Chellie had not even noticed was there, and she found herself being driven downhill between tall hibiscus hedges.

'Where are we?' she demanded breathlessly, and Alphonse pointed ahead to a wooden archway, with the single word 'Arcadie' carved into its overhead timbers.

I suppose that's meant to convey something, Chellie thought with rising vexation. When am I going to start getting some straight answers round here?

They seemed to be descending into a steep valley, plunging into a green tunnel where overhanging foliage almost blocked out the sun. Through the trees, she could just glimpse the lines of a tiled roof.

Clinging on like grim death, as the Jeep lurched and bounced, she gasped out, 'Is that the hotel—the place where you're taking me?'

Alphonse flashed her a grin. *'Oui, mademoiselle. C'est Arcadie.'*

'But I won't be able to stay there.' She tried to speak clearly and concisely above the roar of the engine. 'I'll need my passport to register, and Mr Brennan has it. He forgot to give it to me and I have to get it back. Do you understand?'

Alphonse nodded, still smiling, and drove on without slackening his pace by one iota.

Nuts, Chellie told herself helplessly. He must be. I'm driving round with the local fruitcake.

And if the building below was a hotel, it was a pretty small one, she thought, a frown creasing her brow. There could be supplementary cabins dotted round the grounds, but so far she hadn't spotted any sign of them.

Nor could she see any flash of blue water suggesting that Hotel Arcadie boasted a swimming pool, and that was a disappointment. St Hilaire might not be a leader in the Caribbean tourist industry, but surely whatever hotels it possessed should be expected to have the usual amenities.

And, she realised, she'd been looking forward to a swim.

In her old life in London, swimming had been one of her favourite forms of exercise—apart from dancing. In the pool near her home she'd swum in the early morning, pushing herself almost to the limit of exhaustion. Distancing herself from the devils of boredom and frustration that had plagued her so often.

Here, she had other frustrations to work through—other demons to exorcise—and the prospect of stretching her limbs in cool water—restoring her body to fitness—had been irresistible.

A cold shower wouldn't be the same thing at all, she thought wryly. That was, of course, if the hotel was sophisticated enough to have bathrooms. She didn't even know that for certain.

But when they eventually emerged from the overhanging trees into full sunlight, and she was able to take her first proper look at Arcadie, she had to admit that she'd been unfair. Because it certainly lived up to its name.

It was a gracious two-storey building, standing square and painted white, its roof tiled in faded terracotta. It was surrounded by well-kept lawns of coarse grass and flowerbeds that were a sheer riot of colour.

A shady verandah encircled the ground floor, guarding long shuttered windows, and a balcony with a wooden balustrade surrounded the first floor.

It was very still, only the harsh cry of a bird breaking the welcome silence as the Jeep stopped.

Chellie saw that the main door was open, and an elderly

man with grizzled hair stood waiting in the shade of the pillared portico.

He came forward and opened the passenger door, lifting down Chellie's bag and offering her a hand to assist her descent.

'*Mademoiselle.*' He wore dark trousers and a pristine white linen coat, and his smile was grave and polite. 'My name is Cornelius. Welcome to Arcadie.'

Chellie got down stiffly, resisting the temptation to rub the bits that ached from that headlong journey. She felt hot and sticky, and was aware that the dress she'd worn to impress was creased and dusty.

She took a deep breath. 'I'm sorry, but there's been a mistake,' she began, then whirled round, gasping, as the Jeep's engine roared into life again and the vehicle took off in another swirl of dust, with a cheery backward wave from Alphonse.

'Hell's bells.' Ridiculously, she tried to run after it. 'Don't go,' she yelled. '*Ne me quittez pas.* You can't leave me stranded here. You *can't*…'

'You must not disturb yourself, *mademoiselle*.' Cornelius's voice was soothing as he came to her side. He took her arm and began to urge her gently but firmly towards the door. 'All is well, and you are quite safe. I will show you your room, then Rosalie, my wife, will make you some iced tea.'

Chellie stared at him. 'If you're the owner, then there's something you should know,' she said, swallowing. 'I've been brought here under false pretences. You see, I've no passport or money either, and I needed the driver to take me back to town so that I could sort something out.'

'Neither are required, *mademoiselle*. And I am not the owner of Arcadie, merely an employee. Whereas you, of course, are an honoured guest.'

They were inside now, in a spacious hall kept cool by the gentle movement of a ceiling fan. The walls were painted ivory, and the floor had been constructed from some wood the colour of warm honey.

Apart from a carved wooden chest supporting a ceramic bowl heavy with blue and crimson flowers, the hall was empty. There was no sign of a reception desk, or any of the other paraphernalia of hotel life.

Just a wide curving flight of stairs in the same honeyed wood—which she was being encouraged towards, she realised.

She hung back. 'It's very—quiet. So, how many more are there? Honoured guests, I mean?'

'As yet, you are the only one, Mademoiselle Greer.'

'I see.' It wasn't true, but there seemed little point in hanging around arguing the point, so she followed Cornelius up the stairs, the polished banister smooth under her hand. The only touch of reality in a confusing world, she thought.

She said, 'Has the hotel only just opened for business, then?'

'Hotel?' Cornelius halted, glancing back at her in obvious astonishment. 'Arcadie is a private house, *mademoiselle*. You are here at the invitation of the owner, Mist' Howard.'

Chellie's hand tightened on the rail. 'But there must be some mistake,' she said, trying to speak calmly. 'I don't know any such person. Is he here? I—I'd better speak to him at once…'

'I regret—Mist' Howard is in America.'

'In America?' she repeated, stunned. 'Then how could he…?' Her voice tailed away as realisation began to dawn.

'Ah,' she said softly, between her teeth. 'I think I understand.'

So this was the arrangement Ash Brennan had made, she thought smouldering. Once more he was presuming on his employer's good nature, it seemed. He must be awfully sure of his position in the family to take such advantage. But then he was going to be his boss's son in law—wasn't he?

She forced a smile. 'Tell me, Cornelius, does your Mr Howard own a boat called *La Belle Rêve*,' by any chance?'

'*Mais, bien sûr, mademoiselle.*' He gave her an anxious look. 'There is a problem? You still wish to leave?'

'No, not at all.' Chellie gave an airy shrug. 'Why shouldn't I stay in his house? After all, I've enjoyed so much of his hospitality already in the last few days.' She ticked off on her fingers. 'I've sailed on his boat, eaten his food, and I'm even wearing his daughter's clothes, so what does one more thing matter?' She paused again. 'I presume he *does* have a daughter?' She tried to make her voice casual.

Cornelius nodded. 'Indeed, *mademoiselle.*' There was fondness in his tone. 'Mademoiselle Julie is with him in Florida.'

'How delightful,' Chellie said brightly. 'All the same, I hope I'm not sleeping in her room. I should hate her to arrive and find it occupied.' In fact, I should hate her to arrive, period, she added silently, her memory serving up the image of the smiling blonde in the photograph.

'You have been given the guest suite, *mademoiselle.*' Cornelius sounded faintly shocked. 'But neither Mist' Howard or *Mam'selle* are expected.'

Good, thought Chellie, and meant it.

But, in spite of her misgivings, she could not help but be enchanted by her accommodation. An airy sitting room, furnished with a brightly cushioned rattan sofa and chairs, opened into a large bedroom, with soft turquoise walls and filmy white drapes billowing gently in the faint breeze from the open window.

The low, wide bed had a quilted coverlet, patterned in shades of turquoise and white, and the ivory and gold tiled bathroom held a deep tub, as well as a walk-in shower with glass screens.

Chellie was suddenly aware that tears were not far away. All this comfort—all this beauty, she thought, for someone frankly fraying at the edges.

She said huskily, 'It—it's wonderful, Cornelius. Thank you.'

He inclined his head, looking pleased. He said, 'If you give your dress to Rosalie, *mademoiselle*, she will have it laundered for you.'

Of course, she thought, as the door closed behind him. As her father's daughter, this was the kind of service she had been taught to expect. Yet she'd never really appreciated it until this moment.

She stripped, and had a long, luxurious shower, hoping to wash away the blues, then changed into a pair of cream cut-offs and a black vest top. She slipped on a pair of light canvas shoes, and ventured downstairs.

A large woman in a striped cotton dress came surging to meet her, the dark eyes flicking over Chellie in a swift, shrewd assessment that in no way detracted from the warmth of her smile.

'You would like some refreshment, *mademoiselle*—iced tea, or maybe pineapple juice?' She whisked Chellie through a sitting room replete with large squashy sofas and low tables, and out through sliding glass doors to the verandah at the back of the house, where a table and chairs had been set and a tray awaited, set with covered jugs and glasses.

'It looks lovely,' Chellie said, with a little sigh of pleasure. 'May I have some tea, please?'

She watched as Rosalie poured the tea with a satisfying clink of ice cubes, and took the glass she was offered.

One sip convinced her that it was the best iced tea she'd ever tasted, full of flavour and not too sweet, and so she told Rosalie, who looked quietly gratified.

Encouraged by this, Chellie decided on another tack. 'It's good of you to go to all this trouble,' she said. 'After all, it can't have been convenient to have me dumped on you at such short notice.' She paused. 'I thought Mr Brennan was sending me to a hotel.'

Rosalie dismissed all hotels with a wave of her hand, lips pursed disapprovingly. 'You are Mist' Ash's friend, *mam'selle*, so where else would you stay? Mr Howard would wish you to be here.'

Would he? I wonder, Chellie thought, her own mouth twisting. And is that really what I am—Ash's friend? He wasn't very friendly when we parted.

Which reminded her. She said 'Rosalie, I need to contact Mr Ash fairly urgently. Would it be possible for me to call him on the telephone in St Hilaire?'

'Mist' Ash?' the older woman repeated, setting the jug back on the tray and arranging its beaded muslin cover with minute care. She shook her head. 'I don't know, *mam'selle*. Don't know where he might be.'

'But it isn't a huge place,' Chellie protested. 'Surely you must be able to reach him somewhere.'

Rosalie folded her hands in front of her. 'It's not easy, *mam'selle*. But I ask Cornelius,' she added with the air of one making a major concession.

Chellie sighed in silent perplexity as Rosalie went back into the house. Another dead end, it seemed. Or was she being deliberately blocked? Surely not. Yet Laurent had indicated that Ash had his own place on the island, which must mean an address—a phone number.

Unless he'd given instructions that he wasn't to be contacted—particularly by her. Maybe he'd decided it was time to draw a line, once and for all, under this strange stop-go relationship.

Shaking off the faint feeling of desolation assailing her, she settled herself back against the cushions of her wicker lounger and drank some more tea. A climbing plant, heavy with blossom, was spilling over the balustrade, and a huge butterfly with pale velvety wings was busy among the flowers.

There was a flash of green and gold, and a parrot flew across the grass and vanished into a nearby tree.

Arcadia indeed, she thought, drawing a swift, delighted breath. But she could not allow herself to relax and enjoy it too much. Her presence here was a strictly temporary measure, and she must never forget it.

Another twenty-four hours and I'll be gone, she told herself, and all this will be behind me. And perhaps then I can start to forget—and to heal. And she sighed again, wishing with all her heart that she could believe that.

CHAPTER EIGHT

AT THE time it had seemed like a good idea to go for a stroll. To explore Arcadie beyond the immediate confines of the garden.

Now, with the sun baking on her back, an escort of persistent insects, and an apparently impenetrable wall of greenery in front of her, Chellie was having second thoughts.

But she'd needed to do something, she argued as she pushed forward, parting the thick, fleshy leaves that impeded her, looking for the track which she'd been following but seemed to have temporarily mislaid.

Oh, come on, she told herself impatiently. It's here somewhere. It has to be.

It would have been much easier to stay on the verandah, drinking more tea and finishing the plate of tiny cinammon biscuits that Rosalie had supplied along with it.

But she would only have started to brood—to let her thoughts take her down paths even more hazardous than the one she was now embarked on, which seemed to have led her into the middle of a rainforest.

And over it all hung the mountain. Not the Needle itself, but one of the smaller Pins, yet composed of grey volcanic rock just the same.

It took guts to make a home in such a place, she thought. It was so beautiful, but so savage and unpredictable at the same time.

Someone had once said that volcanoes never really died, but merely slept, and she could only hope that they were wrong.

She found herself almost regretting that she would never

meet Mr Howard, the intrepid man who'd built his house here, daring the dark gods of hurricanes and seismic upheavals to do their worst.

Beyond the tailored lawns round the house the wilderness waited, primitive and still untamed. And she should not be taking any more risks here. She'd undergone enough ordeals lately to last her a lifetime. Now she really needed to step back into civilisation and stay there.

I should turn back, she thought. So why don't I?

Well, for one thing, the walk might do her good. It might even encourage her appetite too. Rosalie had told her when she came for the tray that dinner would be at eight-thirty, and she looked like a woman who took her cooking seriously, and would insist on it being shown due respect.

But at the moment Chellie felt too edgy for hunger. Because Rosalie had also brought the unwelcome news that neither she nor Cornelius had a number where Ash could be reached. *Impasse.*

Arcadie was a beautiful house, and its valley setting was spectacular, but it was in the middle of nowhere.

No one asked me, she thought restively, if I wished to be cut off from the known world. At the moment, my only way out of here is to walk. There are no locks or bolts, but I feel like a prisoner just the same.

But now, like a ray of hope, here was the track again, and somewhere ahead of her, she thought, frowning, was the unmistakable splash of water.

She walked carefully, trying not to twist her ankle on the thick roots which made every step a hazard. She ducked under an overhanging branch, straightened, then stood openmouthed, staring in delight at the scene in front of her.

Her ears had not deceived her. The little waterfall she'd heard sprang straight from the grey rock, spilling some ten feet into a deep natural basin, yet barely ruffling its surface.

Here at last was the swimming pool she'd longed for. And it must be safe, because someone had constructed a small diving board, which waited invitingly. Almost beckoning to her.

One of the accompanying insects grazed her skin, and she brushed it aside impatiently, her eyes fixed on the sky and the light puffs of cloud reflected back by the clear water. Already imagining its caress.

She could, of course, go back to the house and fetch the solitary swimsuit she'd brought with her.

On the other hand…

Impulsively, she kicked off her shoes, then stripped off the vest top, dropping it on to the slab of flat rock beside the diving board. She peeled down the cotton pants, and the lacy briefs she wore beneath them, then walked to the end of the board, positioned herself, and dived in.

The water felt tinglingly fresh and cold against her overheated skin. She let herself go down into the seemingly endless depths, then kicked for the surface, coming up, gasping and laughing, into the sunlight.

She'd never swum naked before, and found herself almost guiltily relishing the intensity of the sensation.

She plunged briefly again, then began to swim in earnest, her body instinctively finding its own smooth rhythm, her muscles working in co-ordination against the strong pull of the water.

Oh, but she'd missed this, she thought, as eventually she twisted sinuously on to her back and floated, staring up at the blue arc of the sky. For the first time in many weeks she felt almost at peace with herself.

If ever I have a boat of my own, she thought, I'll call it *Naiad* in memory of this afternoon.

It was ludicrous in her situation to make any kind of plan, but she had to be optimistic, imagine a future where she was in control and prospering. And owning a boat…

Everyone needs something to aim for, she told herself.

She swam slowly over to the waterfall and pulled herself up on to the slippery rock at its base. She stood upright under the cascade and lifted her face to the pouring water, revelling at the sting of it against her skin, the cold lash of the torrent driving at her stomach and thighs, urgent against her breasts. Chellie, gripping the wet rock to steady herself, was aware that her nipples were hardening in involuntary response.

She was completely, almost voluptuously engrossed in the sheer physicality of the moment, yet some strange, almost animal instinct made her turn her head and glance over her shoulder.

Ash was standing on the other side of the pool, hands on hips and head slightly thrown back as he watched her. He looked casual, but the utter stillness of his stance betrayed him.

And she too was betrayed, her clothes lying in a pile at his feet. Unreachable.

For a few seconds she was frozen, her mind working feverishly. The temptation, of course, was to try to cover herself with her hands. But that was too much of a cliché, and besides, it sent out the signal that she wanted him to go on looking…

And I do, she thought. God help me, but I do.

There was only one other solution, and she took it swiftly and fiercely, jumping back into the pool, then treading water so that only her head and shoulders were visible.

'What the hell are you doing here?' She made her tone challenging.

'I invited myself to dinner,' he said. 'Rosalie's fish stew is renowned throughout the islands, and quite irresistible.' He paused. 'Like so much else at Arcadie.'

Chellie's mouth tightened. 'I mean why are you *here*? Now, and at this particular spot?'

He shrugged. 'Because this is my favourite place on the estate, and somehow I guessed you would find your way here too.' He smiled at her. 'It's a good place to be—isn't it?'

'Wonderful,' Chellie said crisply. 'But getting chilly now. So, I'd like to get out and get dressed. If you don't mind.'

'That's fine with me.' His voice was equable. 'But it can be a scramble when you're not used to it. You'd better take my hand.'

Chellie gasped. 'Like hell I will.'

'Do you have a choice?'

'Yes,' she said, trying to stop her teeth from chattering. 'I can stay here until you have the decency to go.'

'It's a little late to be prim, don't you think?' There was a ghost of laughter in his voice. 'Especially when the image of you standing under the cascade is now irrevocably etched into my brain.'

He paused for a moment, then began slowly to unbutton the white shirt he was wearing with immaculately pressed dark pants. 'Of course,' he said, 'I could always come in and join you. It's very hot today, and a little—stimulation might be pleasant.'

The breath caught in her throat. 'Don't you dare,' she said grittily. 'Don't you *bloody* dare.'

He laughed. 'You mean this pool isn't big enough for both of us? Well, you could be right. But you've also been in there quite long enough.'

He squatted down and held out his hand to her. 'Come on, take it before you get hypothermia,' he commanded. 'I'll even close my eyes if it will make you feel better,' he added caustically.

She swam a little closer. Warily. 'Then will you go—please?'

'No,' he said. 'But I will promise to turn my back.'

Which was like shutting the stable door when the horse was long gone, Chellie realised, fulminating.

She supposed that she could always stay where she was and brazen it out. Call his bluff. Except that she didn't feel very brazen. She felt cold, and shy, and hideously embarrassed. And not too far from tears either. Besides, Ash might not be bluffing.

Biting her lip hard, she swam to where he was waiting, eyes obediently closed. His fingers were warm and strong as they gripped hers, and she felt an unwelcome shock of pleasure at his touch.

She found a toehold under the water, and used it to push herself upwards, landing breathless and flurried on the rock beside him.

She said tautly, 'Thank you. Now turn your back, please.'

'As you wish.' He sounded as if he was grinning. 'May I say you looked much lovelier when you weren't blue with cold,' he added softly.

'Is that a fact?' Chellie said between her teeth, snatching up her clothes and holding them protectively against her. 'Well, you'll still be a bastard, no matter what colour you turn.'

'Tut, tut, Miss Greer,' Ash mocked. 'How very uptight you are. Anyone would think you'd never been skinny-dipping before.'

Chellie, desperately trying to force on her clothes over uncomfortably damp skin, didn't answer.

'That's it, isn't it?' he said slowly, after a pause. 'You never *have* done it—have you, Michelle? Another addition to the long list of experiences I suspect you've missed out on.'

'Then kindly keep your speculation to yourself,' Chellie flashed, dragging on her vest top and noting with alarm how revealingly it clung now, outlining her taut nipples in exquisite detail. 'My life is my own business.'

'You forget,' he said. 'As I told you before, I saved your life, which makes it mine now.'

'Well, I don't believe in ridiculous superstitions, and I belong to myself alone.'

'Alone?' Ash mused. 'Now, there's a chilly word.'

'How odd you should think so,' Chellie said coolly. 'Now, to me all it says is—independence.' She paused. 'And I'm dressed now.'

He turned back, scanning her, his eyes lingering unashamedly on the thrust of her breasts. 'So you are,' he said softly, his mouth twisting. 'But memory is a wonderful thing.'

'My vote goes to total amnesia,' she threw back at him. 'I'd give a lot to wipe out the events of the past few weeks—and especially the last forty-eight hours.'

His voice hardened. 'But unfortunately we're both stuck with them, Michelle, and there's no way out. So why don't we agree to make the best of things in the time we have left?' He paused. 'Rosalie and Cornelius believe we're friends, so I'd prefer to preserve the illusion.'

He held back the leaves of a tall shrub to enable her to pass.

'So, what do you think of Arcadie?' he added in a tone of polite enquiry.

'It's—amazing.' Chellie hesitated. 'This Mr Howard seems to have given you the total run of his house as well as his boat. You must be—lose.'

Ash shrugged. 'We've known each other a long time.'

And Julie? She thought the question, but did not dare ask it. Besides, didn't she already know the answer?

Hurriedly, she changed the subject. 'My passport,' she said. 'You forget to give it to me when we landed. Have you brought it with you?'

'Actually, no. It must still be on the boat. ' His sideways glance was faintly mocking. 'But don't worry. It's in a very safe place.'

'Yes,' Chellie said icily. 'I'm well aware of that.'

'I thought you would be,' he murmured. 'But full marks for trying.'

Chellie, trying in spite of everything to stalk ahead of him with dignity, nearly removed an eye on an intrusive branch.

When they finally reached the lawns, within sight of the house, she wheeled and faced him. 'Tell me something. We've established what you're doing here—you've come for Rosalie's fish stew. But what I don't understand is why

I should be stranded out in the wilds instead of staying in St Hilaire.'

'I'm sorry you feel stranded,' Ash said, after a pause. 'I arranged for you to be brought here because it's quiet and beautiful.'

'Yes, it is,' Chellie agreed. 'But it's also very isolated.'

'Surely that's part of its charm,' he returned. 'It's where I come when I need to chill out—do some thinking—get myself together for some reason. I hoped that was how it would appeal to you too.'

His voice dropped. 'And when I realised you'd found the pool I was convinced of it. Because for me that's the most magical place on the island.' His smile was wry. 'And from now on its enchantment will be doubled.'

Chellie bent her head, avoiding the intensity of his gaze, aware that her heart was fluttering like the wings of a trapped bird. She said, 'Don't—please…'

'Why not?' he asked quietly. 'Because at last I got to fulfil my fantasy? Because you were so lovely—and so vulnerable—that I would have walked across that water to reach you if you'd given me one sign? And because the image of every exquisite inch of you will haunt me for ever? Is that why you want me to keep silent?'

Colour stormed her face. She said in a stifled voice, 'You—must not say these things to me. You have no right…'

'No,' he said, and there was an odd note in his voice that sounded almost violent. 'You're quite correct, I don't. No right at all. But no amount of moral rectitude can stop me wishing. Just remember that.'

Chellie watched him stride away.

One sign, he'd said. *If you'd given me one sign.*

And only she would ever know how fatally close she'd come to doing exactly that. That she'd felt the force of his desire shiver like a warm, sweet wind over her naked body, and that for one brief, treacherous moment she'd gloried in it.

Fortunately she'd come to her senses in time, but every moment she spent in Ash's company represented real danger, and she had to be aware of that.

Her mouth twisted in a small, sad smile. 'But nothing can stop me wishing either,' she whispered, and made her way slowly back to the house.

In spite of the heat, Chellie felt cold and clammy when she reached her room. She stripped off her damp clothing and towelled herself down vigorously until her skin began to glow. She was just fastening the belt on the cream cotton robe that she'd found hanging in the closet when there was a knock on the bedroom door.

For a moment she tensed, wondering if it was Ash outside on the landing. Half-wishing for it to be so, but half-dreading it too. If she kept quiet, she thought, her visitor might deduce that she wasn't there and leave.

But there was a second, louder rap, and Rosalie's voice said, '*Mam'selle*, I have something for you.'

Chellie found herself sighing inwardly, and trailed over to open the door. Rosalie, smiling broadly, was holding a large flat box.

'This is yours, *mam'selle*. Mist' Ash says you left it behind.'

Chellie frowned in bewilderment. 'I think there's some mistake…'

Rosalie shook her head. 'It belongs to you, *mam'selle*. Mist' Ash said so.' Her voice was kind but firm.

'I think,' Chellie said, with a touch of grimness, 'I'd better have a word with Mist' Ash.'

'Oh, he's not here,' Rosalie informed her cheerfully. 'He had to go out, but he'll be back for dinner.' She gave a rich chuckle. 'He wouldn't miss my stew, that one.'

She planted the box into Chellie's reluctant hands and went off, humming a tune.

Chellie put the box down on the bed as if she was expecting it to explode. Everything she owned, and a lot that she didn't, was here with her, she thought, her frown deepening. She had no other possessions, and he knew it. So what was he playing at?

Gingerly, she raised the lid and parted the folds of tissue inside, catching her breath as she saw what was lying there. She lifted out the folds of grey silky fabric and held it against her. It was a dress, its mid-calf skirt cut on the bias, its bodice straight with narrow straps, and as she turned in front of the mirror she saw the faintly iridescent material change from pewter to silver with the movement.

The subtle colour enhanced the creaminess of her skin and the darkness of her hair. It was, she thought, exactly what she'd have chosen for herself.

A tiny voice in her head whispered, Try it on. But common sense told her to put it back in its box and never look at it again. Because she knew if she tried it that it would fit, and that she would not want to take it off again. And one of her main priorities must be to sever even the most fragile contact between Ash and herself.

She sighed, and began to re-fold the dress, her hands reluctant. As she did so, she noticed a slip of paper had fallen to the floor.

She retrieved it, and read the few hand-written words. It said simply:

Chellie, this is no big deal, so please don't throw it back at me.

And under his signature was a PS.

We could always pretend it's your birthday.

Chellie sank down on the edge of the bed and read the note over and over again until the words began to blur.

Where, she wondered bitterly, had Ash acquired this effortless ability to head her off at the pass?

Refusing to wear his gift now would only make her look at best ungracious, and at worst ridiculous, making a great fuss about nothing.

Except that it wasn't nothing, she thought with sudden anguish. In fact, it mattered far too much.

It occurred to her, without self-pity, that this was probably the first present a man had ever bought for her. And that included her father, whose gifts had always come via the nanny when she was little and his secretary when she was older.

Which made this all the more special, she thought with a stifled sigh, smoothing the fabric gently. And all the more taboo.

How could a man she hardly knew get something so completely right? she asked herself with a kind of desperation. Because in so many ways Ash was still a virtual stranger to her, and she must never forget that.

She might have been reticent, but she knew nothing about his own family—if he had one—or his background, which was clearly chequered. Maybe it was best to remain in ignorance, especially if he wasn't prepared to volunteer any information.

Their lives had touched—and that was all.

So why did their brief contact with each other seem infinitely more than that?

What made her feel that length of time, in itself, meant nothing? That in some strange way her whole life had been geared to meeting Ash, and that somehow it didn't matter that their acquaintance with each other could be measured in hours rather than years?

As soon as I saw him I knew, she thought with sudden helplessness. Knew that he was the one I'd always been waiting for. But why didn't Fate warn me that there could be no happy ending? That he was heavily involved with pretty blonde Julie, who probably has no shadows in her life or bitter mistakes to put right?

Why didn't my instincts tell me that, although my life

may belong to him, I never can? Because that's quite impossible, as he's made clear more than once.

He may be tempted, but he's also committed elsewhere. And he's not going to let a chance encounter spoil something good and real for him. A chance to leave the past behind him and establish himself, perhaps.

How could I have looked at him that night at Mama Rita's and not realised this? she wondered. Not seen that he was forbidden fruit? That he would always be prepared to step back out of the danger zone?

Because then, maybe, I could have saved myself a lifetime of heartache.

'"The joys of love",' she whispered sadly, wrapping her arms round her body, '"are but a moment long".'

But if I was offered that moment, she thought with sudden fierceness, I'd take it, and to hell with the consequences. I wouldn't make waves, or demand more than he was prepared to give. And at least I'd have something—some precious memory to take into the empty future.

Apart from this beautiful dress that she could not wear but which she would keep for ever.

She put the lid gently back on the box and tore up the note into infinitesimal pieces. Then she walked out on to the balcony and sat down on one of the cushioned loungers to watch the sunset. And to think.

She stayed in her room until the last possible moment. It was strange, but the black dress she'd brought from Mama Rita's no longer seemed quite so tacky, she thought, viewing herself in the full-length mirror. On the contrary, against the faint honey tan she'd acquired it looked cool and sexy.

But would that be enough? Would *she* be enough?

Well, she thought, straightening her shoulders. This was her chance to find out.

Ash was in the sitting room, standing by the long glazed doors leading to the verandah, staring into the darkness, drink in hand.

As Chellie came hesitantly into the room he turned to look at her, his brows lifting as he scanned the uncovered shoulders and the long, slim tanned legs revealed by the brief skirt. There was a slow and tingling silence. Then he raised his glass, the blue eyes hooded, his mouth smiling faintly. He said softly, 'Not your birthday, after all. But mine, perhaps.' The words lingered tantalisingly in the air.

Chellie shrugged. 'I decided to stick to familiar territory.'

'Very brave,' he said. 'In view of the memories it must revive.'

She lifted her chin, meeting his gaze squarely. 'Oh, they weren't all bad.' She paused. 'But the dress you sent me was spectacular,' she added with assumed nonchalance. 'For someone who sails other people's boats for a living, you clearly know a lot about women's clothes.'

'There's probably a cheap crack just waiting to be made,' Ash drawled. 'But I'll pass.'

'Very wise,' she said. 'And I'm sure you'll find some other lucky lady to benefit from your good taste.'

'I bought it for you.' His mouth tightened. 'It can't have been pleasant—having to wear someone else's clothes all the time on top of everything else that's happened recently. Just for once, I wanted you to have something that was all your own.'

Pain twisted inside her. She thought, *And I want that too—so badly.*

Aloud, she said stiltedly, 'Well—that's—a very kind thought.'

Or is it? she wondered. Could it be that he just doesn't like seeing me in his lady's clothes? That was another distinct possibility and it stung her to the core.

'And here's another thought, even kinder.' He walked to a side-table and picked up a jug. 'Let me introduce you to Planter's Punch—Cornelius-style. It's well worth trying— but strictly in moderation,' he added, pouring some of the liquid into a tumbler and adding ice, sliced lemon and a sprig of mint.

Chellie took a cautious sip, and blenched. 'Hell's bells—what's in it?'

'Apart from local rum, I haven't the vaguest idea.' Ash shrugged. 'Corney plays his cards close to his chest.'

'Corney?' She forced a smile. 'He seems far too dignified for nicknames.'

'Perhaps,' he said. 'But he forgives me a great deal.'

She took another sip, sending him a glinting look from beneath her lashes. 'I wonder what range of sins that covers?'

'Better,' he said, 'not to go there, I think. Although you'd probably be disappointed.'

She ran the tip of her tongue round her lips. 'You're saying that Cornelius has never had a serious strain placed on his loyalty? You amaze me.'

'I didn't think,' he said, 'that I was saying very much at all.'

'No,' she mused. 'You're very restrained. Or do I mean constrained? I'm not really sure.'

'Put that down,' he said, 'to the Planter's Punch. It attacks the brain cells and destroys rational thought, not to mention behaviour. Let me save you from yourself.' He took the glass from her hand and placed it on a nearby table. 'And now I think it's time we were going into dinner.'

Chellie hung back. She said in a low voice, 'Perhaps I don't want to be saved. Has that occurred to you?'

Ash paused, looking down at her, his expression wry. He said, 'A lot of things have occurred to me, and when we've eaten you and I need to have a serious talk. Now, come on, before Rosalie gets cross.'

It seemed, Chellie thought as, subdued, she followed him across the hall to a low-ceilinged dining room, its long table gleaming with silver and crystal, that she'd gambled and lost on the first throw.

But, in spite of everything, the delicious meal that followed was bound to lift her spirits to some extent. They began with a chilled avocado soup, followed by the hot and

spicy fish stew, served with sweet potatoes and a green vegetable that she didn't recognise, but which, Ash told her,
was called callaloo. Accompanying this was a pale, dry
white wine, crisp and clear on the palate to offset the rich
food. To finish, there were mango sorbets, and a wonderful
creamy pudding tasting of coconut.

Ash kept the conversation general, chatting mainly about
the island's history and its plans for the future, the modest
expansion of tourism, making her relax and respond in spite
of herself.

But then he was bound to keep off personal topics, she
realised, in deference to the presence of Cornelius, who was
waiting at table.

Acting as chaperon, perhaps? she thought drily. Looking
out for the interests of the owner's daughter.

But when the meal was over, and coffee and brandies
were served, she was surprised to hear Cornelius wishing
them goodnight.

'Thanks, Corney.' Ash sent him a swift smile. 'And tell
Rosalie that her fish stew still has no rivals.'

Cornelius acknowledged the compliment with a benign
nod, and withdrew.

'And now,' Ash said quietly, 'we have things to discuss.'
He paused, reaching into his back pocket and producing her
passport, which he pushed across the candlelit table. 'I got
you this.'

'Oh.' For a moment she was completely taken aback.
'Well—thank you.' She picked it up. 'Did you make a special trip to St Hilaire before dinner to collect it?'

Ash shrugged. 'It seemed to be an issue. It was time to
resolve it.'

Chellie smiled extra-brightly. 'In time to prove my identity to the consul on Monday?'

'If you want to wait till then.' He was leaning back in
his chair and she could not see his expression.

She said, 'I don't understand. What alternative do I

have?' And felt her heart begin to thud in excitement as she wondered what he was going to say.

'If I lent you some money you could be out of here to-morrow,' he said abruptly. 'You could take a local plane to Barbados or Grenada, and branch off from there to anywhere you wanted.'

There was a silence. Her hands were trembling, and she clasped them together tightly in her lap under the shelter of the table.

'Why would I wish to do that?'

'Because, as you've said, you need to get on with your life. This could help you on your way.'

'It's good of you,' she said slowly. 'But I think you've done enough. I'm a British citizen in trouble, and the consul is obliged to help me.'

'So, what are you going to tell him?' Ash asked laconically. 'Are you going to spill the beans about Ramon and Mama Rita's?' He shook his head. 'I don't think he'll be too impressed. Whereas I already know about your various misfortunes. Think about it. Sleep on it, and I'll come back for your answer in the morning.'

'You're not staying here tonight?' The question was too quick, too urgent, and Chellie felt her face warm.

There was a brief pause, then, 'I decided against it,' he said.

'I see.' Chellie pushed back her chair and rose. 'Please don't let me detain you.'

The sitting room was lit with shaded lamps when she marched in, her head held high, and unexpectedly there was music, with a slow, sensuous, unfamiliar rhythm, playing softly from a concealed system.

'You left your brandy.' Ash had followed her.

'I probably shouldn't have any more alcohol,' she told him curtly. 'Or I might say and do something I could regret.'

He sighed. 'Chellie, I've approached all this in the wrong way. Made a complete mess of it.'

'On the contrary,' she said. 'Everything's crystal-clear.

You need to get on with your own life too, and you can't do that while you still feel responsible for me. So it would be convenient if I was out of the way.' She gave a taut smile. 'So maybe I'll take you up on your offer, after all.'

'Understand this,' Ash said. 'I am not trying to get rid of you. At least, not in the way you think.'

'How many ways are there?' she demanded raggedly. 'Not that it matters. Because I don't have to sleep on it. I'll take your kind offer, and be out of here tomorrow.' She paused. 'And I'll pay you back every single cent,' she added fiercely. 'No matter how long it takes.'

'In that case,' he said, apparently unmoved by her vehemence, let's drink a toast—to the future.'

Chellie shrugged and lifted her glass. 'To the future,' she echoed, and drank defiantly.

But inside her there was pain. In a few moments he would be leaving for St Hilaire, and tomorrow her last sight of him would probably be from the window of some plane.

Why was he making her leave like this? Had he suddenly heard that his girlfriend was arriving, and didn't relish having to explain Chellie's presence in her home?

If that was the case, she had very little time left.

Oh, please, she appealed silently to the listening Fates. Let me have my single moment—my one night—and I'll take the heartbreak when it comes.

Aloud, she said, 'Is it wise to drink if you intend to drive?'

'Obviously not,' he said. 'But Corney will take me, if I ask him.'

'Yes,' she said. 'Of course. How silly of me.' She paused again. 'Tell me something—what is this music? I don't recognise it.'

'It's the *beguine*,' Ash told her. 'We have Rosalie to thank for it. She was born on Martinique, and sometimes her origins come roaring back.' He grimaced. 'Like tonight.'

'Well, I'm with Rosalie,' Chellie said. 'It's beautiful.'

She began to move slowly round the room in time with

the beat, giving herself over completely to the haunting rhythm, swaying her hips gently as she danced, allowing her natural grace full rein, without inhibition.

She did not need to glance over her shoulder to know that Ash was watching her, his eyes locked on her as if mesmerised.

Perhaps, she thought, her heart beginning to bump, the night was not over yet, after all. Perhaps...

His voice reached her softly, but urgently. 'Chellie— whatever you're doing, stop it.'

'Why?' She let the brief black skirt swirl enticingly as she swung round to face him, to challenge him, her emerald-dark eyes heavy with desire. 'You wanted this once—you wanted me to dance for you. So—why not now?'

'For all kinds of reasons,' he said almost grimly. He walked over to her and took her hand, pulling her towards him so that she was in his arms, but not touching. He held her firmly, moving with her in perfect cohesion.

'Dance with me, Chellie,' he directed quietly. 'Not for me. It's safer that way.'

'Why does it always have to be safe?' she demanded huskily. 'You come close, and then you back away. Why is that?'

'Because I always remember, just in time, I have no right to be that near.' His tone roughened. 'Because there are things about me—about this whole situation—that you need to know. Things that we have to talk about because they could change everything.'

'No,' she said, her voice shaking. 'You don't have to tell me—anything. It isn't necessary. Because I already know what you're trying to say.'

'You *know*?' He halted, staring at her. 'Was it Laurent?' he asked sharply. 'Did he say something?'

'No, nothing like that.' Chellie hunched a shoulder. 'He— he was very discreet. I—just guessed. I—I'm not a complete fool.'

'Oh, dear God.' His voice was almost blank. 'You have to let me explain…'

'No.' She spoke on a note of desperation. 'I know—and that's enough. I don't want everything spelled out for me, Ash. Spare me that, please.'

He said heavily, 'If that's what you want.' He hesitated. 'I didn't intend any of this, Chellie—not for a moment. You have to believe that. And I should never have allowed it to happen.'

'And there's something you should know too.' She looked up at him, her eyes pleading as they met his. 'I—don't care.'

He sighed. 'Then maybe you should.'

'Even if I swear that it will make no difference—that I'll leave as planned?' Her fingers bit into his arms through the thin shirt. 'Ash, I promise you I won't be a nuisance. Whatever happens between us will be our secret always, and I'll never pressure you in any way. Or ask you for anything you can't give.' She swallowed. 'You must believe that. No one will suffer because of this.'

'You don't think so?' His crooked smile held bitterness. 'I wish I could be so sure.'

'Unless you don't want me,' she said. Her voice trembled. 'Is that the real truth, Ash? Is it that simple.'

'Oh, I want you,' he said. 'And have done from the moment I first saw you. On the damned boat I hardly had an hour's sleep, and I was fighting all the time to keep my hands off you.'

'Then don't go tonight,' she whispered. 'Stay here. Stay with me—please.'

'Wild horses,' he said softly, 'could not drag me away.'

And he lifted her into his arms and carried her out of the room, through the shadowed hallway to the stairs beyond.

CHAPTER NINE

IIN HER bedroom, the lamp on the night table had been lit and the cover on the bed turned down.

Ash put Chellie gently on her feet. He framed her face in his hands, looking deep into her eyes, his smile faintly troubled.

'You're trembling,' he told her quietly. 'What is there to frighten you?'

I wish my hair hadn't been hacked off. I wish I wasn't feeling so awkward and inexperienced. And, most of all, I wish I was beautiful, with blonde hair and perfect teeth.

'Only myself,' she said. 'I'm scared of disappointing you.'

A faint laugh shook him. He drew her close, resting his lips against her hair. 'Now, how could you possibly do that?'

'Because it's happened before.' Her voice was a thread. 'He said I—I didn't know what to do to satisfy a man. That I was useless—not a real woman.'

'Dear God,' he said bleakly. 'But you must surely have known it wasn't true? Or were your previous experiences equally disastrous?'

She shook her head. 'I didn't have any. Ramon was the first. The only way I can judge myself.'

There was a silence, then he said quietly, 'I'm sorry, Chellie. I didn't know. I thought...' He paused again. 'Oh, to hell with what I thought.'

She closed her eyes, breathing the warm, clean scent of him. 'You said you'd had this fantasy about me, which you'd now fulfilled.' She tried to smile. 'Maybe we should keep it like that and I should quit while I'm ahead.'

'Firstly,' Ash said, very gently, 'do not—ever—confuse me with Ramon again. Secondly, and more importantly, my original fantasy has changed a little since this afternoon. You're still exquisitely naked, but now you're in bed with me, in my arms, and I can touch as well as look. And I dream that you're kissing me—that your body's opening to me. That you're taking me into you so deeply it's almost an agony. And that you're sighing my name as you come.'

'Oh, God,' she said. She was still trembling, but now it was with a longing she had no need to disguise. She could feel the heat rising in her veins, bring a soft, awakened flush to her skin.

She put her arms round his neck, drawing him down to her. Just before his lips met hers, she whispered, 'You dream the most wonderful things.'

'And now we'll make them come true,' he said. 'Together.'

His mouth was warm as it caressed hers, and tender too, his passion carefully held in check. Waiting, she knew, for her.

She responded ardently, her lips parting beneath his, longing for the kiss to deepen, to offer the intimacy she longed for.

She was not disappointed. At once his arms tightened round her, and she felt the hot invasion of his tongue exploring the inner sweetness of her mouth.

When he raised his head the blue eyes were drowsy, clouded with desire. His fingers skimmed her bare shoulders, lingering on each plane and curve as if sculpting her image, then moving down to the first swell of her breasts above the bodice, gently smoothing the warm flesh.

She turned her head, pressing her cheek to his hand with a small, choked murmur of pleasure and need.

His hand moved, found the zip at the side of the dress, and began to release it, letting the bodice peel away from her naked breasts.

His lips found her ear, teasing the lobe with his teeth,

then moving down to plant soft kisses down the vulnerable curve of her throat.

'Just looking will never be enough again,' he whispered. 'I want all of you.'

Her breasts seemed to bloom as his hands stroked them, her nipples hardening in sheer delight under the tender, sensuous play of his fingertips. He cupped them gently, bending to adore them with his mouth, his tongue flickering on the sensitised peaks.

He undid the zip completely, allowing the dress to drift down and pool round her feet, leaving her in nothing but the minuscule G-string. She heard him catch his breath, then felt his hands moving on her in gentle, tantalising exploration, moulding the curve of her hips and the smooth softness of her thighs. Creating a slow, languid torment which ached deep within her.

She murmured something incoherent—pleading—pressing her burning forehead against his chest.

Ash slid down her last tiny covering, then lifted her from the tangle of clothing at her feet and placed her on the bed. He lay down beside her, drawing her close to him, finding her mouth with his.

When she could speak, she whispered, 'You haven't taken your clothes off.'

'There's plenty of time for that,' he returned softly. 'We have the whole night ahead of us—and this part of it's for you.'

He began to caress her again, his mouth following the passage of his unhurried hands down her body, finding every pulse, each soft, secret place. When, finally, he reached the parting of her thighs, his touch was as light as gossamer on her yielding womanhood, the cool, clever fingers creating an alchemy all their own as they stroked the tiny sheltered bud.

Chellie could hear the huskiness of her own breathing, the quickening throb of her heart as her body responded helplessly, adoringly, to the delicate intensity of pleasure that he was building for her.

Her body was writhing in a fever of excitement as he brought her again and again to the brink of the unknown, his lips on her breasts, tugging sweetly at her aroused nipples, circling them with his tongue, then moving back to her mouth, biting sensuously at her lower lip.

The spiral of sensation mounting inside her was suddenly too wild—too consuming—and in some far reeling corner of her mind she understood that this was complete and utter surrender. That she could faint—that she might die—but she would never be able to—stop—because it was—too late, and all control was gone.

And as she reached the ultimate, glittering peak, and pleasure took her like a sea wave, tossing her in endless billows of rapture, she felt tears on her face and heard herself moaning his name.

She lay spent and breathless in his arms, while he kissed her wet eyes and her parted lips, murmuring to her how lovely she was, and how clever. Calling her his darling and his sweet, passionate angel.

When she was capable of speech, she said, gasping, 'So—that's how it's supposed to be.'

Ash kissed her again. 'Only for the lucky people.'

'All the same.' Chellie slid a hand inside his shirt, stroking his warm chest, coaxing the flat male nipples into erection. 'Wasn't it rather—one-sided?'

There was a smile in his voice. 'Just a little, perhaps. But that was quite intentional.'

'Why?'

'Because I needed to prove something to you.'

'Which is?'

He said gently, 'That you could never be a disappointment, sexually or in any other way. Because you, Chellie Greer, are all woman.'

'That,' she said, 'is quite the nicest thing anyone ever said to me.'

'You're welcome,' Ash said gravely. 'And please don't stop what you're doing,' he added lazily. 'I like it.'

She began undoing his shirt. 'But you're going to enjoy this far more,' she murmured. 'You see, I have a few little fantasies of my own to indulge.'

'Oh,' he said. 'And undressing me is one of them?'

'It's a beginning, anyway.'

'I see,' Ash said thoughtfully. 'You're not planning any real recovery time, then? Or even a breathing space?'

She slipped his shirt off and tossed it to the floor. 'You said I was all woman. I have to live up to my reputation.' Her fingers strayed downward to the zip of his pants and tugged experimentally.

He said a little hoarsely, 'So far, it's doing fine.'

'You've seen nothing yet.' She eased the pants down over his hips, and discarded them too.

'I only hope I survive.' His voice was uneven.

'I don't think you're in much danger.' She pretended to consider. 'After all, this may be my first time, but it certainly isn't yours.'

His hands closed on hers, halting them, the blue eyes suddenly serious as they met hers. 'Chellie—I think we should let the past take care of itself. A month—two months ago I didn't even know you existed.'

She bent forward and kissed him on the mouth, running the tip of her tongue across his lips. She said, 'But you know now, don't you?'

'Yes.' In one swift movement, Ash stripped off his briefs and turned on to his back, lifting her over him. And with a soft groan of satisfaction he lowered her slowly on to him.

Chellie stared down at him, eyes widening as she experienced the full heated strength of him inside her at last. As she felt her body close round him and possess him.

Ash looked back at her, his grin wicked, sensuous. He said, 'Well?'

'Yes,' she said, her breath catching in her throat. 'Oh,

yes…' And she began to move, tentatively at first, but then gaining in confidence under his husky encouragement.

He watched her through half-closed eyes as his hands ranged over her, worshipping every slender curve, enticing every nerve-ending into glowing life. He stroked down her back, from her shoulders to her flanks, and she shivered with delight, her spine arching fiercely in response, her round breasts engorged and throbbing.

Their joined bodies rose and sank in complete attunement, in mutual demand.

She could feel the inner tension building in her again. Found herself at once overtaken—pierced by a pleasure so strong it was almost anguish—and sent, her whole body shaking and quivering, into the glory of release. She cried out sharply, in a kind of disbelief that heaven could be there for her once more so soon, and Ash answered her, groaning in ecstasy as his body shuddered into its own climax.

Afterwards, they lay very quietly together, his arms wrapped round her, her head tucked into his shoulder.

He whispered, 'Are you all right.'

'I think,' she said, 'that I'm in a thousand little pieces.'

'Is that all?' He kissed the top of her head very tenderly. 'I'll have to try and do better.'

She realised that she wanted very badly to tell him that she loved him. But that was impossible. It would go completely against the set of rules she had imposed on herself. And, if nothing else, pride should keep her silent. Because, very soon now, she would be walking away from him for ever, and she needed to be able to do it with her head held high. No embarrassing declarations to muddy the waters.

'Is something wrong?' he asked.

She swallowed. 'Not a thing. Why do you ask?'

He said slowly, 'Because one moment you were totally relaxed, like a sleeping baby. The next—not.'

'Imagination can play strange tricks.' She stroked his cheek. 'But perhaps I really do need to sleep for a while.'

'Only for a while?' He captured her hand and kissed its palm. She could feel his smile against her skin.

'Certainly,' she said. 'I don't want to miss anything.'

Ash reached out an arm and switched off the lamp. 'I promise,' he said solemnly, 'not to start without you.'

He slept almost at once, but Chellie could not. She lay in his embrace, not wishing to move in case she disturbed him, and stared into the darkness.

There, in the shadows, was her future, she thought. Without light, and without hope. And she felt frightened, and more alone than she had ever been in her life before.

She dozed eventually, only to be woken by his mouth planting a trail of gentle kisses down her body. She turned to him, her mouth eager, her hands caressing him with total candour. This time their lovemaking was slow, and almost achingly tender.

As if, she thought, their bodies were saying goodbye. Which was no more than the truth.

They did not speak any words. There was instead the intimacy of sighs and murmurs, and infinitesimal changes of breathing to chart their passage to rapture. And when the moment of culmination came, Ash wrapped her close in his arms and held her as if he would never let her go.

Ah, but he will, Chellie thought sadly. He will.

The pain of love, it seemed, had already begun. And when sleep finally claimed her she was glad.

'Miss Greer—*mam'selle*. I have coffee for you.'

Chellie opened unwilling eyes to find the room bathed in sunlight and Rosalie standing by the bed, cup and saucer in hand. In the same instant she registered that she was alone.

The bed beside her was empty, the pillows plumped, the sheet smooth as glass. No sign at all that anyone had shared it with her. No untidy muddle of clothing on the floor. No sound of running water from the shower either.

Ash had gone, and all traces of the night they'd spent together had been removed.

Expertly removed, Chellie thought with sudden bitterness. But why was she surprised? After all, if you were sleeping with the daughter of the house it was bad policy to enjoy another girl in her absence, especially when loyal family retainers were involved.

Ash clearly knew how to cover his tracks—maybe not for the first time.

And if some secret corner of her heart had hoped for a miracle—had prayed that the splendour of passion they had shared might lead to some kind of commitment on his part—then she knew better now.

She sat up slowly, holding the covering sheet to her breasts. 'Thank you, Rosalie.'

'And Mr Ash called. He has a seat for you on the noon flight to Grenada.'

Chellie nearly spilled her coffee all over the bed. 'He called?' she repeated incredulously. 'When?'

'Half an hour ago, *mam'selle*. He also say a car will be sent for you at eleven.'

'I see.' Her mouth was dry. 'Was—was there any other message?' she managed.

'No, *mam'selle*,' Rosalie assured her cheerfully. 'Shall I run your bath?'

'No—no, thank you.' Chellie forced a smile. 'I can manage.'

So, she thought drearily when she was alone. Last night was then, this is now, and what worlds apart they are.

But then what had she expected? She'd appealed to him on a strictly sexual level and he'd taken her. That had been the deal, and it was much too late for regrets.

She stretched, feeling the voluptuous ache in her body, the singing of her pulses. She might be on the floor emotionally, but physically she felt wonderful.

Ash had taught her to be a woman, she thought, and she would always be grateful to him for that. But she had also learned to feel with a woman's heart, and she would never be free again.

She didn't want the coffee, but she needed the boost of caffeine it offered to clear her head and get her moving. After all, she had packing to do. It was time for her, too, to pretend she had never been here.

As promised, Rosalie had washed and pressed the linen dress, and it was hanging on the wardrobe door. But she wasn't going to wear it, or anything else that belonged to Julie. The thought was unbearable.

She would make do with the handful of her own stuff that she'd brought, and buy herself a change of underwear on Grenada for the journey home. Everything else could stay behind.

Except for the dress Ash had bought her, she thought with a pang. She would take that with her—as a salutary reminder of the gulf that existed between sex and love. And a warning never to allow herself to confuse them again.

I don't want to wake up and find the bed beside me empty ever again, she thought, as she pushed back the sheet and swung her legs to the floor. And if that means spending the rest of my life alone, so be it. I've been alone before.

Brave words, but she knew that it would never be as easy as that. Because it would not just be a dress that she would take with her. Ash would go too—the sound of his voice, the unique male scent of him, the taste of his mouth and the controlled drive of his body, taking her to rapture and beyond.

Potent memories, she thought, and also completely inescapable. Something she would have to learn to live with.

She showered, and dressed in her denim skirt and tee shirt. Full circle, she thought, as she set about re-packing her bag.

There was pitifully little to go in it, she mused, frowningly, and then realised why. The black dress she'd worn last night was unaccountably missing.

She hunted through the wardrobe, and even searched under the bed, but there was no sign of it.

Oh, hell, she thought, biting her lip. Rosalie's probably

pounced on it for laundering. What on earth will she make of the G-string? At least I won't be around to find out, she added with a mental shrug.

The last remaining item was the precious passport, which was still downstairs on the sitting room table.

She picked up her bag, gave the room a last, lingering look, then went downstairs.

Rosalie met her in the hall. 'Mr Ash is here,' she announced, sending Chellie's heart into painful free-fall. 'Out on the verandah. I'm making him scrambled eggs. You want some too?'

'No—no, thanks. I'm not hungry.'

Rosalie sent her a disparaging glance. 'You're too thin, *mam'selle*. Should eat more.'

'Ah.' Chellie tried to keep her voice light. 'Someone once said you could never be too rich or too thin. One out of two isn't bad.'

Rosalie snorted and went back to the kitchen, leaving Chellie to make her reluctant way into the sitting room. If she hadn't needed to collect her passport she'd have been tempted to bolt back upstairs again. Even so, if she was quick and quiet…

'Good morning.' The verandah doors were wide open and he was standing there, dark against the brilliance of the sunlight.

Her hopes of evasion dashed, Chellie lifted her chin, trying to ignore the jolt to her senses. 'Oh, hi.' She attempted a casual note. 'I got your message. I wasn't expecting to see you.'

'I wasn't expecting to be here,' he returned. 'But there's been a change of plan. I've found out there's an earlier plane. If we leave straight after breakfast, you can catch it.'

She picked up her passport and stowed it in her bag, aware that her hands were trembling.

'I see.' She forced a smile. 'You—you really can't wait to be rid of me, can you?'

'I've booked you a room at the Oceanside Club,' he went

on, as if she hadn't spoken. 'And I'll join you there as soon as I can. There are issues here that I have to deal with first.'

'Issues?' Chellie repeated slowly. She had a sudden graphic image of Julie, with her bright smile dimmed, her eyes blurred with tears. 'Is that how you describe hurting people—messing with their emotions?'

His brows lifted. 'I wasn't aware that there was much emotion involved,' he said drily. 'But I'm prepared to stand corrected.' He paused. 'Whatever—I think it's better if you're away from here while I sort things out,' he added levelly. 'You'll just have to trust me on this.'

'Ash,' she said. 'We can't do this. We agreed that last night was all there could ever be, and nothing's changed.'

'You don't think so?' He shook his head. 'You're wrong, Chellie. Last night only proved what I've always known— that we belong together.' He came further into the room. 'Darling, I won't let you go.' His voice deepened. 'I can't. And I'll do whatever it takes to give us the freedom to be together.' He came to her, taking her hands in his. 'I thought you'd want that too? Am I wrong?'

'No.' Chellie's voice was wretched. 'I do want it. Oh, so much. But I know that you can't build happiness on the ruins of someone else's life.'

He stared at her. 'Chellie—you can't honestly believe that applies to us.'

She looked down at the floor. 'I think it could.' She jumped as the front doorbell pealed imperatively. 'I—I suppose that's my lift to the airport.'

Ash frowned. 'No, I'm your lift. And I wasn't expecting visitors,' he added with a touch of grimness as Cornelius went past the sitting room to answer the door. 'At least, not yet.'

'I'm here to see Miss Greer.' A man's voice, loud and slightly hectoring, filled the hall. 'Take me to her, please.'

Chellie's lips parted in a gasp of shock. 'My God,' she breathed. 'It's Jeffrey—Jeffrey Chilham. But how can it be? It's impossible.'

Cornelius was murmuring something in reply, but the caller responded with a snort.

'That's nonsense, my good man. I know quite well she's here. And that Brennan fellow too, I've no doubt. Kindly let me pass.'

Ash's hands gripped hers more tightly. 'Who the hell is this?' His voice was urgent.

Chellie shook her head helplessly. 'He works for my father.'

'Dear God.' Ash's mouth tightened harshly. 'So he couldn't even come in person.'

She stared at him. 'What are you talking about?'

He said wearily, 'I think you're about to find out.'

The next minute, Jeffrey Chilham was filling the doorway. He was a tall man, with greying hair and a red face that heat and irritation had rendered brick-coloured.

The khaki shorts he was wearing with a multi-coloured shirt did him no favours at all, and he was fanning himself vigorously with a Panama hat.

'Michelle,' he exclaimed. 'My dear girl. Thank heavens you're safe.' He stared at her, his lips pursed in disapproval. 'But your hair looks terrible. What have you done to it?'

'It was cut.' Chellie faced him unsmilingly. 'Jeffrey, what are you doing here?'

'My dear, do you really need to ask?' His chest swelled importantly. 'I've come to take you home, of course. Although I don't recommend presenting yourself to your father looking as you do,' he added, frowning. 'Perhaps while your hair is growing again you should wear a wig.'

'I did,' she said. 'It didn't suit me.' She realised that she suddenly felt cold. She was still gripping Ash's hand, and quietly detached herself. 'And how exactly did you know how to find me?'

'Well, naturally we have Brennan here to thank for that.' He gave Ash a condescending nod. 'Sir Clive is naturally grateful for your efforts in rescuing Miss Greer, my man, but he is not pleased that you ignored his explicit instructions to bring her back to England. Sending me halfway across the world has cost him time and money, and he has informed your company that he intends to negotiate a reduction in your fee as a result.'

His words fell into a silence that was as deep as an ocean.

Chellie found herself suddenly struggling for breath. When she could move, she swung round and stared at Ash, who was standing stony-faced, his arms folded across his chest.

'Is it true?' she asked huskily. 'What he's saying? Did you know who I was all along?'

'Yes,' he said. 'I knew.' His voice was expressionless. 'You'd been tracked to Santo Martino by other operatives, then the trail went cold and I came to find you myself.'

'Paid—by my father?' The muscles in her throat were taut with pain and she felt physically sick. 'He—hired you?'

Jeffrey Chilham laughed. 'Of course, my dear. Mr Brennan and his partner are businessmen. They run a specialist security organisation. Personal protection, tracing missing persons, negotiating over hostages—that kind of thing. 'Mr Brennan signed a highly-paid contract with us. Or did you think he did it for love?'

'No,' Chellie said quietly. 'I never thought that.' She wrapped her arms round her body, trying to control the violent internal shivering assailing her. She turned back to Ash, still standing rigidly beside her. 'Well, no one can say that you don't earn your money,' she added with icy scorn. 'Does everyone get your particular brand of personal service—or is there an extra charge?'

Ash winced, his mouth tightening. He said, 'Chellie— listen to me. I was going to tell you. To explain. I swear it. I thought—I hoped we'd have more time.'

'We had time on the boat,' she said. 'How long does it take to tell me I've been sold out?'

'It wasn't that simple,' he said. 'Not at first. Because I believed you were just another assignment, and a tricky one at that. 'And I'd been enjoined to secrecy by your father. It was part of the deal. He claimed that you were stubborn, and wilful, and might refuse to go with me or even run away again if you knew the truth.'

Chellie drew an angry, shaking breath. 'Well, he was right about that.'

'But I realised almost at once that you didn't want to be returned to him,' Ash went on. 'You barely mentioned him, so it was clear there was no love lost between you. Everything you said was about making a new life for yourself—finding some kind of independence. And I could understand why. I only met your father once, and it seemed even then that he was more angry than anxious about you. He spoke about you as if you were a parcel that had gone astray.'

He paused. 'He also implied that this wasn't the first time you'd got into a mess. That you were some wild child who'd never done a day's work in her life and slept her way round London, but that Ramon was a scandal too far and he wanted it dealt with quietly and confidentially.'

Chellie caught her breath. 'Oh, God. And you—believed him?'

'He was paying me to find you, Chellie, not to make moral judgements. And I'd seen the newspaper file on you. It seemed to confirm his story.'

He threw his head back. 'But then I met you,' he added flatly. 'And I began to wonder. Because you were a million miles from the cold-hearted, extravagant little tart that he'd described. You were brave and vulnerable, sexy and scared all at the same time. And so innocent you almost broke my heart.

'So that's why I refused to take you to London. I wanted to see your father out of his usual territory—watch how he behaved towards you and then take the appropriate action.' He shook his head. 'I still can't believe he hasn't come in person.'

'Sir Clive is a very busy man,' Jeffrey Chilham put in, his voice shocked. 'And it isn't as if Michelle has been hurt in any way—or locked up and held to ransom. Naturally, under those circumstances, he would have rushed to her side.' He looked uncomfortable. 'But there's been no real harm done. She—she just made an unfortunate choice of man, that's all.'

'I seem to make a habit of it,' Chellie said bitterly. She turned back to Ash. 'So why were you trying to hustle me off to Grenada? Did you plan to hide me so that you could extort some more money from my loving father?' She paused. 'I wonder what my actual market value is? I'll have to remember to ask him.'

Ash moved quickly, almost violently, and took her by the shoulders. 'You know that isn't true.' His voice was low and tense. The blue eyes burned into hers. 'I wasn't going to hand you back against your will to someone who didn't care about you. That's the truth. You must believe me.'

'Why should I?' Chellie lifted her chin defiantly. 'When you've lied to me from the first moment I saw you.' Her derisive laugh cracked in the middle. '*Someone to watch over me?* God, what a joke.'

She shook her head. 'And I made it so easy for you, didn't I—the rich man's stupid daughter? You provided the bait, and I practically dragged you into bed. Why, Ash? Did you decide that your present girlfriend's father had less to offer than mine?'

'What the hell are you talking about?' Ash said roughly. 'I have no girlfriend.' His mouth twisted as he looked down at her. 'Although I did think I had a lover.'

'No,' she said. 'You had a dupe. A blind, trusting dupe. But my eyes are open now, so you'd better revert to Plan A and go on courting the owner's daughter. I hope she finds out what you're really like before the walk down the aisle.'

'The owner's daughter?' His voice sparked with incredulity. 'Are you crazy?'

'I was,' she said. 'But not any more. And please take your hands off me.'

'Michelle!' Jeffrey Chilham's voice was sharp. 'I'm trying to be patient here, but do I infer that you've had some kind of relationship with this man?'

'No,' she said. 'No relationship. He took me to bed last night, that's all. I suppose he viewed it as an unofficial bonus.'

Ash released her and took a step back. He said courteously, 'No, I thought it was a foretaste of heaven.'

He took a deep breath. 'Chellie, my love, you have to listen to me, please. Because you've got things so terribly wrong.' His voice was gentle, almost pleading. 'You have every right to be angry, but I never meant you to find out like this. I thought Grenada would give us a breathing space. Give me time to explain properly.'

'Explain? Or invent another tissue of lies? Thank God I was spared that, at least,' she added with contempt.

'No,' he said. 'So that I could tell you everything and we could start again, with no secrets—all our cards on the table.'

She said slowly, 'Do you know—if this wasn't so hideous, it would almost be funny? But I'm not in the mood for jokes.'

She looked at Jeffrey Chilham, who was standing, his face mottled with shock and anger.

She said, 'I presume that all the arrangements to get me back to the UK have been made with my father's usual efficiency? Then I may as well take advantage of them. Let's go.'

'Very well,' he said stiffly. 'Although you realise I shall have to make a full report to Sir Clive.' He cast a fulminating look at Ash. 'And you'd better start looking for another job—if you can find one. You've made a bad enemy today, my friend.'

'That,' Ash said curtly, 'is the least of my problems.'

He turned on his heel and walked out into the garden.

Chellie watched him go. The numbness of betrayal was beginning to wear off, and she wanted to sink to her knees and howl her loss and loneliness to the smiling sky.

But I can't cry, she told herself with icy determination. Not yet. Because I have to go back, and somehow restart my life.'

A life, she thought, as pain twisted inside her, without love. And which would take every scrap of courage she possessed.

CHAPTER TEN

'DISGUSTING,' Jeffrey said in a furious undertone, his voice shaking. 'Disgraceful. I am lost for words to describe your behaviour.'

'Really?' Chellie sent him a frozen smile. 'I would never have guessed.'

The ride to St Hilaire's small airport had been an uncomfortable one. Chellie, racked by her own unhappy thoughts and still stunned by Ash's betrayal, had hardly exchanged two words with Jeffrey, glum and brooding beside her.

But it had been too good to last. Almost as soon as their private aircraft was airborne, on its way to Barbados, Jeffrey had embarked on a low-voiced barrage of criticism.

Like a wasp, buzzing in her ear, Chellie thought wearily.

'Eloping with that con-man chap was bad enough,' he went on now, warming to his theme. 'But at least you had the excuse of infatuation. Yet now you brazenly admit you've also slept with this Brennan fellow—a man you hardly know. A virtual stranger. Have you no shame?'

'Yes,' Chellie said, lifting her chin. 'I am deeply ashamed that I didn't stand up to my father years ago, and that I ran away instead of confronting him. Will that do?'

'I see no call for flippancy.' He shook his head. 'I also realise that my sister was perfectly correct. All those lurid newspaper stories. She always said there was no smoke without fire.'

'Ah,' Chellie said, conjuring up an image of Elaine, all cashmere, pearls and disapproval. 'What a truly original thought—and worthy of the thinker.' She paused. 'Am I to take it that you've decided to withdraw from the proposed merger my father was trying to arrange?'

'I don't know what you're talking about.' There was faint defensiveness in his voice.

Chellie sighed. 'Yes, you do, Jeffrey. Isn't that why my father sent you to St Hilaire instead of coming himself? And why you agreed to come? Because he thought my ordeal would have cowed me into submission and I'd be ready to fling myself on to your waiting shoulder in grateful tears?'

His mouth tightened. 'I told your father that I was prepared to overlook your original indiscretion, yes.'

'So he dispatched you to kick me while I was down.' She smiled mirthlessly. 'He never misses a trick.'

'However, in view of your disturbing disclosures...'

'You've decided that I'd be more of a liability than an asset.' Chellie nodded. 'Very wise, Jeff. So there is light at the end of the tunnel after all.'

He glared at her. 'There may soon come a time, Michelle, when you will wish you hadn't dismissed me quite so lightly.'

'Jeffrey,' she said. 'As I've tried to explain before, more tactfully, I wouldn't have you if you came stuffed and garnished.'

'Charming.' His smile sneered at her. 'However, I don't think you've considered the full implications of your behaviour. There could be—consequences.'

'Possibly,' she said. 'But unlikely.'

'You seem to take the prospect of giving birth to an illegitimate child very lightly.'

'No,' she said. 'I'm just not prepared to waste time in fruitless conjecture. I'll deal with the situation if and when it happens.' *And I'll care as much as anyone could ever want,* she added silently.

She'd hoped that Jeffrey would be sufficiently offended to revert to sulking, but the damage to his pride was unfortunately outweighed by his sense of grievance. His complaints about her conduct jostled for position with dire prophecies for her future once his report to her father had been made.

'Understand this,' she interrupted him at last. 'I'm on this plane with you only because I'd already decided to return to England. It has nothing to do with any wish or decision of my father.'

'You'll toe his line,' he said. 'If you want food on the table and a roof over your head.'

'Other people earn their livings,' she returned. 'And so shall I.'

'Without any training or references? I don't think so. And none of the companies your father deals with would ever take you on, not if they knew it was against his wishes.'

'All the same,' she said. 'There are still places where his shadow doesn't fall. I'll make out.'

She turned away, pillowing her cheek on her hand and pretending to doze. But inwardly she was in turmoil.

Because there was more than a grain of truth in Jeffrey's unpleasant remarks.

The immediate future was bleak and frightening indeed. But the thought of surrendering meekly to her father's will was even worse.

I ran away once, she thought, but I'll never do that again. I'm not the same girl who thought someone like Ramon could possibly be the solution. I know now I have only my-self to rely on.

There were tears, thick and acid in her throat, but she choked them back.

And Jeffrey had also been right when he described Ash as a virtual stranger to her, she realised bitterly.

On the surface he'd been Sir Galahad, rescuing her from danger. In reality he'd been Judas, selling her out for a lot more than thirty pieces of silver.

I should have realised he wasn't what he seemed, she thought, biting her lip. All the signs were there, but because I was attracted to him I didn't pick up on them. I let myself be fooled

After all, he knew exactly where to find me—and he broke into Mama Rita's desk—and knocked out Manuel. Not the usual skills of any passing stranger, even in Santo Martino.

And when I did ask questions he always had an answer. I see now why he hung on to my passport—to ensure that I didn't get away again.

But he did give it back to you, argued a small voice in her head. And he was planning to send you away from St Hilaire before the trap finally closed.

She stifled a sigh. He'd said he wanted to be with her, she thought desolately, but after all the deception he'd practised on her how could she believe another word he said?

The truth remained that all she knew was his name, and the fact that his lovemaking had driven her to the outermost limits of her soul. Not much on which to base an opinion, let alone the possibility of a relationship, she derided herself.

I allowed myself to dream, she thought soberly, and that shows how much growing up I still have to do.

For one thing, how seriously could she take his denial that he was seriously involved with Julie Howard? Quite apart from the picture beside his bed, there'd been real tenderness in his voice when he'd talked about her on board *La Belle Rêve*. And although he'd appeared shocked at the idea, the evidence was against him.

Besides, would he really be allowed to come and go as he pleased at Arcadie—invite anyone he chose to stay there in the owner's absence—if he was not regarded as already part of the family?

But she didn't have to make any kind of judgement on Ash Brennan or his romantic attachments, she told herself with resolution. Not any more. Because she was out of his life, and the distance between them was widening irrevocably with every minute that passed.

Even though that final image of him walking away from her was etched corrosively into her memory, hideous and inescapable.

Something else I need to deal with, she thought, her heart contracting painfully.

*   *   *

She maintained the illusion that she was asleep until they landed on Barbados. A car was waiting to whisk them from the airport to the Gold Beach Club Hotel where, Jeffrey had coldly informed her, they would be spending a single night, prior to the final stage of their journey back to Britain the following morning.

My last few hours in the lap of luxury, Chellie thought, as the car swung in between the hotel's tall wrought-iron gates.

The hotel was much as she'd imagined Arcadie would be, with the reception and public rooms located in a large low white-painted building, with cool marble floors, soft background music and air-conditioning.

The guests were accommodated in luxurious thatched bungalows nestling in the lavishly landscaped gardens, and there was not just one swimming pool, but three.

They were given a warm Bajan welcome, handed their keys, and told a porter would be along soon with their luggage.

As she turned away from the desk, Chellie found Jeffrey giving her one modest bag a beady look.

'Is that all you have?' he asked.

Chellie clicked her tongue reprovingly. 'Why, Jeffrey, have you only just noticed I'm travelling light?' she returned. 'How very remiss of you.'

'I have had other things on my mind,' he said repressively. He transferred the evil eye to what she was wearing. 'I suppose it's too much to hope that you have something to change into? They operate a dress code here.'

'I'm sure they do.' Chellie put firmly from her mind the thought of Ash's grey dress, neatly folded in the bottom of her bag. She would wear it some day, but it would certainly not be tonight.' She shrugged. 'But I'm afraid what you see is what you get.'

'Then I'll ask them to serve dinner in your bungalow.' Jeffrey pursed his lips. 'You'll be less conspicuous that way.'

'Really?' Chellie looked down at her tee shirt. 'For a minute I thought I had a large scarlet letter pinned to my chest.'

'Very amusing,' he said sourly.

'I wasn't joking,' she said. 'And I'm eating in the restaurant like everyone else. But I'll sit at a separate table if I'm an embarrassment to you,' she added coolly.

Jeffrey's face took on that unbecoming brick colour again, but he turned back to the desk and made a reservation for nine o clock. For two.

'Fine,' Chellie said briskly. 'Then I'll see you later—in the bar.' And she marched off with her waiting porter.

But once alone in her bungalow the bravado slid away. She stood, looking at her glamorous surroundings and the enticing view outside the window. The sound of voices and laughter, and the splashing from the pool area only served to deepen her sudden sense of isolation. And, if she was honest, the sniping match with Jeffrey had left her shaking inside, although a confrontation with her father would have been so much worse.

But how could Jeffrey have ever considered marrying me? she asked herself in bewilderment. My God, he doesn't even like me.

She had a long shower in the tiled bathroom, and hung up her skirt and top to try and get rid of some of the creases.

It's the dustbin for both of them as soon as I get back, she promised, wrapping herself in a dry towel, sarong-style, and stretching out on the bed.

She'd noticed a shop near Reception that sold beachwear, and there were vacant loungers round the pool, but she didn't feel like joining the party. There were too many couples about with eyes only for each other, and she felt raw enough as it was, with the reality of Ash's betrayal heavy in her mind.

But Jeff and I are going to stick out like sore thumbs in the restaurant tonight, she thought, her lips twisting in reluctant humour.

She turned on to her side, letting herself sink into the comfortable mattress. It was a huge bed—bigger than king-size—and certainly not designed for single occupation.

Which brought her back to Ash again, she thought, biting her lip.

Their lovemaking was disturbingly vivid in her mind. Her imagination exploded suddenly, creating an alternative reality where Ash lay beside her, his hands slowly unfastening the towel and slipping it from her body. Soft tendrils of desire were uncurling inside her, making her burn and melt, as she felt his lips possessing her inch by languorous inch, tracing a path from her throat to her breasts, then down over the flat plane of her stomach to the soft mound at the joining of her thighs.

She remembered the slow sensuality of his mouth exploring the sweet secret heat of her, the flame of his tongue bringing her to orgasm, and she lifted her hands and cupped her breasts, sighingly aware that her nipples were hardening irresistibly through the soft towelling.

She groaned, rolling over on to her stomach and burying her flushed face in the pillow.

'What am I doing to myself?' she muttered in anguish.

It wasn't even night and she was already out of control, aching for him, her newly awakened body crying out for the passion he had taught her and its surcease.

I must not recall those things, she thought. I must not remember the lover but the man who deceived me and sold me. The man I can never forgive. And certainly never, ever forget.

And then, at last, she allowed herself to weep for all that she had lost.

Jeffrey was already in the bar when Chellie, outwardly calm and composed, arrived there.

He was wearing cream linen slack trousers and a dark red shirt, with a cravat tucked into the neck, and drinking something through a straw from a hollowed-out coconut shell.

'So here you are.' There was something about the forced geniality in his tone and the faintly glassy expression in his eyes which led her to suspect that this wasn't the first coconut shell he'd encountered that evening, or even the second.

She said lightly, 'Full marks for observation, Jeffrey.'

But how many of me does he see, I wonder? she thought, climbing on to the stool beside him and ordering a sedate cocktail of tropical fruit juice.

When a waiter brought menus, Chellie ordered a Caesar salad, to be followed by red snapper. Jeffrey chose steak, and picked a bottle of red wine to go with it without bothering to ask if she had a preference.

I'll let him do the drinking for both of us tonight, Chellie thought with a mental shrug. Jeffrey Chilham with his hair down. Now, there's a thought to conjure with. And had to suppress a reluctant grin.

The restaurant was large and crowded with diners, the girls showing off their jewellery as well as their tans in skimpy designer dresses which left little to the imagination. A fact not lost on Jeffrey as the meal progressed.

'You'd look good in that,' he said thickly, as one beauty wandered past in an orchid-pink chiffon dress cut down to her navel.

'I know a woman called Mama Rita who'd probably agree with you,' Chellie returned, unsmilingly, as she drank some iced mineral water.

'Never heard of her.' Jeffrey refilled his glass. He paused. 'Not very talkative tonight, are you?'

'I have a lot to think about.'

'Wondering what lover-boy's up to, I dare say.' He smiled unpleasantly. 'Doesn't take much guesswork. His type have women waiting for them all round the world. He won't be lonely.'

'I'm more concerned with the future rather than the past,' Chellie said shortly, putting down her knife and fork. 'As I said, I have a living to earn when I get back.'

'Well, that shouldn't be a problem for a girl of your infinite talents.' He winked at her lasciviously over the top of his glass. 'Do what you do best, that's my advice. Once your hair's grown again you should be able to make a fortune on your back.'

Shock left her speechless. Mounting anger made her dangerous.

'Tell you what,' he went on, leaning confidentially across the table towards her. 'I wouldn't mind being your first customer.' He sent her an owlish grin. 'After all, you're bound to be feeling the lack tonight. You could probably do with some company.'

Chellie pushed back her chair and got up. She said quietly, 'I'll assume that it's the drink talking, shall I? And reply in kind.'

She walked round the table, picking up the bottle of red wine in passing, and poured the remains of it straight into his lap.

'You hellcat.' He was on his feet too, frantically dabbing at his soaked and stained trousers with his napkin as people at the surrounding tables stared and exchanged covert grins. 'Your father's going to hear about this.'

'Yes,' Chellie said crisply. 'He certainly is. And pretty soon, Jeffrey dear, you too will be looking for work.'

And she turned on her heel and walked out of the restaurant.

It was raining, Chellie realised with disgust as she emerged from the office block. There was a time when she'd have hailed a cab at once. Now, she dived into her bag for her umbrella, and started walking to the nearest bus stop.

There wasn't a bus in sight, which meant she was probably going to be late for her duty lunch with her father, she thought with a sigh.

It was a concession she'd acceded to with reluctance. And it had come at the end of a long and bitterly fought campaign to establish her independence. Which she seemed, incredibly, to have won.

It had been a difficult homecoming. Her father had greeted her with the ominous calm which invariably preceded a storm. And the storm had not been long in coming.

Clive Greer had wasted no sympathy on his errant child,

or the risks and dangers she'd endured. He'd dwelt instead on her stupidity, her credulity, and her stubborn recklessness.

'Do you realise I've had to pay out a bloody fortune to get you back in one piece?' he'd roared.

'Yes,' she said as pain slashed at her once again. 'I know.'

'And all to some soldier of fortune who doesn't know his place.' He glared at her. 'Oh, yes, madam. Jeffrey felt obliged to tell me what he'd discovered when he arrived—that you'd lost all sense of decency.'

'Of course,' she said with irony. 'Your good and faithful servant.'

'Not for much longer,' he retorted grimly. 'He's taking early retirement for some damned reason. So I'm losing my right hand, and I've got a daughter behaving like a tart with every unscrupulous bastard who crosses her path. Pretty good, eh?'

There wasn't too much she could say in her own defence, so she bowed her head to the onslaught and conserved her energy for the more important struggle to come.

The moment when she told her father that she was giving up her flat and taking a room in a house with three other girls who'd advertised for a fourth to share. And that, against all the odds, she'd found a job as a receptionist and filing clerk with a firm of accountants.

Sir Clive had resorted to his usual tactics, issuing commands one moment, cajoling the next. Threats, Chellie thought wryly, bribery—he'd tried them all.

Even emotional blackmail had been brought into play. 'I'm not as young as I was,' he'd told her. 'And Jeffrey's decision to leave has been a blow. I need your help, Michelle, your support.'

'And I need a life of my own.' She'd remained rock-solid throughout, steadfast in her determination not to be browbeaten or persuaded back into her old role.

'Then strike out on your own,' he'd shouted, angrier than she'd ever known him. 'But you'll get nothing from me, so don't come whingeing when you find yourself sleeping in a doorway.'

She'd not heard another word from him for almost a month, then he'd contacted her in person, instead of through his secretary.

Sounding oddly subdued, he'd asked if she would join him for lunch at his club.

She'd agreed to meet him against her own better judgement, afraid that he would start wheedling and manipulating, working to get her back into the fold.

Remembering how their previous battles had left her emotionally drained.

I can't start all that again, she thought. I *can't*—even if it does make me a wimp. But I've just managed to achieve some equilibrium, and I don't want to be thrown off balance again.

But the meal had gone better than she expected, probably because they'd adhered rigidly to strictly neutral topics of conversation.

All the same, she was sure that he was biding his time, circling round her, looking for a chink in her armour.

And he'd almost found it with Aynsbridge. She'd enjoyed being at the big Sussex country house more than anything else in her life, and when he'd mentioned almost casually that he was giving a small house party, and asked if she'd care to join it, she'd been tempted.

But then she'd seen it—the small, betraying gleam of triumph—and offered her regrets instead. He'd concealed his chagrin well, but she knew it wouldn't be his last attempt to make her dance to his tune, and that she needed to be wary.

He was sitting at his usual corner table, a buff envelope conspicuous on the white linen cloth. He rose as she approached.

'You're losing weight,' he commented abruptly as Chellie sat down.

'You're clearly not eating properly.'

'I'm fine,' she said. 'And I have three meals a day, including dinner. Everyone in the house has to take a turn in getting it ready, so some of the meals are pretty weird.'

He grunted, clearly uninterested in her domestic arrangements. 'You look pale, too.'

'My Caribbean tan didn't last long.' She kept her tone light, but wondered when she saw his mouth tighten and his fist clench on the envelope.

'So,' he said, as the soup was served. 'Still in that dead-end job?'

She smiled. 'It pays the rent—and for my singing lessons.'

His brows snapped together in the old thunderous way that used to frighten her. 'So you're still going on with that nonsense?'

'It's something I enjoy,' she returned composedly. 'And other people seem to enjoy it too. Jordan, who's teaching me, has managed to fix me up with a couple of gigs. I've actually been paid for them, too. And I'm singing at another tomorrow night,' she added. 'A private party. Someone's birthday.'

His frown deepened. 'Not using your own name, I hope?'

'I call myself Chellie,' she said. 'But I drop the Greer part.' She paused. 'Father—why do you hate it so much? My singing?'

He did not look at her. 'Because it took your mother away from me,' he said roughly at last. 'She was never—just my wife, as I wanted her to be.' He glared at her. 'Satisfied?'

She was silent for a moment. 'They say the more you let people go, the more willing they are to return to you.'

'What Christmas cracker did that come from?' Sir Clive asked with contempt. 'And who's come back to you lately? Not your gallant rescuer, I bet.'

She put her soup spoon down very carefully. 'No.'

'You won't either,' he said. 'I had him fired from that company he worked for. Told them I'd see them ruined if he stayed.' He paused. 'I dare say he wishes now he hadn't been so hasty, sending back his share of the money I paid them.' He smiled grimly. 'An expensive gesture, that, for someone who lives by his wits. It'll be a cold day in hell before he earns that much again.'

There was a sudden roaring in Chellie's ears, and she felt numb. She said, in a voice she hardly recognised, 'You're saying—Ash—sent back the money?'

'Yes.' He pushed the envelope towards her. 'It's all here in the report he submitted before he left, and the final statement from the company. He sent the cheque back himself.'

'Did he explain why?'

'Oh, there was a note with some arrogant comment about blood money. I tore it up.' He paused. 'Do you want to read the report? See what you cost me?'

She shook her head. Her voice was desperate. 'Father— the note—did—did it mention me?'

His eyes narrowed. 'No, and just as well. He's out of the company and out of your life too.'

'And that was your doing.' She closed her eyes, feeling sick. 'How could you?'

'I employed him to save you from the consequences of your own criminal foolishness.' Sir Clive's voice was harsh. 'Not to take advantage of the situation and seduce *my* daughter.'

Chellie stood up, trying to control her unsteady breathing. She said, 'I have news for you, Father. It was the other way round—I seduced him. And there hasn't been a day or a night since when I haven't missed him, or wanted him. And if he was here now, I'd tell him that I loved him.'

As she turned to leave, Sir Clive rose too. 'Where do you think you're going?'

'To find him,' she said. 'If it's not too late.'

'Then you're a fool.' The word cracked at her. 'And I've not time for fools, Michelle, so be warned. I forgave you once, but it won't happen again.

'Is this what you call having a life of your own?' her father demanded scornfully. 'Chasing a man who hasn't given you a second thought since you climbed out of his bed.'

'Oh, but you're wrong,'Chellie told him gently. 'He's given me much more than that. He's given me my life.'

She snatched up her coat, and was gone.

CHAPTER ELEVEN

'HERE are those earrings you wanted to borrow.' Jan wandered into Chellie's room after a perfunctory knock and paused, frowning. 'Hey, you're going to a party tonight, not a funeral. What's the matter?'

'I haven't had a very good day.' Chellie bit her lip. 'I've been trying to trace someone—an old friend—and so far I've had no luck at all.'

'The old friend being a man, of course?'

'Yes,' Chellie admitted. 'How did you know?'

'You've been crying.' Jan shrugged. 'It figures.'

'Oh, God, does it still show?' Chellie gave herself a distracted look in the mirror. 'I've been bathing my eyes too.'

'Well, don't worry about it.' Jan gave her shoulders a quick squeeze. 'Lorna's got some miracle eye-drops. You'll be fine.' She looked Chellie over. 'And that's a wonderful dress. I've never seen it before.'

'I've never worn it before.' The silvery material shimmered enticingly as she moved. 'But tonight I just—thought I would.'

'So who's giving this party?'

'A girl called Angela Westlake—or rather her parents. It's her twenty-first birthday, and they approached Jordan and asked if he'd play the piano during supper, and whether he knew anyone who would sing.'

Jan grinned at her. 'If you're not careful, honey, you could end up famous. Just remember who loaned you the earrings that got you your start,' she added as she went off to fetch the drops.

Left to herself again, Chellie applied blusher without enthusiasm, staring at herself with haunted eyes. She'd really

172

believed it would be so simple to find Ash. That it would take one phone call.

But when she'd finally screwed up the courage to ring the security company she'd been completely blanked by a frosty woman who'd told her they never revealed details about past or present employees.

Her only other hope was to telephone Arcadie. It was the nearest thing he had to a sanctuary, after all, she reminded herself. He might have gone to ground there while he considered his options. And while he licked his wounds too.

But the international operator had been unable to help either. St Hilaire had no listing for anyone called Howard.

So it was *impasse*, thought Chellie drearily. She couldn't afford to hire a private detective to find Ash, or go to the Caribbean and search for herself. Besides, she was unsure what she might find at Arcadie. There was still the unresolved question of Julie Howard, who might now have gained a new importance in his life. Or reasserted her former supremacy.

She might have leapt to the wrong conclusion about the money, too. Who said he'd returned it because of some feeling he still might have for her? Maybe—and more likely—it was simply Ash's way of drawing a line under an episode he now wished to forget. After all, their association hadn't done him much good, so perhaps he was clearing away the debris of the past.

And maybe it was wiser—healthier—for her to do the same.

She picked up her lipstick, put it down again, and closed her eyes.

If only, she thought, it could be that easy. But it wasn't. Ash was in her waking thoughts every hour of the day, and at night she tossed restlessly from side to side of the bed, consumed with longing. Burning up for him.

So she wasn't prepared to give up just yet. Not while there was an atom of hope—another avenue to pursue. And, of course, there was.

Laurent, she thought, her lips quivering into a smile. Laurent Massim. He and Ash sailed together, but they were also friends. He must know where Ash was.

And if he can't tell me, she thought, I'll know that Ash really doesn't want to be found. And, however hard it may be, I'll stop looking.

She looked at her watch. No time to call the operator this evening, of course. She had a party to attend, a professional engagement to fulfil. But tomorrow would be a different story.

She lifted her chin. I will do this, she told herself. It's not over yet.

The party was being held in a tall house in a leafy square. It was in full swing when they arrived. They were greeted by the hostess, a tall, attractive girl with a pleasant smile.

'Hi,' she said. 'So you're Jordan.' Chellie found herself being given a friendly but minute inspection. 'And you, of course, must be Chellie.' The smile widened. 'It's good to meet you. If you put your coats in the downstairs cloak-room, I'll show you where you'll be performing.'

They were taken down to a large basement room, covering almost all of the lower ground floor, where the supper was to be served.

A mouthwatering buffet was already laid out on long trestles, and there was a large tub filled with bottles of champagne on ice standing by. A number of small tables and chairs had been set out for the guests, most of them facing towards the baby grand piano at the other end of the room.

Jordan tried it softly with absorbed satisfaction as soon as Angela had excused herself and returned to her guests.

'The programme's been agreed,' he told Chellie. 'All stuff you know, that we've practised, and space for a couple of requests. I'm going to supply some background noise while the food's being served, then you come on.' He eyed her. 'You look different tonight—glowing, somehow.'

'It's the dress.' She did a half-twirl.

'No, it's more than that.' He paused. 'But put some of it in the performance. Don't hold back, Chellie. Show them what you're made of.'

'Don't I always?'

He shrugged. 'Sometimes I get the impression your heart and mind are elsewhere.'

'Ouch,' she said. 'Then tonight they'll get all of me. They'll have to if I'm to make myself heard over the sound of chewing,' she added cheerfully.

But, oddly, she found she did not have to compete with the chink of glasses and the scrape of cutlery after all. As she started to sing 'Out of My Dreams' from *Oklahoma*, a concert-hall hush fell on the room, and she was greeted with generous applause at the end.

She saw Angela Westlake standing at the side of the room, smiling and giving her the thumbs up.

'We usually do requests at the end,' Jordan announced. 'But we've been asked for a very special song right now— so, if it's all right with Chellie—here we go.'

Is he going to tell me what it is? Chellie thought resignedly as she smiled her acquiescence. Or am I supposed to guess?

Then she heard the opening chords and felt her heart jump crazily. Oh, no, she thought. Not this of all songs—please.

But the introduction was finishing, and there was nothing she could do but launch herself into the haunting first line of 'Someone to Watch Over Me'.

She was halfway through the first verse when she saw him, leaning in the doorway, almost unrecognisable in black tie and dinner jacket. Looking at her over the heads of other people as he'd done that other time. That first time.

Except there were no other people. The room might have been empty as she sang sweetly and wistfully for Ash alone, the slight huskiness in her voice adding poignancy to the words, an emotion that came straight from the heart. Holding his gaze with hers.

When she finished there was an almost startled silence, then the clapping began.

As she took a bow, instinctively her eyes sought Ash again, to see if he was joining in the applause—if he was smiling.

But Ash was turning away, walking to the door, pausing momentarily for a word with Angela Westlake and a swift kiss on the cheek.

Oh, God, Chellie thought frantically. He's going. He's leaving again, and if he does I'll never find him. I know it.

She turned to Jordan. 'I'm sorry,' she said. 'There's something I must do—someone I have to talk to.'

She threaded her way through the groups of guests, forcing herself to smile when a detaining hand touched her arm—to murmur her appreciation for the words of praise. When all she really wanted to do was run. Chase after him wherever he was heading.

He was nearly at the top of the stairs when she caught up with him. 'Ash—wait—please. Speak to me.' Her voice was desperate.

He turned slowly and looked down at her, the blue eyes grave. He said, 'You're wearing the dress.'

'Yes—something made me…' She swallowed. 'You don't mind?'

'How could I?' He smiled faintly. 'You look so beautiful you take my breath away.'

'In spite of my grotesque hair?'

'Maybe because of it.' He touched the silky strands, his fingers feather-gentle.

'But I wasn't asking for compliments. I want to talk…' She paused, her eyes searching his face. 'There are things to be said.'

'But maybe this isn't the right time,' Ash said quietly. 'Your audience will be missing you, songbird. You have them eating out of the palm of your hand.'

She swallowed. 'I wasn't singing for them. I was singing for you. You—must have known that. So why are you leaving? Because that's what you're doing—isn't it? You're going, and leaving me behind.'

'I must.' There was a raw note in his voice that she seized on.

'But why?'

He said gently, 'Chellie, your voice is going to take you to all kinds of places. I'd just get in the way. It's better that I go.'

She said with sudden fierceness, 'If that's how you feel, why did you give back the money?'

He stiffened. 'Who told you I'd done so?'

'My father—who else? He said you were a fool.'

'Yes,' he said. 'I'm sure he did. But I didn't expect him to tell you what I'd done. I thought he'd want to keep that a secret.'

'I'm sure he'll wish he had. Because you're not leaving without me. Never again.'

She lifted a hand, touched his cheek. 'He made you lose your job, Ash, and I'm so sorry. Because he'll probably stop you getting another one.' She bit her lip. 'You have no idea the kind of influence he has.'

'I got a good idea from seeing the effect he'd had on you,' Ash said grimly. He sat on the top step and pulled her down beside him. He said, 'Chellie, no one got me fired, least of all your father. I was already planning to go—it had all been arranged totally amicably, and then I was asked to do this one last job because it was my kind of thing.'

He shook his head. 'At first I said no, particularly when I found out what was involved. I had you down as some rich bitch who liked to live on the edge. My least favourite kind of person. But then your father started offering silly money, and I knew the business could do with a cash injection just then, so—for better or worse—I agreed.'

He sighed. 'I had all these strict rules for myself. Get the job done quickly, and no personal involvement—ever. And I tried my damnedest to stick to them—right up to the end.

'But with you, the ground was shifting under my feet,

and there were no bloody rules. I saw you, and I was lost. Caught up in this incredible, miraculous thing that I'd never really believed in. Knowing that I didn't have to be paid to keep you safe, because I'd lay down my life for you if necessary.'

He paused. 'All this I wanted to tell you, my beloved girl, and so much more. And then that dangerous buffoon showed up a day early and my chance went, and everything descended into chaos. I thought that I'd lost you for ever, that what we had was damaged beyond repair. You had every right to be hurt and angry about the way I'd tricked you, and any explanation I could give was only going to sound like some lame afterthought.

'Anyway, I told myself I'd blown it completely, and consequently nothing else seemed to matter. I made sure Victor got the money for the company, and then I—walked away.'

She said, her voice shaking, 'But that wasn't all of it, Ash. You had another reason to leave. There was Julie. You never really told me the truth about her, did you? And I have to know. Does she love you? Are you in love with her?'

'I should damned well hope not,' Ash said with asperity. 'Or my father will have me arrested. Julie's my young sister, and dying to meet you.'

She drew a deep breath. 'Your sister? Oh, I don't understand any of this. You said she was the owner's daughter. You had her photograph beside your bed.'

'Beside my father's bed, actually. He's the owner in question, and he can be a sentimental old devil, so there's usually one of me too. But I decided to put that particular piece of evidence away for the duration—in a very safe place—along with your passport,' he added, straight-faced. 'Just in case you started putting two and two together at some inconvenient moment. It didn't occur to me, however, you'd do exactly that and make five. Jools and I are fairly alike, if you look.'

'So Mr Howard—is your father?' She tried to unscramble

her thoughts as the joy inside her began to spread like wild-fire through her veins.

'Mr Howard Brennan, yes. I can show you my birth certificate, if you want. And Julie's, too.'

'Oh, God,' she said on a little wail. 'Why didn't you tell me all this? Why didn't you explain at Arcadie?'

'Because in the kind of job I've been doing you keep personal details to a minimum. I learned that in the Army. You don't form relationships with the client. I was trying hard, against tough odds, to be disciplined, and stay away from you until the assignment was over.' His mouth twisted. 'And we both know what happened to that good intention.'

He took her hand. 'Anyway, darling, I thought you knew—that you'd guessed who I was and what I was about. Or some of it, at least. You said so.'

'I was talking about Julie.' Her fingers clung to his. 'I thought you and she were practically engaged,' she added with a little wail.

'And, that being the case, I was still trying to get you into bed?' Ash's tone was wry. 'You can't have a very high opinion of me.'

'I didn't know you. You'd done too good a job of keeping me at arm's length. I was just trying to make sense of it all, and failing miserably. I was so completely wretched I couldn't think straight.' She paused. 'And that's an explanation, not an excuse.'

She hesitated again. 'Tell me something now. Why did you come here tonight—if you meant to walk out again?'

He said with sudden harshness, 'I'm not even sure what I intended. I only knew that I needed to see you one more time. That I was gasping for you like air. But if you hadn't come after me, Chellie, I would have given you back your life and disappeared.'

'And I would have found you again,' she said. 'Some time—somehow.'

There was another round of applause from the basement, and Ash rose to his feet, pulling Chellie up with him.

'I think it's time we were on our way,' he said. 'Any moment Angie's gang are going to be pouring through here looking for the disco, the loos, or more drinks. They could trample right over us.'

'But I can't leave now,' Chellie protested. 'I'm supposed to be here to sing. I've got to see Jordan and explain—that's if he'll ever speak to me again.'

'He'll be fine. Angie's putting him straight at this moment.'

'The Westlakes are friends of yours?' She gulped. 'Of course. They would be.'

He grinned. 'Relatives, actually. Angie's mother and mine were first cousins, and pretty close. Why? Did you think I was gatecrashing?'

'I don't know what I thought. All I could see was you. All I could hear in my head was your name. It was like a miracle.'

Chellie paused suddenly, her eyes widening. 'Except it's nothing of the sort—is it? It's not even a coincidence,' she added on a note of breathless accusation. 'You arranged for me to be here. Ash Brennan—you set me up.'

'Just a little,' he admitted. 'Do you mind?'

'No,' she said. 'Considering I was going to call Laurent tomorrow and beg him to tell me where you were.'

'Oh, my love,' Ash said softly. 'My sweet love.' He paused. 'We could go back to your house, but I'd rather not run the gauntlet of the other girls yet. I need to have you strictly to myself.'

Chellie halted, staring at him. 'You even know where I live?'

He nodded ruefully. 'I asked Vic, my former partner, to keep an eye on you. We were in the Army together, you see, which is where we got the idea for the business, and we went through a lot together, so we've always been close.

'Besides, I was terrified you'd marry that idiot who came looking for you just to spite me,' he added, his mouth twisting. 'And I was hungry for any morsel of information about you—that you were well—that you were happy.'

'And what did he say?'

'Yes, to the first. Not very, to the second.'

'Well, he was right,' she said. 'And, after all, I have said more than once that I need someone to watch over me. So I can hardly complain when it happens.'

'I'm staying at a hotel temporarily,' he said. 'Will you come back there with me?'

'Anywhere,' she said. 'As long as we're together.'

'Oh, I can guarantee that,' Ash said. 'In fact I shall have serious trouble ever letting you out of my sight.'

'Then don't,' she said sedately, and went out with him into the night.

She'd expected a decent room—Ash was too fastidious for anything else—but not a penthouse suite in one of the capital's most prestigious hotels.

'Well?' Ash finished ordering champagne from Room Service and put the phone down.

'Very well.' She gave her surroundings another long look. 'Are you quite sure you gave back your share of the money?'

He shrugged. 'You had it straight from the horse's mouth. And you can always check my bank account later.'

'Later,' she said, 'has a nice sound.'

'Want to check the rest of the accommodation?'

The bed in the adjoining room was king-sized, and it was hard to notice anything else, but Chellie was determined to try.

'Heavens,' she said. 'How many channels on this television set?'

'I've no idea,' he said. 'And I have no plans to find out.'

Aware of his eyes following her, Chellie felt suddenly shy. She walked to the row of fitted closets and flung open a door. 'Oh.' She swallowed. 'You've brought rather more than a shirt and a pair of jeans this time.'

'I came prepared for a lengthy campaign.'

'You certainly did.' Her fingers slid along the rail and met silky fabric. 'And what's this?'

She just managed to catch the black dress as it slipped from its hanger. Turned to him with it spilling from her hands, her lips parting incredulously.

'You—took this?'

'I had to have something,' he said quietly. 'I didn't think you'd miss it. And it had some good memories for me.' He paused. 'Would you rather I threw it away?'

'Oh, no,' she said. 'In fact, I might even wear it again sometimes—birthdays—anniversaries—times like that. Create some more memories for both of us.' She let it drop to the floor. Unfastened the silver dress and sent it to join the pool of black at her feet. Stepped over both of them towards him.

She whispered, 'Darling—do we need champagne? I'm—really not thirsty.'

He stared at her, raw hunger in his eyes, harsh colour burning along his cheekbones.

He said huskily, 'But we might be—later.' And cancelled the order.

An hour had passed before Chellie stirred in his arms, her body sated, her heart full.

She said, 'So you weren't just a figment of my imagination after all. I did wonder.'

'I'm total reality,' Ash returned drowsily. 'Give me a few minutes, and I'll prove it to you all over again.'

She kissed his naked shoulder. 'Do you know, I was actually nervous? Isn't that ridiculous?'

'No,' he said. 'I was nervous too.'

'Under pressure?' There was a smile in her voice. 'What happened to the cheroots?'

'I've given up smoking. All part of the reformation. If I'm going to be a family man, I want to live to enjoy it.'

'Oh,' she said. She paused. 'Is that what you're planning?'

'It was,' he said slowly. 'But now I'm beginning to wonder all over again if I'm being very unfair.'

Chellie sat up and glared at him. 'You gave back a small fortune and went to all this trouble to find me—and you're having second thoughts?' She shook her head. 'I don't believe it. Unless you've decided you don't want me after all.'

'I hardly believe it myself, but I'm trying to be unselfish.' He looked into her eyes. 'Chellie, you have a God-given talent as a singer. I saw suddenly how they reacted to you this evening. You were tearing the heart out of them. And it made me think—how can I take her away from this? Is marriage to me any kind of fair exchange?'

He shook his head. 'Dear God, you've just escaped from your father. Do you really want to replace him with a husband before you've had time to breathe? What the hell have I got to offer in return?'

He took her face gently between his hands. 'I want you to have your chance, Chellie. The life you said you wanted.'

'You're the life I want.' She smiled back at him, her eyes warm and tender, a lump gathering in her throat. 'If you still want me. Singing is secondary. Although I suppose it could be handy as you're temporarily out of work. And spending everything you've got on expensive hotel suites and ladies to go with them.'

'Don't tell Dad I've no job,' he said. 'He thinks I'm his partner in his new brokerage and boat charter business, and is paying me accordingly. Why did you think I packed in the security game? I'd had enough of the high-risk activities and never staying anywhere more than a few days. I wanted a life too.'

He dropped a kiss on her hair. 'You see—you really were my last assignment.'

'So, where do we go from here?' She spread her fingers across his chest.

'How about a crash course in getting to know each

other—no secrets—no half-truths? Just the two of us, talking and loving. And alone.'

'It sounds perfect,' she said. 'What did you have in mind?'

'Dad's looking at this new boat and wants me to give it a trial in the Bahamas. I—I hoped you might come with me.'

She sighed happily. 'It sounds like heaven. And I've been learning to cook too.'

'I'm seriously impressed.' There was tender laughter in his voice. 'But I meant everything I said about your singing. I want you to be free to follow your star. It would be wrong to tie you down.'

'I could be a working wife,' she said. 'At least until the babies come. Then I can sing them lullabies.'

'Ah, darling,' he said. And found her mouth with his.

'We do have one remaining problem,' he resumed, some time later. 'Your father. He's not going to be happy about this.'

'The more you let people go, the more they want to come back to you,' Chellie said softly. 'He hasn't learned that yet, but I have hopes.'

'I have hopes too,' he said. 'And dreams. And you're at the centre of each one of them.'

She drew him down to her and kissed him.

'And we're going to make all our dreams come true, my love,' she whispered. 'You and I—together.' She smiled. 'And now you can order the champagne.'

But Ash's arms were already tightening round her. 'Later,' he said.

A PASSIONATE PROTECTOR

BY
MAGGIE COX

The day **Maggie Cox** saw the film version of *Wuthering Heights,* with a beautiful Merle Oberon and a very handsome Laurence Olivier, was the day she became hooked on romance. From that day onwards she spent a lot of time dreaming up her own romances, secretly hoping that one day she might become published and get paid for doing what she loved most! Now that her dream is being realised, she wakes up every morning and counts her blessings. She is married to a gorgeous man and is the mother of two wonderful sons. Her two other great passions in life – besides her family and reading/writing – are music and films.

Look out for a marvellous new novel from Maggie Cox, *Surrender to Her Spanish Husband*, available in September 2010.

To all my boys: Gary, Conar, Sandy and Luke –
you have my heart.

CHAPTER ONE

Sitting on a wrought-iron bench in Hyde Park, Megan Brand was uninterestedly nibbling at a cheese and ham sandwich when it started to rain. At first she couldn't be bothered moving. It was almost surreal to stay put as the rain gathered strength, streaming in rivulets down her hair and face, drenching her thoroughly as people scurried to and fro before her eyes. Opening umbrellas, pulling coats up over their heads, suddenly directionless, they were like lots of little mice scuttling round a cage, desperately doing their utmost to avoid getting wet.

At some point, almost as if coming out of a trance, Megan decided that being cold and wet and soaked right through to the skin didn't have a lot to commend it and, shivering, she got up and resigned herself to heading home. So much for her grand plan to while away the rest of the afternoon just sitting. Breaking up her sandwich, she threw the remainder to the little grey squirrels that had been keeping her company while she ate. She looped her damp ebony hair behind her ears and strode as purposefully as her limp would allow off towards the park exit and home.

As she turned into the Bayswater Road her eyes scanned the array of art displayed against the railings, a ritual that had taken place every Sunday for as long as she remembered, with artists of every ilk, nationality and diversity displaying their wares to the interested public. As she stopped to stare at an oddly appealing seascape that somehow tugged at her heart, a strong resurgence of need and longing rose up inside her.

Ten years ago Megan had secured a place at one of

London's top art colleges. Her whole future had lain before
her: an unknown, exciting, soon-to-be experienced realm of
limitless possibilities… But that had been before she'd run
into Nick. Confident, good-looking, and a charmer to boot,
he had had no hesitation in applying some of his ruthless
ambition in pursuit of the shy art student who'd never been
the object of such persistence until Nick Brand clapped eyes
on her. Eventually she'd been worn down by his relentless
tactics. He'd charmed Megan into his bed, then marriage,
and finally—his *pièce de resistance*—into surrendering her
precious place at college.

'Time you got into the real world, my love,' he'd said
confidently, secure in the knowledge that his malleable little
wife knew better than to argue.

It hadn't been easy, relinquishing her dream, but in those
days she had operated on the belief that loving someone
ultimately meant making sacrifices. Compromising your
own needs to keep your partner happy. Funny, though, how
it had been her that had done all the compromising. Nick
hadn't sacrificed anything that you could honestly notice.
He'd still acted as though he was a free agent even after
they'd married. What a twenty-four-carat fool Megan had
been.

Her breath escaped in a little cloud of steam as she hovered in front of a seascape, her presence alerting the young
woman with the silver star-shaped nose-stud who was running the display. The girl turned away from adjusting the
tarpaulin she'd been trying to fix in place to protect her work
and placed her hand confidingly on Megan's arm.

'I did that down in Cornwall last winter,' she explained,
gesturing towards the scene. 'A place called Rock.
Smashing surf, if you like surfing.'

Megan felt the heat rise in her cheeks, immediately ill at
ease with the unexpected attention. She felt like the proverbial drowned rat, painfully aware that her hair must look

like rats' tails while her inadequate skirt and jacket were plastered to her body as if she'd just crawled out of a river.

'How much is it?'

She'd already decided she wanted to buy the picture. She'd put it in her room at Penny's flat and maybe think about visiting that place at the end of the summer. Rock— it sounded romantic. As far as Megan was concerned, the coast—any coast—was always best visited out of season. There was a kind of magic about it then, when all the tourists had finally gone and the beaches were more or less bare.

The girl named a figure that was about what she had expected to pay. She slipped her bag off her shoulder and reached in for her chequebook.

'A present for someone, is it?' the girl asked cheerfully.

'For me.' Megan smiled briefly back and refused to feel guilty that for once in her life she was spending her money on herself.

Penny Hallet stirred the pasta again, gesturing towards the postcard she'd left on the kitchen worktop with the long wooden spoon she'd been using to stir. 'I really think you should give him a ring. It could be just what you need.'

Picking up the plain white postcard to examine it, Megan cautiously turned it over to read the advertisement printed on the back.

'Where did you get this?'

Penny's blue eyes were mutinous. 'I "borrowed" it from Mrs Kureshi's noticeboard at the newsagents. I didn't have a pen, so what's a girl supposed to do?'

Glancing up, Megan pinned her friend with a slightly disapproving gaze. 'You mean you stole it. How is the person who put it there supposed to get any business if you come along and steal his postcard?'

Penny's face was a picture. 'Oh, for God's sake, Megan! Don't you ever break the rules?' Rolling her eyes heavenwards, she shook her head and shrugged. 'Never mind. Don't answer that question. I already know what the answer is.'

'Hmm, no name.' Megan's attention was back on the postcard. 'Just initials. "KH". Could be a woman.'

'Could be.' Penny sucked in her cheeks and blew them out again. 'But my money's on a man. Anyway, male or female, what does it matter as long as they know their stuff?'

'But going back to painting—it's been so long... And this—"Let painting open the way to healing and inner peace"—what do you think it means?'

'Why don't you just give the number a ring and find out some more? What harm could it do? If you want things to change you've got to start helping yourself. This could be a good thing for you, Meg, I'm sure of it. You need some pleasure in your life again and I know you'd love to get back into some painting. Besides...' Penny caught the doubt flitting across Megan's face and decided to push her advantage home. 'You hate that tedious job at the bank, working for Misery Guts, and all you do after dinner each night is go to bed with a book. I know sixty-year-olds who have more fun! Right now you're twenty-eight going on ninety!'

'I'm handling things in my own way Pen.' Megan's softly mobile mouth thinned with anxiety.

'Cobblers!' Penny thwacked the wooden spoon on the side of the stainless steel pan that contained the pasta, emotion straining her temper. 'I know you. I don't want to hear excuses. I've been hearing excuses for the last six months as to why you can't do something! Hard as it is for you to hear, sweetheart, your ex-husband's quite happy with What's-her-face, damn him, while you're still walking around like an extra on *Return of the Living Dead*! I'm not trying to be mean to you, Meg, but you've got to realise what you're doing to yourself. Don't write off everything as useless or pointless. Just give things a chance.'

Megan glanced down at the postcard in her hand, staring at the large bold print through eyes that were suddenly stinging with tears. How the hell was she supposed to make such a momentous decision when it was all she could do to decide what to have for breakfast each morning? Pain of one kind or another had dogged her for so long it was hard to see her way clearly. Even harder was finding the energy to take action. She'd racked her brains to find something, some way she could help the healing process, but instead felt as if she was running into brick walls ten feet high.

Well… Perhaps this would be different? Perhaps the mysterious 'KH' and his painting class really did have the answer to all her woes? Yeah. And world peace would suddenly descend on the planet tomorrow—some time around lunch. She sniffed, rubbing at her eyes with the too-long sleeve of her knitted burgundy sweater. *Stop clutching at straws Megan… It's a waste of energy you don't have.*

Crossing the black and white tiled floor to the stainless steel pedal bin on the other side of Penny's immaculate modern kitchen, she put her foot down hard on the pedal. She was about to drop the postcard inside, and almost jumped out of her skin when Penny snatched it from her fingers and tucked it safely into the vee of her powder-blue designer shirt.

'No, you don't! It's my postcard. I pinched it from Mrs Kureshi's and I'll decide when or *if* I want to get rid of it!'

'All right, keep your hair on.' Biting back a helpless grin, Megan watched her elegantly tall friend stalk mutinously back to the cooker. To some, she might look like an aloof catwalk model, in her designer label clothes and her handmade Italian shoes, but to Megan she was the salt of the earth. And they didn't come much saltier than Penny Hallet when the mood was upon her.

'And if you won't ring the blasted number, Megan Brand—then I will!' said the blonde, returning to her stirring of the now bubbling pasta with a vengeance...

Taking her finger off the bell, Megan was immediately consumed by an overpowering urge to turn and run. Not that she could physically run anywhere these days, after what had happened, but still the desire was there. She just prayed this 'KH', whoever he was—Penny had more or less convinced her the initials belonged to a male—was not some crank. At least her friend had the address and telephone number should anything go amiss.

Her heart fluttered a little as she heard the distinct tread of footsteps behind the big black door with the gilded knocker, and she knew with a deepening sense of dread that it was too late to flee anywhere. Instead she took a step back, glancing up the smart little street in a quiet corner of Notting Hill, with its well-tended window-boxes, as if to reassure herself. She told herself the mysterious 'KH' couldn't be a crank because only people with money could afford to live in this area these days. But that didn't mean he couldn't be a wealthy crank, did it?

A frown was creasing her brow as the door swung open, and her unprepared glance collided with the most piercing hazel eyes flecked with gold that she'd ever seen in her life. Astonishingly intense, indisputably sexual, they were the kind of eyes that made a woman sharply, even forcibly aware of the essential basic differences between a man and a woman.

Like a laser beam that could sear through solid metal, that hot glance went straight to the core of Megan's femininity, shocking her with the power of its intimacy. Such a toe-curling glance simply left her with nowhere to go. Which wasn't a bad summation when her feet felt as if they were stuck to the concrete she was standing on.

Her 'Hello there' was slightly breathless—the rapid acceleration of her heartbeat had made her feel suddenly giddy.

'I'm Megan Brand. I believe we have an appointment? If you're "KH" that is? You didn't put your full name on the postcard.'

To her consternation, he merely smiled enigmatically, placed his hands on either side of lean, tight hips, then stepped back into the shadowy recess to let her enter. 'Come in. I've been waiting for you.'

The unexpectedly husky timbre of his voice was like being sensually massaged all over with warm scented oil. Megan tingled with unexpected pleasure. It wasn't just the suggestion of sex in his voice either. The man's appearance rocked her to her toes as well. He was lean, dark and downright dangerous-looking. With his tousled chestnut hair, unshaven chiselled jaw and long angular cheekbones to die for, just looking at him seemed to flout all the rules of convention—because Megan's reaction to him was anything but impersonal. Everything about the man seemed to suggest dimensions of possibility and excitement that a woman could only dream about.

Anxiety locked her throat. 'I'm sorry I'm late but I had a little trouble finding you.' *Liar. You mean you had a little trouble plucking up the courage to come.*

'Don't worry about it. You're here now and that's all that matters.'

'You are the person who's doing the art tuition?' she checked, because just now she barely trusted herself to get anything right.

'Call me Kyle.' He raked a hand through his already mussed hair, a brief flash of amusement lurking in the mesmerising golden depths of his eyes. 'Now the introductions are over, why don't you come inside?'

'Right.' Megan fingered a button on her jacket, pressed

her brown leather tote bag reassuringly to her chest and forced a shaky smile.

'Some time today would be good,' Kyle drawled lazily, holding the door wider.

Her face suffused with heat. She willed herself to make a move. As soon as she did her senses were assailed by the strongly hypnotic scents of sandalwood and patchouli incense. She was instantly transported. The aroma wove its mystery around her, adding to the illusion of somehow stepping into another world. A world of intriguing unknowables, none more intriguing then the man who was currently leading her casually through the portals of the smart terraced house, his long leather-clad legs striding ahead with a compellingly masculine grace that sent a little shiver of exquisite anticipation darting up her spine.

After the contrasting dimness of the hallway, Kyle's living room was an unexpected surprise of light and colour, with patio doors opened wide onto a long deeply verdant garden that, once glimpsed, had Megan longing to explore it. He couldn't be all bad if he loved gardens, she thought wistfully. One day—when she got herself together again, when and if she got her share of the house value from Nick—she'd have a place of her own with a garden, even if it was only the size of a postage stamp.

'Why don't you sit down?'

'Oh. Yes. Of course.' Unbuttoning her cream linen jacket with fingers that shook a little, she lowered herself carefully down onto a large couch draped with an eye-catching terracotta and yellow Moroccan-style throw. The muscle in her thigh was throbbing like a sore tooth with the effort of trying to accommodate her physical discomfort, and she felt awkward and ungainly in front of this disturbing dark Adonis, ill equipped to field her vulnerability the way she needed to. Kyle, meanwhile, had dragged a huge yellow beanbag across the floor, dropping down into it opposite Megan with ease. He positioned himself just bare inches from her san-dalled feet, causing her heart to take a slow elevator ride to her stomach when she realised he had no intention of wid-ening the distance between them any time soon.

'So.' The piercing hazel gaze examined her features closely, hovering for a disconcerting length of time on her mouth before returning at leisure to her startled brown eyes. 'What sort of a day have you had so far?'

The question, so casually asked, put her in a spin.

'What sort of a day have I had?'

'It wasn't meant to be a difficult question.' Humour sur-faced, making his eyes glint more like gold than ever.

In need of rescuing, Megan let her gaze gravitate long-ingly to the lush beautiful garden that beckoned through the patio doors. 'Well, I've been to work, come home, prepared some tea and got ready to come to my appointment. I don't know what else to tell you.'

'How was your day at work? Did you enjoy it? Did it give you satisfaction?'

'It's just a job.' Flustered, Megan tried hard to concen-trate. 'I don't know what you want, what you expect me to—'

'What I want or expect is neither here nor there.' Kyle honed in on her discomfort with the relentless precision of a crack marksman lining up his target. 'What I *need* from you is for you to be honest with yourself. I'm not expecting you to furnish me with answers you think I might be looking for. So I'll ask you again, Megan. What sort of day have you had?'

Megan squirmed. There was obviously going to be no easy way out of her little interview with Kyle. No quick exit route. He had her trapped as surely as if she were a paper butterfly beneath a net. He wanted *honest*. Okay, she'd give it her best shot. Work was a blur. All she'd done for most of the day was stare at a computer screen. Most of the time she'd been on auto-pilot. To her shame, her best shot failed to deliver.

'Nothing special,' she finally replied, because any other answer simply defeated her.

'Really?' His eyes narrowed, a frown creasing the smooth bronzed skin between his brows. 'Goethe said, "Nothing is worth more than this day". Do you really believe there was nothing special about it?'

Put like that, he made her statement sound ignorant and crass. Megan wanted the ground to open up and swallow her.

'I didn't mean that the way—the way it sounded. Look, I don't really know why I'm here. I didn't know what to expect.'

'First of all, you need to relax. This isn't some examination you have to pass or fail. You came voluntarily. You can leave voluntarily. After we've talked a little you can decide whether or not you think it's for you.' To her absolute surprise, he reached forward and with deft fingers slipped her sandals easily from her feet, then placed them side by side on the cool oak floor.

Megan swallowed hard, her skin burning from his unexpected touch. 'And is taking off my shoes compulsory? Or is that voluntary, too?'

A sexy chuckle escaped him that had all Megan's senses zinging like popcorn in response. Heat seared her spine, dripping like slow, heavy molasses into her limbs.

'Bare feet make you more vulnerable—more open to talking about what's real.'

'What's real?' Her voice was a hoarse whisper. What was happening to her? Just a few minutes in this man's company and emotions were stirring inside her that she'd barely known she had.

'The reason you're here. Why did you ring my number and make an appointment, Megan?'

'I didn't—' She flushed guiltily, thinking how Penny had had to coerce her into coming at all. 'I mean, my friend saw your ad and thought it was something that might interest me. She persuaded me to make the call.'

'So it was your friend's idea? You didn't want to come yourself?' His sensual lips quirked in a mocking little smile and a dart of heat exploded in the pit of Megan's stomach like a rocket going off.

'I didn't say that.'

'Okay. Let's put aside the fact that you're not sure whether you want to be here or not, and see if we can touch upon something that's real and honest. Can you tell me about your interest in art?'

He asked the question as if he had his doubts, which made her feel even more defensive. She wasn't trying to deceive him about anything, but she reflected that there were probably a lot of women who would profess interest in the subject if it gained them Brownie points with the hunk sitting at her feet. At least her interest was genuine.

'It's my love.' Her back straightened automatically. 'Ten years ago I had a place at the Slade College of Art. I fully intended to make art my future. Unfortunately…things didn't quite work out the way I imagined they would.'

'Can you tell me what happened?' Kyle's voice was a husky, low-pitched timbre, drugging her senses like the most intoxicating wine. It was almost too hard to reply.

'What happened?' Her tongue came out and moistened her lips. Intensely aware of that mesmerising golden gaze never wavering from her sight, Megan clenched every muscle in her body in a bid to concentrate. 'I'd been at college six months when I—I met someone. He wasn't a student. Nick was working at an American bank in town. He was ten years older than me, confident…very sure of himself. Anyway…' She shrugged as if it were an old record hardly worth the playing. 'We got married. He thought my staying on at college was a complete waste of time. ''What can you do with a Fine Art degree?'' he said. ''It's hardly useful.'''

For a moment, Megan's dark eyes flashed with pain, then, lifting her chin a little to continue, she said clearly, 'Anyway, I gave up my place and found a job in a bank…just like Nick. It was like sealing myself into a coffin. I had no desire or interest in climbing a career ladder. I've been stuck there ever since.'

'What a waste.' Kyle drew up his knees and locked his arms around them. 'What's keeping you stuck, Megan?'

During the long silence that followed, Megan found herself the sole focus of his intensely disturbing golden gaze. *Don't look at me like that…* she wanted to say. *I don't deserve for you to look at me like that…* She had the uncanny sensation that the man had the power to penetrate the secrets of her soul, and the feelings that swamped her as a result had her choking back emotion to stay in control. Self-consciously, she speared her fingers through the soft ebony strands of her hair, her face burning beneath his gaze.

'Me, I suppose. My fears.'

'Of what?'

'Of not being good enough to do anything else.'

'You know what's a good acronym for the word fear?'

Megan shook her head.

'False Evidence Appearing Real. Doesn't mean you're not good enough to do anything else just because you imagine it. It's an illusion, not a fact. What other avenues have you explored to support your belief that you might not be good at anything else? You say you love art. Are you any good at it? What can you do? Paint? Draw? Design?'

Her head spun with his quickfire questions, but even though she felt like a worm wriggling on the end of a pin, she sensed he was trying to get to the root of something. 'I can draw…and paint…a little.'

'A little?' His smile wasn't unkind. 'I can see you have real trouble in promoting yourself, don't you?'

Megan said nothing.

'It must have hurt like hell to give up your college place, to relinquish your dream.' His deep voice was measured, as if he was waiting for her to fill in the gaps.

Megan took a breath, then released it slowly. 'It did,' she admitted, dark eyes round. 'Nick thought being a student was just playing at life, an excuse to get out of going to work. He said I needed to get into the ''real'' world.'

'And now?'

'Now?'

'What's his exalted opinion now?' Clearly Kyle didn't pull his punches.

'I don't suppose he thinks any different. Nick's pretty set in his ways like that. Anyway, we aren't married any more. He left me for one of my closest friends. Shows what a good judge of character I am.' Megan's voice was disparaging.

When Claire had betrayed her with Nick she had really thought the pain would kill her. How could she have known even worse was to come after that?

Wriggling her bare toes against the almost sensuous wooden flooring, she glanced awkwardly at Kyle, waiting for some sort of signal to indicate what was going to happen next.

'Do you paint?' she asked him in a rush, then thought what a stupid question to ask someone who was offering his services in art tuition.

'I do.' He stretched his long leather-clad legs out in front of him, the sensual material creaking a little with the sudden movement, perfectly at ease with himself and with her. 'Like you, it's my love.'

'Are you good?' She blushed as she asked the question, but was immediately reassured when he grinned widely.

His smile lit up his whole face. Tiny lines creased the bronzed skin beside his eyes, making them sparkle with an indescribable sheen that had her whole body tightening in acute awareness. Everything about the man in front of her was so alive and so vital, so absolutely vibrant. Next to him Megan felt like a candle that had been carelessly extinguished.

'I get by. That is, I earn my living at it.' Kyle skirted the subject with his usual dexterity. It wouldn't help the heart-stopping beauty in front of him to know that he'd achieved a certain level of fame in the art world, and he certainly wasn't into blowing his own trumpet.

At best it could be intimidating to someone with such obviously low self-esteem, and at worst—well, it could put her off ever setting foot in his house again. And he really didn't want that to happen—not when he knew he could help her. This new venture had put him on an entirely different path from the crazy sybaritic one he'd been travelling until recently. One he was sure would bring him a level of satisfaction that had so far eluded him.

'I'm very fortunate in that respect. But you're not here to talk about me.'

He leapt up with all the lightning agility of a panther and for the first time Megan registered the fact that his own feet were bare. Long and slender and bronzed, like his hands, with perfectly straight toes, they were inexplicably sexy. There was something indisputably arousing about the look of leather next to tanned bare skin.

'Why don't I make us both a drink? What would you like? I think I have most things.'

'Coffee would be nice,' she replied, 'Milk, no sugar.' Seeing an unexpected reprieve from the butterfly net, Megan eased out a shaky breath. Her gaze settled on a startlingly vivid portrait of a stunning native American Indian in full head-dress with eyes almost the same intense hazel as those of the man she had come to see. An answering tingle ran up her spine as she moved her gaze interestedly round the rest of the room, pleasure throbbing through her as she noted the various prints on the wall.

Degas and Matisse, Da Vinci and Millais—some of her favourite artists, too. Kyle obviously had very eclectic tastes when it came to what he liked, but he favoured simplicity, too. The beautifully cool oak floor was bare apart from a sensuously patterned killim with hues of the same browns, terracotta and yellows that were picked out in the cushions keeping her company on the couch. The whole effect was seductively comforting—conducive to coaxing secrets not easy in the telling.

She heard Kyle clattering crockery and spoons from what she presumed must be the kitchen, and allowed herself to take a deeply relaxing breath and close her eyes.

Bone-deep fatigue washed over her, making her realise she could easily fall asleep at the drop of a hat, and for maybe a minute or two she almost did doze off. Then there was suddenly a touch on her knee and her dark eyes flew guiltily open to stare into a sea of gold. A tantalising waft of some woody male cologne drifted beneath her nose and a sudden wild longing swept through her that almost left her trembling with the ferocity of it.

'Your coffee.' He placed a bright yellow mug in her hands with a measured, almost detached look, then settled carefully back down onto the beanbag.

'Thanks.' She sipped the steaming beverage gratefully, stealing furtive looks his way as he imbibed his own drink.

'How did you come by your limp?'

She almost spilled the contents of her mug into her lap. Nobody ever asked her outright about her limp. Directness like this man's was simply not something she was used to.

Studying her reaction, the interplay of startled emotions

that crossed her strikingly beautiful fine-boned face, Kyle inhaled softly and waited patiently for her answer.

'I—I had an accident.'

'Recently?'

'About—about eighteen months ago.'

'What happened?' He leaned forward in his seat, distracting her a little with the sensually strong definition of his jaw, the muscle that jerked a little in the side of his smooth tanned cheek.

'I fell.'

'How?'

'I think you ask too many questions.'

'We're going for honesty here, Megan, remember?' he suggested gently. 'I know it might be painful, but sometimes it's even more painful to live with secrets than share them with someone who might be able to help.'

'You'd make a good interrogator, you know that?' The urge to come back at him with a taste of his own medicine took her by surprise, but the truth was she was fighting for her life here—did he but know it. She got the decidedly unsettling feeling that he did.

'Yeah, I know. Like a dog with a bone. It's not one of my more endearing qualities, but you don't get anywhere in life by giving up. Come on, Megan, I don't care how long we sit here.' He glanced down at his watch to emphasise the point. 'I've got no other plans for the evening, and I'd much rather stay here and talk to you than do anything else I can think of right at this moment.'

It was a terrifying admission for Megan. It meant he wasn't going to let her off the hook any time soon.

'You're not going to let go of this, are you?' Her voice was a husky broken whisper as she finally met his gaze head-on, and was startled to see something akin to tenderness in his eyes. She didn't see it very often, God knew, but she recognised the response when she saw it. If she'd had a mind to, she could easily have sat there and broken her heart.

'You don't have to tell me anything you don't want to, Megan. As I said, anything you tell me is purely voluntary, and, for the record, will go no further than this room. You have my word on it.'

It was plain he was telling her the truth. He had integrity written all over him. It was there in every exquisitely sculpted line of his indomitable male visage. A quiet yet profound strength and honesty radiating out. Drawing her in. Her secret would be safe with him.

'Nick and I had an argument one night.' Megan wasn't going to tell him that it had been shortly after she'd found him in bed with Claire. That was a wound still too raw to encounter head-on. 'He'd been drinking. He was yelling, and I was too upset to reply. I made the mistake of walking away, which made him even angrier. Nick hated to be ignored. Unfortunately we were at the top of the stairs at the time, and when he shoved me I went head-first down the whole flight. I ended up with a badly broken leg. It—it wasn't an accident. He meant to push me.'

Her throat constricting with pain, Megan remembered the fury and hatred in Nick's eyes when he'd pushed her. He'd been furious because she'd found him with Claire. Told her she had no right to be upset when it was all her fault in the first place. *Her fault.*

Taking a deep, shuddering breath at the shattering memory, Megan glanced at Kyle and managed to force out the wobbliest of smiles. 'Anyway. I've had two operations so far. Unfortunately the bones didn't knit back as they should have. I could be facing further procedures in the future and it's left me with this limp. I know it's not the end of the world, that people recover from much worse…but I'd be dishonest if I pretended life wouldn't be better without it.

Most people are too polite or afraid to ask me outright how I got it.'

'That's the trouble with me, you see.' Dry-mouthed, Kyle stared at her, the air between them thick with the tension of mutual awareness brought sharply into focus by Megan's traumatic revelation. He placed his mug of coffee carefully down on the floor. 'I'm neither polite or afraid. I won't pretend that the lack of those things has never got me into trouble, because on occasion it has. But generally speaking I believe in confronting my fears and working through them. As for politeness—pleasing people is a trap, so beyond the usual conventions it doesn't really signify. But that's me. I'm sorry to hear about what happened to you, Megan. More sorry than I know how to tell you. It was a dreadful thing for any man to do to his woman. An outrage. How are you dealing with it? Did you talk to anyone after it happened?'

'Counselling, you mean? No.' Megan moved her head slowly from side to side, her heart constricting with sorrow. 'I didn't want to talk to anyone. I felt—I felt too ashamed.'

'Ashamed?' Hazel eyes alert, Kyle didn't let his gaze stray for even a second.

'I felt it was my fault.' Even now, in her mind, she could hear Nick calling her all those dreadful names, culminating in his favourite taunt that she was a frigid uptight tease who drove him to have affairs because she was so inadequate in bed, because she wouldn't 'experiment'. She wasn't in a hurry to confess that to Kyle, honesty or not. She already felt as if she'd said too much.

'Sweetheart, let me tell you something—no one deserves to be pushed down the stairs and suffer injury. It wasn't your fault, however much you might tell yourself it was. It sounds to me like your husband was the one who had the problems—not you.'

'Ex-husband. Thank God.'

'I stand corrected.' Kyle's answering smile was beguiling.

Like honey and chocolate. Like a rainbow after a storm, walking on the beach out of season, or listening to classical music with the volume turned up... All Megan's favourite things rolled into one.

'So, shouldn't we be talking about art or something?' She shifted self-consciously in her seat, because simply gazing at this man was completely unravelling her in every sense.

Shrugging his shoulders, he seemed inexplicably amused by her suggestion. 'There are no hard and fast rules about anything, Megan. We can cover just about any topic you want to talk about.'

'I really—' She swallowed hard across the sudden burning sensation in her throat. 'I really do want to paint. Can you help me?'

Riveted by the plea in her voice, Kyle gazed at the lovely brunette, her dark eyes shimmering with hope and longing and everything else in between, and thought fiercely, In a heartbeat, angel. And that's a promise.

CHAPTER TWO

'ONE more exhibition. Is it so much to ask?'

'I've done the exhibition thing for the last five years, Demi. What does it take to convince you I'm not interested?' Kyle helped himself to a handful of peanuts from the little dish on the table, silently calling himself all kinds of an idiot for agreeing to this meeting when he'd rather be home painting or catching up on some relevant study.

But Demitri Papandreou's powers of persuasion were legendary, and he'd caught Kyle in too good a mood to be churlish. He'd wondered how long it would take the wealthy Greek to show up in the UK and demand a meet—and to be honest he'd been surprised Demi had waited as long as two months…well, eight weeks and one day, to be exact.

Now, as Kyle sat opposite him in the plush lobby of the Intercontinental Hotel on Park Lane, he mused to himself that his companion must surely be one of the most slickly polished characters that had ever languished in a five-star hotel lounge. In his Armani suits, revelling in his celebrity connections all around the globe, selling oil to the Arabs was child's play to such a man. He was a natural-born salesman, not to mention an outstanding self-publicist—and, credit where it was due, he'd done an amazing job promoting Kyle's career.

But as Kyle's glance flicked across the tanned broad face, with the deeply liquid eyes that reminded him of two black olives, he knew this time that whatever Demi was selling, however much money it involved, today Kyle had no intention of buying.

'We could have sold those paintings ten times over…ten

24

times! And I know you must have more at home in your studio that you haven't even let me see!'

Demi's jowly cheeks wobbled a little with the force of his feelings, but Kyle was already shaking his head.

'I don't care. I'm not interested in the money.'

'Are you mad?' Demi was practically apoplectic. 'Who in this world is not interested in money? I have made you a rich man, no? Surely you can do me this one small favour? So many people are interested in your work, Kyle. Painting is your life. How can you say you will not paint any more?'

'I didn't say I wasn't going to paint any more,' Kyle replied patiently, running his hand round the faint five o'clock shadow studding his jaw. 'I said I didn't want to exhibit any more. I'm tired of doing the circuit. I want to get back to the simple things in life. That last night in Skiathos was one party too many, my friend.'

'But good, no?' Demi's black eyes twinkled in merriment. A passing waitress in a tight black skirt and fitted white blouse flitted by with a drinks tray, her black stiletto heels hardly making a sound on the sea of plush indigo carpet, and the Greek's amused black eyes were instantly diverted.

Kyle took a sip of his cold beer, then placed it carefully back down on the table. No. Not good. Definitely not good. He was tired of people he didn't know wanting to be his friend, and he definitely didn't want to spend his days—or nights, for that matter—making small chit-chat to the great and the good, all for the sake of making a name for himself.

He'd been so much happier since returning to the UK. Even the rain hadn't had the power to burst his bubble—not yet, anyway. His decision to come home had had a dramatic effect on his work, too. Somehow his painting had suddenly become so much freer, more expressive—better than it had been in years in his opinion…and, more importantly, there was this new venture he was undertaking…

During a surreal conversation at that last party, with an empty-headed little blonde who wouldn't know a Degas from a Da Vinci, with too much champagne coursing through his veins, Kyle had been struck by the awful superficiality of the life he'd been leading. He'd been spending too much time associating with people he didn't care for, people who bid ridiculous sums of money for art yet who had little appreciation of real beauty—people who'd sold their souls for a lifestyle instead of a life.

A distinct feeling of unease and regret had crept up on him, rolling over him like a black cloud of remonstration, reminding him that after all this time he still hadn't fulfilled his promise to his sister Yvette.

Before the car crash that had ripped away her life, she'd often beseeched him, 'Don't waste your talent, Kyle. Do something wonderful with it. You're a good man. You know how to reach out to people. There must be a way you can do that in your work. Promise me you'll try.'

Well, he'd thought teaching was the way. He'd made the discovery that art could offer a place of safety in which to express images that spoke of deep-seated emotions and pain. Images that the artist could reflect on and consider and use as a means of healing even the deepest wounds.

Teaching at art college had made him so sure that he'd finally found what he'd been searching for. Something that Yvette would have been proud of—something that would help assuage his own dreadful grief and heartache at her loss. But he couldn't have been as focused as he'd believed, because when Demi Papandreou had arrived on the scene, visiting the college in search of new talent, Kyle had allowed the Greek's effusive praise of his skill and ability to turn his head.

He'd let himself be swept along by the illusory allure of fame and fortune, and a different road entirely from the one he'd been envisaging for himself. Truth to tell, it had been the perfect excuse to get out of fulfilling a promise he'd felt woefully inept to realise. Perhaps Yvette had thought too highly of him after all? Just because it had been her personal mission to smooth the path of every wounded soul she came into contact with, it didn't mean Kyle could do the same...

God knew, she wouldn't be very proud of him now, he'd thought. He might have created art that sold for ridiculously large sums of money, but he'd nearly lost his own soul in the process. A throb of shame had washed over him. He didn't think his beautiful sister had spent one superficial day in the whole of her life. Somehow she'd approached every moment like the miracle it was. And what had Kyle been doing? He'd been behaving as if he was going to live for ever. More to the point—he'd been behaving as if he didn't give a damn about anyone but himself. Which wasn't true. Underneath that handsome 'don't give a damn' exterior there was a compassionate heart beating, silently crying out for him to take action.

That party had given him a wake-up call and he was going to heed it. Perhaps he ought to drop the dizzy little blonde a thank-you note?

'There must be some other reason you suddenly pack up your bags and jump on a flight back to this cold, rainy country! You were just trying to put me off by telling me you wanted a change of direction. If it is not a better opportunity to make money then obviously it must be a woman.' Demi wagged his finger remonstratively at the younger man.

'Sorry to disappoint you, my friend.' Kyle shook his head and flashed a rueful grin. Instantly, a vivid picture of one gorgeous brunette with velvet brown eyes and a body that would fuel the fantasies of every schoolboy in England—not to mention their fathers—stole firmly into his mind and planted itself there. Then he thought about what she had told him about that louse of a husband of hers and what he had done to her, and every muscle in Kyle's undoubtedly fit, strong body turned to iron as a slow rage burned in his gut.

'You can't fool me, Kyle. I have known you long enough to see when you are lying. Who is she? Do I know her?'

Demi had that look in his eye that reminded Kyle of a bloodhound when his scent was up. The flamboyant Greek was notorious for his many liaisons with the world's most beautiful women—many of whom Kyle also happened to know. It would really stick in the older man's craw if he thought a woman of their mutual acquaintance had somehow slipped through the net.

For some entirely inexplicable reason Kyle suddenly felt fiercely protective towards the reclusive Megan Brand— who, God knew, had no reason to trust any man further than she could throw him right now. Least of all him—a perfect stranger who had inadvertently got her to tell him things that he had the distinct feeling she revealed to very few— if anyone else at all…

'Let me get you another drink.' Kyle caught the eye of another passing waitress, this time a pretty redhead in an equally tight black skirt and white silk blouse, who was only too willing to wait on the two most attractive men in the room. Especially the younger one.

He reminded her of a poster she'd seen of Jim Morrison, who'd used to be in that American rock group in the sixties—the Doors. He could light her fire any day, and that was a fact. She pulled out her pad and pencil from her pocket then dipped down in a fragrant cloud of sensual perfume, her blue eyes darting flirtatiously to Kyle, the smile that raised the corners of her glossy apricot mouth close to intimate.

It didn't take long for Demi to take charge.

'I want a bottle of your best champagne—' He paused from diverting the pretty waitress to raise one luxuriant dark brow in Kyle's direction and scowl. 'Ignore my friend,' he told her, gesticulating flamboyantly with his hand, 'he has taken a vow of abstinence or something. He has forgotten how to have a good time. Now, you, my angel…' He gave the girl the full force of his liquid black gaze. 'Something tells me you know how to have a good time; tell me I am not wrong hmm?'

Megan scrunched up the fashionable pink and mauve T-shirt she'd donned on her arrival home, then flung it unceremoniously into the wicker laundry basket. Turning on her heel, she all but glared at her reflection in the gilt-framed bathroom mirror, furious with herself for agreeing to work overtime when her leg had been aching like crazy all day and she really should have asserted herself and said no.

Now it was a quarter past eight and she was already fifteen minutes late for her second appointment with Kyle. She'd never make it to Notting Hill before eight-thirty at the earliest—and that was only if she was able to hail a cab straight away.

'Damn!' Hands on either side of her curvaceous hips, she found no pleasure in the sight of her svelte but shapely figure in her black, nice but hardly sexy high street store underwear. Just a surge of impotent resignation that yet again she'd said yes to something when she'd really wanted to say no. If anything, her lack of assertiveness had got worse since her divorce.

The pale young woman in the mirror with the dulled brown eyes and turned-down mouth was a poor reflection of the passionate girl with a hunger for life that she'd once been.

Megan brought her hands up to her face. Nick had made her despise almost everything about herself, and it was damn near breaking her heart as well as her spirit…

'Haven't you got an appointment with What's-his-name

tonight?' Penny put her sleek blonde head round the door, taking a loud crunch of the celery stick she held aloft as she did so.

'I'm not going.'

'What do you mean, you're not going?' The blonde frowned as Megan pulled a plain black sweatshirt over her head and yanked it irritably down over her jeans. Even pouting with anger, her glossy dark hair a dishevelled mass of black silk down her back, Penny thought her friend was stunning. Megan Brand had the kind of beauty that needed no further decoration. Her features were strong enough and striking enough to withstand the need for make-up, and add to that glorious hair and a body that couldn't seem to help going in and out in all the right places—well, the men just took one look and fell like ninepins.

Not that Megan was remotely interested. But who could blame her after that imbecile Nick had practically maimed her for life? Why he had even looked at another woman when he was married to the kindest, most gorgeous girl you could imagine was also totally beyond her comprehension. She'd never understand human nature, even if she lived to be a hundred.

'I'm late. I'll never get a cab now. I'll just have to ring him and let him know. He'll probably tell me not to bother next time.' Megan grabbed her hairbrush off the vanity unit and shouldered past her surprised friend into the living room.

Two uplighters on slim steel stems lit the airy, beautifully furnished area while the flat-screened television played softly in a corner. Defeated and despondent, Megan stared broodingly at the two women arguing on the screen but barely registered a word they were saying.

'I can give you a lift, you ninny!' Penny unhooked her Italian leather shoulder bag from where she'd left it behind the door, then rifled through it for her car keys.

'You've not been in long yourself. You know I hate re-lying on you for this kind of thing.' Megan's face was flushed with frustration and remorse as she watched the other girl suddenly take charge. What had she ever done to deserve such a wonderful friend as Penny Hallet? The woman had stuck by her through thick and thin, and then some. It had been Penny who had come and taken her to the hospital that dreadful night when Nick had shoved her down the stairs. Penny who had practically begged Megan on more than one occasion to leave her volatile, handsome husband 'before things got out of hand'.

If only she'd listened. Her leg might not now be scarred from two painful operations and she might not walk with a limp—maybe for the rest of her life… As for the other thing, perhaps the most dreadful thing of all—well, she wouldn't even go there. Not tonight.

'You hate relying on anyone for anything, full stop!' Penny remonstrated. 'But I'd honestly take you to Australia and back if I thought it would help you get out of this damn air of gloom that's been dogging you. And it must be doing you some good seeing this KH—what did you say his name was? Kyle, wasn't it? When you get back tonight I want to know all about it.'

Megan tensed. She didn't know if she wanted to repeat what she'd discussed with Kyle at their last session. All week she'd suffered agonies, wondering what he must think of her after her mostly involuntary revelations about her personal life. Was she mad, contemplating going back to see him again? Could this cool, laid-back, straight-talking handsome man really help put her back on track again? And when was she going to get to do some actual painting?

Oh, what the hell. She'd just have to bite the bullet and take a chance, because there wasn't much else that was help-ful going on in her life right now. Tomorrow morning was already looming large in her mind because she had an appointment with the physio at the hospital and her leg always ached twice as badly after that little session—even though her physio took pains to reassure her it was doing her good.

'Ready?' Penny jangled her cars keys and opened the door.

Snapping out of her momentary reverie, Megan grabbed her suede jacket off the couch and followed her out.

'Glass of wine?'

'No, thanks.' Megan glanced warily round the big modern kitchen with its fashionable stone-flagged floor and bright copper pans stacked from large to small beside the stainless steel oven.

It was like a kitchen that belonged to a show home—not at all in keeping with the more bohemian laid-back style of his living room. There were no obvious signs that much cooking went on there either. No cooking smells lingered, there were no tell-tale stains on the burner, and all the surfaces were gleaming—just like on one of those adverts for 'miracle' cleaning products.

Was she being too presumptuous in assuming that Kyle's artistic talents didn't extend to culinary expertise as well? Oh, well. Perhaps he wasn't a god after all…just a man— a mere mortal with faults and idiosyncrasies and bad habits like everyone else.

Two bottles of good-quality Chardonnay stood on the marble worktop, alongside two elegant stemmed wine glasses and an attractive pale wooden gift box of Turkish Delight. Megan wondered fleetingly if it had been gifted to him by an admirer. A long-time girlfriend or lover, maybe? The thought made her stomach lurch a little. Did this surprising, unpredictable man have a penchant for sweets, then? The very idea filled her with an unexpected burst of warmth. It made him seem more human somehow—less out of reach.

She watched him turn round and lounge against the sink unit, his hazel eyes reflective but impenetrable as he studied her. Brooding almost. What was he thinking? She hoped he wasn't regretting agreeing to see her again. It made her realise that she wanted to be here, had been wanting to see him again since the surprise of that first appointment, wanted to see where their association would lead her—if she would like the result.

This evening his cheekbones seemed even more sharply defined than before, his features all sculpted planes and angles that together created an appearance that was almost soul-destroyingly handsome. His looks were a rare combination of chiselled male beauty and the cool, innate intelligence that shone out from those astute sexy hazel eyes of his, like a beacon beckoning Megan to come home... She caught herself up short, like someone who'd inadvertently stood too close to the fire, hugging her bag tightly to her chest as if to protect herself.

'I'm sorry I was late; I had to work overtime.' As soon as she'd uttered the words she was suffused with ridiculous guilt. There'd been no 'had to' about it. She could have declined if she'd wanted. Lindsay, her boss, would have sulked, as she was apt to, but she would have got over it if Megan had stood up for herself. The trouble was, Megan very rarely stood up for herself.

'You came. That's the main thing.' Kyle raked his fingers through his hair and gave her a lazy smile. The sort of smile a woman could easily fall into and forget to come up for air. Megan swallowed nervously.

'Are we going to do any painting tonight?' she asked.

'Would you like to?'

'Well, if that's what you'd planned. I mean, I—'

'Nothing's planned.' Kyle straightened and hooked his thumbs into the belt loops of his tight black jeans. It dragged Megan's gaze south, to his trim lean hips and long-boned thighs encased in soft worn denim. 'I'm afraid I rarely plan anything very much.'

What was she supposed to make of that? Megan thought wildly. It was all very strange. Kyle still hadn't told her what the lessons would entail, and when she'd tried to pay him at the end of her last visit he'd told her to put her money away because they'd work something out in a few weeks' time, when he saw how things were going. Whatever that meant. The man obviously had income from other sources, and Megan secretly thought he must be wealthy indeed if he didn't need to charge his clients straight away.

'Oh.'

'Does that bother you?' he asked lightly.

It did, if she was honest. But only because her life before her divorce had been so rigidly organised by her husband that in some peculiar, perverse way she'd got used to it—like a prisoner who got used to the four walls that kept him caged.

'It's okay.' She shrugged, unwilling to let him see that she was disturbed by his complete disregard for structure in their sessions. She'd go along with it for a while, she told herself, but if it proved too unpredictable she'd just tell him things weren't working out as she'd expected and move on.

'It's not, is it?'

'What?'

'I'm not a college professor or some sort of schoolteacher, Megan. I don't have a curriculum to adhere to. These sessions are for you to explore exactly what it is you think you need in terms of support and guidance, and for me to help you. Does that make things more clear to you?'

Sensing Kyle move towards her, his intriguingly erotic male scent stirring the air between them, Megan willed her foolish heart to stop beating so wildly so that she could at least make an attempt at some halfway normal remark.

'Give me your bag,' he demanded softly—so softly his

words sounded as though they'd been dipped in honey. Megan shivered, her nipples tingling and growing tight and achy beneath her shirt.

'Why?' She asked the question almost as a reflex, because she was handing it to him even as she spoke.

He laid it to one side, then stood directly in front of her. Determinedly, her dark eyes stared straight at his chin as he towered above her, seeing the slight cleft in the bronzed skin already shadowed by day-old stubble, spellbound by the tantalising shape of his hard, sensual mouth. A different kind of numbness stole over her body. This one made her feel as if she had fallen into some kind of helpless hypnotic trance, because suddenly she found herself incapable of moving...

'Give me your hand.' Clasping it firmly in his own, he laid it against the hard but warm expanse of his chest.

Beneath the plain white T-shirt he wore, which highlighted his exotic tan and drew mouthwatering attention to those silky steel-toned biceps, she could feel the deep steady throb of his heart. Megan's tongue cleaved to the roof of her mouth. The ability to respond to anything in a natural way had completely deserted her. Her senses were jammed, suspended, hijacked...

'Painting engages not just the physical senses, but the soul and spirit as well. Truly, it can work magic. Every brushstroke can be a revelation. So tell me,' he asked thickly, 'what do you feel?'

Oh, Lord, tell me this isn't happening... Megan felt faint with panic. Fear and anticipation were overwhelming her in equal measures. Every cell in her body was thrumming in awareness of this strong vital man who was holding her hand captive against his chest as though he might keep it there for ever, and a series of unstoppable tremors suddenly seized her body and tied her tongue.

'Megan?' he prompted.

'Your heart.' Her voice came out on a croak and a soft crimson blush crept slowly into her cheeks. 'I can hear your heart beating.'

'Good. I'm reassured that I'm still alive, then.' *And haven't died and gone to heaven...* He'd never seen such melting brown eyes or such delectably sultry lips—lips that perhaps unknowingly invited more intimate inspection...

The beguiling scents of her body, her shampoo, her perfume—the sweetness of vanilla and the eroticism of musk—invaded his senses like the delicate brush of velvet and lace, satin and silk, and made him immediately hard. He fought manfully to keep his sudden desire at bay but, Lord, he didn't think his libido had been more severely tested in his life. She was gazing up at him, trusting as a child, her expression a captivating mixture of innocence and fire, wonder and fear...

With a supreme effort she suddenly tugged her hand free and stepped back. Looping her hair behind one ear, she sent him a clear distress signal. *Please don't do this, because I don't think I can handle it right now.*

Kyle slowly nodded his head, as if answering her, but it was several seconds before he could give his thoughts the power of speech.

'What colour would you paint my heartbeat, Megan? Think about it. What did you sense when you put your hand over my heart?'

'Passion, strength—' She glanced away, flustered, staring down at her soft brown leather mules as if seeing them for the first time. Why had she said passion, for goodness' sake? Of all the things she could have told him that was the least safe. But Kyle wasn't going for safe responses, was he? He was trying to psyche her out—uncover the real Megan Brand.

Only he was on a hiding to nothing, did he but know it, because even *she* didn't know who the real Megan Brand was. But, yes, she had felt passion and strength when he'd placed her hand over his heart. In spades. Making love with this man would be like trying to ride the wind or hold back the tide… It was a heady thought that made her weak with wild longing.

'What colours would you paint passion and strength? How would you paint them? Want to have a go?'

Kyle observed her responses with profound interest. Her body language was distinctly ill at ease, and there was a war going on behind those heavenly brown eyes that he longed to put an end to. A soft flush tinted her porcelain cheeks and damn it all if she didn't look close to tears. Beyond her incandescent beauty he saw a woman so wrapped up in her own despair that all he wanted to do was sweep her off her feet, carry her to bed and comfort her in the time-honoured way that could make a man and a woman temporarily forget the troubles or pain that dogged them. He wanted to show her in no uncertain terms that she was a beautiful, desirable woman—the kind of woman that any man with breath in his body would want to protect and treasure…

She was wrestling with her tears and nodding at the same time. Kyle swept past her, taking her hand with him, leading her gently down to the bottom of the garden, to the private temple that he personally worshipped at—his art studio. It was housed in a white pagoda-style summerhouse, with intricate latticework on the cornices and stained glass in the windows, which in the evening twilight looked almost like something from a fairytale.

Megan's despair swept away in an instant. She was enchanted. Enchanted and enthralled. Kyle switched on a light as they entered and Megan felt as if she was entering Aladdin's cave. She couldn't suppress a deep sigh of pleasure. Inside was everything an artist could dream of needing: easels, paintboxes, canvases and everything else in between.

In the air swirled competing scents of turpentine and ink, charcoal and wood.

Stacked next to one opposing wall were several completed canvases, both large and small, and Megan craned her neck to get a proper look. She was dying to see some of Kyle's work—perhaps it would give her some more clues to the man himself? While he was trying to figure her out she was trying to glean some insight into what made this fascinating man tick. Perhaps later, when he had got to know her a little better, he might let her see some of the fruits of his own creativity?

But clearly right now it was Megan's creativity that Kyle was most interested in. With almost breathless anticipation she watched him carry an easel, a canvas already stretched and prepared across it, across the matte wooden floor to the nearest open window. He took a couple of minutes to position it exactly how he wanted it, then looked across at her and smiled. It had been an inclement sort of day, and now a cool breeze drifted in to trail a featherlight touch on the virgin canvas.

'I don't know about you,' he commented conversationally, 'but I work better with some fresh air circulating.'

Megan's chest was tight with excitement and trepidation. Oh, God—it had been so long since she had had the chance to do this. Now, when it came to it, would she be able to do anything at all? If only she wasn't so damned nervous! If only she could rest assured in the knowledge that Kyle wasn't going to judge her on whatever effort she produced. In the past, when she was married to Nick, everything she'd ever done had been with his approval in mind. She had lived in mortal fear of his disapproval. She'd vowed to herself that never again would she subject herself to such tyranny. Only sometimes her own self-imposed tyranny was even worse. She had to cut herself a little slack, but how?

'Do you know your way round a paintbox, or do you

want me to go over it with you?' Kyle had wheeled a trolley across, with a sheet of glass over the top and an opened paintbox on the top. Laid out next to the paints were several high-quality sable brushes in varying thicknesses with polished handles.

Even though she didn't do any actual painting, Megan did know her way around a paintbox. She had three really good art manuals at home—her favourite bedtime reading—and she had those first six months at art college to fall back on.

'I think I can manage.' She gave him a watery smile and was almost knocked off her feet with the dazzling glance he gave her in return.

'Then it's all yours, sweetheart. Paint that passion we were talking about. Don't rein it in and don't hold back. I want to know what that emotion means to you. Take as long as you like. I don't care how you do it; it's not a contest and I'm not judging anything. Just feel free to express yourself in whatever way you feel inclined. In the meantime, I'll go and make some coffee.'

'Kyle?' Her tremulous voice stopped him in his tracks as he reached the door.

His eyes narrowed. 'What is it?'

'Thank you.'

'The pleasure's all mine...really.' He turned and sprinted down the steps.

CHAPTER THREE

'GET me some coffee, Megan, would you?'

Not please, or would you mind—just 'get'. Megan glanced away from her computer screen up at the severe-looking blonde, with her navy-blue power suit and incongruous slash of cherry-red lipstick, and pursed her lips with the effort of remaining calm.

Lindsay Harris was an ambitious thirty-something bank executive, as cool and unemotional under fire as any senior member of the SAS, and in five years of being her assistant Megan had never seen so much as a hairline crack in the woman's impressive armour. She was doggedly single-minded, and her career was everything to her. Anyone who knew her quickly formed the impression that anyone less dedicated was somehow undeserving of respect. The woman rarely smiled—apart from when she was liaising with someone higher up the pecking order in the bank hierarchy—and it was a standing joke in the office that Lindsay had had a sense of humour bypass.

Just Megan's luck to be promoted to her office when sweet old Melvin Harding had retired. Megan's job had been a breeze then. If the work hadn't been as stimulating as she could wish, at least her boss had been kind and fair. It had made it easier to deal with her see-sawing emotions where Nick was concerned, and if Melvin had ever caught her crying or upset in any way he had always been the absolute soul of consideration and discretion. Working for Lindsay had made things tougher all round for Megan.

When she had been in hospital, nursing her broken leg, almost everyone else in her immediate office had visited her

40

with sympathy and commiserations. Lindsay hadn't bestowed her presence even once. Not that Megan had minded. She wouldn't have wanted to deal with her boss's stony face when she was feeling at her lowest ebb. It hadn't taken a genius to detect that Lindsay was sulking because her assistant was away and she 'couldn't be doing with' teaching someone temporary the ropes. Megan's 'accident' had been a colossal inconvenience to her, and she'd let her assistant know it the minute she'd returned to work.

Megan turned her brown eyes up to Lindsay now, striving valiantly to keep her voice level. 'Just give me a minute or two to finish dealing with this report and I'll get one for you.'

'When I tell you to get me a cup of coffee I expect you to do it straight away! Not in a minute or two, not later, not tomorrow, but now!'

Lindsay's pale hands were curled into fists at her sides and Megan stared at the older woman, warring with herself as to how best to respond to this totally uncalled-for fit of pique. One thing was certain: she'd be crazy if she responded to such a demand with head-down acquiescence.

'I'm sorry, Lindsay, but this report has to be faxed across to the New York office as a matter of urgency. Your coffee will have to wait.' When the words came out of her mouth—over a plateau that was as dry as the Sahara desert—Megan could hardly believe she'd said them. From the look in Lindsay's pale blue eyes, she couldn't either. It really was possibly the first hint of dissent she'd received from her meek, hard-working assistant.

Ignoring the tension in her stomach, Megan shuffled some papers into order on her desk and deliberately refocused on her computer screen.

Barbara, a fellow PA from an office down the hall, passed by and called out cheerily, 'Hi, Meg—still meeting after work for drinks? Don't forget it's Sue's birthday. See you then.'

Lindsay spun round with a glare at the young redhead. 'No wonder we don't get any work done around here! You're all too busy organising your social lives!'

'Pardon me for breathing,' quipped Barbara, unabashed, and sailed on regardless out of the office.

Megan bit her lip. She really wanted to laugh and cry at the same time, because Lindsay's behaviour beggared belief. Instead she began typing for all she was worth, determined not to let her boss see that she was rattled.

'Right, Megan. As soon as you've sent the damn fax I want to see you in my office, pronto! I really don't know what's come over you lately, but your professional attitude leaves a lot to be desired!' And with that Lindsay stormed off into the connecting room, slamming the door behind her for all she was worth.

Megan stopped typing and slowly let out a long breath. Something had clearly unsettled her usually cool-headed boss, and no doubt her assistant was going to have to bear the brunt of it. Only she didn't feel like bearing anything she didn't have to today. Today, for some reason, she felt ridiculously rebellious.

Whether it was anything to do with the heady experience of being with Kyle and letting her feelings about passion explode onto the canvas last night, she couldn't be sure. But one thing was certain. Something inside was slowly but surely awakening, like the proverbial sleeping tiger. Something that wouldn't let her stay the same old scared, put-upon Megan Brand. Something that, at last, made her want to stand up for herself and fight back...

Kyle dried his damp waving hair with a towel and for the umpteenth time since Megan had left last night stared at the painting on the canvas in front of him. All of a sudden he wished he hadn't given up smoking, and it had been five whole years since he had experienced such a heartfelt urge. Right now he needed something—anything—to help contain the surge of runaway adrenalin that kept flooding through him like white water every time he glanced at Megan's painting.

He'd told her to paint passion and by God the woman had done just that. He'd left her alone for two hours, save for bringing her in a cup of coffee and leaving it on a small side table by the door. When he'd returned to the summer-house later that night the untouched cup of coffee had still been on the table where he'd left it. For two hours Megan had painted out all the stormy feelings, heartbreak and latent rage she felt inside, and the result was a blinding revelation of hot colour and fire that tore at Kyle's soul and left him questioning his own ability to create anything as powerful. Even to a layman's eye the painting had something magical about it—something hard to imitate that marked it out as special.

Every torrid emotion and sensation was contained in that picture—from sex to love, violence and pain. She had painted a woman in a vivid red dress with her head in her hands, long dark hair shielding her face from view. All around her feet were white roses stained with blood, pulled violently away from their branches, while up above a pale blue sky was rent with thunderclouds coloured grey and black. The woman's feet were bare and a thorn from one of the violated roses was embedded in the bottom of one pale foot. When he'd examined it more closely Kyle had noticed the glint of something gold on the ground, almost hidden by one of the roses. If he wasn't mistaken, it was a wedding ring.

'Mother of God.'

His comment was a savage blend of anger, admiration and awe. He wasn't a religious man, nor given to overly religious expressions, but Megan's painting had moved him deeply on a soul level. He sank down onto his haunches, the white towel draped carelessly round his neck, his hard-muscled torso bare and gleaming with droplets of moisture from his shower. He drove his fingers twice through his tousled chestnut hair cursing softly beneath his breath.

Megan's husband—wherever he was—should be publicly hung, drawn and quartered. If he ever got his hands on him he'd… He had to stop himself from going there. Bad enough that he was eaten up with fury at the thought of him putting his hands on Megan in such a violent way—in any way, as a matter of fact. The thought of her sleeping with such a man damn near drove him crazy.

Her painting had spoken to him. She had shown him in a way that no words could adequately express just how much she hurt inside. Anyone with eyes to see and a heart that was still beating would see it, too, when they looked at her work.

Inhaling a deeply shuddering breath, Kyle got to his feet. Megan had told him she hadn't painted in years, and he had no reason to disbelieve her, but whichever way you threw the dice the woman was a talent waiting to happen. The extent of her ability was almost too scary to contemplate. If she could demonstrate such indisputable skill this fast, with barely any time to prepare or ponder her subject, just what could she achieve under far more conducive circumstances?

Under his tutelage—under any good artist worth his salt—she could go far. Fortunately, Kyle had the connections to make that future for her more than just a possibility and he would, too…if she would let him.

The need to see her again suddenly became an imperative, and the sense of urgency made his heart race. The idea took hold like a match to a fire. Glancing down impatiently at his platinum diver's watch, he saw that it was just after twelve. He wondered what time she went for lunch. He knew where she worked because he'd made a point of asking her. All he had to do was jump in a cab and show up. There were lots of good restaurants and wine bars in the locality, so he'd take her to lunch and…and what?

Damn it all to hell! She was supposed to be a client—would she think his approach just a little unethical? Too bad. He'd never played by the rules in the whole of his life, even when he was at school—he'd be damned if he was going to start now…

'Megan Brand, you dark horse.' Megan glanced up distractedly from her computer at Barbara, who'd balanced her steaming paper cup of coffee on the edge of her friend's cluttered desk.

'What now?' Megan quirked a smile, convinced her colleague was going to rib her about her earlier rebellion against Lindsay. The thing was, she didn't mind in the least—she could stand a little ribbing, the way she was feeling.

Lindsay hadn't even been able to intimidate her during their little 'talk' in her office either. Everything she'd accused Megan of was pointless, trivial and totally unfounded, and her assistant had taken her courage in both hands and told her so. Their meeting had ended with Lindsay sighing like the most misunderstood woman in the world and ordering her to 'Go and do some work…please!' A small victory, then, but a victory nonetheless.

'There is one drop-dead gorgeous man waiting in Reception, asking to see you.' Barbara's eyes twinkled with mischief and admiration and all the blood seemed to rush to Megan's head.

Could it be Nick? A wave of nausea rolled through her at the thought. But Barbara knew her ex-husband so it couldn't be him. Feeling slightly weak as the stab of shock subsided Megan stared mystified at Barbara, not knowing whether she was joking or serious.

'For me?'

'Little old you,' Barbara teased. 'He was waiting in the foyer talking to that man-eater Lucy Draper on the desk, and naturally I wandered over and asked if I could help. Imagine my surprise when he asked for you! No wonder you kept him quiet!'

'Did he—did he say who he was?'

Megan started to get up from her desk. There was only one other man she personally might refer to as 'drop-dead gorgeous'—but it couldn't be him, could it? Once upright, she smoothed a nervous hand down her fitted black skirt, then ran her fingers anxiously over her hair to try and restore some sort of order.

At home she normally wore her long hair down, but at work she tied it back in a black velvet band or butterfly clip. Inevitably, by lunchtime, some of the silky black strands had worked themselves free to drift softly around her face. Lindsay was a stickler for etiquette when it came to dressing for the office, and anything even slightly what she called 'frivolous', such as long hair left loose, was frowned upon.

'Kyle. That's all. Is that his first name or last?' Barbara wanted to know.

Megan hardly heard the question. Every cell in her body was flooded with adrenaline at the thought of her handsome tutor waiting downstairs in the lobby to see her.

Why had he come? He hadn't looked at her painting before she left because when she'd finished she'd suddenly realised how late it was and had had to go. But he'd obviously seen it now. She exhaled a shaky little breath. What if he thought it too much? Too over the top for what he'd asked? What if he'd come to tell her not to bother coming again?

Get a grip, Megan. Scolding herself silently, she limped

across to the coat-stand to retrieve her matching tailored black jacket. Her leg was throbbing as if someone had held a branding iron to it, making her limp slightly more pronounced than usual. She'd had her intense physiotherapy session first thing at the hospital, and the idea of coming face to face with Kyle feeling as she did was really testing her mettle to the limit.

With hands that weren't exactly steady she slipped on her jacket, then turned to her friend. Lifting her shoulders uncertainly, she asked, 'How do I look?'

'Like you're about to break some poor man's heart. But then again, with that face and that figure, how could you not?'

'You're good for my ego, you know that? Not that I believe a word of it for a second.'

Barbara waved her away. 'I speak as I find. Go on. Don't keep loverboy waiting…'

'He's not my—' Megan squirmed with discomfort. Lucky for her Barbara Palmer was a decent sort. Not the type to relay anything Megan didn't want her to to anyone else in the office. That was why they were friends as well as colleagues.

'Anyway, if Lindsay comes looking for me, tell her I've gone to lunch, will you?'

'Sure. I might even tell her you've taken an extended one.'

Kyle did a double-take when he saw Megan stepping out of the lift. Dressed in a dark understated linen suit, with a white camisole underneath, her gorgeous glossy hair pulled back from her face in some sort of elegant ponytail, she looked cool, stylish and unexpectedly efficient. That was until she caught sight of him, blushed beguilingly, then limped slowly towards him.

Kyle's heart went out to her. Every difficult painful step

she took reminded him of how she had come by her injury, and rage filled him anew.

When she drew level he smiled down into her uncertain brown eyes and instinctively touched her cheek with the tips of his fingers.

'I wanted to see you.'

'Oh? That rather makes me feel like a schoolgirl who's about to be ticked off by the head teacher.'

She blushed, hoping she didn't sound as gauche or as out of her depth as she felt, but the truth was her brain had imitated the spin cycle on a washing machine as soon as she'd set eyes on him.

Kyle chuckled, a warm, honeyed sound that worryingly made her think of bedrooms and moonlight, and her mouth went instantly dry.

'Can you take a lunch-break?' he asked. 'We need to talk.'

Megan felt her hand clasped warmly in his and inhaled the clean, tantalising scent of his cologne as she was pulled into closer proximity to that hard masculine body, her senses dulled to anything else but his strong, vital presence and the glint of gold in those gorgeous hazel eyes.

The man looked good enough to eat. He was wearing his black leather trousers with a tan leather flying jacket over a black cashmere sweater, easily transmitting mystery and excitement as well as an undisputed male virility that drew every female eye in the room. Lucy, the trendy young receptionist with a penchant for anything with a designer label, was practically gaping at him with her mouth open, and two female execs from the fourth floor—both in their forties—were stealing the kind of hot glances that you wouldn't find in the boardroom.

Megan retrieved her hand, looking almost everywhere else around the large plush lobby, with its highly polished floor and floor-to-ceiling windows, before finally letting her warm brown gaze drift anxiously back to Kyle.

'What do you want to talk to me about? It must be important if you took the trouble to seek me out at work. It's nothing—nothing bad is it?'

'No, Megan. Don't immediately assume the worst. It can become a habit.'

'Now you're wearing your therapist hat.' She grinned, because seeing him again just made her feel good. As if he cared.

'I wanted to talk to you about your painting. The one you did last night.'

The way he said it seemed to make it abundantly clear it was nothing personal. Sharp disappointment replaced her previous elation, but she did her best to disguise it.

'Didn't you like it?' Almost automatically she fell into the trap of unconsciously needing his approval, and silently cursed the response that had become more like a reflex since she'd met and married Nick Brand.

'You're doing it again,' Kyle admonished, his gaze serious. 'Liking it or not doesn't come into it. I told you to paint what you felt about passion. You did. It was a revelation, and I don't mean that lightly. Let's find somewhere to eat, shall we? Then we can talk.'

He put his hand beneath her elbow and guided her from the faceless glass high-rise that housed the network of offices belonging to the bank, his mind as certain as it could be that the passionate young woman by his side did not belong in such a vast soulless atmosphere any more than he did.

'You've got cream on your chin.' Before she could respond, Kyle reached across the small intimate table, past the melted-down candle jammed into an empty wine bottle, and carefully wiped off the small stain with the edge of his napkin.

Megan wished for the umpteenth time since they'd entered the charming little Italian restaurant tucked away in a little Soho side street that her heart would stop pounding as though she were about to be thrown off the highest diving board into the deep end of the swimming pool.

'If there's an elegant way to eat spaghetti carbonara I'm afraid it's passed me by.' Her lips parted in a self-deprecating little smile.

Elegant or not, Kyle thought, growing hard, it was damned erotic watching her eating it. It had taken an almighty effort on his part to restrain himself from leaning over just then and licking the spot of cream off her chin with his tongue; only he wouldn't want to stop at her chin…

'You're doing just fine.' He raised his glass of ruby-red Chianti to his lips to imbibe a fortifying sip. 'How long have you been working at the bank?'

'Ten years.'

'That's a long time doing something you dislike.'

'Too long.' Eyes cast down, Megan put her fork to the side of her plate and smoothed back her hair. How much she disliked her work had been made crystal-clear to her this morning, after that unnecessary little contretemps with her boss.

'Why do you stay?'

'Apart from my fears of not being good enough to do anything else? Because I need to make a living, of course.'

'You could make a living doing something you enjoyed. Ever thought of that?'

Her eyes grew even darker. 'Of course I've thought of that, but I just didn't have that many options before…' She curled her fingers around the fragile stem of her wine glass and fell silent. She didn't want to talk about Nick, or her disastrous marriage, and she instinctively knew this was where the conversation was leading. She glanced up to see a frown cross Kyle's handsome face.

'You're a beautiful intelligent woman. You could do any-thing you wanted to do if you put your mind to it.'

'You make it sound so easy.'

'It is.' Kyle shrugged. 'It all comes down to choice.'

'Yeah… I could even run the London Marathon if I wanted to!' Megan glanced away, appalled at her outburst when Kyle was clearly only seeking to help. But there hadn't been so much as a flicker of surprise on his coolly implacable face.

'All kinds of people run the Marathon—even disabled people,' he said quietly.

'So you think of me as disabled?' The hot press of tears pricked the back of her eyelids and Megan's hand squeezed the napkin on her lap into a tight ball.

'I was using the term merely to make a point,' he an-swered calmly. 'What I'm trying to illustrate is that people make their own limitations. It's how you think of yourself that matters, not what anyone else thinks of you. If you're staying in a job you hate because you've convinced yourself you don't have any other options, then you may as well lock yourself in a box and throw away the key.'

What he said made sense. She knew it did. But she still didn't see how she was going to change so easily. Marriage to Nick had robbed her of any kind of self-worth. It would take time to rebuild it again, time and patience and probably a lot of hard work.

God, she was sick of hard work! What she really wanted was a rest. No—strike that. What she really wanted was the time and the space to make her dream of being a painter come true. Everything else paled into insignificance against that.

'Your painting blew me away.'

A muscle worked in the side of one smooth bronzed cheek and Megan's thoughts came to an abrupt standstill.

'I had no idea what you were capable of. I know artists—

professional artists—who would give their eye-teeth to create work like you produced last night. Such talent is a gift. I know. I've been around art and artists for long enough to know it when I see it. If you've got all that inside you, Megan, you owe it to yourself to bring it out.' He wasn't just talking about the skilful execution of the painting either; he was predominantly thinking about the power of the message.

Somewhere between breathing in and trying to breathe out again, Megan's breath got suspended. When she did finally exhale the air whooshed out of her in a heated rush. Her cheeks two spots of hectic colour, she stared at Kyle as though he'd just explained to her the meaning of the universe.

'You think I might—I mean that I could—maybe do something in the future?'

'I think you definitely could have a future in painting.'

Once again the unbidden craving came to him for a cigarette. It was excitement, he realised. The pure adrenaline rush of being in this woman's company and wanting so much more than conversation. A woman who had as much passion inside her as the dark-haired beauty sitting opposite him would be a hell of a lover to any man who shared a similar passion.

Kyle felt the sudden demanding heat of arousal in his groin. If he wasn't careful he was going to find it bloody difficult to stand up without drawing unwanted attention to himself. His gaze travelled over Megan's melting brown eyes, with their thick sweeping lashes, down her straight little nose to the sexy mouth—her burgundy lipgloss almost wiped clean—her plump lower lip damp with tantalising moisture from her wine. Further than that he dared not go. Already the quietly maddening effect of her softly floral scent was driving him slowly crazy with want. If it had been any other woman he would have had no hesitation in letting her know that he wanted her, but Megan Brand was not just any other woman. More than that, Kyle really wanted to help her make it as an artist. Forcing a more personal relationship at this stage would probably not be in her best interests.

Damn! He really wished he had that cigarette!

'You don't know how much it means to me to hear you say that I might be able to have a future as a painter. It's like a dream come true. I mean, I know I'll need to work hard and everything, but now I know there's a glimmer of hope I won't ever give up. Do you think—what I'm trying to say is—I mean, would you be willing to help me? I'd obviously pay you; that goes without saying…'

She stared down at the table, suffused with sudden embarrassment at even asking for such a man's help. He must have far more important things to do with his time than spend it helping a fledgling artist struggle to express herself. Especially one as emotionally wounded as she was.

'Do you really think I'd want you to pay me?' Kyle's jaw clenched tight, and any expression of empathy in his gold-flecked eyes quickly disappeared. 'If I were to help you in that way I wouldn't want payment. I'd do it because I recognise a God-given talent when I see it, and everyone deserves a chance to shine in this life. I'd do it because it would give me pleasure as well as immense satisfaction. On that understanding alone I'm willing to extend my time and my knowledge. That clear, Miss Brand?'

Exhilaration and fear swamped her at the same time—as well as remorse that she might have offended him in some way because she'd offered him money for his services.

'I—then, thank you. I accept your offer…Kyle.'

Kyle's heated gaze swept her with a look of such burning intensity that underneath her clothing Megan's stomach muscles clenched tight, as if he had physically touched her.

'I hope you find the rewards are worth it,' he murmured,

unable to stop himself feeling as though he were about to throw her to the lions.

The art world could knock you down just as quickly and as cruelly as it could build you up. But then, Kyle had distanced himself from the need for anyone's approval—let alone an organisation of pompous fat cats who wouldn't know how to draw a straight line across a blank sheet of paper, never mind compose a picture of such exquisite impact as Megan's. Fame and money, he'd discovered, were singularly unhelpful distractions. He'd still paint, even if he lived in a garret without a penny to his name, and it felt good to know that.

Raising his glass to his lips, Kyle tipped it back to savour the rich dry burst of flavour that flooded his mouth, knowing without reservation that if it was Megan's destiny to make it as an artist she'd do it with or without his help. But, all things considered, if she had to have a mentor there was no doubt in his mind he would prefer it to be him than anyone else.

CHAPTER FOUR

MEGAN woke suddenly, her brow and the back of her neck drenched in perspiration. Feeling as if she were suffocating, she kicked back the soft plump duvet that had bunched round her middle, swung herself round to sit at the edge of the bed and almost cried out in agony at the pain that was stabbing through her leg. Excruciating didn't begin to describe it.

'Dear God, please!' Blinking back helpless tears of desperation and pain, she pulled back her modest white cotton nightdress and started to rub both hands up and down her leg in a bid to somehow try to ease her agony.

The raw-looking scars crossing her knee, plus the two others snaking up her thigh, only served to highlight her distress. Megan squeezed her eyes shut in dismay and hung her head. It was still a shock to see them there, and each time she did her stomach took a sickening dive as memories of that dreadful night came flooding back.

'Damn.' Her curse was a grated whisper. She moved her head slowly from side to side and her dark hair slipped like a shroud round her ashen face, as if to ward off further torment.

Automatically, as on every night she couldn't sleep, her bleary eyes sought out the illuminated green digits on the alarm clock that sat atop the pine chest of drawers. The exercise was a form of self-torture, really, and three o'clock in the morning was a particularly bad time for her. It was the time when all her demons came to haunt her. One by one they would confront her, torment her, blinding her to

55

all ways out in a bid to take possession of her mind. Was that why they called the dead of night the Witching Hour? *Nice one, Megan. Scare yourself witless, why don't you?* Ah, God, this pain was making her crazy, its intensity almost unbearable. As much as she hated the idea, she'd have to go and find her painkillers. There was no other way on earth she was going to get back to sleep otherwise.

In the kitchen, she sat at the breakfast bar, her hand shaking slightly as she swallowed down two plain white capsules with a glass of water. They'd make her drowsy, because they were particularly strong, but right now that was no bad thing. She was minus her robe, and gooseflesh dotted her bare arms in response to the cooler night-time temperature, but truth to tell the cold was the last thing on her mind. She'd give anything for this pain just to go away—disappear for good, never to torture her again. God forbid that she might have to face a third operation. Every day she prayed her leg would heal better, faster, so that dreadful prospect wouldn't manifest into a reality, but the way the pain was searing through her right now, things honestly didn't look too hopeful.

The flat was deathly quiet apart from the sound of an occasional car driving past into the night. Too quiet. The kind of quiet that made a person withdraw inside herself even if she didn't want to. Megan stared at her glass of water, her eyes burning with tiredness, her mind racing.

Penny was spending the night with Ryan, her architect boyfriend, so Megan had the place to herself. Usually she didn't mind being on her own but right now, when sleep seemed to be nothing more than a dim distant land that she had no hope of visiting anytime soon—at least not until the painkillers kicked in—she could have done with her friend's cheering company. Penny had a way of dishing out comfort and consolation that was second nature, and Megan had succumbed to her friend's kindness on more occasions than she could possibly recall.

Despondency washed over her. The trouble was, every throb of agony in her leg reminded her why it was there. At this ungodly hour of the morning, with no one else to distract her from such tormenting introspection, it was unlikely that she could hold back the clamouring memories of her ex-husband. Nick. The man she'd once been so enamoured with she'd given up her longed-for place at art college just because he'd told her to. The man who'd turned all too soon from an attentive besotted lover to a philandering, untrustworthy, cruel alter ego. She could scarcely believe she'd contemplated having children with him…

Children. Somewhere inside Megan agony of a different kind threatened. Hardly a day or night went by when she didn't think about the baby she'd lost. But she'd grown adept at forcing the pain away, relegating it to a dim room in her mind, because how else was she going to get through each day otherwise? Discovering she was pregnant right at the end of her marriage, when she'd known there was nothing left worth salvaging, had been a shock—but a secret joy, too.

It had happened one night when Nick had been drunk and Megan at a particularly low ebb. She hadn't had the heart to even fight him off—a fact she was mortally ashamed of. But although the prospect of bringing up a child on her own was nothing to cheer about, she had had the strength of mind and determination to do it. Much better to be a loving single parent than inflict a cruel egotistical bully on her child for a father. She'd deliberately not told Nick about the baby because she'd been terrified he would find a way to somehow take it away from her when the child was born.

But he hadn't even waited that long, had he? He'd taken her child from her before she'd even had a chance at life…

Megan covered her face, numb with pain that was no

longer just physical. It didn't seem right that Nick had made a new life with Claire while Megan was still suffering all the trauma of physical injury, as well as bereavement, with no possibility of recovering from either condition any time soon. The icy cold tentacles of her loss wrapped themselves around her heart, squeezing unmercifully. She gasped out loud at the force of her feelings as wave after wave of unbearable hurt rolled through her.

Losing the precious baby she'd been carrying had been the ultimate devastation. Somehow, a broken leg seemed like nothing in comparison.

'Don't think about it Megan! Not now...not ever!' Berating herself out loud, she pushed herself off the stainless steel barstool, shock eddying through her as her leg gave way beneath her. Her hand reached out in desperation just at the right moment to grab the edge of the breakfast bar. The lightning reaction stopped her from hitting the floor.

Easing herself back down onto the stool, perspiration beading her brow, she took several deep gulps of air to help steady her pounding heart. This wasn't good...it wasn't good at all. She shouldn't be on her own. She should call someone... Penny had left her Ryan's number somewhere. She remembered pinning the white scrap of paper onto the cork noticeboard by the kitchen telephone.

Glancing across the wide expanse of black and white tiled floor to locate them both, Megan wondered how a room of reasonably generous proportions could suddenly turn into the size of a ballroom when she had to contemplate getting to the other side of it with the assistance of just one good leg. But she didn't dare put her bad leg onto the floor—the last thing she wanted to do was to end up face-first, unable to get up again.

Time seemed to pass with excruciating slowness. Every tick of the clock on the wall passed in an eternity of anguish and indecision. She couldn't ring Penny at this hour of the morning. It wasn't right. Saturday was the one day she spent totally with Ryan; the last thing Megan wanted to do was intrude into her precious weekend with her boyfriend.

But who else could she call? Right now, just the sound of another human being's voice at the other end of a telephone would be wonderful. Staving off the urge to cry, Megan gritted her teeth to ease herself gingerly off the stool. With her injured leg hoisted as far off of the floor as she could manage, she started to hop slowly, the pain in her leg jolting a merciless reminder with every step she took.

Finally, her body damp with perspiration from the effort, she reached the opposite counter and the telephone. As she scanned the various numbers scribbled onto odd bits of paper pinned to the board her dark eyes fell almost automatically on Kyle's number. Penny had pinned up the postcard offering his services, with a yellow sticker above saying in red pen 'Remove at your peril!'

Megan cracked a smile, even though it was the last thing she felt like doing. But ring Kyle? Had she totally lost her mind? It was the early hours of the morning. The man was bound to be in bed fast asleep. Maybe he wasn't even alone…

The thought that he might have female company made Megan bite her lip so hard she drew blood. Unexpected jealousy cut a swathe through her insides like a hot blade, stealing her breath. What could it possibly matter to her whether he was seeing someone or not? They didn't have that kind of relationship. Kyle was her teacher. He was going to help her with her painting. He'd offered to tutor her purely in a professional capacity, even though he hadn't actually let her pay him yet.

But, all that aside, the urge to ring the man who had been occupying most of her thoughts since the moment she'd laid her eyes on him was almost too overpowering to resist. If he could just spare a moment or two to talk…

Megan frowned, her hand curving irresistibly round the cream-coloured telephone, her body tense with the effort of propping herself up against the edge of the marble worktop.

'What will I say?' she muttered aloud to herself, hand trembling. 'He's not my doctor—how could he possibly help?'

But that didn't really signify. Suddenly all that mattered was that she heard his voice. That she had access to a listening ear. And if it couldn't be her best friend Penny, then for some inexplicable reason she knew it had to be Kyle.

She punched the number on the keypad quickly, before she chickened out and changed her mind. Hearing it purr at the other end, she didn't know which was louder—that or the erratic pulse of her heartbeat.

'Do you know what the hell the time is?' All of a sudden his deeply sexy voice rumbled like a bear in her ear. She heard something clunk to the floor in the background, heard a further string of frustrated expletives. She almost put the phone down. Almost…

'Kyle.' Megan stared at the nondescript oyster-coloured blind pulled down over the narrow kitchen window, shutting out the dark—disconnecting her from the rest of the world.

'Who is this?' There was a sudden alertness in his voice that overrode the sleepy undertone.

A vivid picture of him sitting up in bed drawing an irritated hand through his tousled chestnut hair flashed up in Megan's mind. Would he wear pyjamas or did he sleep naked? Oh, Lord! Perhaps it wasn't such a good thing to be ringing him after all. A hot stab of pain radiating up her thigh just then reminded her brutally of why she was calling, and brought her nocturnal fantasising to an abrupt end.

'It's Megan. Megan Brand.' She added her full name as an afterthought, suddenly anxious he wouldn't remember who she was. He probably had lots of clients; who was she to think she might be any more special than anyone else?

'Megan. This is a little unexpected.' His voice turned suddenly smoky—intimate, almost.

A little flare of heat exploded in Megan's insides, chasing every notion of coldness away. Winding the telephone lead round and round her fingers until she practically cut off her circulation, she struggled to compose herself. If he'd unleashed another tirade about the time she wouldn't have blamed him. It wasn't as though he was her counsellor or anything like that—someone who might expect to receive occasional distress calls from clients at three in the morning.

'I'm sorry to be ringing you in the middle of the night. I wish I hadn't now.' An embarrassed flush seared her cheeks, along with a sense of futility so acute she thought she might suddenly burst into tears. 'Bad idea,' she added breathlessly.

'Who says? You can ring me any time you want. I mean it. What is it? What's the matter?'

The genuine concern in his voice was almost her undoing. Shuddering helplessly, she unravelled the cord round her fingers, staring blankly at the deep red indentations the flex had left across her knuckles. 'I...I needed to talk to someone.' Her gaze lingered on the postcard pinned to Penny's noticeboard—at the casually signed 'KH' which had told her nothing about the intriguing man who wrote it.

'My flatmate Penny's away for the night and I've woken up with this dreadful pain in my leg. I've taken some painkillers, but when I put my foot to the floor just now it gave way. I—I didn't know what to do...who to speak to—'

'You did the right thing in ringing me. Where are you now?' His tone changed yet again, becoming brisk and businesslike.

'I'm in the kitchen. I managed to get to the phone.' Gingerly, Megan lowered her foot to the floor, then tried to apply some weight to it. As soon as she did, a knife-like pain ricocheted up her leg, almost making her swoon with its ferocity.

Kyle heard her sudden gasp and clamped the receiver to his ear with a grip like steel. 'Megan! What's happening? Are you all right?'

'I tried to put my foot down...not very successfully. It hurts like—like...' Her voice drifted off as hot useless tears coursed unstoppably down her face. She hated feeling so weak and helpless. She hated needing anyone's help, let alone a man she had only known for the shortest time. She had no right to intrude on his time or his consideration like this.

'I shouldn't have rung,' she mumbled into the phone, her mind torn between replacing the receiver or hanging on to illustrate how sincerely sorry she was for being such a nuisance. Somehow she should have just tried to get back to bed, wait it out until the painkillers did their thing...

'I'm coming over. Give me your address.'

'You can't!' Stunned, Megan felt her mouth drop open. 'I mean I—I only wanted someone to talk to... You really don't have to come round.'

'Why don't you let me be the judge of that? Is there any way you'll be able to let me in?'

Megan pressed her fingers deeply against her forehead, rubbing the smooth, slightly feverish skin, her mind racing to be coherent. 'I can probably manage to get to the flat door. I'd never get down the stairs to let you in the main door, but if you go down the fire escape to the basement there's a front door key under the mat by the basement flat door. The girl downstairs is an air stewardess and she's away most weekends. We agreed to leave a spare key under the mat just in case any of us ever got locked out.'

'Not the most sensible thing from a security point of view, but in light of the present circumstances I'm not going to give you a lecture.'

There was a slight softening in his tone, but not much. Megan exhaled slowly. He really did sound like a grouchy bear disturbed from his sleep. 'You don't have to do this,' she said feebly, suddenly too tired to care what he might think of her.

'Give me your address, Megan. I'll be there with you just as soon as I can. Until then, promise me you'll rest, okay?'

She switched on late-night radio, and with her head in her hands at the breakfast bar listened to a string of 'golden oldies', mostly love songs. Some reminded her painfully of Nick, others of her youth—before college, when she was at school... Memories came and went in her head, almost like scenes from somebody else's life.

She longed to make a hot drink but didn't dare risk an accident with a kettle of hot water. She still couldn't put her foot to the floor. Her dark eyes gritty with tiredness, her body aching, Megan wryly conceded a marathon runner couldn't hurt any worse. Finally she switched off the radio and slowly and carefully made her way into the living room.

The ache in her leg gnawed away as if someone had taken a screwdriver and gouged a hole in her flesh, and she gritted her teeth, glanced at the little carriage clock on the mantelpiece and prayed for Kyle or daylight to get there soon. Right now she didn't care which; she was beyond making rational decisions about anything. She struggled across another expanse of carpet to switch on one of the lamps.

It had just flooded the room with its softly filtered glow when she heard footsteps hurrying up the stairs to the landing. Her stomach lurched, emotion making her feel almost faint. Kyle. It had to be. She was hopping slowly across to get the door even before he rapped a loud knock.

'Hi.' Her uncertain smile was anxious with apology and tinged with pain. Kyle saw it immediately in the revealing shadows on her face, in the dark bruising circles beneath her eyes. Against the midnight sheen of her lustrous dark hair her face seemed much paler than usual—almost as if she were standing in moonlight. Dressed in an unbelievably prim white cotton nightdress, her slender arms bare, she presented an almost childlike figure—if it wasn't for the delectable womanly curves that the soft material more than hinted at underneath.

A surge of something fiercely protective, a primal instinct to do with guarding one's own, flared inside him. He saw her holding onto the doorjamb, one slender leg raised carefully off the ground. Tight-lipped, he advanced into the room, a well-worn but clearly expensive black leather jacket thrown carelessly over impressively broad shoulders. A black T-shirt and faded blue denim jeans riding low on his hips without a belt completed the hurriedly put together ensemble.

Megan involuntarily sucked in a breath. He looked like someone who'd just got out of bed, but she couldn't for the life of her imagine anyone else looking as good having just done the same. His square sculpted jaw was shadowed with a full day's growth of beard, his dark hair sexily mussed, as if it hadn't seen a comb for a couple of days. But it hardly seemed to matter—it just made him look all the more appealing. All the more commanding and dangerous. All the more able to wreck any last vestiges of peace of mind she had left. *She must have been insane to call him.*

'You should be in bed,' he intoned huskily. Under any other circumstances he might have suggested he join her there, but it was plain to see that the woman was in considerable pain and practically dead on her feet.

Without further ado Kyle unfurled Megan's fingers from the doorjamb, then swept her bodily up into his arms, holding her tight against his chest, almost knocked off balance by the sheer sense of rightness that rolled over him at having her so near. Her body was soft, warm and deliciously pliant, and as he held her the gentle hint of some intoxicating perfume provocatively wrapped itself round his senses like a whisper of silk rippling seductively over his flesh.

As her beautiful lustrous hair swung round his shoulders—teasing every single nerve-ending he possessed—heat stirred so fiercely in his groin he had to bite down the urge to groan out loud. He had never felt so damn aroused and yet so powerless to do anything about it. All he could do was grin and bear it right now, but as far as Kyle was concerned it merely confirmed what he had already concluded.

Megan Brand was all a woman should be and more. Feminine, soft, and sexy as hell without even trying...

'You shouldn't be doing this.' Her dark eyes nervously met his, their liquid brown depths eliciting a feeling so akin to tenderness inside his chest that the corners of his mouth dragged helplessly upwards in a smile that simply dazzled, did he but know it. Every warm responsive feeling he was capable of was entirely and vividly present in that smile, and it stirred Megan's blood more potently than the most powerful liquor. It was a smile filled with the desire to make more intimate contact as well as comfort and reassure.

'There's nothing else I can think of that I'd rather be doing,' he said honestly, then saw her eyelids droop helplessly downwards. Saw, too, that she was trying to fight it. 'You'd better point out your bedroom to me. You look done in.'

He lowered Megan gently down onto the rumpled bed, and as he drew the lilac-coloured duvet snugly up to her waist he couldn't help noticing how devoid of the usual feminine fripperies the room was.

Apart from an old-fashioned silver-backed hairbrush and comb set and a framed photograph on top of her dressing table, the clean pine furniture was ornament-free. No other adornment was evident except a digital alarm clock and a very nondescript seascape above her bed—otherwise the indisputably plain magnolia walls were left bare. Whether by accident or design the room was fairly minimalist. A plain white terry robe hung on the hook at the back of the door, but apart from that no other evidence of the room's occupant was apparent.

Somehow the thought that Megan had denied herself some of the small luxuries that most women would deem essential moved him deeply. No more than now, when he knew she was in pain. She lay with her head propped up against the plump white pillows, fighting to keep her eyes open, her ebony dark hair a riveting contrast that drew his artist's eye in admiration as well as his male gaze in appreciation.

Every living cell in Kyle's body burned to touch her. He had felt bereft the moment he'd put her down and her long slender arms had slipped gracefully from around his neck, robbing him of her satin-smooth warmth, her beguiling vanilla-laced scent…

'Do you think I should call a doctor?' Kyle's tanned brow furrowed deeply as he stood beside the bed looking down at her. Her dark velvet lashes kept fluttering helplessly downwards as she struggled to focus on him and, concerned, he eased himself down carefully onto the bed, cautiously mindful of her injured leg. Gently, he took one of her pale hands in his.

'Megan? You said you took some painkillers before I came; is that what's making you drowsy?' He was suddenly terrified that she might be losing consciousness for other reasons—reasons connected with her injury that he was powerless to do anything about…except maybe call the emergency services. He could do that. Immediately all his senses switched to red alert, transferring the scene to a hospital bed while he kept an all-night vigil, because he was damned if he was going to leave her alone.

But then she nodded, and—making his heart almost stop—directed the most bewitching little smile straight at him. It hit him somewhere round about the centre of his solar plexus, and want and need slammed into him so hard he actually sucked in his breath.

'It's all right, Kyle. I'm not going to faint on you or anything like that. Painkillers are…very strong. Sorry—can't…stay awake somehow…' Megan felt herself being dragged away on a sea of silky warm darkness as her surroundings diminished to nothing but Kyle's mesmerising golden gaze.

He was regarding her as if he really cared about what happened to her—which was impossible, of course, when they hardly knew each other and she had dragged him out of his bed at three o'clock in the morning simply to succumb to drowsiness practically the moment he arrived. *Oh, Megan, you've done some reckless things in your time—you really have… What were you thinking of?*

She drifted helplessly away, her last conscious thought a fervent hope that Kyle would forgive her for disturbing him unnecessarily. That he wouldn't withdraw his offer of help with her painting. That he would still like her…even if it was only just a little bit…

Megan stirred, sensation gradually permeating the heavy wall of slumber that had closed in on her, opening her eyes to a room flooded with the pale light of morning. Opposite her bed, blue voile curtains moved softly in the breeze from the open window, and she breathed in the sharp freshness of the air with a fervent stab of gratitude for having survived her night-time torment.

The pain in her leg had definitely subsided. All she had to do now was try and walk on it again. Thank God for the painkillers—even though she detested having to take them.

Thank God for…Kyle. He had left his bed in answer to her plea for help and come and helped return her safely to her own.

Shoving herself upwards to a sitting position, she threaded her fingers anxiously through her tumbled hair, biting her lip at the thought that she had exposed her hour of weakness to someone she hardly even knew. She never did that. She even kept things from Penny sometimes, just so that her friend would think she was coping far better than she actually was. Because she didn't want to appear like the failure she really knew deep down she must be. Hadn't Nick reiterated the fact enough times for her? 'You're just a dreamer, Meg—dreamers never amount to anything very much… Just thank your lucky stars you've got your looks to fall back on.'

Feeling the sting of tears behind her eyes too readily, Megan cursed softly, then pushed back the duvet. She had to get up. She had to find out if Kyle had left a note—a note which might possibly indicate that he wasn't too happy with her for hauling him out of bed in the middle of the night to play Shining White Knight to her Damsel in Distress.

But even as the thought surfaced the bedroom door swung open and there he stood, looking like some dissolute raffish pirate rather than the white knight of her fantasy. The day's growth of beard she'd seen in the night had darkened even more round his hard jaw, while his unsettling hazel eyes simmered banked golden fire, making him look…well, making him look aroused.

Beneath her gown, Megan's breasts were suddenly hot and tingly, her nipples peaking to hard, achy nubs of delicious sensual awareness. Her brown eyes widened helplessly as her heartbeat slowed down to a heavy throb.

Leaning against the doorjamb, a mug of coffee in one

hand and a sinful grin on his face that would surely have made a nun rethink her vows, Kyle assessed her at his leisure, just as if he were contemplating having her for breakfast.

Oh, my. Megan swallowed with immense difficulty, then felt her stomach drop as though she was falling into thin air.

CHAPTER FIVE

'I HOPE you weren't contemplating going anywhere without calling for my assistance?'

'I...I didn't think you were still here, to be honest.' Megan's dark eyes slid guiltily away from him, from the too disturbing assault that his piratical dark image was having on her senses. She would do well to remind herself that she was in an extremely vulnerable position. They were alone in her bedroom, for goodness' sake, and she was temporarily incapacitated—at least until she tried to see if she could walk or not.

'Did you think I'd leave you alone after the condition I found you in?' His hazel eyes reflected both confusion and disbelief. He pushed away from the doorjamb and came fully into the room. He easily dominated it with the overwhelming impact of his presence alone, stamping an indelible masculinity on it that Megan knew would linger in her senses long after he had gone.

Cradling his mug of coffee between his hands, he sank down onto the bed beside her, his brooding tawny gaze roving freely over her features as if committing every one to memory.

Heat coiled in Megan's stomach. Glancing downwards, she contrasted the solidly muscular jean-clad thighs beside her with her own, hidden as they were beneath her demure cotton gown. There was a little muscle wastage in her injured leg, but physiotherapy and her exercises were gradually helping to build it up again. Even so, her limbs appeared impossibly fragile and slender next to such a vibrantly healthy specimen of manhood.

Kyle probably had more power in his little finger than she had in the whole of her body right now. He was big and strong and indisputably, irrevocably male. The very air around him seemed to stir in vivid response to his strength, heat and virility. She couldn't deny the almost overwhelming sexual attraction that was buzzing through her body, drowning every sense she possessed in sizzling golden honey, and she knew in the subtle, sudden narrowing of his eyes that he felt it, too.

'I had no right ringing you like that in the middle of the night. I don't—I don't know what came over me.' Tangling her fingers in the soft material of her gown, Megan stole a glance at him. The heat that blazed back at her from those languorous golden depths made her clutch the malleable cotton between her fingers so tightly that it made her palms sweat.

'You did the right thing. I told you.' His voice a disconcerting rasp, Kyle lifted a strand of her hair—his expression intimately intrigued—then wrapped it languidly round his fingers. It not only shone with the fierce sheen of expensive silk, it felt like silk, too.

Profoundly satisfied with the knowledge, Kyle experienced the full, unbridled heat of arousal deep in his groin. He was hard and aching in an instant. Carnal instinct made him long to ravish the beautiful sultry brunette by his side with a reckless hungry abandonment that he could barely recall feeling for any other woman—ever. Right now, self-restraint was a thin veneer glazing a veritable torrent of emotion. A muscle clenched and unclenched in the side of his bronzed cheek, his deeply hazel eyes glittering hard with the sheer effort it cost him to stay in control.

'How's your leg this morning? Are you still hurting?' Furious with himself for allowing the force of his desire to temporarily take precedence over Megan's health and well-being, he unravelled her hair from his fingers, watching it fall away with regret, automatically assuming a distance he knew was necessary to put her at her ease. The last thing in the world he wanted right now was for her to be frightened of him.

'It's not hurting at the moment. I was just going to see if I could stand on it.' He saw relief, mingled with a little flash of regret in her beautiful dark eyes. Satisfaction swelled in his chest—the knowledge that she wanted him too made his blood sing.

'Then let me help you.'

Getting to his feet, he went to put his mug of coffee on top of the pine dressing table, his gaze inadvertently captured by a photograph in a delicately filigreed silver frame. It was Megan and a slim pretty blonde, clearly snapped in happier times. Both girls were beaming at the camera as if they hadn't a care in the world, bare feet sinking in the golden sand of a beach somewhere, sun glinting off the sea in the background.

Kyle honed in on Megan in particular—how could he not? Dressed as she was in skimpy white shorts, revealing long shapely tanned legs and a scooped-neck pink top that left little of her lovely shape to the imagination, she would stir the blood of any male with a heartbeat. He knew it was an outrageous thought but she looked like a *Playboy* centrefold or some seriously gorgeous movie starlet, while next to her her undoubtedly attractive friend simply paled into insignificance. Apart from her luscious physical attributes, Kyle also noted that Megan's lovely face seemed relaxed and more at ease. There wasn't that haunting sadness in her eyes that he detected there now.

'That was taken just before I started college,' she said lightly behind him. But, despite striving to keep her voice even, there was a slight quiver in it that made Kyle pivot, studying her with a laser-like intensity that left her with nowhere to hide.

'Penny and I had a week in Tenerife before we both took up our studies. Penny was doing Fashion and Design and I was doing Fine Art. We had the best time—no responsibilities except to ourselves. I think it was the only time in my life when I felt totally free. No commitments to anyone and no boyfriend to mess things up.'

A shaky smile hijacked her lips, but then Kyle saw the effort even that had cost her as in the next instant she wearily dropped her shoulders. He had to tamp down the sudden, almost overpowering urge to locate her feckless ex-husband and do him some serious damage. He wanted to see the girl in the picture again—the girl she'd been before a destructive relationship with a no-account bully had brought her so low.

'Anyway, I'd better get myself sorted out. I don't want to keep you from anything.'

'You're not keeping me from a damn thing.' Suddenly he was at her side again, supporting her arm and back as she struggled to get to her feet. He breathed in the heady coconut and pineapple scent of her shampoo, the light indefinable something that was purely Megan. He felt the satin-soft glide of her skin beneath his fingers, tightening his jaw in a bid to clamp down an almost uncontrollable resurgence of desire.

'Take it easy. There's no need to hurry things along. Can you try putting your foot to the floor?' His voice was hoarser than it should have been. Being so close and not allowing himself to touch her as he wanted was seriously testing all his powers of self-control.

When her foot nervously made contact with the carpeted floor Megan almost broke out in a sweat because she was praying so fervently that it wouldn't hurt. By some miracle, it didn't. Biting her lip, she tried to relax it a bit and add a little more of her weight. Incredibly, there was still no pain.

She turned her head to smile at the man by her side—a smile of such exquisite delight that it damn near broke his heart.

'It's all right,' she told him, her voice unknowingly breathless. She was like a little girl who'd just been told she was going to get the puppy she wanted after all. Something squeezed Kyle's heart right there and then and wouldn't let go.

'Perhaps you'd better try walking on it?' he suggested, his tone brisker than he'd meant it to be. He saw the smile fade and uncertainty creep back into her huge dark eyes. He could have kicked himself. Still holding onto her arm, he automatically bore most of her weight as she gingerly put her foot forward in a cautious attempt to walk.

She took one step, then another. Apart from the limp that was a given, everything seemed fine. Megan briefly closed her eyes to offer up a quick silent prayer of thanks. The possibility of a third operation receded a little further in her mind, like some ephemeral grey ghost she'd glimpsed out of the corner of her eye, now gone again.

'I think I can manage now.' Blushing a little, she waited for him to free his hold on her arm. When he didn't, she blew out a little sigh, acutely conscious of the fact that she was dressed in nothing but her nightgown, her face unwashed and her hair uncombed. If that wasn't ill prepared, she didn't know what was. Even Penny rarely saw her like that.

'Does it often get as bad as last night?' Kyle asked grimly.

Megan glanced away. Those curiously golden eyes of his were making it difficult for her to think straight, let alone speak.

'Last night was…particularly bad. But, yes, sometimes it's not what you might call pleasant.'

'Can't anything be done?'

'Apart from painkillers, you mean?' She was already

shaking her head, eyes as big as swimming pools. 'The orthopaedic surgeon who operated on me the first two times said it wasn't healing as well as he'd expected. I might be facing another operation if it doesn't improve soon. I really need to get myself into a more positive frame of mind to stop that from happening. One—because it's a hideous prospect, and two—I don't want to have to take any more time off work.'

She could just imagine Lindsay's face if she had to go to her with the news of a further operation—not to mention at least six weeks' recuperation afterwards. The woman was not going to be sympathetic.

'Is there a problem there?' His expression on a knife-edge of self-control, Kyle held onto her arm as if he had no intention of letting it go until he was completely satisfied with what she told him.

With her free hand, Megan tucked her dark hair behind her ear. 'Not a problem, exactly. My boss just doesn't like me taking time off.'

'He knows what happened with your leg, I presume?'

'She. Not the details, but she knows it was a bad break.' Megan sensed Kyle's warm breath skimming across her skin and tried desperately hard not to meet his hungry, questioning glance.

'I don't think you should be working anyway. You clearly haven't recuperated enough. What does your doctor think?'

'More or less the same as you. But I don't want to risk bad feeling at work if I take more time off. It's not worth the heartache.'

'Damn it, woman, we're not just talking about a common cold here!' Finally, the bounds of self-control snapping completely, Kyle jerked her towards him and helplessly, mindlessly, hungrily, crushed her mouth beneath his own.

Megan didn't even have time to protest. Instead, sensation

overpowered her like a sultry summer storm, abandoning her to its primal elemental fury, taking her willing prisoner.

Kyle's chest was a hard granite wall, grinding deeply against her breasts, his hands spanning her waist almost roughly as his arousal pressed hard against her pelvis—leaving her in no illusion as to the depth and breadth of his desire. Meanwhile his tongue was claiming the soft warm recesses of her mouth with impossible heat and sensuality, and a carnal lust so primitive, so hungry that it made her head swim.

Long-suppressed need slammed into Megan with all the finesse of a battering ram—stealing her breath, making her gasp into his mouth, the taste and sheer animal heat of him unravelling every damn thing she'd ever believed about herself. She'd never felt this aroused, this needy, not in all the long, difficult years of her marriage and certainly not before it… Maybe that was why Nick had accused her of being frigid?

With a savage curse, Kyle suddenly wrenched his mouth from hers, pressing her deeply into his chest as he drove his fingers possessively into the long silken strands of her tousled hair. She felt his heartbeat throbbing against her cheek, the warm, impenetrable strength of his hard-muscled torso reaching out to envelop her, to pull her in, to hint at a promise of possible shelter from any storm she might find herself in…

It was almost too seductive to be borne.

'Megan.'

His voice didn't sound like his own. It was gruff and unsteady, composure or any semblance of it totally and utterly gone.

'Yes?'

With her cheek flat against his chest, intrigued by the clean, profoundly sensual scent and erotic contact of toned male flesh against her own softer textures, Megan allowed her hand to play against his back. Her fingers instinctively found the slight indentation just below his waist and massaged it gently through the thin protection of his T-shirt.

Kyle took a moment to steady the sudden rapid acceleration of his heartbeat. The woman was turning him inside out with just a touch.

'You're hurting…and I don't want to take advantage.'

She lifted her head at that, gazing up at him with bottomless dark eyes that tugged at his soul.

'I know that. But you're not taking advantage of me. I— I liked it.' And with that she extricated herself reluctantly from his embrace to limp slowly but determinedly towards the *en-suite* bathroom. When she reached the door, she carefully turned round again, her hands nervously smoothing down the folds of her nightgown, her pink naked mouth wrestling with a smile. 'You don't have to stay. It's Saturday. I know you must have a hundred things to do.'

'You know that for certain, do you?' Kyle's dark brows lifted in amusement.

Megan's heart went bump. The man looked so good he was bad. With his darkly brooding features, tousled just-got-out-of-bed hair and tight-fitting jeans barely concealing honed hard muscle, he looked like a man who knew how to give a woman a good time in bed.

But that wasn't all she wanted, was it? Damn it—she didn't need to go there right now. After last night's agony she had other more pressing things to be concerned about than a potential future relationship. And who said he'd want a relationship with her anyway? Apart from a professional one? Even if sexual sparks were flying between them, it didn't mean Kyle might want anything more than a couple of quick tumbles in her bed, and that was something she'd never been up for—with anybody. But still, that shattering kiss of his had fuelled an ache deep inside that would be nigh on impossible to ignore…

'It was very good of you to come and help me last night, but I don't want to take up any more of your time than is necessary.'

'Did you do that?'

'What?' Megan saw him glance at the little seascape that was hanging on the wall above her bed in its plain undistinguished brown frame—the one she'd been so charmed by in the park. It perturbed her slightly that he was frowning as he stood regarding it, his arms folded, tanned biceps taut as tempered steel.

'I didn't paint it. No.'

'Good. It's terrible.'

Megan's stomach flipped defensively. 'No, it's not. I like it.'

'Terrible is perhaps too kind a description. It's got no soul. It's like something copied from a cheap postcard. Not even a good copy either.' He turned his head and fixed her with a stare. 'I hope your own aspirations are a lot higher than that.'

'You don't pull your punches, do you?' For some reason she felt chastised by his disapproval of the little painting. She remembered the girl with the nose-stud who'd painted it, standing in the rain trying to sell her work to mainly uninterested passers-by, and felt an unexpected kinship.

'Not when it comes to painting. I speak as I find. If you're going to make it as an artist you'll have to be able to take criticism as well as praise.'

'I know that.' Megan coloured a little and glanced away. Did he think she wouldn't be able to withstand a little criticism? After ten years of Nick he couldn't know she was a past master at receiving it. The fact that she was still living and breathing surely said something for her tenacity?

'I didn't mean to hurt your feelings.' His voice dropped to a husky undertone, his eyes eating her up with their golden fire, eliciting a melting ache deep in the very core of her that made her limbs feel outrageously weak—boneless.

'You didn't. If you'll excuse me, I need to get washed and dressed.' Her voice tailed off, every nerve-ending in her body acutely aware of the undercurrent of need that was ebbing and flowing between them like radar.

'Go and shower, or do whatever it is you're going to do. When you're ready, I'll be in the kitchen cooking us some breakfast. I take it you have some food in the fridge?'

Even though he was smiling, Megan lifted her chin a little. No matter how difficult things got, she always managed to put food in the fridge.

'I think you'll find there's plenty of everything. But I don't expect you to cook.'

She thought of his pristine show-home kitchen and tried to give him a get-out. The truth was, she couldn't give a tuppenny damn if he could cook or not. The man had come to her rescue at the drop of a hat and she wasn't about to search for flaws. As far as Megan was concerned he'd played the role of knight in shining armour to the hilt—even staying over until the morning to make sure she was all right. She should be the one making him breakfast.

'Sweetheart, you don't expect a whole lot, do you? Perhaps it's time you did.'

Rooting her to the floor with an indescribably hot glance that stripped her of every stitch, he strode past her, pulling the door softly closed behind him.

Megan showered, wrapped herself in her soft white terry robe, then spent ten hot and flustered minutes drying her lustrous long hair with a dryer that sounded like a jumbo jet taking off. She didn't use hairdryers as a rule, preferring to let her hair dry naturally, but because she knew a certain someone was pottering about in Penny's kitchen—doing

God only knew what—she felt a certain urgency to present herself as soon as possible.

As she sat on the bed, her gaze kept flicking to the seascape that had so charmed her and that Kyle clearly loathed. Perhaps it wasn't as good as she'd first thought?

She chewed her lip, switched off the dryer and sighed heavily. There she went again—worrying in case her judgement was skewed and he was right. But at the end of the day, what did it really matter? Megan had bought the picture because she loved the sea. It didn't have to be a work of art for her to feel a sentimental tug towards it, did it?

There was a sudden loud rap at her door. She went as still as a statue, then called out, 'What is it?' with a thumping heart.

'Breakfast will be on the table in five minutes,' the brisk reply came back.

Megan threw the dryer onto the bed and stood up. 'Okay. Thanks. I'm almost ready. I'm just getting dressed.'

'Need some help?' came the husky rejoinder.

'No. I'm—I'm fine,' she stammered, catching sight of her flushed cheeks and huge brown eyes in the dressing table mirror as she spoke.

She looked just like a frightened doe, she thought impatiently. Any other woman might have laughed off the teasing suggestion, but not her. She didn't have a sophisticated bone in her body when it came to men and the kind of games they played. No wonder she had been such a pushover for Nick. But she wouldn't think about her ex-husband right now. Not with a possible contender for Sexiest Man in the World standing right outside her door.

'Pity.' She heard the smile in his voice as his footsteps receded, and, flustered, tugged the belt around her robe a little too tightly for comfort, so that she had to quickly loosen it again in order to breathe.

Disregarding her usual weekend garb of jeans and sweatshirt, she rifled through her chest of drawers to find the red Chinese silk halter-top that Penny had brought her back from a trip to Hong Kong. It was comfortable, stylish, and extremely flattering to a figure she normally tried to conceal rather than play up, but after the drama of last night she was certainly in the market for a confidence boost.

Teaming the pretty red silk with a brown and red full-length skirt dotted with little gold fleur-de-lis, she completed her ensemble with a touch of kohl around her eyelids and a quick gloss of dark red lipstick. It was early spring and the weather was inordinately mild—almost summery, she assured herself, heading anxiously towards the kitchen. Anyway, she'd be far too warm in jeans and a sweatshirt.

Then she sniffed, her nostrils unexpectedly assailed by the distinct aroma of eggs and bacon. Her mouth watered. When Kyle had offered to make her breakfast, she'd had visions of a bowl of cornflakes and maybe some toast and marmalade—but real cooked food? She got the feeling he was about to blow another ill-judged assumption straight out of the water.

He'd opened both windows to divert the cooking smells, while at the breakfast bar Penny's best blue and white crockery along with Megan's stainless steel cutlery was laid out in readiness for two—side by side. To disconcert her even further, Kyle had tied one of the girls' blue and white striped aprons round his lean hard middle, and was busy ladling perfectly formed fried eggs out onto a hot plate as though he'd been born to the task.

Megan stared. Miraculously, the kitchen didn't look as if a bomb had been dropped on it. It was as tidy as ever, the sink full of hot sudsy water ready for the washing up, the stainless steel drainer wiped clean. Not only could the man cook, he was clearly domesticated, too. In all the years of marriage to Nick, her ex had never so much as boiled an

egg for her—or himself, come to that. What was this astonishing man going to surprise her with next?

'Hungry?' he asked, without turning his head.

Megan's stomach growled in response. It had been a long
time since the bowl of bland vegetable soup and two bread
rolls she'd consumed for dinner.

'Starving,' she said honestly, 'I never could resist bacon
and eggs.'

This time he did look round. He put down the ladle he'd
been using to slide the bacon out of the frying pan onto a
plate, then smoothed his hands carefully, slowly, down the
striped apron. The room was already warm from the cooker,
but in the next few seconds it grew significantly hotter. The
fire in Kyle's hazel eyes all but made her sizzle.

'Funny. Suddenly I'm not hungry any more. Not for food
anyway…' he drawled softly. Megan had never been seduced by a man's voice alone, but she was now.

Dragging her gaze away from him, she nervously crossed
her arms in front of her chest—blazingly self-conscious of
the silk halter-neck she was wearing and the way it emphasised her cleavage. What had seemed like a good idea,
or at least a daring rebellion against her usual conformity,
she now saw could be badly misinterpreted as a deliberate
ploy to arouse his interest. If that was what he thought, then
she wished the ground would open up and swallow her.

'You don't think this is too much? Oh, never mind. Forget I asked.' Angry with herself for yet again searching for
approval, she walked awkwardly past him to the counter on
the other side of the cooker, where she switched on the
already full kettle to boil. Her movements were clumsy and
ill-co-ordinated, her face flaming almost the same shade of
red as her ill-chosen top as she fussed with cups and saucers
from the cabinet above, instead of the usual mugs.

'Megan?'

At the low rumble of his voice she stopped what she was

doing, wincing at the suddenly loud clatter of a cup put down too hastily onto a saucer, and ventured a sidelong look from beneath her velvety black lashes. His brooding sculpted features—hard to ignore at the best of times— seemed even more sharply defined now, when he was regarding her as if he'd like to forget about breakfast altogether and concentrate on feeding appetites of a totally different kind.

'Yes?' Was that barely discernible rasp really hers?

'Just so that you're aware, I have a bit of a problem with my blood pressure…'

'Oh? Is it serious?' Megan frowned, natural concern rushing to the fore, then saw that he was smiling—grinning from ear to ear like a cat who'd got lucky with an extra bowl of cream.

'Only since you walked into the room wearing that outfit.' He blew out an exaggerated breath, then shook his dark head from side to side, his grin even wider when he saw how perturbed she looked.

That was the trouble, Megan thought with discouragement, she always rose to the bait. When God was handing out sharp wits she had obviously been at the back of the queue. As for smart rejoinders to put someone squarely back in their place—forget it.

'Very funny,' was all she could manage. Then, deliberately turning her back, she crossed the room with as much dignity as she could muster—which, taking her limp into consideration, was not the easiest undertaking.

As she moved away in a huff Kyle was left staring at that slim, sexy back, her tiny waist and the mouth-wateringly seductive curve of her hips in the flowing wrap-around skirt. Her hips weren't the only asset the material emphasised, he thought wryly. If he wasn't mistaken she had a derriere worth writing sonnets to as well…

In an instant he'd framed the picture he had in mind of

her: nude, perched on a chair, her back to him as sunlight streamed in from an open window in front of her, one slender hand lifting that gorgeous mass of silky dark hair off of her nape…

He was aroused and enthralled in equal measures, and in agony because of both. There was no question in his mind that he had to paint her and, perhaps more urgently, no question that he had to seduce her—sooner rather than later. Before his seriously inflamed libido made thinking about anything else completely impossible…

CHAPTER SIX

IN THE park where they'd gone to sketch, they sat side by side on the grass in a shady spot beneath an impressively towering oak that stood guard duty, the scent and signs of spring bursting forth all around them. From the pretty yellow and purple crocuses dotting the lush grass to the enchanting haphazard bunches of bluebells growing wild, stirred into a dance by the warm breeze, there was a new optimism in the air that Megan couldn't fail to pick up.

Fingering the good-quality sketchpad Kyle had collected from home on their way over to the park, she picked up her pencil, rolling it around in her hand purely to enjoy the sensation. Touch had always been one of Megan's favourite senses. The texture of a material, the feel of clay between her fingers, the poignancy of a child's small hand clamped in yours—touch revealed so much, yet was seriously underrated in her opinion.

Her gaze drifted idly across the smooth ivory page of the sketchpad, then made a helpless little foray across to Kyle. With his long legs stretched out on the grass beside her, his eyes closed, his back against the sturdy, indomitable trunk of the tree, it was as if the two were silently communing. Two unvanquished spirits locked in mutual admiration and respect.

Megan couldn't help but sigh out loud at her own fanciful notion.

'What is it, Miss Brand? Are you at a loss to know what to do, or was that breathy little sound just then a ploy to get my attention?'

His eyes most definitely open now, Kyle was lazily look-

85

ing her over, amusement and appreciation lurking equally behind his smile.

'I was just thinking…' She flushed, mortified that he might believe she was sighing simply to get his attention—even if it was just a little bit true.

'Is it a private thought, or are you going to share it with me?'

'I was just thinking about how wonderful trees were.'

Picking up the walking cane that lay between them on the grass, which Megan had reluctantly brought along in case she got too tired walking around, Kyle examined the little bumps and knots down the length of it, his attention caught suddenly by some runic symbols carved into the wood.

'This is from a yew tree, if I'm not mistaken,' he mused thoughtfully.

Megan beamed, thrilled that he recognised the fact. 'It was made by a white witch called Dusty Miller. He carved it specially for me.'

'Dusty Miller?' A corner of his mouth twitched upwards.

'He's a white witch…from a family of white witches. Pagans, I suppose you could call them. Anyway, they do a lot of good to help the environment.'

'So you have an interest in magic?' Kyle ran his thumb lightly across the symbols, glancing up to smile into Megan's sparkling brown eyes—wondering if it was really only last night that she had put the fear of God in him with her unexpected phone call.

Today she was a different girl. Out here in the open, sitting on the grass with her long black hair tumbling down her back, wearing her pretty red top and hippy skirt, her long graceful arms bare in the sunshine, he could easily imagine that she hadn't a care in the world. Only Kyle knew different. Behind the bright, almost child-like smile lay a wealth of pain and hurt that he couldn't begin to imagine.

Only the thought of losing his sister Yvette in that terrible car crash came close…

'It's good magic,' she said lightly, carefully dislodging a stray blade of grass from her sandal. 'It's all to do with being in tune with nature. The runic writing is for my protection, so that whenever I use the stick I'll be safe.'

Was she frightened that she might not be safe? The thought left a hollow feeling in the pit of Kyle's stomach. He carefully laid down the stick and dusted his hands.

'Why don't you try sketching some trees?' he suggested gently. 'How about this one for starters?' He got to his feet, moved a few feet away, then stood looking down at her with his hands planted firmly either side of his hips.

Megan's mouth went dry. When he'd stopped off at his house on their way over to the park he'd also changed his clothing and had a quick shave. Not surprisingly, his hazel eyes still looked a little sleepy from his disrupted night coming to her rescue, but just the same his broodingly handsome face was a picture of fierce male beauty and almost wicked sensuality. Practically every time she glanced at him it was like seeing him anew, and the surprise and sheer excitement of it made Megan feel like a schoolgirl hoping for her first kiss from a boy she had long admired.

'What are you going to do?' she asked shyly, her hand fluttering to the vee of her halter-top where she saw his glance was lingering.

He grinned, then jerked his head towards a group of boys kicking a football around nearby. 'Play a little soccer if they'll have me on the team,' he told her.

Privately she thought, Who wouldn't want this man on their team? But aloud she said, 'Fine. Go and enjoy yourself.'

'Sweetheart, if I really wanted to enjoy myself I'd stay here and just gaze at you for the rest of the afternoon…but as that would probably put you off your stroke, so to speak,

I think I'll go for my second option. Take your time…that's unless you had other plans for later on?'

A flash of doubt crossed his face and Megan realised he really did want to spend time with her. She was touched and exhilarated at the same time—not to mention a little unravelled by his previous comment.

'I've made no plans for anything,' she said honestly, dark eyes wide as she met his unwavering gaze.

His sensual hard mouth visibly relaxed. 'Good. I'll see you in a while. Draw the tree. Show me what you can do.'

Megan didn't move her pencil for what seemed like a very long time. As she watched Kyle's tall athletic body jogging effortlessly across the green to the boys playing football she was gripped with such a feeling of intense longing that for a while she couldn't think of doing anything else but looking at him. The boys welcomed him gladly into their game and within seconds he was moving round the field like a born athlete, displaying a natural skill and dexterity with the ball that drew effusive shouts of encouragement from his recently acquired team members…

It seemed he did everything with consummate ease and skill. Would he make love like that, too? Megan shivered at the silent question. She had no business even going there. She had nothing to offer such a vital, dynamic man. Nothing save her love and passion for art—that was the only passion they were destined to share. Anything else was pure fantasy on her part. Because sooner or later cold, hard reality would rear its ugly head and she'd be left facing the fact that, with her injury and her questionable ability to ever bear children, she'd be a poor proposition for any man looking for a partner.

Deliberately snapping herself out of such unhappy reverie, Megan told herself she'd better start applying her pencil and sketch before Kyle came back to see that she'd accomplished nothing. She wanted him to know she was serious about working at her craft. She didn't expect an easy ride just because he'd told her she was talented. And her old skills were bound to be rusty and a little frayed round the edges. The sooner she started to do some real work, the better.

The afternoon drifted by in a pleasant haze, the air permeated every now and then by birdsong or a buzzing insect, along with the unexpectedly comforting sound of children's laughter. Engrossed in her drawing, Megan glanced only occasionally across the grass to where Kyle played his energetic game of football with the boys, content to see him enjoying himself, apparently in no great hurry to pack up and go. The afternoon sun played warmly on her bare back as she drew, and it was a surprise to realise she was the most at ease that she'd been in a very long time.

'How's it going?'

Glancing up with a start, she found Kyle staring down at her, hands on hips, a little winded from his game, a sheen of sweat beading his smooth tanned brow.

'Fine…I hope.' Self-consciously hiding her sketch with her arm, she held up her other hand to shield her eyes from the sun's bright glare.

'Let's see.' He dropped down beside her, speared his fingers through his waving damp hair, then lifted the sketchbook off her lap.

Satisfaction—along with a building excitement, intense and deep—pulsed through him as he contemplated Megan's drawing of the huge oak. He had rarely seen such raw, almost effortless talent—not even in some of the brightest students he had taught in the past—and Megan had done nothing for ten years!

If he had to apply just one word to her drawing of the majestic old tree, it would have to be 'sublime'. Not only had she captured the living physical embodiment of the tree, she'd also managed to endow it with immense grace and presence—a feat not easily accomplished. He should know. Astonishingly, she seemed to possess that extra something that gave her a distinct edge over the competition. He knew he hadn't been wrong about her. That painting she'd done in his studio had been no fluke—not that he'd believed it had. Still, it was a stunning thought to contemplate what a burgeoning talent he had on his hands. He wondered if she had any idea of where it could potentially take her?

Handing back the sketchbook, Kyle casually drew his knees up to his chest and locked his arms around them. 'You say you've done nothing in ten years?'

'Only the odd sketch for my own amusement.' Megan shrugged as if it was of no account.

'And did you keep those sketches?'

'No. I—I threw them away.'

Deliberately skirting the laser-like beam of his searching gaze, she anxiously flipped the cover of the book down over her sketch. Almost reverently she laid it to one side on the grass. Flicking her long hair over a silky smooth shoulder, she stared hard into the distance, noting the boys still playing football, a couple sitting close together on a bench—the young woman gigglingly sharing her apple with her partner as if neither of them had a care in the world.

She didn't want to spoil the day by telling Kyle what had really happened to her precious sketches, but she could tell almost instantly by the sudden stiffening of his shoulders that he knew something was amiss.

'You threw them away? Why?'

'Nick didn't want them in the house.'

'You've got to be kidding? I already gathered that he was a poor excuse for a husband—I didn't know he was an idiot as well!'

'He was jealous.'

Her brown eyes focused on him at last, on the barely controlled anger simmering beneath the tightly drawn features of his face, on the Adam's apple that bobbed in the strong corded column of his throat.

'He didn't want me to have any other interests outside the home…outside of him. I tried to hide them in my wardrobe, but he found them. Then in a temper he ripped them up and threw the pieces into the wastepaper bin. He had no remorse about it. He thought his behaviour was perfectly rational.'

Her throat almost closed over the last few words as with a toss of her head she tried in vain to shake away yet another painful reminder of the hell that had been her marriage.

'Yeah,' Kyle said disparagingly, 'it would be if you only possessed one or two brain cells at most.'

'You won't get an argument from me.'

'And what about when he pushed you down the stairs?'

'What about it?'

'I presume you called the police?'

The question made her stomach jolt sickeningly. Unable to duck the accusation in his eyes, Megan miserably shook her head.

'I didn't get the police involved. They're not interested in what they call "domestics". Besides, Nick was distraught when he realised what he'd done…genuinely distraught.'

It took just one nervous glance at Kyle to know that he didn't believe that for a second.

'He just reacted out of pure temper. He was absolutely terrified when he saw how hurt I was. He begged me not to tell anybody. Only Penny knew what really happened. I got Nick to phone her—he was in too much of a state even to call an ambulance for me. I think he was afraid of what might happen to him if anybody found out. It certainly wouldn't have done his career any favours. Anyway, Penny came straight over and took care of everything.'

Megan paused to tug a blade of grass out of the earth, then stared at it blankly. How did you explain to someone who hadn't lived through such a terrible event the devastation and hurt that crashed in on you, robbing you of everything you ever believed in? Faith, hope, love—not to mention dignity and self-esteem—all had been stolen from her with that one violent act of spite.

His body still and unmoving, Kyle's expression was nonetheless dark with silent rage. 'Had he hurt you before that night? Physically, I mean?'

'Generally his cruelty was of the mental variety.' Her mouth thinning, Megan stared off into the distance once more, but all the colour had drained from her face, leaving her looking like a lost and frightened little girl.

For a moment, Kyle didn't know what to do. He wished with all his heart he hadn't brought the subject up, but the idea of the man ripping up all her work as well as subjecting her to physical and mental torment was almost too much to bear. Yet he had to know the extent of the wrong that had been perpetrated on her. He had to know truly what she had been through before he could even begin to understand how he might help her...

'So when did he leave? When you went into hospital?' he asked quietly.

A slightly more inclement breeze drifted past just then, lifting a few strands of Megan's glossy dark hair, teasing them across her face. As she brushed them aside, she regarded Kyle with a surprisingly steady gaze.

'I was in hospital for a long time. When I came out he was still living at the house and Claire—my one-time friend—had already moved in with him. I was too shell-shocked to think about doing anything about it right then, so I moved in temporarily with Penny. At least, it started out that way. I never meant to stay so long. I thought I'd get my share of the house and buy a small place of my own, but things got...complicated. Nick and Claire had been having an affair for months, and as far as Nick was concerned the house was his to live in or dispose of as he saw fit. A fortnight after I'd moved in with Penny I got a letter from Nick's solicitor informing me he wanted to sell.'

'But surely you owned the house jointly?' Kyle stared at her in disbelief.

Megan swallowed with difficulty. 'It was in Nick's name from the beginning. I never pressed him to put my name on the mortgage. I'm afraid I wasn't very sensible about things like that. I know it probably sounds terribly naïve, but when I got married I—I really thought it would be for life.'

Seconds ticked by. Kyle neither moved nor spoke. Megan shifted uncomfortably, her insides churning at the thought that he might judge her a gullible fool. Even if he did, she thought despairingly, she could hardly be angry with him for being right. As far as her relationship with Nick Brand was concerned, she'd been a damn fool about almost everything—and there was no harsher critic than herself.

'And what about your parents when all this was happening?'

Megan briefly closed her eyes and let out a long slow breath. 'My father left when I was two. My mother remarried and emigrated to Australia when I left to go to college. We're not what you might call close, and we don't keep in touch.'

Rain started to fall—softly at first, blown in on the breeze, then descending with distinctly more purpose. Without glancing at her companion, Megan gathered up her sketchbook and walking cane, then started to manoeuvre herself into a standing position. Her leg throbbed a little, and it wasn't easy to be entirely graceful when she had an audience.

'Let me help you.' Kyle was on his feet in an instant, one hand circling her waist while the other took her walking cane and steadied her arm.

'I can manage. I don't need help!' Feeling desolate, she

tried to shrug him away—faintly surprised when he completely ignored her mini-tantrum and proceeded to help her anyway.

'We need to get you home out of this rain. You're hardly dressed for a downpour.' His speech terse, Kyle refused to return her walking cane, instead tucking it securely under his arm. Then, before she could give him an argument, he swept her peremptorily off her feet as though her weight was nothing to him.

His breath gliding off her cheek, her body held tightly against his hard male warmth, Megan found herself carried without further preamble across the grass, all the way down the gravel path that swept around the park, back to where Kyle had left his car. Ignoring the interested glances of passers-by rushing past in the rain, he was unmistakably a man on a mission. By the time he'd deposited her into the luxurious cream leather of the sedan's passenger seat Megan felt more tense than a sprinter waiting for the sound of the starting pistol. She definitely sensed a storm brewing. She loved the rain, but storms were a big phobia with her. When the thunder crashed and lightning lit up the sky she was usually to be found praying under a table somewhere. But the storm she feared right now was not an elemental one.

Risking a brief glance at Kyle as he dropped down into the driver's seat, she saw that the expression on his darkly handsome face was warningly terse. As if he might snap at any second if she said another thing. So, biting her lip, trying desperately hard not to cry, Megan stared stoically out of the window, just praying for them to reach the flat as soon as possible so she could say thank you and goodbye and escape just as soon as it was polite.

It was clear from her companion's body language that for some reason he was furious with her. If only he hadn't asked her about her sketches. If only it hadn't rained and they could have stayed companionably on the grass, whiling away the afternoon like the friends Megan thought they might be becoming... But now it was all spoilt. And it was all her fault.

'Are you cold?'

Kyle switched on the heating as he drove, glancing across at her with a brief flash of concern in his hazel eyes. His gaze absorbed not just her profile but the red silk top that, since becoming damp, was clinging provocatively, the impression of her nipples clearly in evidence as they pushed against the softly sensuous material with no discernible help from their owner.

Scorching heat slammed deep into his groin, making him bite back a healthy curse. Lord have mercy! How the hell was he supposed to think about anything else but ravishing her when she was sitting there looking gorgeous and dewy-eyed and just about the most desirable woman he'd ever clapped eyes on? For evermore he would associate the colour red with Megan, because he couldn't think of one other woman who suited it more, but what on earth had possessed her to wear that sexy little top this afternoon?

Was she trying to test his resistance, or what? Because, if so, she'd chosen the one test he was bound to fail. At the end of the day he was a healthy red-blooded male, with the same needs, desires and instincts as the next man—maybe more, given his personal proclivity for passion.

He wanted to help her, God knew he did, but first—somehow—he had to get his raging hormones under tighter control. He shifted in his seat as he drove, manfully trying to accommodate his discomfort, resisting the suddenly fierce urge to blaspheme out loud.

Megan, caught in a disconsolate paroxysm of her own, suddenly snapped to—faintly shocked that they were pulling into the smart Notting Hill street where Kyle lived. So he wasn't taking her home first. Perhaps she should have made it clear to him that that was where she wanted to go? Her fingers clutching the sketchbook on her lap, she frowned as he glided the car to a halt in a space just a couple of houses away from his own.

'I didn't know we were coming back here.' She was so nervous her lips were numb when she tried to speak.

'You said you had no other plans for the afternoon.' Having switched off the engine, Kyle turned slightly in his seat, and Megan got an instant charge from the sheer raw unrestrained power of the man. Energy and heat vibrated off him with the unsettling ferocity of some wild thing, making her spine tense so stiffly it could have been made of steel.

There was something unsaid in his voice, in the way he looked at her—those riveting golden eyes with their long dark lashes almost challenging her to look away—to deny whatever it was that was going on between them…if she dared. Megan's gaze moved helplessly down over his hard honed body, her mouth going dry when she saw the evidence of his desire straining against the taut denim of his jeans.

'I—I know I said that, but—'

'But nothing,' Kyle said harshly, releasing the catch on the driver's door. 'You're coming inside and I'm not taking no for an answer.'

Megan heard the distinct slam of the front door as she ventured anxiously into his living room, silently berating herself for not insisting he drove her straight home. Then she realised what a slim possibility that would have been, because she couldn't imagine insisting for a second that Kyle do anything he didn't want to do. She had no idea why he wanted her to stay with him—her mind deliberately avoided the scary, most obvious reason, because the subject had been such a contentious issue in her marriage that, truth to tell, she was too damn frightened to pursue it further.

Her ex-husband had called her a tease when in fact she'd been nothing of the sort as far as he was concerned. 'Cold as the grave' was another taunt he'd tormented her with. 'I'd get more response from a corpse,' he'd said disgustedly when yet again she hadn't been able to satisfy him in the way that he'd wanted. After that she'd convinced herself that when it came to seduction—she just didn't have what it took to please a man.

Forlornly, her gaze settled on the little glass vase of freesias on the coffee table, her nostrils twitching at their much loved fresh peppery scent—and she remembered her surprise at seeing them there when she'd returned with Kyle earlier on in the day and waited while he washed and shaved. They were her favourite flowers. It had touched her in a strange kind of way that such an earthy, virile man should like them, too.

He swept into the room right then, and propped her walking cane carefully against the wall. Straightening, he speared his fingers through his damply waving hair, jerking his head almost curtly towards her clothes.

'You'd better get out of those wet things before you catch pneumonia. Come into the bedroom.'

When he turned his back Megan ran her hands up and down both arms, shivering as she did so, but more from an attack of nerves than damp or cold.

'I'm—I'm all right. They'll dry in no time.'

Kyle pivoted, his mouth thinning to a harsh grim line. 'What the hell is going on with you?'

'What—what do you mean?' Megan stared wide-eyed, her heart beating like a demented tom-tom as she struggled to understand his sudden hostility.

'I'm not your ex-husband. I'm not the bad guy, Megan. I want to help you, but I can't do that if you keep insisting on shutting me out.'

Megan looked everywhere but at him: at the beguiling prints on the wall that she longed to linger over, at the smoothed-out bumps in the cool oak floor beneath her san-dalled feet. She could cope with anything but kindness. People's kindness just undid her. Right now, her insides were just melting over and over at the care and concern in Kyle's deeply sensual voice.

'I'm not very good at accepting help. I appreciate it, I really do, but you're already doing enough in giving me the opportunity to paint again. If you just let me use your phone I can call a cab to take me home…'

'What if I said I didn't want you to go?' He crossed his arms in front of a chest that somehow seemed perfectly designed for maidens in distress to lay their heads on; his biceps, hard and sleek, glistened bronze beneath the sleeves of his T-shirt, his body primed as his eyes burned across the distance into hers. Megan tried to swallow but couldn't. Instead, she pressed her cold trembling hand to the vee of her top, as if by doing so she could somehow still the sudden crazy hammering of her heart.

'You mean you—' She couldn't finish the sentence because her limbs suddenly felt drained of strength, as if all the life force had been sucked out of them with a straw.

'I'm asking you to spend the night with me, Megan. I can't spell it out more clearly than that.'

'It's impossible.'

'Oh?' His mouth quirked in a disbelieving grin, adding to her confusion and embarrassment. 'May I ask why?'

'Because…because I don't know how to satisfy a man.'

CHAPTER SEVEN

HIS answering chuckle was deeply sensual. Like warm syrup being poured over a lush moist waffle…sinful. If she had an ounce of common sense she'd run for cover now, because if she stayed she wouldn't stand a chance.

'I don't believe that for a second…but what about you, Megan? Has any man satisfied you?'

Not in ten long years… She didn't say the words out loud. She didn't dare. All she knew was that the ground she was standing on was suddenly as insubstantial as a cloud and she was sinking fast. Drowning in the molten tawny gaze of a man who could make her want and yearn and beg him to love her—with just a glance.

'I don't—I mean—I'd like to use your bathroom, if I may?' She took a couple of unsteady steps towards him, privately cursing the limp that robbed her of even the simplest dignities.

It didn't make sense that he desired her. A man like him could probably have any woman he wanted. When it came to assets, Kyle had all the aces. Not just good looks, a great body, intelligence and talent, but clearly wealth as well. There was no reason for him to waste his time with Megan. What could she give him but a body that was physically impaired and a disillusioned, emotionally damaged heart?

A moment ago her whole being had glowed in the fierce heat of his all-consuming regard, but suddenly she felt a chill settling in across her bare arms and back that made her long to be warm and dry and safe again—because right now she felt anything but.

'Sure. I'll show you where it is.'

Before she could shut the door to his stylish monochrome bathroom, with its sexy masculine smells of soap and cologne, behind her, Kyle stayed her hand.

'Just wait a second. You'll need some dry clothes.'

His jaw clenched; his glance swept helplessly over her figure with barely disguised longing—so much so that Megan actually found herself holding her breath. But in less than a second he'd turned away, abruptly breaking the spell like a thunderclap at the end of a perfect summer's day.

Releasing a sigh that was more like a rasp, Megan leant her hand against the cool black and white tiles on the wall for support.

He was back in no time at all, handing her a folded clean bundle consisting of a dove-grey T-shirt and black sweats, the look in his eyes no less hot but now with a kind of controlled detachment that hadn't been in evidence before.

Megan took the clothes with a polite 'thank you,' then gently closed the door on his retreating back.

Limbs quaking, she limped across to a black wicker basket chair, dropping down into it with relief. Laying the clothes carefully on top of the lidded laundry basket beside her, she reached for a huge fluffy white bathsheet from the heated chrome towel rail, and started to pat herself dry.

All she could think about was the fact that he'd asked her to spend the night with him. Nothing had ever seemed so tempting yet so terrifying at the same time. Pressing her hands either side of her temples, she let the soft warm towel rest idly on her lap, then briefly closed her eyes.

When she opened them again it was to find herself staring at a rather beautiful water-colour on the wall that she hadn't noticed when she'd first come into the room. It was of a voluptuous young woman stepping out of an old-fashioned claw-tooth bath, tousled blonde hair cascading in soft tendrils around her pink apple-cheeked face, a towel clutched loosely to her breast. There was something very sensual and highly erotic about the picture that almost made Megan feel like a voyeur.

Her distracted mind wondered vaguely who had painted it, at the same time acknowledging that it was really quite exquisite. Was Kyle the artist? And, if so, who was the voluptuous young model? A lover? Maybe the same lover who'd bought him Turkish Delight? And, if so, where was she now?

A deep throb of jealousy reverberated through her insides. Why did things have to be so complicated? Why was she so screwed up and scared when someone like Kyle's young model could confidently strip off, make love, and have her picture painted by her lover as if it was the most natural thing in the world? All right, so it might all be conjecture— Kyle might not have even painted the picture—but the feelings it triggered off in Megan would not be stemmed. Not in the light of the proposition he had made to her just now…

But, oh, the freedom and joy of being able to paint whenever she wanted to! There wasn't one thing she wanted more—well, apart from peace of mind…and maybe one sinful night with the man who had come to her rescue on the strength of one late-night phone call. The same man who had carried her out of the park in the rain, who'd held her close into his wonderful chest, as if it mattered to him that she might not be up to walking after spending a practically sleepless night in pain.

But she was kidding herself if she imagined that one night with Kyle would be enough, and if her heart got involved— what then? Everything came with a price, didn't it? And she'd paid a hell of a price when she'd got involved with Nick. Make a choice and you change the future. Right now, changing her future seemed more than a little dicey, considering her past, and she didn't even know if she had the courage to go through with such a thing.

The problem was she'd only ever slept with Nick, and

Nick had taunted her with less than flattering accusations of being frigid and cold. When you heard those words that often, eventually you began to believe them…

'Megan? Are you all right in there?'

At the sound of his gruffly concerned voice outside the door, Megan sat bolt upright, flicked her hair self-consciously over her shoulder and strove to articulate a calm reply—no easy feat when she could barely hear her own voice over the heavy throb of her heartbeat.

'I'm fine, thanks. Won't be a minute.'

'I'll be in the kitchen, making some coffee. Come and find me.'

Oh, yeah. 'Okay.' Twisting a corner of the towel tightly around her fingers, Megan blew out a soft low breath. She felt like a new addition to the Sheihk's harem, who'd just been invited for the first time into his private quarters.

She knew she should move, finish drying, strip off her cold, damp clothing and dress herself in the warm freshly laundered clothes Kyle had handed her, but somehow she couldn't. Somehow she was caught in a paroxysm of antic-ipation and fear that she could no longer hide. Kyle would see it for sure. Would it amuse him, or perhaps irritate him, that a twenty-eight-year-old long-married woman was acting like some uptight virgin on the brink of her first sexual experience? He was surely used to much more worldly women than that?

Glancing sideways at her reflection in the big Art Deco 'nowhere to hide' mirror, Megan could hardly believe how wild her dewy-eyed gaze was, how scared, yet at the same time how needy. It had been so long since she'd truly felt desire, so long that all she could attribute to it was a distant cloudy memory that was so ephemeral and unreal she might have imagined it.

So, could she satisfy a man like Kyle? The answer clearly had to be no. Psychologically she was damaged goods. Why would a man like him want to involve himself with such an unstable proposition as that? No. She wouldn't inflict that on him—no matter how attracted she might feel towards him. She would finish drying, dress herself, and calmly tell him she was declining his offer to spend the night. He would understand. A man like him would probably shrug, put it down to experience, and get on with his life. There'd never be any shortage of more willing, worldly-wise women to help him get on with it either. Megan was certain about that.

'Hi.'

Kyle swung round at her greeting. He'd been chopping up peppers for an omelette, the radio playing softly in the background—something classical—Schubert, maybe. He didn't have time to really consider it, because one look at the distracting picture Megan made in his too-large T-shirt and sweats wiped all coherent thought clean out of his head.

He let the knife clatter noisily onto the chopping board, picked up a chequered teatowel to dry his hands, then threw it carelessly down on the counter.

The clothes she wore might be too big by a mile, but the shape inside them was far too female to be totally concealed. It was easy to detect that she wasn't wearing a bra. She couldn't have been anyway, because she'd been wearing that sexy little halter top that declared as much to the world, and now her full pert breasts were straining against the voluminous material of his shirt, making him hard just looking at her. So hard and aroused that it was damn near agony to stand there and act as if nothing were amiss.

'Better now?'

'Dry, at least.' Shrugging, she moved uncertainly towards him, her glance wary as she hitched up the sweat pants that were too big even with the tie pulled as tight as she could make it. The cloth pooled around her ankles, and Kyle couldn't suppress the purely male appreciative grin that was tugging at the corners of his mouth.

'Sexy, too.'

'I wasn't trying…to look sexy.' Her lower lip quivered a little as she barely got out the words on a gravelly whisper, her attention hijacked by the hungry longing in Kyle's magnetic hazel eyes. In response, the blood thickened in her veins. Suddenly the question of whether she should spend the night with him or not was immaterial. You might as well have asked her if she needed to take her next breath. Unequivocally yes.

'Sweetheart… You don't have to try to be sexy—you just are.'

Kyle reached her before she got to him, hauling her hard up against him so that her breasts were crushed against the wall of his chest, her senses invaded by his heat and his hardness, by the sheer physicality of skin against skin, by the undoubted animal magnetism he exuded like cologne.

Oh, God, I need this… She melted as his hands slipped easily around her waist, then slid lower to trace the delectable curve of her behind. With a softly muttered oath his mouth found hers, almost instantaneously commanding her response. As his heat invaded her every sense in Megan's body capitulated to his demand as urgently as one magnet attracted another. It was as if their two bodies suddenly fused and melded into each other, so that there was no distinction between where he began and she ended.

His kiss was flooding the delicately soft recesses of her mouth with desire and want and the deliciously erotic flavours of the man himself. Her breasts peaked and hardened, a hot desperate longing flooding her limbs with an ache so deep that Megan gasped hungrily into his mouth. Her soft secret spaces absorbed the erotic little dance of his tongue with another helpless groan as she arched her body into his, exhilarated but scared when she felt the rigid pressure of his arousal pressing urgently into her abdomen.

Dragging his mouth away from hers with a harsh guttural

sound that made Megan's heart thud almost to a stop, Kyle cupped her face between his hands, his gaze burning her with a fire that was all but running out of control. In the side of his perfectly sculpted cheek—intriguingly shadowed by a day's growth of beard—a muscle worked tellingly, the last vestiges of self-restraint hanging on by a mere thread…

'I have to be sure…this is what you want.' His heart racing, Kyle gazed into her fathomless velvet brown eyes and knew himself to be irrevocably lost.

Right then, every feature on her lovely sensuous face became the focus of his whole world. The beautifully rich dark lashes that swept down to the tip of her porcelain cheek, the straight, exquisitely formed little nose, the beguilingly sexy mouth, wet and swollen from his kisses… He was transfixed. Just as if he had been bewitched. As if he had inadvertently wandered into the realms of magic, where reality as he understood it was invitingly suspended, his destiny to be trapped there for at least a hundred years or more.

The thought made him shiver…then it made him smile—because God knew he was a willing captive. Already his lips were missing the taste of hers, desire rolling through him like a rapid that couldn't be stopped—pulling him over the edge as easily as a leaf borne on the wind. He could love her and never stop, and the realisation was a tidal wave hitting him hard.

He stared as her lips moved, need ripping through him as the moist, sultry mouth that he defied any man to look at and not think the most lascivious erotic thoughts—formed words that made every nerve-ending in his body snap to with hungry anticipation.

'I'm sure,' she whispered.

Needing no more reassurance than that, Kyle swept her up into his arms and bore her urgently into his bedroom.

Megan was tremulously aware of being laid carefully down on his big brass bed; the sight of it sent a wave of pure eroticism rippling through her that made her catch her breath. Then she was aware of the slight give of the mattress beneath the darkly masculine navy blue silk counterpane, of Kyle leaving her momentarily to twitch down blinds the colour of café latte.

Her eyes followed him with a kind of wild hunger that she hadn't known herself capable of, devouring him as he languidly returned to join her on the bed, almost deliberately stringing out the tension between them like a bow.

Stripping off his shirt, then discarding it in one easy fluid movement while her gaze thirstily drank in the sight of all that gorgeous bronzed hard-muscled flesh, he was sure, confident, and most of all totally in command. His dark tousled hair grazed his shoulders as he carefully straddled her legs, then reached down to lay his hands on her breasts.

It was like a lightning strike. Megan bit down heavily on her lip as need and passion dovetailed, ripping through her like a thousand volts of electricity—lighting her up from the inside out. Her pelvis arched towards him as she shut her eyes on a deeply languorous groan. Then his thumbs started to work their magic back and forth across the tender aroused flesh of her nipples beneath the soft material of his shirt, and her eyes flew open again to find him watching her with an intensely erotic, almost primeval passion etched on his face.

'Take off your clothes.' The polite veneer was gone. In its place was a need so raw and so primitive that it rocked Megan's world straight off its axis—never to be the same again. All she knew was that there was a wild honeyed heat running through her blood like the onset of a fever.

With shaking fingers she started to comply with his command, struggling as she tried to hike up his too-big T-shirt. Conscious of his powerful muscular thighs placed either side of hers, the lean taut-muscled plane of his stomach, the swirl of coarser dark hair that dipped down from his navel to disappear provocatively behind the waistband of his faded denim jeans, she found it almost impossible to make her fingers do what she wanted them to.

'Let me help you.' In less than a second he had the shirt up and over her head. He jettisoned it carelessly onto the floor as his bold, hungry gaze feasted on the sight of her full, softly rounded breasts with their sensuously dark nipples, her glorious ebony hair falling over her shoulders like some exotically dark waterfall. She was even more lovely than he had imagined, her body supple and curvaceous at the same time—and he ached to possess her with every fibre of his being.

He groaned his appreciation out loud, then pushed her gently back down on the bed. In the next instant, as her hair splayed out like skeins of black silk on the dark blue counterpane, Kyle dipped his head to take carnal possession of her breast, drawing it deeply into his mouth, sucking and laving while his hand greedily caressed its twin.

Biting back a cry, Megan bucked her hips beneath him, and a kind of ragged whisper spelt out her desire.

'Please…'

He lifted his head, placed his hands on her waist and jerked down the sweatpants that were far too big, exposing the black silky triangle of material that—despite being fairly conservative in design—barely covered her hips and drew immediate attention to the flat sexy plane of her stomach and creamy smooth thighs.

Then, before Megan had time to even register his intention, he parted her thighs, pulled the flimsy barrier of underwear aside and drove his finger deep into the hot moist centre of her femininity. Her pupils dilated with shock, her muscles clenching tightly round the sudden erotic invasion and her hands grabbing on to his sleek hard biceps as though clinging on for her very life.

'Kyle!'

At the urgent gasp of his name Kyle sat up, shucked off his jeans and his underwear, then wrenched down the rest of Megan's clothing. At the startled look on her face, he positioned the hot satin length of his sex at her entrance and thrust in deeply.

They both stilled at the urgency and depth of Kyle's possession, Megan experiencing an ache and a yearning so deep that her eyes brimmed over with unexpected tears, long-suppressed emotion unravelling her to the very core. Then Kyle—his expression one of fierce hunger and concentration—started to move inside her, thrusting deeper and harder, until Megan groped desperately for his shoulders and pulled his head down for her kiss.

She was drowning in the erotic taste and flavour of his mouth, issuing desperate little sounds of need and want that she'd never uttered in her life before—carried away on a crest of passion and desire—when the moment of starburst came. It took her like a wave, carrying her away from the safety of the shore, crashing in on her like a torrent, demanding her complete and utter capitulation until she was left shaking and crying in its aftermath—the force of her emotion and surrender almost tearing her apart.

Above her, Kyle's hard-muscled body stilled, the deep musky scents of their bodies mingling as Megan sensed the effort and control it cost him to momentarily curtail his desire.

'I'm all right,' she whispered, tears sliding into her mouth, dark eyes glazed. 'Don't stop.'

'Sweetheart,' he said, gravel-voiced, 'I don't think I could even if I wanted to.'

On the last word he thrust into her deeply, to the hilt, the force of his possession making Megan's hips buck, her eyes closing tight as she felt his liquid heat spill into her with destroying heat, then heard the warrior-like cry that burst spontaneously from his lips as his passion reached its zenith.

Then, shuddering deeply, he eased himself down onto her body—his weight and strength pressing her into the bed, his long hirsute limbs tangling with hers, his breath warm and ragged against her cheek.

Megan kept her eyes momentarily shut, needing those precious few moments to understand the depth and magnitude of what she'd just experienced. To wonder at the recklessness that had suddenly robbed her of every last ounce of common sense and made her give herself to a man who would probably look on their sexual liaison as nothing more than a one-night stand. He would certainly not expect her to regard it as anything more than that, she was sure. After all, she was a modern girl, wasn't she? It went without saying that Kyle would expect a modern attitude.

It didn't matter that her heart said different; it didn't matter that she longed for something far more lasting and permanent...

'Are you okay? I didn't hurt you? I didn't mean for the first time to be over so quickly.' He grinned wryly in the semi-darkness, as if his ego could stand a little humour even at such a critical time. In response, Megan felt her own mouth twitch upwards in a tentative smile.

'I'm fine. It was—it was nice.'

'Nice?' Kyle shook his dark tousled head with a fierce growl. In the dim light filtering through the rolled down blinds his golden eyes burned with a molten glare of disbelief and desire. 'Sweetheart, in all my years as a sexually active male I don't think my performance has ever been accused of being "nice". I'm afraid you're going to have to pay for such a patently unwarranted remark.'

'Pay? How?'

Frowning, Megan let out a surprised yelp as Kyle suddenly grabbed her by the waist and rolled her on top of him. She found herself staring helplessly down into his teasing sexy smile, her long hair brushing against the dark coarser hairs on his chest while the blood in her veins heated and slowed like molasses. Her beleaguered heart raced madly at the prospect of what her supposed 'punishment' was going to be.

'Lady, I seriously hope your stamina can match mine, because the effect you're having on me right now might well mean I just have to keep going all night.'

'Is that…possible?'

'Is that a challenge?'

The look on his face suddenly serious, his hands came to settle round the soft malleable flesh on her hips, easing her carefully yet urgently down onto the smooth satin length of his arousal as if the two of them had been meant for nothing else. Caught up in the spell, his gaze roved hungrily across the slightly stunned, undoubtedly aroused expression on her face with a savage almost primeval male satisfaction—totally consumed with the idea of loving her in every way possible throughout the rest of the night.

He'd been right about the passion in her. The first time he'd taken her hard and fast, but she'd matched him in more ways than one. There was a wildness in her that found a natural home in his own ferocious need to love and possess her.

Megan let out a whimper as Kyle plunged upwards, his rigid shaft filling her so completely she thought she would die from the sheer wanton pleasure of it. If this was making love, she thought dazedly, then whatever it was she had reluctantly shared with Nick all those grimly difficult years was nothing but a pale, sorry imitation.

As Kyle guided her passionately to more demanding, dizzying heights of pleasure with his hands, with his hard warm body, with his wicked, skilful mouth, Megan knew with sudden certainty that all those hurtful accusations her ex-husband had levelled at her were nothing more than a bunch of cruel, resentful lies. Welcoming Kyle's fiercely voracious possession of her body with equal hunger and need, she knew without doubt there was nothing in her that was remotely frigid. All this time she'd just been waiting for the right man to come along and match the insatiable passion she was naturally capable of... Kyle.

Suddenly tilting her head wonderingly to the side, Megan stared down at her lover with wide, glistening brown eyes. 'What is your last name?' she rasped as his hands cupped her breasts and sensuously moulded them.

'What the hell does it matter?' he growled and, shifting position, pulled her round so that she lay flat on her back beneath him. Encasing her hips with his strong powerful thighs, he lifted her arms high above her head, imprisoning her wrists on the silk pillow behind her so that his gaze could look its fill on her supple naked loveliness. 'I'm not hurting you?' he demanded hoarsely, his jaw clenched tight.

'My leg, you mean?' Megan moved her thigh experimentally, mentally blocking the twinge of pain that throbbed inside it as she did so. 'No,' she replied, her lip quivering.

Whatever pleasure he had in mind, she didn't want to dissuade him from it. It would override whatever hurt she was suffering physically from her leg, and besides, she felt as though she'd been waiting all her life for this particular sensual journey—she wasn't going to call a halt to it now.

'I'm fine. Don't I look fine?' she added boldly, a teasing dimple appearing at the side of her lush moist mouth. In answer, a muscle leapt in Kyle's handsome bronzed cheek, his tawny eyes turning lasciviously dark.

'Sweetheart, you dazzle me. A man would have to go a long way to gaze upon anything as lovely as you.' And without further preamble he thrust deep inside her, magically erasing every coherent thought she had in her head irretrievably away.

CHAPTER EIGHT

KYLE burrowed deeper into the cool silk of the pillow beneath his head, determined to linger in the hazy half-world between dreaming and wakefulness a little while longer. Languorously, rather like a sleek cat making optimum use of his God-given ability to just laze, he stretched out his hand beside him.

As soon as it came into contact with empty space his eyes flew open and he jerked upright, his senses immediately alert to the fact that something was amiss. All lingering thoughts of further sleep were swiftly and rudely banished.

There was no sign of Megan. The dove-grey shirt and black sweats he had lent her, which had been so urgently and carelessly discarded in the throes of their lovemaking, were folded ominously on the little Chinese cabinet at her side of the bed. Disappointment and, yes, anger clenched the hard, toned muscles of his stomach. Where the hell was she? She wouldn't have just left without telling him she was going, would she? His stomach felt curiously hollow. No woman had ever walked out on him like that—not when she'd spent the night in his arms. In the past, that particular little trick had been Kyle's, and he wasn't proud of it.

Cursing beneath his breath, he made an irritated grab for his silk boxers and hurriedly stood to pull them on. He yanked up the blinds and blinked as daylight assaulted his gaze, his hazel eyes squinting into the morning sun, dark brows knit in momentary confusion, his senses assailed sharply and irrevocably by the sweet musky scent of his lover's body that made him long for her anew.

Sweeping the room with a cursory glance, he spied his

jeans at the foot of the bed, then, tricky as the manoeuvre was, managed to ease into them at the same time as heading for the door. In the kitchen, the chopped-up peppers he'd been preparing the afternoon before, which he'd left on the well-used chopping board, had been meticulously scraped into a little ceramic dish and covered with cling-film.

The woman had cleared up for him before she'd left but she hadn't been able to bring herself to tell him she was going! They'd spent the entire evening and all night together in bed and she'd left as easily as though they'd been strangers who'd exchanged nothing but a few polite words instead of a passion so profound that Kyle was still reeling from the aftermath.

Frustration and fury gnawed at his gut. Raking an impatient hand through his unruly dark hair, he glared at the coffee pot, momentarily debating whether to make himself a fortifying cup before presenting himself to Megan and demanding to know what was going on.

They'd fallen asleep in each other's arms, for God's sake! Didn't that count for anything? Sated and sleepy in the aftermath of their lovemaking, Kyle had wound his arms round her waist, then fallen asleep with the scent of her coconut shampoo drifting beneath his nose, the soft, pliant curves of her body a seductive combination of satin and velvet beneath his fingers… At no point had she given him any indication that she was leaving early. If she had, he would have done his damnedest to persuade her to stay.

Even now, standing alone and frustrated in his immaculate kitchen, he felt like some godforsaken ship without an anchor. He longed for her in every way it was possible to long for somebody…with his heart, his soul, his mind—not to mention his body. Just the thought of her could make him ache, and right now was no exception. He groaned out loud at the sweet and heavy rush of blood to his groin. He'd never had a more sexy or willing partner. She'd been like wild honey in his hands and he couldn't imagine paradise being any sweeter.

Dammit! He couldn't stand around waiting for coffee, he had to go and find her. Demand that she return with him. He'd promised himself they would spend the day in his studio working, even if his aroused libido said differently. As far as he was concerned it was essential that he demonstrate—intimate relationship or no—that he was more than willing to help her forge an artistic career. It was a point of honour for him. Such a talent should never be wasted and he would personally see to it that she got every bit of tutelage and guidance to help her make her mark.

But first things first. Right now he had to see her and talk to her. Nothing had ever seemed more imperative. He didn't even pause to ask himself why. Instead, he went to his wardrobe, yanked open the doors and rifled through his clothing for something clean to wear before hitting the shower with a vengeance.

The heady, painfully evocative fragrance of Nick Brand's designer aftershave wafted round Penny's bright modern living room like the strong redolence of sweat in a male locker room after a football game. Megan's stomach kept somersaulting like a trapeze artist gone mad every time she sensed it. Painful memories surfaced and melded with the present as she nervously eyed the man who'd so clearly made himself at home on Penny's cushion-laden couch.

In appearance, Nick Brand was as handsome and confident as ever in his stylish but sober designer suit—if a little older. In fact his greying temples had come as a bit of a surprise, but his brown hair was as professionally styled as always, giving the distinct impression that he didn't skimp on his hairdressing bills. Unsurprisingly his expression was totally at ease as he sat absorbing his surroundings—

insolent—almost. As if he were king of his castle and every-one else around him mere peasants.

Nothing much had changed then. He still thought he was better than everyone else.

Megan swallowed hard, trying not to let him see how shaken she was to see him. This man had hurt her enough without her giving him more ammunition to use against her. Right now, his insipid blue eyes were clearly striving to affect warmth, when she knew from bitter experience there was none to be had. On the third finger of his left hand his wedding ring—a single diamond set in platinum, made to complement the one he had bought for Megan—winked back at her as if to mock her.

What on earth? Megan's heart slammed against her ribs as she contemplated the raw fact that he was still wearing it. Just what was he playing at? Their divorce had come through a year ago. There was no reason on earth why he should still be wearing his ring. And why had he shown up out of the blue like this, without warning? He had to be up to something, but what? She'd barely recovered from the shock of finding him at the door just five minutes after she'd got back from Kyle's—let alone had time to ponder the reason for his visit.

Well, she wondered now. Her hands visibly shook as she placed the mug of coffee she had stupidly offered to make him into his hands. Even though she'd made changes in some things, she still found it extremely difficult to be any-thing other than polite. Other women would probably have slammed the door firmly shut in his face, but Megan wasn't as brave. In Nick's presence she reverted to a scared and lonely little girl, and there was no one who despised the fact more than herself.

'Thanks, darling. You still make the best cup of coffee out of anyone I know.'

The slick compliment, so easily paid, made Megan sick

to her stomach. She twisted her hands in front of her long
Indian skirt and glanced angrily down at the floor, garnering
her courage. She remembered what Kyle had told her—that
if she was staying stuck in old behaviour, it was her choice.

'You didn't come here to pay me compliments, that's for
sure.' She raised her chin a little, dark eyes darting to the
door as if mentally willing him to get up and leave. 'I've
got a friend coming round in a minute, so please tell me
what you came for and then go.'

The lie didn't come easily to her, but she had to resort to
such a device out of sheer self-protection. She was on her
own, and if past knowledge of Nick's volatile personality
was anything to go by she had to be prepared for almost
anything. Penny wasn't expected back until the evening and
Kyle—well, Kyle…

Her mind drifted momentarily away from Nick. Her heart
soared and fell almost simultaneously at the thought of the
man in whose strong passionate arms she had spent the
night. What had he thought when he woke to find her gone?
Had he been angry? Would he ever want to speak to her
again?

She had been overwhelmed when she'd woken to find
herself in his bed, and felt almost faint with embarrassment
when she remembered how unrestrained and wild she'd
been in his arms. How reckless. They hadn't used protection. What if she got pregnant? *Don't be stupid, Megan.*
There wasn't any possibility of that. Not given what the
doctor had said after her accident. Anyway, all she had been
able to think about that morning was making herself scarce
as quickly as possible so that she wouldn't have to face
possible regret or embarrassment on Kyle's part if he so
much as indicated it had all been a dreadful mistake…

'I like paying you compliments,' Nick said smoothly
now, bringing her sharply back to the present as he languidly crossed one immaculately suited leg over another.

His gaze travelled up and down her body as if he had the right, and even though she despised the sexual glint employed quite deliberately in his examination of her Megan was glad the she had swapped the revealing red halter-top she'd been wearing for an old comfy ivory sweater that had seen better days. She would have felt vulnerable as hell in the scantier clothing.

'Don't!' Megan's voice cracked in anguish. All of a sudden her resolve not to show even the smallest weakness to this man faltered and crumbled as long-held pain and sheer despair washed over her. He had no right showing up at Penny's flat, intimidating her with his slickly patronising compliments and his paper-thin veneer of friendliness. She wanted him gone. If she never saw him again in this life she would fall down on her knees and thank God.

Startled by the hot rush of tears that welled in her eyes, Megan smoothed her hands nervously up and down the soft material of her skirt. 'You're playing games with me, Nick, and you know it. The difference is, I don't have to stand here and put up with it any more. We're divorced, in case you'd forgotten. You moved in with one of my closest friends, remember?'

'I must have been mad.'

To her shock, Nick rose from the couch, put his coffee down on a small side table next to a carved wooden figure of a laughing Buddha, then stood regarding her with a disquieting pensiveness that made all the hairs stand up on the back of her neck.

Megan felt a trickle of perspiration slide down her spine. Her senses were assailed by the too liberally applied cologne, by the distinct aura of restlessness and threat her ex-husband wore around him like a force-field. What had she been thinking of allowing him to come in?

'Nick, I don't know what you're suggesting, but—'

'I must have needed my head tested to get involved with

a neurotic like Claire. She's nothing like you, Megan. Nothing like my dark and beguiling wife. I even call her by your name when we make love, do you know that?'

'I don't want to know that…and I'm not your wife!'

With a shaky hand, Megan looped some glossy strands of hair behind her ear as her whole body went numb with fear. Had Nick been drinking? She surreptitiously sniffed the air, shocked when she detected the lingering odour of whisky mingling with his aftershave. It was God knows what time in the morning and he'd been drinking already. Why hadn't she detected it before? Where was her mind? Where was her common sense, for God's sake? When Nick drank, he was prone to become slightly unhinged. He'd been drinking the night he had pushed her down the stairs. If he'd been sober then maybe he would have thought twice about committing such a terrible act…

'I think you'd better go, Nick.' Megan was stunned she was able to get the words out. Her own voice sounded strange and disembodied to her ears, but it was hard to talk across a mouth that had turned into a desert. She watched him smile at her suggestion, her blood running cold when he threw back his head and laughed as if she'd said something horrendously funny. It made him look ugly. Ugly and threatening.

'Don't be silly, darling. I'm not going anywhere until we discuss my little proposition.'

'I'm asking you to leave. No, forget that. I'm *telling* you to leave! I don't want to hear any of your propositions, little or otherwise!' In an instant Megan was at the door, holding it open, her heart thumping fit to burst. Please, God, she prayed. Let him go. Make him leave now and I swear I'll never make such a stupid, stupid mistake again…

'I'm no good without you, Meg.' In the centre of her friend's comfortable living room, Nick swept an impatient hand through his carefully styled gelled hair, carelessly dislodging its slick arrangement, his pale eyes darting back and forth from Megan as if he couldn't quite get a grip on his tumbling thoughts.

Megan was secretly surprised. She'd never seen him quite so untogether. Apart from the terrible night when she'd broken her leg—he'd come apart then.

'You're the only woman who's ever really understood me. All the others ever did was make demands... All so bloody hard to please...including Claire. She walked out on me, did you know? I was stupid to let you go, Meg. I want another chance. That's what I came to talk to you about.'

'Another chance?' Megan felt her mouth move, sensed the betraying wobble of her more vulnerable lower lip, registered the numb glide of a tear coursing slowly down her cheek. 'Are you mad?'

His expression hardened at that, a treacherous glint of malice flashing in his eyes that he was either too careless or too slow to disguise. Megan's hand gripped the metal door handle and she felt her palm go weakly moist.

'I didn't mean to push you down the stairs, but you know it was partly your fault,' he said petulantly, jaw jutting forward.

Megan licked the salty tang of tears from her lip, mentally willing her limbs to stop shaking. As if to compound her effort, a torturous spasm of pain shot up her injured leg and burned as though she'd just come into contact with a branding iron. She reached out her free hand to rub at it through her skirt.

'My fault? You left me with an injury I'll probably carry for the rest of my life, Nick. How was it my fault? Explain to me. I certainly didn't throw myself down the stairs! I know I'm a little slow to catch on, but humour me, will you?'

'You can be a bitch sometimes, Megan...I had to teach

you a lesson.' His words distinctly slurred now, he advanced menacingly towards her.

Alerted and afraid, Megan slid behind the door and slammed it shut. With pounding heart she negotiated the stairs, her gaze fixed on the landing below and the front door with its grey frosted windows. With each difficult tread her skin prickled as though it was burning, her mind racing with fear at the thought of what Nick might do to her if he caught her.

Behind her she heard him swear profusely, all veneer of politeness gone as he wrenched open the door and began to pursue her. Megan threw herself on the mercy of the banisters, holding on for dear life as she launched herself downwards, her gaze fixed determinedly on the front door. Miraculously she reached it before Nick, her fingers fumbling with the latch in a bid to open it, crying out as she did so.

Practically at the same moment she was overwhelmed by the sour smell of Nick's breath, and felt his hand on her flesh as he wrenched her arm sickeningly backwards.

'Just what the hell is going on here?'

It all happened in a blink. One moment Megan was certain Nick was going to kill her, the next he was pressed up against the outside brick wall, his expression unflatteringly distorted as Kyle shoved his face angrily into his, his hands gripping the other man roughly by the lapels of his expensive designer suit, rage written all over him.

'Kyle!'

He glanced at her as she rubbed at the arm Nick had grabbed so brutally, his hazel eyes pained and angry at the same time, his trademark tousled dark hair carelessly grazing the broad battered leather shoulders of his jacket. In all her life Megan had never seen a more welcome sight. She was almost dizzy with relief.

Pound for pound, there was probably little difference between the darker man and Nick, but then Kyle's weight was mostly lean, hard muscle, while her ex-husband was clearly not in such good shape. The drinking had begun to take its toll, and the extra poundage had mostly gathered round his middle, where his suit jacket strained tellingly against the pressure. In the pallid light of the morning Megan saw for the first time the tell-tale lines of strain and over-indulgence beneath his eyes, the slightly grey pallor to his skin.

She was furious with him for scaring her so badly, for hurting her yet again. But weaving through her anger and pain was a helpless kind of pity, too. For all his flash posturing and imagined superiority, Nick was clearly a man who had lost his way. Even more than that—a man who clearly needed to get help, and fast, before he hurt another woman as badly as he'd hurt Megan.

'Did he hurt you?' Kyle's voice was thick with fury as he glanced at Megan. He registered the surprise and shock in the liquid depths of her melting brown eyes, saw the way her beautiful hair tumbled in wild disarray down her back, the lack of colour in her cheeks, and felt curiously weak. As if someone had punched him in the middle of his solar plexus and momentarily deprived him of oxygen.

He didn't wait for her reply. Instead his grim gaze swung back to the pale, perspiring, slightly paunchy excuse for a male he was presently helping to get acquainted with the rough end of a brick wall. His grip tightened on the pure wool lapels of the stylish suit—not just to prevent him from escaping but also because he was certain if he let go he would slug the other man so hard he'd never get up off the ground again.

'Usually I act before I think, so all I can conclude is that today must be your lucky day, or else there'd be an ambulance on the way by now.'

As if to emphasise his point, Kyle shoved Nick harder against the wall and glared bluntly into his eyes. He nearly turned away when the distasteful smell of heavily imbibed alcohol practically made him heave.

'I may be jumping to conclusions here, but I presume you must be the infamous ex-husband. Am I right?'

Nick swore. Megan slumped against the doorframe, chilled to the bone. With a shaky sigh she crossed her arms in front of her chest.

'It's none of your bloody business. Just take your god-damn hands off of me, will you? This is an expensive suit and you're creasing it.'

'Is that a fact?'

Megan saw the revealing throb of the muscle in Kyle's cheek and automatically turned away. If Nick got off with a creased suit he could count himself very lucky indeed, because right now the anger emanating from Kyle was a living, tangible thing that would surely strike fear into the heart of even the most foolhardy swaggerer.

'Go inside, Megan.'

The whiplash command made her straighten.

'Let him go, Kyle. He's drunk.'

The look Kyle directed at her in reply made her quake inside. Ice floes were less cold…

'I said, go inside—and stay inside!'

Glancing pityingly at Nick, Megan turned resignedly away to comply. Nick was a grown man. He could take care of himself. If he couldn't—then he only had himself to blame for the predicament he found himself in. Suddenly she didn't have the energy to fight his corner as well as her own.

A good fifteen minutes passed before Kyle followed her inside. Fifteen minutes during which Megan anxiously paced the floor, rubbed frantically at the pain in her leg, speared her hands umpteen times through her already di-shevelled hair and generally came undone. Her ears strained for sounds of a scuffle or a fight, her gaze keeping the telephone firmly in her sight in case she had to call for some sort of assistance.

When Kyle finally appeared at the door, the expression on his fiercely handsome face ominous as approaching thunder, Megan thought she would faint with relief. He didn't appear hurt, thank God. He just looked big and powerful, commanding the room with the sheer force of raw energy that seemed to crackle around him. The black leather jacket and tight black jeans he wore made him look like some dark avenging angel, while his eyes—his eyes all but ate up the distance between them with the wild untrammelled hunger that was in them.

'Are you all right?' He ground out the words as though it pained him to even ask the question.

Megan nodded, then stared down blindly at the carpet, her vision blurring as emotion assaulted her on all sides. He shouldn't look at her like that. She didn't deserve to have him look at her like that when Nick could so easily have struck out in temper and hurt him somehow. Just the thought made her feel slightly nauseous. But she wanted to know if Nick was okay, too, part of her needing assurance that he wasn't lying bleeding in a gutter somewhere. Not because the whole idea was pathetic and appalling, but because she didn't want Kyle to get into trouble because he'd come to her defence.

'He's not hurt,' he said, as though reading her mind. 'If that's what you're worried about. I hardly laid a finger on him. I didn't have to.' His jaw clenched and unclenched with the effort it was costing him to remain composed. Megan raised her head just in time to witness the raw glint of profound fury in his golden gaze.

'We had a little "talk," Nick and I. He won't be bothering you again. If he so much as comes within ten feet of you, next time he really will need an ambulance.'

Instead of reassuring her, his words ignited her temper.

Megan grasped the back of a plump oversized armchair as she pinned him with a furious dark-eyed glare of her own.

'Is that how you men deal with everything? With threats of violence?'

Kyle's head went up at that. The hard, sculpted line of his jaw commanded her attention like nothing else as the action brought the stunning male beauty of his features into vivid and sharp relief.

'He's lucky he got away with mere threats. If I'd gone with my true instincts I'd have taught him a lesson he wouldn't forget in a hurry.'

'And that would have solved everything, would it?' Megan's fingers gripped and ungripped the solid mahogany frame of the armchair.

'No.' Kyle's glance was measured and assessing to the point of coolness. 'But it sure as hell would have given me great satisfaction to know that I'd inflicted pain on the bastard who maimed you for life.'

Megan felt as though all the life had been sucked out of her. She moved round the chair and slumped wearily down onto its plump red cushion. The stark delivery of Kyle's words had brutally brought home to her the gravity of her situation. No matter which way she looked at it, the fact was that Nick could have killed her. In one mindless act of violence he'd inflicted a serious injury that *would* affect the rest of her life. And it could have been even worse. If she'd fallen any more awkwardly she could have broken her neck, and she wouldn't be sitting here now feeling as if she didn't have the strength to get up—never mind carry on with the rest of her life.

'You seem to be making a habit of coming to my rescue.' Glancing up at Kyle, she managed a smile of sorts, but it slid away from her naked pink mouth almost as soon as she'd attempted it.

'Why did you walk out on me this morning?' His voice

hoarse, Kyle walked slowly across to where she sat, glaring down at her with barely suppressed irritation.

All her muscles tightened in response to his nearness.

'I—I just didn't know how to deal with what happened between—between us,' she admitted softly, her mouth trembling.

Kyle dropped down onto his haunches at her feet, his hands reaching out to stroke the gentle folds of her skirt across her knees. 'Why was Nick here?'

He kept stroking her through the material and Megan wondered how his touch simply just didn't burn a hole right through it. 'I don't want to talk about Nick.' Her breath expelled on a tremulous sigh as Kyle suddenly rested his head on her knees, then began stroking his hands up and down the sides of her thighs in a manner that was both sensuous and spine-tingling.

'You shouldn't be alone with him. Ever.'

'I know.' She gasped as he maneuvered a hand beneath her skirt and slid it arousingly up her calf.

'Too many clothes.' He raised his head and stole her breath with his sexy riveting smile. All languorous golden gaze, high cheekbones and even white teeth in a mouth that promised kisses to die for. 'You're always wearing too many clothes, Megan. All I want to do whenever I see you is peel them off, one by one. Like this.'

She'd hardly realised his fingers had worked their way up to the sides of the cotton panties she wore beneath her skirt, so transfixed was she by his outrageously sinful smile. But shockwaves throbbed through her now as he jerked them purposefully down over her hips and discarded them in one devastatingly fluid movement.

'Kyle…!' Mindlessly she drove her fingers into the thick tousled strands of his hair as languid heat poured into her, making her immediately and shockingly moist, her skin flushing as he slid her skirt up over her knees, then started to kiss the soft tender flesh of her inner thighs.

'Oh, God...' She cried out loud when his lips moved downwards to gently kiss the raw, slightly ridged network of scars crossing her knee. 'Please don't.'

'I don't want you to hide anything from me,' he said raggedly as he gently pushed her restraining hand away. 'There isn't one part of you that isn't totally exquisite.'

Tears blurred Megan's vision. She could barely swallow over the egg-sized lump that had formed in her throat. Their gazes met and melded into each other's growing heat.

'I want to be inside you,' Kyle said roughly.

'Yes.'

She found herself urged carefully down onto the floor, her gaze in direct line with the white-painted ceiling and the terracotta shade that swung from the ornate ceiling rose as Kyle deftly undid the button fly of his jeans then thrust himself fully inside her.

Megan's mind exploded with the sensation of heat and velvet hardness inside her body, her tender muscles clenching and unclenching around him as he filled her again and again with his wild hungry possession, his gaze like trapped sunlight, eyes half closed with molten languorous need. Then, just as he bent his head to touch his lips to hers, her pelvis clenched tight as need and desire exploded into unexpected earth-shattering bliss, and she found herself with tears streaming unchecked down her face as Kyle's tongue glided expertly and hotly into her mouth.

As he consumed her body and soul with the destroying devastation of his ardent kiss Megan thought she might just die if she didn't have this wild untrammelled pleasure at least once a day for the rest of her life.

CHAPTER NINE

KYLE paused in the doorway of the summerhouse to savour the arresting sight that met his eyes. Megan was painting. Standing in front of the easel he had carefully positioned for her, caught in the shaft of sunlight that poured through the window. Her eyes were captivatingly dreamy, sooty black lashes framing orbs of a luxuriant, sensual brown. Paintbrush in hand, thoughts far away, Kyle had never seen her look lovelier. The expression on her beautiful face was almost beatific—and there was an incandescent glow about her that was perfectly compelling.

The scene had the kind of soulful presence he strove to bring alive in his work, and a surge of pure pleasure warmed his heart as he gazed at her, silently admitting he would be more than content to just stand and look for the rest of the day. She was wearing one of his old white paint-spattered shirts over her pretty white camisole and jeans, the shirt tails almost reaching the backs of her knees, her rich dark hair falling gently over the soft womanly swell of her breasts. His shirt had never looked so good and probably never would again—unless Megan was wearing it, of course.

Deep in thought, she wrinkled her nose prettily in contemplation of whatever it was she was painting. He'd given her carte blanche to do whatever she wanted, and right now she was totally oblivious to his presence and his silent perusal. So much so that Kyle wrestled with the idea of disturbing her at all.

Then, as if some infinitesimal thing had somehow alerted her, her gaze swung round to collide with his and Kyle experienced the full sensual impact of the ensuing contact like a firework erupting in his stomach. He straightened, shaken by the force of his attraction, swallowing down a deep gulp of air before trusting himself to speak.

'Didn't mean to disturb you, but I've made some lunch.' He grinned as he stepped inside the light airy studio, mainly because he couldn't seem to help himself. Right now life didn't feel as if it could get much better…for him, anyway.

The thought side-swiped him, taking him by surprise. He couldn't remember the last time he had felt either so sanguine or so excited. He certainly couldn't recall the last woman in his life who'd made him feel that way. But something told him this was an entirely new experience.

'Tuna and pasta bake with salad. You are hungry?'

For a moment Megan didn't know what to say. All her faculties for speech suddenly seemed to desert her. When she'd turned just then to find him staring her insides had all but melted with the intensity of her feelings for him. The sensation had been no less than staggering. The unmitigated joy of seeing him, spending time with him, had suddenly become the most essential component of her life, and every living cell in her body was sublimely and intimately attuned to everything about him: from his supremely male yet undoubtedly graceful stride, and the way he could make a smile seem like the sexiest thing you'd ever seen, to the fascinating aura of energy that he emanated that was like a match to the tinder of her heart.

'You really are a dabhand in the kitchen, aren't you? When I first saw how immaculate it was I thought it was just for show, but you can really cook, can't you?' A small dimple appeared at the corner of her mouth as she stole a helpless glance, then became frozen on her face when his own drop-dead gorgeous smile devastatingly deepened.

'My mother wouldn't have it any other way.' He shrugged, hazel eyes emitting a playful twinkle that finished off the complete hijacking of her heart. 'She's a firm believer in ''real'' men knowing how to cook. In a way it's not unlike being an artist. You get all the right ingredients or colours together and hopefully create something beautiful.'

Megan couldn't help but sigh. 'You make it sound so…so straightforward and simple.'

'That's how it *should* be. I didn't say it was exactly like that. Sometimes it can be pure torture.' He was walking slowly towards her, sinewy muscles taut beneath his black sweatshirt and jeans, handsome face reflective. 'Sometimes it's the hardest thing to coax out the vision you have in your mind and transfer it onto the canvas. You live and die in the process.'

Megan shivered. Instinctively she knew what he meant. It was the same with her. There were times when her pencil or brush could flow like a dream, and others when the whole thing was like trying to climb Mount Everest without any climbing gear. That was when disbelief and doubt set in. When that cruel little voice inside her said she was a self-deceiving fool for even daring to dream that she might one day earn her living as an artist. Not that she'd attempted very much in those long years of artistic drought. Not when Nick had heavily curtailed her longing for self-expression. But still she had had her dreams, her own vision of what she might accomplish. And they had never gone away, even when things were at their most dire.

But thoughts of Nick and the disturbing unhappy events of that same morning snatched at the ray of hope that Megan had allowed herself, and her face clouded with unease. Why had he had to show up and take her by surprise like that? She'd been so unprepared to see him, so…so pathetically unassertive. No wonder he had treated her as he had. But even if she had been prepared, would she have dealt with the situation any better?

Frustration and shame crawled up her spine as she silently

cursed the fact that she'd allowed her self-esteem and self-respect to take such an unrelenting battering for all those long lonely years. How could she have done that to herself? A half-choked sound emanated from her lips and her throat tightened in helpless anguish.

Kyle's shoulders stiffened. In less than a minute he was behind her, sliding his arms around her waist in an instinctive bid to offer whatever solace he could. He heard her soft gasp of surprise, felt the muscles in her ribcage grow taut, then sensed her relax against him even as she trembled, her supple body pliant and oh, so feminine beneath his touch, her vanilla-laced scent drifting round him, reeling him in.

Sensation overload. He was instantly aroused. Hell, he couldn't even be in the same room as her without being turned on—let alone stand behind her, feeling the luscious curve of her delectable bottom pressed up close into his groin. But even so he knew she was hurting inside, and that the pain was deep. Soul-deep.

Nick Brand was lucky he had got off with mere words and a warning. For Megan's sake Kyle had kept his hands off him, and only for Megan's sake. If he had had his way he would have demonstrated unequivocally exactly what he thought of a man who deliberately pushed his wife down the stairs and maimed her for life. The thought made the blood pound in his temples.

'Don't be sad.' He lifted her hair, his lips seeking out the beguiling heat of her nape to taste the intoxicating flavour that he was already more than just a little addicted to.

'I'm not sad.' Letting her head drop back against his chest, Megan felt her initial resistance desert her as she absorbed his strong silent strength, his beguiling hardness, his instinctive ability to comfort and console, silently conceding that in his arms was the only true haven she craved. Not just for now, but for always…

The magnitude of the thought hit her like an oncoming

car. She'd fallen for this man just about as hard as a woman could, and in mere days, too…

'I'm just sorry that you had to witness the sorry depths that Nick has obviously sunk to. I wish you hadn't,' she confessed softly, momentarily squeezing her eyes shut at the realisation that she was head over heels in love.

'What I don't understand is how you stuck nine years of marriage with the man. Why did you stay so long?'

'Fear. I stayed out of fear.' Megan trembled as Kyle's lips moved with painstaking thoroughness up to her ear, igniting a volatile trail of lust and longing as his teeth and tongue nibbled and mercilessly teased the tender flesh of her lobe. 'That and the fact that I always thought I could fix things. Stupid, I know. How I deluded myself. I thought most of the fault was mine. If I could just be more organised, more thoughtful, more caring, then maybe a miracle would happen. I thought Nick wouldn't look at other women any more…that he would stop drinking. I thought he might just learn how to be happy with me.'

'He's a lost cause, sweetheart. Make no mistake about that. The man's a fool, but his loss is my gain.' With devastating intimacy, Kyle slid his hands up to her breasts and cupped them in his hands, testing their weight.

The act was destroyingly erotic. Heat sizzled in her stomach, like electricity along a fuse wire. Glancing down, she saw his beautiful slender artist's hands, with their clean square-cut nails, spread out across her chest and a raw little sound of pure desire was expelled from her lips on a sigh. Her body was already tingling and aching with a sweet ferocity from their lovemaking earlier, and it astounded her that she wanted him again so soon, craved his touch with such a wild raw hunger that she could barely think straight.

'I thought—I thought we were going to have lunch?' She twisted in his arms, her limbs turning to water when she saw his eyes grow dark with longing.

'You'd put food before this?' he murmured, his voice thickening like molasses as his mouth hovered bare inches from her own.

'A body's got to eat.' Heart pounding, Megan nonetheless found the strength to push away from him. She laid the slim sable paintbrush on the little shelf beneath the easel, then, turning, smoothed her hands down the sides of her borrowed shirt in a bid to stop them from trembling.

As much as she wanted to make love, she knew she had to engineer a little sane distance between them. If they persisted in falling on each other at every turn they'd probably go up in flames! But, more than that, Megan needed time to think. She couldn't let her life be like a runaway train again. She had to put herself in the driving seat; take stock; think what to do.

'I wonder if the great masters had this much trouble with their protégées?' Kyle quipped, his expression teasing but undoubtedly frustrated as his gaze alighted on her face.

'Am I your protégée, then?'

'Muse, protégée, witch…I don't care. All I know is that you've put under a spell. You intoxicate me, Megan, like a fine cognac that goes straight to my head.' He smiled ruefully.

'Do you pay such generous compliments to all your clients?' She meant the women, of course.

Megan pinned him with a hungry jealous glance, wisps of silky black hair drifting softly round her face as she waited with bated breath for his answer. When he didn't immediately reply, but simply stared at her with equal if not more intensity; she curled her hands into fists by her sides and felt a slow trickle of perspiration slip down her spine like syrup. The truth was she was envious of every woman he had ever known, sick with jealousy at the idea of him having an intimate relationship with anyone but her.

She hadn't even known she was capable of such an extreme emotion. Nick had played around, but her uppermost feeling through it all had been one of wounded pride and hurt. She'd never really been jealous of any of the other women he'd been with, come to think of it. Not even Claire. She'd been more distraught because her friend had betrayed her than because her husband had done the same…

'What exactly are you asking me, Megan?' His expression implacable, Kyle folded his arms with slow deliberation as he studied the dark-eyed beauty in front of him.

'I…I just want to make sure that I'm—that you're not—'

'That I don't make a habit of sleeping with every female client that walks through my door?'

Put like that, it sounded sordid and crass, and Kyle had every right to be angry with her. Megan fiddled with the collar of her borrowed shirt, sensing her face turn crimson.

'I'm not promiscuous, Megan. I've never been a monk, but I don't sleep around. Now that's been established, perhaps we should go and eat. What do you say?'

Turning on his heel, he headed for the door, his back straight, but with a distinct tension in the taut hard line of his shoulders.

Megan sucked in a shallow breath that was barely even there, struggling hard to keep a lid on her sudden temper. 'I don't understand! How can I be having a relationship with you when I don't even know your name?'

Emotion welled in her throat as he stopped in his tracks and did an about-face. Certain that he'd be furious, Megan was completely disarmed by the perfectly wicked little smile that was playing round his lips. A smile that made her feel utterly, devastatingly boneless.

'You know my name.'

'I mean your full name!'

'Why is that so important? You only need one name to call me when we're making love.'

Stopped in her tracks, Megan felt her mouth drop open. 'I—I'd just like to know. Can't you tell me? It seems so ridiculous not to know…'

She recalled the postcard that Penny had hijacked from Mrs Kureshi's newsagent's, signed with a succinct and mysterious 'KH', and wondered if she knew all that much more about him now than she had then. Especially when it occurred to her that he certainly knew a hell of a lot more about her than he had revealed about himself.

'At least you acknowledge that we've got a relationship and this isn't just some hot and fast one-night stand,' he said in a low voice. 'My name's Hytner. Kyle Hytner. Feel better now?'

Somehow the name rang a bell, but she didn't for the life of her know why.

'Did you begrudge telling me? I didn't know it was supposed to be a big secret.' Bewildered by his evasive attitude, Megan frowned.

'It's not a big secret. It's just a name. You're reading far too much into the whole damn thing. Come and eat. At least one kind of appetite will be satisfied, if nothing else.'

He had disappeared through the door, his long stride propelling him down the garden path, before Megan had gathered enough wits to will herself to move.

She was typing out a long, complicated and essentially boring letter to some influential banking CEO in Manhattan whom Lindsay was trying desperately to impress, when the ringing telephone beside her interrupted her already wavering concentration. Staring blankly at her computer screen, she automatically picked up the receiver and sighed.

She was thinking about the painting she'd begun in Kyle's studio, eager to implement some of the techniques he had suggested, her hands itching to pick up a brush and take up where she left off. Right now she wished vehemently that she was anywhere else but here in this soulless air-conditioned office, which had become even harder to endure since she had met Kyle. At least before she could only guess at what she might be missing, but now she knew. Now she knew. And the reality was almost too much to bear. He'd shown her a way out of this half-life she'd been living, a way out that made her want to grab onto it and hang on for dear life.

A frisson of excitement throbbed through her as she spoke into the phone.

'Megan Brand. Can I help you?'

'Oh...I can think of at least a hundred ways...maybe more.'

At the sound of Kyle's unnervingly sexy tones Megan all but melted into a puddle on her seat. Rebelliously, this morning she'd decided to wear her long hair loose, and now she scooped the heavy fall of black silk off the back of her neck as heat unexpectedly drenched her.

'You shouldn't be speaking like that to me at the office,' she admonished breathlessly, then craned her neck to check if any of her colleagues were observing her. Thankfully, none were.

Outside her own little partitioned enclave everyone else seemed preoccupied with work. Computers rule OK. The atmosphere was dense with the silent ticking of human brain cells pitting their wits against machines. One could be forgiven for imagining that none of these people had a life outside of the office. It was a frightening thought, and suddenly Megan didn't want to relegate her own life to such paucity of pleasure. In fact, she was beginning to despise herself for putting up with it when she could be doing so much more...if only she had the courage.

'I like speaking to you like this,' Kyle insisted, his deeply mellow tones reverberating through Megan like a thousand little pinpricks of electricity.

She glanced nervously across at Lindsay's door. Thankfully it remained helpfully closed. 'Our conversation might be being recorded,' she whispered.

'Big Brother, huh?'

Megan heard the smile as well as the irreverence in his voice, and found herself grinning helplessly in spite of the caution that had been so ingrained in her.

'I know it sounds ridiculous, but sometimes they do what they call ''random checks''. Just to make sure we're all busy little worker ants and not wasting valuable working time when we could be making all the shareholders more money.'

'Then let's give them something worth recording, shall we?' Kyle suggested provocatively.

Before Megan realised exactly what he had in mind, he proceeded to tell her in the most graphic terms imaginable just what he'd like to do to her when he saw her next. Something about removing her clothes with his teeth, tying her wrists to the bed with silk scarves, massaging oil into her skin, and finally pleasuring her so hard and so hot that she'd go wild in his arms—cry out and beg him never to stop...

By the time he'd finished Megan was hot and flustered from the inside out. Sitting at her desk, desperately trying to salvage her composure, she knew she was a million miles away from the sensible and conservative Megan Brand. Now she knew why sex lines were such big business. If Kyle ever decided to branch out into something else, as far as Megan was concerned he had the perfect career all ready and waiting.

'Have I turned you on?' he asked silkily into the phone.

Megan automatically brought her hand up to her chest in a half-conscious defensive gesture, catching her breath when she involuntarily stroked it across her exquisitely sensitised nipples. Beneath her skirt her thighs were sticky and damp.

Had he turned her on? If he continued in the way he'd begun she'd soon be demonstrating an aptitude for a new career herself.

'It's very, very naughty of you to do this to me when I'm at work.' Lowering her voice, she cupped her hand around the receiver to ensure she wasn't heard by anyone else except him. A colleague two desks away glanced up and smiled, then continued tapping on her keyboard as though the smile had never happened. Megan felt the tension in her stomach disperse a little.

To her consternation, Kyle laughed at her remark. His rich cultured tones rolled over the telephone line, raising gooseflesh all over her. 'Sweetheart, I can be a hell of a lot naughtier…want to try me?'

Megan gulped. 'No, Kyle don't! Please… You'll get me fired!'

'Good,' he replied emphatically. 'You're completely wasting your time in that glass coffin.'

'I have to earn my living.' It sounded lame even to her own ears.

'Then earn it through your painting. In the meantime, I'll look after you.'

Megan rubbed her fingers hard against her forehead and sighed. He wasn't serious? Her heart dropped like an anchor being thrown into the sea at the idea that he might be. The last thing in the world she would contemplate doing was walking away from her job and letting Kyle keep her. She'd barely known him for five minutes, for goodness' sake. Even if they did fit together like the two missing pieces of a jigsaw. Surely he could see how reckless and irresponsible that would be? It was one thing striking sparks off each other every time they were alone together, quite another letting him bear the financial burden of her welfare.

'I don't want you to look after me.'

'I want to do what I can to help. Believe me when I tell you it wouldn't be a sacrifice, Megan.'

'That's not the point! I put myself in a vulnerable position before, with Nick. I don't want to make the same mistake twice. The cost is just too high.'

Now it was his turn to sigh. Megan imagined him raking his long fingers through his already mussed hair, his expression falling somewhere between fierce and frustrated. But even so, on this occasion she would stand firm. Too much was at stake if she didn't…

'There'd be no strings, Megan. I only want to help you realise your dream. Everything would be at your disposal: studio, equipment, my help whenever you wanted it. There's nothing I want in return.'

Except you. The words came unbidden into Kyle's head, like a visitor unannounced. His heart accelerated a little. He wanted her all right. He'd been roaming round the house like a caged lion since she'd left last night. There was nothing else he could put his mind to but Megan. There was no peace or solace to be found even in his work. He'd picked up his pencil to sketch more times than he cared to remember, but to little avail. He'd stretched a canvas in preparation to paint, but in the end left it alone. He'd done nothing. Accomplished nothing. All he'd ended up with was a colossal headache because his mind was set on a one-way track that he couldn't get off.

As soon as he got the chance he was going to tell her how he felt. To hell with her knowing he had wealth and fame. He'd just have to take the chance it wouldn't put her off or intimidate her—wouldn't make her retreat back into that steel shell she'd so painstakingly wrapped around herself…

'It's a very generous offer, Kyle—'

'But?'

'You know I can't possibly accept it. It wouldn't be fair.'

'Personal integrity is a wonderful thing, Megan, but in your case I'd say it was somewhat overrated. Everyone needs a little help every now and then. There's no shame in that. I'm a wealthy man and I can easily take care of us both. You can paint to your heart's content and I'll be on hand whenever you want as your personal tutor. Does that really sound so terrible?'

'It sounds wonderful.' Megan's hand was damp around the receiver where she was gripping it so hard.

Just at that moment her boss's door swung open and Lindsay breezed purposefully through the outer office to Megan's desk, her heady, almost overpowering scent, like roses past their bloom, ominously stirring the air between the two women. On the older woman's nose, her fashionable black-rimmed glasses were perched schoolmarm-like, her hair escaping uncharacteristically in fine blonde wisps from its severe chignon. There was a letter in her hand, which she unceremoniously slapped down on the desk in front of Megan, oblivious to the fact that her assistant was on the phone.

'What sounds wonderful?' she demanded, a scowl hardly adding to her looks. 'I trust that's not a personal conversation you're conducting during work time?'

Megan stared at the other woman, rage bubbling up inside her at the sheer injustice of such an unwarranted remark. Lindsay made it sound as though Megan spent most of her time on personal calls—a premise that was so far from the truth it was almost laughable. Almost. Because right now Megan didn't see the humour. All she saw was an embittered, totally self-absorbed woman with apparently not the slightest notion of respect for her fellow human beings— unless, of course, they were superior to her in the bank hierarchy. Otherwise she plainly thought good manners were outmoded and unnecessary.

'It *is* a personal call, as a matter of fact,' Megan replied as coolly as she could. Then, nervously running her tongue over her top lip, she continued, 'And I'd like to finish it.'

Lindsay's face reddened, and she made a sound like a kettle blowing off steam. One hand clenched into a fist by her side, the other picked up the letter and gripped it as if she wished it were Megan's throat.

'Come into my office right now! This blatant insubordination has gone far enough, Miss Brand!'

Insubordination? Megan almost choked. The woman was behaving like some petulant prima donna in a dramatic production instead of a professional career-woman in a responsible managerial position.

The only response Megan considered such behaviour deserved was to ignore it. Swivelling in her chair, she lifted the receiver to continue. 'Kyle? I'm sorry about that. I—'

It was snatched from her hand. Before she could do anything about it, Lindsay bellowed into the phone.

'Who is this? For your information this is a professional office, and my secretary cannot afford to have her time wasted with personal telephone calls when she clearly should be working!'

'Lindsay! Give me the phone!'

Megan stared aghast as Lindsay's face grew even redder with emotion. She could only guess at what Kyle must be thinking! It really didn't bear contemplation, and suddenly Megan knew without question what she had to do. What she should have done a long time ago if only she'd had the guts.

'I said give me the damn phone!' Tearing it out of the other woman's hands, she glared furiously at Lindsay, no longer intimidated by a boss who had long ago lost any right to her respect. 'As of now I no longer work for you! I'm going to finish my telephone call, then empty my desk and leave. It's something I should have done years ago, but I gave away my power—first to my husband and then to people like you, Lindsay. People who don't give a fig for other people's feelings just so long as they get what they want. All I can say is that you must be one very unhappy woman to be so mean-spirited. I actually feel sorry for you, but unfortunately not sorry enough to stay.' With that, Megan turned her back.

'Sorry about that.' She glanced briefly down at her watch as her heart pounded like a hammer. 'Can you meet me downstairs in about half an hour?'

'You resigned.' Kyle sounded incredulous.

Megan swirled round at the slamming of Lindsay's door, her face flushed with a new kind of exhilaration she'd never experienced before. 'Yes. Isn't it wonderful?'

CHAPTER TEN

KYLE threw his shaving gear into his tan leather holdall on the bed, pausing when he saw the photograph he carried with him wherever he went in the world nestling amongst his clothes. Reaching in, he withdrew it, his expression fiercely concentrated as he stared down at the beautiful face he missed not seeing every day.

Yvette.

She'd been twenty-five when she died in a horrific car accident, Kyle just eighteen when he'd heard the news that had made him even more resolved to make art his life. *If you have a dream,* his sister used to say, *you should be prepared to move heaven and earth to fulfil it.* There were no half-measures where dreams were concerned. No half-shades.

Yvette had lived life as if she meant it. As if she'd known she would have only a brief stay on this earth. Because she had been beautiful and intelligent and vivacious, men had tried to pin her down in their fascination to possess her, but it had been like trying to capture moonlight or the sparkle in a brook…impossible. Kyle gazed into her beguiling fine-boned face, at the smooth intelligent brows, the twinkle in her tawny almond-shaped eyes that seemed to reflect her belief that life was far too precious to remain serious for long and felt the loss anew. She'd lit up all their lives: their mother's, his, and even his taciturn, workaholic father's.

Briefly running his finger across the shiny creased surface of the photograph, Kyle laid it carefully back inside the holdall, deliberately covering it with a sweater so he could tear himself away from her memory and get on with what he had to do. But as he continued packing he wondered what his beloved sister would have made of Megan.

Yvette would have loved her unreservedly, he was sure. His sister had had a generous heart. It was what had made her choose nursing as a career and become a voluntary worker for the Samaritans in her spare time—anything that would bring comfort to the distressed and wounded of this world. It wouldn't have taken her long to recognise a kindred spirit in the woman who had turned his own life upside down, the woman who had him considering a future that so far had not been even the smallest part of his plan.

Impatience shooting through his veins, he cursed softly beneath his breath. He couldn't wait to see Megan again. He should never have let her out of his sight. What if she changed her mind about going away with him?

The phone rang just as he was zipping up his holdall.

'Kyle?'

'Megan.' Kyle's heartbeat accelerated as a shot of pure adrenaline pulsed through him. 'What's wrong?'

'Nothing's wrong.'

The tremor in her soft voice betrayed her. Kyle's first thought was that her leg was paining her, or worse. Panic stopped him from asking her directly.

'I thought we agreed that I'd pick you up at four?' He glanced speculatively down at the diver's watch circling his bronzed wrist, then edgily raked his fingers through his hair.

'I haven't changed my mind, if that's what you're thinking. I'm looking forward to going away for a while.' Megan took pains to reassure him. 'It's just that…it's just that when I got home there was a letter for me. A letter from Nick.'

At the mention of her feckless ex-husband Kyle's expression darkened, like a stormcloud passing across the sun.

'If he's threatening you in any way I'll—'

'No, Kyle. He's not threatening me. He…he's sent me a banker's draft for my share of the house.'

Kyle's relief was palpable. He dropped down onto the bed and rubbed his hand round his jaw. 'I'm glad to hear it. It's bloody well the least he could do.' It was good to know that his little talk with Nick Brand had produced the desired effect. Now all the bastard had to do was never show his face around Megan again and Kyle would be happy.

'I just—I just wanted to let you know.' Her voice went all wobbly again, making him clutch the receiver a little tighter, feeling an inexplicable knot in his stomach that wouldn't go away.

'I was half afraid you'd changed your mind and weren't coming,' he admitted, gravel-voiced.

'I wouldn't do that. I've almost finished packing. I'll expect you around four, then, shall I?'

Kyle couldn't prevent the smile that broke free as he got to his feet again.

'Kyle! At last!'

Christa MacKenzie maneuvered her generous frame round a reception desk littered with scraps of paper, pencils, a half-eaten chocolate bar and an unfinished cup of tea, to greet the striking specimen of manhood who'd just stepped inside the charming old-fashioned lobby of her small hotel.

Embracing him in a flurry of exotic perfume, generous flesh and jangling bracelets, she placed two loud smacking kisses on either side of his smooth, recently shaven face.

'Hmm, nice…' She appreciatively sniffed the fresh clean tang of his aftershave. 'I've been watching the clock since this morning. You're an hour late and I've been worrying myself stupid. I almost thought you weren't coming.'

'We got held up in traffic. How are you, Christa? You look wonderful.' Kyle dropped his holdall onto the thick royal blue carpet, delivering a smile of such dazzling efficacy that Christa actually blushed like a schoolgirl.

She'd been one of his favourite life models. The two of

them had clicked at their very first meeting, when the blonde had stepped in to replace a girl who'd let him down at the last minute. He'd barely been able to teach at first, because she'd had him laughing so hard with her ribald comments and quaint little anecdotes on life.

Nothing had dented his reputation as a serious artist more effectively than the effect of her presence when he'd been artist in residence at Chelsea. He had laughed easily and readily, no one more surprised than him when he transcended the melancholy that had sometimes dogged him, simply giving himself up to the natural pleasure of enjoying a joke with his students.

Christa just oozed a joy for life, so much so that a person couldn't fail to be uplifted after spending time in her company. Apart from the fact that in Kyle's opinion Megan was in desperate need of a holiday, he knew meeting Christa would be a tonic for her in itself—for both of them.

Glancing round him, he took in the cosy hotchpotch of chintzy mismatched furniture dotted around, a smile pulling irrepressibly at the corner of his lips. The big old-fashioned armchairs, with their overstuffed cushions and mahogany arms; the cosy love seat at the window, upholstered in a rich pink velvet; a plethora of antique lamps with tapestried shades and silk fringes; and—oh, boy. He couldn't fail to notice the veritable gallery of Victorian art on the heavily floral wallpapered walls, suitably hung in fading gold leaf frames that were ever so slightly crooked. He almost felt as if he'd walked onto the set of a Sherlock Holmes film.

'I can hardly believe you're here! It's such a shame that Justin's away on business, because he would have loved to see you again, but never mind. I'm going to make sure you enjoy the best hospitality I can muster or die in the attempt!'

Christa restrained herself from a further hug to note that his dark hair was longer than when she'd last seen him—

suitably unstyled, as was his trademark, but nonetheless gleaming fiercely with flecks of burnished copper beneath the twinkling lights of her beloved crystal chandelier. The man was sexier than ever, with those indescribably wanton tawny gold eyes of his and bone structure to die for. No wonder his classes had been so popular.

In spite of her best efforts, Christa had never been able to progress further than friendship with Kyle. He just hadn't been interested in her that way—no matter how much she could make him laugh. But things had turned out for the best in the long run, because after Kyle had gone to Greece she'd met Justin. He might have been twenty years older and at least a couple of stone heavier than the younger man, but Christa had fallen deeply in love, moving with her new husband to the west of England to set up home and business in Lyme Regis. It was an area famed for its fossil beaches, and Christa had genuinely grown to love it.

Now, as her blue eyes flicked happily over Kyle, she told herself it was about time her former colleague and friend— a man who had made such a name for himself in the art world—had finally relented and come to pay her a visit.

'Megan.' Kyle turned swiftly from his contemplation of Christa, irked that he hadn't yet introduced the reason he had come. But the shapely brunette in the dark brown suede jacket, black ribbed sweater and dark blue jeans was peering closely at one of Christa's Victoriana paintings just inside the door, her dark gaze clearly intrigued by whatever she saw there.

She turned her head as he said her name, faint colour highlighting her pretty complexion as her soft brown gaze bounced from Kyle to Christa.

'Megan, this is Christa MacKenzie. Along with her husband Justin she's the proprietor of the Lady Rose Hotel.'

It was the apple-cheeked blonde from the painting in

Kyle's bathroom; Megan was certain. The lady had grown even more comely since she'd posed for the picture, and was no less lovely for the more generous curves she'd since acquired. Smiling tentatively, because a hot bolt of jealousy had jack-knifed through her, taking her by surprise, Megan registered the shock of scarlet-red lips and nails—not to mention the revealing siren-red blouse with its explosion of frills down the front, teamed with a silky black satin skirt that swished round her ankles and red stiletto heels that made Megan's feet ache just looking at them. It was clear that Christa MacKenzie liked to make an impact—with bells on. *And there was a strong possibility she was Kyle's ex-lover...*

'Megan.' She was holding out her hand, advancing on the startled brunette in a noisy perfumed jangle of bangles and beads. 'I'm sorry, love, but Kyle's barely told me anything about you. Can't say I'm surprised, though. I know that he guards his privacy fiercely, but you must be his best-kept secret! Anyway, the fact that he's brought you with him says more than a thousand words. Believe me.'

Megan's hand was enthusiastically enfolded by the other woman's more fleshy palm, then in the next instant she found herself clutched to her ample bosom as though she were a long-lost friend. Over Christa's shoulder she saw Kyle grinning, and, finding herself unexpectedly and suddenly at ease, she grinned foolishly back.

She'd done her best to resist, practically arguing herself into a standstill, but in the end Kyle had fairly easily persuaded her to join him for a break at the quintessentially English Lady Rose. Now she was absurdly glad he had—even though she had to contend with the fact that he might have had a much more intimate relationship with Christa than he was letting on.

'It's nice to meet you, Christa.'

'And you, too. You're very welcome at my little hotel.' As the blonde released Megan her avid blue gaze swept with unreserved interest over the younger woman. Kyle had been typically tight-lipped about the 'friend' he was bringing with him, but Christa had intuitively expected someone pretty special. There had been plenty of gorgeous fresh-faced girls on the college campus, but as far as Christa knew Kyle hadn't dated any of them. In her book, the odd one-night stand didn't count. The man had needs, just like everyone else, but actually dating someone was infinitely more meaningful. And the girl in front of her had 'meaningful' practically stamped across her forehead.

In her exotic brown eyes there was a dreamy look that even the most cynical male would surely find impossible to resist. Apart from that look of guarded vulnerability, the woman was without doubt stunning, from the top of her glossy black hair to the tips of her small elegant feet in her brown kid leather boots. A girl with looks like that wouldn't have to resort to flashy or expensive clothes to get a man's attention. A girl like Megan just had to smile and the men would run howling round the block—beating their chests to boot! And, if Christa wasn't mistaken, she had a shape on her that no amount of dieting or working out would give Christa a hope in hell of replicating.

Still, to be fair, the woman must possess a whole lot more than eye-catching good looks to keep a man like Kyle Hytner interested for long. The man had an innate appreciation for the beauty of the female form, but he wasn't shallow. Christa knew he was equally appreciative of less physical attributes.

'I expect you'd both like to freshen up and unwind before dinner? I'll get Simon, my young porter, to take your bags up to your room. In the meantime I'll send you up some tea and biscuits. How does that sound?'

The blonde spun round on her impossibly high heels to beam at Kyle, mentally ticking off a list of possible guests whom she would ask to join them at a special dinner she was planning for the following evening. It wasn't every day they had a world-renowned artist in their midst and, while Christa wouldn't dream of actually exploiting Kyle's celebrity in any way, she wasn't exactly averse to making the most of it.

'That sounds good. Megan must be tired after the long drive—she was working this morning, before we made our way down here. Tea is just what the doctor ordered.'

He might have been reading her mind, Megan thought wistfully as his tawny gaze settled with concern on her face. She'd slept for most of the journey—a combination of sheer mental exhaustion from the events of the past few days and the sleek, seductive comfort of Kyle's luxurious Mercedes. The drive had been so smooth she'd burrowed herself deep into the cream leather upholstery and drifted off with practically no bother at all. That in itself had been a miracle. She rarely if ever fell asleep so easily, but then it wasn't every day that she walked out on her job without so much as a backward glance.

Leaving her suitcase next to Kyle's leather holdall, Megan clutched her voluminous brown leather shoulder bag to her chest, then followed Kyle and Christa up the winding wooden staircase, with its red and gold Turkish-style carpeting, to the floor above. As she took her time negotiating the stairs behind them, her hungry gaze couldn't help but linger on every single painting that lined the walls on the way.

'Let's go look at the sea.'

Megan stopped brushing her hair, glancing up in surprise as Kyle came out of the bathroom. He'd taken a shower and all he was wearing were black silk boxers and a smile. Megan's gaze was fixated on the deeply tanned muscles of his biceps and chest, and the way it tapered down to his flat lean stomach. Beyond that she dared not go. The room was hot enough as it was.

Kyle stared back at her, his dark chestnut hair sleek with moisture, his hard jaw dark with five o'clock shadow, an unreadable glint behind his riveting hazel eyes that made Megan long to know exactly what he was thinking.

'Before we do anything else we need to talk,' she told him, glancing quickly away from the sardonic little quirk at the corner of his mouth that told her exactly what he thought about that.

Leaning back against the doorframe, a white towel draped round his toned glistening shoulders, he shot her a look of amused resignation.

'I think women must learn that line before they come out of the womb.'

His gaze pinned her to the beautiful hand-crafted walnut bed where she sat—virginal white linen beneath her jean-clad legs, long hair like a jet waterfall cascading over her shoulders—challenging her to look away. As the air grew thicker between them, Megan's heart thudded in response.

'Even—even so.' She cleared her throat in a bid to shore up her flagging courage, because she got the distinct impression that he was going to be even less forthcoming than she'd hoped. 'I wanted to talk to you about that offer you made earlier…'

'Oh?' One dark eyebrow shot deliberately up to his hairline. 'And which offer might that be?'

Megan blushed furiously at the innuendo, wishing those lascivious sexy looks of his didn't reduce her brain to mush every time he trained them on her. 'The one you mentioned on the phone, when I was at work. About—about using your studio to work in, about maybe you giving me some tutoring.'

'Oh, that.' Feigning disappointment, he dropped down casually beside her, his cologne and the clean sharp smell of soap and man playing havoc with her senses, making her fervently wish she had waited until he at least had some clothes on before instigating a discussion.

'Are you saying you've changed your mind?' Megan's mouth went dry at the thought that maybe she'd got it all wrong, then she silently cursed herself for always waiting for the other shoe to drop—automatically expecting that things wouldn't turn out as she hoped. If she really was going to change her life, then that kind of negative thinking had to change, too.

'Stop putting words into my mouth,' he scolded, looking faintly disgruntled. 'Of course the offer still stands. As soon as we get back to London you're moving in with me. There's no excuse not to now.'

No excuse? Megan's stomach flipped. It was hardly any way to ask her, was it? In fact he hadn't even really asked her at all if she'd like to move in; he'd more or less just told her. Something in her balked at that. She'd had nine years of living with a man who'd told her what to do every day; she was damn sure she wasn't going to repeat that with Kyle—no matter how deeply she cared for him.

Entwining a silky strand of hair round and round her finger, she pulled it tight, then dragged it loose again. 'I don't—I don't think it's necessary for me to move in with you. I'm not far away…there'd be no need.'

His features tightening at every tremulous word she uttered, Kyle glared.

'Not necessary for you to move in? What are we talking about, here, Megan? A cold-blooded business arrangement?

Forgive me if I'm wrong, but I was under the distinct impression that we had a lot more going for us than that!'

'Do we?' she ventured weakly. The truth was she didn't know what he really wanted from her. Did he just want a live-in girlfriend who shared his passion for painting, or was he looking for something a little deeper? Like a life-long partner…a wife, perhaps? Someone who would love him for ever, to the end of her days, and wouldn't hesitate in telling him so at every opportunity?

'I want you to move in, Megan. I want you to share my life. If I was just looking to tutor somebody, hell—I could give you a list a mile long of students who'd jump at the chance!'

His words didn't make her feel any better. Megan pushed off the bed and stood up. 'Then maybe you should do that,' she said nervously, dark eyes darting round the room, trying to ascertain how long it would take her to pack, call a cab to the nearest station and get the next train home. 'I don't want you to offer me anything on sufferance. If you feel under some sort of obligation to tutor me just because we've slept together then we'd better call the whole thing off right now. You won't even miss me. You've got your career, haven't you? A career you've deliberately kept me in the dark about. Damn it, you've played all your cards pretty close to your chest, haven't you? Yet you know practically all there is to know about me!'

Tears had filled her eyes and she jammed her hand impatiently into her jeans pocket, searching for a crumpled tissue to dab at them.

'You're crazy.' Frustration was like a coiled spring inside Kyle's chest, waiting to unravel. Yanking the towel from round his neck, he got up and threw it angrily down on the bed. This wasn't what he'd intended to happen at all. What he'd wanted to tell her was that he loved her, that he couldn't imagine his life without her. Instead he'd fouled up big time. He'd come off as patronising and condescending, and at that moment he hated himself for not having the words to adequately explain what was in his heart.

'Yes, I'm crazy!' Megan threw back at him, distraught. 'I think I have a right to be, don't you? When a woman is deliberately pushed down the stairs by a man who made vows to take care of her and she loses the only thing that made all those horrible years of marriage worthwhile—' She broke off, feeling choked and appalled at what she was saying.

She could hardly swallow over the terrible pain in her throat, in her heart. There was no way she could even bring herself to look at Kyle. The last thing she needed to see was pity in his eyes. It was his love she wanted—not his pity.

'You were pregnant.' He felt as if he'd been sucker-punched. Why hadn't he realised it before?

Megan spun away from him to move across to the window. Lifting the pretty gauze curtain, she stared blindly out at the sea, agitated and furious that she'd been forced to reveal her deepest secret when the man she'd revealed it to didn't even trust her enough to tell her about his own life.

'Yes, I was pregnant. I lost the baby.' Megan uttered the words through lips that were numb with pain. She continued to stare out of the window as Kyle came up behind her.

'So you were still sleeping with him right up until that night?' Kyle didn't know how he managed to grind the words out, because his chest was so tight with jealousy it was suffocating him.

Megan began to cry—soft, desperate sobs that made her shoulders shake and her hands cover her face. Right then, Kyle could easily have hung himself for being such a crass, insensitive oaf. What was his jealousy compared to the inconsolable grief Megan was feeling over the loss of her baby?

'He forced me,' she said brokenly, turning to look at him. 'But I didn't care. All I wanted was my baby.'

As her face crumpled in pain Kyle pulled her hard against his chest and held her there. 'Sweetheart, I'm so sorry…so sorry.'

CHAPTER ELEVEN

'LEG hurting?' Kyle stopped Megan in her tracks as they negotiated the potentially treacherous wet cobble stones of the harbour path, staring down into her rain-dampened features as concern gripped him deep inside.

Around them, the wind howled gustily, whipping Megan's glorious black hair across her face so that she resembled some wild dark gypsy from romantic folklore. Her deep brown eyes were underlined with kohl, glistening like two dark jewels as she met his gaze, the dark fringe of her lashes spiked with the rain, her teeth briefly worrying at her full and naked lower lip.

'No, it's fine. This is a beautiful place, Kyle. I'm so glad you brought me.'

And she was, Megan thought fiercely, as her gaze swept the vast turbulent sea, its waves lapping slate-grey at the sides of the famous Cobb harbour walls. A couple of fishing boats bobbed on the horizon, and apart from herself and Kyle, and the odd seagull or two, there was no one else about on the harbour as twilight faded to dusk. The outside temperature had dropped significantly in the past few minutes, but the change was bracing rather than cutting— just what she needed to blow the cobwebs away.

Taking a deep lungful of air, Megan smiled warmly back at the man regarding her so intensely, wanting desperately to convey to him the depth and breadth of her own profound emotions. She couldn't imagine feeling like this about any other man on earth...ever. Her senses were completely beguiled by the sheer warrior-like beauty of his fiercely male visage: the carved angular cheekbones, the intense golden eyes, the hard yet sensual mouth that made his smile the most lethal weapon she'd ever come across...

There were tiny drops of rain glistening like crystal in his chestnut hair, and, helplessly compelled, Megan reached up to touch a damp lock that had strayed onto his forehead. Immediately she found her hand taken prisoner, then her body hauled hard against his, so that from the neck down she was pressed intimately into the damp smooth surface of his jacket, the smell of leather mingling provocatively with the scent of the rain. The urgency in him was immediately evident, the hard ridge behind the button fly of his jeans straining deep into her abdomen, starting an ache deep inside her that suspended her breath somewhere between a gasp and a sigh.

'Ever made love in the rain?' he asked hoarsely, his gaze a hot flickering flame, hungrily roaming her features.

Before Megan could reply, Kyle traced the shape of her lips with the pad of his thumb, dragging it intimately across her delicate skin in a deliberately erotic little foreplay that made her gasp out loud in surprise and pleasure.

'Do you want me, Megan?' he taunted softly. 'Because I want you. Will you give yourself to me?'

'Always.'

Their lips met in an urgent clash of teeth and tongues, but Kyle quickly took command—ravishing the moist warm inner landscape of her mouth with wild passionate kisses that tasted of wind and rain, salt and sea, heat and desire, all wrapped up in one drugging sensuous package that she had absolutely no defence against. Even as she surrendered to those hot soul-destroying kisses his hand was pushing her denim jacket aside, roughly cupping her breast inside her T-shirt, his thumb restlessly and hungrily stroking across the deep rigid ache of her aroused nipple.

'Kyle!' His name was a naked plea on her lips as Megan allowed herself the briefest glance across his shoulder to ascertain that they were alone, then willingly let him urge her towards the harbour wall.

She was thankful that full dusk was now a shield. Grateful too that the now driving rain was keeping most people safely ensconced inside their houses or hotel rooms. Because it was a cold hard fact that she was powerless to resist what Kyle was demanding. It shocked her to realise what she was consenting to—she'd never made love out in the open in her life. But it thrilled her too—excited her beyond reason to discover that she could be so swept away, body and soul, made almost mindless by the heat of great passion…

There was no need for words as Kyle hustled her against the rough stone wall, dragged her skirt up to her panty line while his body acted as a shield, then ripped open the sides of her underwear with two powerful tugs. He caught the skimpy fabric in his hand and shoved it into his pocket, his expression driven—possessed, almost.

The rain was pouring ceaselessly down, running in rivulets down their faces, but they could hardly have heeded it less. A deep primeval heat was pulsing unstoppably through their veins, making them oblivious to anything else but each other. Desire was a throbbing, drowning deluge, conquering everything in its wake, demanding nothing less than their complete acquiescence. All they had to do was let go to be swept away on its relentless tide.

Megan held her breath at the shock of Kyle's finger insinuating itself deeply inside her core. As a second finger joined the first shimmering sensation exploded inside her. When he withdrew, a helpless little groan—almost a whimper—escaped her, and she held onto the steely muscle in his arms as he raised her hips, his expression a startling combination of deep driving need and yet an almost profound reverence for the woman he held in his arms.

Megan shut her eyes, cradling his pelvis with her thighs

as he penetrated her fully with one deep thrust of his silken shaft. She ignored the nagging throbbing of her injured leg as heat and sensation flooded her, clenching her muscles possessively round him as he withdrew almost completely, then thrust again. His possession was deeper this time, so deep that she was profoundly intimate with every powerful inch of him, their bodies fused as one, both dazed with pleasure and greedy for more. He kissed her hard as his movements became more intense, more focused, and she thought that if she were to die right now there was no question she'd die happy. At least her senses were flooded with feeling, instead of the habitual numbness that had been her natural state for longer than she cared to remember. But there was no pretence at tenderness as profound, shattering need simply consumed them both.

Her mouth would be swollen and throbbing from Kyle's devastating kisses when he released her, but Megan didn't care. How could she when being with him was all that mattered? Her whole life had come down to these few precious moments of deep mind-blowing connection, and she wouldn't have traded it for the world. She had never really thrown caution to the wind, but she was doing it now— almost daring the elements or the powers that be to deny her this savage hungry pleasure. Right now, passion was everything.

Her fingers dug into the hard, honed flesh beneath the damp leather sleeves of his jacket as she suddenly came apart in his arms, trembling and crying his name as incandescent heat poured into her, feeling him thrust even deeper, then suddenly grow still. His breath was rasping clouds of steam into the cold night air as he shook with emotion, his gaze hooded, slightly dazed, as Megan clung to him, her body quivering in the aftermath of what had occurred. Then creeping into her consciousness came the unwanted realisation that they were exposed, out in the open and wet through to their very skins, and she briefly shut her eyes tight, as if to ward off the inevitable moment when they would have to part.

With devastating tenderness Kyle eased her back down onto her feet, letting the creased folds of her wraparound skirt drop safely down to her ankles before pulling the soft damp sides of her denim jacket together over her soaked maroon T-shirt. His palm icy, he stroked the heavy wet strands of her hair gently back from her face, devouring her with his eyes. Without a word, he deftly attended to his own clothing, shoved back a stray lock of rain-drenched hair and grabbed her hand.

'What you need is a good hot shower to chase the cold away.'

His scorching glance sent tremors quaking through every inch of her body as Megan stared, transfixed, suddenly struck dumb by the sheer all-encompassing need she saw writ large in his eyes. For the first time she realised that he had made himself vulnerable to her, too. Her heart accelerated wildly at the mere idea.

'Forget that,' he growled, expression wry. 'What we *both* need is a good hot shower…together.'

'Can I come in?'

'No!' Kyle's reply was curt as Christa rapped on the door. A frustrated sigh escaped him as he watched a stricken Megan grab the large white towel that she'd not so long ago been holding strategically round her lower half, then bolt like a deer into the bathroom. With tight-lipped resignation he threw his sketchpad onto the immaculate white linen covering the bed, then stood up to get the door.

'I didn't mean to interrupt.' Christa stole a less than furtive look into the room across Kyle's broad hard-muscled shoulder, but Megan was nowhere to be seen. The long gold brocade curtains were tellingly drawn against the night, just the single light of one small bedside lamp burning softly, its gentle light casting a mellow glow in the room that was an homage to all things Laura Ashley. 'You were obviously working.'

She was grinning broadly, her teeth startlingly white against the vivid slash of scarlet lipstick that adorned her mouth.

'Obviously.' Kyle bit down his initial rush of annoyance—he hated being disturbed when he was working—then smiled to ease the brusqueness of his reply.

'I wanted to check that everything was okay. I hope you both enjoyed dinner? Alistair is a first-rate chef. I poached him from a really swanky hotel in Weymouth.'

'The food was great, Christa. First class.'

'And you're both...settling in okay?' The blonde sneaked another peek across Kyle's broad shoulder, her gaze briefly alighting on the sketchpad that lay closed on top of the counterpane.

'We're both settling in just fine.' A dark eyebrow shot up towards his hairline at Christa's less than subtle efforts to glean more information. But he could forgive her curious nature—why shouldn't he? It seemed to come with the territory as far as women were concerned.

Of course Megan was right when she'd accused him of keeping her in the dark about himself. A frown settled between his brows as he realised how little he'd personally revealed. She had every right to be angry with him. He knew he was apt to put up barriers where relationships were concerned, but he also knew that maybe it was time to let down a few with Megan. There was no place for mistrust where she was concerned. She hadn't come after him because of his wealth and fame, like so many women had done before. She didn't even know who he was...

'I was hoping you both might join me for a drink in the

bar before turning in? I've got some of that delicious German brandy you used to be so fond of.'

Because he was such an attractive man, and because Christa was such a natural flirt—married or no—she leant a little towards Kyle as she spoke, ensuring he got a generous eyeful of her ample cleavage in the low-necked white chiffon blouse she wore.

He grinned his appreciation even as he shook his head. 'Not tonight, Christa. I think what Megan needs more than anything is rest.'

'I'm sure that's not what would be on my mind if I were in her position.' The blonde dimpled suggestively. 'But even if Megan doesn't feel like a drink, why don't you and I take the opportunity to talk about old times?'

Kyle didn't so much as flinch. 'When did you say Justin was due home?' he asked smoothly.

Rolling her pale blue eyes heavenward, Christa sighed out loud. 'All right, I get the message. I can see you're serious about this one, but you can't blame me for trying. She's a lucky girl—I hope she knows that.'

'You're wrong.' Kyle said quietly as he went to close the door. '*I'm* the lucky one.'

Megan was beginning not to know herself at all. Or maybe she'd just hidden the real Megan so well, out of sheer expediency, that only now was she beginning to get clues about her true potential.

She grinned at herself in the generous bathroom mirror as she tightened the belt of her robe more securely round her. True potential? That was a good one. If she meant true potential for acting like a complete wanton then that was about right, if her behaviour with Kyle at the harbour was anything to go by. Her cheeks burned crimson as she touched her fingers to her still swollen mouth, but the heat that pulsed through her at what she had succumbed to completely submerged the rush of shame that threatened.

She wouldn't be ashamed of passion. She certainly didn't have an ounce of regret about herself and Kyle. Only minutes ago she'd displayed yet another contradictory side to her nature when she'd agreed to pose practically nude, for him to sketch her. Okay, she'd had the benefit of a towel, but still her back had been bare all the way down to the base of her spine, and she knew it was only a matter of time before Kyle persuaded her to discard it completely. But it was stupid to be prudish about the human body when all across the country models like Christa were posing naked for students in life drawing classes as a matter of course.

Christa. She was a beautiful woman—a sensual woman. The way she looked at Kyle, her greedy eyes glimmering with appreciation, Megan was sure she was his ex-lover. She swallowed hard, expelling an uneasy breath. Never mind. She could weather it. Everybody had a past, didn't they? She of all people knew that. It didn't mean because they might have been intimate in the past they'd want to revive that intimacy now, did it? Besides, Christa was married… *Stop it, Megan. Don't even go there.*

She spun round at the sound of the outer door closing and hastily tweaked a couple of glossy tendrils of black silk more becomingly round her face. Kyle had asked her to put her hair up so that he could sketch her body, and now the sheer weight of it was gradually loosening stray strands that slipped away from the initially tidy knot. Opening the door, she peeped out. Kyle was flicking through his sketchpad, expression thoughtful, his pencil momentarily captured between his teeth.

Megan pushed the door wider, causing it to creak. Glancing up, Kyle withdrew his pencil from between his teeth and smiled. Once again the sheer masculine beauty of that devastating smile made her lose her centre of gravity.

Every woman in the world deserved to be smiled at like that at least once in her life, she decided. A toe-curling, purely sexy smile that seemed to say You're the one I want; you and only you. He couldn't possibly look at Megan like that and still want Christa, could he?

'Why did you run away?' he asked.

'I didn't want… I don't feel comfortable with the idea of someone else seeing me undressed.' There, she'd said it. Christa MacKenzie might be perfectly at ease with her body, but Megan wasn't. She was definitely coming out of her shell, but only by degrees. Fiddling with the belt of her robe, she dragged a tendril of hair straight down over her ear and let it go again—anything rather than look up and discover amusement in his eyes.

'Why?'

Megan shifted from one hip to the other, feeling her face grow hotter by the second. 'I don't feel good about—about my body, I suppose…especially since my leg—'

'Do you think your injury diminishes you in some way? Because if you do you're crazy! You've got one of the most arresting female bodies I've ever seen. A man could get eyestrain just looking at your gorgeous curves.'

'You're biased.' Megan dared a glance to see if he was merely teasing, but instead found him regarding her with deadly seriousness.

'Not true. Don't forget I'm looking at you with an artist's eye, and I speak as I find.'

'Was Christa the girl in the picture? In your bathroom, I mean?'

'Yes. That was Christa.' Not a flicker of emotion showed in his face. 'She was a good model. You could be, too, if I didn't get completely chewed up at the mere idea of you posing for anyone else but me.'

'Did you sleep with her?' The question was out before she could check it.

'No. Is this line of questioning leading somewhere?'

A compressed look crept around his mouth, and Megan flinched from the flash of irritation in his eyes. Determinedly she tried to concentrate on her breathing.

'She's a beautiful woman.'

'But we didn't have sex. Next question.'

'You must make—I mean, I imagine you must make a reasonable living from your work?' She advanced as far as the bed, then, holding onto the brass rail beneath the ivory finials, eased down carefully onto the counterpane. Megan prayed her question wouldn't make him angry, but it was driving her crazy to know so little about his life. About him. And surely his work was one of the most integral parts?

He threw pencil and sketchpad back on the bed, then folded his arms across his fitted black T-shirt with something very close to resignation. Megan weathered the suddenly tense expression, seeing the obvious tussle behind those sensual tawny eyes, registering the brief but distinct contraction of muscle in the perfectly angled plane of his cheek.

'I make a good living—some might say an exceptional one. My work's been displayed in galleries around the world, and in artistic circles my name's not exactly unheard of. Is that what you wanted to know, Megan?'

Her fingers flexed a little around the smooth brass bed rail. 'You mean you're well known?' Her expression pained, she cast her face down, staring at the plush gold carpet, the colour swirling in front of her as her brain desperately tried to assimilate the fact that Kyle was a famous artist. Ergo— so far out of her league it wasn't funny. Familiar feelings of inadequacy pressed in on her in a heated rush, threatening to swamp her. So much for her delusional theory that she was finally dealing with her emotional baggage from the past.

'So what if I am?' Placing his hands either side of those

lean tight hips in the close-fitting black leather trousers, Kyle angled his jaw disdainfully towards her. 'Do you think I care whether you know who I am or not? Can you imagine how sick I get of people wanting to know me just because I've achieved some sort of notoriety?'

'But you could have told me!' Megan stared at him with wounded eyes. 'There's so much about you that I don't know. Can't you understand how that makes me feel? I've given you access to the most intimate parts of my life and yet yours is a closed book to me.'

'You've got to learn to trust me, Megan. You came to me for help, remember? I didn't tell you who I was because I was scared you wouldn't be able to handle it. Looking at your face now, I can see I was right to be concerned.'

Her heart hammering, Megan silently conceded he was right. How could she possibly contemplate a relationship with someone who lived part of their life in the public eye? Some women might be totally comfortable with such a situation, but, having gone through what she had, to Megan the whole idea was anathema. She wouldn't want to be scrutinised and discussed like a bug under a microscope because of her association with him.

'I do trust you, Kyle.'

'But?' He knew instinctively there was a 'but'. A big one. His chest was so tight he felt as if his heart was clamped in a vice.

'But you were wrong not to tell me who you really are. You deceived me by keeping something so important about yourself so secret. What if I'd found it out by accident? What if I'd seen your picture or your name in a newspaper? What then, Kyle? Would you have concocted some story to divert me, supposedly to make me feel better, because you concluded that I couldn't handle the truth?'

Her heart was pounding. She was saying words she didn't want to say, making accusations she didn't want to make, but still she couldn't deny the colossal hurt at the idea that maybe he'd thought her too immature, too unstable to be trusted with the reality of his life.

'I thought I was acting in your best interests. Obviously it was a serious misjudgement on my part.'

'You were treating me like a child! I may have been hurt badly in the past, but I'm mature enough and strong enough to handle the truth.'

'Really?' His disparaging gaze poleaxed her. 'Is that why you stayed in a marriage that had long ago passed its sell-by date? Because you could *handle the truth*? You knew your husband was an unfaithful bully, with a predilection for cruelty, yet still you stayed with him until he practically maimed you for life!'

Megan flinched at his words, privately conceding his point and damning herself for her past weakness, but deeply upset that he should speak to her in such a way. Not even speak—he was shouting at her, fury etched deep in his brow, in his eyes, in the mocking tightening of smooth lean muscle in that beautiful angled jaw…

'Everything—everything's happened so fast.' Rising slowly to her feet, she was shocked at how weak her limbs felt beneath her robe. 'I think maybe I've got into this re-lationship without—without really thinking things through. Maybe what I need is some time on my own to work things out. Maybe it would be best for both of us…'

'You're running away.' Kyle glared at her accusingly.

'No, I'm not. For once in my life I think I'm being sen-sible. You obviously don't think me capable of making a smart decision for myself, and that's not how I want to conduct another relationship. I can't afford to make another mistake.'

'Is that what you think this is? A *mistake*?'

'No!' Distressed, she put her hand up to her face. 'I didn't mean— I know you were only trying to protect me by not telling me about your fame, but if I hadn't appeared so weak in the first place you would never have felt that. Well, I don't want to be weak any more, Kyle. I need to sort my life out from a position of strength.'

'Megan, I'm sorry. I shouldn't have yelled or said what I did. I love you. I think I've loved you from the moment I set eyes on you. All I've ever wanted is the best for you. Oh hell!' Scraping his hand roughly through his hair, Kyle shook his head in despair. 'You have every right to be angry with me. It was wrong of me not to tell you the truth about myself, to assume you wouldn't be able to deal with it. But I was scared…'

'Scared?' Megan's brown eyes widened in double surprise. She was still reeling from the idea that he loved her, as well as his stark admission that he was scared. It was almost impossible to imagine the virile and supremely confident specimen of manhood standing in front of her being frightened of anything.

'Scared of losing you, Megan.' The gaze he levelled at her now tore at her heart like nothing else. 'I *am* losing you, aren't I?'

'You're a good man Kyle…the best. You don't need someone like me complicating your life. Not when you already have everything you need.'

'I won't have everything I need if I don't have you.'

His words hung in the air like an anvil about to drop down on her from a great height and crush the living breath from her body. It was almost impossible for Megan to swallow across the huge aching lump in her throat. Tears filled her eyes and spilled unheeded down her cheeks. 'I've got to do this, Kyle. I've got to leave. It would be so easy to lean on you, let you make decisions for me, show me the way…and you've already done so much. But you deserve better than that. I respect you too much to let you settle for anything less than the best. I mean it.'

Kyle found his hand at his throat, his fingers closing around the silver and turquoise amulet on the worn leather lace that Yvette had given him on his eighteenth birthday. His throat burned and his heart ached at her memory, at the void she'd left in his life when she'd died. But that pain was infinitely more bearable now than the pain he was feeling at the thought of losing Megan.

With starving gaze he stared at her, standing there in her robe, her dark eyes huge and shimmering, tears tracking down her face, and it felt as if some gigantic invisible hand had reached down from the heavens, wrenched his heart out of his chest and stamped on it at his feet… He felt weak with the hurt, disorientated, faint, his brain swirling with the implications of her leaving. But even in the midst of his agony, he knew he had to let her go.

More than his loving her, more than his need for her, Megan needed to know that he put her wellbeing first. And part of that wellbeing would be the realisation that she was stronger than she thought she was. Strong enough to stand alone and make a good life for herself. Maybe it was the ultimate gift from their union that he could give her—to let her go with his blessing? If she was meant to come back to him then she would. If she didn't…then he would just have to learn to accept it, just as he had had to learn to accept his sister's untimely death all those years ago…

'Come here.'

She hesitated for only a second before flying into his arms. Tilting her face up towards him, Kyle tenderly stroked back her hair, then wiped her tears with the pad of his thumb.

'Did I ever tell you just how incredible I think you are?'

Megan tightened her arms possessively around his waist, distraught that it might be for the very last time, knowing she had already set wheels in motion that might take them far away from each other…maybe for ever.

'You do what you have to do, baby,' he whispered huskily against her ear. 'If you ever want to come back…you know where to find me.' Pressing her cheek close into his chest, Kyle filled his arms with the warmth of her, her scent invading his senses as evocatively as the honeysuckle on his Greek island after a rainfall, praying he would have the strength to really let her go—but, more than that, praying for the strength to survive it.

CHAPTER TWELVE

HE POACHED a cigarette from a youth lounging outside a pub after closing time, then made his way to a bench by the harbour, hunched into his leather jacket, took a couple of long drags and stared darkly out to sea.

Because he'd given up smoking years ago, the now unfamiliar pull on his lungs, along with the slight giddiness in his head, made him throw the offending smoke onto the cobbled stones, then crush it disgustedly with the heel of his boot.

Pushing himself off the cold slatted bench, he walked head down, grimly resolute against the force of the tremendous gusts of wind that pressed him back as he negotiated a somewhat steep incline in the road. Kyle had no idea where he was going because he had no particular direction in mind right then. All he knew was that he needed to get his thoughts together. To try to deal with the swell of unwanted emotion that was threatening to grip him by the throat as it always did when he thought of Megan, the woman he couldn't seem to forget, no matter what he did…

Squinting grimly into the rain as he walked, he shrugged off the biting cold that lashed against his face and stung his skin. It was summer, but you'd never know it by the weather. He blew out a breath as his long legs strode uphill, dispassionately watching the plume of warmth from his body dissolve in the sharp cold air.

Megan. The thought of her dispersed the icy tension in his belly and replaced it with sizzling heat. He'd never been so enamoured of a woman. So besotted. *So in love…* Neither had he ever experienced such blinding driven need to claim a woman as his own. To be her lover night and day, to imagine her as the mother of his children—loving and working side by side together in their chosen passion, raising their children in a home full of love and joy and never-ending warmth. It didn't matter that Megan couldn't have children naturally. They could adopt.

Except that was where his little fantasy broke down. Icy tension came back, cramping his insides. The lady in question had walked out on him—three months ago, to be exact. Too scared to contemplate deepening their relationship into a life-long union because she'd spent years in marriage to a neanderthal who'd somehow convinced her she wasn't worthy of anything better. Why else would his wealth and fame have bothered her so deeply?

He wondered what she was doing now, if she had started to do something about that sublime talent she possessed. He hoped so. If nothing else came out of that brief intense time they had spent together, Kyle prayed she wouldn't give up on the idea of making art her life's work.

Digging his hands deep into his pockets, he stopped abruptly, glancing back the way he had come. In the distance the dark, barely discernible outline of the sea twinned with the night, while in the street itself the little terraced houses huddled together against the elements as they had done for perhaps a hundred years or more. Each of them furnished with their own enduring stories of the families that had lived and died there and the ones that lived there still. Family. That was what Kyle wanted. But it wasn't likely. Not when the one woman he wanted as the mother of his children had long gone and didn't look like coming back any time soon. *Damn.* He should never have returned to this place, but he was looking for connections. The ghost of Megan's smile, the sound of her voice, the passion that had inflamed them both and driven him to take her out here in the open—uncaring of anything but his desire to lose himself in her completely. But he found none of these things, and his fruitless search only served to remind him more painfully than ever just how much he had lost.

'Megan—another drink?'

'Tonic water with a slice of lemon, please.'

'Boy!' Barbara Palmer's slender brows shot up to her hairline. 'You're pushing the boat out!'

'She's been designated driver for the night,' Penny interjected, with a deliberately sweet smile across a table already laden with empty glasses and dishes of olives. 'Brand new set of wheels outside.'

'I saw. "Compact" is the word I think I'm looking for.' Barbara made a face that transformed into a huge grin as she drained the last dregs of her Bacardi and Coke.

Megan laughed out loud. As far as she was concerned, her new mode of transport was as exciting as any top of the range sportster, and she could cope with a little mickey-taking. The main point was that it was all hers—no more relying on buses or cabs or Penny's goodwill to get her around. Freedom!

Buying herself a car was one more step towards shaking off the shackles that had chained the old Megan Brand to a life without hope. That girl—thank God—had been given her marching orders. Walking away from Kyle might possibly turn out to be the worst decision she'd ever made, but at the very least it had spurred her on to finally change her life for the better. He had been right: everything *did* come down to choice and Megan had at last made the choice to live a different life.

A *very* different life, she mused, as her dark brown gaze roamed the small but select Mayfair nightclub. They had come to celebrate Penny's twenty-ninth birthday, and celebrate they would. But for one or two brief but excruciating seconds Megan recalled what it was like to have woken up

every day for the past three months knowing that the man
she loved more than life itself was no longer hers to love.
Afraid to commit, afraid of her own jealousy, afraid that she
wouldn't be able to handle the demands of his fame—even
vicariously—she had walked away. Her eyes shut briefly
tight with the pain of it.

'Hey, Megan, isn't that your ex over there? At the end
of the bar with the redhead—the one in the leather skirt
with the big—'

'I see her.' More to the point, Megan saw Nick. Propping
up the bar, his face pressed up close to the buxom redhead
with the dangerous cleavage, he still had that swagger about
him that he wore like a tired old suit. As she got to her feet
Megan popped a couple of buttons on her pink coral silk
jacket. It immediately exposed the black lacy edge of her
push-up bra—and a whole lot else besides. Now she had
some dangerous cleavage of her own.

'Meg—' Penny's fingers curled anxiously round her
wrist. 'Meg, what are you doing?'

'I'm only going over to say hello…' She gently extricated
herself, a confounding dimple at the corner of her shimmering peachy lips. 'I'll be right back.'

'I'm coming with you!' A little too intoxicated, Penny
teetered alarmingly on her stylish two-inch heels.

Barbara clamped her arm around the blonde's waist and
yanked her firmly down beside her on the red velvet seat.
Her blue eyes were wide with speculation as she watched
Megan straighten her matching coral skirt, then stroke aside
the slit in the material to expose a tantalising slash of tanned
brown thigh—legacy of her recent trip to Rhodes with
Penny.

'Nick.' Across the other side of the room, Megan raised
her voice a couple of notches to make herself heard above
the sultry sax that was playing on the sound system. When
the man she addressed swivelled at the sound of his name

she registered the stunned expression in his eyes with a deep shaft of purely feminine satisfaction. Good—she already had the element of surprise in her favour. Now to execute part two of her impromptu little plan...

'Fancy seeing you here.' Megan dimpled as provocatively as she could, her little ruse much assisted by the glass of wine she had imbibed earlier, before switching to tonic water.

The redhead beside Nick aimed silent daggers of dislike Megan's way, then slid her arm possessively round Nick's, as if to stake her claim. *You can have him and welcome,* Megan thought fiercely, a slither of revulsion sliding down her spine.

'Well, well. This is a surprise. What? No boyfriend in tow to jump to your rescue and shove me up against a wall?' He gave an exaggerated glance over her shoulder, but Megan stood her ground, even if her heart felt as if it was pounding right out of her chest.

'I'm here with some girlfriends. It's Penny's birthday.'

'Good ol' Pen. Be sure and wish her many happy returns from an old friend, won't you?' His lip curled and a trickle of sweat gleamed on his brow.

Megan stemmed the urge to slap that sneer right off his face, but there was more than one way to skin a rabbit, as she was quickly learning.

Taking a deep swig of his light beer, Nick let his gaze rove across Megan's cleavage with a primitive leer. 'Anyway, I have to say you're looking even more gorgeous than ever. What have you been doing to yourself?'

She replied without hesitation. 'Living, Nick. Something I should have done years ago, when I was merely *existing* as your wife.'

The steadiness with which she held his gaze, her directness never faltering, seemed to faze her ex-husband completely. 'Yes, well. You know what they say.' He tipped back his glass and drained it before continuing. 'Let by-gones be bygones and all that. You got your money, didn't you? I don't owe you a damn thing any more.'

Megan could argue differently but what would it achieve? You couldn't put a price on damaged limbs, or lost babies.

Ignoring the sudden swell of emotion cramping her stomach, she determinedly lifted her chin. 'I didn't come over to ask you for anything, Nick. I agree we should let bygones be bygones. Let me buy you a drink and wish you well.'

'That's more like it.' Loosening his tie, he looked immediately relieved—cocky, almost. *Same old Nick.* 'In that case, I'll have a vodka Martini. Make it a large one, there's a good girl.'

Megan duly ordered the drink from the handsome Australian barman who had been eyeing her and her friends most of the evening. Because she was feeling good she even returned his smile, and saw hope leap in his eyes before turning back to Nick with the cocktail. As he reached out to relieve her of it Megan took a sip, registered the intoxicating burst of alcohol on her tongue, then tipped the entire contents of the glass over Nick's head.

'Bitch!' He lunged towards her with a string of expletives littering the air, moisture dripping from his hair and down his face, but Megan had already stepped back a pace, her heart racing as the young barman vaulted the bar and expertly pinned an astonished Nick heavily against it. With impressive ease he imprisoned one of Nick's flailing arms painfully up behind his back.

The redhead seemed to take it as her cue to promptly retreat into the crowd, clearly concluding her prey was no longer worth the hassle.

'Is he bothering you, love? I'll have him escorted off the premises in two seconds flat if he is.'

Megan looked Nick up and down, tension and long-held resentment seeping from her spine as though an old wound had finally been cauterised, and slowly shook her head. 'For him to bother me I'd have to acknowledge his existence. And as far as I'm concerned this man ceased to exist as a decent human being a long time ago. He's nothing but a bully and a coward. I wasted nine long lonely years of my life on him and I don't intend to waste a second more. Whether he stays or whether he goes really makes no odds to me.'

And with her head held high Megan walked back to her friends through the throng of curious onlookers who parted like the Red Sea to let her through.

The sound of screeching tyres and loud pulsating dance music shattered the early-morning stillness that Kyle had fondly believed to be his right as he sprinted up the steps to his front door with his regular Sunday newspaper. Three young lads in a white sports car were standing up in their seats, whistling and calling to a shapely young woman in red who was crossing the road in front of them. She'd lost a shoe and, intent on retrieving it, was bent over in her tight red skirt, long black hair shielding her face as she struggled to put it back onto her foot. Her neckline plunged as she leant forward, giving a heart-stopping glimpse of voluptuous tanned flesh encased in sexy black lace.

Shock and heat and *got to have* slammed into Kyle's gut as he stood and stared. Megan? *What in God's name…* As the three young lads in the car continued to vie with each other for her exclusive attention his pulse started to race and the blood in his head pounded with a vengeance. His jaw slackened, his mouth dropping open as he watched her reaction to the young men in the car.

Clearly exasperated with their behaviour, her shoe finally cradling her foot once again, she stood in the middle of the road, hands on hips, and told them in no uncertain terms that they should be ashamed of themselves for acting like a bunch of mindless football hooligans. Who did they think they were, causing such an almighty racket on a Sunday morning when most people were trying to relax? Why didn't they do themselves and everybody else a favour and just grow up?

The Megan he had known would never have had the confidence to deliver such a lecture. Astonishment pooled in his stomach. With his mouth clamped tight and his jaw now firmly clenched, Kyle observed the scene with a growing sense of disbelief and admiration as the disappointed young men sheepishly apologised, then finally drove reluctantly away, defiantly blowing kisses her way as Megan walked up the street towards him alone.

Amazingly, she hardly limped at all. That was the first thing he noticed. Followed closely by the fact that the woman was simply—without a doubt—stunning. How could he have forgotten just how stunning? She was tanned, slim, and sexy as hell, and that red suit she wore did everything to highlight the fact. A strange sense of *déjà vu* descended on him. She was the girl in the photo again—the one that had made his blood slow and thicken when he'd seen it in her bedroom.

Kyle sucked in an astonished breath. No wonder the males in the sports car had screeched to a halt in front of her! He could barely swallow over the dryness in his throat. Every night he went to bed and dreamed of her, and for the past three months, after getting over the initial, most immediate shock of her departure, he had been trying to capture her likeness on his canvas. Now he saw that he'd failed, and failed miserably. Not even his clever instinctive brushstrokes could do her incandescent beauty justice.

'Hello.' Her smile was shy and immediately brought Kyle to his knees. There were so many things he wanted to say, but right now he couldn't think of one—except the obvious…and probably the most inane.

'Hello, yourself.'

'I wanted to talk to you.' She pinned him with a surprisingly direct gaze, dark eyes wide.

'It's been three months, Megan. What have you been doing with yourself? Apart from stopping traffic, that is…'

She blushed. *Oh, how he loved to see her blush.* 'I've been painting. I enrolled in a life-drawing class and an art appreciation one. I've also been to some galleries and I've seen some of your work—Kyle, it's amazing!'

Right now, he didn't want to hear her appreciation. Right now, he wanted to know what the hell she thought she was playing at, strolling without warning casually back into his life on a Sunday morning as if she'd just popped out to the shops for a pint of milk. Three months ago she'd left him stranded in Lyme Regis with a heart that was broken in two and not so much as the tiniest clue as to whether she intended to come back to him or not. He'd done the honourable thing by letting her go, but it hadn't eased his pain—not one jot.

'You were hardly limping,' he remarked, the pain in his throat so acute he had to swallow carefully to try and ease it.

'I know! I can hardly believe it myself. I've been having regular reflexology treatments, along with some aromatherapy massage, and what with my painting and my classes and thinking more positively—' She flushed pink, as if embarrassed by her unstoppable flow of words. 'Well—everything just seems to be coming together.'

'I'm happy for you. It couldn't have happened to a nicer person.'

Had she just come to tell him her good news? To demonstrate that her life had taken on a much more positive direction since walking out on him, and please could he just forget the fact that she'd broken his heart and wish her all the best? Kyle was strong, but even his psyche couldn't bear the impossible. The ache in his chest was like a steel band crushing him.

He slapped his newspaper against his thigh, then forced a reluctant smile. 'I knew it would all work out for you one day, Megan.'

'But it couldn't have worked out at all without you!' A pained expression in her dark brown eyes, she looked at him aghast—as if suddenly aware of what he might be thinking. 'You taught me so much. You made me believe I had talent, that there was more to myself than any hurt or condition. And you helped me see that through my art I could get better. I shouldn't have walked away like I did, Kyle. Believe me, I didn't want to. But I was scared too—and so—so jealous.'

He frowned. 'Jealous?'

'Of Christa. Of any woman you ever looked at! I was so scared that if I stayed you would soon get bored with me and look elsewhere. I didn't think I could ever be good enough for you. Especially when you told me you were well known. When I thought about what that might mean I—I just didn't want to let you down—hold you back in any way. I had so many insecurities, Kyle. My past just didn't prepare me for someone like you—' She broke off, biting her lip, her desperate gaze examining him feature by beloved feature.

Kyle was busy trying to absorb what she had just told him. A muscle ticked in the side of his bronzed cheek. What was she trying to say, exactly? That she'd made a mistake? That she wanted to come back to him? He hardly dared hope. Yet hope was the one thing he had held onto in these three long months he had been without her. He would wait, he'd told himself time and time again, when wanting her and not having her had gone way past intolerable. He'd wait for ever if he had to.

He shifted from one booted foot to the other as his hazel

eyes hungrily absorbed her beautiful face, his heart aching. 'Even when I told you I loved you?' he asked huskily.

Megan was caught in a paroxysm of guilt. Her expression torn, she lifted her hand and tucked a few glossy strands of hair behind her ear. They slipped forward again almost immediately.

'I needed to try and put a few things right in my life before I could accept your love,' she admitted softly. 'You did so much for me. I wanted to do something good in return. I wanted to be a person you could be proud to be with—not a self-loathing victim of a disastrous marriage. At the point that I walked out all I could feel was fear. Time and distance helped me see things more clearly. I went to Rhodes with Penny on holiday. I pushed myself. In Lindos I climbed every one of several hundred steps to reach the acropolis and sketch it, and I didn't let my limp stop me. I've learned a lot, Kyle, especially about self-imposed limitations, and it's all thanks to you. Is it—I mean, do you think there's even the faintest chance that we might try again? You indicated there might be...'

Pinning her with an unwavering golden glance for several long seconds, Kyle seemed to be preparing his answer. Megan must have died at least a thousand deaths as she waited for him to reply. Finally, he smiled, and Megan let go of the breath she'd been holding, relief shooting through her system like adrenaline.

'You going somewhere else, or would you like to come in for coffee?' he asked, his tone deceptively casual.

'I'd like to come in, certainly.' Heart racing, Megan took a step towards him, the two thin gold hoops in her lobes peeping through her curtain of dark hair. 'But not for coffee.'

She glanced up at him through lashes so luxuriant it ought to be a crime, and the look she gave him was anything but coy. It was the bold, confident glance of a woman who wanted her man and wasn't afraid to show it. The realisation sent all the blood rushing to his loins.

'You *have* changed,' he said softly in approval.

'If I have, it's because I love you.' Sighing deeply, she climbed up the second stair that brought her right up close to his chest, and without another word laid her head gently against his black cashmere sweater—for just a brief second or two terrified that he might reject her after all. But after everything she had been through she was going for broke, and didn't care who knew it. She loved him. She loved him so damn much she'd risk anything to prove it. Even humiliation.

But Kyle had no intention of rejecting her—not now, not ever. Dropping his newspaper onto the ground, he swept his arms tightly around her. 'I've waited three months to hear you say those words, you little witch, and every day was like a lifetime!'

Burying his lips in her hair, he murmured her name over and over, at the same time fumbling for his key in his jacket pocket like a man possessed. When his fingers finally closed around it he jammed it into the lock and, turning it swiftly, pushed Megan into the shadowy recess of the hallway. Cupping her face between his hands, he urged her up against the wall, his warm breath feathering across her face.

'So what other changes should I know about?' he asked softly, the corners of his beautiful mouth lifting in a smile.

'Well…' Deliberately coy, Megan dipped her head and began unbuttoning her bold red jacket. 'I've started buying much sexier new lingerie. Do you want a peek?'

His hands were already pushing her jacket off her shoulders and his tawny eyes went dark as night as they came to settle on the satiny black camisole edged with lace she was wearing underneath. It was the kind of flimsy wispy slip of a thing that on a body like Megan's could put a man in a serious fever just thinking about her wearing it, and Kyle was already so turned on that if he moved too suddenly he might embarrass himself badly.

'Megan,' he groaned as he drove his fingers through her hair then, lowering his head, slid his mouth across hers and kissed her hard.

Everything melted inside Megan. Desire turned her blood to boiling as his hands slid down to her hips and jerked her towards his pelvis. She bit back a gasp at the extent of his arousal and knew it wasn't likely they'd even make it to the bedroom. Still, what was a good wall for?

Her chest suddenly tight with emotion, she wrested her mouth reluctantly free from his and forced him to look at her. 'I'm sorry I left you. I'll never leave you again. Never! Oh, God, I love you so much!' Her dark eyes shimmered like onyx jewels as she gazed up at the man who meant the world to her. The man who was an answer to a dream she hadn't even known she had until she met him.

'I took a big gamble, letting you go… I just thank God you came back to me.' His voice a grated whisper, Kyle's hands settled round the firm flesh on her upper arms and tightened as if to demonstrate the force of his feelings. 'Will you marry me, Megan?'

'When?'

'Yesterday wouldn't be soon enough.' He pressed a warm kiss to her temple.

'That soon, huh?'

'That soon.'

'Yes, please.' Dark eyes shining, she dropped her own suddenly shy kiss at the corner of his mouth.

'Now we've established the important stuff—I'd like to get back to the other subject you were just discussing…'

'Oh? What subject was that?' Megan dimpled provocatively up at him.

'The subject of your underwear, you little minx.'

'Oh.' She blushed prettily.

'Does what you're wearing underneath match this dangerous little item you're wearing on top?' Deliberately methodical, Kyle slipped one of the silky shoestring straps off her shoulder, his gaze feasting on one full, lightly tanned breast revealed in all its glory with its puckered caramel tip as sheer black satin glided effortlessly downwards.

Catching her breath, Megan chewed slightly on her lip before answering. 'It would if I was wearing it,' she told him breathlessly.

EPILOGUE

A SMALL crowd had gathered round the picture Kyle had labelled *Magic in Mind*, and amidst the chinking of wine glasses, conversational tones and complimentary 'ahhs' Demetri Papandreou slapped his good friend heartily on the back.

'You know you have surpassed yourself with that portrait, huh? Only a man in love could paint such a picture. Such fire, such passion, such beauty in her eyes! A man could die happy loving a woman like that. I am mad at you for finding her first, but so pleased that you have found someone at last. I think it has really helped you as an artist. You are coming into your true potential, my friend, and I find it simply staggering.'

Kyle lifted his wine glass and took an experimental sip of the Dom Perignon Demi had flown in specially from Paris to mark the occasion of what Kyle meant to be his last exhibition. After this he was going to concentrate on art therapy.

Working with art was a fantastic training in building confidence in essential strength and health, and Kyle wanted to impart that to as many people who needed to get the message as possible. Along with that particular venture, he also wanted to spend some time helping Megan fulfil her own dream.

He shouldn't be feeling so self-satisfied but, damn it all, he was! Demi was right. A year into his marriage and he had somehow struck a deep vein of gold in his work that he could only wonder at. But then all he had to do was look at Megan to find the reason for his newfound ability. Every day of his life she inspired him. All he had to do was wake in the morning to find her warm sexy body snuggling up next to his and he was a man on a mission. *Let them look*…he thought magnanimously as he watched the enthusiastic little throng milling round the portrait. *I can go home to the real thing.*

Talking of which—where was Megan? He'd told her to be at the gallery around seven and it was already half past. Glancing anxiously across the heads of people milling round the paintings, he strained to see the glass doors. There were more people coming in, and one of Demi's penguin-suited cohorts was at the door greeting them, ensuring they possessed the right credentials because the exhibition was by invitation only.

Then he saw her. The sheen of her glossy black hair, caught by the carefully arranged artificial lighting, drew his gaze like a magnet. She was wearing a tailored cream trouser suit with a silky camisole to match beneath the vee of her jacket, and Kyle's weren't the only eyes to mark her entrance and stand and stare. But there was another reason besides her captivating beauty that Kyle followed her progress so intently, and that reason was bundled up tenderly in her arms.

Rosy Yvette—their daughter. Born just three months ago, after a textbook-perfect pregnancy and a labour and birth that had lasted just six hours from start to finish. Not bad for a first full-term pregnancy. The midwife had informed them that Megan's second would probably be even swifter.

'I'm sorry I'm late.' Reaching him, Megan angled her cheek for a kiss, startled and pleased when his lips descended on her mouth instead. She clung briefly, heat stirring as it always did whenever she set eyes on her handsome husband, then, conscious they were being observed, blushed becomingly and gave her baby a comforting pat across the soft white shawl that swathed her. 'I know I said I'd leave her with your mother, but she wouldn't settle and in the end I just had to bring her. Do you mind?'

'Give her to me.' Tenderly, Kyle lifted the baby from her mother's arms to cradle her lovingly in his own. A series of approving 'ahhs' fell around him like confetti. Inside, his heart and his chest swelled with pride.

'If little Rosy is destined to be half as beautiful as her mother, then you will have your work as a father cut out for you, my friend.' Demi beamed from Megan to Kyle with glee. 'You will have to chase the boys away from the door with a shotgun!'

Later, when the gallery had thinned of people a little, Megan leaned into Kyle's quiet strength, her senses swirling with the indomitable scent of man and cologne as he cradled their precious babe. Drop-dead gorgeous didn't begin to describe him, she thought. In his black leather trousers, white silk shirt and maroon velvet jacket, his chestnut hair gleaming beneath the lights and making his eyes appear even more golden than usual, Megan was so proud of him she was fit to burst.

'They like your picture, then?' She nodded towards the portrait that still drew an admiring crowd. Every facet of it was known to her in minute detail, from the lovely white antique lace nightgown that the lady wore to the knowing intimate smile on her lips and the loving glance that was purely for her husband alone.

'*Your* picture, sweetheart.' Kyle adjusted his daughter more snugly against his body, then slid his free arm possessively round Megan.

'Are you going to sell it to Demi?' she asked evenly, trying her best to shield her sudden anxiety from his knowing gaze.

The muscle in his cheek jumped as though she'd suggested something faintly improper. 'Are you joking? This one is definitely staying in the family…where it belongs. And next year, Angel—it will be your turn.'

Megan's heart accelerated a little at the thought of exhibiting her work like this, but she had made progress in leaps and bounds during her pregnancy, and with Kyle's guidance knew that one day—and one day soon—she too would be proud to say she earned her living as an artist. But right now, her heart full as she contemplated her adoring husband and baby, she knew she'd already been blessed with more gifts than she could ever have dreamed of.